Serendipity

Sarah Bryant

First edition
Proudly published in 2011 by
Snowbooks Ltd.
www.snowbooks.com

ISBN13 Library Hardback: 978-1907777-06-6
ISBN13 Paperback: 978-1907777-07-3
ISBN13 Digital edition: 978-1907777-47-9

A catalogue record for this book is available from the British Library.

Acknowledgments

A few people deserve special mention for helping me to make this book what it is. Julie, Pete and Adam Hyde for their friendship and their wonderful farm, Gateways, which was my model for Heaven Homestead. Quincy Carrol for reading my Chinese chapters and fixing my many cultural and language mistakes – any still present are mine, not his. Likewise Tristan Le Govic for proofreading the "Queen of the Depths" section. Also for telling me the true story of Ker-Ys and translating the old Breton – he has first dibs on playing Gradlon if I ever sell the film rights! Emma Barnes for loving it and Anna Torborg for finding the glitches. Colin, as always, for picking up the kids, picking up the slack, and his willingness to live with a flighty writer. Finally, and most importantly, Bob Dylan for "Hard Rain" – the roadmap to Meredith's journey, and the catalyst that changed this book from an exercise in post-adolescent navel-gazing into something (I hope) much wider reaching.

To Carl for the sailing lessons
Suz for the riding lessons
and Misty, Meg and Gemma
for the lessons in trust.

Witch Eyes

1

Meredith's first love was the wind.

Pre-speech, she followed it to the shore, a sickle of platinum sand between two granite monoliths, marking the southern boundary of her world. There, its curved arms held her as a mother's might have, as they held the crooning waves and crying birds, the bladderwrack strewn like entrails among beached jellyfish and sanded glass.

On cloudy days, she stood and let its magisterial sorrow wash over her. When the sun shone, she chased it, laughing. When she was old enough, she tied her skirt between her legs and climbed the rocks to feel its heady edge as it tried to tear her down.

Later on, it called to her, sang and coaxed and battered her with a longing she could neither trace nor name. Then she would wade out into the sea until the ancient cold numbed her body, and the wind could do nothing but run jealous fingers through her hair. She would think that she'd escaped it, too young still to realize that there is no escaping a first love. Too young to realize that during those half-forgotten days of her earliest childhood, the wind's soul had blown into hers, rending it to tatters, knotting them again with its own fingers so that it would never quite leave her, although it left her ripe for betrayal.

2

Hunter never doubted that the wind belonged to Meredith, and she to it. It had given her to them, after all: birthed her and sent her shoreward on a solstice tide, just one more piece of flotsam, and hardly the most interesting. That honor went to half a porpoise he'd found the previous summer after a storm, split inexplicably down the middle with the precision of an anatomical specimen. It had afforded him the credibility of the grotesque among the local boys, and a blissful second of Mary-Jane Bluitt's arms around his neck as she shrieked in delighted terror at the unveiling. In contrast, almost everyone he knew had at least one baby girl.

The one thing working in Meredith's favor when Hunter found her was her packaging. She didn't come in a basket like the fishwives' babies, or a papoose like the Indian women's, or even in a spindly-wheeled perambulator ordered from England, like Mary-Jane Bluitt's twin brothers. She came in a miniature boat, carved all over with anemones and mermaids and fish, rocking gently on the morning tide.

Hunter waded into the water for a better look. The baby looked at him, her eyes blue except for three chips of brown decorating the iris of the right one, like stony islands in a summer sea. She looked at him like nothing had ever bothered her and nothing ever would. Her swaddling was white sail-cloth pinned with an awl, which also held a card covered in writing.

Since Hunter couldn't read, he beached the boat, tied it off to a large piece of driftwood, and picked up the baby. Ian's saw was rasping away in the back yard when Hunter finally made it up the hill. He already bitterly regretted his decision to bring the baby to Ian. As soon as he'd lifted her from the boat, she'd begun to wriggle, and then to wail, her face growing redder and her screams louder by the minute. Holding the damp, squirming bundle carefully away from himself, he approached his father.

"Pa, look," he said, and when Ian didn't look, he yelled it.

Ian set down his saw and wiped his drenched forehead with a grimy sleeve, on the verge of a lecture. But when he saw what his son was holding, the words dried up, and the wind whipped them away. After a stunned moment he bent down and took the squalling baby from Hunter, put her over his shoulder in a gesture he thought he'd forgotten and began patting her back, saying, "Whisht...whisht me lass..." until her sobs quieted and finally stopped.

Ian shifted the baby to the crook of his arm, and he and Hunter looked at her. Her face, no longer balled in misery, was like a sweet round apple; as they peered into it, it shifted into a smile. That, to his shock, was when Hunter began to love her, with the almighty love of a lonely child who's waited all his life for a kindred spirit.

"Where," Ian asked at last, "did you find her?"

Hunter pointed down the hill, toward the water. Ian followed him back to the beach. His eyes narrowed when he saw the boat, then darted around the cove as if he expected someone to come out of hiding. But no one did. Ian bent down then to examine the boat more carefully. Only when he'd run his hands over every part of it did he comment.

"Good craftsmanship," he said, as if it explained everything.

Hunter asked, "What are we gonna do with it?"

"The boat?"

"The baby."

Ian looked down at her. She'd gone to sleep, one of her ivory arms draped over Ian's, fragile as a wishbone. Then he stared out to sea, as perfect a cipher as his face.

"It's a she," Ian said after a moment, "and she's called 'Meredith', if she's rightly labeled." He touched the name card, paused, and then said, "Aye, then: first we'll ask in town and make certain that nobody's lost a baby girl. And if nobody has, then we'll keep her…at least until someone with a better claim comes along."

That afternoon they knocked on every door on the way to Bryce's Landing, and every door once they reached it. Nobody knew the baby girl, and nobody had heard of one gone missing. More than one woman offered to take the child off Ian's hands, but Ian politely declined. And so, when they'd knocked on the last door, they turned back toward home with their foundling. The town's eyes followed them, their whispers like the crackle and drag of dry leaves on autumn pavement:

"…like animals…a girl, Heaven help us…another half-breed…a bastard…disaster…remember the motherrrrrrr…."

The wind stretched the final word to a warning sigh. Ian glowered at the eye-level distance and strode on, pretending not to hear. Hunter listened with his eyes on the ground and his heart pounding. But Meredith met every recriminatory eye squarely as she passed, and left silence in her wake.

3

The first thing Ian did, after bringing the dory-cradle up to the house and installing it in his own bedroom, was to consult his book of names. He learned from this that Meredith's name was Welsh in origin, and properly a man's. He also learned that it means "guardian from the sea." What he couldn't explain was how she'd come by such a name. However, as someone had gone to the trouble of giving her one, he thought that it was only fair she keep it.

The second thing he did was to take the old engraving of Botticelli's "Venus" from its nail over the mantle in what passed in his house for a parlor, and hang it above the child's cradle. He already suspected the kind of questions he was going to face when Meredith was old enough to ask them. He knew that a Renaissance image of a defunct deity was hardly an answer, but he hoped that the similarity of Meredith's birth-story to the goddess's might bolster the child against the bitter truth behind it.

Therefore, by the time she was five years old, Meredith knew that the naked lady in the print was the daughter of a god. She knew that this golden-haired woman had appeared out of nowhere one day, floating on the sea in a giant clamshell, and though nobody knew where she had come from, or who her mother had been, she was so beautiful that they let her be a goddess anyway.

Another kind of child might have construed this information – and the uncanny similarity of their looks – to mean that she too was a goddess. Meredith took it to mean that Venus was her mother.

She told Hunter first. It was winter, and as usual they were snowed in. Snow made little difference to Ian's work, or to the parts of it his children helped with, aside from the fact that he moved it indoors. So Hunter and Meredith worked together in the parlor, sanding the hull of a cedar lapstrake ship's boat. It lay upended on two sawhorses between the moth-eaten settee and the roaring wood stove. All around them, sagging bookcases spewed their contents onto the furniture and floor. Exotic junk from Ian's traveling days covered every surface that wasn't already inhabited by the jetsam of his trade, except for the sill of the west-facing window. This was lined with colored glass bottles that had belonged to Hunter's mother, and it was on these that Meredith fixed her eyes when she said:

"I know who my mother is."

"Oh?" said Hunter, carefully nonchalant.

"Yes. She's the lady from the picture. Venus."

"Venus is not your mother," Hunter said bluntly. "She isn't even real."

Meredith looked carefully into his face and then asked, "How do you know?"

Hunter opened out his wad of sandpaper, blew off the dust, and carefully re-folded it. "Because pictures aren't real unless they're taken with a camera, and that picture of Venus is a drawing. Besides, we had that picture a long time before we got

12

you. How would we know about your mother before we even got you?"

"Ian knew *your* mother before he got *you*," Meredith pointed out.

"That's different."

"How is it different?"

"Because..." Hunter answered, wondering how it had fallen to him to explain this, "well, because they were married. That's how it works. First you're married, then you have a baby."

Meredith regarded him with silent skepticism. Hunter sighed.

"Anyway, people knew my mother. They could see that she was real. But Venus...well, I don't think anyone's ever seen *her*."

"Someone drew a picture of her," Meredith said quietly. "There are no pictures of your mother."

Hunter only sighed. She had him there. They sanded in silence for a while, but just when Hunter thought Meredith had finally let the subject go, she asked, "Do you think she's in heaven? Your mother?"

Hunter shrugged. "That's what everyone says."

"Do you think you'll meet her there?"

He scratched harder at the wood. "Of course."

"How will you know it's her?"

"I'll just know."

"But how?" Meredith persisted.

"Because she was my mother. Everyone knows their mother."

As soon as he spoke those words Hunter wished he hadn't. Meredith gazed at him with her speckled eyes unblinking, her fingers turning the sandpaper over and over against her dusty blue smock. Hunter had a sudden clear image of himself and his sister as jigsaw puzzles, both with missing pieces. He knew with certain despair that those pieces would never materialize under the settee, or the carpet, or anywhere. They lay disintegrating at the bottom of the sea – or, in Meredith's case, somewhere more distant still.

He reached into his pocket and took out a tiny, exquisite carving of a sailboat. For weeks Meredith had watched him work on it, perfecting every tiny detail. She had wanted it as desperately as she had known she couldn't have it. Now he was offering it to her. She looked up at him in disbelief.

"That's for Mary-Jane," she said.

"No. It's for you."

"Why?"

"Because," he said, "I'm sorry. About your mother."

She smiled at him gently. "I'm not."

"Why not?"

"Because I'm going to find her." And she pocketed the boat.

4

The following summer, Hunter – still smarting with guilt from that conversation – taught Meredith to sail. He meant only to give her a pastime, to distract her from the hopeless quest to which she'd pledged herself that winter afternoon. He never imagined that he was giving her life its purpose.

Hunter's own tiny dinghy wasn't big enough for two. Ian studiously pretended not to see what they were doing as Meredith helped Hunter drag his mother's boat from the cobwebs at the back of the building shed. He warned her that the sail might have rotted, but it was sound.

Meredith shrieked with delight as they flew over the brilliant water, her hair whipping out like a bright flag. She took careful note of what Hunter was doing with the tiller and sheets, and when she understood she said, "I want to hold it." She listened to Hunter's instructions with quiet patience, until he stopped mid-sentence and said, "Never mind. I think you know what to do."

And she did. When she took sheet and tiller in her hands, felt the ocean tug and the sail resist the wind, she knew why she had been born. The sun shone to light the way out of their cove to the wide bright sea beyond; the wind tore across the water to wind the lines around her wrists and ankles, binding them to itself. The red sail above her, the wooden shell beneath became her world.

When they returned late in the afternoon, Ian saw the beginnings of infection in Meredith's ecstatic face. He had seen it in another once, and he knew where it led. He made Hunter promise to be careful, to make her sit on the leeward side, not to take her into the big waves by the island, to bring her right back if she was cold, or tired, or frightened. He wrung every assurance out of him but the one that mattered most, and was impossible: that Hunter wouldn't let the wind consume Meredith as it had Sweet Angelina. That wasn't a promise anybody could make, not even Meredith herself.

Besides, he told himself, he should have known on the day she arrived that Meredith would return to the sea sooner or later. The best he could do was to mitigate the consequences, and so, for her seventh birthday, Ian gave Meredith a boat of her own.

It was a tiny lapstrake dinghy, the precise color of her hair. The sail arrived a day later from town. Meredith clapped for joy and begged to be allowed to try it that moment. Ian sucked on his pipe and showed her how to rig it, and then helped her push it into the water. Hunter was already out beyond the breakwater, waiting for her. They skimmed the sea like a pair of terns. For the second time in his adult life, Ian fought tears.

5

Meredith thought about her name a good deal as she grew older. At first she clung merely to its ring of significance, holding it as a talisman against the other children's whispers of Witch-Eyes, and Foundling, and worse. Later, as she learned the sea better, she turned to its meaning, trying to tease sense from it. She could not imagine what the sea would need to be protected from.

"I think you have it back to front," Ian said, leaning over the plans for a new boat, making changes here and there with the stub of a pencil. "It's guardian *from* the sea, not *of* the sea."

Meredith sat on the porch swing in the slanting sunset light, chin on her folded arms, rested in turn on her drawn-up knee. She was eleven, her limbs bony and awkward, but the old soul behind her eyes, something sweet and earnest and still ambiguous in the turn of her mouth, promised beauty. A breeze not quite cold but foreshadowing winter caught at long tendrils of hair that had escaped her braids. She rocked the swing gently, almost absently, with one brown, bare toe.

"It must mean *something*," she said at last.

Ian sighed, tired of this rhetoric and his inability to answer it. "Maybe you haven't found it yet," he suggested. "Whatever you're meant to watch over."

Meredith was quiet for a time. Then, abruptly, she said, "I think there's bad things down there."

He set down the pencil, looked at her. "Down where?"

"Under the water."

"Of course there are bad things under the water. Rocks, shoals, sharks…"

Meredith shook her head. "I mean ghosts…demons…things so dark they can't ever come up, but they know about us, and they're jealous of us, and they want to bring us down there with them."

Appalled, he asked, "Is this from the bairns at school?" Ian harbored a deep and secret guilt regarding Meredith and school. He knew that he had to send her, but he also knew she was unhappy there. She was bright enough, but friendless, and he couldn't understand why. Yes, she was a foundling, with all of the potential dishonor that entailed, yet Hunter the half-breed made friends easily. Had he asked, Meredith could have told him that she was indeed unhappy at school, but it had nothing to do with the other children, simply the fact of the four enclosing walls. That she was solitary by choice. That with the wind in her hands, she had more than plenty. But he never asked.

"No," she said. "It's one of those things I think about, when I'm out there." She nodded to the distant water.

Ian was only partially relieved by this answer. He began cleaning out the bowl of his pipe with little, skittish jabs of his knife. "Well then maybe it's you who are to guard us from the dark things. Maybe the sea sent you to us for that." He paused, then added tremulously, "Because, you know, there are angels down there too."

Meredith knew that he was talking about his dead wife. She looked back towards the water. The sun had sunk below the horizon. The sky in its wake was streaked with salmon, lime and periwinkle, but no ghost walked the waves. There was only the wind, blowing cold now from the fading horizon. Meredith got up from the swing and walked down through the deepening shadows to the head of the path to the beach. Behind her, Ian's pipe was a bright orange star in the dim universe of the porch.

*

Mostly Meredith was happy. There were times, though, when she felt the remnant of a memory like an ancient sail, worn to tatters but flapping nonetheless, in the wind it could no longer harness. It bore no image substantial enough to pin down. There was nothing but longing, and the maddening sense of having been shown a glimpse of some deep, gleaming truth, now lost.

She couldn't even name a catalyst. They were as varied as a windjammer's sudden white sails on the horizon, or the beckoning finger of a setting winter sun. There were stirrings sometimes when she ran her finger along the curving patterns cut into the skin of her old boat-cradle. And there was always a shade of it in the deep, bleak longing that took her when she awakened from the dream.

It was always the same, beginning with the disembodied roar of storm waves on the beach. When she opened her eyes she saw the waves rolling a boat's ribs, scored and broken, gashes on the weathered wood as white as bone. Backwards and forwards they tumbled together, never quite reaching the strand. It was only when she saw the sail fluttering in the cleft of a jagged rock that she understood why she was crying: the boat was her own.

She ran along the sea-edge, crying as the waves drew the pieces farther away, the ground from beneath her feet. Down the beach, near the rocks, a group of flint-eyed children cast moldering nets into the water, fishing out the jagged bits. They stacked them inside a cage made of fishnet and seaweed, rotting lobster traps and iridescent mussel shells. And then, as Meredith ran and ran and covered no ground, they locked the cage and tossed the key into the sea.

6

Meredith was almost grown before she began to unravel the dream's meaning. It had left her in peace for many long months: enough for her to wonder, tentatively, if she had finally outgrown it. Then it returned without warning the autumn after she turned eighteen, more vivid than ever. This time it persisted. Night after night she awakened, breathless and heart pounding with inexplicable terror.

Ian watched Meredith's look turn inward as the geese arrowed south, and the leavings of the morning tide bore rimes of frost. He wondered if she'd fallen in love. He hoped not. In fact he would have prayed, had he been a praying man. It wasn't losing her that he feared, but the fact that whoever he lost her to would almost certainly be unworthy of her. Her beauty far outshone that of any young woman on the island, and though he didn't flaunt it his business brought in at least as much money as any other in the vicinity. But he knew that neither her beauty nor his money would be enough to erase Meredith's origins. Put bluntly, the good Christian families of Bryce's Landing would laugh at the idea of a bastard daughter-in-law.

He braced himself for what he knew was coming. Even so, he never imagined the shape it would finally take.

*

Winter hung on that year. Spring was all feints and false starts until summer blew in suddenly at the beginning of June. Meredith went to bed on a sullen, fog-ridden night and woke up to brilliant sun, a sea like a lady's silk, and a promise of heat.

Her first thought was of the Mermaid's Garden, and whether it had survived the winter. She leapt out of bed and, without bothering to dress, ran outdoors and onto the beach path. The moss and pine needles beneath her feet still held the cold of recently-melted snow, but the sun on her face was warm, the smell of the pines sharp and clear, the breeze with its breath of the sea settling into the back of her throat like memory.

Then the woods were behind, the sea spread out before her in audacious blue. A bold wave reached for her, tugging backwards at her heels as it retreated, slipping out between her toes, urging her forward. Meredith tossed her nightdress onto the sand and stepped into the water.

Another wave rolled in, bright as churchglass, and she dove to its roots. Beneath the water she felt the warmth of her skin disperse, as everything took on shades of green. She swam along the bottom, came up for a breath, dived down again and so on, until she arrived at the edge of a sea-meadow covered in fine wavering grass. Among the grass were carefully-placed artifacts, some of which she had found and brought there over the years, others placed by the sea itself. There were giant whelks' shells and algaed bottles, a whale's rib, the remnants of a rusted anchor and, in the center, a rock, every inch of it inhabited by submarine life. There were clumps of barnacled mussels and forests of tiny anemones, their fronds swaying in the currents. Spiny sea-urchins munched slowly through tracts of algae, and in the rock's shadow crab and lobster scrabbled for food. On the top of the rock that morning was a vermilion sun-star bigger than Meredith's hand.

She needed air, swam toward the sun, filled her lungs and then dove again. She didn't return to the rock but drifted, letting the ocean cradle her in timeless arms, in slow green silence that caused her to wonder why she'd been made with the need to breathe air. She wondered too whether it could be unlearned, whether the birth-water could somehow be taken back into the lungs so that a grown woman could return to the medium in which she had begun.

She had almost made up her mind to try it when a shadow passed over her. She looked up. An almond-shaped moon eclipsed the sun. A moment later something dropped into the water beside it: an anchor, hurtling toward her garden. It plunged into the sand just shy of the rock, sending the crustaceans scuttling for cover, and ploughed a strip through the sea grass, smashing a shell and a bottle before it finally found purchase.

Meredith hung for a moment as the lifted sediment curled around her like stormclouds, and then the pull of the gravity was strong again, her lungs burning. She broke the surface gasping, looking up at the boat that had just set anchor in her garden.

Perhaps if the sun had not been behind him, swallowing his face within its bright nimbus, she would simply have turned and swum back to shore. As it was her fear was suspended, her curiosity almost as strong as her annoyance. She treaded water, studying him much as she had studied the sea creatures below. He pushed his hat back, surprised, and the sun hit his face.

The same sun had darkened it, no doubt through hours spent at the tiller of the boat. His eyes were bright blue within it, his yellow hair bleached near white, his smile – when, finally, he recovered from his surprise enough to smile – like the light that comes in sudden, blinding shafts from the chinks in storm driven cloud. A finger of wind slipped across the water and caught the slack sails; they fluttered against his restraining hand like a great, netted butterfly.

Meredith felt something curve around her waist. She looked down to see a line trailing from the boat's stern, moving gently beneath the surface of the water. She looked at it, and then at him, and finally fear caught up with her. She pulled free of the rope and cut out with quick, certain strokes towards the shore. When she reached the beach again, she didn't stop, but pulled her nightdress over her head and ran for the trees.

7

Meredith heard him later that morning, talking with Ian in the back yard. She hid in her room, not daring to go near the window even to learn his business, and then furious at her own timidity when she heard him leave. She didn't ask about him, and Ian – preoccupied with whatever task the man had set him – didn't mention him when she brought his lunch.

She couldn't stop thinking about him though, and by evening the memory of those few moments when their eyes had met had stirred itself into a fever. When the sun had set, Meredith climbed up on top of her dormer window in search of a breeze to cool it. But the wind for once was still, the water serene and murmuring softly to itself. A sliver of moon hung like a smile on the horizon. Meredith had always loved that smiling moon. Beneath it, she never had her nightmare.

She lay back on the slanting roof, turning the little carved boat over and over in her hand. She'd kept it in her pocket since Hunter gave it to her, and now it was worn smooth by years of rumination. She looked for peace in the chaotic order of the stars, but her mind would not be still. In the moon's smile she saw the ghost of the sun's brilliance; in the stars' scattered pinpricks, the specks of light that hover on waves. She could not find the drone of the falling night. Instead it stratified: the bottom layer was the sea's somnolent breathing, then the chatter of water running somewhere back in the woods. There was a high-pitched cacophony of newborn insects, the wind chime over the back door whispering, a whippoorwill somewhere nearby, a ghost-owl farther afield.

The sailor called to her, or so it seemed, with all of the sounds in the non-silence. *Where are you?* implored the whippoorwill. The owl trilled wistfully in response. The brook laughed like a madwoman, the sea hummed and whispered to the sand in its own secret tongue, making her isolation more poignant.

Meredith didn't realize that Hunter had joined her until he spoke:

"You bothered, Witch-Eyes?"

She had never minded Hunter calling her by the children's nickname for her. From him, it came out as an endearment. "It's too hot," she said, her eyes still on the black, jagged silhouettes of trees against the indigo sky.

"Is that all?"

Meredith twisted a piece of hair around her finger. "Hunter..."

He waited for her words, but she couldn't find them. She turned around to look at him. Hunter hadn't cut his hair since he was sixteen, when he'd got tired of ignoring the half-breed comments and decided to embrace the fact that his mother's blood had turned out strongest. Sitting on the ridge-pole, his eyes black in the near-night, he looked every inch the great-grandson of an Abenaki chief.

He also looked sad. Meredith studied him more carefully. For a moment she forgot the blue-eyed sailor. "Were you with Mary-Jane today?" she asked.

Hunter went very still. Then he sighed. "How did you know?"

Meredith shrugged. She hadn't known, in fact, until the moment before she asked. And then, simply, she had.

"Are you in love with her?"

Another long pause. Then Hunter said, as if he'd just that moment come to the conclusion, "No."

That startled Meredith, who was certain that Hunter had carried a torch for Mary-Jane Bluitt as long as he'd known her. "Really?"

Hunter didn't look at her. "It doesn't matter."

"Why would you say that?"

"Because it's what *she* said: 'It doesn't matter whether you love me or not. I can't marry a half-breed.'"

Meredith was shocked, and then furious. "She really said that?"

"I doubt I'll ever forget it."

"You're a thousand times better than any of those Bluitts!" Meredith cried. "And Mary-Jane, well, she's just...she's a..." Meredith waved her hand, casting about for the right word.

"Don't," Hunter interrupted. "It's not worth whatever God-awful word you're swatting at. Besides, I must have been mistaken. I couldn't have been in love with a girl who wouldn't marry a half-breed...could I?"

"I guess not," Meredith said, unconvinced nevertheless.

"Out of curiosity," Hunter said after a moment, "why did you ask whether I was in love with Mary-Jane?"

"No reason," she answered.

"Hm," he said, and his look said an awful lot more. When Meredith didn't respond, he added, "You should ask Pa to tell you about my mother."

Meredith looked up at the smiling moon, now straight over their heads, and not perhaps so sanguine as she'd thought. "Why?"

"Because *that* was love: blind and true."

"I don't think he'll tell me," she said.

"Why not?"

"Because I've asked him before, and he shut right up."

Hunter paused, a handful of half-formed responses in his eyes. Finally, he said, "I think you'd find he'd be willing enough to tell you now."

"Why?" she demanded. "What's changed?"

"I'm still trying to figure that out," he murmured. His face was shadowed now, she could not see its expression, only that he was looking hard at her. "Just be careful. When it's your time… make sure you know."

Meredith nodded.

"Good-night, Witch-Eyes," he said.

She nodded again. He climbed back inside.

*

When Meredith finally crawled into her bed that night, long after the moon had set, the fever was still burning in her. When she closed her eyes she saw the image of a coppery face burned onto the backs of her eyelids. And when she slept, the drone of waves edged into her subconscious with belligerent familiarity.

But this time the dream was different. There were no children, only a man with blue eyes in a sunburned face and sun-bleached hair. It was he who locked up her shattered boat. In the hand that didn't hold the key, he held a severed rope.

8

Meredith tied up Hunter's mother's boat – hers, since she'd outgrown her first – and then loosened the halyards and began hauling the sail down.

"You weren't out long," said Hunter. He was sitting at the end of the dock with his legs in the water up to his knees, splicing line. The heat had not abated over the last few days; if anything, it had increased.

"My mainsail ripped," she answered shortly, examining the burst seam between the lowest two panels. "I barely made it past the jetty."

Hunter's eyes were patient as he took in her sweat-streaked face and uncharacteristic annoyance. "It's a windy day. And an old sail."

Meredith stuffed the sail into a bag and hiked up the blue ribbon holding her hair back. "Do you think the loft's still open?" she asked.

"On a sunny Friday afternoon?"

"That's it, then," she sighed, sitting down on the sail bag. "I can't race tomorrow."

Hunter tucked in the tail ends of the splice, pulled on it to test its strength. "All may not be lost, Witch-Eyes," he said thoughtfully.

"How so?"

He stood up, the water running out of the ends of his trousers and blackening the silvered wood of the old dock. To Meredith's annoyance, he smiled. "Come on. Bring the sail."

After a moment Meredith picked up the bag and followed him. "Where are we going?"

"To see someone who I think can help."

"Who?" she demanded. "Who do you know that can fix sails?"

He pointed to the sailboat anchored over the Mermaid's Garden and untied the dory.

"Hunter," she said in a strangled voice, her stomach having suddenly constricted.

"A problem?" He looked at her levelly.

Meredith shook her head, but she sat very still as he rowed out towards the anchored boat, clutching the sailbag to her chest. As they drew up alongside it she said, "Hunter, I'm not sure – "

But he was already tying the dory to the boarding-ladder, climbing on deck, calling, "Devereaux? You here?"

Meredith heard something clash below decks, and a man's voice cursing. "Just a moment – " the voice called. "MacFarlane?"

"None other," Hunter answered. Then, looking at Meredith, "Well, one other."

"Oh?" Sudden interest, and steps on the ladder of the companionway. Meredith kept her eyes trained on her bare feet as his white-and-yellow head emerged, but she felt him looking at her.

"Jacob Devereaux," said Hunter, "this is my sister, Meredith. Meredith, Mr. Devereaux. I don't know whether Ian's explained, but Mr. Devereaux's come for repairs on his boat, before he sails it to Spain."

Jacob Devereaux nodded. "Pleased to meet you, Miss MacFarlane," he said in a voice the color of his boat, with a soft, slow drawl. When she worked up the courage to meet his eyes, Meredith found that they were laughing. He winked at her. Meredith blushed, but she smiled, hesitantly.

"So," he asked, "to what do I owe the honor?"

Meredith looked at Hunter. With a quick, speculative look in return, he answered: "Her sail blew out. There's a race on tomorrow, and Meredith hoped to enter it. We wondered if you might do a quick repair."

"Of course," Jacob said, extending a long brown hand. Meredith relinquished the sail to him, and he unrolled it on the deck. He examined the split seam, and then plucked at the rest of the stitching with his fingernails.

"It's easy enough to fix," he said, sitting up on his heels and looking at her. "But the rest of the seams are rotting, too. You could do with a new sail."

"No," she said abruptly. "This one belongs to the boat."

Jacob raised his eyebrows. "Very well, then: I never argue with a lady. I'll re-sew all of the seams," his smile budded again, "if you don't object, of course," and blossomed.

Once again, Meredith couldn't look at him, but she nodded. Jacob gathered up the sail and brought it below. Meredith followed him, and Hunter sat down on the top step of the companionway. The cabin was small, containing only one berth, a head and a galley. The rest of the space was occupied by a worktable scattered with plans, tools, offcuts of canvas and rope and, in the center, a shiny black sewing machine.

"It's the latest model," Jacob told them as he cleared a space on the table for the sail, "the same one the best sail lofts use."

He sat down at the sewing machine and began to work the treadle. The needle whirred, flashing in and out of the fabric. Hunter looked down from the top of the companionway, his arms resting on either side. Meredith leaned against the stove, looking at the walls, which were plastered with pictures and newspaper clippings and sketches of sail designs. Directly above the worktable was a tintype of a pretty, dark-haired girl.

Her face shone out from a murky, aristocratic drawing room, her thin lips curved into a smile under wide, dark eyes.

"She was my fiancée," Jacob said, making Meredith jump.

Abashed, Meredith shifted her eyes to the companionway, wondering whether Hunter had heard. He was looking away, though, off over the water. After a moment, he lifted a hand, no doubt greeting a fisherman he knew, and then he climbed up on deck. Meredith heard his footsteps moving overhead, toward the bow, and his voice calling to someone, but the sewing machine was whirring again, drowning out his words.

"Was?" she asked, shocked by her own boldness.

Jacob was bent close to the sail, his hair obscuring his face, but not so completely that she didn't see it darken for a moment. "It didn't work out," he said. Meredith tried and failed to read the tone of his voice.

"Your brother tells me that you're something of a sailing prodigy," he said the next moment, guiding the cloth under the needle. His tone now was warm, uncomplicated.

"Does he?" Meredith asked, startled.

"Well, aren't you?"

"I...never really thought about it."

He smiled, glanced at her briefly. "I suppose a true prodigy wouldn't."

"That was a silly thing for Hunter to say," Meredith added after a moment, "when he's beaten me in every race we've ever sailed together."

Jacob raised his eyebrows. "Has he, now? Well, we can't have that, can we?"

To Meredith's horror, he extracted the sail from the machine, took it between his strong brown hands and ripped. She wanted to stop him, but she was paralyzed, rooted to the spot by the weird, beautiful intensity in his face as he worked.

He tore out all of the seams. By the time he picked up the shears, she was far beyond stopping him. Still, she couldn't look as he began to cut. So she stood with her hands over her eyes until she heard the sewing machine begin to whir again. When she dropped her hands, she saw that the strips of canvas by her feet weren't as wide as she'd feared. She also saw that Jacob was unperturbed by her discomfort.

"What did you do?" she asked.

"Have you ever studied sail design?"

"No."

"Geometry? Physics?"

"Geometry – a little bit. I wasn't clever at math."

He shook his head, and she couldn't tell whether it was negation or disgust. "Never mind. Basically, I've changed the shape of your sail, to better hold the wind."

That, Meredith understood. "Have *you* studied sail design and geometry and physics?" she asked.

His smiled twisted fractionally. "All of them, to one degree or another."

"Where?"

He glanced up at her, and then back down. "Geometry and physics at Harvard. Sail design, everywhere from Halifax to Kingstown and back again."

"You've sailed to all of those places?"

"In this very boat." He clapped a bulkhead.

"Do you do anything but sail?"

He laughed, rather derisively. "That's just what my father asked me the last time I saw him." Then, seeing Meredith's mystified look, he said, "No, I do nothing but sail. As such, I've been rather a disappointment to my family."

Meredith wondered what kind of family would consider a sailing life a disappointment. "I think you're lucky," she said, "to spend your life traveling. I would love to see the places you've seen."

"When you do," he said, "I think you'll find that in the end, all places are the same." He shook his head as punctuation to his cryptic statement, turning the sail deftly under the still-moving needle. "Now I've been wondering," he continued in a lighter tone, "do all girls up here go skinny-dipping in broad daylight? Or are you of a different cut of cloth?"

She turned away, coloring.

"Ah, don't take it to heart," he said, eyes laughing. "I didn't see anything. Well, hardly anything…"

Before she could answer this preposterous divulgence, he whipped the sail from the machine and held it up for her inspection. Meredith nodded, not really seeing it. Feeling his eyes on her face, she raised her own. His were no longer laughing, but opaque with scrutiny.

"Tell me," he said softly, lowering his hands with the sail still in their grasp, "why you ran from me."

His eyes burned like an August afternoon. She couldn't look away. "What else was I to do?" she whispered, clutching her hands together to keep them from shaking.

He studied her. The seconds stretched out. The wind hummed and sang in the rigging, chiming shrouds against spreaders and stays. Meredith didn't see him let go of the sail. She was only aware of its folding slide, its pooling on the floor like a discarded dress as Jacob Devereaux reached for her hands. Heat spread from the knot in her chest, out and into her limbs, her face, suffusing it with something she could only think of as the way beauty must feel. Her thoughts jangled and banged together like the rigging.

And then Hunter's footsteps sounded over their heads, heading aft. Meredith snatched her hands away from Jacob's, clutching at the sail as if to fold it.

"Are you ready yet, Meredith?" Hunter was calling.

"Don't run again," Jacob said.

"I have to go," she answered, tugging and pushing at the sail, trying to force it into a shape that would fit the circle of her arms.

"Yes," he agreed, taking the sail from her shaking hands and rolling it neatly. "But I'll call on you. Your father won't mind."

She looked at him, a tiny voice telling her that these two statements should have been questions. But he smiled, burying the protest. She smiled back, too blinded by his brilliance to notice that her hair ribbon slipped away as she hurried up the companionway, or to see him catch it as it fell, and crush it in his hand.

9

Meredith knew that something was different the moment she opened her eyes the next morning. Every fixture of her room stood out in vivid detail: the tortuous lines between the whitewashed boards of the walls, the dried lavender hanging from the beams, the blue and green braided rug on the floor and the faded quilt sewn by Hunter's mother.

Likewise, when she looked out the window she was amazed at the intensity of the colors, the intricacy of the world spread out before her. The sea swirled with ochres and violets she had never known were there, the sky unfolded in layers of blue streaked with silver and white lines of cloud, the trees' young leaves fizzed against the staid blue-black of the junipers.

Meredith felt that there were eyes on her and moved gingerly to the mirror. The face that looked back at her was both familiar and foreign. Once or twice she'd heard people call her beautiful – grudgingly, and always behind her back. She'd taken little notice, but now, suddenly, she knew that they were right. Abashed, Meredith turned away from the mirror and pulled on her clothes, then went downstairs.

Hunter was in the kitchen making jam sandwiches. He looked up when Meredith came in, then looked again more carefully.

"What did you do?" he asked.

Meredith stuck her finger in the jam jar, licked it, didn't meet his eye. "What do you mean?"

"You look different. Have you put something on your face? Paint? You know Pa won't like that."

"I have *not* put on paint," she said scornfully, and taking one of his sandwiches, she swept out the door, leaving him wondering what it was he'd missed.

The sea was soft and smooth, the wind blowing gently out of the west. Meredith unrolled her altered sail, tied new tell-tails, and then rigged it. She waited for Hunter, despite her annoyance with him, and they sailed on a reach all the way to the breakwater by Bryce's Landing. The course was set just outside the harbor, the racers practicing starts and tacks. Various other vessels, from dories to lobster boats, were anchored around the racecourse, bright with parasols and picnic baskets. In one, Meredith saw Mary-Jane Bluitt in a preposterous mauve picture hat, making eyes at a shopkeeper's son from Bryce's Landing. She also saw Jacob Devereaux's boat, anchored by one of the little islands dotting the harbor.

When the gun fired for the first race Meredith was off the line with clear air, her mind midway between the leech of her sail and the memory of Jacob's haloed face. She knew that there was no one ahead of her, but she didn't think of there being anyone behind. She didn't think at all. The wind had moved inside of her, and she moved with it, shifting to its shiftings, listening to the whispered truths beneath its brazen lies. And she won: that race and all the rest.

Meredith was unaware of the day's passing, only, vaguely, of the change in hue of the water about her. When Hunter told her that the past race had been the last she looked up and around for the first time all day. Like a swimmer emerging from a long crossing, she blinked in surprise at the setting sun.

"Whatever happened to you," Hunter said, half-smiling from beneath his drooping felt hat, "it sure didn't slow you down. Come on," and he turned his boat upwind.

"Where?" she asked.

He nodded toward Jacob's anchored boat. There was a figure standing on deck. A wave of gold and red flecks crossed her vision; her hands shook. For a moment it seemed the wind wailed around and through her, though the evening sea was thick and still as mercury. The bright sky darkened, and she felt the lash of a tattered nightmare sail. She heard the roar of a monstrous wave, smelled salt and wet canvas.

"Meredith?" Hunter said.

She pressed her hands to her forehead for a moment, and the vision was gone. "Yes," she said, and gathered her sheets as Jacob's smile flashed out across the water.

10

"Well," he said to Meredith as he secured her bowline and helped her onboard, "do you believe me now?"

"Believe you?" she asked, her mind still on the dark memory she'd almost captured.

"About the sail. The changes I made. I was right, wasn't I?"

"I didn't doubt you."

"And yet, you couldn't watch me cut it." His eyes laughed at her.

She looked away as Hunter climbed on board.

"So that's her secret?" he asked Jacob. "You altered her sail?"

Jacob shrugged. "Either that, or..."

Or what? Meredith wanted to ask. She still couldn't look at him.

"Well, whatever you did, it worked." Hunter's voice was proud, but also faintly baffled. "I couldn't catch her. No one could."

Meredith was too shy to respond to the compliment, but she was glad that it was true, and that Jacob had seen it.

"A drink, MacFarlane?" Jacob asked. Meredith saw then that he held a glass of amber liquid. "And something perhaps for the lady? Do you take wine, Miss MacFarlane?"

Meredith looked at Hunter, wondering how to answer this given that no liquor had ever passed her lips. Ian kept none in the house.

Hunter said, "We can't stay. Our father's expecting us for dinner." He glanced sidelong at Meredith, who was looking intently at her feet. "But listen – why don't you come with us?"

Jacob looked from Hunter to Meredith, smiling slightly. "I'd love to. That is, if your sister doesn't mind cooking for one more."

"Oh, Meredith won't be cooking," Hunter said. "She's hopeless in the kitchen."

"Hunter!" she cried, flushing scarlet.

He shrugged, grinning at her. "Well, it's no more than the truth, is it?"

Meredith glared at him. Jacob laughed softly, his eyes following her all the while. "Very well," he said. "Why don't we sail my boat back? I'll tow your dinghies." He saw the hesitation in the look they exchanged. "You can take the helm, if you like," he added nonchalantly, to Hunter.

Hunter conceded then, though he wouldn't accept a drink. So they tied their dinghies one behind the other, raised Jacob's sails, and rode the last of the dying breeze home.

"What is your boat called?" Meredith asked Jacob, when the sheets were secure and Hunter ecstatic at the helm. Though he spent his days building them, it was rare that he had the chance to sail his father's yachts. Ian had never kept one of his own.

"Actually," said Jacob, "she doesn't have a name."

Meredith raised her eyebrows.

"Oh, I know it's bad luck or some other nonsense. The truth is, I could never think of one that seemed right." He paused. "Do you have any suggestions?"

Meredith shook her head.

He looked at her, his eyes for once direct. "Do you remember her? I mean, the making of her?"

"Of course I do," she answered, leaning down to run a hand along the smooth silvery wood of the deck. "I remember them all."

His look narrowed. "Truly? All of them?"

"How could I not?" she asked, as surprised as he was. "We live with them for months, sometimes years. They're like family. Brothers and sisters. There's a part of all of us in each of them."

"How so?" he asked, beckoning to her to sit beside him on the windward rail.

Meredith sat, dropping her legs and skirt over the side. The gentle spray wet her feet and hem. "Just that," she said. "Of course the boats are Pa's first and last, but Hunter and I help him with all of them. I spent one whole February on this." She ran her hand again across the decking.

"You? You laid this decking?"

Meredith nodded.

"But this boat is more than ten years old! You'd have been a child then – "

"I was nine."

He gave her a long, appraising look, and seemed about to say something else – something serious – when Hunter yelled: "Need to tack!"

Meredith leapt up to free sheets and wind winches, Jacob following her more slowly. When they were settled on their new tack, he followed Meredith to her place on the opposite rail.

"So you can't cook," he said, "but you can build boats."

"Well…I've never built one by myself," she answered.

"But you could? If you had to?"

She looked at him curiously. "I suppose so. But I can't see why I would ever have to."

He scrutinized her in return. At last he spoke again: "Do you know that you have shoals in your eyes?"

Meredith looked down at the water. "That's a pretty way to put it."

"They're pretty eyes," he said.

Meredith gave a little, deprecating laugh. "Witch eyes."

"I heard your brother call you that."

"They all call me that. He's the only one who doesn't mean it as an insult."

He shook his head. "You're wasted here."

The color drained from Meredith's face.

"I'm sorry," Jacob said when he noticed it, or perhaps it was her silence that he noticed. "I didn't mean to offend you."

"Ian fixed your transom," Meredith said after a moment, carefully keeping her voice neutral, her eyes on the horizon.

"The very day I asked him to, no less."

"And yet you are still here."

"It appears that I am."

Still, Meredith didn't look at him. She didn't want to see his eyes laughing. Instead she rested her chin on the lifeline, pondering all of the questions she didn't know how to put into words. The wind scattered her hair, snatched at her breath.

"Why?" she asked, finally.

"Why!" he muttered. And then, "Do you have any idea how beautiful you are?"

Meredith looked at the water slipping away beneath her feet.

"Nobody in this godforsaken place," he persisted, "has ever thought to tell you."

That startled her into looking at him again. "It isn't our way," she said. "A woman's beauty is of little worth when it comes to salting fish and cutting firewood."

"You don't belong in a place like this."

"And yet, here I am," she answered. When he didn't answer, she added, "And I love this place."

"I wonder if you'll say so five years from now, or ten...when you're out in the cold stacking that wood and salting that fish, with a brood of children you struggle to feed."

Meredith recoiled as if he'd slapped her. "I think that's unlikely," she said after a moment.

His laugh was humorless and his words, for the first time, openly condescending. "Believe me, it's the same up and down this coast, from Maine to Mississipi. I've seen it."

"That may be," Meredith answered, "but as I say, it's unlikely to be my fate, when no one on this island will have me for a wife."

Now it was his turn to look shocked. "What? Why not?"

She smiled bitterly, shook her head. "Witch eyes," she said softly, and there was no time to say more, because they had reached the cove, and Hunter was calling for fenders and docking lines.

But Jacob grabbed her arm as she turned away. "This conversation isn't finished, Miss MacFarlane," he said, his eyes boring into hers. "I mean to learn what you meant by that."

"And when you do," Meredith said sadly, "you'll think the same as everybody else."

11

They found Ian in the kitchen, steaming clams. A clutch of unfortunate lobsters scrabbled on the kitchen floor, leaving dark trails on the worn wood. Meredith corralled them into a washbasin.

"I'd have done the traps for you," Hunter said, but Ian waved a wooden spoon to silence him.

"Mr. Rainey came to pick up his boat today," he said. "I didn't feel like starting on the Wallace ketch just yet. Cooking was a good excuse."

"Pa," said Meredith, pushing the washtub into a corner, "Hunter invited Mr. Devereaux for dinner."

Ian turned and nodded briefly at Jacob. "Pleased you could join us," he said, rather stiffly. "But I thought you were away this morning."

Jacob shook his head. "I only went to watch the races. Weren't you there yourself?"

Meredith cringed: Ian's avoidance of the races his wife used to win was one of the topics no one raised in his house. But he only frowned into a bowl of biscuit dough and said, "Too busy. The bairns understand. Do you mean to stay long?"

Meredith blinked at Ian in surprise. A sideways glance at Hunter revealed his own surprise. Ian was many things, but he was never rude, and yet, that question had certainly bordered on it.

"As long as it suits me," Jacob answered.

Ian nodded as if that confirmed something. He handed the biscuit dough to Hunter, who began to roll and cut it. Then he peered at the clattering washbasin and said, "Lass, you might like to step outside."

"Meredith can't stand to see lobsters boiled," Hunter explained to Jacob.

"And yet, she eats them?" Jacob enquired.

Ian picked up the basin, and with a cry, Meredith ran out the open back door, into the yard.

"Curious woman, your sister," he said to Hunter, and followed her out.

*

The back yard was empty except for y strongback and a few scattered piles of wood shavings in various states of decomposition.

"So this is it," Jacob said. "Where MacFarlane boats are born and bred."

"Did you expect something else?" Meredith asked, rather sharply. Then she sighed. "I'm sorry. What would you like to see?"

Jacob didn't answer. He watched her with the unblinking eyes of a cat. When he saw that she had fallen into their net, he smiled, stepped forward, and threaded her arm through his.

"You show me what you love best," he said.

Meredith looked at him for a moment, then at the gilt-edged woods behind him, branded on the sinking sun. A swarm of backlit insects hummed gyres and spirals against the dark backdrop. She walked toward them, leading him through the sparse stand of junipers that shielded the yard from the wind's headlong assault, to the edge of the cliff where the waves pounded futile fists as they ran from the setting sun.

"This?" he asked, looking down at the furious water. "Why?"

"Because," she answered, "it let me pass."

"I don't understand," he said.

"No?" she asked. "Well, nor do I, Mr. Devereaux. There isn't much to go on, truth be told. But what I do know is this: nineteen years ago, more or less, somebody set a child adrift on this sea in a tiny boat. And the sea didn't take her, but let her pass on into Ian MacFarlane's cove, and the life to which you think I don't belong. So in a manner of speaking, this sea is my mother. At any rate, it's the only one I'm ever likely to know. I thought I might as well introduce you."

For a moment there was no sound but the waves' fugue. Then Jacob said, "I see."

"Do you?" she asked softly.

Jacob gave her his inscrutable look; and then he smiled. "May I kiss you, Miss MacFarlane?" he asked. He didn't wait for an answer. Meredith barely had time to register his words before his lips touched hers, and then there was no time to be afraid, only surprised.

She pulled away after a second, her eyes wide open, his laughter churning the rift between them.

"You're very young, aren't you." His words toppled, slid down the cliff face.

"I'mynineteen," she said, barely above a whisper, feeling her own words shifting like sandbars even as she spoke them.

Jacob shrugged. Nineteen isn't very old. Wait!" For he'd seen her mouth begin to harden. "I don't mean to offend you, though it seems I manage to do so at every turn. The truth is, I'm still here because of you." He took in her blank look and added, "That question you asked me earlier. That's why I'm still here."

"I've just told you, Mr. Devereaux, that I'm a foundling."

"And I'm telling *you*, Miss MacFarlane, that I don't care. I've fallen in love with you."

Shock took her tongue. She could do nothing but stand gazing at him.

He laughed. "That's not the reaction I'd hoped for, but I suppose it could have been worse. I realize that you barely know me; I mean to rectify that. Will you come sailing with me tomorrow? We could circle the island, and that would give us plenty of time to get acquainted."

Meredith paused, her parted lips working delicately, as though she were sounding the thoughts before she spoke them. Finally, she said, "I would like that, Mr. Devereaux. But of course, you'll have to ask my father."

Jacob looked momentarily surprised by this – perhaps even mildly annoyed – but then his face smoothed again. "Of course," he said. "I'll ask him tonight."

"You can ask me now," said a voice behind them.

Meredith turned. Ian was standing ten feet back in the woods, the doomed light making cliffs of his craggy features. There was a challenge in his look, and she was suddenly uncertain where she had been positive a moment past. When Jacob declared himself, he had not looked as Ian looked on the rare occasions he spoke of Sweet Angelina. *It's only because we don't yet know each other*, she told herself.

"In my day," Ian said, "a young man wouldn't have thought of taking a young woman somewhere un-chaperoned."

"With all due respect, Mr. MacFarlane," Jacob said, "times have changed."

Ian looked at him for a long moment. Then he looked at his daughter. "Well, Meredith? Do you want to go with Mr. Devereaux?"

The wind reached for her, pleaded with her, but she ignored it. "Yes," she said, barely above a whisper. "I do."

"Very well, Mr. Devereaux," Ian said at last, visibly diminished. "You may take my daughter sailing tomorrow. Dinner is ready." He turned away abruptly.

Meredith looked at Jacob. "Perhaps – " she began, and got no further.

"He doesn't understand you!" Jacob's anger was almost tangible. "None of them understand you!"

"Do you?" Meredith asked.

"I will," he said.

The wind shrieked. Meredith smiled.

12

For four weeks, she walked the knife blade of a dream.

Or that was how she would think of it later: in terms of precarious, perilous beauty. At the time, she didn't think. She lay daydreaming in the palm of a god's hand, with no desire to look beyond it. Days flicked past, happiness encompassed in a series of snapshots: a hatchway framing a half moon, an attic window open to a summer night full of moths and conjuration. It lay with her in Jacob's arms under the dogwood tree planted by Hunter's mother, while armored insects stalked the grass and cicadas drilled holes in the sea-ridden silence. It laughed with her when he made her open a long, straight package, to reveal a gold-leaf nameplate that read, "Witch Eyes."

Half way through that month Jacob gave her a blue diamond that dwarfed her slender finger, and Ian gave his grudging consent. Afterward, Meredith gave Jacob the last of herself. His pounding heart as he collapsed between her legs seemed to her the pinnacle of happiness.

And yet, there were dissonant notes in it that she couldn't quite ignore. Sometimes she would run down to the cove in the morning to meet him, and his boat would be gone. Sometimes she would wait a whole evening for him on the porch swing, and then spend the night pacing her bedroom wondering why he hadn't come, or tossing sleepless as the rain tapped its soft staccato on the roof.

His absences weren't long, but somehow he always avoided telling her where he'd been. During one of them, she poured a bottle of ink into a bowl beneath the full moon to try to scry an answer. She saw a dark-eyed girl laughing, and threw both bowl and ink over the cliff. Several days later a tiny, wrinkled Abenaki woman stopped her in town and said, "Daughter, I don't know you, but I know your father. He is a good man, and so I must speak: be careful. Your young man is not what he seems – "

Meredith turned and ran before she could say more and told herself that the woman was mad. But when she confessed the meeting to Ian, he gave her a long look and said, "Perhaps, lassie, you should consider what she said. Those old Indian woman have learned by hard experience how to see what the rest of us don't." At which Meredith flew into a rage, and Ian decided against relating what he himself had been hearing in town. It was only rumor after all, and he knew how unjust rumor could be.

So he stood silently by as Jacob filled Meredith's head with impossible dreams. He'd never wished so fervently that he was the kind of man to put his foot down, to tell his daughter that her chosen one wasn't good enough, and expect her to heed him. But he had never known how to speak a bitter truth, least of all to Meredith. Not when she was a child asking him her mother's name, not now when she stood in the splendor of her innocence, her determined certainty bristling around her like a fence.

*

The night before the wedding, Jacob kissed Meredith good-night and left her with his brilliant smile. The rest had been planned for weeks. They would meet at the church in the morning; Ian and Hunter would stand witness; Jacob and Meredith would sail afterward for New Orleans, where his family was waiting to receive their new daughter, his mother being too ill to travel to the wedding.

And yet, Meredith was plagued by cloying doubt after he'd gone. She went to bed early to escape it, but she couldn't sleep. Her room seemed frowning and sinister with all of her things packed away. Her wedding dress hovered on its dummy like a headless ghost. So she got out of bed again and went to the window, looking for his cabin lights to calm her.

She didn't find them. *Perhaps,* she thought, *he's already asleep.* And then something caught her eye: far out on the water, a dim light zig-zagged among the isles and shoals, to the precise rhythm of a boat's tacks and jibes.

Of course there was nothing particularly strange in that. Theirs was an island of men who made their living from the sea, and sometimes that demanded odd hours. It could be a fisherman cheating the tides, or a rusticator from one of the big hotels who'd managed to lose himself on a day-sail. Yet in her heart, Meredith knew that it wasn't. She watched until the light disappeared. Then she lit a storm lantern and made her way down to the cove to wait.

13

When Hunter found her the next morning, she was sitting in the sand by a spent lantern, staring out at the blank water. She was soaked and shivering, her thin night-dress clinging to her skin, and her hair in ochre streaks down her back. A sodden red sail lay rolled by her side.

"Meredith," he said.

She turned slowly, looked at him as if she didn't know who he was. Her eyes were the color of ash. Their gold-brown islands had turned black.

"What happened?" he asked her.

She looked at him.

"Meredith," he repeated, unable yet to believe that anything could have hurt her badly enough to drive her beyond his reach, "tell me what happened."

"He's gone," she said at last, her voice like the grinding of the sea on shingle.

"He'll come back," Hunter said, willing to lie to stop the bleeding.

"He will not come back," she answered, nodding to the sail beside her.

Hunter looked down at it. He had a sudden overwhelming need to push it into the sea. To sink it where he would never have to see what was inside it, where it would never be found, and then take his sister's hand and run. But he knew that that wouldn't unmake its truth. Nothing would.

With a trembling hand he flipped back a corner of the sail, uncovering a girl's face. It was a pretty face, or it had been: smooth-skin, high cheekbones, sickle-shaped eyes and soft, childlike lips. But the skin was gray now, the lips violet, the eyes glazed and still. Hunter knew enough of what the sea did with its dead to judge that she had not been in the water twelve hours.

He covered the girl's face again. "Where did you find her?"

Meredith opened her mouth to answer, but nothing emerged. The words were jammed in a sudden, senseless bundle in her throat. They would have been little help anyway. She could not have told him what made her swim out to the Mermaid's Garden, nor why she had carried a knife; only that it had seemed she had no choice. Nor could she remember how she'd managed to bring the dead girl back to shore in that leaden shroud, though she remembered cutting her free of the anchor to which she'd been bound. The only clear image was the first sight of her because, in the submarine dawn, she had seemed for a moment not only alive but an actual mermaid, with her hair fanned out around her and the sail trailing away like a tail. It had taken several long moments for the truth to penetrate.

So Meredith said nothing, and Hunter didn't ask again. He cut the girl from the sail and, finding her naked beneath it and bruised where no woman should ever be, he wrapped her in his jacket before he carried her up to the house. There, he laid her on the hearth-rug, called Ian, and then went back for Meredith. She was still sitting where he had left her, but now she was methodically ripping the sail to shreds and feeding them to the wind, which was rising with the light. It snatched them from her hands, whipping them into the trees and the crevices of the rocks, until the grey beach fluttered with bloody banners.

When he tried to take the last of the fabric from her hands, she fought him. When he lifted her, she tried to scream, but no sound came. And then, at last, she began to cry, with sobs that seemed they'd shake her to pieces, though they never broke her sudden silence.

14

Nobody expected the silence to last, least of all Meredith herself. But day after day she found herself unable to make a sound. She could not answer the questions of the Abenaki elders who came to claim the girl's body, nor those of the indolent sheriff who arrived with his notebook and wrote only six words, despite what Ian and Hunter told him: Indian girl found dead. Case closed.

But silence was not the extent of Meredith's transformation. She stopped sleeping. She ate only when her father and brother forced her. She couldn't bear anyone's company, nor could she bear to be near the sea. Instead, she walked into the woods at dawn and came back at night with her face scratched and bleeding, her hair matted with pine-sap and bracken. She would go upstairs just as she was, then get up at dawn and go through the same ritual again.

Meredith was only half aware of what she did. It seemed to her that she'd become a ghost, voiceless and paper-thin. She moved to the rhythm of a vague belief: that if she could only walk long enough, she could fall like last year's leaves beneath the burgeoning trees, lie down among their murmuring masses and join in their slow, unconscious disintegration.

Then, on the last day of August, Ian awakened to wind pounding the casements, and a quicksand feeling at his core that he'd had once before. He leapt out of bed, bounded up the attic stairs, but when he reached Meredith's room, he found it empty. Even her wedding dress was gone. He didn't call for her or try to follow. He knew already that he would never find her.

He sat down on that empty bed, and for the second time in a quarter century he cried: not because he'd lost his daughter, but because he had not learned from losing his wife. His tragedy had repeated itself, and he had no one but himself to blame. He'd let the sea be Meredith's solace, as he'd let it be Sweet Angelina's. Was it any wonder that in the end, its scream was the only sound wide enough to fill her crushing silence?

And then he remembered his son.

Hunter wasn't in the house, and Ian ran down to the cove through the grim, grinding morning, clutched by a new terror. Mountains of slate-gray water slid and crashed into the shore, tearing rents in the decaying dunes at the foot of the cliffs, then, perversely, covering them again. Hunter was standing in the water with the waves breaking over him, screaming her name at the rampant sea. In his hands, he held a shredded scrap of bridal lace.

When he turned and saw Ian's face he cried, "She's not dead! She isn't!" and Ian caught him as his knees buckled. He dragged his son back onto the sand, beyond the waves' grasp, clutching him in a convulsive embrace while he wept and ranted.

But Ian had already spent his tears. As he listened to Hunter cry, he watched the ocean's furious body writhing against the shore, and he thought about what the preacher had said when they set up the memorial to his wife: "The Lord giveth, and the Lord taketh away." He began to laugh, because it was true. He had never answered to any god but the sea; the sea had given them Meredith, and now, finding him unworthy, it had taken her back.

Ian had no patience for a god like that. He had still less for his own self-pity. So that night, when the tide flung the gnawed bones of her boat onto the beach, Ian burned them along with every piece of lumber on his property. And when he threw the ashes into the sea, for the first time in his memory, it fell silent.

Laying Down

1

Deep in a landlocked hollow, Silence Ogden dreamed of flying. By night, he skimmed the surface of a world without trees and hills and fields, without tumbledown fences or meltwater creeks or neighbors squabbling over a six-foot strip of earth. In his dream world, there was only a blazing blue expanse beneath a windscoured sky, unbroken except by the white wings above and the wooden vessel beneath his feet.

"He's out of his mind," his grandfather muttered the first time the child voiced these dreams, or an approximation of them. And Silence might well have believed him, skewing the entire current of his life, had Annie Newcombe not heard him speak.

She looked up from the eggs she was picking over and said, "You're wrong, John Ogden," in her soft, incontestable way. Then, to Silence's mother: "He has the sea in his soul, that's all. He's not the first boy born that way, and he won't be the last. Don't you let them make a madness of it, Esther."

Esther Ogden bobbed her head, the awe with which she regarded Annie mitigated for a moment by gratitude. Annie nodded back and took up her basket of eggs. But she touched Silence's head on the way out, and her lips turned upward into the barest fraction of a smile.

*

Annie was right, but she was also wrong. The sea was already a madness in Silence, but there was no evil in it. It was the madness of a man in love, and rather than fading with childhood, the dreams grew with him. In his sleep he navigated cats' paws and wind-shifts, the dark lines of opposing currents and whitewater shoals. He knew the angles of precarious beauty, the upended scope of a man who's spent his life on the waves. In another place, he might have skipped the tortuous path to his destiny that was already being mapped.

But Silence lived three hundred miles from the sea. Neither he nor any of his friends and relatives had ever seen the ocean. He had never sat on a grandfather's knee, listening to tales of naval battles, or an immigrant's hard sea crossing. He hadn't heard of Melville or Stevenson; in fact the only novel he had ever read was "Oliver Twist", in its original serialized form in back-issues of "Bentley's Miscellany", which he'd found moldering in the attic. There was simply no good way to explain Silence's obsession. Whatever his mother might have taken from Annie's admonition, by the time he was ten years old, Silence Ogden was firmly established as the town eccentric.

2

In those days, the town of Heaven consisted of fourteen smallholdings, one general store, a tattered Confederate flag whose rebellious colors had long since faded to orange-gray-violet, and a church of contestable denomination sporting a peeling billboard thate proclaimed "He is the Savior and the Light" to anyone who might not have heard. In short, even if he hadn't been an Ogden, Silence would have been in little danger of being cast out to beg on his town's single street.

But Silence *was* an Ogden, and that single street originated at his front door. As the town's founding family, they were universally respected. Plus they had money – more of it, anyway, than anyone else in town – and money will erase stains in a small town just as well as a big one. The bottom line, though, was that Silence was simply too charming ever to be an outcast. He was blessed with his mother's fine face and down-turned dark eyes, his father's affability and brilliant smile. He headed his school class effortlessly, made friends with equal ease, and he had been made to understand by Jenny Lindquist – age eight, the uncontested town beauty – that once he came of age, she would marry him, and no one else. With so many golden tickets in his hand, it was easy enough for everyone to ignore his single quirk.

Besides, Esther's friends said, smiling indulgently and ruffling his curls, what could reasonably be expected of a boy called Silence? Which always elicited a smile from Esther, albeit a wistful one, which was the most commentary she ever offered on her son's preposterous name.

Another kind of woman might have blamed her husband, and thereby poisoned her marriage. Esther knew though that John had been equally disappointed by the turn of events. Besides, Esther was honest enough to recognize that she herself wasn't blameless in the matter. She and John hadn't discussed names until she was well into her final month of pregnancy. Esther had naively assumed that the child, if it were a boy, would take the name of his forbears.

"Absolutely not!" he'd cried, when she told her husband how she looked forward to meeting little John Isaiah Nathaniel Ogden IV.

"But why not?" she'd asked, stunned.

"Yell 'John' in this house and you get three answers. Do we really need a fourth?" Seeing her distress, he'd added, "Don't worry. I'm sure it's a girl, anyway." Esther was not so sure, but she thought that once the baby arrived, her husband would see sense. And if not, there was always the next baby.

That guileless certainty would haunt her for the rest of her life. For, although she'd been right in guessing that her baby was a boy, there would never be a next one. That was what the midwife had said, or near enough, when the afterbirth failed to show itself in Silence's wake.

John III had shaken his head at her dismal canting. He'd never seen his wife look healthier or happier than she did with her newborn child at her breast. But that was before the blood and the fever, the weeks when his son screamed for the mother who didn't know him, and subsisted on goat's milk he sucked, foul-faced, from a rag. It was before Esther's womb closed in on itself like a blighted flower, saving her life but proving the midwife's grim prediction.

"It's all the more reason to give him the family name," said Esther when she recovered.

"It's all the more reason to lessen his burden," John contradicted.

Neither would give an inch. It was the first and only battle of their married life. The stalemate stretched out across one week, then two. By the third, no one really believed that the child would ever be called anything but "him" or "it," or that his parents would ever speak to each other again.

It was Silence's great-grandfather who settled the matter. In church on the Sunday marking the end of the third week of the Ogdens' stony silence, just before the minister announced the Peace, John I stood up, cleared his throat and, like the venerable patriarch he was, pointed one admonitory finger at his grandson and another at his granddaughter-in-law.

"You," he said in a voice that brooked no argument, "and you: stand up!"

John III was mortified, Esther in paroxysms over the sacrilege, but both were too terrified of John I to disobey. They stood and followed him as he strode from their front pew up to the altar under the astonished eyes of their neighbors. Even the minister backed, open-mouthed, into a corner to give the old man center stage.

John I glared at the warring couple with rheumy blue eyes. "I'm old," he announced flatly. "I don't want to spend the last of my time on earth listening to the two of you squabble. As I see it, you're damn lucky to have that child – pardon me Pastor, but it's the truth, and I've no doubt God himself would say the same!" Turning back to the couple as the minister passed a hand across his eyes, John I continued, "Moreover, you're even luckier to have nothing worse to worry about than what to call him. So you are going to decide on a name right now. Then the good

Pastor is going to wet the boy's head to make it official, with all of you as witness." He threw an expansive arm toward the congregation. "After that, you are going to shake hands. And then, you will never bring the matter up again, come hell or high water. You have five minutes. I'm counting."

"He *looks* like a Johnny," pleaded Esther.

"He looks like an individual," insisted John III.

This started off a whole new round of arguing, to which the congregation listened with interest, and the elder Ogdens with deepening irritation. At last, near apoplectic, John I yelled, "Silence!"

And silence reigned for one perfect moment. Even the infant stared at his great-grandfather in wide-eyed wonder. And then, like an old door swinging in the wind, John I began to laugh. "Silence," he chuckled, looking thoughtfully back at the baby. "I believe there was a Silence away back on my mother's side…a Puritan, came over from England…" John I took the baby from the stunned Esther before she could protest, handed him to the minister and said, "Do the deed, Father."

It was done before either of the child's parents had recovered their wits enough to protest. Thus the last of the Ogdens, and future town eccentric, was christened Silence.

3

Silence seemed to take the name to heart. He was the kind of baby other mothers called "good" while his own worried herself sick. He rarely cried or complained, never spoke a word until he was well past two, at which point the women stopped telling Esther that he was good, and started telling each other that he was simple. Nevertheless, as solitary heir to the Ogden homestead, Silence's agricultural education began as soon as he was old enough to keep up with the plough, though long before he could tell his father that he had no interest in it whatsoever.

"This one will be tobacco," his father shouted over the suck-and-drag of the horse's hooves in the mud, nodding at the field prostrate beneath the pendulous springtime sky. Silence looked obediently at the stretch of grizzled earth, with its cover of scraggly weeds. "The two on the right and left, and that big one by the road, they'll be corn."

Silence stopped and watched the furrows unraveling behind the ploughshares, thinking of the troughs between the waves in his dreams. He was three; he'd never spoken a complete sentence in his life, but he already knew without a doubt that the deep and fundamental Something which awakened hope and excitement in his father at the sight of the somnolent fields was missing in him.

Esther Ogden knew it too, in the unassuming way that mothers know things. She never said it outright, but sometimes her questions were less than innocent. Once Silence started school and his aptitude for it became apparent, the questions also became more frequent. For instance, "Do you like going to work with your Papa?" Which he couldn't bear to answer. Or, "You don't have to go, you know." Which he didn't believe for a moment. Or, "You don't have to like it." Which he knew, unfortunately, to be the truth.

But it wasn't until Silence came home on the final afternoon of his first year at school with the prize for the best boy – a brand new book of poetry rather than the usual dictionary – that Esther got to the point. She'd been standing at the kitchen table when he came in, her hands moving rhythmically in a lump of bread dough. But when she saw the book she hugged her son and then sat down, clutching his shoulders with sticky hands, leaving the half-kneaded dough to settle across the floured board. Her eyes had a furtive, defiant look, which both excited and frightened Silence.

"Did I ever tell you," she began, her voice low and intent, "that I won all of my school prizes, too? I even beat the boys."

Silence shook his head, shocked more by the thought that his mother had ever been a schoolgirl, than that she had been a keen one.

"Those books in the attic? Most of them are mine. I went right through high school and took a diploma. Our teacher held special sessions at the end of the day, just for me, and when I finished she got me an application for a college up north. I meant to learn to be a school teacher myself…"

"You were a teacher?" Silence asked, further stunned.

Esther's face changed then. It wasn't quite bitter, but the light suddenly went out of it. "No," she said. "I got the place, but…well, it was complicated. In the end, I married your father instead. And Silence, I've never regretted that for a moment, but still…" She trailed off, looking at the grey sky through the window.

"Do you want to be a farmer?" she asked, turning back to him abruptly.

Silence thought of his father's face, joyous at the plough. He thought of his mother's thwarted desire. He thought of Jenny Lindquist's bright blue eyes, and of the road at the bottom of the mountain that he had never traveled.

"I don't know," he said at last, wary of whom he might betray with the truth. But the water inside of him wouldn't be still. It swirled in protest, and his mother cocked her head, listening. He held his stomach in his arms, pleading with it to be quiet.

Esther studied him and then nodded once, almost imperceptibly. Her face was still troubled when she went for a cookie from the stoneware jar. But when she handed it to Silence, she was smiling again: a mother's smile, encompassing fervid hope and infinite forgiveness.

"Whatever it is you choose, Silence, I will love you," she said, and he believed her. But he also knew that love didn't preclude disappointment.

4

Silence's parents argued that night, though they waited until he ought to have been asleep, and they did it in whispers. The next morning at breakfast, Silence's father stunned him with the announcement that as of the next school year, he, Silence, would be excused from farm chores three afternoons a week, so that he might devote more time to studying.

Silence wasn't averse to the idea of spending less time in the fields, but his ambivalence about extra studying was compounded by guilt at being the source of his parents' strife.

"I got plenty of time to study as it is," he objected.

"You surely don't, if you're still saying 'I got,'" his mother said crisply, putting his plate in front of him.

Silence looked from his mother to his father, as starkly as they avoided looking at each other. Then he looked at his grandfather, but John Jr. was lost in a copy of the *Farmer's Almanac*.

At last, John III broke the silence. "Your mother says that you're mighty clever, and if you wanted to, you could probably go to Trinity. Get yourself a degree. You could learn to be a doctor, or a lawyer..." He trailed off, not so much lacking enthusiasm as the belief that anyone he knew might become one of these things, never mind his own son.

Silence was equally stunned by the suggestion. He knew nothing about justice or medicine, except that there was no apparent adventure connected with either one. In fact both, thanks to Dickens, suggested days shut up in grim, windowless rooms, hunched over desks burgeoning with closely printed documents, tuberculine corpses, or both. But Silence saw the glint of hope in his mother's eye, and he couldn't bear to dash it any more than he could the one in his father's, whenever he rhapsodized over a harrowed field. He opened his mouth to speak, with no idea what words would come out of it.

However, John Jr. had not been as lost in the *Farmer's Almanac* as he'd appeared, and now he came to Silence's rescue. "These plans are all mighty fine," he said, "but has anyone bothered to ask the boy what *he* wants to do?"

Silence's parents looked at each other, startled, and then at him.

"I...I don't really know," Silence said, though the shifting sea in his gut was telling him otherwise.

John Jr. laughed ruefully as he went back to his griddle cakes, "Well, boy," he said, "you better make up that gold-plated mind of yours, before someone else makes it up for you."

*

Silence spent the rest of that day and most of the following night considering his grandfather's words. John Jr. opinined frequently, but he seldom mandated, and when he mandated, he was always right. The problem was, Silence had no idea how to choose a direction for his life, because the only direction it had ever had – namely, seaward – was as senseless as it was tenacious.

Then, quite suddenly, it came to him: the way to choose the right path must begin with eradicating the wrong one. He would seek the source of his watery subconscious obsession. He would find it, and he would subdue it, and then he would know what it was he was really meant to do. Thus resolved, Silence turned over and went to sleep.

The next morning after breakfast, he walked to the river. It seemed as good a place as any to begin, given that somewhere, somehow, it must lead to the sea. A few years back he'd discovered a cave in the riverbank: a hole left where a tree had uprooted in a winter storm. It was just big enough for Silence, a few journals and a fishing rod. Outside the cave, the bank plateaued briefly before its steep drop to the riverbed.

Now he sat on this narrow shelf, watching the water flow over the stones and trying to direct his thoughts backward. Recollection followed a clear progression so far, and then, abruptly, there was nothing. Or next to nothing: his very last clear memory regarding his watery affliction – or his first, depending how he counted – was of the morning his grandfather had called him crazy, and Annie Newcombe had come to his defense. But neither offered an explanation for the plight itself.

There Silence's anchor caught, and there it might have stayed, if he hadn't heard a rustling then on the far side of the river. He looked up and saw Annie looking back. She looked at him long and hard for a moment before she hitched her berry-bucket up her arm, nodded to him, and turned away. But there'd been something in that look that made Silence wonder if the answer hadn't likewise been staring him in the face all along.

5

However, what seemed simple and clear that morning by the river became muddied and complex as soon as he turned toward home. Never mind how he would phrase his questions to Annie; he had no idea how he might be in a position to ask them in the first place. One didn't just go and demand answers from Annie Newcombe. In fact, as far as Silence was aware, nobody ever asked Annie for anything. It wasn't that she was unfriendly, though she was undeniably circumspect. Rather, she was solitary; so utterly solitary that her isolation was sacrosanct. As far as Silence knew it had not become, but had always been that way.

Annie had been a fixture in Heaven for as long as Silence could remember. He'd known for just as long that she came from somewhere else. Of course, everyone in Heaven had come from somewhere else not too long since, but Annie had an air about her of being once-again removed, as definite as it was difficult to pick apart. For one thing, she looked nothing like the other village women. They uniformly bore out the coloring of their Scots-Irish, Scandinavian or German ancestors. Even Esther Ogden, the town's only brunette, had ivory skin that burned in a half-hour's sunshine. But Annie's long plait was jet-black where it wasn't white, her eyes startlingly blue in a face the smooth, hard, secret brown of a pecan shell.

"That woman's a quadroon," Silence's grandfather whispered to him once as Annie negotiated with Esther for produce, "mark my words."

He marked them himself with a conspiratorial wink and chuckle, which made little sense to Silence even after he'd looked up "quadroon" in the attic's putrefying, bug-riddled dictionary. Appalachia, even their southern corner of it, was a long way from New Orleans; Silence was a postwar baby, and Heaven, despite its Confederate flag, was too far from anywhere ever to have bothered much with any racial politics but its own. Heaven's racial politics were simple: as long as a man pulled his weight and didn't bother anyone, no one cared what fraction of Negro blood might run in his veins.

True, Annie was no man, but she pulled her weight at least as well as any in town, and she had never asked anything of anybody in all the years she'd lived in Heaven. She'd even built her house herself, politely refusing the help of the men who stayed to watch, dumbfounded, as she felled the trees and split the logs and hauled the river stones for the hearth. When at the end of a week she'd hammered the final tack into the tin roof, two bachelor farmers had proposed on the spot. She'd refused them both as politely and firmly as she'd refused their building help.

Though it made talk, it also made sense to those whose heads had not been turned by Annie's peculiar beauty and formidable strength. She was clearly capable of looking after herself, but more clearly even than that, she'd chosen Heaven. Likewise, she'd chosen to build a house exactly big enough for one. Annie wasn't looking for charity, said the sensible ones, and she certainly wasn't looking for a husband.

Within a few months, she'd proved them right, planting a garden and chopping a winter's worth of wood. The rest of the time, she made quilts. Most women in Heaven made quilts, but they were nothing like Annie's intricate, pictorial tapestries, built of minute snips of cloth, with stitching so tiny it was almost indiscernible. Some showed mountains and lakes and rivers populated with fantastical creatures. Others portrayed farms or towns or fairytale cities. More than once, she replicated the giant oak tree that stood in the center of Heaven, beside the church. She did it in summer greens, and again in brilliant flaming autumn reds and golds and browns. Once she sewed it bare for winter, in the deepest blues, with watered-silk snow on its branches and the ground beneath.

Silence, who had come with his mother to deliver a packet of needles Annie needed to finish it, thought it was the most beautiful thing he had ever seen. But it also unnerved him, and Annie's sharp eyes saw it.

"You don't like my work, then, young Ogden?"

Her face was serious, even stern. But there was a slight twist to her tone as she spoke; something that gave the words more meaning than they appeared to have. Silence was too young to recognize irony, but old enough to realize that she intended him to answer truthfully.

"It's as good as a painting," he said. "It looks just like the tree after a snowstorm…"

"But?" asked Annie, pinning him with her brilliant eyes.

Silence knew that his mother wanted him to be quiet. She was clenching his hand hard enough to stop the blood. But he also knew that Annie required an answer.

"Well, it's *not* a painting, is it?" he answered at last. "It's a blanket. And I only wondered who would buy it, because I don't know who could sleep under such a cold quilt."

Esther was looking daggers at him, and beneath Annie's circumspect gaze, Silence wished he'd kept his mouth shut. Then, to both of their surprise, Annie laughed. She threaded one of her new needles with fine silver thread and went back to work, saying, "Well, you needn't worry on that count, young Ogden."

She liked to address him by his surname, and she always did it with that same twist in her voice. "It's sold already. It was a commission. It's to be a wedding gift, from a mother to her new daughter-in-law." And she laughed again, with inexplicable delight.

Silence could tell that Annie's words and her laughter had shocked his mother, though it would be a long time before he understood why. But he did understand why Annie sobered when she saw Esther's confusion, why there was no twist in her words when she thanked her for the needles, and why Esther's answering smile was warmly sincere. Even a chosen seclusion has its limits, and the only person in Heaven whom Annie had come anywhere near forming a relationship with was his mother.

Esther in turn, for all her prim respectability, seemed to take pride in having been so chosen. Whether or not this unspoken understanding between the two women went far enough to be labeled friendship, it included certain imperatives. One of these was that Annie would buy her eggs and butter from no one but Esther Ogden, despite the three miles of farms in between her house and Esther's that would happily have supplied her. Her Saturday afternoon visits were as punctual as the school bell and so, on the Saturday after his epiphany at the river, Silence was waiting for her.

He had no intention of actually speaking to her. Or he thought he didn't; but he would have had little to say to anyone who asked what he intended by hiding in the rhododendron by the porch as Annie conducted her business with his mother. He had never hidden from her before. Then again, he'd never wanted anything from her before.

Five minutes into his covert non-operation, he realized how ridiculous it was to be hiding in a rhododendron bush from a woman he'd known all his life, but there seemed no way out of the predicament without losing face. He waited, desolate, for the sound of Annie's hobnail boots on the old stone steps. But when at last he heard them, they weren't on the steps. They clacked purposefully down the old creaking boards of the porch until they reached the rhododendron, and then they stopped, six inches from Silence's face.

"Well, Silence Ogden," Annie said, parting the glossy leaves to look down at him, "are you going to come out of there and tell me what's on your mind, or should I go on home?"

Cobwebbed and dusty, Silence backed out from under the bush. He looked up at Annie, who looked down at him with eyes glittering brilliant in her smooth, inscrutable face. Her look was stern enough that Silence might have made his excuses and run, if he hadn't looked closer and seen that rare quirk of a smile on her lips. It looked, he thought, like the twist in her voice when she called him "young Ogden". This gave him courage.

"I wanted to know," he said, "how you knew."

"Knew what?" she asked in a way that told him she didn't need an explanation, only wanted to make him say it.

He drew a breath. "You were the one who told them that it was the sea I was dreaming of. That day when I was little, you said I was dreaming of sailing on the sea."

She waited.

"I want to know why."

"Why and how are two different questions," she said.

Silence sighed. Clearly, she wasn't going to take pity on him. "All right. *How* did you know?"

She snorted a chuckle. "The real question is, how did the others *not* know? Meaning no offense to your family, of course – but there wasn't much else you could have been talking about."

Which, Silence thought, *doesn't really explain anything.* "Why, then?" he asked.

"You mean, why are you dreaming of the sea?"

Silence nodded. She turned from him, frowning as she looked out over the fields and shook her head. "That's anybody's guess."

Silence sighed again. "Do you think I'm crazy?"

"Do *you* think you're crazy?"

"I must be," he said dejectedly, "to spend all my time dreaming of something impossible."

To Silence's surprise, Annie laughed. "Oh, you're in good company there, Silence Ogden. Everyone dreams the impossible. You just happen to be honest about it."

"It doesn't help," he said bitterly.

"With what?"

"With choosing whether to be a farmer or a lawyer."

Annie scrutinized him. "Those are your choices, are they?" she asked. There was no twist in her voice now, and she spoke softly, as if she realized he wouldn't want this conversation overheard. Silence nodded, and Annie sighed, her shoulders slumping. He had the feeling that she was suppressing other words when she said, "Why on earth do you think I can help you with that?"

Silence looked at his feet, kicked miserably at the dirt. "Because I can't choose," he answered, "until I get the sea out of me. But how can I do that when I don't know why it's in me in the first place? I mean, I don't even know anyone who's seen it, or a sailboat, or even any kind of boat bigger than a canoe, unless…"

Finally, he looked at her. She looked back: an unblinking dare.

"Unless *you've* seen it," he said, as steadily as he could. "But even if you haven't," he added before she had a chance to deny it, "you must know something about it – about those sailing ships I dream of – or else how would you have known what I was talking about that day? So if you know something about it, and you tell me, then I can figure out why it's in me, and get it out."

Annie shook her head and muttered, "Lawyer."

"Excuse me?"

"Never mind." She studied him a moment longer and then, with a nod as minute as her smiles, she said, "I was being flippant a moment ago. The truth is, I can't tell you how I knew you were dreaming of sailing. Dreams just make sense to me… like building, or sewing. But for what it's worth, I don't think you're going to get very far trying to exorcise your sea demons, so to speak."

"Why?"

She sighed. "We are what we are, Silence Ogden," she said. "And believe me, we none of us can escape ourselves."

He was about to turn away in disappointment when she said, "Still...it so happens I do know a story about the sea. It's a story about choices, too. I don't know whether it will mean much to you – "

"Yes!" Silence cried, his heart suddenly pounding. "Oh, yes, it will!"

"Very well, then," she said. "Walk home with me, and we'll see how far that gets us."

Annie was down the steps in two strides, and Silence had to run to catch her up.

6

"Way up north on an island in the sea," Annie began without preamble, "where the summers are short and the winters kill strong men with no apology, there's a place called Juniper Barrens. It hasn't always been called that, and it hasn't always been barren. Once it was a forest of trees a hundred feet high, and home to people who respected them. But then other people came who had no respect, and they cut the trees down to build a town, and masts for your beloved sailing ships, and who knows what else. With the trees gone, the wind blew too mean for anything but nettles and Chickweed and a few stunted junipers ever to grow there again. No good for farming. No good for anything. So they called it Juniper Barrens, and no one bothered with it for a hundred years and more. Not until Sweet Angelina moved in."

"Sweet Angelina?" Silence interrupted. "What kind of a name is that?"

"The same kind of a name as Silence," Annie shot back, which shut Silence up. "In fact," she elaborated, "Sweet Angelina Loring was a woman named after a boat. Well, a half a boat, to be precise. She was the bastard daughter of an Indian woman called Mary Loring, and a drunken Irish shipwright called Josias Flynn. Flynn had been working on a fishing boat called 'Sweet Angelina' for as long as anyone could remember. If he looked near finishing, he'd take a sledgehammer to it."

"What?" Silence cried. "Why?"

"I guess," said Annie, "it made him look like a tragic perfectionist. In fact, Flynn was just a lazy ass."

Silence blinked at the epithet, delighted and shocked. He'd seldom heard anybody swear, and never a woman.

"He had no money," Annie continued, apparently oblivious to his reaction, "but he had soulful eyes: the kind that make some women want to mother a man. He lived off of the idiocy of those women." Her tone left no doubt as to her opinion of this talent, or those who fell prey to it.

"He'd had a lot of them in his time, but he liked the Indian girls the best. Said they didn't complain as much as white ones. And the Indian girls – well, some of them – liked white men better than their own kind. Said they were more fun. That was how Mary and Flynn ended up together, though she was a malcontent, and he had no money for fun.

"Still, he said he'd marry her when he found out she was expecting, and maybe he'd have actually done it, if he hadn't killed himself first. He fell off the 'Sweet Angelina' on a drunk the day before his daughter was born. Broke his neck. Mary went crazy with grief and died not long after – though not before she saddled her child with that unlucky name. And the child, being a half-breed no one wanted, grew up in the Female Orphan Asylum on the mainland." Silence, recalling Dickens, shivered at the words "Female Orphan Asylum".

Annie walked on for a few moments, her eyes on the violet evening sky, before she continued. "By the time Sweet Angelina came of age, there wasn't much sweet about her, and even less angelic. She was lonely and miserable and furious with the world that didn't want her. Not knowing what to do with herself, she went back to the island where she'd been born. She built herself a little driftwood lean-to on the one piece of land on the island that no one wanted."

"Juniper Barrens?"

The twitch of a smile surfaced again. "You're a whip, Silence Ogden."

"But I thought there was nothing there?"

"There wasn't," said Annie ruminatively, picking a sassafras leaf and chewing on it. "And that's why it suited Sweet Angelina. She could live up there and never have to meet another soul, if she didn't want to. And for a while that's how it was. It's how it might have stayed, too, if it hadn't been for Ian MacFarlane.

"He was a Scotsman, born in the Glasgow shipyards. He'd barely set foot on land since he took up with the Merchant Navy at sixteen. By the time he saw Juniper Barrens, he was nearing forty. He was tired of wandering, but the sea was too much in his blood to leave it behind. He spotted the Barrens from the deck of his ship one morning as they were coming into Goose River, and he knew it was as close as he would come to a sea life on solid ground. He bought it that very day."

"But Sweet Angelina…?"

Annie shook her head. "Ian didn't know anything about Sweet Angelina, and I guess no one thought to tell him. Or maybe the land owners didn't know she was there either."

"But she'd been living there for – well, for some time, hadn't she?"

"Yes," said Annie. "But she was a half-breed, and that's even less worthy of notice than just plain Indian." She paused for a moment, spat out the hard parts of the leaf and continued, "So when Ian went up to the Barrens the next day with a canvas tent and a load of lumber, the last thing he was expecting to find was a house. He knocked on the door, but no one answered. He went inside. There were embers in the stove, but no one was home.

"He was half way down the hill to the cove when he saw her. She was picking mussels on the rocks below, wearing a red dress tied up around her knees, a man's oilskin, and nothing at all on her legs and feet, though it was only March.

"'Ahoy!' he called down to her. She looked up, scowled and yelled, 'Go to hell!'

"Being a sailor, Ian had been sworn at by his fair share of women, but never one who looked like Sweet Angelina. In that instant he was smitten. He couldn't do anything but stand on top of that hill staring at Sweet Angelina like an idiot, which only made her madder.

"'Stop looking like that,' she told him.

"'But I'm looking at you,' he said.

"The truth was, Sweet Angelina was looking at him, too. He was a nice-looking man, even if he had a strange accent and was past the flush of youth. But then he said, 'Why don't you come on up here so we can speak proper, like?' and Sweet Angelina knew enough about what went on between white men and dark girls to guess the meaning of 'talk'.

"But Ian was a foreigner, and he'd meant just what he said, which is why he pushed it: 'Would you rather I came down, then?'

"Sweet Angelina said, 'I guess you'll do what you like. Though if I'm lucky, you'll break your neck first.' Ian only laughed and said, 'Very well. I'll leave you to it.' And he turned around to go.

"Well, that made no sense at all to Sweet Angelina, so she did something that made even less. She called, 'WAIT!' and ran up the hill. When she got to the top, she could see that Ian was older even than she'd thought, but he didn't look at her like other white men looked at her, and so she said, 'What are you doing here?' and he shrugged and said, 'I live here,' and she said, 'No you don't. I live here.' And Ian said, 'Aye, then. We'll be neighbors.' And Sweet Angelina said, 'I don't want neighbors.' And Ian said, 'I'm very sorry tae hear it, but there's nae much I can do about it the now. I spent the last of my pay on this place.' And then he took out the deed with its map of the Barrens and showed it to her.

"Sweet Angelina took it pretty well, all things considered. She read the whole thing through before she slapped him, and then she sat down on a rock and burst into tears. And Ian took *that* better than well. He folded the deed back into his pocket and said, 'I never meant tae offend you, ma'am. There mustae been some mistake. I'll go tae town the noo and return your property.'

"But Sweet Angelina just shook her head and said, 'Don't bother. Someone else will buy it sooner or later. Give me a day, and I'll be gone.'

"'Och,' said Ian, 'surely that isnae necessary?' But Sweet Angelina said, 'Yes, I believe it is. The Barrens is yours, and I won't live here on charity.'

"Ian looked long and hard at her. He was probably measuring up the probability of her slapping him again, or further hysterics.

But Ian had never been a coward, and so he said, 'Ma'am, I believe I have a proposition. Only first, will you tell me your name?'

"Sweet Angelina couldn't see any reason not to, so she told him. 'Well, then,' said Ian, getting down on one knee. 'Miss Sweet Angelina Loring, will you marry me?'

"As you can imagine, that was the last thing Sweet Angelina had thought to hear. But she was calm enough when she said, 'Why on earth would I do that?' Ian said, 'Because then it willnae be charity.' And Sweet Angelina said, 'Suppose I want to marry someone else?' and Ian said, '*Is* there someone else?' Sweet Angelina didn't know what to say to that, because of course there wasn't, and chances were there never would be. She started to cry again.

"Ian was horrified. 'Miss...ma'am...there's nae call for greetin'!' he said. 'It would be in name only – just so we'd be on equal footing, ken. You can keep your house, and I'll build mine, and we'll live as we please, and the world be damned!' And Sweet Angelina said, 'You mean that? Really?' and Ian said, 'I'm a man o' my word.' And Sweet Angelina wiped her face, put her arms around his neck and kissed him."

"Why?" asked Silence, for whom these strange characters' motivations were proving more than difficult to follow.

Annie shrugged. "It's a foolish woman who'll turn down a good man when she's lucky enough to find one, and whatever else she was, Sweet Angelina was no fool."

"Oh," he said, though this hadn't really clarified anything.

"They were married two weeks later by a Justice of the Peace on the mainland, since the island had no such person, and Sweet Angelina refused to set foot in a church. Ian had bought her a gown of pale blue sateen, and no one who saw her on her wedding day could bring themselves to utter the nasty words they'd been thinking since she took up with Ian MacFarlane.

"After the wedding, Ian brought his bride to the cabin he'd made of her lean-to in the intervening fortnight, while she'd slept in the tent and he under the stars and rain and fog. The house had only expanded by the space of one room, but it had a fresh coat of green paint, a tight cedar-shake roof, and a second stovepipe. To a girl who'd resigned herself to living off of other people's leavings, it was heaven."

"That's what my great-grandmother said when she first came here," offered Silence. "That's where the town got its name."

"Is it, then?" asked Annie, seeming honestly interested. "Well, you see, it takes a woman to see the value of something."

Which seemed to Silence yet another an odd thing for her to say, since it was John Ogden I who had first chosen their hollow to settle, just as Ian had chosen Juniper Barrens. But he kept his mouth shut, and hoped he hadn't distracted her from her story.

"So," she said slowly, as Silence held his breath to see where it would lead, "they set up housekeeping, Ian and Sweet Angelina. But their marriage nearly ended on its very first night, when he told her what he planned to do for a living. Sweet Angelina had been carving their wedding roast when he told her. 'Please,' she said, pointing the carving knife at Ian, 'say that I heard you wrong.' And Ian repeated in a tiny little voice, 'You didnae hear wrong. I intend tae build boats.'

"Sweet Angelina flew into a rage the like of which Ian had never seen, that ended with her driving the knife into the table two inches from his right hand. She drove it in so hard she couldn't get it back out again, which was probably lucky for Ian. When he was sure that she wasn't going to kill him, he asked her to explain her objection to boats. And Sweet Angelina, realizing at last that Ian probably hadn't been on the island long enough to hear the stories, explained about her father. And then Ian explained that he meant to finish his boats. Which got Sweet Angelina bothered all over again.

"She said, 'Do you mean to tell me that you've never *actually* finished one?' And he said, 'Well, that would be difficult, seeing as how I've never even started one. Not on my own. But my father was a shipwright. I grew up helping in the yards.' And she said, cold as a winter sea, 'How long ago was that?' And he said, 'Ach…round about the fifties, it would hae been.' And she said, 'I see. So these yards you grew up helping in, they'll have been building – what – clippers?' And he said, 'That's right,' pleased that he had secured a wife who knew her ships.

"But Sweet Angelina was not pleased at all. 'I think you will have noticed,' she said, 'that clippers are not much in demand these days.' Ian smiled, thinking that he'd got to the heart of the problem. 'Dinnae worry about that,' he said. 'I dinnae mean to build clippers. I mean to build pleasure boats. Yachts, I believe they're calling them. They're all the rage with the rich folks that holiday at the shore.' And Sweet Angelina said, 'There are no rich folks on this shore.' And Ian said, 'Nae matter. Once they see my boats, they'll come.'

"'So you'll build on speculation?' she asked him. And Ian said, 'Aye - tae begin with,' glad that they had reached an understanding. But he realized soon enough that her understanding wasn't the same as his, because she started to pack. So he said, 'Very well, here's a bargain for you: I'll start building a boat tomorrow. If it isnae sold in six months' time, then I'll make over the deed tae the Barrens tae you, and leave you in peace.' Sweet Angelina stopped packing and looked at him, knowing with her new wife's intuition that the catch was yet to come. 'But if it *is* sold,' he went on, 'then the next boat I build will be yours, and you have tae learn tae sail it.'

"'I don't sail,' she said, each word dropping like a pebble off a pier. And Ian said, 'Nae – not yet.' And he smiled."

Annie smiled too. Silence had to prod her to continue: "Then what happened?"

"Well, Sweet Angelina considered being angry at his arrogance, but she was a wise woman for nineteen. She knew enough about men to believe that even if she lost the bet, she'd never have to set foot in a boat if she didn't want to. Of course she didn't say so, but she couldn't help adding a smug smile as she shook on the deal over the knife stuck in the table."

Annie laughed quietly, with little humor. "The only possibility she didn't consider came along nine months later. By then, though, she was the owner of a mahogany gaff-rigged dinghy, and a passion for sailing even she would never subjugate."

Mahogany gaff-rigged dinghy, Silence repeated to himself. The words were as meaningless and magical as a spell. "Then what?" Silence demanded. "Did her baby dream of the sea? Did Ian get rich from his boats?"

Annie stopped walking and looked at him in surprise, as if she'd forgotten he was there. They were standing at the head of the path to her house, and it was nearly dark. "I don't know," she said.

"You don't know?" he cried. "But it's your story!"

"No," she said. "A story is always its own. Hurry home now, Silence Ogden. Your mama will be worrying."

Without so much as a good-bye, Annie hiked up her basket of eggs and butter and walked off into the thickening twilight.

7

A less trusting child might have wondered how Annie came to speak in such detail about a place and people so far away. A more perceptive one might have picked up on the odd nuances of her expression when she told her tale. But Silence had never had cause to take the world at anything other than face value, and so he was twelve before he realized that Annie's story about Juniper Barrens might have been more than a story.

Even then the discovery came out of the blue. Or, more accurately, the gray: the thick, mossy gray of a rainy summer mountain afternoon. Silence was in the attic's sleeping loft, lying on John I's ancient, rough-hewn bedstead, peeling newspaper from the walls as he waited for an end either to the rain or the afternoon. Which makes little sense, without understanding the Ogden attic.

In fact it wasn't an attic at all, but John I's original cabin. Each successive generation had added to it, the building gradually telescoping outward into a long, rambling farmhouse. In the process, the cabin became a sink for four generations' worth of family detritus of the type that people generally store in attics, and thereby earned its name. By the time Silence was peeling newspaper from its walls, it was a madman's archive of broken furniture and china and glassware. A fretful, stuffed buzzard perched on a worm-riddled highboy, flanked by a case of mounted butterflies slowly crumbling to dust. A grotesque, carved wooden head, allegedly a piece of an ancient totem pole, occupied one corner. In another, a box of decrepit guns and knives lay rusting, among them a saber that, according to family legend, had seen service in the War of Independence.

There were also towering piles of paper: old agricultural journals and *Farmer's Almanacs* and *Godey's Lady's Books*, campaign posters fifty years out of date, war propaganda and advertising handbills and every other conceivable type of outdated paper media. These had at times been raided as insulation for the walls, pasted on in layers to keep out the weather that came in between the ill-fitting boards. Now this makeshift wallpaper was slowly falling away as the wheat paste disintegrated, leaving thousands of mangy ribbons fluttering in the wind they were meant to block. Irresistible fodder for a bored little boy; rich ground for an epiphany. And so, beneath five layers of frail yellowed newsprint, Silence found one.

It was the front page of a Glasgow broadsheet, dominated by an engraving of a two-masted ship under full sail. "America Rules the Waves!" its headline declared. The story continued underneath: "Britain is reeling from the defeat of fourteen of her best vessels by the upstart New York-built schooner 'America' in a race around the Isle of Wight. 'America', not content with victory alone, crossed the finish line an hour before the rest of the fleet, putting paid to the rumored inferiority of Yankee ship builders. Docking amidst universal shock, the captain of the second place boat declared…"

But Silence didn't finish the article, because in the meantime something else had caught his eye. Down at the bottom corner of the page was a tiny advertisement: "Do You Dream of the Open Seas? Follow in the footsteps of the World's Greatest Sailors in your very own 'America', scaled down and modified for pleasure sailing. Full blueprints and sail plans available." At the bottom were a name and address for one Ian MacFarlane, care of Hill's Shipyard, Port Glasgow, Scotland.

For a moment, the attic tipped and whirled. When he'd steadied himself at last, Silence carefully peeled the paper off the wall and read the advertisement again. Then he sat staring out at the rain through the loft's single window, his initial excitement slowly ebbing. After all, it might not mean anything. Perhaps Annie had seen that newspaper too, and it had inspired her story.

Yet how could she have, when it had been covered by a corset pattern and an advertisement for Dr. Bentley's Miracle Powders until that very afternoon? A duplicate was stretching credibility too far; strange enough to have one foreign newspaper in a place like Heaven. Which meant that Annie must have learned about Ian MacFarlane some other way.

Well, and so what if she had? Silence asked himself. Even if this Ian MacFarlane happened to be Annie's Ian MacFarlane – even if all she had told him about Juniper Barrens was true – in the end, it changed nothing. He was still Silence Ogden, farmer's son, future lawyer. He told himself so firmly three times, knowing it was the truth.

And yet, that truth didn't quite drown out the little, insistent voice in the background, which was telling him another one: that it was possible to buy a set of plans and build a sailboat all by oneself. He held the proof of it in his hands. And if one happened to be twelve years old? Well, Annie had single-handedly built a cabin and a life for herself in a place wary of strangers and self-sufficient women. If she could do that, then surely a boy could build a boat.

Maybe, said the future lawyer. But this advertisement is decades old. Even if one managed to track down Ian MacFarlane, Annie's version or otherwise, it was unlikely that he would have any of those boat plans left. And if by some mad fluctuation of fate one happened to procure such a set of plans (never mind the wood and canvas necessary to realize them), if one managed to shape them into something that would float and harness wind… well, one was still three hundred miles from the nearest coast. And so would one's boat be. Impossible, the future lawyer told himself, and bent to drop the paper on the pile of peelings.

But Silence's hand wouldn't open. It shook, but remained resolutely shut. *Why?* he demanded silently of his clenched hand. Why torture himself when his course was clearly plotted on the chart of his life? His father had finally, if reluctantly, embraced the idea of his son as a university man. The schoolmaster, Mr. Marsh – fresh out of Trinity himself – promised the Ogdens that Silence would have no trouble winning a place at his *alma mater*. Once there, it was only a matter of studying hard. The bench loomed before Silence, almost as solid as the bed beneath him. There was no room in that plan for sailing ships.

Yet lawyers must not spend *all* of their time at desks with stacks of paper. Farmers rested; lawyers must too. And surely there was a call for lawyers in coastal towns? Maybe, just maybe, Silence thought, his own dream and his parents' weren't entirely at odds after all.

He laid the newspaper on the ticking mattress in front of him, and smoothed it carefully. In that moment, beneath his tender hands, his old dream ceased to be a dream. It took on shape and solidity, morphed from a possibility to a living entity. Yet he'd learned his lesson. He would keep it close, until he had worked out just how to make it happen. But it *would* happen, and then everyone would be happy.

With a feeling of profound relief, Silence folded the page carefully, stuck it in his trouser pocket, and went to study his Latin grammar.

8

When he was still alive, John Isaiah Nathaniel Ogden I had been fond of telling people that he was not the oldest resident of Heaven. That honor, he said, went to the oak tree that stood at the center of the hollow. It had been this tree that had caused him to stop there in the first place. He'd been caught in a fearsome rainstorm one afternoon on his quest for his fortune, and run under the tree for shelter. Sitting out the storm, he had a good long time to look around him and enumerate the valley's virtues. When it was over, he decided to stay. "And so," he used to conclude, when he told this story, "that tree is at least as much to thank for the existence of our fine town as I am, and it deserves far more respect."

His first thought was to build his homestead beside the tree by way of honoring it, but the ground there was too rocky for farming. Instead he chose a lush swath of bottomland adjoining a wide, shallow river in the south of the valley, and staked his claim to it with the cabin that would one day become the attic. Yet John I was a religious man, and he fully believed that the storm and the tree and the ensuing epiphany had been God's work, and the tree deserved some kind of recognition. So he built a cross and hammered it into the ground where, later, he and his neighbors would raise their church. Then he built a bench and set it up against the tree trunk, so that he could contemplate God's mysteries while in direct communion with one of His holy vehicles.

Even after the crude wooden cross had given way to the white clapboard church, the tree remained the true center of Heaven's little world. There was a churchlike solace about sitting on the bench beneath it. The wind in its branches whispered truths; its deep-running sap pulled like a tide. Branches soared, beamlike, holding up the sky, and sunlight filtered through leaves like colored glass. With one's back up against four hundred years' worth of living wood, the tree's mute, ponderous wisdom was palpable. Countless hearts had been given on that bench and, no doubt, more than one of Heaven's citizens conceived. It's hardly surprising, then, that that's where Fate scheduled her next appointment with Silence.

9

It was October, and he was on his way home from school. He walked ponderously, his satchel heavy with the books Mr. Marsh had piled into it, his head with the thought of all of the new lessons they entailed. The only bright spot on his present horizon was the awed admiration with which Jenny Lindquist had stared at him as he conjugated Latin verbs for the teacher while the others worked out of their primers. That, and the pink candy heart she had pressed secretly into his hand as they filed back into school after their dinner break, printed with the sugary mandate "Be Mine".

Silence intended to keep this token forever, or at least until Jenny was the lawful wife of Heaven's first lawyer. He turned it in his pocket as he passed between the store and the church of fickle denomination, his own heart rising and sinking by turns as he considered, alternately, Jenny's bright blue eyes and the mountain of books that stood between him and possession of them. And then something came at him from beneath the shedding branches of his great-grandfather's oak, knocking the dreary rumination flat. It was a sound: music, he realized after a few stunned moments, but unlike any music he'd ever heard. It sounded like a cross between a fiddle and a banjo, its low, wrenching melody full of slides and half-cadences.

The sun was behind the church and the tree, so Silence could make out no more than a dark figure on the bench, with shoulders rounded down over something on its lap. He wasn't aware of how long he stood there. He only recalled himself when the sun was swallowed abruptly by quick autumn cloud, pitching the world into gloomy chill. Then he found himself staring the musician in the eye, across an equally abrupt silence.

The man raised a beckoning hand. Silence looked behind him, certain that the gesture was meant for someone else, but he was alone on the road, aside from a handful of skittering leaves. When he turned back, the man was still beckoning. Silence took a few steps toward him and then stopped again as the man's face came into focus. He was a Negro man, the first Silence had ever seen, and this made him uneasy. He considered excusing himself, walking away again. The pull of the music, though, was stronger than his fear. Drawing a deep breath, he stepped forward.

The man was old, lean-framed and gangling, his mahogany skin sagging off of him like limp, wet leather. His clothes were ragged, his boot soles worn down almost to nothing. In the lines and creases of his face was a sadness as old as time; in his eyes, the circumspect patience of a good horse. On his lap lay a dark blue guitar at least as battered as he was. He held a knife in his left hand, while his right rested on the guitar strings.

"No use standing away over there," he said, "if you mean to speak to me. My ears ain't what they were." He spoke with a strange accent, not the German or Irish inflections that prevailed in the hollows, though Silence thought he heard faint traces of Scots and French. For all he knew, though, this was the way that all Negroes spoke.

"Was it the guitar, making that music?" Silence asked.

"Yep."

"I never heard a guitar sound like that before."

The old man smiled, but still he looked immeasurably sad. "I don't suppose you have. Not many folks have. But that's all about to change."

With no idea what this meant, Silence wasn't sure how to respond. Instead, he said, "So – how do you do it?"

The man raised his eyebrows and looked down at his instrument. He turned the knife so that the flat of the blade lay on the strings. And then, with the blue guitar still prostrate, he began to play. Once again, Silence found himself ensnared by the weird, whining music. This time, the man sang along:

"Be easy, now; don't you fade away,

Be easy, now; don't you fade away.

I'm goin' back where that Southern cross the Dog

An' this time I'm gonna stay…"

The old man sang on through verses hinting at wandering and grief, while the music told them plain. At the end of each one, he repeated the phrase about the southern crossing the dog. Silence had no idea what it meant, but it struck at something deep inside of him, a near-memory, as if the meaning were something that he'd been told once as a child, or dreamed and then forgotten.

He stood transfixed until the man had finished, and laid his hand back over the belly of the guitar, the knife on the bench.

"What does it mean?" Silence asked after a moment. "That part about the southern and the dog?"

The man gave him a frank, quizzical look. "The Dog I'll give you. But surely you've heard of the Southern Railway? Runs from Florida clean on up to Illinois, and passes not too far from here."

Silence shook his head, smiled ruefully. "I've never been outside of Heaven."

The man shrugged. "No shame in that. You're a child, still. First time I left the plantation where I was born, I was twenty."

His look was distant, inscrutable, for which Silence was glad; it gave him time to recover from the naïve shock of the realization that this man had been a slave. After a moment, the man shook his head, looked back at Silence and continued as if he'd never started down this intriguing tangent.

"The Southern Railway crosses the Yella Dog – that's the Yazoo and Mississippi Valley Railroad – at a place called Moorhead, Mississippi. Most folks who know anything about it will tell you that's where this kind of music started."

"Was that where your plantation was?" Silence asked, hoping that it wasn't a rude question.

The old man shook his head. Far from offended, he laughed. "Lord, no, child! I'm sorry, there's no way you'd know – but Moorhead's about as far from a plantation as you could get, even if it's surrounded by cotton fields. The town was founded a few years back by a man called Chester Pond. He built up some mills along the Southern Railroad –factories made staves, cotton, oil and such. But he also built houses for his workers and he let them live there for free, so long as they worked hard and stayed sober. That's more than anyone might expect of a rich man, but then he went on and started up a college for Negro girls. His sister ran it, along with some Yankee missionaries. Yep, Chester Pond was a good man…about as far from a planter as they come."

"Did you work in one of his mills?" Silence asked.

A strange look crossed the old man's face then, part regret and part anger, with other things in the mix Silence couldn't tease out. "I never worked for Chester Pond. But for a time I did live in one of his houses…" The intense look dissipated, leaving his face wistful, and he shut his mouth down tight around whatever story that house held.

To break the ensuing pause, Silence stuck out his hand. "Silence Ogden," he said.

The man peered at Silence's hand as if it might conceal some trick, and then, hesitantly, he took it, squeezed it once, and let go. "Pascal McCune," he said. "Pleased to make your acquaintance."

Night was coming down with the dry leaves, and the wind was beginning to bite. "Do you have somewhere to stay tonight, Mr. McCune?" Silence asked.

The old man shrugged. "Right here seems all right."

Silence peered at the bench. Aside from a guitar case, the man had no luggage. "You're welcome to come home with me. We've got plenty of beds."

Once again, Pascal looked surprised. Then, hesitantly, he smiled. "That's kind of you, *P'tit*. But I've slept out in worse than this, and truth be told, I've been doin' it so long, I don't know if I'd remember how to sleep under a roof."

"All right, then," Silence said reluctantly. "But if you change your mind, it's Heaven Homestead, at the end of the road. That way." He pointed. "I'll tell my parents you might come."

"And I thank you kindly for it," said Pascal. "Good night."

"Good night," said Silence, and still feeling that he shouldn't, he turned his back on the old man and started walking home.

10

"I've heard that kind of music once or twice," Silence's father said that night at the dinner table, after Silence related the story of his meeting with Pascal. "Comes from down in the Delta, I think. But I'd be willing to bet it came from Africa before that."

"What's it called?" Silence asked.

John shrugged. "I don't suppose it has a name. Or if it does, no one tells it to white folks." Esther shot him a warning look. John winked at her. "What did you say that man was called?" he asked Silence.

"Pascal McCune."

Esther raised her eyebrows. "That's a funny name for a Negro."

"Funnier than Silence for a white boy?" Silence challenged, inexplicably protective of the old black man.

"Don't you sass your mother!" John said, but under the sternness in his eyes was a layer of covert laughter. "Anyway, I'm not surprised he impressed you. Some of those old colored musicians have an uncanny talent. I suppose because they had little else of their own, on the plantations…" He shook his head, and Silence wondered what he was negating. Nobody in the

Ogden family ever spoke a judgment on the peculiar institution, or its bloody defeat.

"Some of them are so good," John continued, "they'll pick up a tune from a tone-deaf whistle and play it back to you like nothing you've ever imagined."

Silence wondered when and where his father might have heard a Negro musician, but his mother's lips were set in a line of disapproval, and he didn't dare ask.

"We could go back tomorrow," he said instead, cutting his eyes tentatively at his mother. "Then you could hear him."

John looked at Esther. She sighed, shrugged. "Suit yourselves. I have plenty to occupy me here." She got up, and pointedly began clearing the dinner plates.

"All right, then," John said to his son, ignoring his wife's tacit objection. "We'll go and see what we can see. Only don't get your hopes up. Like as not he'll be gone by tomorrow."

*

But when John and Silence reached town the next morning – a bright-washed morning after the night's wind and rain – they found a small crowd gathered around the tree and music coming from somewhere in its midst. This time it wasn't the metallic whine of the knife-blade on the metal strings, but a softer, finger-pad sound, tied up in the latticed shadows thrown by the oak's bare branches.

Silence hung back at the fringes of the group, watching the others listen. His heart beat fast, and a lump came into his throat, though he couldn't have said why. When the guitar finally fell silent, there was a scatter of applause and calls for other songs, but Pascal ignored both. He looked straight through the crowd at Silence and smiled.

"Back for more?" he said.

A few people looked curiously at Silence. Some, clearly, were adding his acquaintance with the old man to the case for his eccentricity. Most were wondering what he knew that they didn't, and how they might find out.

Silence nodded. "And I brought my Pa. He wanted to hear you too."

"You're a mighty fine player, Mr. McCune," John Ogden said.

Pascal smiled faintly. "Your son has a good memory for names. But Pascal will do just fine."

John smiled. "What brings you to Heaven, Pascal?"

The old man shrugged, running a hand along the strings of his guitar. "I was on the road through the valley and saw the sign. Had to have a look at a place called Heaven."

Some of the crowd had wandered away, sensing that this talk might take a while. A few lingered to listen, but neither man paid them any mind.

"And what do you think?" asked John.

Pascal looked up through the wind-stripped branches at the pale sky beyond. "I think whoever named it wasn't too far off."

"She'd have been pleased to hear you say so."

Pascal and John looked each other in the eye. Then Pascal gave a slight nod, and John a slight smile, and Pascal began to play again. This time he played with the knife, and after listening for a few disconcerted moments, the rest of the crowd dispersed. Even John looked discomfited by the strange music. Silence stared at Pascal's hands, entranced.

"I need a few things from the store," John said to his son. "You can stay and listen until I come back, all right?"

Silence didn't hear him. He and Pascal were in a world one step removed from the wider one, a fragile globe spun from the bewitching music and the branches' crosshatched shadows. He stood unmoving, barely breathing, watching Pascal's hands move until Pascal finally put the guitar aside and patted the bench beside him. Silence sat down, and together they watched the children playing in the weedy yard beside the store. Every once in a while, Silence stole glances at the guitar. It winked on the bench in the windy light, daring him to ask. At last he mustered the courage.

"Is it hard to learn?"

Pascal didn't ask what he meant. He only shrugged and said, "Harder than some things, easier than others."

"How long did it take you to pick it up?"

The old man laughed out loud. "Pick it up!" he repeated, slapping his knee. "Oh, *P'tit*, that's priceless! I'm sorry, I don't mean to laugh at your expense…it's only, I've been playing for twenty years, and still *I've* barely started…"

When his laughter died down, he saw that Silence was still waiting for an answer. He sighed. "Didn't take me long to learn my way around the strings. But I already knew the fiddle, and the guitar's a damn sight easier than that."

"You play the fiddle too?"

Pascal's lips made a thin line, not unlike Esther's did when she wanted everyone to know that she was displeased, but didn't want to say so. "Not anymore."

"Why not?"

"Things change." Pascal looked away, pain making mountains and canyons on his face. He kept on looking at the children by the store, as if for an answer to some unspoken question.

Abruptly, he turned to Silence said, "All right."

"All right – what?"

"I'll teach you." He rapped on the top of his guitar.

"But…I didn't ask you to."

"Not out loud. But you've been looking at this guitar since the first time you saw it, as love-sick as that little tow-headed girl over there's looking at you."

Silence's eyes darted to the store's dooryard. Jenny Lindquist turned away almost as quickly, but not fast enough to hide the fact that she had been watching him.

"Your sweetheart?" Pascal asked, grinning.

"No! I mean yes…I mean maybe…" He broke off, flustered, and with a needle of guilt he realized that he hadn't even noticed that Jenny was there until that moment.

Pascal shook his head, still smiling slightly. "Well then, commiserations, congratulations, or get a move on, depending on which of those answers was true. But back to the matter at hand…?"

"Yes," Silence said, glad that he could at least be clear about something. "I do want you to teach me. But I never played anything in my life. Will you be here long enough for me to learn?"

"Who said I was leaving?"

"Well, no one, I guess," Silence answered, mortified by his unintentional rudeness. "Only, it's near winter, and you can't keep living on this bench, so I thought…"

Pascal shrugged. "It wouldn't be the first time I wintered out." Then he sighed. "But you're right: I'm used to flatland winters, and I'm not as young as I was. Truth be told, I could do with keeping still for a spell, and this seems as good a place as any to do it."

"You can stay with us," Silence said hopefully.

"That's kind, *P'tit*," said Pascal, "but I think your mama would have a thing or two to say about that."

Silence said nothing, because this was true.

"Don't you worry, I'll figure something out. And to answer your question: yes, one winter's long enough for you to learn, if you go at it like you mean it."

"What if I'm no good?" Silence asked.

"Oh, you won't be," Pascal told him. "No one is when they begin. But you got music in you. You wouldn't be here talking to me if you didn't. You'll get there, if you want to."

Silence thought about the hours of practice standing between him and that music – assuming it was even achievable by hours of practice. He thought about his Latin grammar and his farm chores, about Jenny's wistful blue eyes when he stayed behind in the schoolroom for his extra lessons, and the threadbare newspaper advertisement folded carefully in his desk drawer. He wondered whether there was space in a lifetime for all of them. He knew that he would have to make it.

10

Nature tested Silence that first week of his musical instruction. After the cold weekend, the wind shifted around to the south, granting Heaven a rare Indian summer. The children shucked their winter woolens and brought their kites and fishing poles and baseball bats to school in anticipation of a glorious dinner hour. But Silence and Pascal had decided that the best time for his music lessons would be this same dinner hour, Silence bringing lunch as payment.

It was hard for him to walk on past the schoolyard that first noontime, particularly when both baseball teams pleaded with him to bat for them, and Jenny looked at him hopefully from beneath a crown of Black-Eyed Susans. But Silence Ogden was nothing if not resolute. He waved to his friends and turned. When he arrived at the tree and heard the soft music spilling from beneath it, he knew he'd chosen rightly.

Silence hurried through his lunch, eager to begin. Pascal ate carefully, considering every bite, and when Silence, still chewing, reached for the guitar he shook his head.

"Why not?" asked Silence.

"Because you can't possibly play 'til you've learned how to listen."

"I've already listened to you play."

Pascal shook his head. "I don't want you to listen to me. I want you to listen to *that*." He pointed upward, into the branches of the tree. Silence's eyes followed his finger. Seeing nothing, he looked doubtfully back at Pascal.

"See," Pascal said, "I'm not like those traveling players your daddy told you about." He looked up at the clattering branches with their last few lonesome leaves, smiled as if they'd told him something amusing, then amended, "Well, maybe I am. The difference is they walk the highways in search of money, whereas every step I've taken, it's been for love."

"Of music?" Silence asked.

"These days, yes. But also, love of God, and His good green earth, and being free to walk on it as I please…"

"And a girl?"

Pascal gave him a wry smile. "No. I can't say I ever walked anywhere for a girl." Silence didn't believe him, but he kept quiet so that Pascal would continue. "If I stop somewhere it's because I hear something worth stopping for. It just doesn't happen too often."

"So you stopped in Heaven because of this tree?" Silence asked, feeling that the point was eluding him.

But Pascal nodded affirmation. "It speaks, this tree. If you listen hard, you'll hear it. And once you hear it, well..."

Pascal had picked up his guitar as they spoke. Now he began to play a murmuring little tune that did indeed resemble the sound of the breeze in the tree branches. Likewise, the breeze in the tree branches had begun to resemble the sound of whispering voices, the words they spoke too faint to decipher. But the tone of them – subdued, pitched to the coming winter – was clear enough.

"See, son, this is no ordinary tree," Pascal said, abruptly clapping his hand over the strings. "There's power in it, a will to live I felt in but a few creatures before. I think," he continued, looking upward, "this tree knows God."

"Because it's beside a church?" Silence asked, trying not to feel impatient.

"No. Because it stands so straight and tall, reaching its fingers up to Him, singing praise. Besides, God must have something to do with a tree stranding smack in the middle of Heaven."

He smiled at his own joke and handed Silence the guitar. Silence accepted it carefully, holding it as he might have held a baby, if anyone had ever offered him the opportunity. Pascal poked and prodded the guitar and Silence's hands until they formed some semblance of the right position. Then he gave a curt nod of approval.

"Got that?" he asked.

"I think so," Silence said, waiting with tremulous excitement to begin.

"Good," said Pascal. "Now give it back."

"What!"

"Trust me, that's plenty for one day."

Glumly, Silence handed it over.

Revenants

1

Meredith was dead.

Or perhaps she wasn't. Perhaps she knew with that very thought that if she could think it, she couldn't be. Yet if she wasn't dead, she didn't know what to call the senseless state in which she found herself. No hope or memory sullied her absolute present. There was nothing behind it but a dim memory of pain, nothing ahead but the next involuntary breath. She knew that she lay curled into herself, but she could not feel the texture of what she lay on, nor tell whether she was warm nor cold. She heard nothing but the echo of the wave that had drowned her, a faint ghost of its roar hovering in the perfect, crystalline silence. She saw nothing but the black of the floor of the nighttime sea.

And yet, that wasn't quite right. There were faint gray lines against that black, and with them came a sluggish understanding that would certainly have crushed her if the job hadn't been done already. That gray was the gray of dawn, and if she was seeing it, then her bid had been rejected. She had begged the sea to take her, and instead it had thrown her back, consigned her to the horror of a life gutted of meaning or purpose.

Please, she thought.

But there was only silence and the growing light as her heavy lids opened against her will, just as her lungs continued to fill and empty and fill again in spite of her. With the light came the pain of a salt-scoured nose and throat, grazed skin, limbs the raging waves had tried to tear apart. Yet these things seemed to exist somewhere to the side of her, as if the sea had managed to shake her soul half-loose from her body before it lost her to the shore.

The shore. Her eyes, now fully open, were apparently still functional, though everything seemed oddly washed of color. She saw that she lay on a hard wet circle of sand, sheltered from the reach of the waves by an arm-like curve of rock. She didn't wonder how the sea had managed to place her there so precisely, when that little haven was clearly beyond its reach. She didn't wonder anything at all.

Mechanically, she sat up. She examined herself and noted that she was drenched. She wore nothing but a tattered shift and a ring with a dull, faceted stone. She saw that her skin was pimpled with cold, and her bare feet were white. She knew that if she were going to live, she would have to rectify those things, but that was the extent of the impression they made on her.

By placing two hands on the encompassing stone, she managed to stand. Her legs felt wooden and waterlogged, but by sheer force of will she managed a step, and then another. In this way she turned her back on the still, black, blown-out sea, and began to walk.

*

She kept moving all through that day, with no other purpose but to put the sea as far behind her as possible. She took little notice of the landscape, except when it provided a sudden, rutted road out of the midst of a blueberry thicket. The road was rocky and crooked, but it pointed in the right direction, so Meredith took it, walking while her legs held, crawling when they gave out, until darkness fell, and she was forced to stop.

The sullen rain that had fallen on and off throughout the day set in with a vengeance, then. Meredith, lying a little way off the road, was aware that she'd begun to shiver, and she had a sudden, sidelong hope: that the rain would finish what the sea had begun. She closed her eyes, comforted a little by the thought that she wouldn't have to open them again.

And so she felt a certain anger, though little more potent than the previous night's hope, when she woke the next morning to a shaft of sunlight piercing the forest canopy. *How?* she thought dismally. Sitting up, she had her answer. A blanket of dry leaves had blown over her in the night. They fell away from her like loose patchwork squares, showing skin no longer pocked with cold, a shift nearly dry.

Very well, thought Meredith, and she took once more to the road.

It was several hours before she finally identified the gnawing in her gut as hunger. She'd drunk water from streams when her tongue felt hot and filled her mouth, but it hadn't occurred to her that she might require food. Now, though, the need for it overwhelmed her. She stopped and looked around. The early autumn forest was bright in the morning sunlight, but still drawn in gray, like a tintype. It occurred to her that there ought to have been berries and nuts at this time of year, yet if she'd

101

passed any fruit-bearing bushes since the blueberry thicket at the road head, she didn't remember it. Of course, she might not have noticed them in this weird, grey world. Her hearing had not returned, nor could she smell anything in particular.

Sighing, she walked on. She hadn't walked far, however, before she came to the road's first fork. The left one, lined with shivering birches, turned sharply east. The right one ran narrowly into a stand of hemlocks and seemed to lead upward, though the forest was so dense that it was difficult to tell. Meredith chose the right one with barely a pause. She could not bear the possibility of coming back to the shore.

Before long, the road she'd chosen rose steeply and narrowed to a stony path. Meredith's head swam with exertion and hunger. Before long she was crawling again, partly from weakness and partly because her feet had been so badly cut by the stones that they would no longer carry her. It seemed she'd been climbing for days when the ground finally leveled, and the forest thinned. She collapsed onto a soft carpet of fallen pine needles, lying for a long time before her heartbeat and her breathing evened.

When at last she was able to sit up, she saw that she had arrived at a circular clearing shaded by hemlocks and white pines. In the center of the clearing was a little clapboard shack stained dark by time and damp, its door hanging by a single hinge. Behind the shack, the path continued up a gentle slope to the hill's bald top.

Despite Meredith's bleeding feet and light head, she had a sudden driving need to reach the top of that hill. She tore strips from the tattered hem of her shift, bound her feet, and then began once again to walk. It seemed to take her hours to reach the top, though her perception had by then been pried apart by hunger and pain. When she finally stood on the bald, though, she knew she'd been right to climb it. From the hill's stony crown she could see for miles across a limitless expanse of evergreen forest, unbroken by so much as a wisp of smoke. Nowhere, no matter how hard she squinted, could she see the ocean.

2

Meredith fell asleep on the hilltop. By the time she awakened, it was near dark. Her feet had bled through their bandages and her sweat had cooled, giving way to shivers. When she reached the soft pine needles she wanted nothing so much as to curl up on them and sleep again, but a fog was chasing the falling night. It touched her cheek with a cold and fatal finger, and she recoiled. She was beyond examining her reasons. She simply got up again on her hands and knees, and dragged herself into the mossy cabin.

There was enough light left to find her way to the hearth. There was no stove, just a crude fieldstone recess, but whoever had last occupied the cabin had left the makings of a fire in the grate and a small pile of wood beside it. Meredith felt around on the floor and mantle, but she found no tinderbox or matches.

She did, however, find an old tin box half-full of stale crackers. The crackers weren't much in the way of sustenance, but they were enough to clear her head a little, enough that she realized an image was struggling against the sea wall her mind had made against her past. A moment later it slipped through: a pair of slender, sinewy brown hands striking two flints above a pile of twigs and dry leaves. Two fish hung from green sticks above the kindling.

Meredith went back to searching with her hands. At last she turned up a couple of small stones fallen from the fireplace, and with them she managed to throw a spark. It was enough to light the bone-dry kindling, which caught and flared. She added sticks quickly, and when they ran out, she put in logs. Luckily the wood was old too and very dry. Meredith stoked the fire as high as she could, and then she curled up on the floor before it and fell asleep.

*

She woke shivering to murky light. The fire had burned out, leaving only a few glowing embers, and the fog that had risen the previous evening wafted in through the hanging door. It was the kind of thick, linty fog that so dirties the daylight that time loses its way, and everything seems possible.

Meredith, however, was in no mood for possibilities. Her feet throbbed excruciatingly. She tried to peel the hardened bandage off of one of them, and if she'd still had her voice she would have screamed. As it was she had to sit for several moments with her head between her knees to keep from fainting, though this dragged at the knotted muscles of her back and neck. It seemed that every part of her protested in one way or another, from her throbbing head to her furiously empty stomach. She knew that she needed to get the bandages off of her feet, to clean and dress them properly, or she would face a fate too grim even for her. But she had no idea how to go about this. Even if she could bear to pull them off, she thought she might cause herself worse damage in the process. All she could think of was to soak them, and for that she would need to rebuild the fire, and find water.

Choosing the easier task to begin with, she stirred the embers, carefully feeding them twigs and scraps of bark until a little flame licked up from the ash. When it was steady she added the last of the wood. It smoked and fretted and finally caught, and Meredith released a breath she hadn't realized she was holding.

Next, she dragged herself to her feet, fighting another wave of dizziness as the pain stabbed upward into her legs. She turned slowly, surveying the cabin's interior. There was little enough to see, but in the shadows by the far wall she caught a glimmer of what might be metal, and a darkness with the form of a hanging garment. With one hand on the wall, she hobbled in their direction and found that the darkness was indeed a garment: a heavy, tartan hunting coat. She took it down, and found beneath it a pair of woolen trousers and a collarless work-shirt. Beside these, on another peg, was a felt hat.

They were men's clothes, but she was a tall woman. Meredith pulled on the jacket, and found it fit her well enough. As it settled around her, something knocked against her hip. She reached into the pocket and her hand closed around a knife. It had a patterned handle and a small curved blade made of something that wasn't metal, bearing the patina of great age. She would have said stone, except that it didn't seem hard or cold enough. Meredith slipped it back into the coat pocket.

The metallic glimmer she'd seen from the far side of the cabin turned out to be a half-dozen rusted tins on a raw board shelf. They were labelled: Flour, Sugar, Coffee, Jerky, Beans, Salt. She expected that they would be empty, but on picking up the first she found it half full of weevily flour. There was a quarter tin of sugar left, half a tin of coffee, a few strips of desiccated meat, and full tins of both navy beans and salt.

As well as the tins of dry goods, the shelf held a tinderbox, a cracked stoneware pitcher, a large tin pot and a wooden pail. Beneath it was a bare ticking pallet, along with a small blanket-box. At the head of the pallet were a zinc washtub and a pair of black hob-nail boots.

Meredith thought that the boots might be a decent fit, but she couldn't bear to try them on her wounded feet. Instead she looked into the blanket-box, and found a rough woolen rug and several cotton sheets. She took one of the sheets and put it in the washtub with the pot, the pail and the salt, and limped back to the fire. Laying everything down but the pail, she made her way to the door.

With the fog so thick and lacking her sense of sound, she was prepared for a long search for water. But she had moved only a short distance beyond the cabin when she saw a shape looming in the close, cottony distance: a dark dactyl thrusting up from the earth. Approaching it with cautious hope, she was rewarded by an iron pump over a capped well. It was stiff, creaking as she began to work it, but when the water came the bucket filled quickly. She carried it back to the house with painful care and emptied it into the pot, which she set up on three stones over the fire. Then she went back for a second bucketful.

When she returned, with the last of her will, she retrieved the pot, and the beans and the dried meat from the shelf. She poured most of the simmering water into the washtub, and added the rest to the pot with the meat and beans. She put the pot back on the fire, hoping that that it would result in something edible, and then looked grimly at her feet. They stung and throbbed now after her exertion, but if they'd bled beneath the bandages it had done nothing to loosen them. Working on instinct or perhaps some buried memory, Meredith mixed salt into the hot water in the tub. She waited, stirring it with her hand until she thought that the temperature would be bearable, and then she lowered her feet into the water.

The heat and the salt seared the raw and swollen tissue. But gradually, the pain diminished until she thought she could try again with the bandages. She lifted her left foot from the dirty water, took up one of the strips of fabric and began to unwind it. It stuck in places, but most of it came away easily. It was only when she reached the last layer that she found it stuck fast again. So she put the foot back in the water, and repeated the process with the other one.

Slowly, she worked at the bandages until she had them off. Her wounds were worse than she had realized. Most of the skin was gone from the soles of her feet. They were red and weeping, and she knew that it would be a long time before they would bear her weight again. She would have cried, if she'd remembered how. But the sea had taken her tears along with the rest. So she picked up the sheet, and began to rip.

3

The next morning the fog was still thick around the cabin. Meredith's feet felt hot and tight in their bandages, while the rest of her shivered despite the hunting coat and the woolen rug.

The fire was out, and she needed more wood. She tried to stand, but the pain sent her sprawling, so she crawled to the hearth and fed the last of the kindling to the embers.

Hunger was gnawing at her again. She checked the pot. The meat had softened to an edible consistency, but the beans remained hard and bitter. Meredith ate the meat and the broth, and she was still hungry. She sat staring at those evil, shrivelled beans, wondering whether they had gone bad or she had done something wrong. Quick as a minnow, another memory slipped the net: speckled beans in a crockery bowl, covered with water.

Meredith poured some of the beans into the pitcher with what was left of the water, and then there was no more excuse. She had to bathe and re-wrap her feet or give up altogether. How, though, was another question. She willed herself upright, but the best will couldn't force the limits of her body. Though she managed a clumsy forward movement by leaning heavily on the wall, she would have to cross ten yards of thin air to reach the well, and then again with a heavy bucket.

You'll find a way, she told herself, *or sit here and wait to die.* So she took up the bucket and inched along the wall to the door. She stepped outside and then she stopped short, clinging to the doorframe. Something was there in the weird hanging murk: a dark, solid shape, swelling periodically with the minute movements of breath. For a long moment Meredith hung there, her pains forgotten and her heart in her throat. It was a bear, she thought. It had to be. There was no other creature of that size and color in those woods. And with that thought, Meredith realized that there was still another way that she would prefer not to die.

With little choice, she waited for the teeth and the claws, hoping that the bear was hungry and wouldn't make a game of her. It didn't come. The shape simply hovered there in the mist.

And then, shocking herself, she moved forward. As the animal came into focus, Meredith didn't know whether to be relieved or terrified. It wasn't a bear, but it was nearly as bad. She had always been afraid of horses, and this one looked monstrous to her: a great black beast with huge, white-feathered feet, a white crescent-moon mark on its forehead, and a matted mane hanging to its shoulder.

Meredith backed toward the cabin, but the horse followed, stopping a few feet from her, its ears flickering back and forth, its great nostrils flaring. It had a rope around its neck with a long frayed end, and where the rope had rubbed, there was a red weal that blazed against her monochrome world. Meredith waited for the horse to do something, but it only stood staring at her, its ears swiveling to sounds she could not hear. Gradually, her heart stopped racing. Likewise, her awareness of her pain returned. So, doing her best to ignore the horse, she clutched her bucket and laid a firm hand on the outer wall of the cabin, and began once again to move toward the well.

The horse followed her. She could not hear it, which made the sensation of the great moving bulk matching her steps all the more horrifying. She turned, heart pounding, and swatted the air with her hand. The horse brought its head up and around, fixing her with a wide black eye, but it stood its ground. Frustrated and frightened, Meredith turned away and kept moving.

When at last she reached the corner of the cabin, the fog stretched out before her, vast and taunting. If she could have cried then she would have. She might have found a way, crawling, to reach the pump and regain the cabin, but she would not go down on her hands and knees with the horse so close. She stood there, despairing, and then she felt a warm breath on her neck. The horse's head was inches from hers, lowered so that it looked her in the eye. She had no choice but to look back, and when her heart had slowed enough to allow her thoughts to move in file, she realized with a panicked wonder that the horse was speaking to her.

Why are you afraid of me? it asked.

She thought, *I don't know.*

I mean you no harm, the horse said. *I have run a long way. I am thirsty, and this rope hurts my neck. Will you help me?*

Don't, said Meredith's shattered mind.

But the horse's eye bored into her, deep and steady. The horse shifted a little, so that its shoulder was level with hers. She saw then that the horse's body was not all black. On its side was a white mark, wide as Meredith's hand, with a scatter of smaller marks trailing from it. And in the mark was another memory: an island on a map that lived somewhere in that place she'd forgotten, with the cooking fish and the bowl of beans.

Her arm came up despite her. It came up, and it moved across the horse's broad back, the black sea and the white islands until it bore her weight. Meredith took a step. The horse matched it. And so, in that slow, ponderous way, they crossed the yard until Meredith sank to her knees by the pump. She leaned there for a long moment while the pain and dizziness subsided. Then, with shaking hands, she filled the bucket, and pushed it toward the horse. It looked at her for a moment, then lowered its nose to the water and drank the bucket dry.

Meredith filled it again, offered it to the horse, but the horse turned its head away. So she got to her feet, and put her arm once more across its back, and the horse guided her to the door of the cabin. When she had set down her bucket inside, Meredith turned to the horse. It looked at her, its broken rope dangling. Slowly, her hand shaking again, Meredith reached out for the rope. The knot wasn't tight, but it was too much for a horse. She slipped it, and the rope fell away. The horse lowered its nose and sniffed it. Then, shaking its head, it turned and galloped off, leaving Meredith with an inexplicable feeling of desolation.

4

The next day, the beans had softened enough for cooking, and Meredith's feet were feelinglooking better. They were still sore and raw, but the swelling had gone down, and she was able to make several trips to the pump, walking slowly. It was just as well, for the horse had not returned. The rope she'd taken from its neck had likewise disappeared. There wasn't even the mark of a hoof on the clearing's soft pine-needle floor to show that it had been anything more than a figment of her imagination.

Meanwhile, the fog held on. Meredith's feet healed faster than she'd thought they would, and on the morning she wakened to sunlight and the last of the weevily flour, she knew that she would be able to walk on them, if she was careful not to go too far or fast. She boiled water and bathed in the washtub. She put on the clothes from the peg. Then she wrapped her feet well, pocketed the last of the bandages, put on the boots and the felt hat. She wished she had money to leave in their place, but she had nothing.

Or she thought she had nothing. As she wadded her ragged shift to throw it on the fire, two things clattered to the floor from its pockets. First, a little wooden carving with the shape of a sailboat, though it was worn now almost beyond recognition. She picked it up and held it as she might have held a talisman, while she examined the second object: the ring with the baleful diamond. It was blue now rather than grey, the color of a winter sky, and under its gaze she felt something powerful, unfathomable – anger or grief, she wasn't sure. She weighed the two objects, one in each hand, and she knew that only one of them belonged in that cabin. Slipping the ring back into her pocket, she set the carving on the mantle. Then she left the cabin behind her.

*

The track ran west through unbroken spruce forest. It was smooth and for the most part flat, winding through the trees with only gentle drops and rises, never offering a clearing or vista. Meredith saw no sign of life aside from the twitching of birds in the treetops and the occasional white flicker of a deer's retreating tail. Aside from the remembered red of the horse's wound and the steely blue of the ring in her pocket, the world remained colorless.

It grew so monotonous that Meredith began to wonder if she had died after all, and was wandering some monochromatic purgatory. She might have believed it, if it hadn't been for the pain of her feet. Walking worried the scabs, never quite allowing the skin beneath to heal. Worse still was the hunger. Since the rations in the cabin, she'd found nothing to eat but a few early nuts and late blackberries, and she knew that if she didn't find something more substantial soon, she would starve.

It was the horse, once again, who saved her. She would have walked right past the camp in the evening gloom if the horse had not turned to her, its white islands showing clearly in the dim light. It stretched its neck toward her unperturbed, as if it had expected her.

Greetings, it said.

I thought I had dreamed you, said Meredith.

Perhaps you did.

Meredith shook her head, stymied still by the impossibility of the horse's voice inside it.

You are hungry, said the horse. *You are in pain.*

Meredith knew then that the horse was female, that she had been a mother at least once in her life. Washed by a sudden, silent need, she went to sit down by her.

No, said the horse. *You need to go inside.*

Inside? Meredith asked.

The horse turned her head toward the back of the clearing. Meredith followed the movement, stumbling forward until a building hovered out of the gloom. It was a long, narrow cabin, many years abandoned. The door was gone, torn oilpaper fluttered in the windows, but the walls, made of notched spruce logs chinked with mud and moss, were still solid. The roof's cedar shakes also seemed intact. Meredith moved toward the door and then she stopped, looking back at the horse. Her white moon marked her in the fast-falling dark. Meredith reached out; the horse closed the distance.

Will you be here in the morning? Meredith asked her.

The horse pressed a damp, sweet, grassy nose into her hand and said, *Do you want me to be?*

I do, Meredith answered, surprising herself with her conviction.

Then I will be, the horse said, and she went back to cropping grass.

*

Inside the cabin, Meredith found a fire pit. There was no wood or kindling left, but she had kept the tinderbox from the hilltop cabin, and despite the dark she was able to gather enough pine needles and twigs to catch the sparks. Once the fire was burning, she found old crates and broken furniture with which to feed it. When it was bright enough she began to search for food.

The camp had been primitive even before it was abandoned. There was no stove, only the fire pit and a square hole in the roof to let out the smoke. What appeared to be a single long bed ran along one wall, with a half-hewn log laid at the outside that seemed to double as a footboard and a bench. The bed had no mattress, only the disintegrating remains of balsam boughs and a very long, very dirty woolen blanket.

Along another wall was what passed for a kitchen. In place of a sink there was a hollowed log with an open drain running out beneath the wall; a dented tin pitcher hanging from a hook above had been the water source. There were a number of empty barrels that had once held food. At last, though, Meredith discovered a tin of dry beans on a corner shelf, along with some musty tea and sugar. She also found a small, unopened barrel of crackers, and a kerosene lantern not quite empty.

With a mouthful of crackers, she took the pitcher, lit the lantern and went outside to search for water. She found the horse drinking from a little stream not far into the trees. Meredith filled the pitcher, patted the horse, and then went back inside. Before she slept, she put the beans on to soak.

The next morning, after she'd changed her bandages and put the beans on the fire to boil, Meredith searched the camp again. She found an old grindstone, a pair of boots with outworn soles, a small and dented tin pot, a rusted hunting knife, and a woolen blanket in better condition than the one on the bed. She found no more food. Once she'd eaten, she packed the remaining beans, the tea and sugar, the pot and the knife and what crackers she could carry, and rolled them into the blanket. She tied it tightly with a bit of old rope she'd found in one of the barrels, and made two loops so that she could wear it like a pack.

When she stepped outside, the horse was waiting. When she began to walk, the horse walked beside her. They had not gone far when she said, *Your feet are not healed yet.*

They will carry me, Meredith answered.

It would be easier if I carried you.

Meredith didn't say, *I'm afraid to get on your back.* She didn't say anything. But when the horse looked away, she knew that she had heard her thought, and that in thinking it, she had hurt the horse. She was sorry, but not sorry enough to quell the fear.

5

Meredith lost count of the days. They traveled mostly through dense forest, sometimes spruce, more often newer growth. It was a watery landscape too, but not in the way of the nightmare shore. This water was sweet and still. Sometimes they walked for miles just to round a black, brooding lake, or to find a place shallow enough to ford a lazy river. As well as deer tracks, they walked on logging roads and packed-dirt thoroughfares lined by fences and fields and old, stone walls – roads, in short, with the mark of human hands all over them, but no one in sight.

As the empty world unfolded mile after mile, the strangeness of it finally penetrated Meredith's solitary keep. It seemed that she and the horse were the last beings left on earth. This might not have worried her if she hadn't been so hungry. As it was, hunger pressed its way into her present-tense, until she found herself rationing and counting days and longing for some human settlement, even if it was only another abandoned logging camp.

Two days after the beans ran out, they finally found one. By then Meredith was so lightheaded with hunger she thought that it was an illusion when the forest ended abruptly at the margin of a field, the wide spongy leaves of its plants beginning to pale and shrivel with the advanced season. But the horse saw it too. She stopped at the edge of the field, hanging back in the shadow of the forest, her ears swiveling, her head low and sniffing.

At last the horse turned to Meredith, perhaps for direction, but Meredith didn't see it. She was in the grip of another anchorless memory. This time, though, it was more than a flicker. She knelt in a dim room with a steeply sloped ceiling, by a window with a curtain half drawn. Beneath the window, in neat rows inside wooden crates, were dozens of little shriveled potatoes growing green sprouts. As she watched, the eyes became spongy green leaves and yellow flowers, bent in a strong sea wind.

Understanding, Meredith stepped toward the field. Now she saw the little brokenbacked house in the distance; the barn with so many chinks in its walls that the soft morning light came through them like a lace curtain; the weeds among the rows of potatoes. She knew there had been no farmer here in years. Bending over the nearest of the plants, she pulled. It came up easily, trailing shallow roots and stony soil and a few tiny, waxy tubers. She put them carefully aside as the horse looked on, silently vigilant. Then she put her hand into the soil where the plant had been and lifted out a handful of egg-size potatoes.

After that she worked faster, lifting another plant and another, digging around in the soil until she had enough potatoes to feed her for a week. As she was putting them into her pack, though, the wind suddenly stilled. A shadow crossed her, and her breath caught. She looked up into dark, narrowed eyes in an ancient face. A man's face. He studied Meredith for a moment, and then he reached out with a gnarled and spotted hand. Meredith scrambled backward, pushing the potatoes toward him. But the man ignored them, reaching through the late-morning light that made his hand brilliant and insubstantial. He plunged it into the turned earth.

Meredith wanted to run, but she felt the horse's warm breath on her neck, telling her to wait. And so she waited, hardly daring to breathe, until the man's hand came back up out of the earth, holding a stone. He brushed the soil off of it and then turned it toward Meredith. Its back was rounded, fitting his cupped palm. Its front was rough, as if it had been broken from another piece of rock.

There was a tree on it. It wasn't a carving, but seemed part of the stone itself. A twisting trunk ran up the center, with branches angling off of it. There were flecks like bits of twigs that had fallen into the picture and frozen there. In one corner was a delicate, feathered cinquefoil with one of its appendages broken off: a blossom turned to stone, its grooves in the rock glassy and ancient. The old man pressed the stone into Meredith's hand. Then he turned and slipped away, melting into the wavering margin of the field.

The horse gazed after him, ears pitched forward as if she could still see him. Meredith saw nothing but the swaying plants. She shivered and shook her head, then quickly packed up the potatoes and the fossil stone and hurried back into the forest with the horse at her heels.

6

Not long after the potato field, the land changed. They forded a stream, the scrubby forest on its far bank thinned, and all at once they were in farmland. The track ran between little homesteads, their people working hard to bring in the harvest. At first Meredith was hesitant about drawing attention to herself, but when the horse walked out onto the road no one gave her a second glance, and they paid no more attention to Meredith when she followed.

The road grew wider and smoother as they traveled. By that, and by the way the horse's ears pitched forward, Meredith knew that something significant lay ahead. It was evening, though, before they reached it. Meredith's feet were hurting her again, but when they came to the top of a rise and looked down into the valley below, Meredith forgot her pain and exhaustion.

A wide river ran through the valley. On its far shore rose the smoke and steeples of a large town, but Meredith didn't see them. Her eyes were fixed on the river, where boats of all shapes and sizes moved to and fro. The sight of them churned the still, black water inside of her, disgorging images that tore through her like a ship's fractured beams: an anchor plowing a sea meadow; lobsters scrabbling in a zinc tub; purple bruises on brown skin; eyes like ice in a sunburned face. Beneath them was a sinkhole of unfathomable pain; at its vortex, a mind-wiping panic.

In the grip of it Meredith turned and ran. She didn't feel the pain of her feet, or the thud of the horse's hooves as she trotted to keep up. She didn't see, didn't think until she collided with something sharp and solid. She came back to herself then and collapsed beneath the huge old white pine she'd run into. Her head hurt where she'd hit it, but at least the blow had shaken the jagged memories down again below the surface of her hidden sea.

The horse was breathing quickly. Meredith reached out and stroked her muzzle. *I'm sorry*, she said.

What spooked you? she asked.

What indeed? Meredith wondered. She took a tremulous breath, and then she looked again at the river. It was wide as it had been when they'd first seen it, but the town was far behind, and with it the sailing boats. There were smaller craft here and there – rowboats and canoes, some with little sails – but Meredith felt no panic when she looked at them.

She also saw that the sun was setting behind the river. It ran north to south. To continue on her course away from the sea, she would have to cross it.

It looks deep, said the horse, hearing her thought.

We have to try, Meredith insisted.

The horse trundled down the bank, stepped into the stream. The current made waves around her feathered feet. Hand wrapped in her mane, Meredith coaxed her forward. A few yards from shore, the water had already risen to the horse's belly.

It is too near night for this, the horse said.

Meredith didn't argue. She too had felt the fierce pull of the current. *Tomorrow we'll find a place to cross,* she said.

The horse didn't answer, only lumbered back up the bank and put her head down to the scrubby grass.

*

Meredith woke to a drizzling dawn, still fenced by that wide, silent river. She peered into it as she washed her knife and pot after breakfast, hoping for inspiration, but the black water showed her only her own face, thin and white and dead-eyed. So she packed up her things, kicked dirt over the fire's embers, and began once again to walk north.

It was slow going. Her feet were swollen and throbbing again after her panicked run the previous evening. She tried not to think about them, to concentrate on the river and where it might let them pass. It was a busy river, but not as it had been by the town. Anglers fished from shore or from boats in the stream. All of them ignored her, as the farms' people had done. She began to wonder whether they could see her at all.

After a time, the road curved away from the water, and the ground began to rise. It crested a hilltop, and that was when Meredith spotted the islands. They were close to the far shore, tucked into a dip in the riverbank as if once they had been a part of it. Just to the north of them, the far riverbank jutted out in a sharp point, halving its width. The day was still grey, the water opaque. It was impossible to tell how deep it might be, even at that narrow point. But by another instinct or memory – she had given up trying to distinguish which – Meredith knew that where there were islands, the riverbed was likely to be shallower.

There, she said to the horse.

The horse said nothing, but she followed Meredith as she zig-zagged down the hill to the water's edge. It lapped at the shore, dark and inscrutable. The horse stood at the brink of the stream, her ears flickering in intricate communion with it. She leaned down, sniffed the water.

There is artifice in this water, she said at last.

What kind? Meredith asked.

I don't know.

Meredith looked at the horse, and then at the water. At last, slinging her boots around her neck, she said, *I will go first.*

The horse snorted as Meredith stepped forward, and then she followed, her feathered feet slopping mud and water back at Meredith. She didn't notice. She was concentrating on the water's rise. It was gradual, but it was definite. When it reached the horse's belly, Meredith wound her fingers into a handful of mane. Beneath the covert slip of the surface the current was strong, but the horse moved steadily onward.

Then the ground fell away. Meredith gasped and clung to the horse. The horse's legs were churning, and Meredith tried to keep her own out of the way. She tried to kick, to make herself less of a burden, but her boots and heavy clothes made it almost impossible. The horse was panting, struggling to hold her head out of the water. Meredith could no longer see the point they were aiming for.

When the horse's legs stopped their frantic kicking Meredith thought that she had given up, that the water would claim her after all. The irony almost made her smile, until she realized that the horse had stilled because she'd found solid ground again. A moment later, Meredith felt it beneath her own feet, and then she was dragging herself onto the muddy spit at the tip of the larger island she'd seen from the hill. The horse's sides heaved. Meredith retched murky water. But there was only a shallow channel of water left to cross to reach the far bank. The river had spared them.

7

The forest closed in again. Heavy clouds caught in the treetops, skimmed the surface of the fir-rimmed lakes. Sometimes it drizzled, and sometimes it didn't, but the air was so sodden and heavy with moisture that it made little difference either way.

Meredith had no strength left for pretence. She stumbled along on feet wrapped in strips torn from her trousers, because they had swelled beyond the confines of her boots. She stayed upright only by virtue of one arm across the horse's back, and the horse matched her slow, stumbling pace without protest. Meredith knew that they needed shelter and food, dry clothes and bandages. But though she passed numerous farms, she could not bring herself to knock on a door. She told herself that it was because she had no voice with which to plead. It was easier than facing the fear that had been growing in her since the potato field, moreso since the river had failed to kill her: that she was a spirit already, and if she knocked on a door, no one would hear it.

Darkness came quickly to a sky half taken already. They were walking at the margin of a small pond, its surface so smooth it seemed they might walk straight across it, when the horse stopped. She didn't startle or shy; she simply planted her feet and would not move. Meredith slipped her arm off of the horse's back, limped a few steps on her own, but the horse didn't follow. Instead she looked out across the water, leaning toward the far shore, her ears pitched forward.

What is it? Meredith asked her.

The horse didn't answer. Meredith stood still, looking where the horse looked. The dusky world was utterly still. No birds fluttered, no breath of wind ruffled the trees. Even the soft, steady drizzle had stopped. The horse took a step toward the water, stopped again. Then she turned abruptly and resumed walking. She did not wait to see if Meredith followed, though the girl could barely keep up.

Please, Meredith called to her, but the horse didn't listen, only trudged on, determined and unstoppable as time. As they rounded the far side of the pond, Meredith saw a small building. It was little more than a shed, with a ramp running from its door into the water. Only an icehouse, but she didn't care. Any shelter at this point was better than none, and at this time of year, there was unlikely to be any ice left inside.

She picked up her pace, wanting nothing more than to lie down somewhere out of the wet. But the horse had stopped again and wouldn't come to Meredith's call. Instead, she lowered her nose to the ground, sniffed, and flattened her ears.

What is it? asked Meredith.

The horse took a step backward.

You brought me here, and now you don't like it?

I don't understand it. I hear one thing, but I smell another.

Meredith looked at the icehouse again. Though it was hard to tell in the dying light, it looked like it had not been used in some time. She was close enough now to see that the door stood ajar. The dark interior was as still as the rest of the landscape. Meredith started for the door, but her hand went involuntarily to her pocket, to the odd little knife she'd found there on her first night in the cabin. The horse watched her for a moment, then she tossed her head, wheeled around, and trotted off, but she stopped again fifty yards away.

Meredith unslung her pack and took out the tinderbox. She lit one of the pitch-pine sticks she'd collected for kindling. With the light in one hand and the knife in the other, she approached the door, pushed it wider open with her foot. She still couldn't see into the dark confines, but she could feel that the air was warmer than it should be in an abandoned shed. There was also the unmistakable smell of something living. It was not a human smell.

A chill ran down Meredith's spine, colder even than her wet numb limbs, but she didn't turn away. She told herself that she had nothing to fear. If she were a spirit, then whatever was inside the shed couldn't hurt her. And if she weren't, well, she was willing to face her fate. Or so she told herself, over and over again, to try to drown out the little voice crying protest beneath her insistent nonchalance.

She took a deep breath and stepped inside. At first she could make out little but a pair of eyes illuminated by the flame. As her own eyes adjusted to the darkness, though, she realized what she was looking at. She stood transfixed between wonder and horror. In the corner of the shed, on a bed of old sawdust, lay a rawboned silver she-wolf. Tucked into the curve of her body were three nursing pups. In between two of the pups was a human child, not more than two years old, sucking along with them.

The child was dirty and tangle-haired, with calluses on her hands and feet. As Meredith stood gazing, the child broke away from the wolf, looked up. Her eyes were the same color as the wolf's, like maple sap half boiled down. She looked at Meredith for a long moment, and then she turned back to the animal. She pushed at the wolf's jaw with her head, and at last the wolf broke Meredith's gaze. She looked down at the child, licked her face, and then nudged her back amongst the others, where the child curled up and appeared to fall instantly asleep.

The wolf looked back and Meredith. Her eyes said, *Well?*

Meredith's pine stick had almost burned out. With the last of its light, she nodded to the wolf, then turned and left. She carefully pulled the door to its original position and walked back to the horse waiting for her in the darkness.

Well? said the horse.

You were right, said Meredith, and she slept that night in her wet clothes, after all.

8

Meredith woke dry and warm, lying between the embers of the fire she had built the night before and the horse's breathing back. It was a frosty, sunny morning. While she stirred the fire, the horse stood and shook herself and then walked off. Meredith turned to see what had taken the horse's interest, and saw her eating apples from an ancient, wind-bent tree. The apples were a brilliant red against the dying yellow leaves, the leaves blazing contrast to the blue sky. Meredith stared for a few moments, arrested by the sudden colors. That tree seemed the most beautiful thing she'd ever seen, and her heart ached with an emotion she could not name.

Meredith sat down beneath the tree and ate with the horse. When she was full, she packed as many apples as she could carry, and they set off again. Her feet hurt less that day, despite the beating they'd take on the previous one. For two days they wound their way slowly through a landscape of red autumn hills and blue-laked gaps, of falling leaves loosened by the nighttime frosts and the occasional farm. They were potato farms mostly, and Meredith watched the people's activity with half a mind on her stomach. She noticed that they didn't bother bringing in the smallest potatoes, but left them in the turned fields, and so she felt no compunction stopping at dusk and picking up these leavings for her dinner.

On the afternoon of the third day in potato country, the horse's ears began to flicker. Meredith had come to understand that this meant something out of the ordinary lay ahead; she had come to dread it. She slowed her pace, but nothing she did would make the horse change direction. That evening they arrived at a low town of clapboard houses and smoking brick factories, dark against the setting sun. A river ran through the town. It was no wider than the one they had crossed before, but it ran harder, raging over great boulders into a spectacular fall. A railroad bridge spanned the rapids, joining the two sides of the town.

There will be somewhere to cross further north, Meredith said, involuntarily clutching the horse's mane. *Let's go on.*

The horse only stood, her nose stretched toward the town and the roaring water.

Please, said Meredith.

But the horse's feet remained firmly planted, her nostrils widening at the cacophonous scents of civilization. It was too late in the day to argue with her, too late, in truth, to go on. Sighing, Meredith lit a fire, cooked her potatoes and then lay down. Even in the darkness, she could sense the horse leaning toward the water.

*

Dawn came boiling with river mist, and a round patch of blue overhead, promising it wouldn't last. As Meredith shouldered her pack, the horse began to walk toward the town.

I can't go that way, Meredith said.

There is no other way, the horse answered. *This river would not spare us.*

Looking across its roiling expanse, Meredith knew that she was right. She consoled herself with the thought that it was still early; the town still slept. She followed the horse along broad streets lined with trees and neat houses, some of them grand, all of them proudly kept. The horse twisted and turned as if she'd walked this way a thousand times before, drawing ever closer to the falling water.

When at last they reached it, Meredith saw that the river had been dammed at the site of a natural falls, the pent water raging first over the man-made lip, and then over a series of natural stone steps until it swirled into a black pool and away to the south. She could feel its pounding beneath her feet, and the railroad bridge suddenly seemed terribly flimsy, but the horse strode boldly toward it. Meredith's heart beat hard. She'd thought that her apprehension was for the size of the town and the people it contained. Now she knew that it was in fact for the falling water, though she could not have said why.

A sidewalk had been built in the lower cords of the bridge. The horse stepped onto it without apparent apprehension, but Meredith clung to the railing as she moved, her eyes fixed on the river below. The sight sickened her, yet she couldn't look away. The falling water beat at the dam of her memories, and images tumbled through. A little boat driven into a soaking pier by waves twice its size. White, wrinkled fingers fighting to knot sodden lines. A worn, red sail torn to streamers. A wave, black and ravenous, its embrace curiously warm.

In the middle of the bridge, the horse stopped abruptly, jerking Meredith from the memories' spell. The horse started to turn back, but the bridge shuddered, signaling an approaching train. Meredith put a hand on the horse's trembling neck, clung to the railing against the certain death of that raging water fifty feet below. The shudder came again, so hard that Meredith knew the train must be upon them, but when she looked up at the track, there was nothing. She peered, confused, down the empty track in both directions.

Then she looked at the horse. She stood quivering, her black eye showing a rim of white. She looked not at the rail tracks above, but down into the pool at the falls' foot. Meredith followed her gaze. Something indistinct was moving in the mist. Slowly it rose, resolving into a human hand. Yet it was all wrong: colorless and insubstantial as the river's spray. It reached up from the pool, settled on the first of the fall's spurs of white water. And then another hand emerged, and a head, and two legs and slowly, the man made of mist began to climb the falls, as if it were a ladder.

Meredith felt the horse's terror, but curiously none of her own. She kept a steadying hand on the horse's neck, and the horse stood her ground, by courage or simply the flummoxing fear of moving either forward or back. At last the gray man reached the top of the dam. He strode along its surging lip, and with a great leap, he caught the underside of the bridge, swung himself up, and then stood there for a moment, looking down at the water from which he had emerged.

His form blurred, shifting like a net curtain in a breezy window, then hung still again. He turned then and saw Meredith. He tipped a misty hat over sad grey eyes, offered her a wan smile. Then he turned and began to walk to the far shore, but he never made it. At the second to last pier, the bridge shuddered again, and he was swept up as if by a strong wind, though the morning remained still. His head struck one of the bridge frame's uprights and he fell forward, turning languidly as a feather until he met the water and vanished.

Meredith watched, transfixed beyond any reason, though the horse was beginning to dance and turn. When she took off for the far shore at a quick trot, Meredith finally tore herself away. Just before she put the water behind her, though, she caught a final glimpse of the dark pool, and a gray hand emerging from it again, to reach for the first rung of a watery ladder.

9

Meredith and the horse spent a couple of quiet days moving steadily west. They had to dip south once below two long lakes, and then north again around another so vast that it reminded Meredith of the sea. She put her back to that one and didn't turn south again until it was well out of sight.

During the day she gathered nuts and windfall apples, and at dusk she collected cast-off potatoes. Sometimes, if the farms looked prosperous enough to spare them, she took a piece of cheese from a dairy or bacon from a smokehouse. The farms were fewer and farther between, though, as the terrain grew hillier. Mornings broke to ever-thicker coatings of frost, giving way to luminous days that wore at Meredith's determined present, until the threadbare pocket where she kept past and future began to leak speculation. As the leaves fell faster, and each sunset showed more clearly between the disburdened branches, she found herself wondering what she would do when the apples ran out,.

Her brooding deepened as they passed out of farmland and back into forest. The loggers had been at work here, too. At first the scars were old ones. Birch, beech and ash had reclaimed ground where pine and spruce had been decimated. Meredith and the horse walked along an old logging road bordered with bracken and berry bushes and the occasional pile of abandoned trunks, too crooked or knotted to bother dragging them from the woods.

Though the devastation was long since past, Meredith felt its echo within her silence. It grew louder the further west they walked, the signs of destruction more recent as the day faded. There was no longer enough regrowth to hide the scars. It seemed some primeval beast had rampaged through the forest, devouring trees, leaving torn stumps and a few sad, dying saplings in their place.

Meredith kept walking long past the point when she should have stopped, hoping to camp somewhere other than that ruined forest, but there seemed no end to it. She took off her pack in the last of the light and sat down beside it, exhausted and dispirited. Her feet throbbed; she knew they had swollen again, and she could feel the slip of weeping sores.

We should not stop here, the horse said. *This is a bad place.*

Meredith looked up and around. The last of the light showed a clearing. It seemed to be a natural one; at any rate, it predated the loggers, for there were no stumps within it. Instead there were little stone cairns, and the whole of it was circled by an ancient, crumbling dry-stone wall.

There's no light left to find another, said Meredith.

A horse does not need light to see. If you get on my back, I will take you to a better place.

I'm too tired to ride, said Meredith, not caring whether the horse heard the truth beneath the words. She would have to live with it, as Meredith would have to live with the horse's disapproval. It was only one night, she told herself as she slipped into sleep.

*

That night, among the stones, a village grew. Barely a village: a half-dozen round huts built from wooden frames and sheets of birch bark. The snow reached nearly to their roofs. Only three of the huts had smoke rising from them. Outside, a handful of people clustered over something. By the drops of blood on the snow, Meredith thought that it must be the spoils of a hunt, but there was something wrong. The people were silent, their movements were furtive, and they avoided each other's eyes as they divided up their kill. When one young man turned to enter one of the huts, Meredith saw that his face was emaciated, his eyes sunken and vapid. She also saw what he carried: a human arm, dripping blood into the snow.

She clawed at consciousness, but the nightmare wouldn't let her go, nor even turn her focus from that horrific village. She could only watch as darkness fell, and the faint lights in the huts' doorways went dark. It began to snow. The silence was complete.

Then a sudden howl sounded through the stillness, like the first gust of a nor'easter through stripped winter trees. There was a shriek and crack like breaking bone, the shudder of a heavy footfall. No lights came on in the huts, but Meredith knew that those starving people were awake, listening and shaking as she was. The footsteps drew closer, ponderous and inevitable. A creature emerged, towering about the tallest trees, a great, emaciated, grey-skinned beast, with fangs like hunting knives bared between ragged lips it had chewed away in its voracious hunger.

Wendigo, Meredith thought, and she knew that was the name of this creature, though she didn't know how. It walked into the middle of the village, raised its ruined head to the sky and screamed. Then it bent down, lifted the lid off of the young man's hut. It plucked a dark struggling shape from within, and swallowed it whole. When it had done so it grew by the height of the man it had consumed. And so it picked its way through the village. When the huts lay in ruins, it stalked off again into the forest, uprooting trees as it went.

Silence settled again, uneasily. Dawn came, and with it the snow melted. The remains of the bark houses rotted. The earth shrugged and sighed and gave up the bones of those who had been consumed first by their own hunger, and then by their people's. Scavengers carried off the best of them; the sun bleached the rest, pitted and hollowed them until they turned to dust and rose again as a swarm of ghosts, howling with the voice of the winter monster. They took stones from the earth and piled them where their bones had lain, and sat down on them to shriek out the agony of their limitless purgatory.

In her dream, Meredith heard them crying out, and it was bad enough. But the horse, scared and sleepless, saw the wraiths. For a fleeting moment she, too, was sorry, but she could do no more than obey her nature. She wheeled and ran, on and on into the night, until that terrible place and its ghosts were far behind her.

10

Meredith woke to a buzzing in her ears, and no sign of the horse, aside from a trail of hoof-prints. She followed this trail for several hours, trying to ignore the buzzing, which seemed to be growing louder, trying to convince herself that the horse had not really abandoned her. Around the next corner, she told herself, she would find the horse browsing grass. On the crest of the next rise, or the next dip in the road…

As the day wore on, though, the road turned muddy, cross-hatched by wagon tracks that erased the horse's trail. Then, at last, Meredith accepted what she had known since she had wakened alone in that restless graveyard: she had asked too much. She had not trusted the horse, and so proved herself unworthy of the horse's trust. The horse had cut ties, and Meredith didn't blame her.

And so she wandered for some days, first west, then south, always aimless and despondent. She walked simply because she didn't know what else to do. She didn't even know which way she was heading, her sense of direction having abandoned her along with the horse. At the same time the buzzing in her ears was growing louder, and her food once again running low, increasing her disorientation. Her neglected feet began to bleed again, but she barely noticed. She began to wonder, once more, whether it might simply be better to die.

And then one morning Meredith woke to a shriek.

She sat up shaking, a roaring in her ears like a storm. It took her several terrified minutes to realize that this was not the sound that had roused her. This roar was an amalgam of the wind in the tops of the spruces; the birds crying out to the new day; the rush of water somewhere back in the forest. It was what she had once taken for silence, and it seemed monstrous to her only because it was so long since she had heard anything.

Then the shriek sounded again. This time she knew it. It was the horse, and it was afraid. Meredith stood. Her feet hurt, her head was light from hunger and the suddenness of sound, but the horse was calling her and she had to answer. She stepped off the path and began to push her way through the dense forest in the direction from which the cry had come. She wasn't sure that it was the right direction; she wasn't sure that she wasn't simply walking around in circles. But her newfound hearing was keen, her instinct true, and before long she saw light ahead.

The forest ended abruptly in a swath of felled trees. It was as if a scythe had cut through it, leaving a trail of stumps and a wagon track with ruts of dried mud as high as Meredith's knees, stretching off as far as she could see in either direction. But there were hoof-prints in the mud. She turned to follow them.

She hadn't gone far when she heard human voices. Men's voices. She ducked into the trees again, followed the sound to a clearing. It wasn't a natural clearing, but its trees had been cut so long ago that the stumps had rotted almost to nothing, and young birches thrust up among them. A dozen men ranged around the clearing, some stripped to the waist and leaning on the handles of crosscut saws, others in jackets like Meredith's, standing by a wagon loaded with logs. Hitched to the front of the wagon were two horses, and one of them was the black one.

A young man with a felt hat pushed back on his brow was admonishing the horse with the help of a stripped birch switch. The horse turned toward Meredith as she approached and called out again.

"Shut up and get on, you Godforsaken nag!" yelled the driver, swatting at the horse's flank with the switch.

The horse shook her head and didn't budge. The other men jeered and hollered, "You're a fool, Morrison! That horse ain't gonna pull."

"She'll pull," the young driver spat back. "Or else."

"Or else what? You'll send her back to the circus she came from?"

"She ain't no circus horse! This here's a Spotted Draft." He tapped the recalcitrant mare with the switch. "I seen her papers."

One of the older men snorted. "Papers! What good are papers but for lighting a stove?"

"Shut up!" said the young man grimly, casting a look at the horse that made Meredith creep forward again, despite her fear. The horse's ears flicked in her direction, but no one seemed to notice, least of all the driver. "Now," he said, taking a pistol from his pocket, "you'll pull, or you'll be dried and salted against next winter."

The mare didn't move, but she rolled her black eye back to meet that of the driver. He put the gun to her temple.

"Aw, hell, Morrison," called one of the men. "Leave her be. She'll be all right once she settles in."

"I ain't got time for a horse that needs settling in," the driver retorted.

The horse looked at the driver with a calm and absolute despair that Meredith understood implicitly. With that look, something inside Meredith that had been slowly thawing broke open at last. Before she had time to think about it, her bleeding feet had taken her to the center of the clearing, to the side of the doomed horse. Without hesitation, she slipped her arm around her neck, shielding her from the pistol. The horse blew and leaned into her.

"Who in the hell are you?" the driver demanded.

Meredith looked at him along the barrel of his gun. His arm dropped. The driver pulled his brows together, clearly trying to make sense of the woman's face and man's clothing.

"I beg your pardon, ma'am...only this ain't no place for a woman. I suggest you take yourself away from here, right now."

Meredith continued to stare at him.

The driver narrowed his eyes. "What's wrong with you? You deaf?"

Meredith shook her head.

"Well, you might think you got some claim on this horse, but I bought her fair and square! I got papers!" He pulled an envelope from his breast pocket.

Meredith paid him no attention, but looked into the horse's dark eye, which was level with her own. *Well?* She asked.

The horse said, *He does not own me.*

Clearly.

I am not a bad horse. I didn't mean to run from you.

I know that.

I am not meant to pull these trees from this forest.

Nobody is, said Meredith. And she began to unbuckle the horse's harness.

"What are you doing?" the man cried. "You can't just take my horse!"

"What's the difference, if you mean to shoot her?" asked the oldest of the loggers.

"I paid good money for that horse!"

"Ain't the horse's fault nor the girl's if you're a damned fool. I say, if she can move the beast, let her have it."

The horse slipped her harness. The driver brought his gun-arm back up. Meredith stepped into the space between them.

"Time was," Morrison said grimly, "no one bothered if you shot a horse thief."

"Well these ain't those times," said the old logger.

"She pays me for that horse," Morrison said grimly, "or neither of them leaves here."

A perfect hush descended over the clearing. Nothing moved but a single scarlet leaf, jettisoned by its branch, angling earthward. The sky behind it was a frigid blue. It reminded Meredith of something. She reached into her coat pocket and took out the ring. She studied it for a moment, and then she walked toward the man with the gun, the ring cupped in her palm.

The gunman's mouth hardened when his eyes lit on it. "You trying to tell me that's real?"

Meredith caught his eye and held it. When his shifted, she laid the ring at his feet. Morrison laughed. "You've gotta be kidding me! Every small-town dime store's full of rings like that."

Meredith barely heard him. She was looking at the horse, who was looking back. With an unmoving eye and a ponderous grace, the horse dropped one foreleg, then another, and then her hind legs until she knelt upon the ground. And Meredith, knowing that this had taken a courage she would never better, swallowed her own fear. She stepped back, and then back again, until she stood by the horse's withers. The gun still stared her down. She took a fistful of black mane in her hands. Then she threw her leg over the horse's back, and held her breath as the horse unfolded herself, and stood.

Morrison's hand was shaking. "I'm warning you. Take one step…"

"You asked for payment," said the old man, picking up the ring and passing a finger over it, "and she gave it."

"A worthless piece of glass!" he scoffed.

"You sure about that?" the old man persisted calmly.

Morrison cocked his gun.

"You pull that trigger, and it's murder. Not one of us will testify for you." The old woodcutter didn't need to look around to know that every one of his fellows nodded agreement. "I tell you one last time: let them go."

Slowly, as if aware of how precariously their lives were balanced, the horse turned. She lifted one tufted foot, then the next. Meredith counted each pace, waiting for the moment when the bullet would rip through her chest. But it didn't come. There was only the silence of the autumn forest, the muted fall of the horse's hooves on the leaf mold and pine mast. When at last they had passed out of shooting range, Meredith drew a breath. And that was when she knew that she intended to live.

Diamond Highway

1

The horse walked along the logging road with quiet assurance and a measured gait, while Meredith sat tense and taut on her back, tipping and sliding as her knees failed to find purchase. She stayed on only because she had no choice; she didn't know how to stop the horse, and she didn't dare jump off. But when the horse turned abruptly onto a narrower path, Meredith nearly lost her seat.

Enough, she said.

The horse ignored her.

Please, let me down. I cannot ride.

You are riding.

I'm holding on. Barely.

Your feet will never heal if you keep walking, the horse said.

Despite her anger, Meredith knew that the horse was right. She also knew that what had passed between them in the loggers' clearing had become a tacit pledge when they rode out of it together. So she wound her fingers grimly in the black mane and willed herself not to fall.

At first it was a battle. As the miles passed, however, Meredith began to relax. She stopped thinking that the horse would rear or run, and so, unconsciously, she settled into the curves of the horse's back and shoulders, and believed that she would stay there. She began, at last, to ride.

*

The woods were quiet as Meredith had begun once again to know quiet: neither human voice nor machinery interrupted the drone of birds and wind and falling leaves. Yet she was uneasy. This forest hadn't been pillaged as recently as the one where she had found the horse again, but the scars were still raw. Saplings stood trembling amidst the tombstones of the giants: gray rotting stumps three and four and five feet in diameter.

Then, as afternoon slid toward evening, the young trees went still. The shadows stretched and grew branches until they became a ghost forest. Every living thing fell silent before that vast, grey recrimination. Meredith thought of the Wendigo, and her legs tightened involuntarily around the horse. The horse, keened already to danger, needed no more permission than that. She took off in a choppy trot, with Meredith clinging on desperately. Then her gait changed again, speeding up but smoothing out. By instinct Meredith leaned forward along the horse's neck, clinging to her mane as she fled that haunted wood.

When it was finally behind them, the horse slowed again to a trot. This time, tense and exhausted, Meredith lost her balance. They were back into spruce forest by then. The ground was soft with needles, the fall barely hurt, but it was one insult too many. Her head raged with pent-up tears, and she swatted at the horse's muzzle when she came sniffing.

The horse blew and then walked off. Meredith forgot her wounded pride then, terrified that the horse would leave her again. She got to her feet and stumbled after her. The horse hadn't gone far; she was browsing grass in a clearing a little way into the trees. She didn't turn to Meredith, though Meredith knew by her swiveling ears that the horse was well aware of her.

I'm sorry that I blamed you, Meredith said.

There was a long pause. At last, the horse said, *You will learn not to fall.* She blew again and then pressed her nose into Meredith's chest. Meredith lowered her cheek to the horse's forehead, and stood like that until her legs stopped shaking.

*

The next morning, Meredith's whole body ached, as it had when she'd first come out of the sea. She had a bruise as wide as her hand on the hip where she had fallen. It hurt even to think about riding, but she knew that she had no choice. Not only her feet but the horse's pride must be spared at any cost.

Still, she ate her boiled potatoes slowly and washed her dishes in a nearby steam with meticulous care. Then she approached the horse, who was quietly chomping grass. The horse raised her head, ears pitched forward, grass roots and earth falling from her mouth. Meredith waited, but the horse appeared to have no intention of lowering herself to accommodate Meredith this time. Had she been so inclined, she could have rested her chin on the horse's withers. Climbing up from the ground would be impossible.

How is it done? Meredith asked.

The horse stopped chewing and looked at her. Then she turned and began walking down the path. Meredith followed, feet throbbing and joints grinding beneath her pack. They'd gone no more than a hundred yards when she had to stop. She sat down on a rock by the side of the road, sore and frustrated. The horse stepped up beside her and stood waiting, one back hoof tipped up so it rested on the toe.

It took Meredith a few moments to understand. Then, she stood up on the rock. It would still be a stretch, but she thought she could get her leg over the horse if the horse didn't move. Clutching a handful of mane, she dragged her clumsy weight onto the horse's back.

Walk, now, said Meredith when she was settled.

The horse gazed into the middle distance. The wind parted around them.

Why won't you speak to me? Meredith asked.

The horse blew. Meredith sighed, considering what might make the horse move. She thought of the previous night, when fear had made her clamp her legs and the horse had shot forward. She had no desire to repeat that experience; on the other hand, she had no desire to sit stationary on the horse's back all day. Gingerly, she squeezed with her legs. The horse took a step forward. Meredith squeezed again, harder, and the horse took another step. She closed her legs around the horse, and this time she didn't release them. The horse took a step, and then another, and a third, and Meredith stopped counting.

2

The next afternoon, skirting a hill at a lake-head, Meredith found herself looking across a valley at the backlit steps of a mountain range rising to the northwest. They were spectacular, and utterly foreign, and so she knew that she had never seen mountains before. The horse stopped, and they both stood looking toward the distant peaks.

If there is a God, Meredith said at last, *he is there.*

You have not crossed them yet, said the horse.

Have you?

The horse only blew and walked on.

The ground rose all through the day. That night Meredith dreamed of a highway unraveling along a mountain chain's knotted backbone, beneath a gold-ringed moon. She woke to a falling sky. It took her several long moments to make sense of it: snow.

The squall blew itself out before she'd finished breakfast. The sun crested the hill on which they'd camped, burning away the cloud and igniting a brief, searing brightness before the thin snow melted. Then the world settled back into shades of green and brown except for the mountains hovering blue on the horizon, their peaks incandescent with snow.

That day the logging roads gave way to rocky meadows and deep ponds, hills bristling with grizzled pines. The hills had been plundered for their old wood, but they didn't have the haunted feel of the earlier forests. It seemed the remaining trees had soaked up the granite heart of the hills, and grown stoical rather than vindictive. They knew that they could outlast fate.

All of that country had the same unbending feel to it, as if no human action could quite leave its mark. At one point, hearing a pounding of water, the horse followed it until she and Meredith stood at the foot of a great cascade, where a river had driven through rock with the undulating motion of a screw, to descend a series of stone steps until it plunged over a lip and into a basin below. Not far from there, they found the same river running through a hole in the rock so deep that the tops of the trees growing on its banks were level with the ground on which they stood.

Then, in the afternoon, they found a road. It was a proper carriage road, furnished with split-log bridges where it crossed streams and gullies, but it looked as if it hadn't been traveled in a long time. They followed it through a world whose population seemed to have dwindled once again to the horse and the girl on her back. Meredith was glad not to encounter any more towns, but she still felt uneasy about the pristine emptiness of the abandoned road. She didn't want to stop on it overnight, but as the sun set, there was no end in sight.

Finally, the horse refused to go on. Meredith slid down from her back and looked around. Just off the road was a little birch grove cross-cut by a stream, which gurgled as it fell from a lip of rock into a small, round pool. Sighing, she put down her pack by the stream and began to make camp.

She'd just lit a handful of kindling when she heard the snap of twigs, the rustle of movement. She froze, thinking of the wolf in the icehouse. Though the silhouette that eventually emerged from the shadows was human, Meredith was no less frightened. She crouched in front of her embryonic fire, shielding the light with her body and hoping that whoever it was would turn before noticing her. Instead, the figure kept moving toward her.

Now she could see that it was a child – a boy of perhaps ten or twelve. His face was just visible in the light of the lantern he carried. His clothes were ragged, his feet bare, and he carried an old satchel slung across his body. Stopping at the pool beneath the little waterfall, he set the lantern down. By its flickering light, he pulled a loose-woven reed basket from the pool. Meredith saw the flash of silvery bodies as he emptied the trap, and her stomach constricted with hunger as the boy knocked each fish on the head, gutted them, and packed them into the satchel.

He turned then to go, but the light of the lantern caught Meredith's face. His initial fear was replaced by curiosity when he realized that Meredith was as terrified as he was. He took a few steps toward her, and then stood looking at her, his head cocked to one side. Meredith could see the freckles on his thin face, the wide gray eyes and overlong red-brown hair. She could see kindness beneath the curiosity in his expression.

At last, he nodded to her. "I'm sorry, ma'am," he said. "For a minute there, I thought you were a ghost."

Meredith had to smile at that.

"Don't mean to be rude, ma'am, but what are you doing away out here by yourself?"

The horse blew; the boy jumped. Then, realizing what he had heard, he laughed in self-deprecation and held the lantern higher. It gleamed in the horse's eye. "Ah – not quite alone. Still, it's a funny place to stop, with our town just over the rise."

Meredith shrugged. The boy's eyes narrowed.

"You a mute?"

The word made her flinch, but it was no more than the truth. She nodded.

"You ain't simple, though."

She shook her head.

He studied her again. "You look hungry."

145

Meredith showed him her handful of potatoes. It was the last of them. The boy screwed up his face. "I don't mean no offense, ma'am, but taters ain't a meal. Here." He stepped across the stream, took two fish from the satchel, and held them toward her.

Meredith shook her head.

"Go on. I know you're hungry, and there ain't nothin' worse."

Meredith pointed to him, and shrugged. The boy smiled a sweet, brilliant smile.

"Oh, I got plenty. Ma'll never know there were two more." He paused, studied her again. "You know what to do with 'em?"

Meredith knew. She'd kept that memory of the brown hands lighting a fire beneath twig-skewered fish. In fact, it seemed that each memory she recovered stayed put. She wondered, briefly, if they would ever amount to a whole, or if she would go through the rest of her life with only a half-pieced jigsaw awareness of its beginning.

The boy was still looking at her. She nodded. He made to turn away, but she waved her hands to stop him.

"Eh?" he asked.

She'd meant to thank him for his open-handed kindness. Too late, she remembered that this was impossible. He was giving her that cocked-head look again. In a moment he would turn away, and suddenly, desperately, she didn't want him to go empty-handed. She put her hand into her pocket, and came up with the knife from the cabin.

The boy's face lit up when he saw it. "That's an Indian knife!" he said. "Real old, too. I bet it's worth something...only if it was mine, I'd never sell it." He blinked at her earnestly. Meredith held it toward him. "Oh, no. I couldn't."

Meredith indicated the fish.

"That knife's worth a lot more than a couple of fish!"

Meredith could see that he wasn't going to take it. Hesitantly, she extended her free hand toward his. The boy watched, perfectly still, as Meredith's hand closed around his. It was a gesture so ordinary it should have been near meaningless, but Meredith had lost all memory of the touch of another human being. The boy's warm, damp hand was charged with all that she had lost, and it pushed at her like a sea current. Willing back the overwhelming images, she put the knife into his hand and closed his fingers around it. Her own hands fell away from his, clutching each other.

The boy grinned and shook his head. "Well all right, ma'am – if you're sure. Thank you." He turned to go, but he said over his shoulder: "Good luck."

Meredith nodded. Raising his hand once, the boy stepped back across the stream, and away into the dark.

3

The next morning, for the first time, Meredith woke without the dull ache of loss. What startled her most was that she had not realized until she felt its absence that she'd carried it with her. Everything looked cleaner, brighter. When she mounted the horse, it was with anticipation. She wondered if this would be the day they finally reached the mountains.

It was difficult to judge, since often they could not see them. The road they traveled was a low one, following the base of the hills, but Meredith sensed the mountains all the same. They seemed to be pulling her onward, toward them, and every once in a while a valley would open up or they would crest a rise, and she would be rewarded with a glimpse of the jagged gray-and-white peaks against the brilliant sky.

The town took Meredith completely by surprise. One moment they were riding through silent woods, the next they rounded a bend and found themselves in the middle of a village. Meredith's eagerness evaporated into panic. Her gut in her throat, she tried to turn the horse, but the horse ignored her, walking calmly forward. Meredith waited for somebody to call out, to stop her, but no one did. When her heart had stilled at last, she realized why: the town was empty.

It was a strange emptiness, different from desertion. It held no menace or expectation. If anything, it seemed deliberate, as if the whole town had decided one day to go somewhere else. The houses were closed up carefully; what windows weren't shuttered were neatly curtained. In the overgrown yards, Meredith could still see the distant work of garden shears. She had no doubt that if she were to enter one of the cottages, she would find the beds made and the stoves blacked beneath however many years' coating of dust.

Meredith, however, had no desire to open any of those doors. The idea of sleeping in a bed or eating in a kitchen that had been purposely, efficiently abandoned was more horrifying to her even than a night in a stripped forest. Dark was fast closing in, and with it big, bruised clouds promising further snow, but she nudged the horse onward. Reluctantly, the horse moved. She was sluggish though, her heart stepping back as her feet moved her forward until finally, she stopped.

I won't stay here, said Meredith.

There is no danger here, the horse answered. *There is help.*

Help for what? asked Meredith.

But the horse had lapsed back into silence and would not move. When Meredith kicked, she horse only dropped her head and began browsing for grass.

Please, said Meredith.

Still the horse said nothing. Meredith sighed, slid to the ground and looked around her. At first she saw nothing but the empty houses and dead gardens. Peering up the road ahead, though, she discerned a dim, red beacon: a tiny spot that flared bright for a moment, then faded, only to burn bright again a moment later. It moved slowly toward her, and she felt not fear but an inexplicable a wave of warmth, cut abruptly by regret and a longing that almost brought her to her knees. She clung to the horse, her heart fixed on that approaching light. A push of wind brought with it the faint scent of pipe smoke. Her eyes filled, and her throat burned.

"All right, there?" a man's voice called from the direction of the red glow.

Meredith clung to the horse. Her mind was stilled by the poignancy of the pipe-smoke. She could not have spoken then, even if her voice had not deserted her. At last the man's shape emerged out of the night. He was an old man, small and sinewy, with a hard-weathered face and kindly, intelligent dark eyes set back in its folds. His clothes were patched, his hat worn, but he looked too healthy to be destitute. He stood, studying Meredith, drawing ruminatively on his pipe.

"I'm real," he said at last.

Meredith looked at him.

"What I mean to say is, you don't need to be afraid. I'm no ghost. Most folks come through here – not that there's many

– they figure I'm a ghost, seeing as I live in a ghost town." He chuckled to himself. "But I'm just as real as you and that horse."

Reluctantly, Meredith nodded.

The man peered at her closely. "Can't you speak?"

She shook her head.

"Huh. But you can hear all right?"

She nodded. He nodded back, with what looked like approval.

"Well then," he said, "you're the first woman I met who's got *that* the right way 'round!" He chuckled again, and then, seeing that Meredith hadn't followed suit, he added, "Come now, Miss – I don't mean nothing by it. You got somewhere to go tonight?"

Meredith was poised to nod when the horse shoved her in the back with her muzzle. She righted herself and swatted the horse, but the old man only laughed again. "Looks like your horse has sense, anyway. Wherever you're going, you aren't going tonight. We're fifteen miles from anywhere, and there's a storm coming. Better come home with me."

He turned and began to walk back the way Meredith had come. Meredith hesitated. The horse followed the old man without a backward glance. As the man reached out to pat the horse's shoulder, a handful of windblown snowflakes stung Meredith's cheek. Sighing, she turned and followed the horse.

*

The man's name was Joseph Chapman, and he lived in a tiny house on the outskirts of the village. The house had a barn behind it, in which he installed Meredith's horse beside a milk cow and two lugubrious, elderly sheep.

"Pip and Squeak," he said, pitching fodder into a manger for the horse as he nodded to the sheep with a fond eye. "They would have been chops ten years back, but Jessie got her hands on them first. She was a soft soul, my Jessie. She never could turn her back on a crying baby, never mind the species. These two were orphaned twins, born too early. She kept 'em in a crate by the range for two days. I never thought they'd make it, but I came down one morning and there they were, running around the kitchen, bleating for their bottles…well, how could I butcher them then?"

For a second, Meredith imagined lobsters scrabbling on a wooden floor, and her heart constricted. "Your horse will be fine," said Joseph, misinterpreting the look. "Come on in now, or supper will burn."

Meredith followed Joseph back to the house through swirling snow. He cocked an eye to the black sky before he shut the door. "There's going to be some weather, all right."

Meredith felt a restless urge to contradict him, but she knew she might as well contradict the snow-riddled sky. She followed Joseph into the kitchen, where the sudden smell of real food cooking brought up another wave of half-memories. She staggered at their onslaught and was glad that Joseph had his back to her.

"Jessie was the cook," Joseph said apologetically as he ladled chicken and dumplings onto two plates. He handed one of them to her. "Since she's been gone, I've learned enough to get by – no more."

But to Meredith, who'd existed for so long on the brink of starvation, Joseph's dinner was far more. She cleaned two plates and could have cleaned a third, except that common sense told her she would regret it if she pushed her shrunken stomach any further. So she covered her plate with her napkin despite Joseph's urgings, and accepted a mug of strong black tea.

"Well then," he said, eyeing her across the table, "I suppose it's no use asking you where you're going, though I bet there's a darn good story in it."

Meredith shrugged apologetically.

"I know one thing, though: you came from the coast."

Meredith looked up sharply, clattered her mug onto the table.

"Jessie came from the coast. You have the sea in your eyes, just like she did."

Meredith shook her head emphatically.

Joseph raised his eyebrows. "All right, have it your way. But you don't have to worry. Whoever you are and whatever you're running from, I got no one left to tell. I've been the only man in town for five years now."

Shakily, Meredith lifted her mug again and took a sip. Joseph watched her carefully, just as he might have watched her if she'd made a spoken response.

"You're wondering why I'm alone here," he said. Meredith nodded, and reached for his plate. He pushed it across the table to her without protest, for which she would have liked him if she hadn't begun to already. As he spoke, she washed the dishes.

"The simple answer," he said, "is stubbornness. The honest one is that the world's changed, and I've dug in my heels. It's silly, I know, but I just couldn't face it. Motor wagons and electric lights – it all sounds dangerous to me. Maybe if I'd had children…they ease you into the future, I guess…" He sighed. "No good speculating. As it is, I stayed here when the others moved on, and now it's too late to do anything else. Me and Larchton, we're both relics, and there's a kind of justice in that I guess, because I was the first child born here, and I'll be the last to die."

He paused until Meredith looked over at him and shrugged.

"You really want to hear all this?" he asked.

She nodded.

"Well, all right. But you tell me to shut up when you get bored. Let's see now…I guess if you've never been here before, you won't know that Larchton was a purpose-built logging town. There were a lot of them back at the beginning of the century. Like as came up from the ground overnight. Most of them didn't even have names. When this town was built, it was just called 'Township A'. I guess it was never going to be much good for anything but logging. Most of it's hills, and even where it isn't, the growing season's too short to make a go of farming anything more than hay and a few potatoes.

"My father founded the place. That was back in the '30s. There was no road then, only a footpath through the Notch. But he saw lumber and plenty of it, so he built this house and married my mother and brought her to live here, and it wasn't long before others followed. He dammed the river and built a sawmill, and with the money he made, he built a bigger house – the one you passed when you first came into town. He and my mother, they lived a life grand enough for these parts, though they both worked hard. He always ran the sawmill himself – said he didn't trust foremen – and my mother cooked for the lumber crews. She was the one that named the town. 'Larch' was her maiden name, you see.

"By the time I was seven, there were nine children in town: enough to warrant a schoolhouse. Oh, didn't we hate it! Winters were so bad, most folks couldn't get to town, so we had our holiday then and sat in school all summer. They taught us well, though. They sent more of us to high school than any other town around these parts, and it was in high school I met my Jessie…"

Meredith had long since racked the dishes and cleaned the basin. Now she leaned against the kitchen counter, watching the old man look deep into a past that was clearly as real to him as the room around him. While she pitied him for all he'd obviously lost, she also felt an unexpected twinge of jealousy. It confounded her. She didn't want a love like Joseph's for his dead wife. She felt no need to belong to a place or people. Nevertheless, the force of Joseph's emotion echoed in the hollow where her grief had been. What had seemed that morning a blessed emptiness now looked like the place where a great tree has fallen. A wound streaming earth and torn roots like a bleak, black cry.

"I married her," Joseph said at last, recalling Meredith from her rumination. "It was the day after we took our diplomas. I brought her back to this house. Mother wanted to build a new one, a grand one, but Jessie said the house where I was born was good enough for her. And it's well enough that it was, because even then, the town was dying.

"First there was the war. You wouldn't think politics could make its way up here when it took the mail three weeks in a dry season, but it did. Half the men in town enlisted, and less than half of those came back. I didn't go. Jessie and my mother begged me not to. I still don't know if I did right, but I guess there's not much in it. Those Negroes got their freedom without me, didn't they?" He shook his head, unconvinced.

"But what really finished us was the railroad. They extended the Berlin logging line up here in the seventies. The first year it ran, we shipped out twenty-million board feet of soft wood, and so it went: a few years of boom the like of which no one here had ever imagined, and then all the easy wood was gone. And if it wasn't easy, it wasn't worth the company's time. Ten years after they built it, the Berlin line stopped running up here, and one by one the logging families left. What was there to keep them?" He asked in a beseeching way that made Meredith wish she had an answer.

"Even my mother and father left in the end. They came back to summer at the big house until he died, and she lost heart. Then it was only me and Jessie left. We never did have any children, though she wanted them desperate enough. I thought she'd be lonely here, but she said, 'This is our home, and I intend to die here.' And so she did. The last funeral held in that cemetery was hers." His voice shook, near breaking. "Well, the last but one. When I die, I'll be buried beside her, and Larchton will be officially finished."

He sighed, and looked up. He seemed startled to see Meredith standing there, but he covered it with a smile. "Forgive me. I've been rambling. These days, the past seems more real to me than the present." He looked at her. She made no gesture of understanding. She couldn't, when she had no past at all.

"I guess that's hard to imagine, when you're young," Joseph said, shaking his head. "Oh, well, it's time for bed anyway. It's not much, but I keep the spare room made up on the off chance it's needed. It's through that door, to the right." He pointed the direction.

Meredith nodded.

"Sleep well," said Joseph, and tapped his pipe out on the grate.

4

It snowed all night and on through the next day. Meredith had a memory of snow, but not snow like this. This was so thick, so quick-driven by the wind funneling through the deep valleys that she couldn't see her hand if she stretched it to arms' length. It felt like walls closing in on her, and she didn't like being confined with another person – even one as amiable as Joseph Chapman. But he seemed to recognize this and kept a respectful distance. In fact, he only asked her two questions in the course of that long day, the first in the morning, when he came back from the barn with a washtub full of snow and set it on the range.

"When it snows," he explained, "I wash. Myself, my clothes, the house…you got anything you want washed, Miss?"

Meredith peered down at her filthy clothes and nodded.

"Well, then," said Joseph with a faint smile, "you can have the first tub of water. I don't suppose you have any other clothes… I'll find you something to wear while yours dry."

She nodded again.

Joseph gave her a speculative look and then asked his second question: "Can you write?"

Which Meredith answered, to her own surprise, with a nod. Joseph rummaged in a drawer, came up with a piece of paper and a stub of pencil. "If you see fit," he said, laying them on the table, "you can write your name on there. You don't have to. Only it seems funny, calling you nothing but 'Miss'."

He turned and went upstairs then. Meredith heard him moving around above her head. She looked at the tub of snow on the range. It would take a long time to melt and warm. At last she sat down at the table, looking at the blank piece of paper. In all of the time since she'd awakened on the beach, it had never occurred to her that there might be a simple antidote to her muteness.

She picked up the pencil in shaking fingers, and made an experimental mark on the paper. Her hand felt clumsy and the line wavered, but it was dark and definite, nonetheless. She drew another, downward and right-sloping, then its mirror image, and finished the letter with a second vertical. After that it was easier. By the time Joseph returned with an armful of clothing, the eight letters of Meredith's name stood stark and clear on the crumpled bit of paper.

Joseph glanced at it, and his eyebrows raised a fraction. "Meredith. That's a strong name. You know, there's a town of that name on Winnipesaukee. That lake almost seems like the sea, it's so big…I was only there once, as a boy – " Seeing Meredith's face cloud over, he stopped abruptly and laid his armful of clothes over the back of a chair along with a faded towel and a wash cloth. "There, now. These things are mine. I don't suppose they'll fit, but it'll be better than anything of Jessie's. You're a good head taller than she was. I'll set another tub on to heat, and then I'll let you be. You just take your time."

Joseph lifted the first tub, now warm, to the floor. He set another on the stove, and then retreated back upstairs. Meredith looked for a few long moments at the tub of water, and then she began to peel off her clothing. She'd lived in it so long, it had become like another skin, and without it she felt more than naked. Flayed. The image was compounded by her emaciation, which made her seem more bone than flesh. She could count the ladder-rungs of her ribcage, her knees and hipbones protruded like those of a corpse half-buried in sand. Her belly was concave, her breasts flattened.

She dipped the cloth in the water and brought it down on her arm. Though the water was barely warm, its touch was painful, as if she were bruised all over. She didn't stop, though, not now that she saw how filthy she was. The dirt on her hands stood out starkly beside the white of her arm where her sleeve had covered it. Her hair was a tangled, matted mess, dull and full of pine needles and burrs. She no more belonged in this house than the horse did, and in a sudden rush of shame she scrubbed herself violently.

Within minutes the water was murky and gray. She took the second tub from the stove. It was barely melted, nowhere near warm, but the cold was less shocking to her newly-bared skin. She washed her hair and her body all over again, and when she was done she stood shivering by the range, looking frankly down at herself. It was almost worse than when dirt had covered her. Her stark, purplish, pimpled limbs reminded her of nothing so much as a plucked chicken.

Sighing, she dried herself and dressed in the clothes Joseph had left. There was a pair of cotton long johns; an old flannel shirt and trousers, worn to softness by years on the washboard; a pair of woolen socks, much-darned but warm; and a thick, grey, woolen sweater. Meredith felt better when she was dressed, though still vaguely raw, as if she'd washed off a portion of herself with the dirt. She tossed the dirty water out the back door and filled the tubs again, putting one on the range to heat. Then, having no way to call to Joseph and no inclination to go upstairs and look for him, she sat down to wait.

5

That afternoon they sat together in the humid kitchen washing clothes. Since Meredith had only the one set, she helped Joseph with his own washing. While they worked, he continued his monologue from the previous evening.

"Do you know," he began, "the first white folks to come here came for diamonds?"

Meredith said nothing, but Joseph continued just as if she'd exclaimed surprise.

"That's right: diamonds! Not right here, of course. They were meant to be a bit further west, in the mountains, but of course to get there you had to go through the Notch, which meant coming through Larchton – or whatever the red men called this spot.

"It was an English settler called Field who started the rumor. He climbed White Hill way back in sixteen-thirty-something. He brought down some rocks from the top he was certain were diamonds. They turned out to be no more than crystal, but it was enough to get the rumors started. Pretty soon they grew into the full-fledged legend that there was untold treasure hidden in the hills.

"So folks came out here looking for it. They brought their ropes and their picks and their packhorses for hauling all those diamonds back to civilization. Of course they didn't find any. They didn't even find any decent farmland – just mountains, each one bigger and harder than the last." He shook his head. "Still, a few of them stayed. Maybe they didn't have the money to go home. Either way they managed to scrape out a few farms, and over time they moved farther west, built a road through the Notch...but this never stopped being wild country. You ever heard the story of the Willeys?"

Meredith shook her head and wrung out a shirt.

"They had a place in Crawford Notch, right in the middle of the mountains. These days there's a railroad running through it, but a hundred years ago, there was no more than a dirt track, barely wide enough for a wagon and team to scrape through. Scrape through they did, though. They had to, so the settlers in Lancaster could reach the ports on the coast. By the turn of the century, there were enough teams passing through the Notch that they needed a lodging and stable there, especially in winter. You think this is a bad storm," he nodded to the gray, snow-blown window, "but it's nothing to what you get in the mountains. The old teamsters had a saying: when a winter nor'wester blew through the Notch, it took two men to hold one man's hair on." Joseph laughed. Meredith smiled.

"The first inn was built in the 1790s, but it wasn't til '25 that the Willeys took over the tenancy. They spread out a bit, added on, with the plan to entertain tourists as well as teamsters. It was no foolish dream, either. There's some beautiful country up there: wildflower meadows and rock maple, the Saco bubbling away and the mountains all around...sure, it must have seemed like heaven on a summer afternoon."

Joseph paused, a shadow on his face. Meredith realized that her hands were hanging slack in the cooling water. She fished a forgotten shirt from the bottom of the tub and began scrubbing again, hoping that her lapse hadn't distracted Joseph from his story.

"Trouble was, the inn sat at the foot of a mountain known for slides. The Willeys saw their first one in June. It's said Samuel and his wife were looking out the back windows of their house when a huge chunk of that mountain gave way, and came sliding toward them. Can you imagine that? Earth and boulders coming down a mountain so fast and furious they uprooted hundred-year-old trees like they were garden weeds, and all of it headed straight for your back door.

"Well, it missed them – just – but it scared them all right. At first they planned to move away. But when they thought it over, it seemed unlikely to them that something like that would happen again. So they built themselves a slide shelter below the house, and went back to their business.

"That was a dry summer. By August, the mountain soil was like a desert. Then, at the end of August, it began to rain, and this was no common rain. The Saco rose twenty-four feet in two days. The feeder streams swelled to rivers. Houses and livestock and fields all washed away. Valleys turned to lakes. And of course, there were slides. With the soil so dry, there was nothing for the rocks and trees to cling to, and down they came with the water.

"Once I met a man who'd seen it. He said that when the storm finally blew out, it looked like a mad beast had been at the mountainsides with its claws. The trees were gone, along with the boulders and the soil. The rock at the inside of those mountains lay bare as bones." Joseph sighed, as if he'd seen it himself.

"It was Tuesday night before anyone reached the Willey house. He was a traveler, determined to get through the Notch that evening. When he reached the inn, he found it still standing. It was a miracle, he thought. The mountain behind the house had been torn apart, the meadow around it was buried under tons of sand and rock, yet the inn had not a scratch on it.

"Then he went inside, and found the house deserted. The beds looked as if they'd been left in a hurry, and there was a Bible open on a table, as if the family had been praying just before they left.

That traveler figured that they'd escaped to a neighbor's house lower down the Notch, and so he slept the night there, and the next morning he went on his way.

"It wasn't until the next night that the Willeys' neighbors realized that something was wrong. No one had seen the family since the storm. A party went up to investigate. They found the empty house and the buried land around it, and they read in them what the traveling man hadn't. They started to dig." Joseph paused. He'd forgotten his washing, and Meredith's shirt had disappeared into the murky water again as she stared at the old man, transfixed by this terrible story.

"They found one of the hired men first, near the top of a pile of earth, with his hands still clenched around a broken tree limb. Next came Mr. and Mrs. Willey, barely recognizable. They kept up the search over the following days, and recovered more bodies, but not all of them. There had been five Willey children. Three of them were never found."

Joseph paused. "It's still a custom," he said at last, "to place a stone on the spot where the family were buried. If you should ever go that way, you'll see it: a monument made of the leavings of that slide." He paused again, his rheumy, dark eyes hard on Meredith's. It seemed he was looking into her, and she felt suddenly light-headed.

"The Bible they'd left on the table," he said, "was open to the eighteenth Psalm. Do you know it?"

Meredith shook her head.

"It's the one where the earth shakes and the mountains tremble, and so on. Fitting reading for that night, I guess. But do you know, it's never that part of the verse I remember."

Meredith didn't blink. She didn't breathe.

"I always remember that verse for the part about the water. 'He drew me out of many waters...the Lord was my stay.'"

Meredith's mind was suddenly full of the scream of tearing wood and rigging. The thunder of black waves on a gray beach, like the roar of a riven mountain. She began to shake.

Joseph watched her for a moment more, and then he said, "I guess you aren't much of a church-going woman – begging your pardon if I'm mistaken – but look up the verse sometime, if you can. And if you ever go up by the Willey's Notch, you think of it, and lay a rock on their cairn, and remember, Meredith: no tragedy is ever irredeemable."

6

The next day, the sun rose on a silent, glittering world. Joseph loaded Meredith's pack with provisions and a second set of clothing, despite her gestured protests. He also gave her a rope halter for the horse, and a second loop of rope to use as reins. The horse accepted them readily enough, but when Joseph rummaged in the barn and re-emerged with a lumpy old saddle, she laid her ears back and danced away from him. Meredith put a hand on her shoulder to still her and shook her head at Joseph.

He shrugged. "Seems the two of you have got on well enough without one. Besides, I always said a man who can't ride a horse bareback's got no business sitting in a saddle." He paused, then grinned. "I suppose the same goes for a woman."

His smile turned gentle, wistful. They stood looking at each other across the clouds of their breath. Meredith wanted to thank him, and cursed her voicelessness. Then, pulling her jacket around her, she felt a slight weight in her pocket. She drew out the stone with the tree in it, and offered it to Joseph.

He looked at it for a long time before he said, "Now, I've heard of these, but I never thought I'd see one in my lifetime."

Meredith tried to put it into his hand, but he closed his fingers. "Don't you know what this is?"

Meredith shrugged.

"It's a tree preserved in stone. A tree more ancient than you or I can imagine. This is valuable."

Meredith knew that what he had given her paled against any value the fossil could have. That anyone who tended the past as carefully as he did deserved to have it. But she could only continue to proffer it. At last, hesitantly, Joseph took it.

"All right," he said, smiling slightly. "You take care, young Meredith. You're no shrinking violet, but the way you're headed is a hard one."

Inwardly Meredith shivered, but outwardly she smiled at him.

"If you ever come back this way…well, you know where to find me."

She nodded again. Then she shouldered her pack, let Joseph give her a leg up onto the horse, and with a wave, they were off.

*

Though there were deep drifts in places, the wind had kept the snow from piling too high on the road. The horse skipped and tossed her head, and Meredith's spirit lifted too as they rode through this bright, clean world.

An hour or so after they'd left Joseph, the horse stopped at the top of a ridge. There was nothing before them but coruscated silence, the snowy road unfurling toward the mountains in the distance. Meredith imagined the ghosts of prospectors on that brilliant highway, grasping at faceted snowflakes that melted in their hands. She wondered if those men had stayed long enough to learn the wealth of the foothills' winter beauty, or if disappointment had blinded them to it, sent them chasing the specter of riches they would never find.

There are diamonds here, after all, Meredith said.

The horse snorted and began to walk again.

As before, they rode west and south, skirting mountains now rather than farms and lakes. As the day wore on, the mountains gradually closed in around them, blinding white giving way inch by inch until they rode almost entirely in violet shadow. It seemed they had wandered once again into an unpopulated world, though once, far to the south, Meredith heard the scream of a train's whistle.

The road inclined gradually until, near evening, they came to a great stony gate – two massive boulders twenty feet apart, a doorway minus its lintel cut from the solid rock. After the gated mountain pass, the road ran steeply downward, with cliffs of speckled grey stone towering on either side. It was nearing dark, but Meredith had no desire to camp in that claustrophobic place, with the wind whistling through.

Finally, the cliffs gave way to a little stony valley with a river running through it. It was a wild, lonely place, and the Willeys' fate loomed in Meredith's mind. But it was almost dark, the mountains stretched as far as she could see in any direction, and the horse seemed untroubled. Meredith found a sheltered dip of rock on the bank of the river and lit a fire, trying not to think of the mountains rearing up on every side. Still, she couldn't help imagining the thunder of a landslide in stormy darkness, a mountain's roared warning. She wondered what had made the Willeys leave their house, and whether she would have done the same, or if cowardice would have sent her under a bed or a stair cupboard and so saved her.

Stop it, she told herself, and opened her pack to look for supper. Her hand met something hard among the wadded clothing and parcels of food. She pulled it out. It was a careworn Bible with a marker sticking out of it. The front cover fell back on its threadbare binding. At the top of the flyleaf, in neat, faded copperplate was the inscription: "Jessie Armstrong." Meredith turned to the marked page, and she felt a welling in her eyes as they skipped to the verses of which Joseph had spoken:

"He sent from above, he took me, he drew me out of many waters.

He delivered me from my strong enemy, and from them which hated me: for they were too strong for me.

They prevented me in the day of my calamity: but the Lord was my stay."

Meredith closed the book, clutched it to her breast.

7

The mountains grew as they followed the road south and west. They lost their distant, ethereal beauty and gained a terrible kind of grandeur. Peering up at their cloud-quilted tops,

Meredith knew she would have been at a loss to put words to the emotions they stirred in her, even if she'd been physically able. It seemed that the earth had grown walls, and in all her solitary wandering, she had never felt as cut off from the living world as she did in their still, grey midst.

Often now the footing was bad. When the horse began to stumble, Meredith got off and walked beside her. They inched along that poor, pitted road, skirting old slides and fallen boulders. They crept along the feet of mountains brooding with mist, their sides raked by old avalanches; mountains snow-scoured and bleak. They saw them in the magisterial purple of the setting sun, in the pale pink dawn, and they saw them erased by cloud.

Sometimes they passed gaps leading to drops of thousands of feet, into valleys full of rocky rivers. Once they found themselves on a wide stone shelf, surrounded by nothing but cloud and air. They stood there for a long time, leaning into the icy wind, and rather than vertigo, Meredith felt a wild elation, as if she had gained the top of the world.

The next storm came when they were in a valley so deep and narrow it had never been logged. It was full of funereal black spruce, a contrasting scatter of balsam thrusting rich green spires toward the roiling sky. The trees grew so close together that their lower branches had died from lack of light, and beard moss hung like ghosts' garments from the bare branches. Between the forest and the thickening snow, Meredith quickly lost the path. She knew that she should stop, but the narrow valley and the tight-packed trees seemed to close in on her with menace. So she carried on, her fingers wound in the horse's mane as the horse dipped herdnose, pushing against the headwind as if it were a harness.

This time, Meredith's stubbornness paid off. Around a bend, the valley opened out abruptly into a clearing with a pond. On the pond's far bank, a little hut shaped like an upended bowl huddled beneath the branches of an old, gnarled tree. A dim light shone at its door, and a sweet snatch of wood smoke came over the frozen water with a gust of wind.

It wasn't lost on Meredith that the hut looked very like the ones in her nightmare of the cannibals' graveyard. However, she was learning to trust the horse's instinct, and the horse showed no fear. In fact, she walked eagerly toward the hut, her ears forward and alert.

By the time they reached it, someone had come outside. She was a young woman, roughly Meredith's age but a good head shorter, dark-skinned, sweet-faced, with wide, intelligenk eyes. She wore a strange mixture of clothing: a beaded leather tunic and moccasins with a blue tartan shawl and a sprigged calico skirt. When Meredith dismounted, The young woman nodded to her and smiled. Meredith nodded back, her face too cold to smile.

"You are welcome," said the young woman. "Go inside and warm yourself. I will see to your horse."

Meredith hesitated, looking at the horse. The horse blew and pushed against the woman with her muzzle. The woman laughed and patted her and said to Meredith, "Don't worry. Even if I meant to steal her, I wouldn't get far in this." She gestured to the whirling snow. "But as it happens I have no cause to steal her, for I have my own horse, and he is all the horse I need. They will be glad of each other's company."

Meredith remained uneasy, but the horse was looking toward the edge of the forest, where there was another building. This one was a more conventional wooden square – in fact it looked more like a human house than a stable. Meredith heard a faint whinny from within, and her own horse's head rose, her ears flicked, and she called shrilly back.

Meredith turned toward the hut, and then, abruptly, she stopped. There was a dark patch in the snow by thetdoor. Meredith bent down to look, her guts as cold now as her skin. The stain was blood, fresh and unmistakable. Meredith stood up again, reaching for the horse's halter with a shaking hand.

The woman smiled at her calmly. "Don't fear it. It is a sign, but not an evil one." She pointed up at the overhanging tree. Warily, Meredith followed her finger to an ancient, blackened branch, which reached from the crotch of the tree and ended just over the door of the hut. The blood dripped from the tip of this branch, as if from a severed limb. Hard as Meredith looked, she could not find its source.

Echoing Meredith's thought, the woman said, "You won't find it, because there's nothing to find. The blood comes from the tree itself, sure as its own sap. It's all that's left of an old, old sadness. I will tell you about it, but first, let me see to your horse."

Meredith looked from the bleeding branch to the woman. The woman smiled again, and with a faint nod, she turned and led the horse toward the wooden house. The horse went willingly. Sighing, Meredith stepped over the bloodstain, lifted the heavy leather flap serving as a door and ducked inside.

8

Inside, the hut seemed something between a house and a tent. It was about twelve feet in diameter, its supporting frame made of slender poles bent and tied into shape, its walls made of animal skins. Wooden benches ran around the walls, covered with blankets and quilts and cushions. At the center, an open fire burned inside a fieldstone ring, the smoke rising up through a hole in the roof. This, along with a couple of small kerosene lanterns, provided the room's light.

As Meredith walked toward the fire, something she'd taken for another pile of blankets moved. She was half way out the door again when she realized that it wasn't a pile of blankets at all, but an anciend man, so swaddled that his face was barely visible among the quilts and skins. As it was, all that Meredith could make out were a shriveled face, two milky white eyes and a hand like a tree root.

"Welcome, daughter," he said in a voice like the creak of the wigwam's poles in the wind. "I did not mean to frighten you."

Reluctantly, Meredith came back and took the extended hand. It was surprisingly warm and strong. Still holding it, the man guided her closer until she could see his gentle smile. She also saw that his white eyes were fixed somewhere beyond her. He was blind.

"We have been expecting you," he said, at which Meredith tried to back away again. He held her fast. "There is nothing to fear. There is no evil here, just as Anis told you, and no sorcery but nature's. The tree is bleeding again. When the tree bleeds, we know to expect a visitor."

Meredith had no idea what he meant, but his voice was gentle. She stopped trying to pull away, and the man released her. "There, now." He patted her hand, his milky eyes so nearly resting on her own that for a moment she wondered if she had been mistaken about his blindness. Then they shifted away again. "I suppose it would frighten me too, except that it's been bleeding as long as any of my people remember."

He paused. Then, as if Meredith had spoken the obvious question, he said, "No one really knows why. Sometimes it goes for years without spilling so much as a drop of sap. Then it will start up again – no warning, no regard for the time of year. But heartbreak isn't seasonat…"

He trailed off, shaking his head as the young woman, Anis, came inside. Having heard his last words, her brow furrowed. "Ah,

N'mahom!" she scolded. "Let the poor girl sit down before you start in on that."

"I only wanted her to understand," the old man said. "She was terrified."

"Well, I'm glad you've set that right," Anis said wryly, glancing at Meredith's dubious face as she hunp her wet shawl on a rack by the fire. "I'm sorry if my grandfatheruis too hasty with his information," she said to Meredith. "It's because he's been waiting for you all the last week."

Meredith looked at her.

"Ever since the branch started bleeding."

Meredith shook her head. Anis smiled. She had a kindly face, which Meredith couldn't quite distrust. "Let's begin again. I am Anis Brisebois, and this is my grandfather, Tomah."

Meredith nodded, waiting for the questions, but they didn't come. Instead, Anis held out her hands. "Give me your wet things, and I'll hang them to dry. The trousers too – don't worry, *N'mahom* is completely blind. Cataracts. There is a doctor in Portland who can remove them, but *N'mahom* won't allow it."

"White doctors are imbeciles!" the old man interjected.

Anis shrugged. "And there you have it." She took the clothes that Meredith gave her and hung them with her shawl by the fire. Meredith put on the extra set of trousers that Joseph had given her.

"Still," Anis continued, lifting a pot from one of the benches and setting it on three stones so that it balanced over the fire, "he always knows when the tree bleeds, whether he can see it or not – eh, *N'mahom*?"

"If I didn't," he said, "I'd have no right living here."

"He is its guardian," Anis explained, stirring the contents of the pot. Her black braid slipped over her shoulder, and she twitched it back again, out of the reach of the flames. "And I am his, now that he can't look after himself."

"So you say!" Tomah complained. "I looked after myself well enough before you came and started fussing."

Anis rolled her eyes at Meredith. "Our family has always guarded the tree. Ever since the lovers were buried."

"She doesn't know what you mean," Tomah said.

Anis sighed. "I suppose not. Why don't you tell her."

Tomah nodded in satisfaction, as if he'd expected this prompt. "It was a long time back," he said, "just after the white men came, but before their pestilence began to kill our people. It was all wars in those days: the English fighting the French, the tribes fighting the English, the English fighting the tribes...and yes, sometimes, the tribes fighting each other."

He shook his head, frowning, and took the plate of stew that Anis handed him. She handed another to Meredith, took one herself, and then sat down by her grandfather and began to eat. After a moment, Meredith joined them. The stew didn't look like much, but it was delicious, with chunks of fresh meat and vegetables.

"It's a wonder," Tomah continued between bites, "that every tree in these hills doesn't bleed, with all the blood they must have taken up in those years." He shook his head. "It was brutal. In that kind of war – the kind that lasts year after year, when no one has a clear idea anymore whom they're fighting or why – men forget mercy. Sometimes they forget basic decency. That was what happened here. There was a battle in this valley. A terrible, bloody battle between our tribe and a group of English settlers. It is said that the very mountains wept to witness it..."

Tomah's blankets had fallen back as he ate, revealing the wizened, battle-scarred skin of his shoulders. His eyes were no longer fixed above the doorway, but on the fire, as if it burned through his blindness to show him these visions of the distant past.

"The English won that day," he continued, as Anis silently refilled Meredith's plate. "At the end of it, one of their officers was walking the field, looking for wounded men who might have been left for dead. I don't know that he found any, but when he came to this spot – " he tapped the packed-earth floor of the wigwam " – he noticed a Pequawket warrior lying dead beneath a young cherry tree, overlaid by the body of a beautiful woman. "The English man turned her over to see whether she might still have breath. It was then that he saw that both she and the warrior had been shot through the heart. The only explanation he could imagine was that the woman had put herself between her beloved and the white man's gun, and the single bullet had killed them both."

He paused. Meredith's refilled plate lay untouched by her side. Anis gazed at her grandfather with a half-smile as the wind whistled around the hut.

"Well," Tomah continued at last, "this white man was so moved by the young woman's bravery and the strength of her love that he ordered their bodies be kept from the fires and given back to their own people, so that they might have proper funeral rites. An unusually honorable Englishman." Tomah shook his head. "Word was sent to the tribe, and they came. It's said that all of the surviving Englishmen came as well, to see them buried.

"Have you ever been to an Pequawket funeral?" He didn't wait for Meredith to answer before continuing, "Like you, we bury our dead, but not beneath cold stone markers. Instead the men of the tribe sway a young tree – they bend it down until the roots turn up – and the body is placed in the cavity beneath. Then the tree is released, and the earth replaced around it. As the tree grows it takes sustenance from the body, extending the dead one's life by its own. And so the lovers were buried beneath the cherry tree where they'd fallen."

Tomah faced the wall behind which the tree stood. "That very first spring, the tree began to bleed. At first the tribe thought that it was a reminder of the brave woman who gave her heart's blood to save her beloved. A reminder of the strength of love." He paused again, chewing thoughtfully on a tough piece of meat. "No doubt it is that," he said at last. "But if that was all, then I suppose it would bleed all the time. And it doesn't." He turned his white eyes on Meredith. "It bleeds in sympathy with those who have been wounded in love. It bleeds when they come near it. And that, daughter, is how we knew to expect you."

9

Meredith expected questions on the heels of Tomah's revelation, but neither he nor Anis asked her anything, not even the reason for her silence. In fact, they seemed not to notice it. It went beyond a failure to mention it. It was as if they had unconsciously accepted her muteness as soon as they met her and immediately shifted their interactions to accommodate it.

Still, Meredith couldn't settle in their house. She kept twitching the skin door back to see if the snow had let up, but it raged on, too heavy for her to think of going anywhere further than the stable. She went there every few hours on the pretense of checking the horses' fodder, but they were never more than halfway through the pile of sweet hay she kept topping up. Anis's horse – a giant, heavy-boned chestnut with a six-pointed star on his forehead and beautiful, white-feathered feet – gazed at her with eyes that seemed to wonder why she could not leave them alone. Meredith's own horse didn't even bother to look.

"They have made friends, your horse and Alakws," Anis said when Meredith came back from one of these trips. Meredith raised her eyebrows at the strange name. "It means 'Star'," Anis explained, not looking up from the garment she was stitching. "It's not the most creative name. But then, I was only five when I gave it to him. He answers to it happily enough."

As Anis sewed and Meredith fiddled with the little chores Anis gave her to occupy herself, Tomah talked. He told stories about the past, mostly about the Pequawket. He told her about clans in the neighboring valleys, about the struggles amongst them, and the times when they gave them up to unite in wars with the Iroquois. He talked about the infiltration of the white men, who brought further strife along with the pestilence that killed three-quarters of his ancestors in a few short years.

"They call us savages," he said, "but we were never savage until they taught us the meaning of the word." He said this conversationally, and Meredith wondered, as she chopped winter squash, if one could grow old enough to let go even of justified bitterness.

"We'd had a code of honor," he said, "laws defining right and wrong. But there was so much suffering after the white men came, and every year seemed to bring more: war, sickness, starvation, with never an end in sight. Even the strongest laws will break under enough pressure." He shrugged, and Meredith studied him. He could not be old enough to have lived through those things, she thought, and yet in his voice she heard the soft regret of threadbare memory.

"There is a story," Tomah continued, his white eyes fixed once more on the doorway, "about a village in the woods far to the east of here. It was a village made up of the ragged remnants of ten others, which had been destroyed by illness and fighting. Their first winter together was long and bitter. With the young men gone to the wars, they had not been able to put in the stores to survive it. And so they ate each other."

"*N'mahom!*" Anis cried in horror.

"Ah, but she knows this story already, don't you, daughter?" Tomah answered mildly, turning his blind eyes on Meredith. From deep in the heart of that awful memory, Meredith met them. "I thought so," he said, nodding. "It's haunted you. It was a terrible thing…but not quite as terrible as what you imagine.

"They didn't kill each other. They knew before autumn set in that they could not all survive the winter, and they made an agreement – a pledge to sustain one another. To keep their brothers alive, in order to take revenge on the invaders in the spring. But," he sighed, "it was still forbidden, what they did. They offended the Great Spirit, and so the Great Spirit punished them – sent the *wintiku* to devour the savages as they had devoured their dead. But I wonder, did the *wintiku* also come for the men who had made them savages?"

He shrugged. Anis shook her head in disapproval. Meredith, however, was fascinated, and Tomah sensed it. "You understand," he said, pointing a bony finger at her. "I knew you would, even if you're a white girl."

"Oh, *N'mahom…*" Anis groaned.

"Mr. Lincoln laughed at that story," Tomah said, ignoring her. He spoke as if Meredith should know Mr. Lincoln. She was wondering if he had known the murdered president – she would have believed Tomah capable of just about anything after what he had just told her – when Anis interrupted.

"Lincoln was the governor of Maine," she said. "He liked Indians, or so he said. He wandered around these mountains with a notebook and a pair of field glasses, looking for any of us who might still live out here. He came to us one summer – oh, a few years back – and he stayed for a week." She frowned into her pot of beans.

"Anis did not like him," Tomah explained.

"Why would I like him? He called our house 'rude' and you 'the old, blind red-man'."

"He never said such a thing!"

"He wrote it in his book," Anis insisted. "I saw it."

"Well, you should not have been reading his book without his permission! It serves you right you didn't like what you found there."

Anis lapsed into wounded silence, and Tomah continued, "He was a good enough man, for a white one. I took him down the river. He paddled well, and he knew a number of our words for birds and beasts. He said he would write about us in a book."

"Yes," said Anis crisply, "so all the world will think that we live in a 'rude' hut."

"Never mind, Anis," he said, patting her hand. "I will die soon, and then you can get married and live wherever you like."

Anis shook her head at his beatific smile and returned to her sewing.

10

When Meredith awakened the following morning, Anis was gone, and Tomah was still sleeping by the fire. She pulled on her coat and hat and stepped outside, where she stopped still in awe. For two days she'd seen nothing but the snow-scribbled gray of the icy pond, an indistinct line of trees, and the white ground beneath her feet. Now she stood at the center of an amphitheatre of mountains, their craggy foothills green-and-white with snow covered trees, the main range unfurling above in transcendent blues to bright blazing summits.

She looked away only when Anis called to her, "Good morning!"

She was leading the horse by her rope halter. The horse skipped and danced through the powdery snow, delighted to be out again at last. She whinnied when she saw Meredith, and when Meredith reached out her hands the horse dropped her muzzle into them and blew, filling Meredith's heart.

When the horse lifted her head again, Anis pushed a burlap bag into Meredith's hands. When Meredith looked inside and saw that it was filled with grain, she tried to push it back. Anis wouldn't accept it. "Where you are headed, there won't be much forage," she said. "Take it for the horse's sake, if not for your own. Though I've packed some things for you, too."

Meredith saw then that her pack rested by the door, considerably bulkier than it had been before. She looked back at Anis, raised her eyebrows.

Anis sighed, and when she spoke wistfulness colored her tone. "I am not trying to drive you away. Lord knows, I've been glad of your company."

Meredith was surprised at this. She would not have thought that she provided any kind of company at all. But she knew enough about Anis after the days she'd spent with her to know that she wasn't a woman to say what she didn't mean, which made her next words troubling: "This weather will not hold. You must take advantage of it while you can."

Meredith nodded, her eyes already drawn back to the mountains' mesmerizing beauty. Anis watched her for a moment, and then she said, "I am glad that you came." The sadness in her voice was clear. "I'm glad that you met *N'mahom*. I would tell you to come back and visit us when your business is done, but unless that is soon, I'm afraid it will be a cold welcome."

Meredith looked at her, questioning.

"*N'mahom* was not being flippant when he spoke about marriage," Anis said. "I am engaged. John is Pequawket, but he is a modern man. He is an overseer at a mill; he would never live out here. When *N'mahom* dies, I will move to town. We are the last of our people to live in this valley."

Meredith felt the words like a blow. It must have showed on her face, because Anis sighed and said, "I know. Sometimes I wish that John was different. That I was. That I had my grandfather's conviction..." She shook her head. "But the old ways are past. I was raised a Christian, and I'm glad of it. I love my grandfather, and I respect his beliefs, but I cannot share them." She looked at Meredith, her eyes uncertain. "Do you think that it makes me a bad grand-daughter? A bad woman?"

Meredith shook her head and meant it.

Anis studied her, and then she said more quietly, "Do you think that God will forgive him?"

Meredith didn't known how to answer this. If she'd ever believed in God, she didn't now. Still, she felt she owed Anis something after all of her kindness. Comfort, if not affirmation. She dug into her pack and brought out Joseph's Bible.

Anis's face lit up, and she eyed the book longingly. "I've never had a Bible of my own…"

Meredith held it toward her.

"Oh, no – I couldn't!"

Meredith nodded, pushed it toward the other woman.

"But won't you miss it?" Anis protested.

Meredith shook her head.

"I suppose you know it off by heart."

Meredith had to smile. She shook her head again.

Finally, Anis accepted the book, hugged it to her breast. "Thank you. You don't know what a gift this is. I wish I could say that I will read it to *N'mahom*, but he would never allow it…" A shadow crossed her face. She paused, then added in a low voice, "I fear for him. That he will not be saved – "

Meredith touched Anis's hand, wishing to stop her worry, and Anis laughed ruefully, shook her head. "You are right. And I suppose we deserve each other: he fears for my soul, too. I've abandoned the old faith; by his beliefs, I am damned. And there are times when I wonder whether he might be right. After all, I have never seen a man walking upon water or raising the dead, but I have witnessed a tree bleeding…oh!"

Anis had glanced up at the tree, and her gaze had frozen there. Meredith turned to see why, and then she too stood staring. The blood no longer dripped from the branch. The snow beneath it was clean and white. There was still a spot of red, however, bright against the black and white of the tree and snow: a single cherry, full and ripe, hanging from the end of the once-bleeding branch.

"Now *that* has never happened before!" Anis said. Tentatively, she touched the cherry. It fell into her palm. She blinked at it for a moment, and then she handed it to Meredith. "This must certainly be yours."

As Meredith stared at it, Tomah emerged from the wigwam, trailing blankets and leaning heavily on a stick.

"I hope," he said gravely, "that you will not forget us." He closed her hand over the cherry and patted it twice. Meredith slipped the cherry into her pocket.

"Good luck," Anis cried as Meredith mounted her horse and turned off down the valley. And Meredith raised her arm in farewell.

Offsets

1

Nobody expected Silence's fascination with Pascal McCune to last, least of all Pascal. But Silence returned to the bench under the tree every day of that brilliant autumn week. At the end of it, even Esther had to accept that Silence was as serious about this new passion for what she called "Negro music" as he was about his others. It worried her as much as his sea dreams, but since he slacked on neither his farm chores nor his academic ones, she had no grounds to forbid it.

Likewise, at the end of the week Pascal was certain that the tenacity he'd first sensed in the white child was true as the heart of the tree behind him. Silence also showed a degree of talent that surprised and intrigued him. So when the weather finally turned, Pascal knocked on the minister's door to see if there might be a chance of exchanging winter accommodation for some upkeep work at the church. By the following Sunday, Pascal's meager possessions were ensconced beneath a borrowed cot in the sacristy, and the man himself, scrubbed and shining, stood at the back of the congregation.

Heaven absorbed Pascal in that way peculiar to small towns and their interlopers – simply by ceasing to notice him. He worked hard at the task the minister had set him: clearing the lot beside the church of weeds, in order to use it to extend the cemetery. He taught Silence diligently. And when Silence left, he took up the guitar himself, and played on into the night. Over the winter, Heaven's residents found themselves coming to town more often in the afternoons or, if they lived near enough, out onto their porches on still evenings. They told themselves that hearing Pascal's music was only incidental, but by the time spring came, they had stopped trying to stop themselves humming his music.

Pascal didn't much care whether they listened or not, He stayed on in Heaven for Silence, and Silence alone. It wasn't simply that he'd come to love the child, though he had, despite himself. It was the fact that that love was cut by a persistent premonition of disaster. It was clear to Pascal that Silence's true heart lay not in his mother's Latin grammar or his father's fields, in the pretty blonde girl he thought he loved or even in the music he'd taken to so readily. It lay somewhere next to impossible, and Pascal knew too well how impossible dreams could break a man.

He watched Silence grow into a young man, knowing that he could neither save him from himself, nor abandon him to the fate he saw taking shape. He smiled when Silence showed him the ring with the diamond chip he'd chosen for Jenny, and when she accepted it. He congratulated when Silence read him the letter offering him a place at Trinity's college of law. He held his tongue as he watched the ghosts of Silence's dying dreams take shape around him, hoping for a miracle and steadily losing faith until the day he realized that nothing could keep the boy from his fate.

Yet fate doesn't tip her hand even to the wisest of men, and fate was about to deal Silence Ogden a card that would change everything.

2

It happened the summer his mother was dying. Nobody talked about it, but everybody knew it. Death was written in the hollows of Esther Ogden's face, in her dull hair and the dark half-moons under her eyes. It was a presence at her shoulder when Silence came into the kitchen to find her seated at the table, head in her hands and a bowl of bread dough at her elbow, forgotten and fermenting. The inscrutable nearness of it colored everything, driving Silence and John into a frenzy of activity intended to make Esther happy, when all she really wanted was for them to be still.

She couldn't tell them that. To tell them would mean speaking the truth, and no one in Heaven ever spoke a bitter truth. So she wore her best dress and smiled when Silence brought his fiancée to tea, though she wanted to tell him not to tie himself down so young; not, at any rate, to a girl like Jenny Lindquist, who could not keep her hands from her hair or her eyes from the mirror over the mantelpiece. Esther schooled her face to pride when

Silence showed her the letter from Trinity, though she had long since come to fear that she had been mistaken to push him that way. And she agreed with her husband that a steam-powered thresher was exactly what they needed – that it would indeed revolutionize farming in their town – though the thought of a machine that ran without the sweat of a man or beast carved her gut into a deep, cold pit.

Silence shared his mother's antipathy regarding his father's new contraption, but it was from guilt rather than fear. The feeling was so familiar by then that it was perversely comforting. Still, he wished that he could share something of what his father felt when the team of draft horses came up the road, hauling the thresher and the engine that would drive it. Instead he felt sorry for the horses, made to haul the machinery that would replace them.

When the men had put the engine and thresher where John wanted them, he took his son on a tour of its wonders, oblivious – or perhaps simply impervious – to Silence's disinterest. Silence, meanwhile, wondered how he could be fluent in a dead language and yet be flummoxed by a modern invention that wasn't even particularly new. Hard as he tried, though, he couldn't keep the words in his head. They turned like bright stones in a riverbed as his father spoke, gleaming for a moment before they rolled again and were lost: Tuxford design; cylinders and firebox; crankshaft and smokebox; flywheel and boiler. He wondered, dismally, why he couldn't be enthusiastic just this once, for his father's sake.

"You'd have to go four counties east to find another machine like this," John said, repeating with shy pride the words of the man who had sold it to him.

"That's right," Silence agreed after a pause, surfacing from his rumination and trying to remember what he had just agreed to. When he couldn't, he added, "It will change everything for us."

"For all of Heaven," his father amended. "It would be wrong to keep it to ourselves."

All of this was territory they'd crossed before. John intended to loan out his machine to Heaven's other families for a small fee. As such, they'd been as impatient for its arrival as John had. They were already lining up by the yard fence to see it, a day ahead of the official unveiling.

"Silence...son..."

Silence looked at his father and saw that he anticipated a negative answer to the unspoken question. He resolved to say yes, whatever it was.

"I wonder...well, would you help me tomorrow? Oh, I know that farm machinery doesn't much interest you, but this may well be the last time you're here for the harvest. Of course I could hire a man, but really – "

Silence put a hand on his father's shoulder, stopping him before he pleaded. "Of course I will," he said, smiling. "It would be an honor."

His father beamed, and a pang went through Silence. It took so little to make him happy; he wondered how many opportunities he'd missed, with his head buried in his schoolbooks. In the wake of the thought, he was struck for a moment by a paralyzing doubt.

3

Silence had walked out with Jenny Lindquist almost every evening since their engagement. Jenny's parents had long since waived the pretense of a chaperone, and if Silence's mother didn't like it, she didn't have the strength left to go to battle with Mrs. Lindquist. Still, she couldn't stop herself admonishing Silence to be careful every time he took his hat and stepped out the door.

He'd laughed the first time she said it. "Of what?" he'd asked. There had never been anything in Heaven to be careful of.

"Of that girl," she'd said after a moment's deliberation.

"Jenny?" Silence had asked, now entirely baffled.

Esther had nodded grimly, her eyes pleading with him to understand.

"I thought you liked Jenny." Which Esther could not bring herself to answer. "Besides," Silence laughed, suddenly anxious, "what could a little thing like her do to me?"

His mother had given him a long, incisive look. "A little thing like her," she'd said at last, her frustrated schoolteacher's voice making cut crystal of every word, "could take away all you've worked for without lifting a finger."

Which had baffled Silence until the first time Jenny led him past the end of the road at the top of the hollow, into the shadows of the forest. He didn't have much time to wonder what she intended before she showed him, her lips finding his, and her small soft hands moving over him with astonishing conviction. He'd pushed her away, gasping, before they did what he knew they shouldn't. He'd spent the rest of the night tossing in his bed, flung between bewilderment and the knowing look in Jenny's eyes as she'd straightened her skirt, echoed in her mother's when he took her home.

He'd told himself that it had been a misunderstanding, but the next time was just the same, as was every night that summer. They walked, seldom talking, and in the damp purple evening woods they battled each other, fighting for ascendancy in a territory that Silence barely understood. So it went until the night before the harvest, when once again he pushed Jenny away before he lost control and this time, instead of a simpering smile, she burst into tears.

Silence, horrified, wondered if he had hurt her. It hadn't occurred to him that she might suffer the pangs of unsatisfied lust as he did. He'd believed what he'd been told by the other boys: that it was different for women than it was for men. That they didn't feel the same urgency, and had to be coerced. Yet Jenny's behavior all summer flatly contradicted this advice; perhaps his other beliefs about women and sex were equally unjustified. Tentatively, Silence reached across the falling dark and rested a hand on Jenny's shoulder. Immediately she fell on him, sobbing into his chest.

"Jenny," he spluttered, "I'm sorry...I don't quite understand –"

"Of course you do!" she cried with astonishing vitriol. "My mother said that any man would understand...that a girl like me wouldn't even have to try. But I've tried and I've tried, and you still push me away. Don't you think I'm pretty enough? Don't you...don't you love me?"

Gradually, hazily, Silence began to understand the meaning of the frantic charade they'd been playing every night. Still, his logic rebelled against it: "Your *mother* wants us to...to..." He couldn't make himself say the words to her, despite what had passed between them. Jenny nodded. He felt himself flushing bright red and was glad of the dark that hid it.

"But…why?" he asked.

Jenny drew a shuddering breath. "Because then you couldn't leave me."

Silence shook his head in confusion. "I gave you a ring, Jenny. Why would I leave you?"

"Because you'll go to town, and you'll meet lots of girls – fashionable girls. It won't be long before you forget about me."

Silence looked off into the dark, astounded and suddenly furious. He had to remind himself that the anger wasn't for Jenny; that this hadn't been her idea. Still, his voice sounded unnaturally hard to him when he said, "I admit I don't quite see how having had you – so to speak – would make me any less likely to forget about you, were I as fickle as that." He felt her cringe at the words.

"Because," she said tremulously, "because it wasn't just that. If…if there was a baby, then you'd have to marry me now. You'd have to take me with you."

Silence thought of Jenny's mother's hungry eyes. The Lindquists were no worse off than any other family in Heaven, but Mrs. Lindquist had always been ambitious, or so his mother said. "That woman aspires to be a snob" – those had been Esther's exact words. For the first time, Silence believed them. He felt a surge of disgust and had to remind himself that it wasn't for Jenny, that this wasn't her fault.

"Jenny," he said, turning back to her at last. She was no more than the faint glint of the hazy moon in her eyes. "I'm going to ask you something, and I want you to tell me the truth."

He felt her shudder, but she answered, "All right."

"Do you love me?"

There was a heartbeat of a pause, but it was enough. Silence only half-heard her answer: "I've always known I'd marry you, Silence. Everyone has. It's the way it's meant to be."

"The way who means it to be?" he asked quietly.

"If you think I don't mean it," she said in a stronger voice, "then I'll prove it. I'll marry you now, go with you to Trinity. I'll keep house for you – "

"And live on what?" Silence interrupted. "Air, and your mother's aspirations?"

Immediately he regretted the words. She was only a girl: a good girl, trying to please everyone. He felt a surge of pity for her, and a tenderness that must be love.

"I'm sorry," he said, reaching out for her hand. It was wet with tears he hadn't realized she was weeping; he felt even worse, and so willing to promise her anything. "That was cruel, what I said. I'm only stunned – angry, to be honest – that your mother would think all of this was necessary. That I'd go back on my word.

"But Jenny, we can't get married yet. It wouldn't be any kind of life for you – scraping by in a place you don't know, without family or friends. No," he said more firmly, "we'll do what we'd planned to do and marry when I've graduated. In the mean time though, you have to promise me you'll stop listening to your mother. I mean no disrespect to your family, but if she thinks she needs to push you to…to *that*…in order to keep me, then she doesn't know much about either one of us. All right?"

Sniffling, Jenny nodded.

"Besides," he said in what he hoped was a mollifying tone, "I'm the one who should be worried."

"How so?" she asked.

"Well, here I've got the prettiest girl in town to agree to marry me, and I'm making her wait. Who's to say you won't up and marry someone else while I'm gone?"

She giggled. "You know I wouldn't, Silence!"

"So you'll wait for me?"

"I'll wait for you."

"Let's go home, then," he said, helping her up. "Tomorrow after the reaping, you can help my mother serve the tea. That will show everyone my intentions. No more of these walks, all right?"

"All right," she agreed, and put her hand, soft and pliant, into his.

It was only much later, lying in his bed and looking into the darkness, that Silence realized she had never answered his question.

4

Harvest day dawned with razor-edged clarity, colors leaping like kaleidoscope beads in the bright sunlight. Silence stretched and smiled and remembered what Jenny had said rather than what she hadn't and thought, *This is happiness.*

But when he came into the kitchen, his mother leveled him with sharp-eyed scrutiny. His spirits deflated; she knew. In self-defense, he pretended not to see her look, took a piece of toast and a cup of coffee and turned to go. Esther, however, put a hand on his arm to stop him.

"Silence," she said, and he turned back, the blush already beginning. But Esther had something different on her mind. "You saw the man," she said. "The dealer."

It took Silence a long moment to realize what she was talking about. When he did, he knew that the look he'd taken for grim determination was in fact her attempt to master her fear.

"For the thresher?" he said, and she nodded. "Yes, I did."

"Did he tell you where that machine came from?" she asked. "Or how old it is?"

Silence wracked his brain. The truth was, though he had gone with his father to buy the machinery in a show of guilty solidarity, he had barely listened to what the salesman had said. "I don't rightly know its age," he answered, "but it looks to be in good condition. And it came from...ah...I think it was Tennessee?"

Esther didn't look appeased by this information. "Silence – do you think it's safe?"

"Oh, yes," he said, glad that he could at least answer this question with confidence. "He showed us an inspection certificate only a few months old."

Esther nodded, placated if not convinced, and went back to making lemonade and cookies for the neighbors who would come to see the machine in use. Outside, Silence found his father feeding wood into the engine's firebox. He could feel the heat coming off of it from several feet away. His father turned, wiped sweat from his forehead with one arm, and then went to look into the water barrel by the boiler. The feedwater pump was running. John lifted one of the water buckets sitting on the ground and poured it into the barrel.

"I was thinking," he said as Silence came up beside him, "it'll be a right nuisance, going back and forth to the well to keep this barrel filled. I wonder, could we use a hose to bring the water direct to the barrel?"

Silence considered the machinery, thinking how little he was qualified to answer this question. But his father knew no better. "If the hose reaches," he said at last, "then I don't see why not."

John poured another bucketful of water into the barrel, and then he went to help Silence with the hose. It was an old, mildewed canvas pipe, but it didn't leak much. They tied it tightly to the pump spigot, and then unfurled it. It just reached the water barrel. John grinned, and Silence smiled back, watching through the engine's wavering heat as their neighbors beginning to collect by the house.

"Well," said John, "we'd best begin, if we're going to finish today."

Silence eyed the golden sheaves of wheat stacked by the thresher and sighed.

"Better get the pump going," John continued, patting the hose. "We don't want to run out of steam when we've just begun. I'll see if we have any volunteers." John turned to the knot of people back by the house, smiling to himself. He knew that his friends would be clamoring to help. They all wanted to be the first to see the new thresher in action.

Silence turned his back on the hissing engine and returned to the pump. He began to work it, watching as the hose slowly filled. He was hot already. He wiped the sweat from his eyes, looked over toward the house. His father stood at the center of a knot of men, while the ladies crowded around his mother, sipping cups of lemonade. He saw Jenny among them, resplendent in a new hat with bright blue ribbons. The breeze lifted them, and they seemed to disappear against the sky. Silence raised his hand to her, although he was too far away to see whether or not she saw him. He felt a twinge of the past night's antipathy and told himself firmly, *We will be happy. We will be –*

There was a deafening crash, a blinding light that rent the sky before it went black. Silence was flung onto his back as heavy things thudded into the earth around him. There was no sound. His vision was hazy with smoke and with something hot and wet, but he could see the well pump, wavering and too far away, before charcoal spots took his sight.

I have died, Silence thought without emotion. But then there was a fall of light, a chaos of motion, dark shapes moving in the half-dark above him. He saw the vague image of his father's face, and then his mother's. He thought he saw Jenny's blue ribbons, but they had turned grey as the sky. Then for a moment he saw her clearly: her eyes wide, her hand over her mouth, gaping with a scream he could not hear.

There was another spell of darkness, and when it cleared again, he was moving, lying against his father's chest as he hadn't since he was a child. There were disjointed images: smoke-smudged people whose names he couldn't remember; a shaft with a spoked wheel driven deep into one of his mother's flowerbeds; bits of metal, singed and torn, scattered around the once-neat yard; and behind them, the wheat sheaves on fire, sending red tongues lapping at the smokestained sky.

That was the memory Silence would keep: not the encroaching pain, nor the horror as the beginnings of understanding penetrated his shock, but the image of his father's harvest burning, red as his own blood seeping into the ruined earth.

5

They brought a doctor – the first ever to visit Heaven – but by the time he arrived, Silence had slipped into unconsciousness, missing the novelty. It was just as well, because it took two men to wrench his shattered leg into place for the splint, and hours of intricate stitching to close his torn cheek.

"He was lucky," the doctor said to Silence's parents when he was finished. "Not many men survive a boiler explosion, and those who do usually lose most of their skin."

John winced, but Esther's eyes never moved from her son's patchwork face on the blood-spattered sheet. "Will he live?" she asked without looking up.

"If he survives the infection," the doctor said, and then, since no one had offered him dinner or even a fortifying brandy, he took his own leave.

Before the next day was out, Silence's face swelled and suppurated, his blood raged. He lived for weeks in a world populated by monsters, screaming and thrashing through nightmares he would never remember. In his brief lucid moments, he tried to cry without moving his face, without spilling the tears that seared the weeping wounds. John paced the kitchen, leaving his neighbors to reap what remained of his fields. Esther kept vigil at Silence's bedside, hunched around her own expanding pain, bargaining with God.

God or not, Silence lived. The infection burned itself out, and by winter the wound had dried, the bones of his leg knit back together. But his right cheek bore a star-shaped, cranberry-colored scar that reached from chin to temple, and his left leg healed shorter than the right. The first time he limped to the parlor mirror his mother drifted behind him, wringing her hands. She expected tears and fury; what she got was worse. Silence stared blankly at his ruined face for a few unblinking moments and then turned away. There wasn't even resignation in his expression. There was nothing at all.

Esther's worry deepened when Silence tossed aside the apologetic letter from Trinity with equal impassivity. When he dropped Jenny's into the kitchen stove, unopened and including her jettisoned engagement ring, Esther had to accept that the months of pain had pushed her son to a frigid remove, far beyond sorrow. But she also knew that he couldn't stay there forever. Sooner or later he would have to react to all that had happened, and the longer he left it, the worse it would be.

Esther prayed for the strength to help him, but nothing could stop the rampant onslaught of her own illness. At last she had to accept that she didn't have the strength for both fights. She barely had the strength for one. And so Esther Ogden spent her final days watching her only child become a ghost. The flesh ran off of him like water. He barely spoke. He stayed inside, kept away from the windows, walked in restless circles that Esther thought would drive her mad, until his neurosis took a more insidious track and she wished them back.

She found him one morning sitting on the parlor floor, the mirror from the mantle piece propped in front of him, staring at his reflection with an intensity of loathing that ran through her like icy water. For days he sat there looking into the mirror and then, with no apparent provocation, he tore it apart. He pried out tacks with his fingernails until they bled, peeled off the brown paper backing until he came to its black reverse and scratched away at it with a hunting knife. When he'd cleared the last of it and found nothing but his own hand beneath the scored glass, he threw it into the grate, battered the pieces with a fire-iron until his father pulled him away, still raging, and locked him in his bedroom.

While Silence sat looking at his bleeding hands and his mother cried outside the door, John took down their other mirrors and threw them one-by-one down the well. By the time spring came, Silence had forgotten his own face.

It was spring, too, when Esther died. Silence conceded to leave the house to see her buried, and John thought that perhaps, finally, the ice was breaking. But Silence shed no tears on his mother's grave. He stared across the mound of earth at Jenny Lindquist, who stood by Thomas Marden and wouldn't meet his eye as the sunlight glinted balefully off the emerald on her finger. Afterward, Silence retreated to the attic, leaving his father and the now-senile John Jr. to face the town's sympathy on their own.

His father planted only three fields that year: the bare minimum he needed to feed the family through the following winter. The rest of the land quickly reverted to the wilderness it had been not so long ago. No one ever said a word about it. Even John Jr. went to his grave without comment on the frittering of his inheritance. It seemed the Ogdens' ruin was complete.

6

At some point during his adolescence, Silence had stopped dreaming of the sea. He couldn't remember the last time he'd dreamed of wings and water. Perhaps, he thought (when he thought about it), there hadn't been a last time. No line to cross, only a gradual fading, like a photograph forgotten on a sunny wall until the day someone realizes that the frame is empty.

The summer after the accident, the dreams returned, but they weren't what they had been. Instead of sun on water, there was a wasted beach battered by storm-driven waves. Instead of white sails billowing on the blue, tattered red flags whipped a charcoal sky. The sea rolled splintered driftwood on the shingle, which might have been the bleached ribs of a boat.

This new dream dogged him without respite or explanation, infecting him with a despair that might very well have consumed him if his father had been a lesser man. As it was, John Ogden knew something about his son that Silence didn't know himself: with no love, no purpose, no passion to outweigh his own self-loathing, he was nearer death than he'd ever been in the gangrenous grip of the past autumn. He also saw that there was a new element to his son's unhappiness. Silence didn't speak about his nightmares, so John didn't know the source of the suffering, but he did know that whatever it was, it was close to breaking him.

That simply couldn't happen. Silence was all John had left, and the need to keep him was powerful. More powerful still, though, was the promise he'd made Esther when he put her in the earth: that he'd see her son a happy man if it was the last thing he did. And so one night when the leaves were just beginning to turn, a year and a month after the accident, John extended a brown-paper package across the silent gulf of their kitchen table.

"What is this?" Silence asked, looking dully at the parcel. He couldn't think of anything he needed, much less anything that he wanted, so John's answer shocked him.

"It's your birthday present."

Silence was stunned: not that he'd forgotten his own birthday, but that anyone would remember it. Birthdays were something that happened in the world to which he no longer belonged.

"Open it," John said with what passed in a quiet man for authority. When Silence didn't react, he said, "I know you don't want it. I know you wish you'd died that day." John met his eyes bluntly, and Silence said nothing. It was no more than the truth. "But God spared you," John continued, "and today you turned nineteen. By anyone's reckoning, you're a man now, and a man needs a purpose."

John drew a breath and let it out slowly, looking suddenly uncertain. "It seems to me, son, that you've spent your life doing what others wanted you to do. That's as much my fault as anyone's. Think of that as me trying to make amends." He nodded to the package. "I hope I've got it right…" He shrugged, already trying on defeat.

Silence stared at him, feeling something he hadn't felt in a very long time: pity, for someone other than himself. When he recognized it, he had the sudden, powerful urge to weep. To stop himself, he looked down at the package and then took it in his hands. He slipped the string off slowly, a cold ball of anxiety in his stomach.

When the paper fell away, though, his face smoothed with astonishment. He looked up at his father. He couldn't find the words to form the questions that suddenly invaded his mind. A pulse beat in his temples like a netted fish. Finally, he asked, "How did you know?"

John, meanwhile, had begun to smile; even, in his background way, to beam. "Silence," he said, "you've kept that tatty piece of paper on your desk for seven years. Even I couldn't fail to notice."

Silence shook his head, staring down at the envelope in his hands, still clearly in shock. "But…how did you ever find him? It was so long ago…so far away…he can't still have been there…"

John was nodding. "He wasn't. Apparently he immigrated to America quite a while ago. But his father still lives at their old address in Glasgow, and he had a box of these plans. Never sold a one of them, it seems. He wouldn't take money for this one, either – said it was enough for him that someone was interested. He also said his son was only a boy when he drew these up, so he couldn't guarantee their accuracy." The light in his face faded a bit. But Silence knew with sudden clarity that the plans would be true; that Ian MacFarlane, even as a boy, would not have made mistakes.

"We'll clear the barn," John continued, looking hopefully at his son. "There's not much in it anymore anyway, and I doubt the cow and the horse will mind keeping company with a boat. I'll get you started, such as I can. It's a long time since I've built from scratch, but I helped my father raise half of this house – I dare say the knack will come back. If you want my help, that is…if you even want to build the boat at all…"

He looked at Silence with a face full of hope and doubt. Silence thought, *Dear God, he means it. He means to build a sailboat in the barn.* He wondered which of them had gone mad.

"Yes," he heard himself say, "I do." And he thought wryly that he had his answer.

7

Silence regretted his decision the next morning, when he and his father moved the long oak table from the dining room into the cleared barn and laid out the plans on it. There were far more of them than he'd ever imagined, leaf after leaf of drawings and instructions and charts. They words were English, but they might as well have been Japanese for all he understood. He looked at the list of "Required Tools" on the first sheet of paper: *Panel saw, 16 in., 5 teeth to the inch; Rip saw, 28 in., 5 teeth to the inch; Jack plane, double iron; Smoothing plane, double iron; thumb plane; claw hammer; riveting hammer…* His head swam, his leg ached. He sat down on the table, shaking his head with a bitter smile.

"What is it?" his father asked, looking up from a page he'd been studying.

"This is madness," Silence said. "We don't have these tools…I don't even know what most of them are! Never mind the wood and brass and canvas and the…the 'molds and stocks' – " he pulled the word from the page beneath his hand " – and God only knows what else."

His father's blue eyes were distant and thoughtful. "Well, I have a claw hammer all right," he said slowly, "and I reckon I've got a saw or two that will serve, though I can't say as I've ever had cause to count their teeth." He looked at his son's dubious face and sighed. "It'll be hard, Silence; I don't argue that. But it's possible – if you want it to be."

Silence looked back at him, hating himself for his pessimism but unable to contain it. "And if it is, if we really go ahead with it, build this thing – where would we even sail it? It may not be as big as the real 'America', but it'll be too big by half for the Blackbottom River."

John shrugged. "I reckon it'll take us long enough to get it built, we'll have thought of something by the time it's finished."

Silence looked at his father. Light from the little dirty window slanted over his shoulder, illuminating half of his face and throwing the other half into shadow. *If I stood there, just so,* Silence thought, *my face would look whole again.*

"I reckon what we don't have for tools, we can borrow," John continued. "And what we can't borrow, we'll buy. I have money saved."

Silence sighed, shook his head. "Why are you doing this, Pa?"

John gave a slight, indeterminate shrug. "What else would I do?"

"Take the farm back," Silence answered. "Smoke with your friends outside the store. Who knows, maybe you'd find another woman to keep time with you – "

"No," said John, with a firmness that wasn't anger, but which startled Silence nonetheless. "Your mother was the only woman I ever wanted, and her dying doesn't change that." He sighed, softened. "And I don't care about the farm. Not anymore. I'd rather spend my time to see you happy."

Silence smiled sadly, stopped when he felt how his scar twisted it. "What if that isn't possible?"

"I don't mean to condescend to you, Silence, but you're too young to make that decision."

Silence saw no purpose in arguing the point. Instead, he asked, "And you really think that building this boat will make me happy?"

John sighed. "Not in itself, no. But I do know that you've wanted this all your life. I heard what Annie Newcombe said all those years ago: the sea is in your soul. Well, I've learned to trust Annie's hunches." He paused, as if uncertain about his next words. "It's more than that, though. You see, I don't think you're unhappy because of the accident. I think you've never been really happy in your life. At least not since you saw this boat, and knew you couldn't have it." He gestured to the plans. "Now you do, and that's a beginning."

Silence shook his head, but once again he found that he couldn't argue with his father. And a tiny, buried kernel of his old self even wondered whether his father might not be right. "Well then, what happens now?" he asked.

"Now," said John, brightening in his gentle way, "I take this list of tools to the neighbors and see what I can rustle up. Meanwhile, you go see your old friend the schoolteacher and ask if he can't find you some books that might help."

Gloomily, Silence went to get his hat.

8

Silence hadn't seen Mr. Marsh since before the accident. He knew that his old teacher had called at the house more than once in the first months of his convalescence, bringing armfuls of books and journals to help Silence pass his time. Esther had continually sent the man away, as Silence had insisted. But Silence had heard the regret in his voice each time Mr. Marsh took his leave and had known he hadn't made those calls out of duty. Even at his lowest point, Mr. Marsh's sincere tenacity had given him twinges of guilt.

Now, as he walked toward the schoolhouse, the unread books under his arm for an excuse, the guilt revived and spread, leaden in his guts. School had been out for an hour when Silence arrived, but he knew that Mr. Marsh would still be there. The sad fact was he had nowhere else to go. Though he was one of the town's more eligible bachelors, he had never found a woman to suit his tastes. He confessed to Silence once that Heaven's women were far too docile. He didn't want a compliant farmer's wife, raised to work hard and smile and agree. He wanted a woman with ideas of her own, a woman who could argue with him and win. Even as a child, Silence knew this was too tall an order for Heaven.

"Unless you marry Annie," he'd suggested once.

Mr. Marsh had offered him a serene smile and said, "Annie would be a challenge, all right. But I don't think Annie has much mind to marry."

With which Silence had had to agree. And so Thomas Marsh accepted inveterate bachelorhood, meandering toward middle age alone in the little cottage that came with the schoolmaster's post. If he regretted it, he never said so to anyone, not even Silence. He seemed content with his solitude, the novels he ordered from England, and his fat tabby cat named Beatrice.

But having no wife to return to meant he often stayed late at the schoolhouse, marking students' work or planning lessons. So Silence found him on the evening after he opened his boat plans. When he saw Silence standing in his doorway, Thomas Marsh's long, thin face lit visibly, which was a painful reminder to Silence of his terrible behavior during his illness. Nor was there any hesitation when the teacher leapt up to shake Silence's hand, not the slightest hitch of his eyes on the scar, which made Silence feel even worse.

"Mr. Marsh, I have to apologize – " he began, but Mr. Marsh only waved a hand at him.

"No, you don't. I understand perfectly, and I'm so glad you've finally decided to visit." He reached for the chair he kept in the corner for disobedient pupils, hooked it with a long finger and set it by the desk. "Have a seat…excuse the provenance."

Silence gave him a stilted smile and sat. "It's all right. But I can't stay long."

Mr. Marsh's face fell again. "That's a pity."

Silence put the pile of books on the desk. "I'm sorry I've kept these so long. You ought to have come to the house to get them back…but I guess after the way I behaved – "

Mr. Marsh waved his silencing hand again. "I don't blame you for it. I can't imagine how I'd have reacted, in your situation." He peered at Silence frankly, thoughtfully, through his small round spectacles.

"That's kind of you, Mr. – "

"Thomas," he interrupted. "You're no longer a child, and besides, two Trinity men should address each other as equals, no matter the age gap."

Silence smiled sadly. "I'll call you Thomas if you like, but we both know I'm no Trinity man."

Mr. Marsh gave him another incisive look. "They accepted you."

Silence saw the hope in his eyes. It fed the bitterness in his heart. "And then they thought better of it."

"Silence – "

But Silence didn't want to hear it. He stood up, wishing he'd never come. Mr. Marsh sighed, leaned back in his chair with his hands laced behind his head. His eyes never left Silence's, and Silence couldn't quite make himself walk out the door.

"I've been back and forth over this more times than I can count," Mr. Marsh said when he saw that he hadn't quite lost the younger man yet. He reached into his waistcoat and took out a heavy cream envelope with a typewritten address beginning: Silence Ogden, c/o Thomas Marsh. "I wanted to give you this, but not until the time was right. I suppose this is as good as any."

Silence didn't need to open the envelope to know what it contained. Rage and guilt and sadness thrashed in him. "Why did you do it?" he asked.

Mr. Marsh gave Silence a wan smile. His eyes, though, stayed steady on Silence as he answered, "Because somebody had to. You were in no position, obviously, nor were your parents. You worked hard for that place, Silence. I couldn't let them believe that you were simply a fickle country boy who'd give it up on a whim."

"I don't much care what they think of me," Silence said sullenly.

"Very well," said Mr. Marsh. "But what about me?"

"You?"

"My reputation is tied up in this too – or hadn't you thought of that?"

In fact, Silence hadn't. He considered the boy who'd spent his childhood looking firmly ahead at the next obstacle. It seemed now that he'd dreamed that person; that that version of himself had never really existed. "I'm sorry," he said.

Mr. Marsh shook his head. "I don't want you to be sorry. In fact I don't care whether you ever go to Trinity or not. But whatever you do, I want it to be a conscious decision."

Silence turned back to his old teacher, who still proffered the expensive envelope. He reached a shaking hand across the desk and accepted it, and then the paper knife. The letter wasn't long or complicated, but it seemed to take Silence hours to process the words. At last he folded it back up. He replaced it in the envelope and held it toward Mr. Marsh.

"It's yours," said Mr. Marsh.

"I'm not the boy they offered the place to," Silence said softly, bitterly.

"I made them aware of that. And they're still offering it."

Silence shook his head. "Mr. Marsh...Thomas...I don't want you to take this the wrong way. I'm more than grateful for all you've done for me – even this." He laid the envelope on the teacher's desk, next to the pile of books he'd returned. "But the accident made me see things differently. Clearly. I know now that I was never meant to go to college, or be a lawyer, or marry Jenny Lindquist."

Again, the incisive look. At last Mr. Marsh said, "Very well, Silence; I won't say I like it, but I can accept that, if it's the truth. Still, if you're going to give up on one vocation, you'll need to find another."

Silence smiled wryly. "Have you been speaking to my father?"

"Not about your career choices. Why?"

Silence wondered what Thomas Marsh and his father *had* been talking about. Too afraid of the answer to ask, he answered the question instead: "He's on a mission to find me a purpose."

"Oh? I hope he's had better luck than I have."

"Actually, I think he's gone mad."

"Children will do that to you." Silence bristled at "children", but Mr. Marsh just smiled. Propping his elbows on the desk, steepling his fingers he said, "Coming back to the point: why did your father send you here?"

Silence sighed. "To ask you for books."

"On what topic?"

"Boat construction."

Mr. Marsh blinked behind his glasses, and Silence couldn't help feeling a twinge of triumph at having surprised him. "Pardon?"

"You heard me right."

Mr. Marsh nodded. "What kind of boats are we talking about? Rowboats? Canoes?"

"Schooners," Silence sighed.

Mr. Marsh looked at him quizzically. "Schooners, in these mountains? Shall I start collecting pairs of animals?"

Silence had to laugh. "Not yet. It's just...an experiment."

"I see. Well then, allow me a few days to do some digging. I'll come to the house when I have something for you. Unless...?"

Finishing the question in his head, Silence felt a sudden shame. "Yes," he said too quickly, and then, with a steadier voice, "yes, please. Come to the house. We...I...would be glad to see you."

"Likewise," Mr. Marsh answered. "You know, this job has become positively tedious since you graduated."

Silence shook his head. "Thank you, Mr. – Thomas." He raised a hand in farewell, and let himself out into the twilight.

"*Ad astra per aspera,*" Mr. Marsh said to himself, as the door closed. *To the stars through difficulty.*

9

John Ogden was too impatient to wait for Mr. Marsh's books. The boat plans had come with detailed drawings, so Silence and his father began work the following morning. With the help of the attic's dictionary – which they'd since moved to the barn – they managed to decipher enough of the instructions to realize that Ian MacFarlane had already done the drafting for them. He'd also supplied something called a Table of Offsets, a rectangular grid full of numbers and intriguing terms: stem, rabbet and sheer, breadth and deck and diagonal.

"That looks like math," Silence observed doubtfully – it had never been his strong subject.

"It is, I suppose," his father answered, studying it alongside the cross-sections. "But more to the point it's a map. It tells us how to scale these drawings up to the actual size of the finished boat, so that we can use them as patterns."

Finished boat, thought Silence, and he realized that he could no more picture this than he could answering that letter from Trinity. But he refrained from saying so. He nodded when his father told him that the first thing they needed was a workbench, and not just any workbench: though it would be of normal depth, it had to be long enough to hold the longest piece of wood they would be working on.

"I reckon," said John, "it's going to have to run the length of the barn."

Silence watched incredulously as his father cleared one side of the barn of accumulated farming detritus. When he went on to demolish the three empty stalls that stood at the far end, Silence finally believed that his father was serious about this project and reluctantly joined in. They spent several days clawing the wood from the stalls apart to build the bench, and several more erecting it. When it was secure they went to the attic, where John unearthed an old spice cupboard. The woodworms had long since done their worst, but John said, "Perfect." With Silence's help he shifted it to the barn, and installed it under the near end of the workbench.

"We'll store the fastenings in here," he said when it was in place. "We can label the drawers and keep from getting confused that way."

Next they ran a board along the back of the bench, put in pegs and hung their tools. John built two sawhorses and then drilled two holes into one of them, an inch in diameter, an inch and a half apart. He took a piece of oak from the woodpile and carefully carved two pegs. Finally he drove the pegs into the holes so that they were flush with the surface of the sawhorse.

"What's that – practice for plugging leaks?" Silence asked.

"No," John answered, half-smiling. "I might be jumping the gun, but I expect we'll be splitting boards before we're through. You lay the board across the sawhorses, drive the pegs up to wedge one end of it, and split from the other. That way the board doesn't move."

Silence nodded, chastened by the realization of how much unspoken knowledge his father had. In all the years he had dreamed of building Ian MacFarlane's boat, Silence had never thought about the process. Now it seemed absurd to him that he could have failed to realize he would be as out of place working wood as he had been working the earth. It terrified him. If it hadn't been for his father, he would have shut the barn door on this folly and never looked back.

As it was, guilt was more potent than fear, and so Silence stayed put as his father made one more trip to the attic. He couldn't help but be intrigued, however, when John emerged with a dusty saloon stool. He promptly cut the legs down to eighteen inches, then he wrenched off the top, cut it in half, nailed one half back on and connected it to the other with two hinges. He boxed in the space under the seat, and then opened the hinged half.

"For storing fixings and tools and whatever else might otherwise find its way onto the floor," he explained.

"How do you know all of this?" Silence asked, shaking his head.

John shrugged, wiped his forehead with the back of one hand. "So far, it's not much different from raising a barn."

*

After that, though, the process became too complicated to continue without some kind of reference. The Ogdens closed up the barn to wait for Mr. Marsh's books. When the schoolteacher finally came up the road, however, he had a single, slender volume in his hand. Worse still, it bore the uninspiring title "Canoe and Boatbuilding for Amateurs by W.P. Stephens".

"I'm sorry," he said, taking the seat and the glass of tea John offered him. "I thought I'd find stacks of books on the subject, but it seems shipbuilders are a taciturn lot. Either that, or they all learn the craft as apprentices…" He shrugged. "Anyhow, this is the only book I could find that offered any kind of instruction, and I had to send to Asheville for it."

"Don't apologize," said John, accepting the volume. "It's sure to be better than nothing. What do I owe you for it?"

Mr. Marsh waved the question aside. "Consider it a congratulatory gift."

"What for?" asked John.

"For Silence choosing a new path."

The two older men exchanged a complicit smile, as if Silence weren't sitting between them. Irritated, Silence said, "Indeed. Here's to the way forward! Have you begun collecting the animals?"

"Animals?" asked John, frowning.

"Mr. – I mean, Thomas thinks we're building an ark."

"Does he, now?" said John, looking hard at Silence.

"Of course not!" cried Mr. Marsh. "Silence, I said that purely in jest – "

"Come on, Marsh," John interrupted, smiling as he stood up, "let's set the record straight!"

Silence trailed behind them as they walked to the barn, regretting his flippancy. When John rolled back the door, though, Mr. Marsh stood for several long moments in what might be interpreted as awe. Finally he said, "From my talk with Silence I guessed the nature of your project. But I had no idea you intended something quite so *big*."

Silence was impressed not so much by the comment as the fact that Mr. Marsh could formulate any conclusions at all out of the chaos in front of him. So far, his boat consisted of a pile of windblown charts, reams of discarded drawing paper and a stack of anonymous lumber that had lain in the barn for at least twenty years.

"Oh, it'll be big, all right," John said with quiet certainty. "It'll be the biggest thing that Heaven's ever seen."

"If we ever finish it," Silence muttered.

"*Dimidium facti qui coepit habet[1]*," said Mr. Marsh mildly, raising his hand as he turned to go. "I'll keep an eye out for more books."

"What did that mean?" John asked Silence when the teacher had gone.

Silence sighed. "It means we have a long way to go."

Which is why he was surprised – indeed, shocked – when he opened Mr. Marsh's book that night and found that so far, they were on the right track. Ian MacFarlane had already completed the drafting process: what W.P. Stephens called "laying down". It appeared that they had correctly interpreted the offset table, and collected the proper tools, more or less. When he began to read about making frames, though, Silence's doubt was vindicated.

"...the lines are laid down full size on the paper," said Stephens, "each distance being measured off on its proper frame or water line, and a long, thin batten of pine run through the spots thus found."

As far as Silence knew they had no battens of pine – only the heap of bone-dry lumber in the barn. Even if the pine could be procured and the necessary battens constructed, translating them into frames was no simple matter. "...all errors are increased in the same ratio," Stephens warned, "and though the small drawing may have been accurate, there will be some errors in the large one, and to correct these the same process of 'fairing' is necessary...running in the water lines, frame lines, and diagonals with the battens until all the curved lines are fair and regular, and the breadths and heights of every point are the same in all three plans."

Silence shut the book, and lay down to dream of infinite error.

---

1 He who has begun has the work half done. (Horace)

10

There were tides to Pascal's music, surely as there were tides on the sea. When he'd first decided to stay in Heaven, he'd made sure to figure out what its people liked to hear. For the most part, that was the music he played: folk songs brought from far-off countries, shaped by time and the bony mountain landscape into a music that belonged to it alone. People always stopped to listen to these songs, and often to lend their voices, awed that this old colored man from somewhere else could tell their stories better than they could.

In the evenings, though, the tide turned. The retreating water uncovered a seabed strewn with shapes wetly black and baleful in the fading light. These were the forms of Pascal's night music – a music that resembled nothing Heaven had heard before, full of melancholic piquancy that few of them could stomach.

In fact the only people who sought it out were Silence and Annie Newcombe. Annie took it as poker-faced as she did everything else, but the consensus was that she enjoyed it, because she always seemed to sense when the mood would take Pascal and show up with a pail of supper that they would share when he'd played himself out. Silence listened with a furrowed brow, trying to understand the creeping unease the music made him feel, and the paradoxical need for more of it. A drinking man would have understood his fixation well enough, and that was why, when Silence asked Pascal to teach him that music, Pascal said, "Absolutely not!"

His tone was harsh and unfamiliar. It was also the first time Pascal had ever refused him anything. Silence took it for anger and, hurt, avoided Pascal for several days. Meanwhile Pascal ached for the loss of the boy's company. Given it all to do again, though, he'd have done the same, because it wasn't anger that had made his voice hard; it was fear.

Pascal had a second talent at least as prodigious as his music, and it was a secret he'd intended to die with until he met Silence Ogden. Sensing an affinity in the child, he'd tipped his hand during their first lesson. He'd watched Silence's expression change to wonder as he heard the voices in the tree branches, but it stopped short of understanding. Silence could not decipher them, and despite his disappointment, Pascal knew it was just as well. Better to let the child believe the tree made the music, than the ghosts.

Or spirits, or souls, or the long memories of the dead, cut free from the moorings of chronology and conscience – Pascal had never been entirely certain what they were, only that they belonged to the deceased and they liked to roost in trees, and Heaven's oak had more of them than he'd ever seen in one place. They flapped ragged wings in the branches, telling the twilight truths that Pascal later translated into the music no one wanted to hear.

That would have been enough for any man to bear, but Pascal's gift plumbed deeper still. Sometimes he heard the silent voices of the living, too. Throughout his life, these living voices had come to him only rarely, when a mind was unlocked by madness or illness, profound grief or joy. In Heaven, though, they rang out like church bells all the night through, as the town dreamed. All through those nights, Pascal lay on his cot in the church and listened to what the waking town left unspoken. He absorbed hopes and worries, pain and exaltation into the quiet dark behind his closed eyes. And these too became music that no one wanted to hear.

After Silence's accident, all of this changed. Other voices faded to a background murmur as Silence's agony shrieked out. Pascal had no choice but to listen. At first, in the days when Silence hovered between life and death, Pascal was grateful for it. No one thought to keep the old Negro man alerted to the boy's condition. At least if he could hear his spirit scream, Pascal knew that Silence was still alive.

But Silence's voice didn't recede when he began to heal, as Pascal had assumed it would. He kept crying out for help, in terms that made no sense to Pascal: storm-ridden beaches and wide, dark water, red canvas and rent white lace. He didn't worry about it overly much. He was certain that Silence would explain the images to him when he was well enough to come asking in person for whatever it was he needed. He held that certainty against the terrible void Silence's absence had left in his life.

Pascal waited patiently through the months when Silence turned away all visitors and most of his old friends gave up on him. He knew that the spirit takes far longer to heal than the body. He followed its subtle ebb until it spoke little louder than the other voices, and so he wasn't surprised to look up one evening from his musical ruminations on the tree's bench to see a man coming toward him with a hitch in his step and his hat pulled down low. He kept playing as Silence sat down beside him. Only when the song was finished did he lay the guitar flat on his lap and look up.

Pascal thought he'd prepared himself, but Silence's face still came as a shock. It wasn't the starburst scar so much as the hollow cheeks, the thin bitter lips, the eyes like holes bored straight through to the night behind him. There was nothing left in this melancholy man of the golden boy he'd been. Pascal wanted to weep; he wanted to hold him. Instead he waited, and was rewarded with a crooked, joyless smile.

"That bad, eh?"

"It's bad, Silence Ogden," he said softly, "but not in the way you mean."

Silence looked out across the road. "Well?" he said.

"You look like your own ghost," Pascal said.

Silence smiled again, this time with a little humor. "That pretty well sums up how I feel." He paused. "I'm sorry."

"What for?" Pascal asked.

"For not coming sooner."

Pascal shook his head. "It's all right, *P'tit*. I know you couldn't."

Silence raised his eyebrows. "You're the first, then. Everyone else just thinks I'm ornery."

"You sure about that?"

Silence didn't answer.

"Well, it don't much figure, I guess. You are where you are – and just now I'm glad you're here."

They sat unspeaking for a long time. Then Silence said quietly, "I'm not."

Pascal clamped his mouth shut on the welling protest and listened.

"I might as well have died that day. Sometimes I think I *did* die...Silence Ogden died...and I'm some kind of..." He shook his head, lifting a hand toward his scar, but he stopped short of touching it. "Everything is disconnected. As if I don't quite live in the world anymore. I...I think I've gone mad."

"You haven't gone mad," said Pascal.

"You sound pretty certain."

"I *am* certain."

"How?"

"Because I've heard madness plenty, and it doesn't sound like you."

Silence looked at him. There was a flicker of interest in his eyes. "What do you mean?"

Pascal tipped the guitar up, regarded its face. "Remember when you were a child," he said, "and you asked me to teach you to play that music no one wants to hear?"

"Of course. It's the only time I was ever angry at you."

Pascal nodded. "I shouldn't have hollered at you," he said. "You couldn't know what you were asking...that it would be a sin to teach a child to play like that."

"It's all right."

"I wish it was." Pascal paused, then said, "Look up. Tell me what you see."

Silence looked up into the tree's tangled branches. They were barely distinguishable at first against the dark sky, but they came clearer as his eyes rested on them. Yet there was something strange about them. Although the tortuous black lines were solid at the center, their edges seemed to shiver and shift, blurring into the sky's lesser dark as if colonies of tiny birds were fluttering among the branches. Silence passed a hand across his eyes, and then looked at Pascal.

"You see them," said Pascal.

"What are they?"

"I don't rightly know. But grief makes them visible, and the way I figure it, if you can see them, then you're ready for the blue music."

"Blue music?"

"That's what I call it – that music no one wants to hear."

Silence sighed. "I don't even know if I remember how to play."

"It's not something you'll ever forget." He handed Silence the guitar, and as he'd predicted, Silence's fingers found their places unguided.

"Now what?" he asked.

"Listen," said Pascal. "And when you can hear it, play it."

Silence listened. At first there was only the breeze, the night insects, the soft rustle of dying leaves hanging on against winter. Then, just as he had on that day so long ago, he began to hear a chorus of whispers. But the whispers changed as he concentrated, became a single low voice singing a wordless sadness, old as time. Silence listened for a moment longer; then he stretched his fingers and began to play.

11

When Silence woke the next morning, something had changed, too subtle for him to name. He didn't necessarily feel happier or more hopeful, but at the same time he was certain that he had discarded something he hadn't wanted and didn't need. His mind had cleared, if only a little bit.

He hadn't looked at Mr. Marsh's book since the afternoon the man brought it, now almost a week past. Nor had he been to the barn, though his father went out doggedly every morning. Now Silence reached for the canoe-building manual, determined to show at least a pretense of enthusiasm for the project, but it wasn't where he'd left it on the bedside table. It wasn't anywhere in his room at all.

Silence pulled on his clothes and went downstairs. His father wasn't in the kitchen, but there was a pot of coffee on the stove. He poured a cup and went outside. As he'd suspected, the barn door was open, the rasp and drag of a saw carrying across the warm, still morning. Silence found his father standing in the center of a low wooden box, saw in one hand and canoe book in the other. The resident pile of elderly lumber was gone, and after a moment Silence realized that it had become the box in which his father stood. He also realized, when he looked more closely, that the box was roughly boat-shaped, with crossbeams at regular intervals of roughly two feet.

"Silence," his father said without looking up, "I'm glad you're here. Joe Neville delivered the spruce boards for the frames this morning, and I'm going to need your help to cut them." John indicated the wood, lying in a rectangle of sunlight under the window. The boards looked newly milled, clean and white and expectant as an artist's stretched canvases.

"If you haven't made the frames yet," Silence said, indicating the box, "then what is that?"

John looked up from the book, his eyes still lost in whatever he'd been reading. "The strongback."

"The what?"

"The frame for the frames. To hold them in place while we plank them." Seeing that Silence was still lost, he added, "It's because there's no mold."

Silence sighed and shook his head, wondering if he was doomed always to disappoint his father. John, however, seemed unperturbed by his ignorance. "Now Stephens here," he said, twitching the book so that the pages ruffled, "goes on and on about molds without saying much about frames, while

MacFarlane's plans are the opposite. I admit that's had me hung up for a few days, but this morning I realized what the problem is: molds and frames serve the same purpose. Well, more or less. The only difference is in the planking. Molds are taken out and thrown away once the planks are on, while these frames of MacFarlane's become a part of the finished boat, which means less waste – that's a Scotsman for you!"

"Right," said Silence, finally catching hold of what his father was saying. "So we – what – trace MacFarlane's plans onto that new wood, and cut them out?"

"Near enough," John agreed. "I had to scale them up first using those offsets, which was a hell of a job – you see, math wasn't my strong subject either! But I think I've finally got the patterns right." He moved to the worktable, Silence following dazedly, and picked a piece of paper from a neat pile. The paper was cut into an elongated "C" with a notch in the center.

"This one will go at the bow end, where the hull is narrowest, so it was small enough to cut it in one piece. A few of them are, but the larger ones, the ones that take more of the weight and strain, will be made from three pieces of wood bolted together." He picked up another piece of paper, this one only half curved, and nearly as tall as he was. "We'll cut two of these ones, and a straight piece to join them – do you see?"

"I think so," said Silence, surprised to find that he did, and even more so to realize that he wanted to see what the cut frame would look like.

They spent all that day drafting and cutting frames, and the next bolting the larger ones together. After that they began to lift them into position and clamp them to the strongback, but it quickly became clear that this would only work with the smallest, lightest ones. There was no way that two of them alone could lift the larger frames, let alone clamp the ends to the strongback's cross-beams. The two of them sat looking forlornly at the carefully-cut and constructed frames that they couldn't lift. At last they got up and shut the doors on the boat. There was nothing else to do until they solved the problem.

*

A few days later, as they sat sipping coffee on a dismally drizzling morning, John's face lit up. He ran toward the barn without a word. Silence limped after him and found him peering up through the rain at the rusty old block and tackle above the hayloft door. It stood out, a brilliant orange against the weathered wood.

"If we take that down," said John, "and attach it to the roof beam above the boat – "

"You think that rope will hold the frames?" Silence interrupted doubtfully.

"No," John answered. "We'll need a chain, and something to fasten it off to." He looked at Silence. "You want to get that block down or go into town for the supplies?"

Silence wondered what change in him his father thought he had sensed, that he would ask a question that would have been a foregone conclusion a few weeks back. A part of him wanted to be brave, to face down the newly-married Jenny behind the counter at Marden's store, but he knew that that part of him wasn't yet the stronger one. "I'll do the block," he said. John shrugged, nodded, and started for town.

By the end of that day, the pulley was working. By the end of the week, all eleven of the boat's ribs were clamped in place. On Friday night, John opened a bottle of Esther's apple wine. It was old and mellow, and he and Silence passed it back and forth, sitting on the worktable admiring the product of their efforts.

"You do realize," John said when the early dusk had deepened to night and the wine loosened his tongue, "that it's going to happen."

Silence took a deep swallow of wine in lieu of an answer. He knew what his father meant, and that there was no reason why it shouldn't be true. Yet since the night that he'd heard the sorrowful voice in Pascal's tree and allowed it to sing through his fingers, he'd had an uncannily accurate sense of things. Clairvoyance, he might have said, if the very thought of the word hadn't so terrified him.

Whatever it was, this was a prime, if unwelcome example of it. All week as they'd raised the frames, a conviction had been growing in him that the boat was much farther from finished than he or his father could imagine. Now, looking at the frames standing smooth and true, he knew with deep and inexplicable conviction that his father would not be the one to midwife his old dream. That many more things had to happen first.

"It's going to happen," he said with a defiance he didn't feel, and he drank to stymie the truth and told himself that anything was possible.

That night, though, he dreamed of the boat's ribs clothed not in varnished planks but in dust cloths, the barn swathed likewise in cobwebbed shadow. And without quite meaning to, he began to steel himself for whatever it meant.

Laughing Gift

1

For days after Meredith left Anis and Tomah, the weather remained clear. She and the horse rode out of the mountains and into a region of low hills and broad lakes. They passed one so wide and windswept it looked like the sea, and Meredith turned her cheek to its persistent call until it was well behind her. They passed farms in the valleys shut down against winter, their animals folded close, their fields somnolent black between the furrowed crusts of snow. Often the wind was tinged with the smoke from curing-houses. They tempted Meredith, but not enough that she would approach any of those farms. The people she had met so far had been friendly, but she saw that as luck – or at best, fate's leniency. And so they rode on; their pace was steady, the road uneventful until the dead forest.

They reached it at dusk. It wasn't another logging casualty. The trees were old growth and still standing, though they'd been dead a long time. They reached up from the ground like skeletal hands, bleached white by wind and water and sun. It didn't matter to Meredith that the horse walked calmly through their midst, with none of the skittishness she'd shown in the felled forests weeks before. They seemed to grope blindly for Meredith, and panic bloomed. She clamped her legs around the horse, thinking better of it only when the horse began to run.

This time, though, she didn't slip, and gradually she realized that the horse was speaking to her: *You will not fall, if only you believe you won't. If only you don't draw your legs up in fear. If only you give yourself over to me. And you see, like that, we will outrun it, whatever it is that frightens you...*

Meredith let her legs drop down and curve around the horse's barrel. She wound both hands in the wiry mane, pressed her face into the horse's neck, and trusted her. The horse, feeling her surrender, leaned into the wind of her own speed and ran as she'd been made to run. Meredith felt the great heart pumping beneath her, the horse's joy flowing into her, and she thought, *Thank you.*

2

When the weather was fine, they rode on into the night. The full moon blazed in a cobalt sky; the snow cast its light back, until the world was almost as bright as day. The horse followed the moon's path through thickets of shadow and across the silent white oceans of slumbering fields. They passed through aisles of glittering tree-trunks like temple columns in the mooncut dark. One night they passed a vast, frozen waterfall: a hundred feet of carved marble, hung from a frame of rock. On another, a flock of white birds circled a clutch of snowy firs like the spirits of dancers. Once they followed a frozen stream until it toppled abruptly into a hole in the ground: a vast circular cavity hollowed out of the bedrock. Meredith could hear a river rushing somewhere far below, and the grinding of the rocks it flung against the sides of the cavern, digging it slowly deeper.

Then, at last, the fine weather broke. Meredith woke one morning to a dense, frozen mist. She could see no more than a few feet ahead, but the horse plodded on with silent assurance, refusing to answer questions. Meredith could only have faith that they weren't riding in circles, or straight toward another watery hole in the ground. What finally emerged from the deepening afternoon murk, however, was a different kind of horror. They passed through a gate-posted gap in a stone wall, and before Meredith could think to turn the horse, they were in the middle of a settlement.

Four large, whitewashed houses loomed in the mist; behind them, the suggestion of fields and outbuildings. In the center of the square formed by the houses, was a smaller, single-storey building with three black doors across its front. It had the look of a schoolhouse, though it lacked a bell. The tiny village was silent. No light shone in its windows; no one moved in its dooryards. Meredith was about to write it off as another ghost town when she caught a sudden, sharp drift of wood smoke.

She stopped the horse and sat listening. The horse too was alert, looking from right to left, with her ears flickering. After a moment she walked on unprompted, and stopped in front of the schoolhouse with no bell and too many doors. The right-hand one stood slightly ajar. Meredith peered through the gap into a single large room. The room was full of people sitting on benches made of pale wood. *Birch*, Meredith thought, and wondered briefly where the knowledge had come from. But only briefly; her mind was occupied by the people.

They sat with their backs to her. There were perhaps fifty of them in all, of various ages. The men and the women sat in two distinct groups, separated by an aisle. From the smallest children to the frail elderly they were dressed alike: simply, in sober colors, the women with neat white caps and the men with their hair brushing their shoulders. Heads bowed, they faced another bench that ran along the wall to the left of the black doors. Two men and two women sat on this bench, their hands folded in their laps and their eyes cast down.

The stillness of the congregation was perfect, even profound. It held Meredith mesmerized, though part of her wanted to run. Then one of the women in the back row turned. Meredith withdrew, hoping that the woman had not been seen her, but it was too late. The woman appeared in the doorway, reaching out a work-roughened hand with a sweet, grave smile.

"You are welcome," she said, and Meredith knew that it would be a terrible thing to refuse that hand. So she allowed the woman to lead her inside and accepted a seat on the bench beside her.

Her arrival didn't seem to penetrate the serene meditation of the people around her. Even the children didn't look up. There was no sound but the wind in the building's eaves and the occasional creak of a bench when someone shifted. Meredith wondered who it was that they worshipped and what it was they prayed for. She hoped that the horse would not wander away. She tried not to fidget, though her muscles, used to riding, chilled and stiffened on the hard bench.

And then one of the children began to sing. He was a little boy, and his voice wasn't strong, but in such perfect silence it was plangent as a church bell. Meredith waited for the words to make sense, but they didn't. She wondered if he was singing in another language. Perhaps, she thought as the others began to join in, they were a community of immigrants. Yet the woman who had taken her inside had spoken in English, without an accent, and now she too was singing the strange words.

After a few minutes, still singing, the people began to get up. They pushed the benches back against the walls. The woman who had led Meredith into the hall met her eye, nodded, and smiled, but Meredith drew back against the wall, huddling on the end of a bench as they began to dance. Though it wasn't much of a dance: more a kind of circular march, a ring of men surrounding a ring of women. In itself, the movements were mundane, but the senseless words gave the scene the feel of some arcane ceremony. This impression deepened for Meredith when the first song led into another, and the dance changed. Now the congregation held out their hands. They turned their palms to the floor and began to shake them. Soon they were shaking so violently that their bodies and their music trembled too.

Meredith looked at the doors, far away across the sea of writhing dancers. She had no idea how long she had been sitting in the meetinghouse, but it was long enough for the horse to be miles away. Panic took her then, and she stood up, ignoring the hands that reached to draw her into the dance. When she arrived at the door, though, panic turned to despair. The square outside the meetinghouse was empty except for thick violet swags of mist.

Meredith ran outside. She didn't hear the following footsteps; she didn't hear anything but her own heart beating the beginnings of grief, until a hand closed gently on her arm. She whirled.

"Do not be alarmed," said the same woman who had led her into the meetinghouse, looking at Meredith with clear, kindly grey eyes. "It looks strange, no doubt, to an outsider. But it is our gift...our way of worshipping God. If you had not chanced upon us on a Wednesday – saving Sunday, of course – you would have found a farming village more or less like any other."

Meredith tried to listen to her, but she couldn't stop thinking of the horse. Her eyes flickered left and right, searching for a shape darker than the falling night.

"What is it that you have lost?" the woman asked.

Meredith opened her mouth, thinking, *Surely this is the time.* No sound emerged. She felt the tears build behind her eyes, wished she knew how to let them spill.

"Can you not speak?" the woman asked.

She shook her head. The woman looked at her thoughtfully for a moment. Then she asked, "I thought I heard a horse's gait, before I saw you at the door. Is that what you are missing?"

Meredith nodded and clutched the woman's arm, forgetting the weirdness in the hall in the flush of relief at being understood.

"Well, I doubt it will have gone far. I will help you find it. I am Sister Grace."

Meredith nodded and followed Grace as she set off toward one of the houses. Grace went inside and came out with a lantern. Then they set out again toward a building behind the house. As they approached it, Meredith heard a familiar whinny. She ran forward, and once again felt the pressing tears when the familiar dark sea with its white islands emerged from the dusk. A black eye reflected the lantern light, a warm nose blew sweet breath into her neck. She put her arms around the horse's neck, leaned into her mane.

"So," said Grace, her voice warm, "you have found your horse. You can put her in the barn for the night, supposing you mean to stay."

Meredith looked around at her, uncertain.

"It is your choice, of course," she said. "But this is no night for traveling, and visitors are always welcome here." She smiled at Meredith's continued uncertainty. "I promise that there will be no more dancing or singing."

Finally Meredith nodded, and allowed Grace to lead the horse into the barn. When she had seen her safely bedded in an empty stall, with a tall draft horse on one side and a geriatric grey pony on the other, she followed Grace back toward the houses.

"As I am Deaconess of the North family," she said as they walked, "you may join us."

As they made their way through the dark, Meredith wondered what it might mean to be deaconess of a family. The fog bound the lantern light, so that they walked within a tiny glowing bubble in the vast, quiet dark. Grace said nothing, but there was no awkwardness in her silence, no despair of words. She seemed content that all that needed to be said had been.

This time when they reached the house, there were lights in the lower windows. Meredith noticed now that the house, like the meeting hall, had a peculiar entrance. A single flight of steps led to two doors, side by side. Grace opened the right-hand door. Meredith followed her into a corridor with whitewashed walls and a wooden floor polished until it shone like glass. There were no pictures on the walls, no furniture or vases of flowers or curtains on the windows, only a peg-board painted grey-blue and hung with women's cloaks.

"You may hang your things here," said Grace, indicating them.

Meredith took off her hat and coat and hung them by the neat black cloaks. She was immediately ashamed of their grubby shapelessness, but Grace didn't appear to have noticed. She led Meredith through a door at the end of the corridor, into a bright, warm room lit by fat beeswax candles. A tall, wooden desk stood in between two windows at the far side. Drawers and cupboards had been built into one wall; another held a large fieldstone hearth with a well-stoked stove. The floor was covered with a plaited rug, and the chairs' seats were woven from strips of colored canvas.

Grace indicated to Meredith to sit by the stove. Reluctantly, she chose a stool with a red and grey woven seat, painfully aware of the travel dirt on her boots and clothing. But Grace seemed to take no notice of it. She only said, "I will fetch the Eldress for you now."

Meredith had only a few minutes to wonder what an Eldress might be before the door opened again, admitting a stout older woman with a brisk air. Meredith was certain she was one of the four who had sat at the front of the meetinghouse.

"Good evening," she said, nodding to Meredith. "I am Eldress March."

Meredith began to stand, but the woman gestured to her to keep seated. She herself remained standing, looking at Meredith for a moment with incisive hazel eyes before she said, "You are not able to speak."

Meredith shook her head.

Oddly, the woman chuckled. "Well, that will serve you well enough here. We are not given to idle conversation." Again she paused and looked at Meredith. "This is your first visit to a Shaker village?"

The word "Shaker" dredged the image of a clean-lined wooden chest from Meredith's jumbled memories, but nothing more. She nodded.

"So you did not come to us intentionally?"

Meredith shook her head.

The woman looked mildly disappointed, but she said, "Very well. It is all part of His plan." She smiled faintly, frank curiosity still clear in her eyes. "I suppose you are wondering about what you have seen this afternoon."

Meredith nodded.

"I will do my best to answer your questions, but it is supper time now. Come and eat. We will speak afterward."

Eldress March was already in the doorway. Meredith scrambled after her. They walked along another spare, spotless corridor, passing a staircase running up into darkness. Then the Eldress opened another door, which led into a room nearly as large as the meeting hall. It was furnished with two long tables, each lined with ladder-backed chairs. Only a handful of the chairs were filled, but despite this the women kept to one table and the men to the other.

Eldress March indicated to Meredith to sit. She took a chair beside Grace, who nodded to her with a small smile and then resumed looking at her folded hands. Everybody looked at their hands, silent and still as they had been when Meredith first looked into the meetinghouse. In all the time since her words had fled, Meredith had never been so conscious of silence.

After a few minutes, two women came in through a door on the far side of the room, carrying steaming dishes. They set these on the tables and went back for more. They brought bowls of stew, buttered greens, fresh bread, cheese, canned peaches and cake. It was more food than Meredith ever remembered seeing in one place.

Finally, the serving women sat down with the others. By some unspoken cue, the people began to sing. This time, though, it was a simple song with English words, which seemed to be a prayer of thanksgiving. When it was finished, the people began to pass the dishes around. They did it wordlessly, with the precision of familiar ritual, nodding thanks to each other as the food passed from hand to hand. Meredith accepted the bowls that Grace handed her and took helpings the same size as Grace's.

The Shakers ate, as it seemed they did most things, in perfect silence. Meredith was conscious of every scrape of her fork against her plate, every clatter of her knife, and grateful that they didn't linger over their dinner. When the meal was finished, the men stood up and left by a door opposite the one through which Meredith and Eldress March had entered. The women began to clear the table, to hang chairs from the ubiquitous peg-board, and to sweep the floors.

Meredith stood to the side, uncertain whether she should try to help or not, until a girl of about ten beckoned to her from the doorway through which the food had been brought in. She followed her into a vast kitchen. The girl rolled her sleeves back and led Meredith to a sink full of steaming water.

"I am Martha," she said. "Will you dry the dishes for me?"

Meredith nodded and took up the cloth Martha offered. The child went about her work cheerfully enough, though she made no attempt to talk to Meredith. There were three other women cleaning with them in the kitchen. They spoke to each other in low voices, even laughed now and then. Meredith wondered if Martha's silence was a reaction to her own, or if it was somehow obligatory.

When she had wiped the last plate, Martha finally spoke: "Thank you for your help. Come now; we will go to the sitting room."

Meredith followed the child back through the refectory, into the hallway and then to the sitting room, where the Eldress had spoken to her earlier. The other women from the dining table had gathered there, taking chairs from the peg rail and opening work boxes. They were elliptical in shape, made of a single sheet of wood lapped round. They had carrying handles and trays inside to hold needles and thread, pins and scissors. The trays lifted out, showing knitting wool or patchwork fabric neatly packed at the bottom.

Out of those women's boxes came another memory: a similar box, though darkened by time and use, sitting beneath the whitewashed eaves of an attic room. Inside it, beneath the needles and cotton spools, were the beginnings of a quilt – wavering strips of fabric in greens and blues and violets, some of them pieced with precise, tiny stitches, others lying just as they had been cut, beneath a pair of rusting shears. All bore the scent of old wood, mildew and unfulfilled promise.

A gentle hand came down on Meredith's shoulder. "Would you like a piece to work on?"

Meredith looked up from the unmoored memory into Grace's kind face. She wanted to oblige her, but she had no recollection of this kind of work. She pointed to the sewing box and shrugged, hoping that her meaning was clear.

"You do not know how to sew?" Grace's voice was puzzled.

Meredith understood: even the smallest child in the room, a girl of perhaps five, was sewing diligently. This, like cooking and knitting and no doubt much else, was the work women did, whether they were farmers' wives or religious sisters. Grace didn't understand how a grown woman could be ignorant of it, nor did Meredith herself. She knew only that this ignorance was somehow shameful.

But Grace didn't press the point. She only said, "I will show you."

Meredith nodded gratefully, and Grace took two little piles of calico squares from her box, one cream colored, one a muted blue floral. She also took out a quilt section made of nine squares in alternating colors, and laid it on a table between them. She threaded a needle, took up a square of each color, and began to stitch them together. She turned the work so that Meredith could see how it was done.

Meredith watched her for a few moments and then, doubtfully, picked up a needle and bit off a length of thread. She sucked the thread-end as she'd seen Grace do, aimed it at the eye, but she could not put it through. Her fingers were clumsy, the skin too hardened by her outdoor life to feel the fine thread properly. Mortified, she put them down again.

But Grace wasn't willing to give up so easily. She took up Meredith's needle and thread. With a flick the thread was through the eye and the end knotted. Sighing, Meredith picked up two fabric squares and began to piece them together. Hard as she tried, though, she could not make her stitches as neat and tiny as Grace's. When she pulled on her seam to test it, she could see light between the stitches. She pulled them out in despair. Grace took them from her gently. Meredith couldn't look at her.

"Don't be ashamed," Grace told her. "You have tried your best, and that is all that He asks." She looked at Meredith's hands and then continued, "Your fingers seem nimble enough; I don't doubt that your sewing would improve with time. But I think perhaps you have worked at something else. What is it?"

Meredith didn't know. But then, with an involuntary movement, her hand went to touch the smooth wood of Grace's workbox. There was a tingle of recognition in her fingers; her fickle memory told her *cherry*. She looked up at Grace, who looked back with earnest eyes.

"You cannot have failed to notice," she said, "that the brethren and sisters of our families lead separate lives. It is the same with the work we do. The brethren see to the heavy labor, the sisters to the light; brethren to the hard materials, sisters to the soft.

Sisters do not work wood." She paused again, with the same thoughtful look. "And yet, you are not a sister; not yet, anyway. If wood is your gift, surely it is fitting that you share it. I will speak to Eldress March."

Meredith wanted to tell her that she didn't know how to work wood, and that she wouldn't be staying long enough to employ a "gift" even if she had one. At the same time, though, she thought of the benches in the meetinghouse. She thought of the workboxes, whose spare beauty still intrigued her. She found herself nodding.

"Good," Grace said, and then went back to her sewing.

Not long after that the women began packing away their work. Taking candles, they left the room. "Martha," said Grace, "please show our visitor to our retiring room. I will be up when I have spoken to the Eldress."

"Yea, Sister," the child said, taking up a candle. "Come," she said to Meredith, who followed her out into the dim corridor and then up the stairway she had seen earlier. It ended on a wide hallway, with doors opening off either side. Meredith saw men emerging from another stair at the far end of the corridor and disappearing into doors on the left-hand side. The women entered the doors on the right.

"This way," said Martha.

Meredith followed the child into a room with four beds. All four had wooden frames, made up with quilts and crisp sheets. There was a braided rug on the floor and a stove on the outer wall, but it was still cold compared with the sitting room. A young woman was washing at a stand in the corner. When she had finished, she undressed, hung her clothing from the peg-rail and pulled on a long flannel nightgown. Without a word, she opened a dresser, took out a similar gown and handed it to Meredith, who nodded her thanks.

"This will be your bed," Martha told her, indicating the one nearest the door. "We keep it made up in case there are visitors."

Meredith laid the nightgown on the bed.

"Here is a flannel," said Martha, handing her a clean folded cloth. "You may use the basin before me."

Meredith nodded again, and then took off her boots and trousers. Shivering in her shirt, she washed her hands and face and neck, and then quickly pulled on the nightgown. The other woman was already in bed, so Meredith turned back her own covers. Grace came in as she pulled the quilt up to her neck. She smiled at her, but there was a strange turn to it. Not quite sadness; perhaps regret.

"I have spoken to Eldress March," she said. "Tomorrow morning you will join Elijah in the wood shop."

Meredith nodded, hating herself for her duplicity. By tomorrow morning, she planned to have put this strange village far behind her.

3

Once again, nature foiled her. She awakened to bright sunlight and the tolling of a bell. Her breath plumed despite the roaring stove. Martha and the young woman were up and dressing, Grace already gone. Meredith stood, and with arms wrapped around herself, she looked through the window's frosted panes.

The road stretched away from the village in a band of beaten silver, a screaming brightness where the past day's fog had settled and frozen solid.

Meredith might not have mastered the urge to climb back into bed and pull the quilt over her head if she'd had a cold cotton shift and petticoats to negotiate. But she had the warm woolens from the cabin, cleaned and dried by Anis. She washed quickly and put them on as Martha watched her curiously.

"Why do you dress like a man," the child asked, "when God made you a woman?"

"Martha!" the older woman chastised.

"I'm sorry," Martha said, eyes downcast.

"She is still learning," the woman said to Meredith.

Meredith shook her head, smiled a little.

"Very well," said the woman. "I am Sister Anna. Come, it is time for breakfast."

And so once again Meredith found herself at the sparsely populated table, facing a bountiful, silent meal. After the women had cleared the table and washed the dishes, they filed out into the hallway and put on their cloaks. Then they went out into the frosty morning, holding onto each other as they shuffled along the icy path to the meetinghouse.

When she realized where they were going, Meredith hung back. A moment later Grace caught up with her. "It is your choice whether or not to attend Morning Prayers," she said. "But if it heartens you, this will be a quick and quiet service." There was a smile in her voice and eyes. Meredith went with her.

Someone had lit the stove in the meetinghouse, and it had dispelled the worst of the chill. Meredith sat between Grace and Anna, half listening as one of the men at the front of the room read a Psalm. She thought that he must be the minister of the sect, but then he sat down, and Eldress March stood up, taking his place to read another verse. After that the other woman at the front of the room read from a Gospel, and then the congregation sat for a long time in silent prayer.

Meredith's attention drifted. She watched the wavering shadows the bare branches threw across the floor. She looked at the bent heads of the children, wondering how they had been trained to sit so still. As her eyes ran over the little group of boys sitting at the front of the men's section, she noticed a young man sitting at the end of their bench as if they were in his charge. He had a serious face, dark hair, hazel eyes from which he looked sidelong at Meredith. He averted them as soon as he saw that she'd noticed. Meredith also looked away. Then the people began to sing a hymn. It stirred no memory in Meredith, but at the same time, she was taken by its words:

"Who will bow and bend like the willow, who will turn and twist and reel

In the gale of simple freedom, from the bower of union flowing

Who will drink the wine of power, dropping down like a shower

Pride and bondage all forgetting, Mother's wine is freely working

Oh ho, I will have it, I will bow and bend to get it

I'll be reeling, turning, twisting, shake out all the starch and stiff'ning."

As the Shakers sang, Meredith looked across again at the dark-haired man. He was not singing, but looking gravely at the floor. She noticed then that his hair was not long like the other men's, but cut above his collar. She was not entirely surprised when Eldress March came up to her in the yard after the service, leading the dark-haired man and two little boys.

"This is Elijah," the Eldress said, nodding to the man. "And his apprentices, Jonah and Peter. Elijah is our finest box-maker."

There was a note of regret in Eldress March's tone, in the too-long look she gave him. Then she said to him, "And this is the woman I told you about. You may take her to your shop, and she may assist there, if He should so move her."

There was unguarded curiosity on Elijah's face, but he bowed his head and said, "Yea, Eldress. Come, Miss…?" He looked at Meredith expectantly. Meredith looked back, mortified.

"Our guest has, I believe, taken a vow of silence," said Eldress March. "We, of all people, can respect that."

Elijah bobbed his head again, then repeated, "Come," and started carefully down one of the icy paths. Meredith hung back, looking toward the barn.

"Do not worry," said the Eldress. "Your horse will be well looked after." Meredith nodded, gave her a hesitant smile. The Eldress smiled back briefly and then turned back to the house.

Elijah walked slowly, but even so Meredith nearly fell twice. The second time he caught her by the arm, releasing her abruptly when she was upright again, as if the touch had burned him. The two boys studied her when they thought she wasn't looking, but they didn't whisper or chatter as most children would, faced with such a strange addition to their party.

At last they arrived at another white clapboard building. Elijah held the door for Meredith and the boys, then shut it firmly behind them and went to stir up the stove. The workshop wasn't much different from the other rooms Meredith had seen, with its whitewash and peg-board and smooth wooden floor. Still, its purpose was clear. In the center there was a big worktable, holding strips of wood and half-finished boxes. Various tools hung from the peg-board, along with extra chairs.

The little boys sat down at the table and went straight to work on two of the boxes. Elijah stood beside Meredith, clearly uncertain how to proceed. She wished she had words to assuage his discomfort.

"Have you ever made a curved box?" he asked at last.

Meredith shook her head.

"That's just as well, because our building methods are different from most others. I'll show you their making, if you would you like to learn it."

Meredith did want to learn it, but more than that she wanted to stay in the workshop. There was a familiarity to the hanging tools, to the smell of the shavings littering the floor that was comforting. When Elijah picked up one of the strips of wood and handed it to her, the resonant feeling of recognition returned to her hands. *Cherry*, she thought again.

"It's cherry wood," Elijah confirmed. "The last of it."

He didn't elaborate on the statement, though Meredith looked at him with questioning eyes. After a ruminative moment, he shook his head and continued, "It's quarter-sawn…you see, the grain runs straight this way…" He ran his hand from one end of the thin board to the other. "And here, at the ends, it's vertical. If it's not cut along the grain, it will split when we bend it."

His words were a half-remembered song, some of them leaping at her with crystalline images attached, others meaningless. Of the wood, though, she was certain. When Elijah tried to take it back, she held on. He smiled, bemused. The little boys exchanged a look.

"All right, then," he said. "But you will at least have to lay it flat, if you mean to do anything with it."

Meredith laid the wood on the table. Elijah opened a drawer and took out a flat piece of metal with two tongues cut into the end, and laid it on the wood. He traced around the tongues, and Meredith recognized the swallowtail pattern of the workboxes' single joint. Elijah put the template away, and made little marks on the traced tongues. Next he took a fine-toothed saw from another drawer, and while Meredith held the wood, he cut out the first of the swallowtails. When the waste wood dropped, he handed her the saw.

The wood was so thin and fine that Meredith felt sure she would break it, but her hand never doubted. In a few minutes she was brushing the dust from the finished cuts. It earned her another serious smile from Elijah, and the unconcealed admiration of Peter and Jonah, who left their work and came to watch.

Elijah brought out a drill and a fine bit. "Drill here," he said, indicating the marks he'd made on the swallowtails. Meredith took the drill and again, with a confidence that surprised them both, she made two holes in each of the three tongues, and seven in a row at their base.

"Perfect," said Elijah. "Now we'll sand it down. The join can't be too thick." He handed her a piece of sandpaper, and she went to work on the wood, while he herded the boys back to their own projects. When the tails were thin enough, Elijah said, "Now we bend it."

It was another word Meredith knew, and this time the image it unearthed was more than a flicker: a cluttered room with a frame like a ribcage standing in the center; her own hands tacking warped boards to the frame.

"...Miss?"

She looked up into Elijah's bemused eyes, shook her head, and then handed him the piece of wood. He took it, shaking his own head, and brought it over to the stove. The boys had put a tub of water on to heat, and now it was simmering. Elijah fed the wood carefully into the water, and then pushed it down with a pair of tongs.

"It has to soak for twenty minutes," he said when it was positioned properly, "which is just time for a cup of coffee." He ladled some of the water into a coffee pot and set it on the stove to percolate. Then he took two chairs from the pegboard, offered one to Meredith and sat in the other.

"Where did you learn your craft?" he asked, and then flushed. "Oh – pardon me – "

Meredith shook her head, went to the table and picked up the pencil Elijah had used to mark the wood. She mimicked writing with it. Elijah nodded, got up and rummaged in another drawer. He took out a sheet of yellowed paper. It had box plans drawn on one side, but the other was blank.

Meredith laid the paper on the table, took up the pencil and wrote, "My name is Meredith. I did not take a vow of silence." When she looked up at Elijah, he raised his eyebrows, smiled and said, "I see. I think this will require coffee." He went to the stove, poured two cups and set them on the table, then pulled the chairs up to it.

"First of all," said Elijah, sitting down and lifting his cup, "may I say I am pleased to make your acquaintance, Miss…Meredith? Is that your given name or surname?"

"Given," Meredith wrote. It was the first time she'd thought about it. She tried now to recall her surname, but it flitted just beyond her reach.

"Very well, Meredith. Forgive my impertinence, but if you haven't taken a vow of silence, then why don't you speak?"

Meredith wrote, "I don't know." She paused. From Elijah's look, she knew that he wouldn't let the matter rest there. "At the end of the summer," she wrote, "I awakened on a beach. I suppose I had been in the sea and washed up there. But I do not remember why I was in the sea, nor anything else before that."

"So you don't know how you learned to work wood."

"No," she wrote, thinking that she was not being strictly truthful: she had, after all, that image of her hands tacking bent planks to a wooden ribcage.

"Well," said Elijah, "it seems you learned it properly, however you learned it." Meredith shrugged. Elijah sipped his coffee thoughtfully. After a moment he asked, "Why did you come to us?"

Meredith wrote, "I didn't. The horse did. I go where she chooses."

He smiled again. "And your horse chose a Shaker village on a Wednesday evening at prayer time. That must have been a shock!" Meredith nodded. "I cannot imagine how it would look to an outsider. I mean all of this – not just the prayer meeting." He gestured to the shop around them. "All I can say in defense is, they are sincere in their faith."

Now it was Meredith's turn to scrutinize him. Except for the short hair, he looked no different from the other Shaker men. But still: "They?" she wrote.

Elijah sighed. "In two days I will turn twenty-one, and I will leave the community."

"Why?" she scribbled.

"Because I am not called to lead this life." Meredith waited, sensing more. At last Elijah rewarded her: "My mother left me here as a young child. She told the Eldress nothing but that she was alone and destitute and could not care for me."

Meredith saw a baby rocked improbably by the sea in a floating cradle. Her breath came suddenly in short, shallow bursts, but Elijah didn't notice.

"I suppose her story is easy enough to guess," he said solemnly. "But the people of this community do not judge as harshly as those of others. They do not believe that a child born in sin is cursed by it forever. They see him no differently than they see that piece of wood." He indicated the softening plank on the stove. "I suppose you have been here long enough to realize that the brethren and sisters design and make their material objects with great care. That is because they believing that making something well is an act of prayer. Well, they look similarly on the making of a man."

He looked up at her then. Without turning, he said, "Jonah, Peter, go fetch more water."

Meredith expected the children to protest being sent away, but they only said, rather regretfully, "Yea Elijah," and took their buckets and went. Meredith waited, watching Elijah. In his hazel eyes was a fathomless sadness. In Meredith's, all of the questions that she could not ask and the memories she could not piece together.

"It is not right that I influence the boys with my views," Elijah said at last. "And yet, I feel that you deserve to hear the truth." He paused, sighed. "The truth is this: the Shakers take us in when nobody wants us. They feed us and school us and love us. But the truest gift they give us – and, to me, the surest sign of their holiness – is choice. When a boy or girl turns twenty-one, he or she is asked to decide whether they wish to enter the community as an adult brother or sister, or to leave it."

"And you have chosen to leave," Meredith wrote.

"Yes."

Meredith looked down at the paper for a long moment before she wrote, "You do not seem contented with this choice."

Elijah smiled ruefully. "That is because I wish that I could choose differently. Their numbers decline every year. The last thing they need is to lose a brother. The last thing I want is to be the one they lose." The question was obvious. Meredith didn't bother to write it, and Elijah duly answered, "I am also unhappy because I am ashamed of my reasons." Finally, he looked at her.

"You cannot have failed to notice that men and women lead separate lives here. In this, they are absolute. Shakers do not marry."

He paused again, and then repeated, "Shakers do not marry. But I long for a wife, and children, and so I cannot be a Shaker. I will turn my back on these people who have given me everything, in favor of a woman I might never meet, a dream that might be no more than the devil's whisperings. Where is the sense in that?"

Meredith didn't know. She couldn't remember ever thinking about marriage or love or family. On the other hand, she'd developed a keen eye for the truth in the time since she'd awakened on the grey beach, and so she wrote, "It seems to me that your people are, first and foremost, forgiving. Grace saw last night that I could not sew. Instead of trying to make me a seamstress, she sent me here. Is this so different? You recognize that you do not want to live a celibate life. That doesn't mean that you won't still be the man that the Shakers have made you."

Elijah looked at the paper for a long time. As he opened his mouth to reply, though, the boys came back, red-cheeked and trailing cold into the steamy heat. Elijah took the paper, closed it in his fist and put it into the stove, but not before he'd nodded once, earnestly, at Meredith.

"It's ready," he said then, poking at the boiling wood with a pair of tongs. He put on a pair of padded gloves and handed another to Meredith. "Now," he said, "we will have only a minute before the wood cools too much to bend. Jonah, please bring the form."

Jonah set an oval-shaped block of wood on the table, while Peter waited with another piece of wood to soften. Elijah lifted the plank from the water and then quickly wrapped it around the form.

"You must be careful," he said, "when you come to the swallowtails. They are so thin they can snap easily, and then all of this work is for nothing." But under his expert fingers, the swallowtails bent perfectly. Elijah held the wood in position while it cooled and took its shape. "Do you still have the pencil?" he asked Meredith. "Good; now trace around the swallowtails." Meredith traced them onto the other end of the wood strip, while Elijah held it tight around the mold. "There," he said. When he let go, the curved wood sprang away from the frame, but it kept its bend.

Elijah brought it to a small anvil. Beside the anvil was a dish of copper tacks and a diminutive hammer. "I will hold the join in place," he said to Meredith. "You take a tack, and put it in a guide hole we drilled earlier. Good. Now tap it with the hammer – gently." Carefully holding the tack in place, Meredith did as he'd instructed. The tack turned on the anvil beneath, making a tight cinch. She put a tack into each of the drilled holes like this, and when Elijah lifted the finished oval, she felt a rush of delight.

"It has to dry overnight before we can do any more to it," he said, and smiled at her obvious disappointment. "Don't worry. We have all day to make others!"

Elijah put shapers into the oval and then set it on a shelf to dry beside other bent bands of varying sizes. He took two of these from the end of the row, and brought them to the table. "These are ready for lids," he said, and so they repeated the process with thinner bands of wood, which would form the rings of the boxes' lids. After that they worked on pegging in the tops and bottoms, bending handles and making trays for workbaskets. It seemed only a few minutes had passed when Elijah said, "It is time for midday prayer."

The sun had melted the top of the ice-slick, making it even more treacherous than it had been before. They picked their way carefully along to the meeting house, and Meredith was almost glad to reach it, if only for the stable footing. There followed a prayer service not unlike the morning one, and then all of the brothers and sisters filed out again through their separate doors, back to their dwelling houses for dinner.

When Meredith returned to the workshop afterward, Elijah was waiting with a slate and chalk for her. He told her about his childhood with the Shakers, and she told him about the journey that had brought her to them. He took particular interest in the story of Anis and Tomah and the bleeding tree.

"I would love to see that tree. Fruit trees seldom live so long." His look turned sad. "We had a very old cherry here. It was planted by the brethren who founded the village. But it came down in a storm a few years back. This is the last of it." He nodded at the box.

"It's beautiful wood," Meredith wrote.

"But the tree was more beautiful still." He paused. "Sometime I cannot help but see these boxes as gravestones."

"Why not consider them an afterlife?" Meredith wrote, with the strange feeling that she'd once heard someone else speak the words.

"A living tree," Elijah said, "strives toward heaven like a prayer. A box is merely a shell."

"No," Meredith wrote. "A boat is the vessel of a dead tree's memories."

"A boat?" Elijah asked, looking up at her quickly.

But Meredith was looking down, paralyzed by the word that had slipped out. There wasn't even the possibility that she'd misremembered it; it was right there, stark white on the black slate. The corners of the shop swam with images: an iron blade tearing through wavering, watery grass; a shadowed face stamped on a blue sky; the carving she'd left in the hilltop cabin months before.

"A boat?" Elijah repeated. "Is that how you learned wood? You built boats?"

"I don't remember," Meredith wrote at last. "But it would explain some things."

After a moment's consideration, Elijah said, "A boat does indeed seem a fitting vessel for a tree's memory. Another kind of prayer." He gave the lid a last brush with the sandpaper, fitted it to the box. He looked at it, and then at Meredith. "Perhaps you are right about the boxes, too," he said at last. "And yet, of what value is a store of memories which cannot be spoken?"

Meredith shook her head.

"Don't you know why Tomah's tree bled?" he said softly.

Again, she shook her head.

"Because it could not speak."

4

Meredith brought the slate with her to supper. There was no opportunity to use it there, but afterward, in the women's sitting room, she sat down by Grace and wrote, "Thank you for introducing me to Elijah."

Grace smiled. "I am glad that you enjoyed his company, Meredith. Yes – Elijah told me your name, and a bit of what you told him about yourself. I hope that it does not bother you?"

Meredith shook her head.

"Was the work to your liking?" Grace asked, taking out her patchwork squares.

"Very much so," wrote Meredith.

Grace nodded. She sewed for a few minutes, while Meredith wondered whether she should offer to help. But then Grace said, "I have a favor to ask of you, Meredith." Meredith nodded. "Elijah will have told you that he is leaving us on Saturday, when he comes of age. I know that you don't intend to stay with us; would you be willing to let him travel with you when you go?"

Meredith blinked. It was the last thing she had expected Grace to ask. "I do not know where I am going," she wrote at last.

"Nor does he," Grace said. Meredith looked up at her, surprised, and Grace smiled ruefully. "Elijah dreams of love. He believes that he will find it if only he goes looking." She shrugged. "Perhaps he is right. But then, he knows very little of the world."

She sighed. "There was a time when the life we live here differed little from the lives of those around us. But the gulf has widened. Fewer and fewer join us each year. Fewer of the children we raise choose to stay. Yet at the same time, joining the modern world becomes ever harder for them. It is especially hard for dreamers like Elijah." She paused, searching Meredith's face. "Something tells me that you've already learned this lesson – that you might be able to soften it for him."

Meredith doubted it, but she didn't want to disappoint Grace. "The journey has been hard," she wrote at last, "but not without its merit."

Grace nodded. "And that is why I hope that you will agree to travel with Elijah, until he finds his feet."

And will I ever find mine? Meredith wondered. She didn't even know what it would mean for her, but she wrote, "He is welcome, if it's what he wishes."

"You are a good girl," said Grace.

Once again, Meredith wondered.

5

The next morning dawned bright and icy again. At the prayer meeting Meredith's mind drifted to the boxes and the day ahead, until Eldress Williams stood up and began to read the psalm. Then her dreamy half-attention froze into sharp awareness of the words: "'They that go down to the sea in ships, that do business in great waters; These see the works of the Lord, and his wonders in the deep. For he commandeth, and raiseth the stormy wind, which lifteth up the waves thereof…'"

The sunlit meeting room was gone. Meredith stood at the end of a wooden dock, her face to the teeth of a northeast storm. Waves crashed around her legs; rain pelted her face and plastered her sodden dress to her body. She shivered, but she felt no cold. She felt nothing but the raw hollow where her heart had been.

"'They mount up to the heaven,'" the Eldress read, her voice cold and clear as a bell on a winter dawn, "'they go down again to the depths: their soul is melted because of trouble. They reel to and fro, and stagger like a drunken man, and are at their wits' end.'"

On the sea-swept dock, Meredith fumbled with the knot in a boat's painter, but the wind and the driving waves had turned it to a cold pebble. She flung open a storage chest bolted to the dock, tossed out its contents until she found a knife, and then cut the line. She stepped into the boat, hoisted the sail, and turned its nose into the storm, forcing it onward by sheer force of will. She passed the dark smudges of the harbor islands and came into open water.

Now the waves reared up in earnest. They snapped the rudder like kindling, but the mainsail held, cleated by both sheets while the mast screamed in protest and the stays groaned. The boat fought its heart out for her, but it could not win against that sea. And when at last the sea came for them – a wave rising like a black wall – there was no fear, only relief.

And then Meredith was back in the Shakers' meeting hall, clinging to the first concrete memory of her life before the beach. It was a bitter, blighted thing, but it was her own. She laughed as she held it, laughed until her sides hurt, and she thought she could not draw another breath. One by one, the Shaker Brothers and Sisters knelt, until they formed a ring around her.

"'They cry unto the Lord in their trouble,'" the Eldress said softly, "'and he bringeth them out of their distresses…he bringeth them unto their desired haven…'" Then she put the book down, and knelt with them.

6

Before she left the Shakers, Meredith went to the orchard. It was easy enough to find the place where the cherry tree had fallen. The cherry Tomah had given her was soft now and shrivelling in her pocket. She buried it in the hole left by the old tree, pressing frozen earth around it, and hoping that there would still be Shakers in the village to gather its fruit.

After that, she went to the workshop and collected the box that she had made on her first morning. When she gave it to Grace, the woman turned it reverently in her hands. With tears in her eyes she said, "This is a true gift," and embraced Meredith. "I hope you will come and visit us again," she said.

Meredith was surprised to find that she hoped so, too.

*

The horse was overjoyed to be out of her stable again. The weather had turned mild; what ice was left was pitted and rotting and broke easily beneath her hooves. She danced on the road, ignoring the reproachful glances of Elijah's staid bay gelding which, he told Meredith, he had paid for in boxes.

They rode through a country of rolling hills and valleys. The air was clear; the wind carried snatches of wood smoke from the little farms they passed. Here there were only faint traces of snow. The landscape's soft greens and browns were strange to Meredith after so many days of white.

"How do you decide where you are going?" Elijah asked when they stopped at midday to eat and let the horses rest.

"The horse decides," Meredith wrote on her slate.

"How far do you travel each day?" Meredith underlined her first answer, and Elijah raised his eyebrows. "There are plenty who would tell you that's the fastest way to ruin a horse."

Meredith put a protective hand on the horse's shoulder.

"Don't worry. I'm not one of them. After all, she brought you to the village, didn't she?" When they rode out again, he let Meredith take the lead.

Late in the afternoon, they came to a lake. The road ran close to the shore for a time, until it arched up into a rough board bridge over a culvert, where the lake narrowed to a wide stream. Someone was fishing from the bridge, perched on a barrel. The figure was so tiny that Meredith thought at first she was a child. As they drew nearer, however, she saw gnarled hands and a thread of smoke. The figure was in fact an old woman, dressed in a filthy skirt and apron and a man's cable-knit sweater of a shade made indistinguishable by dirt. She had a woodsman's cap pulled low over her forehead, and a pipe clenched between her teeth.

The fisherwoman didn't look up until Meredith and Elijah stopped in front of her. They had to stop: the bridge was too narrow for them to cross as long as the woman was sitting there. She looked them up and down and then reeled in her line, put the rod aside and stood up. She couldn't have been more than five feet tall or younger than eighty. A miasmic stink hung around her, a conglomeration of fish and smoke and sweat.

"Evenin'," she said, pipe still clenched firmly in her teeth. She reached across a bucket of gaping fish to shake their hands.

"And to you," Elijah answered politely.

"I don't suppose," the woman said, "you got a spare twist?"

"A what?"

She dislodged the pipe from a gap-toothed mouth and tapped out the cinders. "Tobacco. I'm clean out."

"I'm sorry," he said. The woman sighed mournfully, fished around in the pocket of her voluminous apron, and finally came up with a few linty brown strands. She stuffed them into the bowl of her pipe, lit it, drew on it, and exhaled a cloud of sweet smoke.

"Not plumb out, yet," she said. "And I got plenty of fish anyhow. You come with me, and I'll give you dinner."

Meredith could see that Elijah was intrigued by the old woman. She put a supplicating hand on his arm – a gesture the woman took in with keen dark eyes.

"The girl dumb?" she asked.

"She can't speak," Elijah said, "if that's your meaning."

"Simple?"

"Not in the least," he answered.

The woman gave a curt nod. "Come on, or I'm going without you." She began to walk away. Elijah followed her, and grudgingly, Meredith followed him.

Despite her age and stature, her bucket and tackle, the woman kept abreast of the horses easily. The road curved around into a stand of conifers, and without hesitation she plunged into these, following a barely-discernible path. A hundred yards in, the path ran up against a windowless wooden shed, with "Connecticut and Passumpsic Rivers Railroad" stenciled on the side in peeling red paint.

The woman stopped, looked at the horses and said, "Can't bring them inside."

Meredith looked anxiously at Elijah. "They'll be all right," he said, "if we tie them here. It's not too cold, and we'll give them grain."

Sighing, Meredith went along with him. When they came into the shed, they found the woman sitting at a table consisting of a board on two empty barrels, gutting fish between swigs from a bottle marked "W.H. Darling & Son". Behind her, a glowing stove leaked smoke from a leaning pipe. Beside the stove was a disintegrating cane chair, and beside that a bed whose clothes were as filthy as the woman's own. The far wall was piled to the eaves with split firewood. The whole place smelled strongly of pipe smoke and fish.

"Have a seat," the woman said, tossing fish guts into a pail. Elijah sat on a barrel; Meredith, gingerly, on the chair. "Name's Maggie Hanlon."

"Elijah Ellis. And this is Meredith."

"Ellis?"

"Nay. She's a friend, not a relation."

The woman looked up at him with narrowed eyes. "You one of them Quakers?"

"Na – no," Elijah answered carefully, coloring. "I once belonged to the United Society of Believers in Christ's Second Appearing."

"The United *what*?"

Elijah sighed. "The Shakers."

Maggie's eyebrows raised in interest, her knife drooped in her hand. "That so? You leave because of her?" She jutted her chin at Meredith.

Meredith frowned, and Elijah blushed more deeply. "No. I left because I was ready to leave. Meredith was passing through, and we decided to travel together for a time."

Maggie nodded as if this explained everything and went back to her fish. "I left my family, too," she said. "Both my parents came from Ireland. Had a farm in the north of the state and seven big boys to help run it. Then they had me: scrawny Maggie, not big enough for farm work and no patience for women's work." She shook her head. "But fishing – that, I could do, and that I've done ever since. Drink?" She proffered the bottled in slimy hands.

"Thank you, no," said Elijah. Meredith shook her head. Maggie shrugged, and drank.

"Can we help you?" Elijah asked.

"Now he asks!" Maggie cackled, tossing the last gutted fish onto the pile. "No: if there's one thing I do know, it's how to cook fish."

To prove it, she stood up, put a massive skillet on top of the stove, scooped a lump of lard into it and stirred it around with a pair of fire tongs. When it was melted she put three butterflied fish into the pan, where they smoked and sizzled.

"So where are you headed, Elijah Ellis?" she asked as she poked the cooking fish.

"I don't rightly know," he answered.

"Does *she* know?" she asked, glancing at Meredith.

Elijah paused, exchanging a look with Meredith. "I suppose we're both looking for our rightful place in the world."

Meredith assumed that this would earn a snort or cackle from the old woman, but instead she nodded as if the answer made perfect sense. She lifted the fried fish onto a plate, handed it to Meredith. Against all reason, the fish was delicious.

"I hope you find your place before winter sets in honest," Maggie said, adding more lard and fish to the pan. "This ain't no country to be wandering in snow season."

"Indeed not," Elijah agreed.

"If I was you," Maggie said, serving Elijah and then putting in the last of the fish to fry, "or even if I was young again, I'd go south."

Meredith looked up and found Maggie's eyes already waiting for hers. "That's right," she said, sitting down at the gut-strewn table to eat. "You could go straight on down to Florida, eat oranges every day and never have to worry about chopping wood. Don't know why it took me so long to realize it was that easy. It ain't like there's water to cross. You just keep on walking til you're there."

Thinking of her narrow escape from the river, Meredith had to disagree about the water; nevertheless, Maggie's words intrigued her.

"It's only when you're too old to do anything about it," Maggie sighed, swigging hooch, "that you realize all the things you might have done with your life." She chewed for a while, spat out a bone, then shrugged. "But then, my life hasn't been too bad. Got all I need right here. All except tobacco, and even when that runs out, well, there's ways and means. Are you sure you haven't got none?"

Meredith smiled and shook her head. Elijah said, "I am sorry."

Maggie twitched a shoulder, pushed her plate aside to make room for the bottle. "Don't suppose you have any stories to tell?"

"I'm afraid my story is a plain one," said Elijah. "What you haven't heard of it, you've no doubt guessed."

Maggie chuckled at him, but her eyes were on Meredith. "*You* got a story, though. I'd bet my last twist on it."

Meredith's eyes settled on her lap.

"Meredith doesn't remember her past," Elijah explained. "She suffered some kind of accident at sea. She awoke on a beach a few months ago, and her memories had gone."

Meredith looked up at him. Then she opened her pack, and took out the slate and chalk. She wrote, "I remembered something. In the meeting hall, when I laughed…it was because I remembered how I came to be in the sea. I didn't tell you before now, I didn't tell the others because – " She stopped with the chalk suspended over the slate, realizing that she had no good explanation for keeping the memory to herself – only irrational fear.

"It's all right," Elijah said gently. "You were under no obligation to tell us. You are under none now."

"But I want to tell you now," Meredith wrote.

"What is she saying?" Maggie demanded.

"Meredith?" asked Elijah. She nodded. To Maggie he said, "She says that she's remembered something else. How she came to be in the sea." And he read to Maggie as Meredith wrote out her memory of the storm, of the wave that had destroyed her boat and nearly drowned her. When she'd finished, he gave her a searching look. "And do you know why you did it? Sailed into that storm?"

"Because I wanted to die," Meredith wrote without hesitation. She saw the shock in his eyes; nevertheless, he read the words out faithfully to Maggie.

Then he asked, "What could have made you want to take your own life?"

Meredith shook her head, rattling the half-images of a face against a blue sky, bruises on brown skin. But Maggie answered, "Oh, there's no mystery there." They looked at her, equally surprised. "She had her heart broken."

Broken? Meredith thought. Clawed out, perhaps. Shredded. That recovered memory of pain left no doubt that violence had inflicted it. Yet on the heels of that certainty came another: there was no hollow in her chest anymore. There was a numbness, an absence, even a kind of regret, but somewhere in the midst of it her heart was beating.

Given the way Elijah was looking at her, she knew that the epiphany must have showed on her face. She wanted to explain it to him – the pain, and the unexpected reconciliation to it – but she didn't know the words.

Maggie did.

"Mo bhrón ar an bhfarraige
Is é tá mór,
Is é gabháil idir mé
'S mo mhíle stór…"

She sang the peculiar words in a cracked old voice. Still, the sea was clear in the rhythm and cadence of the song, along with a tireless grief and a congruent acceptance of it. So Meredith was not surprised when Maggie finished singing, and spoke the words again, this time in English:

"My grief on the sea,
How the waves of it roll!
For they heave between me
And the love of my soul…"

Meredith didn't try to hold onto them; she knew that she couldn't. But they spoke to something deep inside of her, beyond thought or even memory: a longing and a grief that were as much a part of her as her blood and bone. They went far deeper than whatever insult had driven her to the sea that night. They brought a tide rising, both familiar and terrifying.

"It's an Irish song," Maggie told her. "My mother used to sing it when she was homesick for Clare. Said she'd learned it when she was a child from a woman of one hundred and three, who lived in a hut in a bog near her family's farm. Folks round about had it that woman knew a song for every year of her life. That may be, but I doubt she knew any more beautiful than that one." Maggie looked hard at Meredith with her liquor-bright eyes. "Of course, who could say? It's the only one my mother remembered, and that old woman is long since rotting in her pauper's grave – she and all of her songs with her…"

"Sing it again," Elijah said, taking Meredith's slate. "I want to write it down. To remember it."

"I'll sing it again," said Maggie, "but don't you write it down. It's a song from another time. It's meant to be forgotten."

Reluctantly, Elijah put the slate down. Maggie began to sing again. In Meredith, the tide overflowed, and at last, she wept.

Queen of the Depths

1

It snowed intermittently for the first few days after Elijah and Meredith left Maggie's shack. The horse tended more south now than west, heading into a hilly region thick with trees and brooding winter silence. The farms were few and far between, the villages small and sullen and hemmed in by forest. They rode into one of them one noontime with a plan to buy supplies, but they found the shop closed. Likewise, no one stirred behind the houses' windows, though smoke drifted from their stovepipes and chickens chattered in backyard coops.

At the far end of the village was a white clapboard church, its steeple rising up from the black-and-white woods like a naked knife. A chill went down Meredith's spine when she looked at it, and the horse slowed, ears pitched back. Elijah coaxed his own horse forward, his eyes fixed on the church like a beacon. Though Meredith didn't like it, she liked less the thought of going back into those dark woods without him.

By the time Meredith caught up with him, Elijah had dismounted and tied his horse by two others at the church's hitching post. She could hear the drone of a man's voice behind the closed doors, feel the presence of a roomful of listening people. She slid to the ground, keeping a tight hold of her horse's rein as Elijah stepped up to the door. Just as he grasped the handle, three knocks came from within – wood on wood, with the resonant finality of gunshots. The droning voice rose, and Meredith clearly heard the words, "Court adjourned."

A sudden tide of whispers swelled to chatter. Elijah stepped back as the door flew open and people began to pour out. There was a secretive sullenness about them that Meredith didn't like. They whispered and cut their eyes at her and Elijah, trailing menace like shadows. Last to come out were three men in judges' black, followed closely by another man and a woman. The man was tall, with a handsome, ruddy face and grey hair. But his blue eyes, fixed on the woman, were cold.

She was easily the most beautiful woman Meredith had ever seen: small and soft-featured, with fair hair and eyes the color of robins' eggs. Her face was tear-streaked, and her head hung like a rainsoaked blossom. Her hands and feet were shackled. She looked up as she passed Elijah and Meredith: a look of such desperation that Meredith's heart clutched. Elijah looked as if he'd been struck a blow.

"Afternoon," said the handsome man in a voice that almost managed the joviality he attempted. "I guess you've come to see the trial?"

"Trial?" Elijah asked. "Of whom?"

The man looked hard at him. "You haven't heard?"

"It's been days since we've stopped in a town."

"Well, you've picked yourself a historic day to stop in this one. We're in the middle of our first murder trial." He said it proudly, jutting his chin at the chained woman. Meredith felt sick.

"This woman has murdered somebody?" Elijah asked dazedly.

The man looked around, apparently to see whether the judges had retreated. Then he leaned in to answer Elijah, but before he could speak the woman cried: "*Ils se trouvent! Je n'ai jamais blessé quiconque!*"

"What is she saying?" Elijah asked.

The man snorted. "God only knows; but I can guarantee it's lies."

Elijah looked from the woman to her jailer. "You don't understand her?"

"Never learned a word of French." He said this as if it were a badge of honor.

"Does she speak English?"

The man shrugged. "A few words."

"Is she being tried in French?" Elijah asked, his frown deepening.

The man laughed. "Now why would we do that? We're all Americans here! All except *her*." He jerked the woman's wrist-chains.

Elijah tried to catch the woman's eyes, but they rested stonily on her feet. "Who did she kill?" he asked quietly.

"Her husband," the man answered. "My brother."

"I don't mean to be impertinent," said Elijah, "but if she speaks no English, and none of you speak French, how is it possible to know the facts?"

The man gave him a long, hard look. There was no pride in it now, only grim determination. "The facts are clear enough."

"Why then try her at all?"

Meredith put a hand on Elijah's arm, warning him, but he didn't seem to notice.

"Because," said the man, in the tone he might take with a child or an idiot, "the law says you can't hang a murderer without a trial." Seeing that Elijah meant to protest, he held up a hand. "Listen to me, young man: don't you let her fool you. She might look like an angel, but this woman is evil right through. By tonight, the court records will say the same."

Elijah considered the man and the woman for a long moment. Then he said, "Perhaps we will stay to see the trial." Ignoring Meredith's pleading eyes, he added, "Is there anywhere in town we might buy dinner?"

The man considered him for a moment, then he said, "You go on back to my place. First house on the right when you came into town. Tell my wife I sent you. Name's Ellory Smith, town sheriff." And with a tip of his hat, he led his captive down a lane and out of sight.

2

The Smiths' house was the largest in the village. It sat beside the closed-up dry-goods store. A pinched-looking child answered Elijah's knock, and called for her mother when he explained his business. A thin-lipped, dark-haired woman came to the door then, wiping her hands on her apron. She was as small and retiring as her husband was expansive, and accepted Elijah's explanation for their presence on her front porch without comment.

"Jesse!" she called. A teenage boy appeared. He was a younger version of his father: handsome, but with a furtive, sullen look that dulled its brilliance. "See to their animals," his mother said, and the boy went out without a word. Meredith wanted to protest as he led the horse away, but she saw the determination in Elijah's squared shoulders. Sighing, she followed him inside.

After raising her eyebrows at their dirty coats and boots, the woman seated them in a parlor with a dead fire and a lugubrious grandfather clock, and then left them in the frigid, ticking silence. When she was gone, Meredith cast Elijah a reproving look.

"I know," he said softly. "But I cannot believe that that woman is guilty of murder. If I leave here without trying…" He trailed off, and Meredith wondered what could be tried with any degree of success in a village that had clearly made up its mind. She knew that this was exactly the kind of situation Eldress March had meant her to protect him from, but the determination on his face looked implacable.

They seemed to sit for an eternity, with nothing to do but watch the sun creep across the faded carpet. Finally they heard the front door open and shut. Ellory Smith spoke indiscernible words to someone in a low, harsh voice, and then the parlor door opened. He stood in the doorway, smiling brightly. Inwardly, Meredith shuddered.

"I'm sorry that Mary put you in here without a fire," he told them. "I've spoken to her about it. Come now and have something to eat."

Elijah and Meredith followed him to an over-decorated dining room, in which a long table took up most of the space. Six children were seated around it, including Jesse and the girl who had answered the door. Mary sat at one end, Ellory at the other. A chair had been hastily shoved in beside each of them. Elijah took the one beside Ellory and Meredith squeezed in beside his wife, who assiduously avoided touching her. An older girl said a flat if lengthy grace, and then Mary began to pass the dishes around the table.

"So you've really heard nothing about the case?" Ellory asked Elijah, his eyes and tone full of the arrogance of a big man in a small town.

"I imagine I would have remembered if I had," said Elijah, thanking the girl beside him as she handed him a plate. She didn't acknowledge him.

Ellory shook his head, cut into his meat. "I warned Emmett," he said. "I told him not to marry a Canuck. They're never anything but trouble." Then, turning to Meredith, "Begging your pardon, ma'am, but they're a bunch of lying, thieving savages to the one. I told him, 'Emmett, that girl will put a knife in your back the minute it's turned. All she wants is your money.' But he wouldn't listen. He never would listen."

Ellory frowned at his plate. Meredith counted five seconds of studied regret before he delved back into his dinner, and his story. "He was well off, you see, Emmett was. Our great-great-something or other was town founder, and the Smiths have always owned the store. When Daddy died, he left me the store and this house, and he left the farm to Emmett. It's down the valley a ways. You might have passed it."

"Likely we did," Elijah agreed. Meredith could see how carefully he was trying for neutrality. No doubt he feared an argument would derail Ellory's story.

"Well, Emmett could have had any girl he wanted," Ellory continued, "but instead he took up with that Evangeline. Don't even know where she came from, aside from north of the border. He met her at a market in Barre last summer and brought her home that very day, though they'd only just met. Love at first sight, he said. I told him, 'Emmett, you're a fool! Take her right back to where you found her and run.' But he never would listen. Married her a week later. Stuck up thing, wasn't she, Mary?"

Mary nodded affirmation. "That little hussy never would speak to me," she said in a bitter voice.

"Perhaps because she couldn't speak English?" Elijah suggested.

Ellory only shrugged. "She understood Emmett well enough, didn't she?"

Elijah said nothing. Meredith pushed her food around her plate.

"She was freeloading off of us," Ellory said, re-filling his own, "and Emmett was too bewitched to realize it. New dresses, new boots – the best of everything. And she didn't even trouble herself to show gratitude." His face flushed suddenly in anger, and he pounded a fist on the table. The children went on eating, as if oblivious. Mary started fixedly at her plate. Meredith saw that she had eaten hardly anything. The cold creeping in her spine returned.

"And then, two weeks ago, Emmett disappeared," Ellory continued at last. As abruptly as it had surfaced, the anger had turned to misery. His eyes looked into the distance over his wife's shoulder, and his voice wavered with emotion. "Who knows how long he'd been gone before that little witch thought to tell us? Luckily, as it happened, I'd stopped by the farm that night to see Emmett. That's when she let me know he'd gone out to see to the cows the night before and never come back.

"Well, that wasn't like him. We set up a search party. Found him a few days later in the cellar hole of a ruined cabin in the woods, chest blown wide open by a shotgun. We also found an empty cartridge in the farmhouse kitchen."

Elijah's face was white. "And Evangeline admitted to shooting him?"

Ellory snorted. "Even a Canuck isn't *that* stupid! But she was the last one to see him alive, and she couldn't even come up with a decent alibi. All she'll say is that she was home that night, alone."

Elijah considered this information carefully for a few moments. Then he asked, "Why would she want to kill her husband?"

Ellory shrugged, pushed his plate away. One of the older girls got up and began to clear the table, though not everyone had finished eating. "The money, I guess," he said. "The farm's worth a lot. She could have sold up, gone home a wealthy woman…" But his look was anticipatory.

Elijah obliged: "You think there was another reason."

"I know it," Ellory said, knocking the table with his knuckles. "She's expecting."

"That's not a sin for a married woman, is it?"

Ellory leaned forward conspiratorially. "You can see here I've got six children of my own. Mary never showed so early on."

Mary's lips pressed tighter together. Her eyes bored into her husband. *She hates him*, Meredith thought, and her chill deepened.

"I'd put money on it that Evangeline was carrying that child when she met Emmett," Ellory said. Abruptly, Mary stood up and retreated to the kitchen, but Ellory didn't seem to notice. "Then two weeks ago he found out the truth, and he didn't much like it. I expect he told her to pack her bags and go, and she took matters into her own hands, as they say."

"As they say," Elijah repeated, his voice odd and thick, as if he found it difficult to breathe.

Ellory nodded, then looked at his watch. "And I reckon that's also what the jury's going to say in about fifteen minutes. The judge, he's from the city, but he's a second cousin of Mary's. He'll do what's right."

"What about the child?"

Ellory paused for a moment before he answered. "We'll wait until it's born, of course, to hang her."

The pause wasn't lost on Meredith; nor, she thought, on Elijah. His face was calm, but there was a cold rage in his eyes that Meredith had never seen there before. She only half-heard him ask to accompany Ellory back to the courtroom. When Ellory asked whether the lady would like to join them, it took Meredith a moment to realize that he was referring to her. She shook her head.

Ellory shrugged. "Suit yourself. You can stay and talk to Mary."

Meredith threw Elijah a desperate look. "Meredith doesn't speak," he said.

Ellory looked at her, eyebrows raised. "Oh? I hadn't noticed." He peered at her a moment longer, as if she might prove Elijah wrong. She looked steadily back at him.

"You ask me, that's a blessing," he said to Elijah behind his hand. "I've never heard a woman say anything that might not as well have been left unsaid." He laughed and didn't seem to notice that no one joined him. Then he stood, pushed back his chair and gestured for Elijah to follow.

3

Night had fallen by the time the men returned. Elijah looked haggard, Ellory perplexed as they came into the parlor where Meredith sat with Mary and her daughters, before a paltry fire.

"Well?" said Mary – the first word Meredith had heard her speak since dinner.

Ellory shook his head, sat down. "The jury found her guilty, but the judges wouldn't charge her. Said they couldn't convict her when she couldn't testify properly. We have to wait for the city to send a court-approved translator! Court-approved translator: those were his very words. Have you ever heard the like?"

He spoke loudly enough, but his tone fell short of outrage and his eyes roved the room wildly. He reminded Meredith of a caged animal. She looked at Elijah and raised her eyebrows.

"We ought to see to the horses," he said in a hard, flat tone. "Mr. Smith has kindly offered to let us stay the night, seeing as it's so late."

Mary's head whipped around at that, but it was Meredith she glared at rather than her husband. Meredith turned her head away, and found that Ellory too was looking at her: a speculative look.

"Very well," Mary said in a voice frozen with suppressed rage.

"Meredith," Elijah said. She stood up quickly and followed him out. Once outside, though, Elijah turned away from the barn, toward a cluster of trees. When they were hidden in its shadow, he took Meredith's slate and chalk from his pocket and handed them to her.

"I need your help," he said, his eyes wide and his voice afraid. Meredith nodded once. They had been together long enough now for him to understand that this was not agreement, merely a signal to continue. "After the trial today, I heard Ellory talking with some of his friends. Obviously, they're angry about the judges' decision. They don't intend to wait for that translator."

This didn't surprise Meredith, but she felt sicker and colder to hear it. "What are they planning?" she wrote, and then tipped the slate toward him.

"To finish it – those were the words they used."

Meredith thought for several moments before she finally wrote, "What if she is guilty?"

"She isn't," Elijah answered with cold vitriol. "Ellory is."

"How do you know?"

"Because she said so."

"If you speak French – " Meredith began to write, before Elijah cut her off.

"I don't. I didn't need to. For every question they asked her in that courtroom, she gave the same answer, and pointed at Ellory. The way she looked at him...I would give anything to know what he's done to her."

Meredith thought of the way that Ellory had looked at her in the parlor, and the way his wife had looked back at him, and she knew. But she didn't dare stoke Elijah's rage any further. She wrote: "What do you meant to do?"

"Get her out of here," Elijah said vehemently, "as soon as possible."

Meredith realized then that Elijah had fallen in love with Evangeline. It shocked her, but the feelings it dredged were far more complicated than that: regret; a strange, faded longing; and the certainty that once, she had felt what he felt, though she could no longer recall its object.

"I will help you," she wrote. Before he could answer, though, a commotion erupted in the street nearby them. There was shouting, and the sound of running feet. Elijah turned toward them, his eyes wild.

"It's begun," he said grimly. "Get the horses and our packs. I'll meet you by the church." And he was off into the night.

With shaking hands, Meredith tacked Elijah's horse and fitted his saddle-bags, then put on her own horse's rope halter. She put a pack over each shoulder, and then led the horses outside. There was more noise from the street now, and the acrid smell of burning. The horses shied at the noise and the smoke, but finally Meredith managed to get them onto the road and moving forward.

A knot of people passed her, carrying shotguns and farm tools. A group of children followed them, their hands full of stones and kitchen knives. One little boy held a tarnished army sword with belligerent resolve. Meredith followed them toward the church, feeling as if she were walking into a nightmare. They didn't stop there, but turned down the lane where Ellory had led Evangeline that morning, and then disappeared into the thick smoke gathering there. Meredith couldn't see beyond it.

She tethered the horses by the church, hid the packs nearby and then followed in the footsteps of the armed children. The lane wasn't very long, though the billows of red-tinged smoke made it feel longer. At its end was a small snowy yard with a shed in the center. The back of the shed was burning. The front had a door with a barred window. Evangeline's face was pressed up against it, her hands clutching two of the bars as Elijah addressed the gathering crowd.

"This is murder!" he cried. "The woman in there has not been convicted of any crime, and she is carrying an innocent child!"

"She's bewitched you, son," said Ellory, shaking his head with slit-eyed regret as Meredith pushed her way forward, "just like she did poor Emmett."

"Witchery?" Elijah said, looking at him squarely. "Is that how you excuse what you've done?"

"What *I've* done?" Ellory cried, his face florid with heat and anger and, Meredith thought, a shade of fear.

Rather than answer Ellory, he turned to the crowd. "Two weeks ago, this man went out to his brother's farm. He knew that Emmett would be away – that his sister-in-law would be alone. It was the perfect opportunity to have his way with her – " he swallowed hard " – as he'd be trying to do since they met. But Emmett came home early." Elijah fixed Ellory with merciless eyes. "He fought to protect his wife. And for that, you shot him."

Ellory's eyes were wild as he turned to his neighbors, who looked back at him doubtfully. "I told you that bitch had a lover!" he cried, pointing at Elijah. "I should have known, when he came into town on this of all days. I say, let him burn with her!" He shoved Elijah up against the shed door, but nobody moved to help him. They only stared, dumbstruck, at the two men and the encroaching flames and the barred window, which was now empty.

Elijah saw it too. Shoving Ellory aside, he scrabbled for purchase on the door. There was no handle, Meredith saw then, only a keyhole. Ellory took a gun from his coat pocket, aimed it at Elijah's back as he began to kick at the door's wooden planks. At last, the crowd broke from its stupor, beginning to murmur, and then to fall back. But it wasn't Ellory's gun or the burning shed they retreated from. They were parting to admit a small, dark figure. It was Mary Smith, her face fierce in the firelight, and she held a key.

"What are you doing?" Ellory screamed at her.

Mary didn't look at him, just handed the key to Elijah. The crowd stood watching, transfixed, as he wrenched the door open, disappeared into the smoke and flames and re- emerged a moment later, carrying Evangeline. She hung limp in his arms, her skirts blazing. He laid her in the snow, beat out the flames with his coat. Nobody moved to stop him or to help him.

Meredith pushed futilely against the impenetrable crowd. She could do nothing but watch as Elijah bent over the woman, imploring her to breathe. And then a gasp went through the crowd as Evangeline drew a wrenching breath, which gave way to a fit of coughing. She turned onto her side and vomited, and then spat, and then, slowly and deliberately, she sat up and looked at Ellory. She pointed a trembling finger.

"Him," she said.

Ellory gave her a look of abject hatred. Then he put his gun under his chin and pulled the trigger. As he fell, the burning shed collapsed with a whoosh, driving the crowd back. One by one they retreated, until only Meredith and Elijah and Evangeline were left.

Evangeline flexed her singed fingers, and gingerly pulled Elijah's coat around her. "Tank…you…" she said, and then she put her hands to her face and began to weep. Elijah reached out, and she leaned against him, sobs wracking her. Over her shoulder, Elijah met Meredith's eyes. Slowly, solemnly, he nodded. She needed no words to know that he was releasing her. With a pang she had not expected and a hotness in her eyes, Meredith turned and walked back toward her horse.

4

I hope, said Meredith as she lay that night looking up at the cold cast of stars, *that it was not wrong to leave him there.*

It was his destiny, said the horse, huddled beside her.

I'm afraid for him, said Meredith. *He knows nothing about the world.*

Nor did you, when you began, said the horse.

It didn't matter. I wanted to die, then.

You never truly wanted to die.

Though Meredith thought the horse was wrong, she didn't say so.

After a moment the horse said, *He knows how to coax wood to his will. He knows how to treat a horse kindly. He knows a true woman from a false man. He has all that he needs to make his way in this world.*

And still, said Meredith, *I'm afraid for him.*

That's because you loved him, said the horse.

Meredith turned to look at her. The horse looked back, her black eye riddled with stars. Meredith put out her hand, buried her fingers in the soft fur beneath the horse's wiry forelock. *You will not leave me?*

The horse was still for a long moment. Then she said, *A horse is born to run away; a human to stand her ground.*

Meredith said, *I have not seen the ground that I would prefer to running with you.*

Not yet, said the horse. *But when you do, I will not grudge you it. And when it's time for me to run, I hope you will not grudge me.*

Meredith couldn't bring herself to answer this. At last the horse blew, and shut her eyes. Meredith looked back at the sky. But she didn't let go of the horse's mane all that night long.

5

For days after Meredith left Elijah, the weather was dry, with never more than a dusting of snow, and the horse moved quickly. They saw few people, and Meredith lapsed into the familiar silence of the time before the Shaker village. They crossed out of the mountains and then over a great river on another railroad bridge. After that the ground rose to mountains again, higher and rockier than any she'd seen since Tomah and Anis's country. There were towns in the valleys, but Meredith rode through them without looking to the left or the right.

One morning she came to a little huddle of houses at the foot of a hill with a signpost that said, "Hunter." She studied that sign for a long time. The village looked no different from any of the others she'd passed in the last few days, yet the sign filled her with a poignant loneliness that stayed with her even after the town was miles at her back. That night she lay down shivering and wept inexplicably while the horse blew its concern on her with hot, grainy breath. She fell asleep finally on a blanket stiff with frozen tears and dreamed of brown hands threading fish onto green sticks, a melonseed cradle rocking on a sea swell,

277

scaled creatures reaching up from a primeval depth. But the brown hand reached her first, closing around her white one. The warmth between their joined palms spread until the bad dreams faded, and at last she slept peacefully.

When she woke, it seemed for a few drowsy moments that she lay beneath a pile of quilts. When she opened her eyes, though, she realized that it was snow, deep and thick and still falling. She sat up, shook it off. The horse shook too, sending a white shower flying from her shaggy coat. After breakfast, Meredith got up on the horse again, but the going was slow. A few hundred yards along the road, the horse stopped. Meredith nudged her with her heels, but the horse only swished her tail.

When Meredith got down she saw the problem at once. Snow had filled the hollows of the horse's feet and built up until she was standing on balls of ice. With the help of her knife Meredith was able to knock them out, but they hadn't ridden far before the horse stopped again. Sighing, Meredith resigned herself to a long walk.

The snow kept on, and every few minutes Meredith had to stop and knock the packed ice from the horse's feet. She thought of stopping, but they were in desolate country with no obvious shelter. The hills were steep, covered with huge trees knotted together by age and time and windfalls to make a forest as good as impenetrable.

It was afternoon and already darkening when the horse refused to go on.

I have just cleaned your hooves, Meredith said.

It makes no difference to the pain, said the horse.

We have to go on, said Meredith. *There's no shelter here.*

Look harder, said the horse, and hung her head, and would say nothing else.

Meredith stood looking into the snowy silence. She saw nothing but rock and ice and dark tangled forest. She turned in a slow circle, searching for any kind of gap in the trees. And then, unbelievably, she saw a faint light farther up the hill to her right. When she was certain that it was no illusion, she took the horse's rein and went to look for a path. The horse followed slowly, her head bobbing down with each step.

At last Meredith located a break in the trees, and a track leading upward. The path culminated in the dooryard of a little round hut not far beneath the summit of the hill. The hut had been built in a deep angle of the mountainside, with a sheer rock face rising above it. The better part of it was its thatched roof, which rose at least twice the height of its low, circular wall. A single lit window shone like a dim eye in the midst of the storm.

Meredith looked at the horse. She had stopped at the edge of the yard, her head down and legs splayed. Fear went through her, colder than the wind-driven snow. She had never seen the horse look defeated – not even when she was hitched to the cart in the logging camp – but that was how she looked now. Meredith ran, such as she could, through the deep snow toward the lit window. It was oilpaper; she could see nothing through it. She followed the curving wall around and finally located a wooden door near the rock face.

She knocked and then stood waiting as the blowing snow blanketed her back. She knocked again. This time she heard a horse's whicker, followed by a slow approaching step. The door opened. A man stood in the smoky light. He was on the far side of middle age, though not quite old. He had long black hair streaked with grey and slate-blue eyes. He wore a jacket of rough-woven red wool, cinched with a wide leather belt. The belt had a ring at one end, and attached to the ring was a small leather pouch, apparently full of something heavy. Under the jacket, he wore a pair of short trousers; under the trousers a pair of thick woolen stockings. His feet were wrapped in pieces of sheepskin tied with leather thongs.

A pipe protruded beneath his grizzled moustache. Its smoke reached out and wound around Meredith's heart, and suddenly he was another man: a tall man with a red-brown beard and dark eyes warm as a home hearth. He knew her, too. He leaned forward, his face a mixture of shock and cautious joy. He took the pipe from his mouth and said, "*Dahud? Ma Dahud eo?*"

The voice was not the one that Meredith had expected, and she didn't understand the words, though the plea in them was clear enough. The illusion faded. She was looking at a stranger. Likewise, the man took a step back, the light draining from his face. "I am sorry," he said in careful, heavily-accented English. "I thought that you were…" He shook his head. "It does not matter. How may I help you?"

Meredith showed him her slate, on which she had written about the horse's feet. But the man only glanced at it and shook his head sadly. "I am sorry, *Dimezell*," he said, "but I never learned to read or write in English. Do you not speak?" Meredith shook her head; he sighed. "We will work something out. Come inside. It is a dreadful night to be out, and you will never find a town before dark."

She shook her head again, and pointed behind her. The horse was just visible against the snowy trees in the fading light.

"Ah – a horse!" he said, brightening. "Well, that is lucky."

Meredith wondered how he could possibly see luck in the horse's abject stance, but his expression didn't change when he walked toward her. He called to the horse: "*Deus 'ta!*"

The horse crossed the short distance between them, head bobbing, and stopped in front of him. The man leaned down and lifted her feet one by one, inspecting them in the light from the doorway. "This is the problem," he said, tapping one of them. In the dim light Meredith could barely see the horse's hoof at all, let alone anything that might be considered a problem. "They are *goloet gant ar struzh*…ah, how do you say it in English? Grown over? Overgrown! *Ya 'vat!* You see, the shoe is grown into the horn. Come."

He turned and led the horse through the lit doorway. Startled, Meredith followed. She was even more startled when they were greeted by a shrill whinny. A great black horse stood knee-deep in straw at the far side of the hut. The man didn't even notice her astonishment, let alone attempt to explain the horse in his house. He was entirely focused on his work as he tied Meredith's horse to a strong stick in the hut's wickcr wall and then opened a heavy, iron-strapped wooden chest and began rummaging inside it.

Meredith stood with her hand on the horse's withers, unable to stop staring at the other horse a few feet away. Even apart from the peculiarity of his being in the house, he was an arresting beast, with a neck arched like a half-moon, wide bright eyes, a well-muscled back. He lifted his fine head and whinnied at them again.

"*Peoc'h*, Morvarc'h!" the man growled as he returned to Meredith's horse, his hands full of tools. The black horse gave a low grunt and blew, then he lowered his head to a manger standing against the wall.

"Now, *Bihanig*," he said, patting the horse's shoulder, "we shall see to your desolate feet."

Desolate? Meredith thought, as one by one he lifted the horse's hooves, and with a pair of large pliers he pulled off her worn shoes and tossed them by the doorway. Then he took another tool, a cruel-looking set of pincers, but the horse stood quietly as he used them to cut away the ragged bits of horn where her shoes had been. He worked at this for a long time, and when at last he was satisfied he took a file, and setting each hoof in turn on a little iron stand, he smoothed them off. When he was done he nodded and patted the horse's shoulder again.

"Good girl," he said. "We shall put on new shoes when the storm ends. The smell of burning horn is one thing I cannot abide in my house." He untied her rope rein, led the horse to the manger, and tied her again by Morvarc'h. Seeing Meredith's anxious look he said, "Do not worry. He will be gentle with her." Which seemed true enough: the black horse sniffed the mare, and then stood aside to give her access to the manger.

"Now come," the man said to Meredith, smiling wanly. "You too look in need of feeding." He turned to the fire-pit at the center of the hut, where an iron pot hung from a tripod over the flames. He stirred whatever was inside it, dumped in a bowl of something else, stirred again. After that he filled two big cups from a tapped barrel behind him, set them by the hearth, and stuck a poker into the flames. All the while he stole glances at Meredith, as if trying to convince himself of something.

At last, he could not contain his thoughts. "Does the name 'Dahud' not speak to you at all? Even in a whisper?"

Meredith heard the hope in his voice, and felt cruel shaking her head.

"Ahes?" he persisted. "Perhaps you remember that one?"

Again, she shook her head.

The man peered at her over the pot, with a look that was almost apprehensive. "What of 'Gradlon'?" he asked in a low voice. He seemed relieved when Meredith declined recognition for the third time. He held out his hand. "I am Gradlon." Meredith took his hand to shake it, but instead he brought her hand to his lips and kissed it. She snatched it back, then regretted it as a plangent sadness crossed his face.

Gradlon shook his head, smiled wearily, took the poker from the fire and plunged its heated end into one of the cups. Meredith jumped back as the contents sizzled and spat, convinced now that she was in the presence of a madman. She looked toward the horse, trying to gauge how long it might take to free her and run, and whether there was anything to hand to use as a weapon. She was so intent on this that it took her a moment to realize that Gradlon was offering her a steaming cup of something that smelled of burnt sugar, and to realize, at last, what he had been about.

"If you fear poison," he said, "I will drink first."

Feeling suddenly foolish, Meredith accepted the hot drink. Gradlon put the poker back in the fire, then smiled as Meredith took a sip. The drink tasted of spices and apples, and it had a distinct alcoholic bite, but it warmed her immediately. *Poison couldn't taste so good*, she thought, and turned to examining Gradlon's home.

It was a spare kind of a house. Aside from the horses and the fire pit, there were only a few stools, the chest from which Gradlon had taken his blacksmithing tools, a second, similar chest, and a bed on the floor with wooden sides like a box. There were shelves of provisions and various tools and a few clothes, tack and brushes for the horse, and above her head, legs of meat and other game curing slowly in the smoke of the fire.

When Meredith looked at Gradlon again, he was drinking from the other mug and dipping a spoon into the pot. He tasted his concoction and shrugged. "It's not lobster stew," he said, sighing, "but it will suffice."

Lobster, thought Meredith; it was another of those sudden, laden words. She saw slick green-and-brown creatures scrabbling in a zinc tub, and then threw off the memory in a shudder of revulsion.

Gradlon motioned for her to sit on one of the low, three-legged stools by the fire. He ladled stew into a wooden bowl and handed it to her, along with a slice of dark bread thick with nuts and dried berries. Meredith lifted her bread, ravenous, but Gradlon bent his head over his own bowl and spoke in a low voice. The words meant nothing to Meredith, but they were clearly a prayer. She set her bread down again and bent her head as he did, until he stopped speaking and began to eat.

Meredith bit into the bread, which was as dense and dry as it looked, but welcome enough after the long, cold trudge up the snowy mountain. The stew consisted mainly of some kind of meat she did not recognize, with a subtle, smoky flavor. She wished that she could ask Gradlon what it was.

"I wish," he echoed, fixing her with his sad eyes, "that you could tell me what has brought you here." He continued to look at her as he chewed a tough piece of meat. "Or perhaps there is no need to ask. Nothing but grief would have brought you to my door, and I think it is a sea-grief, like mine."

Noting Meredith's surprise, he explained, "I am an expert of grief, for I have lost everything that a man possibly could." There was nothing boastful in his words, no vie for pity. There was only a truth as bleak as the storm-emptied sea of his eyes. He put his bowl aside, peered closely at Meredith. "I feel," he said, "that I must know your name."

Meredith looked back at him for a long moment. Though she knew that she couldn't tell him, this strange man made her want to try. She pressed her lips together, poised her tongue to form the first, hummed consonant – but even that was too much. She lowered her head in despair.

"Do not be unhappy, daughter," Gradlon said softly. "Try with your stylus and your stone. Perhaps the gods will intervene."

Meredith thought this unlikely, but she took up the slate and chalk and wrote her name on it, as boldly and clearly as she could. Then she handed the slate to Gradlon. He looked at the word for a long time, and then he said, "Yes. This is a name that I know." He took the chalk from Meredith, and beneath her name, in a painstaking, spidery hand he wrote, *Meredydd*. "It is an old name," he said. "It comes from the *Brythoniaid*."

Meredith looked blankly at him.

"The ancient history of Cymru. That does not speak to you? No? Well, it is a country far from here, I cannot recall the name by which they call it today…but the Vikings called its people Waelisc."

"Wales," Meredith wrote, guided by the faint memory of a map of an island country, and the westernmost of its divisions.

Gradlon studied the word at length. Finally, he shrugged. "I suppose so. This name…your name…it has belonged to princes of that land. Meredydd, Maredudd, both great men. Great lords. They say that is what the name means, 'Great Lord.' But that is only would-be kings rattling their shields, eh? The name as I know it means 'Lord of the Sea'."

Lord of the Sea, Meredith repeated to herself. The phrase was familiar, and yet it wasn't.

"Like Morvarc'h – that is 'Horse of the Sea.' He was a gift from my wife."

Meredith had seen no evidence of a wife, but she looked around inadvertently anyway.

"She is long since dead," Gradlon answered her unspoken question.

How long is long since? Meredith thought. Morvarc'h looked to be in his prime. Once again she wondered if Gradlon was mad; then she became aware of his keen eyes resting on her. She realized how she had been staring at the horse, how transparent her thoughts must have been. She flushed, but Gradlon only gave her a faint smile.

"I will tell you all that you must be wondering," he said, "but first, your cup."

Meredith looked down at the cup in her hand. It was empty. When she thought about it, she felt hot and light-headed – the drink had been as potent as she'd suspected. Nevertheless she handed the cup to Gradlon, resolving to drink more slowly.

"Once I was a king," he began matter-of-factly, as he repeated the ritual with the hot poker and the cider mugs. "I ruled the land of Cournouaille, which was in the country of Armorica." Seeing Meredith's blank look, he added, "Very far from this mountain," and handed her her cup. "More important, I was a king with a fleet of war ships. The people who knew me said that I was the greatest sea captain of my time." He shrugged, sipped. "That is the kind of thing people say to kings. For certain, I can say only that I was a very good one.

"In those times kings who were sea captains used their ships to plunder the lands of other kings. I was very good at this, too. I grew wealthy, but I was like any man with the sea in his soul: I lived for the voyages, not the spoils. A well-trimmed sail against a blue sky was to me the very heart of happiness."

The image arrested Meredith; the longing in his voice as he spoke of it was something she knew that she had once shared. "But that is a king's luxury," he continued, sighing. "My men thought differently. They tired of war and the lonely waves. They missed their wives. I had no wife, no understanding of what they longed for, no desire to learn. I was young and arrogant and foolish. I ordered them ever northward, to attack another petty fortress and then another…"

Once again, he sighed. "I do not like the word 'mutiny'. It is too often put upon men who had no choice. Mine didn't, although it took me many years to know that, and many more to forgive them. I had driven them so hard that they chose probable death – if not at my family's hands, then by the cruel homeward journey on a winter sea – rather than go on. They left me in a dinghy and took my ships and fled for home.

"I sat all night against the mast of my boat, as desolation bound me and a freezing mist rolled in. I knew that if I did not do something to help myself, then I would die there. I did not think that the idea was such a bad one. But as I began to accept it, I felt a presence. I looked up to see the most extraordinary being. The people of Ériu have a goddess called Mór Rígan, the Queen of the North, who comes to dying heroes…I thought that she had come to take me. I did not care. She was so beautiful – as pale as the moon, with great dark eyes like the wide sea around us, and copper hair that fell to her knees. She took me by the hand, lifted me to my feet. She told me that she was indeed a queen, but she was a human one. Her name was Malgven, and she knew mine by the stories of my exploits.

"Now you will have heard," Gradlon said, his voice suddenly anxious, his eyes imploring as he looked up at Meredith, "that Malgven was a sorceress, an evil woman, that she came to me that night by magic in the middle of the sea." Meredith shook her head, less out of negation than bewilderment. "Indeed, those are lies! Malgven did not tread upon water; my boat had washed up on the beach upon which she was walking. She had no magic but her own clever mind, and what she proposed to me – what we did – it was an act of mercy. Only time and cruel tongues have made it into murder…"

Gradlon looked up at Meredith, his eyes stricken, pleading for affirmation. Anxiety renewed, Meredith nodded with what she hoped looked like sympathy. Apparently it did, because Gradlon offered her another fractured smile and then continued his story.

"We pulled the boat up onto the shingle. Malgven put her warm cloak over my shoulders and then she said, 'You, Gradlon, are the answer to my prayers, for I came to walk on this beach tonight to pray for guidance.' I did not think that a captain whose men had abandoned him could offer much in the way of guidance, and so I told her. She said, 'I think that you can. I am married to an old man, but a kind one. He has treated me well, and I would do the same for him. Yet what he asks of me now is beyond me.

"'For a year,' she said, 'he has suffered from a wasting illness. For the last half of it, he has not been able to leave his bed. Now the pain is so very great, he begs to be delivered. His doctors have refused, as have his sons. They do not want his blood on their hands. And so he has turned to me. Put a knife in his heart, he says, or poison his drink, if the blood would unnerve me. But how can I do this? I am a young woman married to an old man. I would be branded a murderess, thrown out to starve, or worse…'"

Gradlon sighed, looking back at Meredith with resignation rather than regret. "The rest has been told countless times: Malgven and her young lover kill her husband and run away. But no one tells how the old king lay disfigured by the tumors that were killing him. No one tells how he blessed me and bid me do it with his own blade, or how Malgven kissed his lips and held his hand until it was over. No one could, because no one knows but the two of us and the old king's ghost, if it remains somewhere in the North country. For we fled afterward. We had no choice."

Gradlon paused to drink, and when he began again, his voice had lost some of its sadness, warmed with fond memory. "We took to the sea in one of his ships. We brought nothing but Morvarc'h and a chest of gold, which was Malgven's own. I did not want to take the horse – they are well known for dangerous cargo – but Malgven assured me that he knew the sea and would be calm. But no such promise can be exacted of the sea itself. The very next night a storm came up, and we were blown farther north than I had ever been before. They say that we were lost for a year on that sea, but it is as false as the stories of the king's murder. The truth is that we were shipwrecked on a desolate island, and there we spent the better part of that year, as I repaired the boat.

"Malgven spent her days foraging for food, and I for driftwood, but we were happy there. Not so long before the boat was complete, Malgven told me that she was with child, and when at last we set sail again for home, it seemed my happiness was whole too." But Gradlon's smile faded abruptly. When he spoke again, his voice was bleak and broken.

"Malgven's time came when we were still at sea. Her blood flowed like a black river, and before our daughter had lived a day, she was motherless. Dahud – that is what we called the child – would certainly have died too if I had not happened upon an island with an old woman and a flock of goats. She helped me to bury my wife, and showed me how to feed the baby with a rag and a bowl of milk. She sent me on my way with a nanny-goat and a pile of clean rags, and by the grace of the gods we came back to Cournouaille at last."

Gradlon paused and refilled his cup before he continued. He indicated Meredith's. It was empty, and her head was swimming to prove it. She covered the cup with her hand, and Gradlon shrugged, taking a long drink of his own.

"I was a dreadful father," he said flatly. Meredith raised her eyebrows, but Gradlon shook his head. "It is true. No sooner were we home than I locked myself in my castle with my grief. My daughter's care was given to whoever could be found to take it on – and who that was, I still do not know. It is my greatest shame and my greatest sorrow, for it was the foundation of our tragedy, and I have no one to blame for it but myself." He shook his head.

"I did come to my senses, but it was far too late. I remember that I looked out of my window one day to see that Dahud had become a young woman. She was as beautiful as her mother had been, though very different. She was fair and tall like Malgven, but her hair was golden and her eyes...they were strange. Light, but with dark spots in them. Like yours." He studied Meredith for a long moment. "More than once I heard them called witches' eyes."

Meredith started, her heart beating quickly with the memory of gold letters on dark wood. But Gradlon didn't notice; he had fallen back into his story, his eyes fixed deep in the past. "From that day Dahud became the meaning of my life. She was so often charming, I could overlook the times when she wasn't. I gave her whatever she wanted because it delighted me to see her happy, but also, if I am honest, because I could not bear her vile rages, which took her when a thing she wanted was denied her. It was too late to discipline her, too late to change her. I said to myself, it was better to keep the peace, and hope the good in her nature would win over the bad in the end..."

Gradlon sighed, stirred the fire with a charred stick. "But it did not work so. The more I gave, the more she wanted. She was like the sea wearing at a rampart, subtle and relentless, until I had lost the power to refuse her anything. And so on the day when she asked me to build her a city of her own, I agreed. Ah, I see your look, Meredydd! I know that it sounds preposterous... it *was* preposterous, and even more so than you realize, for this was to be no ordinary city. Like her mother, Dahud loved the sea. She also loved novelty. What she wanted was a city set in the middle of the sea."

Meredith no longer believed a word Gradlon was saying, but she was so absorbed in the strange story that she didn't care. She leaned forward, eager for him to continue.

"It was madness," he said. "*She* was mad – I knew it for certain when she asked for this impossible thing. But when she saw me hesitating, the storm came up in her eyes, and so I called in the architects and the engineers, the stonemasons and carpenters and blacksmiths and everyone else who would be needed to give Dahud the impossible. I chose a spot in a bay off the coast of my country – a spot that was partially exposed at low tide, for even a king cannot command the sea to draw back for the laying of foundations. We began to build.

"First came the wall that would hold back the sea at high tide. I was a fool, but I had not completely departed from my senses: I knew that the safety of this freakish city – and of my daughter – depended on that wall. I also knew that Dahud was far too flighty to be its keeper. And so I allowed only one door to be built, a great door of bronze, embossed with scenes from the adventures of the sea gods, which was I admit a plea for their favor. I cast a single key, and hung the key around my neck by a chain, and I never took it off from the first time that door was shut against the tide.

"The city grew quickly, and Dahud loved her new home. She called it Ker-Ys, which means 'the city of the depths.' And because it was hers, she called herself the Queen of the Depths. I told her to be wary of what she said. Her city stood only by the sea's grace, and he could easily take it back again. But she laughed at me, and said that the sea would never do anything to harm her. She said she had stood on its walls the first night and pledged herself to him. She said that he was her beloved, her true consort, and that was why he had allowed her her strange queendom.

"Who was I to argue with that? Why should the sea not make my daughter his queen? In fickleness and obstinacy and beauty, there was certainly no human man who could match her so well.

She found plenty of subjects, too. You could not come upon that city, rising from the waves as if by magic, and *not* believe that its lady had some special power. Pilgrims came and knelt before her, offering gifts and prayers.

"One northern prince brought her a cloak he'd had made for her, he said, by a great sorceress. He said that it would make its wearer invincible. Magical or not, it was a magnificent thing, made of watered silk which shone green in some lights and blue in others. It was embroidered with sea creatures and plants in colored silks, with gold and silver and pearls. Dahud wore it when she met her subjects and supplicants, and in the evenings when she walked the ramparts, singing her love songs to the waves."

Gradlon sighed. "She could be charming in her fancies, but she was what I had made her. She lived only for pleasure. Ker-Ys became a place of endless feasts and games, of free-flowing wine, and every other indulgence you could imagine. It is not true, as the rumors have it, that Dahud took a new lover every night and flung him into the sea in the morning. But she did take her share of lovers, and she did discard them cruelly. Until *he* came."

The words, the tone in which Gradlon spoke them, sliced straight to Meredith's heart. She did not want to hear what he would say next, but he was already saying it. "He rode in on a black horse almost as magnificent as Morvarc'h, dressed like a lord, in a crimson cloak. He had eyes as blue as the sea, hair brighter even than Dahud's, a smile that could have charmed a locked door open. As soon as she saw him she was determined to have him.

"But he paid her no heed. Dahud was unused to being slighted. She was furious, but she was wise enough to realize that a tantrum would not win her this prize. So she arranged for a feast that evening, and made certain that the handsome stranger would sit by her. She thought that she could charm him this way." Gradlon's mouth was hard and bitter on the rim of his cup as he sipped. "But he was not there to be charmed. He was there to charm her – to win her utter devotion – and he knew that the quickest way to secure it was to scorn her. For Dahud always wanted most what she could not have." Gradlon shook his head.

"I did not trust him, but I never imagined the extent of his arrogance…his greed. He played Dahud to perfection," Gradlon continued, weary now rather than bitter. "First he paid her no attention, but then as the night wore on he showed her more. He made her believe that she was captivating him, until he looked at no one but her." He paused, drank. "I wanted to draw my sword and challenge him! But I had long since given up the right to do any such thing. I had never been her father…"

Meredith studied him as his eyes wandered the past. In the dim light, his face became for a moment that other, dark-eyed, bearded face. Then the illusion faded, and Gradlon spoke again. "All the time they were feasting, a storm was brewing. The wind wailed in the ramparts, and the waves could be heard pounding like a drum on the sea-gate. Dahud's new friend asked, 'Will the gate hold?' pretending anxiety. 'Oh, yes,' she said. 'The doors to my city are stronger than the sea, for my father built them himself, and he carries the only key.'

"I saw him look at me then, and he saw me look back. He drew Dahud away from the table and spoke to her. I did not know then what he was saying, though it is easy enough now to imagine. If you knew how often I have imagined his words! It is as if a demon whispers them in my ear…" He shook his head, as if trying to clear it of those whisperings. "But I didn't imagine then. I assumed that he would steal her jewels and be gone when she woke. I even – " his voice cracked " – I even remember thinking, as I went to bed that night, that it might teach her a lesson."

He smiled bitterly through a long silence. Then he sighed and said, "I do not know why I did not wake when she took the key from around my neck. Perhaps her lover had drugged my wine. Perhaps I simply slept soundly. I do not even know whether he meant to rule the city or destroy it – but destroy it he did. As soon as Dahud put the key into his hand, the sea rose up in a jealous fury. It formed a monstrous wave, higher than this mountain upon which we sit, and crashed down upon the city. The walls crumbled, and my great bronze door was torn from its hinges and flung aside like a scrap of dirty cloth.

"It was the roar of that wave that wakened me. I opened my eyes to see my daughter standing by my bed, shaking like a terrified child. She said to me, 'Father, I have done a terrible thing…I have taken your key, and the sea has breached the walls…' And she began to weep." Gradlon's eyes too were wet, but he did not seem to notice. "I did not allow her to tell me the rest, although she tried. It did not matter, and there was no time. I took her hand and ran with her to the stables. The other horses were gone – run off or stolen by those attempting to escape the water. But no one had dared touch Morvarc'h. He stood in his stall, up to his knees in water. I bridled him, got on his back, and pulled Dahud up behind me. She seemed too heavy, and I saw then that she had loaded herself with jewelry and her sea-cloak, which had grown heavy with water.

"'Leave it,' I told her, but she refused, and there was no time to argue. The water was licking my boots. I gave Morvarc'h his head and he lept out of the stable into the storm. He proved his name that night, somehow finding a path through those flooded streets. But he could not outrun the tide; not, at least, with the great weight on his back, which seemed to be growing ever greater. In a flash of lightning, I looked behind me. Dahud still clung to me, but her waterlogged cloak hung down to the waves, tripping poor Morvarc'h. 'Daughter, you must drop that cloak!' I cried to her. She said, 'I will not!' And she clung to it. I drove my heels into Morvarc'h again. He tried, but the rising water and the dragging weight were too much for him. A few more minutes, and the water would be too deep for us to cross to the mainland.

"I told Dahud again that she must give up that cloak, or we would pay with our lives. She cried, 'The sea would not harm me!' But the water surged up over our legs, and I think at last she understood that it was as fickle a lover as she. And so she tried to remove the cloak, but the clasp was a great, jeweled thing, far too complicated in the cold and dark. The next wave reached right up to Morvarc'h's neck, and swept Dahud off of his back. She clung to my waist for a moment, crying, 'Save me, my father!' I tried to hold her, but the sea was stronger. The next moment she was gone, as if she had never been, and I had nothing but that sodden cloak in my hands."

He paused again, and then he said, "I might have followed her if it had not been for Morvarc'h." He gave the horse a strange glance, part pride, part antipathy. "I still do not know whether he saved me or damned me, but there is no doubt that he preserved my life on that night. With the dragging weight gone, he began to swim. It was not long before his feet met solid ground, and then we were up on the beach and he was running. I could not stop him. He ran until even the smell of the sea was gone, and then, at last, he stopped.

"It was dawn. That was the first day of my penance. Where it will end…well…" He shrugged.

Meredith gazed at him over the dying fire, the images of the story churning in her like wave-rolled stones. At length Gradlon spoke again, slowly and carefully, as one might speak to a horse on the brink of bolting. "Even now," he said, "fishermen on the Bay of Douarnenez tell of still nights when the bells of Ker-Ys can be heard, very faintly, from beneath the waves." He paused. "They also tell of a *morverc'h* – a mermaid – who appears sometimes at the full of the moon, sitting on a rock, combing her golden hair and singing a love song to the sea."

Gradlon looked at Meredith's face, reading it. "You do not believe me," he said and then, smiling faintly, he turned to open the second chest. He leaned into it, digging for something, and then he turned back to her, a dark bundle in his arms. He shook the bundle so that it unrolled, pooling on the floor around his feet. "Well? Now what do you say?"

Meredith came toward him despite herself, her hand out to touch the brittle blue silk. A sea-meadow spread across its expanse, aquatic grasses wavering upward in faded shades of green. There were whelks' shells in ivory and coral, a whale's rib outlined in tarnished silver, a dull, golden anchor half-hidden among the weeds. On pearl-studded rocks, clumps of mussels clung inkily, interspersed with the carmine flashes of swaying anemones. There were crabs and lobsters, silvery minnows, vermilion sea stars, but the crowning glory was the golden-haired mermaid who swam through the sea garden, her scaled tail so artfully sewn that it seemed to slip and waver as the fabric moved.

A log collapsed on the dying fire. Meredith came back to herself with a start and realized that she was kneeling, clutching the sides of the cloak in her hands as she studied the picture she already knew by heart. She looked up, mortified. But Gradlon met her eyes with his calm, sad smile.

"Do not be alarmed, child," he said. "Of course you know it."
He paused, studying her. At last he said, "My people believed
that the soul is a traveler. That it does not go on to what I suppose
you would call 'heaven' until it has completed its journey on
earth. If the soul has not finished its journey when its body dies,
it moves to another." He paused again.

"It is a lovely story, but the world has changed, and I've
changed with it. I do not believe that my daughter's soul has
migrated to the body of a mermaid. I also do not believe that it
has migrated into yours. And yet I know that the sea is in your
soul as deeply as it was in hers. In some way, somehow, you and
she are connected, and that is why you are here."

Meredith turned away.

"I am sorry if these words upset you, but I must speak them,
or I would fail you as I failed my daughter." Seeing Meredith's
wary glance, he sighed. "Do not misunderstand me. I would
never presume that I am in a position either to give or to receive
absolution…but perhaps it is enough for you simply to believe
this story I have told you, to believe that you carry a piece of
Dahud in you, and to hear me say that I loved her, even if it was
not enough to save her. "

All at once, there were tears in Meredith's eyes. She didn't
know why, though the grief was plaited into the memory of pipe
smoke, dark eyes, a faint red glow through the falling dark.

"It is late now," said Gradlon. "You must be tired. Please, take
the bed."

Meredith pointed to him, shrugged.

"No – I won't sleep tonight, not after telling that story. But
listen: the storm has eased. I will shoe your horse now. In the
morning you will be ready to go. And when you do, I would like
you to take this with you."

He folded the cloak and held it toward her. Meredith shook her head. She could not even begin to calculate its value, or the battering it would endure in her rough pack.

"Yes," he insisted softly. "It was meant for a queen of the sea."

Meredith took it, thinking that she could always leave it behind when she went. Gradlon smiled, but his face seemed to her suddenly, immeasurably old. "One more thing: pay attention to your dreams tonight. Whatever they tell you, you must heed them."

He is raving, Meredith thought as she nodded; *he must be.* Yet his eyes were clear and steady when she finally met them.

"Good night, Meredydd," Gradlon said gently. "Sleep well, and may your journey bring you peace."

Meredith lay down on the bed as Gradlon untied the horse. Admonishing herself to stay awake, she fell asleep to the sound of Gradlon's first hammer blows.

*

She woke in the pre-dawn dark, shedding confused dreams. She thought of Gradlon the previous evening, telling her to remember them. The only things she remembered, though, were a white ship with blue human eyes, a lament sung in an ancient tongue, and a thatched hut burning against a blue sky.

She tried to get her bearings, but the darkness was complete. There was no remnant of the past night's fire, no sound of the horses. She panicked then: the old man had deceived her. He had lulled her to sleep and then stolen everything. She stood, trembling, searching with her hands for the door.

She found it just as the sun crested the mountains. It shone straight through the doorway, dazzling her. But when her eyes adjusted, she was more dazzled still. Overnight, Gradlon's hut had changed. He had broken up all of his furniture and belongings and stacked them in a pile along with dry wood and kindling, aligned precisely to the shaft of light coming through the door. He lay on this strange bed, wrapped in a tattered green cloak. A thin gold band circled his head, and his hands lay on his breast, clasped around a spring of mistletoe. A tinder-box sat at his feet. Morvarc'h was nowhere to be seen.

Meredith knew at once that Gradlon was dead, though she checked perfunctorily for breath and heartbeat. She also recognized the purpose of the tinder-box. Slowly, she put on her coat and hat, picked up her pack – heavier now than it had been – and the rolled sea-cloak. For a long time, she looked down at Gradlon's still face, hoping that he had found the deliverance he wished for. She wished she knew what prayer he would have spoken.

The sun rose higher; the line of light faded. Picking up the tinder-box, Meredith set a corner of the kindling alight. She watched until the flames took the hem of his cloak, and then she fled. She found the horse tethered to a tree at the edge of the yard, munching on a pile of hay. She wore shoes made of bronze, with scalloped outer rims – very different from the shoes Gradlon had taken off of her.

Sighing, Meredith opened her pack to put away the cloak. She found it full of dried fruit and meat, dark bread like that Gradlon had given her the night before, even a little flask of the lethal cider. There was just room amongst it all for the blue cloak. She mounted the horse and turned her onto the path down the mountain without looking back at the hut. She wasn't sad for Gradlon – she couldn't be, if any of his strange story were true – but she still couldn't bear to watch his pyre burn. When she reached the valley, though, she could not help seeing the funeral smoke. It wavered and condensed, galloping across the sky in the shape of a black horse for a moment before it shifted again, thinning until it was swallowed at last by the blue.

Deadwood

1

They'd put in the keel and transom and begun to rip the planking when Silence's father died. A heart attack, the doctor said, a diagnosis with which Silence concurred. He also said that it had been sudden and that John had felt no pain, both of which Silence knew to be lies. However well he'd hidden it, John Ogden's heart had been under attack since his machine maimed his son; fatally by the time he put his wife in the ground. His remaining days had been a long, dirty war with guilt, and when it came to the laying out, no amount of stretching and prodding would wipe the smile of blessed relief off of his face. So that was how God got John Ogden III back.

For Silence, his father's death marked the discovery of a whole new shade of loneliness. It lay so thick in the house that it was like another presence, but the barn was even worse. Its obstinate hush was a constant recrimination, for Silence had neither the knowledge nor the inclination to continue building the boat on his own. And so he rolled the door shut on it, ignoring the supplication of its reaching ribs.

It didn't haunt him as he'd thought it might. He had the odd moment of guilt when he remembered how hard his father had worked on it, but it was the half-fond, distant guilt with which one thinks of a long-abandoned love. In his heart, his old dream was dead. Likewise he let the weeds take the fields and the kitchen garden, and set the animals free in them to fend for themselves. For a time, well-meaning women brought him dinners in pails and on covered plates he forgot to return, and so in the end they stopped bringing them, leaving Silence to subsist on whatever he could dig out of the garden and the store cupboards.

If his father had died in winter, he would certainly have starved. As it was, John had done his son the final service of postponing the inevitable until the spring's new crop was in the ground, and with only a cow and a horse for competition, Silence managed to take a fair amount from the neglected garden. He didn't need much sustenance. He spent his days sitting on a cane chair on the porch, sipping apple wine and glowering out at the burgeoning spring, and his nights on the first John's patriarchal bed, reading his way through the attic's contents. He existed within each moment, having forgotten the preceding one by the time it lapsed, and without a roadmap for the next. He was neither happy nor unhappy. He was finished.

2

The wine had run out by the time Mr. Marsh came to call. It was a Sunday morning. Silence sat morosely in the porch shadows, watching rain fill the holes in the road beyond the front fields. At first he didn't know the spindly, grey-haired man who emerged from the trees, dodged the puddles and turned into his yard. When at last he recognized his old teacher, he was so stunned that he was shaken for a moment out of his misery. Mr. Marsh seemed to have aged years since the autumn day when he'd delivered the book on canoes. Silence wondered how it was that he hadn't noticed, and what it was that had caused the change. It never occurred to him that he might have had a hand in it.

Mr. Marsh stopped a few paces from the porch steps. He held a small stack of books, a prayer book prominently on top. "Good morning, Silence," he said.

"Morning," Silence answered.

"I hope you don't mind my stopping by." He offered a tentative smile.

"Of course not. Come on, sit down." Silence gestured to the empty chairs around him.

"Thank you," Mr. Marsh said, choosing a rocker. "I won't stay long." He paused then, studying Silence. Silence could tell that he was trying to decide how best to word a request, and he braced himself to reject it.

At last Mr. Marsh said, "I can't help but notice that you've never come back to church."

In fact, Silence hadn't set foot in the church since the accident. He wondered why Mr. Marsh would choose to bring it up now. "That's true," he said.

"I can't help wondering whether it's because you're angry with God."

This surprised Silence. He would have thought that Mr. Marsh had better things to worry about. "No," he said. "I'm not."

"I'm glad to hear it."

Silence smiled ruefully. "I'm not angry with him, because I don't believe in him."

"Very well," Mr. Marsh said, as if he'd expected the answer. "It still vindicates my bringing these."

He proffered the books, minus the prayer book. Silence took them. They were old, their leather so darkened by time that it was difficult to make out their titles. He opened one to the flyleaf. *The Republic* it said, and under that, "Plato".

"What is this?" he asked.

"An apology," Mr. Marsh answered.

"What for?"

"My own arrogance." The teacher sighed. "When you were my student, I deliberately withheld the philosophers from you. I believed that you weren't mature enough to understand them…no, worse. I thought that no one in a place like this was mature enough. That a boy from here would need to see 'civilization' before he could understand. I reasoned that they would give them to you at Trinity; that there, you would be in the correct environs to make use of them, and so on…" He waved a deprecating hand. "At any rate, I've done you a serious disservice, and I fear that it's in good part to blame for your current despair."

Silence considered contradicting "despair". In the end, though, it seemed as accurate a description for his state of mind as any. "The boiler would have exploded whether or not I'd read Plato," he said.

"Perhaps. But you'd have been better equipped to face the consequences."

Silence smiled again, bitterly, looking at the wet, empty road. "I don't believe there's a book out there that can account for losing everything."

Mr. Marsh was quiet for another few moments' consideration. Then he said, "Sometimes what looks like a loss is really the opposite."

Silence gave him a wry look. "Don't tell me these books are full of advice like that."

Mr. Marsh laughed. "They contain no advice at all – at least not in the way that you mean. I was speaking of myself."

Uncertain whether he could stomach another anecdote, Silence didn't reply. After a moment, though, Mr. Marsh said, "I don't suppose you've ever heard how I came to be your teacher." Silence realized that this was true. Like most schoolchildren, he'd taken his teacher for granted. "In fact," Mr. Marsh continued, "I was never meant to be a teacher at all. I was to be a lawyer, like you."

"Really?" Silence asked, sincerely surprised and beginning to be interested, despite himself.

Mr. Marsh nodded. "Just like you, my mother had me a lawyer from the time I could talk. My father was a tobacco merchant, solidly middle class, and I could have stepped right into his shoes. But I was bright, and my mother was ambitious for me." He sighed, with what sounded like annoyance rather than nostalgia. "And like you, by the time I won a place at Trinity, I had a pretty sweetheart whom I believed loved me. I saw my whole, bright future stretching ahead like a wide, straight road."

He smiled with soft bitterness. "And then we went to war, and everything changed."

"You fought for the Confederacy?" Silence spoke the words softly, hesitantly, uncertain whether he wanted to know the answer. But Mr. Marsh shook his head, his smile widening and its bitterness deepening.

"That's the irony of it: I was never a soldier. I was at college when the southern states seceded, reading the Transcendentalists and full of righteous fire for the downtrodden Negro. I refused to fight to own other human beings. In fact, I talked about joining the Unionists, fighting for justice and freedom..." He sighed. "It never occurred to me that in the convoluted way of the world, it was this same downtrodden Negro who was funding my education, in growing the tobacco by which my father earned the money to pay my tuition. Nor did it occur to me that the Union army was made up of men, just like the Confederates, that very few men are idealists, and even idealists are human." He sighed again, shaking his head.

"My father couldn't have lasted long in his business once the plantations collapsed, but as it was, he never had the chance to try. A group of drunken Union soldiers torched his warehouses one night. The entire stock was ash within hours. There was no money left for my education, and so I had to leave Trinity without a degree. I was lucky to take a teacher's qualifications, luckier still to find a job in those days, never mind if it was in a hill town in the middle of nowhere. And that, Silence Ogden, is how I came to be here."

There was a long pause. Then Silence said, "I'm sorry."

Mr. Marsh looked at him with quick, bright eyes. "In that case, you've missed the point entirely."

"Which is...?"

"That I wasn't meant to be a lawyer any more than you were."

"What?" Silence cried, pushing out of the chair. "Then all of those years...all of those lessons...they were for nothing?"

"No! Learning is never for nothing. Besides, you're jumping to conclusions. I still think that Trinity would have been – could be – a wonderful place for you. But I never agreed with your mother about your course of study."

Silence walked to the end of the porch, his uneven gait creaking iambs on the old boards. He stopped with his hands on the railing, looking down into the rhododendron bush in which he'd once hidden from Annie Newcombe.

"Silence," Mr. Marsh persisted gently, "if I had said this to you before...if I'd told you that the choice you thought you'd made wasn't really your choice, and that it was the wrong one... would you have listened?"

Silence wanted to hate his old teacher, but he couldn't. Moreover, he knew that he was right. "No," he said softly.

"Very well then: there's been no waste, not even any true loss." Silence turned to him with a baleful smile. Mr. Marsh met it unflinching. "I don't deny you've suffered, Silence. I don't claim that it was fair. But in the end, it isn't a question of suffering or justice. Disaster was what it took to open your eyes, just like it did mine." He held up a hand to stay Silence's angry protest, and his next words, though spoken gently, had the hard edge of truth. "You're at a crossroads, Silence. God or Fate or whatever you believe in has given you an opportunity."

"By maiming me?" Silence asked incredulously.

"Maybe it took that to stop you barreling headlong into a worse disaster." He sighed as Silence turned away again, his face hard with anger. "Whatever you think about it now, try to remember that Fate is too far-reaching to deal in absolutes. I can say with complete honesty that it was looking after me the night the drunken soldiers burned my father's tobacco. One day you'll say the same about the day it blew up your father's machine.

"Oh, I know you hate me for saying that. Feel free to hate me for as long as is necessary. But in the meantime, read these," he patted the books. "If nothing else, they'll give you ammunition for our next discussion. A word of advice, though: don't begin with Schopenhauer."

3

The books sat on the kitchen table for five days before Silence finally gave in to their mute allure. He started with Plato, for no better reason than that it was on top of the pile. But he hitched up a single chapter into *The Republic*. The next evening, when he was certain the children would be gone, he took the books back to the school.

Mr. Marsh looked up from his work and smiled. "Really, Silence Ogden," he said, "I thought you had more tenacity than that!"

"I have no use for a treatise on right and wrong," Silence answered grimly, putting the books on the teacher's desk.

"I told you not to start with Schopenhauer."

"I didn't. Plato. Chapter one, *The Republic*. Cephalus and Socrates are arguing about money, which somehow becomes a discussion about the wisdom of returning a borrowed axe to a man who's likely to use it for murder, neither of which seems particularly relevant to my life." Silence was aware that he sounded cranky. He felt cranky, taking Mr. Marsh's books for condescension.

"You haven't read far enough," Mr. Marsh said mildly. Silence sat down sulkily on a desk and waited for more. The teacher, recognizing the same petulance with which Silence had once approached geometry, took off his glasses and wearily began to polish them on his handkerchief. "Rhetoric isn't fiction," he said, "and it isn't straightforward. After all, it's only opinion, however convincing the language."

"Then what use is it to me?"

Mr. Marsh's mouth compressed to a thin line. "Silence, you disappoint me."

Silence stood up, anger flushing his face. "Well then I apologize – and I won't trouble you any longer."

"Don't be a fool, Ogden!" It was the first time Silence's old teacher had addressed him as a man, and it stopped him in his tracks. "Surely I've taught you better than that."

Silence turned. He didn't need to speak his challenge.

"I know that you've given up," Mr. Marsh said, meeting his eye. "I even understand why. I can't make you take the place a Trinity, and I can't make you finish your boat, but you've got a first-class mind, and I'll be damned if I'll let you waste it!"

Silence could not help being reminded of his father's similar words, on a birthday that already seemed immeasurably distant. Slowly, he returned to the desk and sat down. "How do you mean to do that?" he asked, still sullen.

"Honestly, Silence," Mr. Marsh sighed, rubbing his eyes, "I don't know. You sure don't make things easy. But what I *do* know is that you can't be an educated man without learning to consider the world from all sides. If you won't go out into the world, then I'm going to do my best to bring it to you. I owe you that much."

Silence didn't understand the last statement, but it defeated his anger nonetheless. "You really think I should read these books?" he asked.

"Would I have brought them to you if I didn't?"

Silence sighed. "All right. I'll give them another try."

*

It wasn't until he reached the Neoplatonists that Silence began to warm to his new field of study. Recasting God as the Prime Mover Unmoved and creation as a consequence of its existence satisfied the space left by his demolished Sunday-school faith, without the need to defend a sentient deity's apparent injustices. More than that, the idea of the True Human seemed a decent rejoinder to those people in his life determined to make him give up his self-imposed exile. But what really convinced him that there was truth in Plotinus's words was that he provided the only explanation Silence had encountered for the things living in Pascal's tree.

"'In the Intellectual Kosmos dwells Authentic Essence,'" Silence read to Pascal one close July evening as they sat under the tree, waiting for a breeze, "'with the Divine Mind as the noblest of its content, but containing also souls, since every soul in this lower sphere has come thence: that is the world of unembodied spirits while to our world belong those that have entered body and undergone bodily division.²'"

Pascal slung him a suspicious look. "What the hell is that s'posed to mean?"

---

2 Plotinus, the Fourth Ennead

Undaunted, Silence read on: "'Soul, there without distinction and partition, has yet a nature lending itself to divisional existence: its division is secession, entry into body.'" He held up a hand to stop Pascal's protest. "But 'something of it holds its ground, that in it which recoils from separate existence. The entity, therefore, described as consisting of the undivided soul and of the soul divided among bodies, contains a soul which is at once above and below, attached to the Supreme and yet reaching down to this sphere, like a radius from a centre.'" Silence closed the book and looked up at Pascal. It was the nearest he'd felt to excitement in a long time. "And that explains the tree."

Pascal picked up his guitar and thumbed the strings, looking up through the leaves at the cross on the church's tiny spire. The left side of his mouth was curling upwards, in annoyance or humor, Silence couldn't yet tell. He only knew that it wasn't the reaction he'd expected, and it doused the spark of enthusiasm the reading had kindled.

"Well?" he asked, despite it. "What do you think?"

"I think you're thinking about it too much," Pascal said.

"But it all makes sense!" Silence cried. "If individual souls are really just offshoots of the same soul that separate for a while to animate a body, and they leave part of themselves behind when they do it, then it makes sense that they'd go back to the one soul when the body dies. It also makes sense they'd congregate along the way."

"I didn't hear anythin' in all that gobbledygook about a tree."

Silence shrugged. "You can't expect he'd have covered every eventuality." Pascal gave him a dubious look, and Silence answered with an exasperated sigh. "Maybe it's some kind of stopping place. Maybe they need to rest on their way home."

Pascal ruminated on this as his thumbing became a sprightly tune. "It's a good idea," he said at last, "except for one thing."

"What?"

"Those souls don't move on. They live in the tree."

"How do you know that?"

This was a question Pascal didn't particularly want to answer. He still hadn't admitted to Silence how well he knew those flapping shadows. He hadn't even told him that each blue tune was a story. So he dodged the question with another: "It's all well and good philosophizin' about souls and way stations on the road to heaven," he said, "but does this fellow Plotinus tell you anything about what to do while you're here on earth?"

"Of course," said Silence, glad to find himself back on firm rhetorical ground. "See, there's the Prime Mover – that's like God, except it doesn't get involved in human affairs. It creates everything, and all of us in living bodies are trying to get nearer to the best creations of the Prime Mover."

"Like what?"

"Well…like pure intellect."

"Intellect?" Pascal scoffed. "What about love, and joy, and beauty?"

"Plotinus talks about those too," Silence admitted reluctantly, "but he says that the only real way to be happy is to live the life of the mind. He says true happiness isn't physical, and what happens to us in our worldly lives doesn't have any bearing on it. See, it all goes back to the way our souls are divided. One part walks around on earth with us, while the other is with the Prime Mover, in its greatest capacity for Reason.

"But it's more than that, too," Silence argued as Pascal shook his head. "Even in our human bodies, we can overcome things like sickness and hunger if we control reason and contemplation. To be happy, we only have to stop thinking about worldly things. '…The Proficient's will is set always and only inward.[3]'" Silence had found that phrase particularly compelling, and it had been knocking around his head since he read it.

But Pascal still looked unimpressed. "That's all well and good, *P'tit*," he said, "and I'm real happy for you that you found somethin' to light your fire again. Trouble is, it ain't got much to do with real life – the hurtin' and lovin' that goes on every day. You live too much in your head, you'll never really live."

Silence closed his book and stood up.

"Aw, son, don't be angry," Pascal said. "I only want to keep you from some of my mistakes." That surprised Silence enough that he turned back to look at Pascal. "You and me, we're more alike than you think," he said. "I used to do a lot of my own kinda philosophizing. All I learned is, you can't dodge God's will for long."

"There is no God."

"Fate, then. Your Plotinus have anything to say about fate?"

Silence sighed, wondering why all of his conversations of late seemed to come down to a choice between the two. "If fate's in charge," he said, "it's not done much to recommend itself to me." Pascal's pity was obvious. It only made Silence more determined to prove him wrong. "Sorry, Pascal, but I'm finished with God, and I'm finished with fate. From now on I'm a man of free will."

Pascal only smiled. He knew that God and fate were far from finished with Silence. He also knew there was no point trying to tell him so. "Just don't try to read and walk at once, Silence Ogden," he said as Silence stood to go. "You never know what's waitin' in the road to trip you up."

---

3 Enneads I.4.11

4

Many years later, Silence overheard someone ask Celia how she'd ended up settling in Heaven. She considered the question carefully and then answered, "Well, Silence and me, we got to talking." Which was one way of putting it. Silence's memory of their meeting was rather different.

It was June, and it was evening: the kind of mellow, burnished, early-summer evening whose stillness is so thick and lush, it begs something to break it. Young girls leaned on window frames, dreaming up that something as dark eyed and smooth tongued and rich. Old men tried to ignore its sepulchral pallor. Women unpinned limp sheets from damp lines, thinking as they folded them, *This one, or perhaps the next; behind one of them, it will look different.* And all of them held their breath.

All of them except for Silence Ogden. He was sitting on the porch as usual, eating a handful of snap-peas, waiting for nothing. He half-watched the cow and the horse, knee-deep in green oats, eating as if founder were their goal. His eyes rested beyond them on the empty road, where it bent sharply out of its covering of trees and down toward the bottomland.

And then, all at once, it wasn't empty. Something was moving in the shadows by the bend, something that didn't fit into the rhythm of the town he'd known all of his life. Silence leaned forward, trying to bring it into focus. There was a short, sharp thrust of breeze. The trees filled like lungs, and then sighed. The world stilled again except for the flicker of movement, which had resolved into two children pulling a cart, one in a deep red dress, the other in sky blue, each of them holding one of the shafts that should have hung from a horse's harness.

As they reached the fence by which Silence's horse stood gorging himself, the girl in the red dress stopped and set down her cart shaft, the one in blue following suit. It was only when she stood and stretched that Silence realized the girl in the red dress wasn't a girl at all. Though she was small and slender, she had a woman's figure and long, full skirt, and the girl in blue hung by her in clear deference.

The woman approached the fence separating the road from the oat field and peered over it at the horse. She watched him eat for a few long moments, and then she raised her hands and clapped them together three times. The sound was like shots in the still evening. The horse wheeled and trotted a few lumbering steps before dropping his nose to the oats again. At that the woman looked up, straight across the field and into Silence's watching eyes. She climbed over the wall and strode toward Silence. He was half aware of the child straggling along in her wake, but only half aware, the majority of his attention focused, rapt, on the woman's fury. It preceded her like a billowing spinnaker, and he knew he was about to take the brunt of it.

She stopped a few feet short of the porch, and without preamble she demanded, "Is that your horse?"

"Yes'm," Silence answered, staring at her in wonder. He had never seen a woman quite like her. She put him in mind of Annie, though he couldn't say why, since she looked nothing like her. She looked even tinier close up, almost impossibly tiny. She should have been overwhelmed by her thick, dark, coiled braids and cranberry calico, except that she had a birdlike strength about her, the kind made of muscle and bone, filling her out as no amount of fat could. Her face was fair-skinned and fine. She had no doubt been a beauty not too long since, and might be again if life dealt gently with her – for Silence could see very well that it hadn't of late.

"Well, you don't deserve him!" she snapped.

"No doubt you're right," said Silence.

Clearly, the woman had been expecting a fight. Her dark eyes widened, and some of the spit went out of them. "What's wrong with you?" she asked.

Silence, having momentarily forgotten about it, turned the scarred side of his face away from her. The woman clucked impatiently. "I don't mean *that!*" she said, gesturing to his scar. "I mean, what kind of farmer lets his livestock loose in a field of green oats?"

Silence smiled sadly. "I never said I was a farmer. As for the animals…well, they seem happy there, and God knows there isn't much happiness in a farm beast's life."

The child had caught up to the woman by then. She looked like her, but also not like her. She was perhaps six or seven years old, with her mother's dark hair and white skin, but her eyes were bright blue, and the sense of her solid, rather than flitting. Her head reached her mother's shoulder already.

"Mama," she said.

"Not now," said the woman, without shifting her eyes from Silence. "Listen," she said to him in the same tone with which she'd spoken to the child, "if you're hell-bent on killing that horse, perhaps you might consider selling him to me instead."

"Our horse got stolen," the child interjected, ignoring her mother's shushing eyes.

"I'm sorry to hear that," said Silence.

"Just two days ago. Taken right out from under us in the night. She was the prettiest horse you every saw."

Silence couldn't help smiling. It wasn't often that children would even look at him, let alone address him, yet this one had done both without apparent reference to his monstrous face.

"It's not funny," the child said sharply.

"No," he said, "it isn't. I'm sorry." Then, to her mother, "Charlie is old, but he's surely strong enough to pull that cart to wherever you're going. If he's of use to you, then take him."

But the woman shook her head, speaking before the child could. "I don't accept charity. How much do you want for him?"

Silence shrugged again. "I have no idea. Besides, it isn't charity. I have no use for him. You do, so you should have him; it's only logical."

"Logic," the woman said to her daughter. "Logic, says the man who turns his horse out in the green oats!" To Silence: "Just you tell me how much, and if I have it I'll pay it, and if I don't... well, either way I'll leave you in peace."

Silence studied the woman for a moment. Perhaps because he hadn't looked hard at anyone in so long, his perception was keen, and he took in a number of things at once. First, though her dress and the child's were clean, they were very nearly threadbare. Both woman and child had hunger's hollowed eyes and cheeks. Though the woman spoke boldly of paying him for the horse, it was clear that she had very little to offer. More than that, he had the sense that she wanted the horse more for the animal's sake than her own; to save him, perhaps, from his negligent owner.

"Tell me," Silence asked, "what's wrong with feeding a horse green oats?"

The woman gazed at him for a long moment, as if not quite believing that he was serious. Then she said, slowly and meticulously, "They're too rich. Green *anything* is too rich, this time of year. He's already going lame. It was clear when he

317

trotted. If he continues to eat like that, he'll founder, and then he'll die. So will the cow, but it will take longer for her."

Once again Silence studied the woman. "You know a lot about this," he said.

"I hope so," she said, laughing humorlessly. "I'm a farmer's daughter."

"And I'm a farmer's son," said Silence, "but as you can see, I know nothing about it." He paused, his mind full of an idea he couldn't quite bear to hear rejected. But the woman was looking toward her cart, and he knew that in a moment she would give up and go away, so he said. "I don't need money."

"How very fortunate for you," muttered the woman, her look darkening.

"At least," Silence continued, "not as much as I need help. If you could stay for a few days, show me how to set the place in order…"

She gave him a hard look. "Why?" she asked.

"Look at it," he answered, gesturing to the overgrown fields.

"I meant, why me? Is there no one in this town who will help you?"

Silence laughed sadly. "I'm afraid they've long since given up on me."

The woman scrutinized him, not bothering to hide her distrust. Then she said, "Happy?" and it took several moments for Silence to work out that she wasn't questioning him, but speaking to the child. The little girl stepped out of her mother's shadow and looked up at Silence. It was a long, unblinking look, and yet Silence had no compulsion to hide his scar. Perhaps it was because he had the sense that the child was not looking at him at all, but around him, and into him. After a moment, she gave Silence a flashbulb smile, and her mother a nod.

"Celia Gagne," said the woman hesitantly, offering Silence her hand. "And my daughter, Happy Moon."

"Silence Ogden," he said, taking it. "Pleased to make your acquaintance."

*

The first thing Celia did, after catching the horse and the cow and putting them in the bald paddock, was wash all of the dishes. Silence dried and put away those that belonged to him. The others Celia stacked by the door, admonishing Silence to return them in the morning. After that, she inspected the pantry, sighed, and went out with Happy to see what could be salvaged from the garden. Silence followed at a forlorn distance, making half-hearted attempts at apology. In spite of him, within an hour Celia and Happy had a pot of beans and bacon on the stove, another full of greens ready to steam, and a sheet of biscuits in the oven. Silence knew how to make tea, at least, and when Celia stopped for a moment he gave her a glass, sweetened with sugar and mint.

"Thank you," she said, looking up at him in surprise.

"It's the least I can do," he answered, handing another glass to Happy. Once again the child offered him a brilliant smile and Celia's brow, which had drawn again towards worry, relaxed.

They sat for a few long moments in the silence of the falling night before Silence worked up the courage to ask, "What brings you to Heaven, Mrs. Gagne?"

"It's Miss," she answered curtly.

"I'm sorry," he stumbled, glancing at Happy. "I thought…"

"What everyone thinks," she said bitterly. And then, "Happy, go set the table."

"But Mama – "

"Happy."

"But I don't know where he keeps his – "

"You're a smart girl," said Celia. "You'll figure it out."

Happy huffed, but she went. When they heard her rummaging in the kitchen, Celia looked at Silence with hard, brave eyes and said, "I don't believe in whitewashing the truth, Mr. Ogden. The truth is, I found out the hard way that a man can be more of a bastard than the child he abandons to namelessness. The truth is also that I am not a whore, and I won't be treated like one."

Silence blinked at her, stunned speechless by the words and by what she'd imagined to be his intentions.

"I'm telling you this," she continued, "because, however decent a man you might be, there aren't many things you can think of a single woman who has agreed to stay in your house, with only a girl child for chaperone."

"I…see," gulped Silence, though he didn't.

"So now you're wondering why I agreed," she said, her fingers white around her glass. Without giving Silence a chance to deny it, she continued, "It's because Happy said she approved of you. She's never wrong."

"No?" said Silence, who was by this point completely lost.

"Never," said Celia. "She sees the light around people," she added, fondness and pride softening her careworn face for a moment. "Yours is white. The cleanest light she's ever seen, she said. Like the light that comes off of water…" Celia's expression turned strange and secret and backward-looking for a moment. Then it was businesslike again. "And that, Mr. Ogden, is why we are still here."

"I see," Silence repeated, and at last, he was beginning to. He waited for Celia to say something else, but her lecture apparently was finished. She was staring off into the dark, her lips a thin pink line under her wide, worried eyes.

"Miss Gagne," said Silence. She looked at him. Her eyes were the eyes of all the world's women, faced with an unknown man: poised between hope and distrust. "Thank you."

"For what?" she asked.

"For telling me the truth. And don't you worry. I intend to sleep in the attic."

"The attic?"

Silence pointed to the old homestead. "You can lock me in if you like."

Hesitant as the new moon cresting the treetops, Celia smiled. "Thank you, Mr. Ogden. But I don't think that will be necessary. I believe that we understand each other."

"Please call me Silence," he said, offering his hand.

"And you may call me Celia," said Celia, accepting it.

When Silence stepped out of the attic the next morning, the sun was barely over the horizon, but he found the kitchen spotless, a covered plate of bacon and grits on the table. With a gut-punch, he realized that Celia had thought better of Happy's assessment – he could not bear to think that the part about the light had been a lie – and they'd gone. Forlorn, he made a pot of coffee and took it out onto the porch to resume his survey of nothing. But he never drank it, because the horseless cart was still in his yard, and far off amidst the tangled weeds of what had once been a cornfield, he saw two dark heads bent together.

By the time he reached, them Happy had wandered off to the margin of the woods, leaving her mother alone, thoughtfully eating earth. Celia nodded to Silence when she saw him approach and carried on chewing. Silence watched her for a minute, and then he asked, "What are you doing?"

Celia opened her palm, the invitation clear. Silence decided then that she was either completely out of her mind, or she was trying to make a point. Maybe both.

"Ah...no, thank you," he said.

Celia shrugged, tipped the dirt out of her hand, wiped her hand on her skirt, and spat. "The best way into the mind of the earth in a given place," she said, "is to taste it. Didn't your father ever taste the earth?"

She knew to ask this because Silence had told her a little – the barest little – of his history the previous night. In return she had told him that she and Happy were traveling to Virginia, where they hoped to find seasonal work in the tobacco fields after a spring spent in the Louisiana cane. But that was, as yet, the most he knew about her.

"I don't know," he admitted.

She shook her head. "Well," she said, "your earth is tart."

"I'm sorry."

Celia laughed. "There's no cause for 'sorry'. All of the soil is tart in these hills. But – " she held up an admonitory finger " – yours is more so than most. It's been neglected. For that, you can apologize."

But he saw that her thin lips were turned into a hint of that new-moon smile, so he didn't. Instead he asked, "What does it mean, that it's tart?"

She sighed. "It means you have no chance of a corn crop this year. The apples will be small and sour, if they stay on the tree long enough for you to tell. If you can afford quicklime, though, you'll save the garden. And if you start spreading your ashes and bone-meal on the fields, then you might just be able to raise corn next year…" She trailed off, looked out over the fields, her eyes full of what needed to be done; full also of a look Silence remembered well enough, though it hadn't lit his father's face since before the accident. Likewise it woke in Silence the old, familiar remorse. This woman was in her element here, as his father had been – as all of Heaven's people were. All except him.

Celia must have seen some of this on his face, because she asked, "What's the matter?"

Silence sighed. "Nothing," he said, "except that you've reminded me why I never liked farming."

"Perhaps," she said, her voice as acidic as Silence's soil, "that's because your life never depended on it."

"But – " he began and then went no further, because she was right. They stood for a while listening to the wind in the trees. He couldn't see Happy anymore, but he could hear her singing in a high, sweet voice. Celia heard it too. Like a sunflower, her face clocked to the light of her daughter's song, and it was the face of the girl she must have been before life started teaching her hard truths. Silence felt as far from her then as he'd ever felt from anyone, her absolute love for her child waking in him a sharp, bitter envy, quite different from the inert loneliness he'd become accustomed to.

"If not this," Celia said after a moment, turning that soft face to him and gesturing to his fields, "then what is it that you live for?"

"I don't know," he said, sorely tired of the question.

"There must be something."

Because Celia didn't know any better, Silence said, "Before the accident, I was engaged to be married. And I was going to college to be a lawyer."

"And yet you're still single, and still here," she challenged. "Why?"

Silence sighed. "I guess I don't know what else to do."

"So that's it? For the better part of two years, you've sat here and watched a damned good piece of earth go to waste?"

She spoke the truth too bluntly for him to be angry. "Not quite. When my daddy was still alive, we were working on something."

"What kind of something?" asked Celia, relentless.

Silence looked at her, uncertain. She already had enough cause to think him crazy. But by the look in her eye, he knew that she wouldn't back down, so he turned toward the barn and began walking. He didn't hear her follow, but when he reached the door and turned, she was there. Happy had shown up too, drifting back from the woods with a child's infallible instinct for something imminent and interesting. Silence took a deep breath, unlocked the door and rolled it back.

A shaft of sun lit the boat's dusty skeleton. Celia's look clouded over, but Happy ran delightedly into the barn and began clambering around the frames, until her mother called her sharply back. Celia's reaction didn't surprise Silence. What did was the way that his heart leapt to his boat's mute reach.

"I see," Celia said at last, with a bitterness in her voice he couldn't quite fathom.

"I doubt it," he said.

"The sea is a madness in some men."

Silence laughed humorlessly. "I know that. Or I used to."

"If you've got it," she said, "I don't think you ever get over it."

"Well, I stand as proof that you're wrong. At any rate," he added, his smile dying, "there isn't much in it one way or the other. With my father gone, I don't suppose I'll ever finish it."

"No?" asked Celia.

"Not unless you know anything about boatbuilding?"

"No," she answered grimly.

"That's it, then," said Silence, rolling the barn door shut again, a little wistfully.

But Celia said to herself, "We'll see."

5

When Celia had been in Heaven for a month, Silence proposed.

"Absolutely not," she answered, with neither affront nor apology.

"Of course not," he answered glumly, fingering his scarred cheek and tucking his bad leg under him as he sat down on the porch step.

Celia sighed, and her eyes softened. "You misunderstand me. It's not your looks or your leg that I object to. Indeed, why would I? You're a good-looking man, and you pull your weight these days, limp or not." Silence raised his eyebrows, but Celia, not much given to compliments, let alone repeating them, ignored him and began enumerating her reasons on her fingers. "First of all, I'm thirty years old, which makes me – what – ten years older than you?"

"Roughly," Silence muttered.

"Very well. A ten-year gap isn't always a disaster, but the odds are too high for my liking. Second, you and I are philosophically opposed."

"I didn't know that you read philosophy."

Celia smiled, shook her head and said, "That's exactly what I mean."

"But I get along with you as well as anyone I've ever met!"

Celia sighed. "That may be true. But that's partly because the boundaries are clear. Start erasing them, I think you'd find we're far less compatible than you believe. And to be married, we'd have to erase them all."

"Is that it?" Silence asked bitterly. Celia gave him a long look, and then she looked away, coloring. Intrigued, Silence said, "What else?"

Celia didn't meet his eye, but her voice was steady when she said, "The truth is, I couldn't marry you even if I wanted to, Silence, because I'm married already."

"But you said – "

"I lied!" she snapped.

"Why?" he persisted.

"Because I'd rather be a fallen woman with a bastard child than own up to being my husband's wife." Her voice was hard and determined, just as it had been on the first night when she laid out the margins of their relationship to him. "But don't you ever tell anyone I told you that – especially not Happy!"

"All right," Silence said dubiously. "But if you feel that way, couldn't you get a divorce?"

Celia sighed. "If I could find him. If I had the heart to look… but that's all beside the point. Even if I was a free woman, and all the other things didn't figure, there's still one big problem we'd never get around."

"Another one?" Silence asked with grim irony.

But Celia nodded earnestly. "That boat in the barn."

"I've told you – that's all over."

Celia couldn't help smiling. "Please don't take this the wrong way – believe me, I'm in no position to patronize anyone – but you're too young to know that."

"Oh, Lord," Silence groaned. "Now I'm a child, too?"

"Of course you're not, and I didn't say you were! But I can't help having lived ten years longer than you, and what I've learned between twenty and thirty is that you never really escape the original path fate put you on. Your heart and your mind might change, but your soul – or whatever you want to call the pole your flag is hung on – that never shifts. If what you've told me is true, Silence, then the sea's been in your soul for as long as your soul's been in your body. Believe me, you won't escape your destiny by shutting a barn door on it."

"Building that boat was my father's idea."

"It was yours, first."

"Well then," Silence said, unable to resist a final defiance, though he knew that he was beaten, "how do you know the boat's not *your* destiny, too?"

Celia laughed again, but she looked immeasurably sad. "If there's one thing I'm certain of, it's that I do not belong on the sea…though it's an irony and a bitter one, given that I'm plagued with men who can think of nothing else."

"What?" asked Silence, forgetting his wounded pride at the intriguing words. "Who do you mean by that?"

But she only shook her head. "At any rate, I am not going to marry you or anyone else just to stop tongues wagging. If I'd wanted an excuse, I'd have kept my ring."

"What? I never – "

"Come on, Silence Ogden," Celia sighed. "I've heard them talking too, and we both know that's why you really asked me."

Once again, Celia was right. The talk had started the morning after she arrived, when Silence had gone to town and returned all of the dishes that had been moldering in his kitchen since his father died. No one could have known Celia and her daughter were staying with him; nevertheless, the women knew immediately that something was afoot. A solitary man couldn't bring a shine like that to a plate, never mind Silence Ogden.

"Look," added Celia, taking Silence's ruminative stare for heartbreak, "if I had any desire to get married again, you're the first man I'd pick."

He shook his head, but he couldn't help the rueful smile. "You're a woman of backhanded compliments."

"No," she said. "I'm a woman who tells the truth. And one day, you'll thank me for it."

6

If Heaven was whispering before they found out about Celia Gagne, it was buzzing like an upturned hive afterward – buzzing with fury at Silence Ogden. Since his father's death, people had just about managed to forget him and his freakish bad fortune, consigning him to a life of hermitude. But they couldn't ignore him once he began cohabiting with a decent-looking single woman, and it rankled them to have to wonder why she would take up with him, and not one of the hollow's far more eligible bachelor farmers; to wonder what exactly went on in that house at night; and to see her prove herself more than capable of reclaiming the fallow farm they'd all been eyeing up for months.

What galled them most, though, was Celia's child. Heaven had never produced anything but pretty, proper, born-in-wedlock babies, every one of whom slept through the night from the first, if you believed their mothers. Amongst them, Happy Moon Gagne was more than an anomaly: she was an offense. She made parents look sin in the eye and explain it to their children in the starkest of terms. Worse still, those parents couldn't simply forbid association with her. Though they might speak the words, Heaven was too small and too isolated to allow them to enforce their law.

And Happy was irresistible: a wild, lawless, brilliant little fairy who drew Heaven's children from their mother's pious bosoms like the piper with his rats. She walked ridgepoles with laughing nonchalance, ate green apples without a sign of colic. Bareback, she rode the old plough horse Charlie as if she'd been born to it, exploring deer paths in the wooded hills or coaxing her friends into races that she always won.

One listless, muggy afternoon she tied a rope to a bucket and hauled herself up a bee tree, cleated the rope around a broken branch, and caught two-dozen bees in a canning jar, along with a sizeable chunk of honeycomb. She fed the bees through the window of Jesse and Jamie Reiss's parlor, where their mother was hosting a meeting of Heaven's Ladies' Moral Improvement Society, and then shared out the comb among her friends while they observed the results.

Another day she showed her rapt audience how to light a fire with Indian sticks, and then set one under Eva Hauser's grandfather's drainpipe. She climbed up on the roof and made smoke signals using one of Eva's starched white aprons, stolen from the washing line, until both apron and drainpipe caught fire. She turned their jeers to stunned silence when she planted a kiss firmly on Silence Ogden's scarred cheek and failed to catch his affliction. And she hammered home the last nail in their scandalized adulation on the day that she fearlessly took up a dare to knock on Annie Newcombe's front door, and Annie let her in.

After that, Happy forgot the other children. Her sudden lack of interest in her playmates would have delighted their mothers if her indifference had not compounded her appeal, and the addition of Annie to the mix had not likewise compounded their despair. By July it was a commonplace to see Annie Newcombe walking along in her serene unawareness, with Happy tagging beside her talking nineteen to the dozen and a straggling handful of fascinated children following several paces behind.

Silence watched these processions partly with interest, partly with envy. It was years since he'd exchanged more than a passing nod with Annie, yet since his conversation with Celia about the boat, he found himself thinking about Juniper Barrens again. He wondered if Annie was telling Happy those same stories. He waited for Happy to say something about it, but she didn't. In fact she didn't mention Annie at all. And so at last Silence realized that if he wanted answers from Happy, he was going to have to ask the questions.

*

Early on in her tenure in Heaven, Silence had shown Happy his old cave in the riverbank, and she had been quick to co-opt it. It was where she hid her treasures, where she retreated from her cloying celebrity, and where she went when she quarreled with her mother. Now, in late August, in order to avoid being put to work in the harvest, she had more or less taken up residence.

When Silence arrived at the cave he knocked on the ground outside the mouth, though Happy's bare feet were clearly visible sticking out of the dim recess. Happy was acutely sensitive to condescension, and Silence knew from past experience that if he didn't formally announce his presence, she would sulk and pout and his trip would have been in vain.

"Yes?" she said crisply, tossing a plum pit into the river.

"You open for business, Happy?" Silence asked.

Happy leaned out of the hole to look at him. Her blue eyes were distant, her face thoughtful. "Not officially," she said. She blinked, and tapped her cheek with a broken pencil. In the other hand she held a feed merchant's bill, its back covered with close writing. "But you can stay – as long as you aren't going to try to make me come home and shell beans."

Silence's heart swelled at the throwaway certainty with which she spoke the word "home". For his empty house to have become Happy's home felt the way he imagined it would feel to gain the trust of a wild horse. But to comment on it would only rile Happy, who didn't like sentiment any more than her mother did. So he said, "I wouldn't presume. But you know, your mama's working hard. She could really use your help."

"No, she couldn't," Happy said. "She'll get on much better without me interfering."

Silence blinked, trying not to smile. "What makes you think that?"

Happy shrugged. "That's what she said: 'Happy, I'll get on much better without you interfering.'"

"Oh? Do you want to tell me what happened?"

He knew that she wanted nothing more. But he kept a straight face as she pretended prevarication, and finally said: "All right. When we were at the store earlier, Mama saw Mr. Marden was selling daffodil bulbs half price. She said, 'Lord knows I have enough to do already, but it would look real cheerful come spring to have daffodils growing up the path to the house.'"

Silence was as thrilled to think of Celia planning for spring in his house – for something frivolous, no less – as he had been to hear Happy call it "home". But he knew well enough by now that saying so would only embarrass Happy and derail her story. Happy continued, "So I said, 'That would look real nice, Mama. You go on and buy them, and I'll help you plant them.' And Mama hemmed and hawed, and then finally she bought a sack of bulbs. Well, we brought them home, and I said, 'Can we plant the daffodils now?' and she said, 'No we can't, Happy. There's work to be done,' and she made me go pick beans. But there weren't too many, and when I was done, I saw that sack of bulbs, and I knew Mama wouldn't get to it today, and then she'd make us do something else tomorrow, and in the end she might forget all about them. So I planted them myself."

Happy gave Silence a grim, expectant look. "That doesn't sound too bad," Silence said, "though you might have asked her first if she needed any more help."

"It *was* bad, though. It took me hours to plant all those bulbs, Silence. And then, when I was down to the last few, Mama came over to see where I'd got to. For a minute she didn't say anything, so I thought she was glad I planted them after all. And then she yelled, 'Hap*pyyyy!*'"

"How come?"

Happy sighed. "Because I put them in upside down."

"All of them?"

Happy nodded mournfully. "Every single one of them. I thought the scraggy parts were what makes the flower, but really it's the roots."

"Well," said Silence, "I guess that's an honest mistake. I wouldn't know which way up to put a daffodil bulb, either."

"Well that's not what Mama thinks. She said that now she'd have to dig them all up and turn them around, and she'd get on much better – "

"Without you interfering," Silence finished for her.

Happy nodded. "So I came here. Silence, why don't you ever come in this cave with me?"

Over time, Silence had grown used to Happy's flying conversational changes. With barely a pause, he said, "Because I barely fit in there without you."

"Annie can fit in with me."

Hardly able to believe his luck, Silence said, "Annie visits you here?"

"Sometimes." Happy was looking at the trees on the far side of the river in the same way that she looked at the light around people. Silence wished, not for the first time, that he could see what she was seeing.

"You sure spend a lot of time with Annie these days," he said, trying his best to sound nonchalant.

"Yep."

"What do you do?"

Happy turned those through-seeing eyes on him, along with her astonishing smile. "We don't talk about you."

"Did I ask if you did?" Silence cried, trying to hide his mortification with annoyance. Happy only smiled again. "When I was little, Annie used to tell me stories," he prompted after a moment.

The smile flattened. "Seven is *not* little!"

Silence sighed. "Sorry. I just meant, littler than I am now." Happy nodded, but her giddy mood had deflated. "Does Annie tell *you* stories?" he prodded.

Happy considered him for a moment, and then she said, "No. But sometimes I tell her some."

"Oh yeah? What about?"

Happy shrugged. "Where we've been, me and Mama. The other day we threw pinecones in the river to see how long it would take them to sink, and I told her stories about the swamps in Louisiana, how they can suck you up like the river sucks up those pinecones, but she didn't say anything. I asked Mama how come sometimes Annie doesn't say anything when you talk to her, and Mama said she's a sentrick, but I don't know what that is. I even looked in the dictionary but it wasn't there, so I think she just made it up."

Stifling another smile, Silence said, "She didn't. But the word is '*ec*-centric' – with an *e* and a *c*." He knew that he was treading thin ice: her own ignorance enraged Happy, as did anything that reminded her of it. Gingerly, he ventured: "Do you want to look it up, or should I tell you?"

"You tell me," she said after a moment's pretended consideration.

"Right. 'Eccentric' means not quite like everyone else. A bit different, but not so different that you're crazy."

"Oh," said Happy. "All the girls are scared of Annie, and all the boys say they're not, but they are. I'm not scared, though. Even if she's a – I mean, ec-cen-tric – she isn't a witch, like they say."

"Is that what they say?" asked Silence, wondering what they said about him. Eccentric, he suspected, no longer even began to cover it.

"Yes. But she isn't a witch. She's got gold light."

"Gold," he repeated. It wasn't what he would have guessed, but when he thought about it, he had no idea what he would have guessed.

"It's a good light. But they don't believe me. One day I came here, and Annie was here already, and she was bleeding from her head and crying. But she stopped when she saw me and said she was okay. Well I told her she wasn't okay, she was bleeding. So I took her home and she was real brave – lots braver than me. She didn't cry anymore after I told her it was okay, not even when I put iodine on it and a plaster."

"Did she say how she got cut?" Silence asked, with the leaden certainty that he didn't want to know.

"No," said Happy, unperturbed. "Just that she was running, and she tripped and fell."

From what? he wanted to ask. Silence had never known Annie to run, and he couldn't imagine her falling.

"She's all right," Happy concluded.

Silence forced a smile. "That was nice of you, to take care of her like that."

Happy nodded, then reached behind her into the cave and brought out two handfuls of wild plums. She set one down beside Silence and began eating her own, spitting the pits into the river.

"Guess what else," she said after a while. "Jamie Reiss says Annie used to be a colored lady when she was young." Silence nearly choked on a plum. "I don't know if it's true, though," she continued. "You can't tell something like that from someone's light, and when I asked, Annie didn't answer."

"You didn't," Silence groaned.

"Yes, I did," insisted Happy. "I asked her, but she answered something different. Have you ever noticed how when you ask Annie a question, she usually answers a different one?"

He laughed. "Actually, yes."

"Sometimes when she comes here, I'm not in the mood, and I tell her to go away."

"Happy!"

"Sometimes she brings me berries, or crowns made out of flowers."

"Oh, Happy. Please tell me you say thank you!"

Happy shrugged, and Silence, suddenly anxious, made himself ask: "So she's never told you about Juniper Barrens?"

"Juniper *what*?"

Silence sighed.

7

Not long after his interview with Happy, Silence's sea-dreams changed again. He was still on a grey beach beneath a cloud-ridden sky, but it wasn't the beach of the bleached bones and red rags. This one was long and straight and rocky, its bordering sea black and still, the sky low and brooding. More than that, for the first time in all of his sea dreams, he wasn't alone. A girl knelt at the water's edge on a hard circle of sand within a bony arm of rock. She wore a torn and sodden dress that must once have been white, and her long, pale hair hung in clumps down her back, as if she'd recently come out of that dead ocean. Her face was beautiful and bleak, her feet and her lips purple, but none of this was as disturbing as the despair that radiated from her like a storm cloud.

Silence wanted to comfort her, but when he spoke to her, she didn't answer or even seem to realize that he was there. After a moment she got unsteadily to her feet and began to walk away from the sea, toward a black tract of woods lining the beach. Silence knew that there was danger in those woods, but though he ran until his lungs burned and his heart screamed, he could not reach or stop her.

*

When he'd dreamed the dream relentlessly for a week, Silence decided that it was time to speak to Annie. It wasn't as easy a feat, though, as it had once been. Annie never came to Heaven Homestead anymore. There had been no point after Esther died and the cow went dry and the laying hens feral. Still, Silence couldn't help wondering if there were more to it than that; if Annie, regardless of her own oddities, could no more bear to look at him than anyone else could. He hadn't dared to find out.

Now, though, the dream-girl's despair gave him courage. Annie might slam the door in his monstrous face. On the other hand, she might not, and if not she might be able to explain the girl, who in the course of that week had become a haunting at least as potent as the sea had been.

Annie was sitting on the front step of her cabin when Silence arrived, beneath a clatter of birches already surrendering their leaves. It had rained the night before, staining the birch bark rose and violet. Drops of water still shivered in the yellow foliage. Annie had her eyes closed, her face to the sun. The years since she had told Silence about Juniper Barrens had been heavy on her – there was more white in her hair, more lines on her face – but in that light, in her calm, she looked not aged, but ageless.

Ready for any excuse, Silence turned to go. But Annie opened her eyes then. They were level on him, unsurprised. "I've been waiting for you," she said.

Silence took a few steps forward. "Since when?"

She only shrugged and shifted to make room for Silence on the doorstep. After a moment he sat down beside her.

"I'm sorry," Annie said, "about your mother. She had a rare heart."

"She did," Silence agreed, and it didn't seem strange to him that Annie would offer this condolence when his mother had been dead so long, or that she would say nothing about his father.

"And for what happened to you." She paused, looking at him carefully. "You've borne it well." Silence gave a small bitter laugh. Annie shrugged again and said, "Why are you here, Silence Ogden?"

With a smile more genuine than the laugh, he said, "You know that my father and I were building a boat before he died."

"I had heard that," she agreed.

Silence gave her a hard look. She looked back, unflinching. He reached into his pocket and took out the old piece of newspaper, worn now almost to air. "This is my boat."

He handed it to her. Annie looked at the paper for a long time, her hand quivering almost imperceptibly. "Surely," she said at last, "you've had this for years."

"I have," said Silence.

"Then why do you bring it to me now?"

"Because I've started dreaming again."

Annie nodded, waited, her blue eyes still resting on his face. As Silence began to speak, though, her own face took on a peculiar look – as if she were tasting something she didn't much like but knew she had to swallow. When he'd finished, she sat for a very long time saying nothing at all. Finally, she sighed and said, "That is a very bad dream."

Silence knew that already, but hearing her say so made him despondent in a way he hadn't anticipated. "Who is the girl?" he asked.

Again, Annie sighed. She shook her head, but not, he thought, in negation. So he pressed: "She's the baby Sweet Angelina was carrying at the end of your story about Juniper Barrens. Ian MacFarlane's baby."

To his surprise, Annie said, "No. That baby was a boy." After a long pause: "They named him Hunter." And she continued in that same way, full of halts and staggers, telling him about the sourceless despair that took Sweet Angelina after her son's birth. How the light went out of everything. How she loved her child, and at the same time couldn't bear him. How the guilt of it ground her down until it killed her.

"Killed her?" Silence repeated. He couldn't hide his shock. He had thought that he understood.

"That's what I said," she answered curtly.

"But – "

"No buts. It's my story, and I'm telling you that Sweet Angelina died on the night she left her husband and son. She sailed her boat into a storm, and the sea took her."

"I...don't understand," Silence said at last.

"I don't suppose you do."

"So the girl in my dream...is she Sweet Angelina's ghost?" Somehow, he couldn't believe that. In his mind, Sweet Angelina, had always been dark.

"No," Annie confirmed.

"Then who is she?"

"She's her daughter."

Silence looked at Annie, wondering if she'd gone mad. But her eyes were earnest, lucid.

"You just said that her child was a boy."

"He was."

"And that Sweet Angelina died."

"She did."

"So...she had another child first?"

"No."

"That makes no sense!" Silence cried.

"Not much," Annie agreed. "And yet it's the truth. I'm sorry, Silence Ogden, but that's the best I can do." She stood up then, went inside and shut the door. The last Silence heard from her that day was the sound of the wooden bar falling into place.

9

That night Silence finally admitted to Celia the reason for the purple shadows under his eyes – and with it the whole long, tangled history of his sea dreams. Rather than the skepticism he had feared, she offered him a theory that no one else had:

"Maybe," she said, "they aren't your dreams at all."

"What?" Silence asked, less because he'd misunderstood than that he couldn't believe that anyone – but particularly someone as pragmatic as Celia – would speak such a thought out loud.

"Have you ever considered that these sea dreams might be someone else's? That you've got them because someone's misplaced them – even abandoned them?"

He gave her a long look to see whether she was teasing him, but her dark eyes were deadly serious. "No," he answered at last, "that's something I've never considered." He paused. "Do *you* think that's what they are? Because honestly, that sounds a whole lot more like something Pascal would say, than something you would."

Celia looked out over the paltry wheat field which, such as it was, was nearly ready to harvest. She drew on her cigarette – she smoked when she couldn't sleep, and lately she'd been as sleepless as Silence – and then handed it to him.

"Well," she said at last, pulling her shawl close against the early autumn chill, "I can't say I've ever borrowed any dreams myself. But I sure have lost some."

"Lost some?" he asked, stubbing out the cigarette. He no longer coughed when he smoked, but despite Celia's coaching, he didn't much enjoy it.

She nodded. "All of them, in fact. I haven't dreamed since the night Happy was born."

"Not at all?"

She shook her head.

"And you think…what? Someone stole your dreams?"

She smiled. "Now that would just be crazy, wouldn't it? No, I think they got pushed out along with Happy, and the earth soaked them up."

Silence had no idea how to answer that, so he didn't. After a moment, she continued, "Happy was born in a dirt-floor shack in Georgia that belonged to an old witch of a midwife. It wasn't much to talk about, but if it hadn't been for that woman and her shack, we'd both have died. I thought the birth water had been something," she continued without pause, or bothering to see if Silence understood, "until I saw the blood. There was more of it than I thought any one body could hold, never mind lose and go on living. Once Happy was out, the midwife made me drink something. It brought the pains back worse than ever, but it stopped the blood.

"Or I guess it did. The midwife said it wasn't the medicine but the moon that saved me. It was a crescent moon. It caught the blood like a cup, she said. If it had been new or full the blood would have kept coming until there was nothing left."

"Is that true?" Silence asked, appalled.

Celia shrugged. "We both lived, didn't we? Either way, that's how Happy got her name. 'The crescent moon is the happy moon,' that midwife told me, 'and that's what you've got to name your child. To honor the moon, to keep the child safe.' I agreed, God only knows why…it must have been the blood loss. I couldn't have been thinking straight, to give the poor child a name like Happy Moon!" She shook her head. "Anyhow, I never dreamed after that night. I think the dreams slipped out with my blood and the earth hoarded them away."

"That's no kind of logic, Celia," Silence argued, disturbed to find her slipping further into Pascal's territory. "Why would you even think a thing like that?"

"Because sometimes," she said, looking sidelong at Silence, "I find pieces of them when I dig."

Mad as it sounded, Silence believed her. The vulnerable bravery of her voice proved her words. "Here?" he asked. "On this farm?"

Celia nodded, lighting another cigarette. "Here…anywhere. It's like the bits of old glass and china you sometimes find in a plough furrow: I know they're pieces of my dreams, but they're too small to work out the whole they belonged to. So you see, Silence," she concluded, "I'm tied to the earth by my dreams, and I guess I will be until the earth decides to give them back. As for you…well, if I had to guess, I'd say that your sea dreams are leading you to whoever has lost them. But as for who that might be – " she shrugged, blew smoke at the indigo sky " – heaven only knows."

Tabula Rasa

1

Meredith descended from Gradlon's mountain onto a snowy plain dotted with homesteads, their smoke violet against the searing white, the white crisscrossed by somnolent stone walls. The towns she passed each clustered around a stream and its ubiquitous lumber mill. They all boasted a church, a handful of carriage sheds, two facing rows of houses and, increasingly, a railroad station.

She saw in the new year from a clutch of woods on a hill above such a town, chewing on venison jerky and the last of Gradlon's dark bread as the people below built a bonfire and danced around it until the church bells tolled the turning year. Meredith had shadowy memories of such festivities. She wondered, without emotion, if she would ever again feel the urge to join them.

*

Not long after New Year, the scenery began to change. There were still snow-covered hills, but rather than farms and mill towns, they were populated by stark little hill villages of modest frame houses, mostly painted red. Despite the bright paint, they had a ramshackle look to them, as if they had been constructed quickly and with no expectation that they would last. They reminded Meredith of the logging camps she'd passed farther north, but though the hills around the towns had the torn, ravaged look of those stripped for lumber, there was no evidence of wood cutting. There were no log piles or sawn boards, and most tellingly there were no rivers to float them to market.

Instead, the towns were built around high, angular buildings that seemed extensions of their setting, all dark slopes and jagged peaks, and flanked by vast, black piles of what appeared to be earth. Their hidden orifices spewed clouds of dust that covered the villages in a fine grey haze, and even from a distance, Meredith could hear the roar of machinery from within them. Once she rode close enough to one of these buildings to see the train tracks that ran beneath it. A locomotive sat steaming moodily farther down the track; behind it trailed a row of lidless cars. As she watched, a load of glistening black rock was released from the bowels of the dusty factory above, filling the waiting car. Then the train inched forward so that another empty car stood beneath the building, and the process was repeated.

Meredith didn't make sense of it until the night she made camp at the edge of one of these towns, and found a little pile of the dark stones in the snow at the side of the path. She picked one up. It was shiny and hard. As she turned it over in her hand, staining her fingers black, the word came: *coal*. She knew at the same time that it was meant to be burned, but though she waited for a memory to follow the recovered knowledge, nothing came. Even the coal's resinous smoke, when she threw it on her fire, stirred nothing but mild repugnanelt,It only confirmed her suspicion that a fire should be made of wood, not rock.

Tomorrow, she told the horse as she lay down, *we will leave this country*, and she tried to take heart from the fact that the horse didn't disagree. Another day of riding, however, brought no change to the farmless landscape. She even stopped a dust-blackened man on the road outside of one of the villages and presented him with her slate, on which she had written, "Which way out of coal country?"

He only shrugged, and answered her in a chopped, vowel-filled accent that ely strangely familiar, "Sorry, Miss – I dinnae ken me letters."

Meredith nodded to him, though she felt suddenly exhausted, and unjustly angry at his ignorance. Another day passed with little change. On the morning of the third, Meredith began to wonder whether they should change direction. But when she pulled at the horse's reins to turn her head, the horse jerked them back and plodded stubbornly onward. A while later Meredith tried again to turn her, this time using her legs. The horse's ears went back, and she kicked out with her back legs.

You are a stubborn tyrant, Meredith said to her, reclaiming her seat.

The horse said nothing, but feeling that Meredith had relented, she relaxed and picked up her pace again. They had not gone far when Meredith saw something on the path ahead. At first she thought that it was a bundle of old clothes or blankets that somebody had dropped, but as she came closer she saw a pale splash within it: a face, still and white and lifeless as the snow on which it rested.

The horse stopped, and Meredith slid down, knelt by the prostrate form. The face belonged to a girl who looked to be barely into her teens. She was wrapped in threadbare clothing in muddy shades of blue and black. At first Meredith thought that she must be a beggar who had succumbed to the cold. Yet there was nowhere out here for her to have come from other than one of the coal villages, and surely, she thought, they were too small and isolated to support beggars. Somebody, somewhere must be missing her.

Sighing, Meredith put her arms under the girl's head and legs, and lifted. It was easier than she'd imagined: the girl's bulky form was mostly clothes. No wonder she had frozen to death, Meredith thought, with so little flesh to protect her. She slung the body over the horse's withers, preparing to ride back to the last village she'd passed and leave the girl there.

As she mounted the horse, though, the girl opened her eyes. They were wide and green and blank, and they so shocked Meredith that she nearly let the girl slide to the ground. Catching hold of her, their eyes met for a moment. Then the girl's, having taken in Meredith's face, rolled back again into her head.

Sighing, Meredith gathered the reins with one hand and the girl with the other, and turned back the way she'd come. It seemed they traveled hours before the coal tower finally showed over a rise, but when it did Meredith realized that she had no plan. She had meant to leave the body by the nearest house and flee; now she would have to make sure the girl was delivered into somebody's care, and this meant explaining how she had found her. She rode slowly up the town's single street. The houses all seemed lifeless, despite their smoking stovepipes; she had no idea which one to choose. Then, at the end of the row near the coal yard, Meredith came to a large building with a sign reading, "Store". She tethered the horse, shouldered the still-unconscious girl and brought her insiA sharp-faced woman stood behind the counter in a well-cut calico dress and steel-rimmed spectacles. She was weighing flour for another woman in patched homespun, with a shawl wrapped over her head and shoulders. Both turned when Meredith entered. The woman in the shawl took a look at the girl Meredith was carrying, uttered a cry and then ran out the door, calling something unintelligible to the woman behind the counter.

"Finally dead, is she?" the shop woman commented, looking over her spectacles at the girl's face with far more interest than sympathy.

Anger flared in Meredith's chest. She shook her head and brought the unconscious girl to the stove glowing in the corner. The calicoed shopkeeper followed her, admonishing, "You can't leave her here! She ain't *my* responsibility! Ain't *my* fault if those Russians can't look after their brats!"

Meredith ignored her, pulling off the girl's wet outer garments, exposing a drab cotton dress, much worn and mended but spotlessly clean. She also pulled off her boots – a good size too small – and began to rub her feet.

"You can't – " the shopkeeper began again, but she was interrupted by the crash as the door flew open, admitting another woman dressed like the first, though her shawl had slipped back onto her shoulders and she breathed hard, as if she had been running. She had large, dark-fringed green eyes, and smooth, dark hair braided and coiled neatly around her head. She wore a white, wide-sleeved blouse, a full back skirt, and a faded red sash. She was perhaps thirty and ought to have been pretty, but there was no light in her face or eyes, and their expression seemed far too careworn for her years. She walked to the place where the girl lay and then stood looking down at her, shaking all over. Meredith thought that it was shock or fear, and she stepped toward the woman with a hand outstretched to reassure her. But when she saw the woman's face, she realized that the emotion that had seized her was rage.

"You get your brat out of here!" the shopkeeper said to the woman.

The woman ignored her and slapped the girl across both cheeks. The girl opened her eyes, and the woman knelt, pushing her to a sitting position as she spoke to her in a long string of foreign words. The girl looked for a moment at the woman's face, and then she burst into tears.

"Out!" cried the shopkeeper. "This ain't a hospital or an orphanage – all of you, go home!"

Despite the shopkeeper's rudeness, the dark-haired woman bowed to her and said in careful, heavily-accented English, "I thank you, Mrs. Gaverly, for your kindness. We trouble you no further."

"Haverly!" the shopkeeper growled. "It's *Ha*verly! No wonder your daughter is an imbecile!"

The woman only smiled coldly at her. Then she turned to Meredith. "You have brought my daughter, yes?" she asked.

Meredith nodded.

"Then please, come with me. In my house, you tell me what happened."

Meredith tried to gesture to the woman that she couldn't speak, but the woman had already lifted the girl to her feet and begun guiding her toward the door. Meredith had to rush to catch up with her, untying the horse quickly and dragging her after the woman and her daughter.

The woman stopped by one of the red houses, opened one of the doors – there were two, side by side – and went in. Meredith wanted nothing but to get on her horse and leave the grim place behind, but she felt she should try to explain to the woman what had happened, if only to spare the girl her wrath. She tied the horse to a spindly tree beside the house and followed the woman inside.

The dwelling consisted of a single room with a narrow open stairway leading to a second storey. Meredith assumed that the other half of the house belonged to someone else. The room was dominated by a step stove with a cast-iron kettle on top. Against one wall were a cluttered deal table and bench. The only other piece of furniture was a rough-hewn rocking chair with a quilt hung over the back. The woman pulled the chair close to the stove, seated the girl on it. The girl didn't protest or comment, just stared at the stove's vent, which was open on the glowing embers.

The woman bent to add wood to the stove. In the sudden light from its open door, Meredith saw what had been hidden in the gloom: the entire wall above the table was covered in paintings. They seemed to have been made on blocks of wood, none bigger than a man's hand, but brilliant as a rainbow against the dim light and dark wood. The clutter on the table consisted of more paintings, as well as brushes, jars of pigment, and various other materials she couldn't name.

"Go – look at them," the woman said behind her.

Meredith turned, her eyes apologetic, but the woman only gestured toward the paintings in exasperation. "Go on," she said. "Is what they all come for."

Having delivered this cryptic bit of information, the woman lit a lamp and handed it to Meredith, then took the kettle from the stove and went outside, presumably to fill it. Meredith put the lamp amidst the painting supplies on the table and leaned toward the pictures. They were detailed and lifelike, but there was also an exuberant naïveté to them that convinced her they had not been made by the bitter woman.

Each one focused on a central figure, with smaller details around it, apparently placing it in a context. One showed a young man riding a horse, looking down at a bird's feather on the ground, the color of flaming autumn leaves. Another one showed the same young man seated on a brilliant carpet spread with a feast, in front of a gold pavilion. In the next the man stood on the shore of a lapis sea surrounded by lobsters, which seemed to be listening to something he was saying. Meredith looked away from the lobsters with a shudder to find herself staring at her own face, painted on a girl standing on a rock by that same deep-blue sea. She held a white dress toward the reaching waves. Meredith turned away in blind panic, and found the dark-haired woman at her shoulder again, her face fixed in a joyless smile.

"Yes," the woman said with resignation. "We all show up in Vasilisa's pictures, sooner or later."

Meredith wondered how the woman could so calmly disregard the fact that the girl – if Vasilisa was the girl she spoke of – had never seen her before she rescued her from the freezing woods. But the woman only gazed at her unapologetically, proffering a steaming mug, and in the end Meredith saw no option but to take it. The woman nodded then, picked up a mug of her own from the table and sat down on the bench. Meredith sat beside her.

"*Za vashe zdorovye,*" she said to Meredith with a bitter smile and then drank deeply from her cup. Meredith sipped her own. The tea was sweet and fruity, and the surprise must have shown on her face because the woman's smile thawed a bit.

"Jam in place of sugar," she said. "Is how we make tea at home."

Meredith wondered where "home" was and why, if this sad house wasn't it, the woman and child lived here.

"I am Lyuba Petrovna Kaminskaya," the woman continued. "I not know how to thank you for bringing Vasilisa back to me."

They were the words Meredith had expected to hear, yet the ambivalence with which Lyuba spoke them made her question what she had taken for granted: that she had done Lyuba a kindness by returning her daughter to her. She wanted nothing so much then as to be away from that strange, cold house, but Lyuba was speaking again.

"Forgive me," she said, "but I forget your name."

Meredith put the cup on the table among the dishes of paint, took her slate from her pocket and wrote: "I have not told you. I cannot speak. My name is Meredith." She handed it to Lyuba with little hope that she would understand the message. But Lyuba took the slate and looked at it for a long time, following the words with her finger. Then she nodded and handed it back to Meredith.

"Vasilisa also cannot speak," she said. "We manage." Lyuba saw Meredith's surprise, and guessed the reason. "Mrs. Owens, on other side of house, is Welsh. She teach me to read and to write. I am still very slow."

Meredith shook her head. Lyuba lowered her eyes in embarrassment, but she also smiled. It was a true smile, transforming her face like a cloud break on a snowfield.

"I thank you. I am no scholar, but now, thanks to Mrs. Owens, I can at least see when Gaverly try to cheat me. If only the same was true when Petya – " She cut herself off abruptly, hands over her mouth.

At first Meredith didn't understand. Then she heard a strange sound, a low whine that grew in pitch and volume until it was the screech of a trapped animal. It came from Vasilisa. Meredith sat stunned by the terrible cry, but Lyuba didn't seem surprised. She stood up, took the girl by the shoulders and shook her, shouting more foreign words at her. Vasilisa roared back at her, flung her tea mug at the stove where it shattered, the spilled tea sizzling away with the smell of burning sugar. She lunged at her mother, but her mother pushed her back, slapped her across the face. The girl collapsed back into the chair, silent and trembling.

Lyuba watched her for a moment, apparently to make certain that she meant to stay there. Then she returned to the table, sighed, and said, "I am sorry. I should know better by now than to speak her father's name in front of her. It always make her…" She trailed off, gesturing for the lost word that Meredith couldn't supply. They both sat silently for a moment, watching Vasilisa watch the fire. Then Lyuba asked quietly, "Where do you find her?"

Meredith wiped the slate and wrote, "On the road some miles from here."

Lyuba nodded, as if this was what she'd expected to hear.

"What was she doing out there, by herself?" Meredith wrote.

"Looking for him," Lyuba answered, sighing.

Meredith let the non-answer dangle. She knew that Lyuba wanted her to ask about Vasilisa's absent father, but she was uncomfortable with the other woman already, and wary of the binding power of confidence. Instead, she wrote, "Why is she mute?"

Lyuba looked at the words for so long that Meredith thought she had not understood them. But at last she answered, "I do not know. She hears, but she does not look when someone speaks to her. She does not smile when someone is kind, or cry when he is cruel. It is as if we are not real to her." Lyuba gestured between herself and Meredith. Then she paused again, studying her daughter.

"Sometimes, also, she fits," she said at last in a low voice, as if she didn't really want Meredith to hear her.

But Meredith didn't understand. She raised her eyebrows, shook her head.

"She shakes or lies stiff," Lyuba explained, "and cannot be woken. At home, old women would say such person is possessed by demon. Sometimes I wonder, is it true?" Without giving Meredith the chance to respond, she continued, "Once, special doctor came here. Not company doctor. He came to listen to men's chests. To dust in the lungs, from the mines. He call himself...ah, what is the word? Form? A former?"

"Reformer," Meredith wrote.

"Yes! Reformer. I asked him would he examine Vasilisa when he finish with the lungs. I did not expect him to say yes." Another pause. It occurred to Meredith that Lyuba might be translating the words in her head, testing their accuracy before speaking them. It tired her even to think about it.

"'Schizophrenic introversion,'" Lyuba said slowly, carefully. "That is what doctor called it. He said she was not idiot. That she understands, but that she will never speak. She lives in her head, not in world. He said also that he was sorry, and I believe that he truly was. He said if we took her to New York...but of course, that was not possible. And the fits..." She shrugged. "He did not know. In time, he said, they might improve."

Meredith waited.

"They have not improved," Lyuba added grimly. "Since her father died, she has begun to scream also. You heard. When I hear, I think doctor was wrong, and there is no understanding in her. But then she make these." She nodded to the paintings. "And still sometimes I wonder, would be better if she did not? If she made nothing and knew nothing?"

Lyuba met Meredith's quick upward glance without flinching, her eyes daring the younger woman to judge. "You think it is gift." She gestured offhandedly to the paintings. "They all think.

They bring her paints to make more. They do not understand that it is not gift but curse. It goes against God. Do you know what is *ikon*?"

Meredith shook her head.

"Is religious painting. Portraits of saints, or stories from scripture. They look like these." She nodded to Vasilisa's paintings. "But Vasilisa does not paint God's word. Not *ikons* – something against God."

"I don't understand," Meredith wrote.

Lyuba sighed, her hands moving as if to pull the right words from the air. "These pictures, they are from the tales of our home…the stories grandmothers tell to children. Stories about magic and people who never were."

Meredith wrote, "Fairy tales."

Lyuba nodded. "Yes – but one tale only. Once, she paint other things. Even, sometimes, holy things. But since Pet– since my husband died," she caught herself, leaning toward Meredith so that she could speak softly, "is always the same story. Is the story he told her the night before accident. All these," she rounded the paintings up with a pointing finger, "are from tale of *Vasilisa Prekrasnaya* – Vasilisa the Beautiful. Perhaps she believes that painting it will bring him back…"

This time Meredith gave in to curiosity: "What happened to your husband?"

Lyuba shrugged, her mouth bitter. "What always happen here: greed wins." They both turned as Vasilisa suddenly stood up, reached for her mother's shawl and tied it around her neck like a cloak. "Mine gas meets flame," Lyuba continued, "or coal pile slumps. Tired man robs a pillar one time too many and tunnel collapses. Sometimes I think if there was gravestone to show her…"

Lyuba was quiet for a moment. "Petya was farmer at home," she resumed as Vasilisa swirled the shawl like a ball gown. "But times have changed in Russia, same as here. We are tenants only. The owner take land back to build houses, paid us off with tickets to New York. It is generous – many farmers not paid at all. But what is potato farmer to do in New York?"

There was a long silence, and then Lyuba began again in her low, bitter voice: "Petya saw opportunity, but I saw death climb up on his shoulder when he took tickets. And when we arrive in this village, when I see how many women wear black…in my heart I begin to mourn him then.

"You think I am hard woman and bad mother," she said, looking abruptly at Meredith. "I was not always. But life here is only long wait for steam whistle saying 'disaster'…for the Black Maria that stops at all of our doorstep, one day." She shrugged, her grief both obvious and matter-of-fact. "Or not, because there are no bodies to bring. They are buried already. A widow is made with no grave to tend, no work to keep family, nothing but debt to company. And that will turn softest heart to stone."

Meredith allowed the silence to stretch and settle before she wrote, "I am sorry for your losses. I will leave you in peace."

She stood up, handed the slate to Lyuba. Lyuba read the words carefully, and then she looked up at Meredith with eyes widened by panic. "No! Please, you must stay – let me cook for you. It is least I can do."

Meredith didn't know how she would bear more of Lyuba's bitterness. But she saw Vasilisa peering at her from behind the rocker's woven cane back. Despite what Lyuba had told her, Meredith could not help thinking that she saw a glimmer of interest in her eyes. Sighing, she sat back down.

"Good," said Lyuba, and turned to rummage in the single, pitiful cupboard that served as a pantry. Meredith watched her for a moment, and then she opened her pack, unloaded her provisions onto the bench. Lyuba turned to see what she was doing, and her eyes widened. Meredith read the look, its bitter core of privation and hunger, before Lyuba could hide it. When the woman collected herself and began to protest, Meredith shook her head stubbornly, gathered the food and dumped it on the tiny kitchen worktop.

Lyuba looked at her for a long moment, and then she lowered her eyes, nodded and said, "*Da blagoslovit vas Bog.*[4]"She picked out a piece of dried venison, an onion and a few wrinkled potatoes, holding them for a moment with a look of abstracted wonder. Then she shook her head, put them on a chopping board and was instantly absorbed in her cooking.

Meredith watched Lyuba for a moment, and then she turned to Vasilisa. The girl had moved to the table and turned up the lamp. She leaned over the painting of the woman on the seashore. Meredith crossed the room to stand behind her. Vasilisa looked up, and Meredith smiled at her. Then Vasilisa sat down on the bench, pushed the unfinished painting aside, and picked up a blank piece of wood the size of a church hymnal. She stared hard at it for a moment, and then she took up a brush and began to paint.

The picture beneath the girl's hand rapidly took on the proportions of a ship. She painted with quick assurance, never pausing to consider her choice of color or to squint at a proportion. Meredith watched with horrified attention as Vasilisa completed the ship and began on the figure standing in it: a woman's figure. But when Vasilisa began to paint the woman's hair in yellow ochre, Meredith turned away abruptly.

---

4 God bless you.

Lyuba was just setting the pot on the stove to stew. Meredith handed her the slate with the question: "What happens in this story your daughter is painting?"

Lyuba raised her eyebrows but made no comment as she walked toward the wall of *ikons*. She pointed to the young man on the horse. "It begins with young archer on wise horse. This feather, by horse's hoof, belongs to Firebird. The horse warns archer not to take feather, because it bring bad luck. But archer does not listen. He takes it and gives to king."

Lyuba pointed to another picture, which showed the young man presenting the feather to an older man seated on a throne. "King is delighted, but he is greedy. The feather is so beautiful that he desires whole bird. He says archer must bring him Firebird, or else lose his head." She made a chopping motion with one hand, into the palm of the other. "Is like the company," she said grimly, "always wanting riches at expense of someone else..."

She frowned, sighed, and indicated another painting showing a brilliant red bird with a peacock's plumage, one wing caught beneath the horse's hoof. "Here, wise horse helps foolish archer to catch Firebird, and archer brings Firebird to king. But king is still greedy. He think, 'If this archer is so cunning to catch Firebird, surely he can capture Vasilisa the Beautiful, who lives in land where sun rises.' And so he sends foolish archer out again, on pain of death."

Lyuba pointed to the unfinished painting of the girl with Meredith's face. "Archer comes to his horse in despair, but horse saves him once again. He says, 'Ask king for golden tent, and food, and drink.' King gives them, and archer sets off. When they come to land where sun rises, there he find a wide sea, and upon the sea is beautiful girl in silver boat with golden oar: Vasilisa the Beautiful.

"Archer make tent and lay out king's feast, and Vasilisa come to eat. After, she fall asleep from drinking too-strong wine. Then archer carries her to the king, and so it goes," Lyuba waved her hand at the rest of the paintings, rolling her eyes heavenward.

"Pretty princess does not wish to marry ugly old king; she sets him task and more tasks to postpone wedding. He must find her wedding dress hidden at bottom of sea; he must bathe in boiling water; and so on. King makes archer perform tasks in his stead, and wise horse saves him every time. And of course, all ends well for archer, despite foolishness. Horse outsmarts king into boiling bath, and archer is made king in his stead. He marry Vasilisa the Beautiful, and they live happily ever after."

She paused, then said ironically, "Though I think Vasilisa would do better to marry horse." Lyuba looked into space for a moment, and then she shook herself, smiled at Meredith without joy. "So that is story of Vasilisa the Beautiful. You can see my Vasilisa has been exact in her paintings."

She looked over her daughter's shoulder then, at the painting beneath her hand. Meredith looked too. On the painted plank she saw her own face, as she'd known she would. The painted woman smiled as she stood on the deck of a sailboat, her arms outstretched as if toward an unseen beloved. Meredith's mouth dried, and her eyes prickled with tears. There was a rushing sound in her head like the sea filling a cave.

"What is this?" she heard Lyuba ask, as if from far away. "The princess had rowboat, not sailboat."

Vasilisa ignored her mother, looked up at Meredith. And, with her back to her mother, she smiled.

3

The meat, being dry, took hours to stew. Meredith, too unnerved to stay in the cramped room, spent the time chopping wood for the stove – Lyuba refused to burn coal. As she worked, she tried to devise a way to refuse the woman's invitation to spend the night. When the daylight failed, though, she was no closer to her goal.

She brought the horse into a little shed behind the house, gave her grain and a pail of water and then watched her for any signs of unease. The horse just snuffled on the floor for more grain and then, finding none, dropped into a doze with her eyes half-lidded and one back hoof tipped up. Sighing, Meredith left her there.

Back in the house, Lyuba had moved Vasilisa's painting materials to one side, clearing a space at the table for the three of them to sit. She set out bowls of stew and a loaf of dark bread, three battered spoons and three mugs of tea. Vasilisa still sat on the bench, staring at the table in front of her. Her hands, bereft of work, hung listlessly by her sides. When she heard Meredith come in, though, she looked up. Slowly, she raised a hand to her, palm upward – an unmistakable invitation. Meredith smiled and took the place beside the girl, only then noticing the intense look Lyuba had fixed on her.

"I am sorry," Lyuba said, looking quickly away. "I have not seen her do this before – to invite someone."

Meredith looked at Vasilisa, thinking of her earlier covert smile. The girl was already eating, apparently oblivious to her mother's words.

"I think you have charmed her," Lyuba said, sitting down at the head of the table.

It was a compliment, but it sounded like a condemnation. To hide her discomfort, Meredith began to eat. The food was good, and she tried to concentrate on it rather than on Lyuba's constrained silence. When they had finished, Lyuba began to clear the dishes, but Meredith put out a hand to stop her, took them from her. Lyuba raised her eyebrows. There were dark half-moons beneath her eyes.

"Thank you," she said simply. Then, as Meredith took the dishes to the basin and poured water from the kettle, Lyuba climbed the stairs. The thin boards bowed beneath her steps. After a few minutes, she came down with another quilt and a pillow. She put them on the chair by the fire.

"There is barely room in the bed for two," she said.

Grateful for this, Meredith nodded.

"We go to bed now," she said. "It is long day for us…"

Meredith nodded again.

"I thank you for bringing her back," Lyuba said. This time, there was a shade of sincerity in her tone.

The silence eased a little when Vasilisa and Lyuba had gone, but the room seemed to grow ever colder, despite the roaring stove. Therefore Meredith was shocked when she opened the door to throw the wash-water out. The air that came through the open door felt soft on her skin: balmy compared with the ghost-ridden atmosphere inside the cottage.

Meredith knew that she would never sleep in that sad little room. It was a clear night, the moon near full. Drawing a breath of the clean air, she went back inside. She took more food from her pack and put it in the store cupboard. Then she pulled on her boots and coat and hat, shouldered the pack and turned to go.

Vasilisa stood at the foot of the stairs. Her eyes were wide, her face as white as her threadbare nightgown. She held her hands in front of her, clasped tightly around something. Slowly she walked toward Meredith. Inadvertently, Meredith backed toward the door. When she reached behind her for the latch, though, Vasilisa's hand shot out and closed over her wrist with surprising strength. Meredith had the sudden, panicked thought that the strange girl and her mother meant to keep her prisoner.

Then, Vasilisa pressed something into her hand. Meredith looked down, and saw herself looking back. It was the painting of Vasilisa the Beautiful in her boat. Meredith barely glanced at it before handing it back. But Vasilisa clenched her fists and shook her head. Meredith sighed, and looked down at the painting again. Now she saw what she hadn't at first: the woman in the boat wore a long blue cloak, figured with pearls and colorful embroidery. On her head was a golden crown, shining against the rainbow sky of a summer sunset.

Vasilisa opened her mouth. It took her several tries to form the words, but at last she got them out, two painstaking syllables: "For you."

Meredith gazed at her, disbelieving. Once again the girl opened her mouth, and drew breath, and repeated: "For you," and then, her face contorting with the effort, "Princess."

Meredith's eyes filled and burned. She put the painting in the pocket of her coat. Then she unslung her pack, opened it up, and took out Gradlon's sea cloak. Vasilisa'a eyes widened, her mouth slackened with wonder. Gently, Meredith shook it out and put it around Vasilisa's shoulders. The girl's slight figure was swamped by it, the fabric pooling around her on the floor. But as she looked down at its lustrous blue folds, Vasilisa's pale little face bloomed into a smile.

Meredith smiled back at Vasilisa, but the girl's eyes were fixed on the intricate embroidery, her fingers stroking the pearls. And when Meredith rode past the door, she was standing there still.

4

Over the next few days, a mild wind softened the snow banks, and the afternoon sun felt almost warm, but Meredith could not shake the chill of Lyuba's bitter grief and loveless home. With every coal town she passed, it weighed more heavily, until at last she gave up her south-west path and turned east.

Within a couple of days, she had put the coal hills behind her. They gave way to lowlands where the snow didn't lie, and the ground was harrowed into iron-red fields or mulched with winter rye. The few people she came near enough to hear spoke with broad, flat accents and gave her no more than passing glances. It was a pleasant enough place to ride through, and the horse liked grazing the ryegrass, but Meredith couldn't shake the feeling that they were going in the wrong direction.

One evening she passed a great burial ground, its headstones circling some kind of monument: a figure on a stone pillar, with other figures at its base. The headstones were identical, rising like teeth from the dun colored grass. Meredith couldn't stomach graveyards since her night in the cannibals' clearing, so, although it was nearing dark, she kicked the horse into a gallop and didn't pull her up until the cemetery was miles at her back.

But as soon as she lay down to sleep that night, in a little stand of pines at the side of a wide field, she knew that she hadn't gone far enough. She heard the drums first: a strange, hollow sound like the echo of a distant parade. The figures too were insubstantial when they appeared, pale grey shapes with edges as tattered as the uniforms they wore. They materialized from the darkness at one side of the field, beating a furious march on their drums, their hands moving faster and faster as they approached the far side. For a moment they blazed against the dark, flaring like burning photographs for a moment before, one by one, the night re-captured them.

5

Meredith took it as a warning: when the horse turned her head south-west the next morning, she let her. By the end of that day they were back amidst rolling hills, with dark mountains on the horizon. Meredith was relieved and anxious at once. She knew that she was down to the last measure of Gradlon's grain, and her own food supplies were nearly gone.

There is a town not far from here, the horse said when they camped that night.

No more towns, Meredith answered.

We are hungry, said the horse.

We have no money to buy food.

When have we needed money?

Thinking of Lyuba's foolish archer, Meredith let the matter lie. Still, she was uneasy. She could feel the weather poised to change, and she tossed in her blanket until morning crept across a moody sky. A bitter wind blew through the valley where they camped, and she was glad of the horse's warmth beneath her when they started off. Once again she let the horse choose their path, which for a time ran straight uphill. The horse puffed doggedly onward, and Meredith kept her head down against the wind, resigning herself to a long, grim day of climbs and drops. But it wasn't yet noon when they crested a hill to find themselves looking down on a town sprawled in a river valley.

The buildings were mostly made of red brick. Railroad tracks radiated outward from its edges, and horseless trolleys plied its streets. Parallel to the river ran a wide canal, with flatboats tied up at its edges and a towpath on one side. Most of the boats were loaded with coal, though some seemed to hold other goods. A clutch of cylindrical chimneys marked a district of mills or factories. No smoke came from them, which puzzled Meredith until the bell in one of the church steeples began to ring. It was Sunday.

We can't go down there, Meredith said to the horse.

We are meant to, the horse answered.

How can you know that?

The horse didn't answer, only tugged at the reins. Sighing, Meredith gave her her head, and they descended toward the town. The closer she came, though, the more she balked. It was a long time since she'd been to a town of this size. It might be a Sunday, but there were plenty of people on the streets as the churches let out, and their hum and bustle made her head swim.

Perhaps sensing this, the horse turned off into a quieter side street lined with two-storey buildings, most of them with businesses at ground level and living quarters above. Turning a corner, they came into a narrow lane with cottages on one side, and on the other, some kind of factory. There was a burnt-grain smell in the air and the horse's nostril's widened, her ears flicking back and forth. As they passed the building Meredith saw a sign: "Queen City Brewing Co."

For a long while, they wandered the outskirts of the town. They passed other breweries and mills, a glass factory, iron and steel works, all with their gates shut tightly. The horse slowed to peer through each gate they passed.

What are you looking for? Meredith asked at one of them. The horse didn't answer, though she stepped out again eagerly. Meredith saw no explanation for it. They were on yet another nondescript street, lined by nondescript cottages with postage-stamp yards. The cottages were quiet, the yards empty, and no lights showed in the windows, though the afternoon was turning toward evening.

Abruptly the horse stopped and stood in the middle of the empty street with her ears swiveling. Up ahead the road ended at what seemed to be a factory wall. The horse fixed her attention on this and began to walk toward it. Then she stopped again, her ears cocked toward some sound beyond Meredith's hearing. Meredith sat as still as she could, listening. She thought she heard a faint strain of dance music coming from somewhere beyond the factory wall. But there was something else too, incrementally closer: a low moaning that might have been no more than the wind in the eaves of the houses, except for its persistence.

Meredith leaned forward, straining to hear better. The horse took a few steps and then stopped again. The sound was louder now. It had the unmistakable timbre of a human voice, a chilling note of despair. Meredith wanted no more to do with misery. She pulled on the rein to turn the horse, but the horse dug in her heels, and when Meredith slackened her hold the slightest bit she snatched the reins and began to trot back toward the factory wall. Meredith wondered if she intended to run straight into it, but the horse turned abruptly right into a narrow alley formed by the wall and the end house of the row.

Meredith could see little in the high-walled gloom. The horse's shoes on the cobbles sent echoes cascading from the high walls, drowning out both the music and the moaning. When a dark figure unfolded from the shadows at the alley's end, the horse broke again into a trot. Meredith yanked at the reins and the horse yanked back, nearly unseating her. Furious, Meredith jerked the reins again, but it was too late. The horse pulled up beside the moaning man.

He was a Negro man, the first Meredith had ever seen. He was short and heavy-set, though not quite fat. He wore a gaudy plaid suit, a bowler hat with a red felt flower, and shoes that looked a good two sizes too big. Strangest of all, though, was his face. His hands and neck were the color of a ripe hazelnut, but his face had been painted coal black except for two round patches around his eyes and a wide, ludicrous grin around his miserable mouth.

"Oh, thank God!" he said, reaching a hand toward her.

Meredith swung down off the horse's back and began rummaging in her pack for her slate.

"What are you doing?" asked the man, his eyes and voice panicked. "We have to go now, or else – "

Before he finished the sentence, a door in the wall behind him opened. A middle-aged woman stood in a frowsy cloud of light, music and raucous laughter leaking out around her huge body.

She, too, was a Negro, and dressed as strangely as the man, in a gaudy skirt, wide-necked white blouse and scarlet headscarf. Her face had been blackened like his, and her mouth was furious inside her false smile.

"What the hell you doin' out here with some white tramp in the middle of the show?" she hissed. "You get yourself back in here *now*! And you," she said, glancing at Meredith, "you pay at the front, or you get on your way. We ain't no charity show."

Another gust of laughter came from the building's smoky interior. The young man looked at her, his face stricken and his eyes desperate. They were amber, Meredith noticed now: almost golden against the black of his face. Tear-tracks traced muddy patterns from their corners into the paint on his cheeks. Without thinking, she put herself in front of the man and looked the woman squarely in the eye. The woman went rigid with fury.

"What the *hell* is this? A white *woman*? Have you clean lost your senses, Sox? You wanna get us all hanged?"

"It's not like that," the man, Sox, answered, stepping out from behind Meredith. "I never saw her before she came riding down this alley five minutes ago. Don't waste your breath," he continued, holding up a hand as the woman opened her mouth. "I'm coming." He turned to Meredith. "My apologies, ma'am," he said, nodding to her. "I don't know what I was thinking. You go on your way, and I'll go on mine."

He stepped toward the door. But Meredith couldn't forget that desolate cry. Seized once again by an inexplicable protective urge, she reached out and laid a hand on his arm. He looked at her. The sadness in his eyes was bottomless; once again, they brimmed with tears.

"Oh, Sweet Jesus!" the woman cried, flinging up her arms in exasperation. Then, to Meredith, "Come on in then, but you keep out of sight, and don't you make a peep. As for *that* – " she jutted her chin at the horse " – it stays outside."

Meredith tied the horse's reins to a drainpipe and followed Sox into a tiny room full of old crates, sectioned off from a larger one beyond by a black curtain. "Stay here," he said to her, then he wiped his eyes, further smudging the black paint, and followed the woman up a set of makeshift steps and through a gap in the curtain. His entrance was met with wild applause.

"Thank you," Meredith heard Sox say – or she assumed it was Sox. His voice had taken on a strange, high, laughing edge. "I thank you most kindly, kind ladies and gentlemen, for excusing me for a moment…"

"He one lazy nigger!" cried the woman who'd brought him back. Meredith heard the sound of a swat, and then another, and then uproarious laughter. "I think it time for a song. What you say?"

Noisy approval.

"This little ditty is one of my favorites," she said. "It's called 'Carry Me Back to Old Virginny'."

A banjo took up a melody, joined after a moment by a piano and some sort of percussion. The woman began to sing in a low voice of surprising sweetness. Meredith couldn't make out many of the words through the heavy dialect, but she took the opportunity of the covering noise to cross the anteroom and climb the steps. She sat down on the top one and peered out through the gap in the black curtain.

The steps led up to a platform serving as a makeshift stage. It had been set up in the main hall of the factory, which was apparently derelict. Light came in through high, barred windows. There wasn't much in the way of stage sets, only a semi-circle of chairs in front of a crudely painted backdrop of a plantation. Sox sat at the far end of the semi-circle, holding two pairs of curved sticks, one in each hand. Next to him was an empty chair, presumably belonging to the singing woman. The banjo player sat in the middle chair. He was somewhere between thirty and forty, dressed in a black tail suit and top hat. He wore no make-up, and his skin was so light that he could almost have passed for a white man. His smile had a hard, fixed quality.

There was another empty chair beside the banjo player, and Meredith guessed that it belonged to the girl at the piano. The girl looked roughly the same age as Sox. She was dressed in purple taffeta, high-hemmed and low-necked with absurdly puffed sleeves. She was light-skinned like the banjo player, tall and slender, with a face so beautiful it transcended the whore's dress. In the last chair was an older man, rail-thin, with a grizzled beard and a face blackened like Sox's. He played a tambourine. When the song was finished, the two women returned to their seats. The banjo player laid his instrument aside and addressed the older woman.

"Why, Bessie, that was just beautiful!"

The singer exaggerated embarrassment.

"No, truly: there is nothing I like better than a love song. I say, Bones, were you ever in love?"

Sox grinned and answered, "I wasn't nothin' else, old hoss."

Meredith was puzzled. Sox had spoken clearly enough in the alley, so the heavy dialect was a part of the show. Yet she couldn't understand why it should be, when the banjo player spoke properly.

"What kind of a girl was she?" the banjo player asked.

"She was highly polished," answered Sox – or Bones. "Yes, indeed. Her fadder was a varnish-maker, and, what's better still, she was devoted to her own sweet Pomp."

The audience laughed.

"What do you mean by that? She must have been a spicy girl."

"Yes, dat's de reason she was so fond of me. She was a poickess, too."

"A poetess, you mean."

"Yes, she used to write verses for de newspapers."

"Is that so, Bones?"

"Yes, saw," said Sox, grinning. "De day I went to de house, I – golly! – I dressed myself to kill, and my ole trunk was empty. Well, just as de gal seed me, she cove right in – she was a gone coon. When I left, she edged up to me and whispered, 'You're too sweet to live.' Next day I got a billy-doo."

More laughter from the audience.

"How do you know it was a billet-doux?" asked the banjo player.

"'Cause Billy Doo was de name of de boy dat brought it." He waited for the laughter to subside before continuing, "It smelt all over like a doctor's shop. I opened it, and found dese words:

'What lub is, if you must be taught,

Thy heart must teach alone!

Two cabbages wid a single stalk,

Two beets that are as one!'"

Snickers from the audience. When they died down, the banjo player said, "Well, Bones, you responded?"

"Yes, sir."

"What did you say?"

"You see, her fadder was a gardener, so I wrote what I call very appropriate lines:

O you sweet and lubly Dinah!

Dare are nofin any finer;

Your tongue is sweeter than a parrot's.

Your hair hangs like a bunch of carrots,

And though of flattery I'm a hater,

I lubs you like a sweet potater!"

Uproarious laughter.

"That was very nice, Bones," the banjo player said.

"Yes, I thought so," said Sox. "So delicate was her constitution, dat it nearly killed her. So terrible was de concussion, dat de next time I went to see her she was dissolved in tears."

"What! Weeping?"

"Yes, wid tears in her eyes and a big knife in the other. She raised it as I approached."

"Rash girl!"

"Yes," Sox agreed.

"What was she about to do? Commit suicide?"

"No; she was peeling onions to stuff a goose wid!"[5]

After the audience's laughter subsided, the banjo player turned gravely to the tambourine player at the other end of the semi-circle. He said, "Brother Tambo, I understand that you would like to address the audience this evening on a matter of utmost importance?"

"Oh, why, yes saw!" the older man exclaimed, leaping to his feet. The pretty young woman got up and dragged an apple-crate from behind the piano to the center of the stage, and Tambo, after offering her an exaggerated bow, climbed on top of it. He cleared his throat, blew his nose on a spotted handkerchief, and when the audience had stilled again he began:

"Feller-feller and oder fellers, when Joan of Ark and his broder Noah's Ark crossed de Rubicund in search of Decamoran's horn, and meeting dat solitary horseman by de way, dey anapulated in de clarion tones of de clamurous rooster, de insignificition of de – de – de – de hop-toad am a very big bird – du da – du da day – does it not prove dat where gold is up to a discount of two cups of coffee on de dollar, dat bolivers must fall back into de radience of de – de – anything

5 "Ethiopian dialogue" by J. Harry Carleton, from "Minstrel Gags and End Men's Hand-Book" (New York: n.d., Dick & Fitzgerald, Publishers)

else, derefore, at once and exclusively proving de fact dat de afore-mentioned accounts for de milk in de cocoa-nut!"[6]

And so he continued, declaiming for several more minutes on – as far as Meredith could tell – absolutely nothing. She was rapidly growing weary of this entertainment, but the audience seemed to love it, whistling and calling for more. It went on for another half hour, culminating in a skit in which the beautiful girl spurned the bumbling advances of all of the men in turn. Afterwards the five actors returned briefly to their seats to sing a song that seemed to be about sweet ham, and then they filed off the stage and down the steps, which Meredith had rapidly vacated.

As soon as they left the stage, the grins they had held throughout the performance collapsed, and their wild energy fled, leaving their faces worn. When they saw Meredith hovering in the shadows by the door, their looks turned wary as well.

"Who she?" the banjo player demanded.

"Ask *him*," said the older woman, jutting her chin at Sox.

"I told you," Sox began, "I don't *know* who she is – "

Meredith stepped forward and held up a hand to silence them. During the last part of the show, she had written out a brief explanation of why she was there. She offered her slate to the banjo player, assuming that he was the group's leader. But the man's expression darkened.

"You mocking me, girl?" he demanded. He stood blocking the door. Meredith's heart pounded, her hand trembled as she raised it to touch her mouth. She shook her head and then touched the slate, praying that he would understand. But it was the big woman who took her meaning first.

She squinted at Meredith for a moment, and then she said, "Sweet Jesus – the child can't speak!" The sharpness was

6 Robert Toll, 'Blacking Up'

gone from her look and voice, replaced by guarded curiosity. She turned to the banjo player. "Just you stop glarin' at her, Josiah. Sure, she didn't mean no insult. You, honey," she said to Meredith, "you give that slate to Sox, and we'll see if we can't get somewhere."

As Meredith handed Sox the slate, he gave her a quick, pleading look. He read what she'd written, and then he said, "She says her name's Meredith. She's looking for a friend who belongs to a minstrel troupe. She thought we were them."

Meredith stared at him, dumbfounded by the lie.

"How's a white girl like you got a minstrel friend?" Josiah asked.

Meredith took the slate Sox offered her and wrote furiously, "What are you trying to do? I've never even a met a Negro until today!" She shoved it back at him.

Sox read the words with a composed face, and then he said smoothly, "It's her old nanny's daughter she's looking for. They grew up together, til the girl fell out with her mother and went off to join a troupe. But the old lady's just died, and before she went Meredith promised her she'd let her daughter know."

"You pulling our leg, Sox?" the older woman asked dubiously.

Sox shrugged, perfectly sanguine. "I'm only telling you what she wrote."

Meredith stared him down. He looked back with eyes that clearly begged her not to contradict him. Meredith realized then that Sox was the only one of them who could read, also that the horse had been right: Sox needed something, and he'd lied to his people to buy time to ask her for it. But it didn't make her any happier about the story he'd just concocted, which she'd now have to corroborate.

"So what troupe is your friend with?" asked the young woman, looking intently at Meredith. Meredith glanced inadvertently at

Sox, but he gave her nothing back. She shrugged her shoulders and then waited, barely breathing, as everyone's eyes appraised her.

Finally, the man who played Tambo broke the fraught silence. "Could be Anderson's, I guess," he said, finally relaxing his stance. "I hear they got a new actress not too long ago."

"If so she's got a long trip ahead," Josiah said. "They headed out west two weeks back. Same reason as always," he added, as if Meredith had asked why. "Not enough work on the eastern circuit anymore. Pretty soon, these shows'll be a thing of the past."

Meredith nodded with what she hoped looked like regret, then wondered if it was the right response – none of the others looked particularly upset by the prospect.

"Why don't you come have supper with us," Sox said, before anyone could question Meredith further.

The girl cut him a sharp look, but the older woman smiled and said, "Sure, honey – it's the least we can do after treating you so cold."

Meredith held out a hand to protest, but the woman ignored it, ushering her toward the door. "Name's Clem," she said, "and she's Chloe," indicating the younger woman. "You got Sox and Josiah, and old Tambo here is my husband, Sox's daddy, Abel. You say you're name's Meredith?"

Meredith nodded.

"That your given name?"

Meredith nodded.

"Damn strange name for a woman," Chloe muttered. "But then, she looks like a damn strange woman."

"You watch your mouth, girl!" Clem said, swatting her and then, to Meredith, "Don't you pay her any mind. That dress always puts her in a mood."

Chloe shook her head and opened the door to the alley. The others followed, Meredith last of all. The horse greeted her with a whicker.

"Now that's a fine animal," said Abel, looking the horse up and down. "Clydesdale or Percheron?" Meredith shrugged; likewise when he asked, "She yours?" because she couldn't imagine that the horse considered herself anybody's.

But Abel interpreted the shrug differently, laughing, "That's the way, child. No one gonna hand you what you need in this world – you just gotta take it! Come on."

Leading the horse, Meredith followed him down the alley. It let out into what must once have been the loading yard for the factory. Two green wagons stood on the snow-rimed cobbles, their sides painted with foot-high black and red letters reading "Jo's Minstrels". Four mules were picketed nearby, browsing piles of hay.

At the far side of the yard a set of padlocked iron gates let out onto the street. Meredith looked from the wagons to the locked gate, wondering how the troupe had got their wagons into the yard. Seeing where her gaze rested, Sox guessed her question.

"The lock's ours," he said. "Sometimes after a show, the audience gets ugly."

Meredith looked at him, raising her eyebrows.

Sox looked back, his eyes sober over his absurd painted smile. "They like us up on stage," he said, "but off it, we're just five more niggers." She recoiled at the word, taking its meaning from Sox's tone, though she couldn't recall ever having heard it before. "Sometimes they come complaining, asking for their money back. Sometimes they want a private audience with Chloe. If you argue with them, they pick a fight; if you fight them, you hang. So if the next town's too far to make before nightfall, we lock ourselves in for the night." He smiled grimly and walked off toward the wagons.

Rattled, Meredith looked at the horse, but she was relaxed, snuffling among the cobbles and old snow for anything edible. Meredith untied the bridle, and the horse ambled toward the mules, who called to her with their odd, braying whinnies. The horse whinnied back, and keeping a wary eye on them, she began to browse the windblown remnants of their hay. Meredith watched her for a moment, then she turned and followed the others.

In the sheltered space between the wagons and the wall, someone had built a campfire. Chloe, now in a high-necked black dress and blue shawl, was feeding it with bits of broken crates. The others had also changed into ordinary clothes. Clem sat beside Chloe, measuring cornmeal into a pan, while Sox and Abel washed their faces in a bucket of water and Josiah counted the afternoon's take, swigging from a bottle wrapped in a brown paper bag. Meredith opened her pack, took out the last of Gradlon's cured meat, and handed it to Clem.

"I believe this is venison," she said, looking up at Meredith, who nodded affirmation. "Why, I ain't tasted venison since I was a child!" She made no show of polite refusal, for which Meredith's estimation of her grew considerably. She set the meat frankly on a board and began cutting it into chunks, which she then put it a bowl of water to soak.

"You just made her night," Abel said. "Old Clem, she'll forgive just about anything if you give her a good cut of meat." Meredith saw Chloe's mouth tighten for a moment, though she didn't look up from the carrots she was peeling.

"Well, Miss Meredith," said Josiah, putting the money back in the box and locking it, "you mean to keep chasing this Negro girl, now you know she's gone west?"

Meredith was careful not to look at Sox, though she could feel his eyes on her. She knew that if she did, she would blush and betray them both. Instead she took the slate from her pocket, wrote, "You have to make them stop asking me about this!" and then handed it to him. She watched as he read, certain that she could actually see his mind racing ahead with his concocted story.

"Meredith says that she owes it to her nanny to try," he said.

Chloe looked up at Meredith, her black eyes intent. "That seems mighty risky, Miss Meredith," she said, with an unmistakable twist of irony in the "Miss", "when you don't even know your runaway joined Anderson's – and when you can't ask after her. How is it that you lost your voice, anyhow?"

"Chloe!" cried Clem, but it was half-hearted. Obviously she was just as curious to know the answer, however rude the question.

Sighing, Meredith sat down on an empty apple crate beside Sox, reaching for her slate. He handed it back to her. "Even you," she scribbled, "can't do better than this!" He raised his eyebrows as she swiped her hand across the slate to clear it, and then began to write again. Sox went very still as he read, and Meredith thought that she'd finally confounded him. Then, once again, he began to fabricate:

"She says she comes from…up north. She…and her parents were in a river-boat accident. They were killed, but she survived, only she lost her voice." He glanced at Meredith, apparently to see how he was doing. Suppressing a smile, she wiped the slate and continued.

"There was no family to take her in and no money left after her father's debts were paid. She had nothing but a few of his old clothes, and their horse."

"And her sweet Negro nanny?" Chloe asked drily.

"No," Sox said evenly, "her nanny left years ago. But since she had no one else, Meredith went to see her – and found her dying. And seeing as she only just lost her own parents, when that woman asked her to find her daughter – "

"The one with Andersons," Chloe interjected.

"That's right," Sox answered nonchalantly. "She decided to help. But she couldn't find her, and now…well…here she is."

Meredith looked up. The actors were studying her with varying degrees of skepticism and interest. At last, Josiah broke the silence. "That's a mighty strange story."

Meredith met his eyes, and shrugged.

"It'll be a hard road for a lone woman," Josiah said. There was a challenge in his voice, but also, she thought, a touch of envy.

"I've come this far," she wrote. Sox read it out without editing.

"You gotta stop sometime," Clem said.

"I'll stop," she wrote, "when I find a place worth stopping."

"Hm," said Clem, when Sox had translated. Then she shrugged, and with that, all of them seemed to lose interest in her fabricated history. Josiah went inside one of the wagons, and after a moment Meredith heard him playing softly on his banjo. Abel dozed off. Chloe and Clem turned their attention to cooking.

"Come on," Sox said to Meredith. "You can help me feed the mules."

She followed him to the back of the other wagon. He went inside and came out carrying a bucket of grain, set off toward the animals. When they were far enough from the others, he said, "Sorry about that story. It was the best I could do on short notice."

Meredith shrugged, but she couldn't help smiling.

Sox smiled back. "Besides, they never would've believed what you wrote. It all true?"

Meredith nodded. He shook his head, began to scoop grain into little piles, far enough apart that the mules wouldn't fight. He poured grain for Meredith's horse last of all. She lapped at it greedily.

"Thank you," Meredith wrote, indicating the grain.

Sox shrugged. "Thank *you*, for not telling them what happened back in the alley."

Meredith wrote, "What <u>did</u> happen in the alley?"

He chuckled grimly. "I guess the sorry truth of my life got the better of me."

"I don't understand," Meredith wrote.

Sighing, Sox answered, "I thought you were the answer to my prayers."

"What prayers?"

He looked at her, his mouth suddenly bitter. "Didn't you watch that show today?"

"Yes. And I understood none of it."

Bitterness changed to incredulity. "Haven't you seen a minstrel show before?"

Meredith wrote, "Until today, I had never even seen a Negro."

Sox blinked at her for a moment, stunned. "No kidding?" he asked, and when Meredith shook her head he said, "Damn," and began to laugh. "Well, Miss Meredith, if you're heading south then you better get used to it. There's a whole lot of us down that way."

Meredith looked at him, wondering why it sounded like a warning.

"Anyway, I'm sorry."

"For what?" Meredith wrote.

"For that show. What you saw on that stage today was the dregs...the worst of us, and the worst way to introduce you to our people. I'm shamed to have been a part of it."

Meredith wrote, "And people really find it entertaining?"

He gave her another quick, disbelieving look. "You mean you didn't?"

"What is entertaining," she wrote, "about a smart man acting like an idiot?"

"Well," he answered slowly, after a moment, "I guess it's not that simple. See, Minstrel shows started during slave times. White folks liked to see Negroes as stupid and happy and lazy. It made them feel better about owning us."

Meredith was both horrified and fascinated by the matter-of-fact way Sox spoke the words. She was ashamed, too, of the bare few facts she could call to mind about the war and its causes.

"Funny thing is," he continued, "in the beginning it was white folks corking their faces and playing the clowns. In those days a black man wasn't allowed on stage – not even to cut himself down."

"And now?" Meredith wrote.

Sox shook his head. "Now, the world's a different place. We're all free, and the white minstrels, they're long gone. There's no more than a handful of troupes left at all, and those can barely scrounge an audience. I'd say the world's coming to its senses, except that clowning's my bread and butter."

"There must be other acting jobs," Meredith asked.

"Oh yeah, there are. But they're all in vaudeville, and vaudeville's white."

A long silence followed, broken only by the sound of the animals chewing. Night had closed down over the factory yard, and the firelight barely reached far enough for Meredith to see Sox beside her. She watched the mules' dark shapes shifting, turning over all that Sox had told her.

"My name isn't really Sox," he said suddenly, out of the darkness. Meredith turned to him. He was looking at the ground, kicking at the icy rime on the cobbles with one worn boot. "I was christened Abel," he said, "just like my daddy. 'Sox' is short for Socrates. They call me that because they think I'm so smart…because I can read, and they can't, and no one knows how I learned. Mama says I was born knowing my letters, and for all I know, she's right. Sure I can't remember not knowing. She calls it a gift."

Finally Sox looked at Meredith. His eyes caught the light, but it was too faint for her to read their expression. "Maybe, for them, it is," he continued. "It sure helps them out, me knowing how to read. I don't know how they'd get by now without me. I don't mind it, not really. But still sometimes it turns into a collar around my neck. It comes on me with no warning; it's just there, getting tighter and tighter until I can't breathe, and my heart goes like a train, and I think I might die…"

He shook his head. There was a long silence, which Sox broke at last with a sigh. "Anyhow, that's why you found me crying in the alley today. Crying and praying, if you want the truth – for someone to deliver me from my gift, from act two, and all of the other acts that will make up my life…because every time I get up on stage, I justify another room full of white fools in thinking they're better than I am. And because of my 'gift', I got no way out."

Meredith studied him, trying to think of a way to help him. Finally, she wrote, "I guess you've tried to teach the others to read?" and tilted the slate towards the flickering light.

Sox smiled bitterly. "Oh, I've damn near killed myself trying. But since I can't remember learning, I can't break it down. I can't explain it. I got Chloe to recognize a few words, but that's all. It's why she's so sour. She's angry she doesn't have what I got. And here, I'd gladly give it to her – "

"Sox!" Clem called from the campfire. "Dinner!"

Sox seemed to shake himself, like a dog coming out of deep water. "Look here – I'm sorry for troubling you with all of that. Sometimes I forget myself…"

"Sometimes we need to," Meredith wrote.

He smiled sadly. "A black man can't afford to forget himself – not ever."

*

As she ate Clem's stewed venison and cornbread, Meredith watched the family, comparing what she saw with what Sox had told her. They carried on a lively conversation, punctuated by laughter, and Sox's unhappiness didn't keep him from joining in. Despite his frustration, he belonged to them; or maybe, she thought, it was part and parcel. Maybe belonging was the source of his despair: as much as Sox wanted his family to stop needing him, he needed them, and he saw no way to separate that need from the life he hated.

It was such a little thing, Meredith thought, standing between Sox and liberation: the ability to understand a mark made on paper. A little thing or a vast rift, depending on which side of it you stood. Meredith looked at the slate beside her, suddenly ashamed of taking it for granted. She'd pitied herself for her missing voice when it had never really left her, simply shifted to a channel of chalk and slate, ink and paper. She certainly hadn't seen her grasp of it for the gift it was. It shamed her too, to realize that somebody, sometime, had painstakingly given her this gift, and she couldn't even remember who it had been. But when she thought about it, she realized that she did remember how.

Picking up the slate, she wrote, "I know how to help you. I need paper and a pen or pencil."

She gave it to Sox, who read it, then put his plate aside and went into Josiah's wagon. Sox's parents and uncle were still eating and talking among themselves and didn't pay any mind to the exchange. But Chloe had watched it all with bright, cold eyes. She stared at the slate for a moment after Sox left, and then she picked it up and brought it down on her knee. With a resounding crack, in broke in two.

Everyone stared at her in stunned silence. At last Josiah ended it, speaking in the implacable voice with which he'd first addressed Meredith, "That's an evil thing you've done, Chloe."

Chloe stood up, shaking with fury. "Any more evil than letting that white bitch mock us?" Throwing the pieces of the slate at Meredith's feet, she stormed off into the dark.

The silence stretched out for a few more moments, and then Clem turned to Meredith. "Honey, I apologize," she said. "I don't know what's got into that girl. We'll pay for your slate – "

But Meredith shook her head emphatically. Sox came down from the wagon, holding a sheaf of handbills advertising a show now six months past. He also held a pencil.

"You still want these?" he asked Meredith.

Meredith was acutely aware of the others watching her. She had the sick realization that they watched her with fear. "I want them now more than ever," she wrote on one of the pieces of the slate. "Tell her...tell all of them I'm sorry."

"You got nothing to be sorry for," Sox answered bitterly.

"I made her angry."

"She envies you. That's not your fault."

Meredith saw Clem and Josiah exchange a look. "Well," Meredith wrote, "now she need not. I am going to give her the gift. I'm going to give it to all of them."

"You're going to teach them to read?" he asked. This time the look Clem exchange with Josiah was skeptical, but also the barest bit hopeful.

Meredith shook her head and wrote, "You are."

"I told you, I don't remember learning – "

"But I do," Meredith said, and switching to a blank sheet of paper as the family gathered curiously to watch, she began to write the alphabet, as carefully and neatly as she could, down the side of the page. She wrote upper case and lower case, and then a simple sentence for each one: "A is for apple...B is for boat..." And so on through all that she remembered of her grade school primer.

Gradually, the actors got tired of watching her and went back to other tasks. Abel dried the dishes Clem washed, while Josiah lit a pipe and took up his banjo. Chloe came back after a time, marched into her father's wagon and didn't come out again. Only Sox stayed with Meredith. From time to time he got up to feed the fire or to refill their cups of chicory coffee. The rest of the time he watched her, transfixed.

At last Josiah put his banjo away and retired into his wagon. Not long afterward, Clem and Abel went into the other. Meredith looked up at Sox. His eyes were ringed, his eyelids drooping.

"Go to bed," Meredith wrote on a blank sheet of paper and handed it to him.

"What about you?" he asked.

"I want to finish this."

He nodded. "You need anything else?"

Meredith looked down at her stack of finished pages, then at the two halves of the broken slate. "An awl, if you have one," she wrote. "A file, and a drill with a fine bit. A darning needle and strong thread."

Sox nodded, went into Clem and Abel's wagon, and came out a few minutes later with all of the things she'd asked for.

"Thank you," she wrote.

"Thank *you*, Miss Meredith," he said. "And good night."

Sox went into his parents' wagon, and Meredith went back to work. When the pages of the primer were finished, she picked up the awl and carefully drove four holes through them. She threaded the needle, and sewed the pages together through the holes. Then she filed the sharp edges off of the two halves of the broken slate, and drilled four holes at the edges of each, to align with those in the pages. Finally, she sewed the slate covers onto the book. As she bit off the final thread, the first light was coming into the sky.

Meredith sat looking down at the book for a few moments. The bare stone cover looked oddly forbidding, so she picked up the chalk and wrote, "Sox's Primer" on the cover. When she looked at it, though, it seemed too mundane a title for a book that would accomplish so much. She wiped the slate and sat sifting though her deepwater memories. When she thought about books a single image came into her mind, of a tattered old volume, its page-edges softened with wear. She could not recall its title, but a handful of phrases came to her: *that way madness lies...her beauty hangs upon the cheek of night...when the hurlyburly's done, when the battle's lost and won...* Nothing that seemed right, until one of them did.

"To thine own self be true," Meredith wrote carefully on the cover of the book, and then she placed it, along with the borrowed materials – minus the pencil and the rest of the handbills, which would be a temporary replacement for her slate – on the top step of Chloe's wagon.

Meredith stood for a moment watching the sky brighten. She was tired, but her mind was too full to sleep. She heard a ringing step behind her, felt warm breath on the back of her neck. Reaching up, she stroked the horse's nose.

Its time to go, she said.

The horse pressed her nose into Meredith's palm. Meredith put the handbills and pencil in her pack, then shouldered it and bridled the horse. She led her to a piece of fallen masonry and mounted, hoping to get away without waking the others.

As she turned the horse toward the alley, though, she saw a figure standing in front of the wagon. She seemed to float in the early-morning mist, her face luminous as a spirit's. She clutched the stone-bound book to her breast.

Meredith raised a hand to her. Gravely, Chloe nodded back; at her mouth, the wingtips of a smile.

Stella Maris

1

After the city, there were mountains again. They were higher and bleaker than the ones in which Meredith had met Lyuba and her daughter, but it seemed they were equally full of coal. Little villages clustered on the hillsides, houses huddled around the breakers and vast culm piles of rich mines. One full-moon night, Meredith followed a glow on the horizon until she came to a village whose culm pile was on fire. Low flames of brilliant blue and orange licked the glowing red embers, radiating a warmth so seductive that she considered camping beside it. When she slid down from the horse's back, though, her foot came down on something pliant. It was a man's hand. Stumbling back in horror, she saw that he was a tramp with a long, grizzled beard. No doubt he had been lured by the warmth of the fire; no doubt he was now dead. She didn't know whether one fact bore on the other, but she didn't care to find out. She didn't stop again until the glow of the burning pile had faded from the sky behind her.

*

After that, she rode into a valley with a winding river. Its water was covered in a viscous slick that threw the light back in prismatic colors. Gradlon's food had finally run out, but Meredith didn't dare eat any fish from that water. She noticed too that the mining structures on the hillsides had changed. Wooden obelisks replaced the breakers and coal piles; the dust clouds and the muted roar of machinery disappeared. The trains no longer pulled coal cars, but piles of barrels. It seemed that whatever the people mined here was a liquid, and no doubt accounted for the state of the river. She didn't want to know what it was. She was finished with mining villages.

Two days later, Meredith woke to a symphonic dripping. Her clothes and bedding were damp, the horse's coat silvered with dew. Over the next few days the remnants of snow melted, leaving behind a world of sodden brown and green. The horse's feathers were heavy with mud, the ground so slippery that she walked with her nose only inches above it, as if she could sniff out any treacherous patch before she stood on it. Meredith wondered if this could be the beginning of spring. She had long since lost track of time, so as she rode she scanned the trees for the telltale leaf buds, the ground for the first shoots of flowers and new grass.

She was gazing up into the latticed branches, trying to decipher their language, when the horse stopped abruptly. Looking down again, Meredith found the road ahead blocked by a child. She was perhaps twelve years old, with a thin, dark-complected face framed by black hair under a red hood trimmed with white fur. She looked up at Meredith with inky eyes, whose expression wavered between terror and determination.

"Are you the one?" she asked in a faintly accented voice.

Meredith's surprise turned to pity when she heard the desperate hope in the child's voice, knowing that she had to dash it. To her surprise, though, the child brightened when she shook her head.

"Can you not speak, Miss?" she asked.

Again, Meredith shook her head. Incongruous joy washed over the girl's face. "Please forgive me for contradicting you, Miss, but if you cannot speak, then you *are* the one! She said that I would meet you on this road, and I would know you by your silence."

Sighing, Meredith took pencil and paper from her pocket. "Who," she wrote, "is 'she'?"

"Our Lady," the girl answered without hesitation, as if this ought to have been obvious.

Meredith wrote, "And who is it that you think I am?"

"The one who will save us," the child answered without irony.

"From what?"

The girl sighed. "You would not believe me if I told you; you will have to see for yourself. Besides, I have left them too long already."

Meredith considered the girl. She was well spoken and well dressed, if a little unkempt – as if, used to having help, she'd suddenly had to dress herself. Her words made little sense, but they were sincere; and then, she was only a child.

"All right," Meredith wrote. "I will come with you. What is your name?"

"Gabriella Marinelli."

"I'm Meredith. Where are we going?"

The child pointed to the top of the hill above them. Up beyond the tree line, Meredith could see the pointed head of a piece of the new mining machinery. Sighing, she shoved the paper and pencil back into her pocket and walked the horse toward a flat rock, beckoning to the child to follow.

The child watched anxiously. "You want me to ride?"

Meredith nodded.

The girl looked up the hill, twisting her hands in front of her. "All right…but only if you promise to hold on to me and don't let me fall."

Meredith nodded. The child climbed reluctantly onto the rock, and Meredith pulled her the rest of the way onto the horse's back. When they were settled, the horse turned unprompted onto a deer-path and began to climb the hill.

"How did it know where to go?" the child asked, surprised.

Meredith shrugged. The horse followed a barely-visible path up the mountain, zig-zagging over the steeper places and picking her way carefully over wet or rocky ground. Finally they joined a wider track. It bore the marks of wagon wheels, though none of them were recent. Gabriella saw Meredith looking and guessed her thoughts.

"Nobody has come here since the plague began," she said sadly.

Plague? Meredith thought, alarmed. But it was too late now to turn back. She could only hope that once again, the horse knew what she was about.

At last the road let out into a village with a signpost reading "Belmonte". The village was nothing like Lyuba's. It was nothing like any village Meredith had ever seen before. The houses weren't made of wood, but, apparently, whitewashed mud, their roofs shingled in reddish tiles. They sat in neat little yards with planters by their doorways, full of evergreen herbs and the remnants of summer flowers. At the far end of the central street that divided the rows of houses was a tiny, whitewashed church with a pointed steeple housing a bronze bell. It might have been a cheerful place, if it had not been so still and silent.

Gabriella slipped gratefully to the ground. "Your horse can stay in Giuseppi's stable," she told Meredith. "Just there, behind that house." She pointed to the house nearest them. "He keeps a cow. She will not mind the company. Come."

Meredith followed her to a small building behind the house. A baleful lowing came from within.

"She needs to be milked," Gabriella said apologetically. "It is so hard, looking after all of them…"

She opened the door. Inside was a piebald milk cow, her bag full and hard. As Meredith led the horse inside and found hay for her, Gabriella drew up a milking stool and pail and set to work. Clearly, though, this was not work she was familiar with. She struggled to pull the udders properly, and when the cow switched her tail, stinging her face, her eyes filled.

Meredith indicated then that she would take over. She thought that this might be another unknown skill that would come back to her when she put her hand to it, but there was nothing familiar about the feel of the cow's udders or the hiss as the milk streamed into the pail. In fact it took her a few moments to work out how to make the milk come at all. Gabriella watched her without comment until the bucket was half-full, and then she said, "Thank you. That is enough."

Meredith was certain that the cow had more to give, but she was sick of the work by then and glad enough to give it up. Gabriella picked up the pail, and Meredith followed her outside. Calmly, the child tipped the milk into the muddy grass behind the house.

Meredith glared at her. Gabriella met her anger with sad eyes. "There is nobody to drink it but you and me," she said, "and I already have more than enough for both of us. I milk them only because they will be ill if I don't."

Them? Meredith thought.

The question must have showed on her face, because Gabriella sighed and said, "Come, I will show you." She upended the pail by the wall of the house and then led Meredith around to the front. Inside was a single large room with a set of wooden steps leading to a second storey. The inner walls were whitewashed like the outer, and dark wooden beams ran across the ceiling with bunches of dried herbs hanging from them. A well-worn deal table stood against a wall with four wooden chairs, and on the opposite wall was a washstand with a colorful ceramic bowl. Instead of a pitcher, there was a tap for running water. Likewise there were sconces on the walls of the type used for gaslights.

It should have been a warm, inviting room, but the air inside it was like that of a sea-cave: cold and dank and tinged with decay despite the semi-circular fireplace with its basket of glowing embers. An elderly couple lay on a pallet in front of the fire. They looked like bodies at a wake, their arms limp at their sides, with none of the tossing and muttering of sleep. If it had not been for the faint rise and fall of their chests beneath their blanket, Meredith would have assumed they were dead.

Gabriella walked calmly toward them and knelt by the pallet. "*Buongiorno* Giuseppe, Maria," she said, laying her hand on each wrinkled cheek as she greeted them. The man and woman did not stir, but this didn't appear to surprise Gabriella. Formalities dispensed with, she turned to build up the fire.

"It ought to be bigger," she said to Meredith, looking at the little flame that sprang up among the armful of sticks she laid down, "but with no one to cut more, I am afraid that I will run out of wood before they are cured."

Meredith crouched down by Gabriella, felt the old people's foreheads and the pulse at their necks. Their skin was clammy and too cold, their pulses weak and slow compared with her own, but Meredith didn't know what these observations meant.

"Put your ear to his chest," Gabriella said, when she saw that Meredith was at a loss. Reluctantly, Meredith lowered her head to Giuseppe's breast. She listened for a moment and then drew back, wide-eyed with shock against Gabriella's calm, sad gaze.

"You heard it, didn't you," the child said.

"What is it?" Meredith wrote.

"The sea."

Meredith balked at the words, but she couldn't deny them. The sea was exactly what she had thought she'd heard in the old man's chest: the wash of waves on a shore, the suck and drag of their retreat. Inadvertently, she shook her head.

Gabriella sighed. "I didn't believe it at first, either," she said. "But they're all the same. Come and see."

It was true. Every house that they entered was full of the breath of a rank sea cavern, the occupants, young and old alike, lying like death by hearths that could not warm them. In each of their chests, Meredith heard the reach and retreat of the tide. They visited every cottage, stoking the fires and tucking quilts and blankets more tightly. It was only when they left the last of them that Meredith thought to wonder which had been Gabriella's family.

"I've kept them for last," Gabriella said softly, when Meredith wrote the question. She led Meredith along a path through the woods, which let out on the front yard of the biggest house Meredith had ever seen. It was big enough to be called a mansion, and though it was built of the same materials as the cottages, it was embellished with swags of stairs and long windows and filigreed molding.

"This," said Gabriella, "is our house."

Meredith followed her up the center set of steps, through a carved wooden door and into a grand entrance hall full of side tables and dark paintings. Gabriella didn't linger there but moved quickly through its echoing silence toward the back of the house, into a kitchen packed with recumbent people. Meredith counted six women in humble clothing, who must be servants. By the stove, a man and a woman lay on a large feather mattress with a small boy and girl between them.

"My parents," said Gabriella, bending to smooth the hair back from her mother's face, "and my brother and sister."

"We must find them a doctor," Meredith wrote.

Gabriella shook her head. "The doctor has been and gone already. Only half of them were sick then, but he told us to stay up here until everyone was better. He told us not to call him again, or to come down the mountain at all, or we would risk killing thousands. I did not like to disobey him," she said unhappily, looking up at Meredith with eyes rimmed violet by exhaustion, "but what could I do? Especially when She told me to go…"

Ignoring the final comment, Meredith wrote, "Did the doctor tell you what was wrong with them?"

"No," Gabriella said. "He said that he did not know himself, that it must be some kind of immigrant plague." She frowned at the memory. "He laughed when my father told him it is not a plague at all."

"What do you mean?"

"It's not a plague," Gabriella repeated. "It is a curse."

Meredith raised her eyebrows, but Gabriella's eyes were fixed on her family, her brows drawn with worry, and she didn't see. Meredith touched her arm, showed her the paper on which she had underlined her previous question, "What do you mean?"

Gabriella looked at her for a long moment, then she answered, "I will show you."

Checking that the stove was well stoked, she led the way back through the house to the front door. Meredith followed her back to the village, where Gabriella turned toward the church. She stopped in front of its closed doors, apparently steeling herself for something unpleasant. When she opened them, Meredith understood why. The pelagic air that had invaded the houses where the villagers lay ill was nothing to the rank draft that came from the church. For Meredith, it bore a tide of ghosts: a girl in a blue skirt and hair ribbon; a cobwebbed boat, forgotten, drying to tinder; a memory of bliss rotting with past summer's leaves beneath a bare dogwood tree; and then they were gone. Meredith didn't know what Gabriella had seen in those moments, but when she came back to herself, she found the girl white and shaking. Meredith took her hand, and Gabriella's closed gratefully around it. Together, they entered the church.

Given the smell, Meredith half-expected the floor to be puddled with water and the pews festooned with rotting kelp. In fact the church's interior looked as it must have done the last time the parishioners left it. The polished wooden pews shone dully in the grey light from the thin arched windows; the hymnals and embroidered kneelers were neatly stowed beneath them. The brass candlesticks on the altar were untarnished, the cloth beneath them crisp and white, except where the muted colors of a round, stained-glass window fell upon it. A Bible lay on the priest's lectern, open to Psalms. Meredith glanced at it apprehensively, and caught a single phrase: "I will bring my people again from the depths of the sea…" She realized suddenly that they hadn't visited a priest on their rounds.

"Who presides over this church?" she wrote.

Gabriella shook her head, frowning. "No one, anymore," she said, walking slowly down the aisle. "And that is where all of this began." She stopped by the wall to the left of the altar, where there was a niche about three feet high. It was painted cobalt blue with silver stars, and beneath them, an azure sea frothing with waves. Curving around the arch, gold letters spelled, "*Ave Maria, Stella Maris.*"

Gabriella reached out a hand, as if to stroke the empty space. "This was where Our Lady stood until three weeks ago, when Father Vincente stole her." She considered her words, and then amended, "Well, we thought he did. What else were we to think, when both he and she went missing on the same morning?

"My father was certain that Vincente meant to take her back to Calabria, that he believed it was her rightful home. Most everyone else thought that he took her for her gold and pearls, to sell them and then, well, who knows what?" She shook her head. "Either way, he did a bad thing. The first of us fell ill that very afternoon."

Meredith wrote, "I don't see the connection."

"I will tell you the whole story," Gabriella said, "but not in here." She led the way back up the aisle, and when they were both outside she shut the church doors tightly. Then she sat down on the step. Meredith looked at her pinched, pale face and hoped that she was not about to fall ill as well.

"All of us in this village," she began, "except a few of the youngest children, were born in the other Belmonte – the one in Italy, on the heel of the boot. It was a fishing village, just like all the others around it, except that we had Stella Maris." Gabriella paused, sighed, looked at her fingers. "It was my father's grandfather who found her. He thought he had caught a *tonno* fish, but when he pulled up in his net he found instead a beautiful statue of the Madonna. It looked bright and new, not like something that had been in the sea. He took Her straight to the village priest, who set Her up in the chapel. That very day the priest held a mass to thank the Holy Mother for coming from the sea to grace us with her presence. From then on we called her Stella Maris."

Meredith looked blankly at Gabriella.

"Star of the Sea. It is one of the Madonna's titles…?"

Meredith shook her head. Gabriella looked at her curiously, but refrained from questioning her ignorance. "There is a beautiful prayer to Her. It starts: 'If the winds of temptation arise; If you are driven upon the rocks of tribulation look to the star, call on Mary…'[7] Our village took this prayer to heart. Whenever we were faced with trouble, we prayed to Stella Maris, and She helped us.

"It did not take long for word to spread. Soon people were coming from miles around to pray to Her, but Her first miracle came sometime later. There was a cholera epidemic. People were dying in scores. Only our own village was spared. We knew that it was by the grace of Stella Maris. Then our priest realized that Her benevolence might be shared. He took Her on a pilgrimage through the stricken villages, and wherever She passed, there were no new cases of the disease, and those who were already ill recovered.

"After that, many people wanted to buy Our Lady. Some of them offered enough money to make all of us wealthy. But She had chosen us; we could not sell Her. Besides, what price can you put on a miracle?"

What indeed, Meredith thought, caught between fascination and disbelief.

"There were other, smaller miracles after that. Lulls that allowed the fishing boats to return to harbor before a squall; storm surges that stopped a hand-span from our doorsteps.

---

7 12c, Saint Bernard of Clairvaux

Nothing that anyone beyond the village would notice. Not until my father's time."

She paused, and then, drawing a breath, she continued, "My father wasn't born wealthy. He was a fisherman, like everyone else he knew. But he was not content with that life. He had heard that there were fortunes to be made in America, and he had no doubt that he could make one himself, if only he had the means to get there. But he had a wife and a baby – me. There was no money to spare.

"Then one night he dreamed of Stella Maris. She took him by the hand and led him to the sea. They walked across the waves, to a rocky shoal where he often fished. She pointed downward, and then She vanished. The next morning Papa took his boat to the shoal, and dove into the sea at the place where Our Lady had stood. Right away he found a gold coin, and so he thought that Stella Maris had led him to a shipwrecked treasure. But he searched for hours, and found no more. He went home thinking he'd failed."

Gabriella gazed at the sky, the fondness for what was clearly a familiar story warming her sallow face. "The coin was not one he recognized, and so he brought it to the priest. This was the priest before Vincente," she added, frowning. "He told Papa that the coin was an ancient one, that it was likely to be worth quite a bit. And it was: my father sold it for more than enough to buy a ticket to America. But it was not enough for three tickets, and so he gave the rest of the money to the priest who had helped him and went to seek his fortune. He promised to send for us as soon as he had earned enough.

"When he arrived in New York, he was hired by a mining company looking for soft coal. They sent him here, but they couldn't find a seam. The company decided to close the patch and move the workers elsewhere. But the night before they were to leave, Papa dreamed again of Stella Maris. She sat in a boat on a black sea, and She told him that if he left he would die a poor man, and he would never see his family again. But if he trusted Her and kept digging on that hill, he would be rewarded.

"Papa had a little bit left of the money he'd brought from Italy. The company boss laughed at him when he offered to buy the mountain, but since it was worthless to him anyway, he took the money. The others left, and Papa dug up here alone for many days. The ground was rocky, and by the end of each day he had barely scratched the surface. He began to doubt that the dream had been prophecy. But since he had nothing now besides this mountain, he kept digging. And Stella Maris rewarded him with another miracle.

"He was looking for coal, but he found oil. At last he understood the meaning of the boat on the black sea: he had uncovered the biggest oil well in the state. He hired workers, and with the profits from the first few months of drilling he bought his own equipment. He also bought more land, and on that land he found more oil. By the end of a year he could afford to bring not just his family, but his entire village to America. And so he offered to pay passage for anyone from Belmonte who wanted to come.

"In the meantime he built this village, as like the old one as he could, except that he put in modern conveniences. He also re-created the church. He asked the others what they thought about bringing Stella Maris with them. Everyone wanted to bring Her – everyone except the priest, Vincente. He was a new priest, and he had not planned to follow us here. But when he found he could not stop us taking Our Lady with us, he changed his mind. He said that it was his duty to protect Her, though it was She who protected us." Gabriella frowned. "She led us here, to a new world and better lives. And until Father Vincente's greed overcame him, we were happy."

Gabriella fell silent. The sun had set; the sky was an incandescent violet above the black hills. The plumes of smoke from the village's chimneys drifted up until their blue smudges dispersed into it. It would have been a scene of perfect tranquility, if it had not been for the darkened windows, the preternatural silence.

"Why would the priest steal the statue?" Meredith wrote.

Gabriella had to hold the paper close to read it in the failing light, but when she had, she smiled sadly. "Because the old priest had used the money my father gave him to adorn her in gold and pearls and other precious things."

"But if this – Stella Maris is so attached to your people," Meredith wrote, when Gabriella handed the paper back, "why would she curse all of you for something you didn't do? Why not curse Vincente?"

Gabriella shook her head. "We prayed to Her from the night that She was lost and the first people fell ill, asking why. We continued to pray every day, as more of us fell ill, until I was the only one left." She sighed. "Some thought that She had stopped listening. Others thought that She was too far away to hear, or that Vincente had done something so terrible to Her that Her power deserted Her. Papa thought that God was testing us, as he tested Job."

"What do you think?"

"I think that I have to find her and bring her back."

"And what is my part in this?"

"I cannot look for her and look after them." She gestured to the village. "Besides, he must be far away by now. Too far for me to walk alone. And then last night, I dreamed of Her. She told me to go down to the road and help would come to me."

In the form of a mute woman dressed like a man, Meredith thought wryly. There was no light left to write a response, but Meredith could still see Gabriella's pleading eyes, fixed on her. She drew a breath, breathed a sigh, and nodded. Gabriella's pinched face softened into a smile.

3

After stoking the cottages' fires, they returned to Gabriella's house. When they came into the dark hallway, Gabriella lit a taper, moved to the wall, fiddled with something for a moment, and was rewarded with a bright blast of light.

"It's gas," she said to Meredith's look of surprise. "Papa loves inventions. He says change is the only way forward. He wanted electric lights, but they were too expensive, so he ran gas lines to all of the cottages. We're the only ones who use them, though." Meredith thought of the empty sconces she'd noticed in the first cottage. "It comes from the ground, like the oil, but they all think that it isn't natural. Against God – that's what Father Vincente used to say. Even Mamma didn't like the idea, but Papa only laughed and told her God created progress, like everything else."

She smiled sadly and lit more of the lamps, until the hallway was almost as bright as day. Then she went back to the kitchen, and lit the ones there. "*Sono spiacente*," she said to one of the prostrate servants. Then she explained to Meredith, "Cook never lit the gas lights in here, but now that it's only me – well, kerosene and candles make too many shadows. Are you hungry?" She asked abruptly, opening a door to reveal a well-stocked larder. "I hope you can cook, because I can't."

Meredith looked into the cupboard. It was full of intriguingly unfamiliar items, but among them she saw eggs and butter and bread. While she fried these, Gabriella plied her with delicate slices of cured meats and hard, salty cheeses she had never tasted before. The child rattled off their Italian names, but Meredith quickly gave up trying to remember them, and merely appreciated the diversion from her bland diet.

Stoking the stove after supper, Meredith thought that it was a shame to waste all of the heat. She asked Gabriella if she might boil water for a bath.

Gabriella smiled and said, "There is no need. Come."

Meredith followed her down a hallway and into a tiled room at the back of the house. Gabriella lit another lamp, illuminating a bathroom complete with a flushing toilet, a basin with two brass taps, and a huge clawed bathtub with two more. She put a plug in the bath's hole, turned the taps and laughed delightedly at Meredith's look of awe as water rushed in.

"Hot and cold," she said, indicating which tap controlled which. "I will bring you towels, and clothes too."

Meredith nodded vaguely, still stunned by this unimagined luxury. Gabriella came back in a moment with a bundle in her arms, put it down, and turned off the water.

"I will wait in the kitchen," she said.

Meredith shed her filthy clothes and stepped into the steaming water. Within a few minutes it was murky with dirt, so she pulled the plug, re-filled the bath and then began to wash in earnest. It took another tub-full before she felt clean, and then she lay in the hot water for a long time, merely marveling at it.

At last she recalled her little hostess and dragged herself sleepily from the water. She dried herself with a towel the size of a blanket, and then she put on the clothes Gabriella had brought her: a man's fine linen shirt and woolen trousers. They were too big, but they were clean and soft. Looking at her own beleaguered clothing, she re-filled the bath, added soap, and then threw the lot in to soak.

She found Gabriella back in the kitchen, reading to her family in Italian from what appeared to be a Bible. It might have been a trick of the light, but the sleepers seemed to have more color in their faces than they had in the afternoon.

"You're back," Gabriella said with obvious relief.

Meredith nodded. The child looked exhausted. Meredith hoped that she was not sickening as well. "You should get some sleep," she wrote. "We'll start early."

Gabriella nodded and stood up, putting the Bible on the table. "I haven't slept in my own room since they fell ill," she said. "But I think, if you will stay in the one beside it, I will go there tonight."

Meredith nodded. Gabriella checked the stove, shut off the kitchen lights, and then led the way upstairs. "Here is my bedroom," she said, lighting a lamp in a pretty room at the front of the house. "My mother's is just there. She would want you to have it."

Gabriella lit another lamp, and Meredith looked into the grand bedroom. It was dominated by a tall, lacy bed. She knew that she could never sleep in such a bed, but she did not want to hurt Gabriella's feelings.

"Thank you," she wrote, and smiled.

"Thank *you*, Miss Meredith," said Gabriella. "I am more grateful than you can imagine." She paused to yawn. "Please wake me as soon as you are up."

Meredith nodded. Gabriella went into her bedroom and shut the door. After a moment, the light went off, and silence descended. Meredith looked around her own bedroom and sighed. She would have preferred to sleep in the stable with the horse, but she could not break her promise to the child. So she turned the light down low, picked up a stack of *Godey's Lady's Books* she found on the floor by the skirted dressing table, and settled herself on a chaise longue to wait out the night.

4

She woke, disoriented, to a brilliant morning, her head on a pile of magazines and her feet hanging off the end of the dainty chaise. She sat up slowly and then, remembering, she stood. She swayed in a spangle of dizziness; her head felt thick and strange. She forced back the panicked thought that she was coming down with the villagers' illness and went to wake Gabriella. But when she opened the child's bedroom door, she saw Gabriella lying like a china doll against her starched pillowcase. Meredith didn't have to touch her to know that her skin would be cold and clammy, and her chest would echo the sea. She lifted her and carried her downstairs to the kitchen, tucking her in with the other children between her parents. And then she went grimly to keep her promise.

*

Since there was only the one road connecting the hilltop to the valley, and she had seen no signs on it of recent usage, she began by circling the village on foot. She had little idea of what she was looking for – she didn't even know whether the priest had taken a horse. It wasn't long, though, before she found a trail of bent branches and saplings. It was so obvious that she wondered why the villagers hadn't found it themselves. Perhaps, she thought, they had already been sickening then and lacked the energy. It was easy enough to believe it: though her head had cleared a bit in the fresh air, she still felt as hazy as she had the morning after drinking Gradlon's cider.

Trying not to think about the implications of this, she followed the trail in to the woods. It was a peculiar trail, zigzagging through the trees, as if the priest had had no clear idea where he was headed. The wide swath of crushed underbrush confounded Meredith until she realized that he must have been dragging the statue behind him. It seemed he had simply decided to grab Stella Maris and run, without a plan or even forethought.

At last, the trail joined an established path along a wooded ridge. She followed it until it petered out among a stand of old-growth Red Spruce, the carpet of needles so thick beneath them that even the priest's heavy burden hadn't left a mark. At the far side of the copse Meredith could see a rock-strewn clearing, and she heard running water. She made her way toward it, thinking she'd drink and rest for a while, then go back for the horse to continue her search. But the smell stopped her several yards before she reached it: the same sulfurous smell that had been in the villagers' houses and the church.

She found a handkerchief in the pocket of her trousers, and putting it over her nose and mouth, she continued toward the clearing. By the time she reached the rocks, she was swaying on her feet, but she pressed on, certain now that she was near the source of the villagers' illness. Among the rocks was an opening, a kind of natural well leading to an underground stream. Near the mouth of the well, she found three pea-size pearls and a long strip of black fabric wedged in a crack in a rock. Along with sulfur, she smelled corrupted flesh, and she didn't need to see into the well to know what had happened to the priest.

Still, something urged her to look. Holding her breath, she peered over the lip of the well. There was no sign of the priest's body, but on a ledge a few feet down, she could dimly make out a woman's face – except that it could not be a woman's face. It was too small, too hard and perfect, glinting with enamel and gold leaf. Stella Maris.

And yet: the statue's eyes seemed to plead with Meredith. They were blue as a summer sea, except for three brown spots of tarnish on the right one. Or was it tarnish? Meredith wondered. Was it even there at all? She stretched one arm down toward the statue. It was within her reach, but her hands were wooden and clumsy with the poisonous fumes. She grasped at the hard wooden hand, uplifted in a gesture of benediction, and for a moment the statue's face seemed to smile. Then there was a loud crack and a clatter of falling rock. Meredith watched the blue eyes receding until she lost consciousness amidst the roar of sliding stone.

5

When Meredith awakened it was almost dark. For several minutes she could not remember where she was or how she had come to be there. Then she saw the fluttering strip of black fabric, and the three pearls shining in the dirt, and she remembered.

Yet she didn't quite trust her memory. She recalled reaching into a hole in the earth to save Stella Maris, and now there was no hole, only a circumspect pile of stone. There was, however, a remnant whiff of sulfur in the air. Meredith had no understanding of the workings of the earth, but she knew that there had to be a connection between the fumes from the well, her loss of consciousness and the villagers' strange illness. She suspected that the cave-in had saved her, but there was no guarantee that the poisonous breath of the well wouldn't find some new outlet. So she pocketed the strip of fabric and the pearls, got unsteadily to her feet, and made her way as quickly as she could back along the path through the woods.

As she walked, she tried to formulate a plan to bring Gabriella's people down the mountain, away from the poisonous miasma infecting their village. She resigned herself to days of grueling work, a search for a sympathetic doctor, and the very real possibility that she would succumb again to whatever had overtaken her at the well. So when she saw a light through the trees and heard the sound of voices, she thought that she had lost her way. She was about to turn back and wait out the night in the forest when another light sprang out of the darkness: a brilliant mandala of jewel colors.

Meredith crept around the wall of the church and peered into the open doorway, wondering whether she was still dreaming. The sight of the gathered congregation did little to convince her otherwise. Their pallor was ghostlike in the light of the candles. Some of them trembled; few seemed to have the strength to remain standing. Even the speaker leaned heavily on the lectern in front of him, but he straightened when he caught sight of Meredith. His face lit with wonder and relief. Meredith recognized him then – he was Gabriella's father.

"Behold," he said in a thickly-accented voice, reaching an arm toward her, "our savior!"

Meredith's instinct was to flee, but a small figure stepped out of one of the front pews and ran to her, nearly toppling her as she flung her arms around her waist.

"Oh, My Lady!" she cried. "You've returned to us!"

To Meredith's bewilderment, the congregation began to cross themselves and then to fall to their knees amidst a murmur of prayer. It took her many moments to realize that they were praying to her. Meredith looked down into Gabriella's shining eyes, wishing for the paper and pencil she had left with her pack. She shook her head, gestured to the gathered people to ask what was happening.

"They are offering you prayers of thanksgiving," Gabriella said. "For delivering us."

Meredith was lost. They could not know what had happened in the woods, and she hadn't even managed to recover their statue.

"I know," Gabriella continued, her eyes earnest, "you would have preferred that they did not realize who you are. But when I woke, you were gone, and I was worried. I had to tell them about you. They looked through your pack, and they found the painting."

Painting? Meredith thought. She shrugged, hoping that Gabriella would understand. After a moment, the child nodded. She pointed toward the front of the church. Meredith followed her finger to Stella Maris's empty niche. But it wasn't empty any longer. Vasilisa's painting of the princess in the boat hung in the center, with a bank of candles burning underneath it. At last, Meredith understood the villagers' preposterous conclusion. She shook her head frantically again.

"I understand," Gabriella said gravely. "You didn't want us to know. But what's done is done – and very well done! We are all here tonight." She looked proudly at her people, and then she looked back at Meredith with sudden anxiety. "You did mean for us to have it? The painting? To replace the statue?"

Meredith looked helplessly at the villagers. They looked back at her in adoration. She sighed, and then nodded, and turned to go.

"Wait!" Gabriella's father cried. He climbed down gingerly from the pulpit, hobbled toward her. He paused once on his trip up the aisle to pick something up: a pack, but not her old makeshift one. This was a proper army knapsack with a thick new blanket strapped to the top. It seemed to be heavily loaded.

"My daughter tells me that you cannot speak," He said when he reached her. Meredith shook her head. "The priest – he is dead?"

Meredith reached into her pocket for the pearls and the strip of cassock, put them into his hand. He let the rag fall with a look of distaste when he realized what it was. He rolled the pearls across his palm for a moment, then pressed them back into hers.

"These are yours," he said, and clasped his hands so that she could not give them to him again. Meredith nodded and pocketed them. "Please forgive my impertinence – but you are now appeased? The plague will not return?"

Meredith thought of the sealed hole in the ground, and she shook her head again, hoping that it was true.

Gabriella's father gave her one more incisive look, and then he said, "The lights, I suppose, are the sacrifice?"

Meredith looked questioningly at Gabriella.

"The gas lights," she explained. "They have stopped working. My father now believes that the others were right: the lights were against God. He thinks that the plague was punishment for his arrogance…that the lights were the sacrifice we had to make, to be cured."

Though she couldn't explain it, Meredith knew there was a connection between the hole in the ground and the villagers' miraculous recovery. If there was no way to dissuade them of her divinity, she thought, she could at least use it to keep them safe in the future. So she nodded emphatically.

Gabriella's father sighed regretfully, but then he smiled. "Really, it is a small sacrifice. Besides, my wife will be delighted. She did not trust them." He handed the pack to Meredith. "We made this ready, in case you returned. We do not have much to offer, but what we have, we have put in here as thanks to you. And of course, you will have our prayers forever."

Meredith bowed her head to him. She hugged Gabriella. Then she put on her coat and hat and went to find her horse, to a chorus of whispered prayer.

6

The warm weather continued after Meredith left Belmonte. Over a string of mild days, she felt her body ease into acceptance that the harsh winter really was over, and if spring hadn't quite come yet, it wasn't far off. For most of each day she rode without her coat. The horse trailed a drift of black hair as her own coat began to molt. In the mellow mountain sunshine, they both let down their guard, and for the first time, the horse's judgment failed them both.

They were high on a ridge when the storm struck. There was no warning but a sudden, cold blast of wind. They emerged from a thick stand of trees to see a black cloud racing across the sky from the south. Within a few moments, that cloud had extinguished the sun, and the air was full of snow.

Meredith had been in the mountains long enough now to recognize snow that meant business. She hadn't met a storm so heavy since the night she'd spent with Gradlon. By the time she buttoned her coat, she could barely see the horse's ears in front of her. They needed shelter, but the woods here were new growth, not thick enough to provide it. Meredith thought back along their road. She remembered looking down from the ridge earlier in the afternoon, into a valley dotted with white houses and red barns. They had looked so far away, dreamlike and remote in the watery, false-spring sunlight, but she knew now that she had to find them.

She turned the horse toward the western slope, but the ground was a mire of rock and mud from the recent thaw, now uniformly white and impossible to decipher. The horse slid and stumbled and finally bunched herself up, refusing to move. Meredith got off and tried to lead her, but the horse was shaking, terrified by the uncertain footing and the blinding snow. So they climbed the hill again and moved painstakingly through the trees just below the ridgeline.

Snow blasted Meredith's face when she tried to raise her head, stinging into her eyes so that she couldn't see where she was going. But, she thought, it hardly mattered. If the horse would not go down the hill, then there was no hope of finding shelter, and without shelter, the only thing they could do was keep moving so they didn't freeze. They walked for what seemed like hours, inching along as the snow piled up and the murky light failed. At last Meredith could go no further. She slumped down against a tree, into a deep snowdrift. The horse stood over her, her head hanging and legs splayed. Meredith shut her eyes, though she had a memory of somebody telling her once that to go to sleep in the snow was certain death. *Well*, she thought, *so be it*. She was too tired to care. She stared into the dizzying white, her hand buried in the sodden feather of the horse's foreleg.

I'm sorry, she said.

The horse said nothing. But after a moment she lifted her head a fraction, her ears twitching. Meredith's heart leapt with irrational hope. She looked up and around. At first she saw nothing but snow and the looming grey shadows of tree trunks. As she stared into the murk, though, she began to make out something blacker than the forest's twilight. It moved toward them slowly, almost stealthily, and for the first time Meredith wondered what wild creatures stalked these hills. For all she knew, there were wolves here still; no doubt there were wildcats and bears. The shape looked too small to be a bear, but a cat was bad enough. Even the horse could not outrun a predator in these conditions.

She stood still and waited as the black shape approached, increasingly baffled by it. It was too bulky for a wolf, its movements wrong for a cat – oddly stilted and choppy. But when the creature finally came close enough for her to see it properly, she was no nearer guessing what it was. It looked like some kind of fantastical lion: coal-black, with a dense, heavy coat to which the snow seemed incapable of clinging, and which thickened into a mane around its head. Its tail curled over, lying on the base of its back.

It stood motionless for a long moment, looking at them with invisible eyes, and Meredith had the feeling that she was being appraised. At the same time, her fear had left her. The horse, too, seemed to have relaxed slightly. Meredith took a step toward the creature. It took a simultaneous step backward, its eyes intent on her. It's tongue came out of its mouth, and it began to pant. Meredith understood then that it was a dog. It's condition was too good for it to be a stray, so when it turned and trotted off into the trees, she stumbled after it.

The black dog moved diagonally down the eastern side of the mountain. This time the horse did not balk at descending, though she slid and stumbled so that Meredith could not hold her reins, only trust that she would follow. The dog, however, was sure footed, moving over the snow like a shadow, despite its bulk. It didn't stop or turn to look at Meredith and the horse, but it kept within their sight no matter how many times they stumbled. And they stumbled often. Meredith's eyes were stung and swollen from the blowing snow, her legs leaden, and she could no longer feel her hands. Her breath came in short, painful rasps as she struggled against the drifts than seemed to grow visibly in front of her. She could hear the horse breathing hard, sense by her gait that her hooves were caked with snow and ice.

Then, abruptly, her body gave out. Her legs buckled beneath her, and she sprawled in the snow. She knew that she was about to die, but the thought didn't move her. The last thing she heard was perfect silence, and she was grateful for it.

7

When Meredith opened her eyes, a specter leaned over her. She thought that it must be the spirit of the storm, because its hair and eyebrows and eyelashes were white as the snow that had claimed her, its face smooth and pale as a pearl against its dark jacket. The only pigmented parts of it were its lips, which were pale pink; its long eyes, which were pale blue; and a patch of slabby, livid skin on its forearm, which was revealed when it lifted the arm and the sleeve of its jacket fell back.

It held a long, silver needle between its thumb and first finger. Meredith struggled weakly as the creature lifted her limp hand. It was red and swollen far beyond its usual size, but she forgot her misshapen hand as the demon inclined its head to her – an affirmation? A gesture of respect? – and then plunged the needle between her own thumb and forefinger. It didn't really hurt, but the shock of it was enough that she tried to rise. Pain tore through her body.

"Please," said the demon in a gentle, curiously accented voice, "you must lie still."

Meredith obliged by losing consciousness again.

*

The next time she awakened, the white figure of her fever dream was nowhere to be seen. She felt limp, wrung-out, but the pain she remembered from her previous waking had dulled to an ache in her limbs when she moved them. Slowly, she sat up. Her vision filled with colored lights, but after a few moments sitting still, it cleared again.

The bed where she had been lying was set beneath a small window. The window framed a group of snowy firs, and the weathered shingles of a lean-to joined to the house by a door in the wall at the foot of her bed. The ubiquitous stove stood against the wall beyond the lean-to door, with split wood stacked around it right up to the ceiling. Two pots were simmering on top of the stove, releasing a pungent steam. Beside it was a washstand, and next to that a large cupboard, its open upper shelves stacked with plates and cups and cooking implements.

In the wall across from the bed, there was a door, apparently leading outside, with pegs on the back of it. Her own coat and hat hung from two of them. To the right of the door was another window, a large twelve-pane one, with a dark wooden table and chairs beneath it, clean and mundane in the early morning sunlight. Through the window she saw a sloping yard and snowy hills. There were tracks in the yard's snow, but no one in sight.

On the other side of the door was some kind of shrine: a low table covered by a red cloth, with a small, carved wooden cabinet sitting on it. The doors of the cabinet stood open. Inside it were a figurine, several framed pictures, and a handful of objects whose purpose Meredith couldn't guess. In front of the cabinet stood an urn with a number of half-burnt tapers emerging from it, a few dishes of pooled wax, and another dish holding what appeared to be printed paper.

The final wall of the cabin had shelves built from floor to ceiling, except at its center, where there was a small table with a set of brass scales and several measuring jugs, an oil lamp, a sheaf of paper. On the shelves were dozens of labeled crockery jars. Meredith could also see her knapsack leaning against the bottom row of shelves. She swung her legs over the side of the bed and put her feet on the floor, and then realized that she was no longer wearing the clothes Gabriella had given her. Instead she was dressed in a plain blue robe that opened at the front, crossed over and tied with a red sash. The thought that someone had undressed her was disturbing, but not as much as the sight of her bare hands and feet. They were red and swollen and covered in weeping blisters. When she tried to stand, pain shot up her legs, and she toppled back on to the bed, her eyes filling with tears.

The door opened then. The black dog stood in the doorway, along with the demon from her dream. Except that he wasn't a demon, simply a peculiar looking man. His skin was uncannily white, except for the touch of pink at his lips and cheeks. His hair beneath his black cap was equally pale, falling to his chin in thistledown wisps. By contrast, all of his clothing was black: baggy trousers, felt boots, the quilted jacket with its short, round collar and braided toggles running down the front, and a pair of round, smoked glasses. Meredith looked for the scars she remembered, but his sleeves hid his forearms.

The white man and the black dog stood in the doorway for a moment longer, looking at her with similar, subdued curiosity. Then, with a faint shake of his head, the man smiled and took off the glasses. Behind them, his eyes were slate blue. He came inside and shut the door. "Good morning," he said in a light, friendly voice, nodding his head to her.

The dog lay down on a carpet in front of the stove, tongue lolling as it stared at Meredith. Its tongue was violet.

"I did not imagine that you would wake so soon," the man continued as he unbuttoned his coat and hung it beside hers, along with his cap. The accent was very faint, more a deliberateness in the way he spoke. "I am Jyu Siu Fai," he continued, bobbing his head again. "You may call me simply Siu Fai. And you are Meredith, who cannot speak."

Meredith shrank back, wondering if he was some kind of supernatural being, after all. Seeing this, he laughed and shook his head, then took something from the desk by the shelves of crockery and handed it to her. It was a handful of playbills, their backs full of one of her conversations with Gabriella – the one in which she had introduced herself. Meredith took them, and then gestured for a pencil. Siu Fai gave her a look, tinged by worry she didn't understand until he obliged her, and she found that her swollen, blistered hands could not close around the instrument. She tossed the pencil and pages aside, her eyes filling in frustration.

Siu Fai sat down beside her and put one of his smooth white hands over her blistered red ones. "Do not despair, Meredith. They will heal – that, I can promise you." His face and manner were untroubled, the touch of his hand devoid of expectation, and Meredith felt the tension leaving her. Siu Fai seemed to sense the precise moment when she relaxed. He stood up then and went to look into the pots on the stove.

"I have just come from your horse," he said. "You will be glad to know that she is well."

Though the horse had not been foremost in Meredith's beleaguered mind, she was more than glad to hear this. She was also suddenly worried that the horse might have been damaged by the cold as she had been, but Siu Fai continued, "She was sorry for herself for a day or two, but a horse's heart is like this stove. It can withstand a good deal if it is well stoked, and hers is stoked with love for you. I told her that you would not recover if she didn't. That roused her…that, and a few doses of *baak coek* and *dong gwai*. You could do with some yourself." He filled a cup from the pot he was stirring and brought it to Meredith. She took it, then sat looking dubiously into the brown, foul-smelling liquid.

"I know that it looks strange to you," Siu Fai said, "as all of this must look strange." He gestured to himself, and the dog, and the room. "But it is by virtue of this medicine that you have kept your hands and feet. This, and the needles. Your outer limbs were nearly dead when I found you."

At the mention of needles, Meredith recalled more of her fever dream. She put the cup down abruptly and turned back the sleeves of her robe. The marks were hard to see against the damaged skin, but she found them at last: faint bruises like thumbprints, with red pinpricks in their centers. There were two on the back of each hand, where the thumb and first finger joined it. Meredith tried again to stand, and when the pain drove her down again she glared up at Siu Fai. Sighing, he went once again to the desk. He took a small, flat wooden box from a drawer, and then opened it for Meredith. It was lined with white silk. A row of gold and silver needles, ascending in size, were held against the lining by fine silken loops.

"They are for *jamgau*," Siu Fai said. "My people's medicine." When Meredith made no response, he shut the box again and put it in the pocket of his tunic. "We use them to correct the flow of energy in the body. Sometimes, also, the blood. When Siji brought me to you, your body was dying. The blood had left your arms and legs to rush to your heart, because the body will save its core at any cost. If I had been a few minutes later…" His polite, serene face wrinkled for a moment into a frown, and then it smoothed again. "But happily, I was not. Siji saved you." He nodded at the dog. "Siji and your horse – she lay by you and kept you warm. So, with the *jamgau* and the teas, I have made the blood return to the places it had forsaken."

He paused, studying her. When he saw her lingering distrust, he sighed. "I am sorry. I cannot imagine how you must feel, to wake here, like this."

Meredith herself didn't know, beyond the fact that she wished she was riding a snowy ridge instead.

"I will not force this on you," Siu Fai said at last, picking up the cup of liquid. "But you have eaten nothing in days. There is chicken broth on the stove. Will you take some of that, at least?"

Meredith realized then that she was hungry. She was also suddenly ashamed of herself. Clearly, this man had saved her life; quite possibly her limbs, too. If his methods were strange to her, they were nevertheless effective and offered in kindness. So when Meredith nodded assent to the soup, she also held out her hand for the cup of medicine. Siu Fai smiled and inclined his head as he handed it to her, then he went back to the stove. Meredith shut her eyes and swallowed the contents of the cup, trying not to gag. She opened them again when she heard Siu Fai laughing softly. He was standing by her with a small, steaming bowl in his hands.

"Well done," he said. "I promise that this will taste better."

He took the cup and handed her the bowl. There was no spoon, so Meredith sipped straight from its rim as Siu Fai watched. It was, as he had promised, plain chicken broth, though there were also flavors in it that Meredith didn't recognize. None of them were unpleasant, though, and she drank the soup greedily. When the bowl was empty, Siu Fai took it and refilled it. As Meredith sipped this second bowl, she looked at the dog. It lay on its rug by the stove, facing her, alert and dignified. It might want her soup, but it wouldn't stoop to begging for it. She decided then that she liked it.

"Siji has bewitched you," Siu Fai said.

Meredith looked up. Siu Fai was leaning against the table, studying her as intently as she had studied his dog.

"She has that effect. All Chows do. It is the noblest of all dog breeds."

Siji turned to look at her master, as if she understood every word he was saying and took it as her due. He smiled fondly at her.

"Do you know, the stone lions that guard Buddhist temples were modeled on Chow dogs?"

Meredith shrugged. She knew nothing at all about China, except that it was the origin of silk and tea, and its inhabitants were meant to be black-haired and yellow-skinned, not pure white.

"When Buddhism came to China," Siu Fai continued, "no one there had ever seen a lion. But the descriptions they heard reminded them of these dogs, and so they made their guard lions to look like them. It is why I named her Siji."

By which Meredith could only assume that the name meant "lion". Her head swam with questions that she couldn't ask, and her eyes teared again with frustration.

Siu Fai took it all in. "It must be infuriating," he said, "not to be able to communicate."

Meredith nodded.

"I think," he said, "that you have not always been mute?"

Meredith hesitated. When she'd awakened on that grey beach, her speechlessness had seemed a sudden and recent affliction. She did not think that she could have lived the life she half-remembered if she had been mute. Nevertheless, she could not recall a single conversation, or even the sound of her own voice. There were only images, and even those had an overexposed, dreamlike quality.

Siu Fai's blue gaze rested gently on her as she ruminated, as his hand had rested earlier on her wounded one, easing the anxiety. "I would give a good deal," he said softly, "to know what has happened to you." He looked at her for a moment longer, and then he shook his head. "I'm sorry. I did not mean to say that aloud. But to answer my own question, if you cannot: no, I do not believe that silence is your natural state. I have met a number of mute men and women in my life, and there was a quality to their silence…an acceptance, but more fundamental. There was no battle in them, as there is in you."

Meredith raised her eyebrows.

"There is nothing otherworldly about it. I know it the same way I knew where the cold had attacked you. You see, in my kind of medicine, I approach the body as a whole, rather than a series of separate systems. So if someone comes to me with a pain in the bowel, I do not merely examine the lower abdomen. I examine the whole body, the way that the energy flows through it, to try to determine the root cause of the illness.

"You…" he paused, as if weighing his words, and then continued, "you came to me with frostbite and severe hypothermia. Of course, I treated these conditions. But I also examined you for those weaknesses that might make you susceptible to them."

Meredith shrugged.

"Are you asking me what I discovered?"

Meredith nodded.

"To be perfectly honest, I'm not quite sure. Your flow of energy has been damped by something, which of course one would expect to find in a patient suffering from over-exposure to cold. But even after you warmed up, and your blood began to circulate properly again, the energy remained sluggish. In fact, it is very nearly static. It is as if your body lives, but you spirit is somewhere else…" He shook his head. "That, however, crosses over from medicine into philosophy, or theology perhaps… either way, not my area of expertise. All I can say is that at some point, not too long ago, you suffered a tremendous shock. A shock characterized by cold and wet, and from which you very nearly did not recover."

Meredith thought of the girl in the red shroud and her own deathlike waking on that bitter beach. She nodded.

"I am sorry," Siu Fai said, and because he said it sincerely, she nodded again.

She looked at him for a few moments, wondering how to ask what she wished to know. She touched her hair, her eyes and her face. He gave her his small, ironic smile.

"You are asking me why I am white?"

Meredith nodded. He thought for a moment, and then he went over to the shrine and picked up the photographs. He brought them to the bed and sat down beside her, moving the unfinished bowl of soup to the floor. Siji came and began to lap at it.

"I will tell you all about it," Siu Fai said, "but please, lie down and elevate your feet. They are collecting too much fluid."

He picked up a bolster and put it under her legs when she lay down. Then he handed her the pictures. The first was of a man dressed much like Siu Fai, with similar features, except that his hair and eyes were dark. He stood on a beach in bright sunlight, holding up a fish as long as his arm. The second picture was a hand-colored studio photograph of a woman in an intricately embroidered blue robe with voluminous sleeves. She had a pretty, delicate face and a spray of flowers in her dark hair. The final photograph was another formal portrait taken against the same backdrop as the woman's, though it had been left in its original sepia tones. It showed two children in robes similar to the woman's, though shorter, with trousers underneath. The younger child had dark hair and eyes like the adults'. The older one had hair and skin so pale that the camera's flash had almost erased his features.

"My father, Jyu Tou Waa," said Siu Fai, pointing to the man. "My mother, Jyu Gam Jyun; my sister Jyu Wai Ling; and of course, myself. You can see that they looked as all of my people look. I was the only white one in the family, in the village where I was born...very likely in all of the villages of the Jyugong Delta.

"As you can imagine, my birth created a sensation. Some called me a miracle, but many more an abomination. As I was my parents' first child, my father was advised to put my mother aside and find another wife. My mother was advised to have no more children. Luckily for me, and I suppose for Wai Ling, neither of them listened to these suggestions.

"My parents weren't superstitious people. They treated me as they would have treated a child of the proper color, and for a long time I did not even realize that I was different. But this could not last. My father was a doctor, and there had never been a question that I would be as well. When I was five, he began taking me on his rounds with him. That was when the trouble began. A man died in a house I had visited. He was an old man, and ill, but people said that it was my influence. White, for us, is the color of mourning. It was no great stretch for people to decide that I brought death with me.

"My father began losing patients, and those who kept him on asked him bluntly not to bring me into their homes. My parents tried to reason with them. They were friends, relatives – people they had known all of their lives. But fear is often more powerful than love, or even blood. My village did not want me, and my parents were faced with the choice between locking me away like a shameful secret, or destitution. My father could not stomach either of these options, and so he searched out another. Within a week, he'd sold everything we had, and bought tickets to America.

"It was not unheard of. In those days many Chinese men went to California to work in the mines or on the railroads; some from our own village had gone. But those were poor men, peasants and fishermen desperate for employment, and they did not bring their families. People were shocked. They told my father that he was mad to choose such a life rather than send me away. But he knew what he was about. He had seen an advertisement offering work for doctors in the railroad camps. The Chinese laborers refused to be treated by American doctors. To keep the camps running, some of the companies had resorted to hiring Chinese doctors."

Siu Fai paused, studying the picture of his father with an unreadable expression. "I do not remember much of the journey," he said at last, "only that we spent most of it shut in the dark, stinking hold of a cargo ship. My mother was sick; my sister was an infant, and she wailed ceaselessly. But we came out of that ship into what seemed to me a paradise. The air was warm, but there was none of the cloying humidity of the river delta we had come from. The sun shone in a clear sky, the sea was an unpolluted blue, the land more wilderness than town. I decided then that I loved America." He smiled sadly to himself. Meredith wondered what had changed his view.

"We lived in the railroad camps for about a year. I think that for my father, it was the happiest time of his life. There was plenty of work, and his patients were grateful for his services, but most of all, nobody objected to my presence. Of course I still stood out, but the men of those camps had seen far stranger things in their travels than a white boy. Besides, they were too tired for superstition, and too glad of my father's services to risk angering him.

"But it wasn't an easy life for my mother and sister. We moved constantly; our houses were little better than shacks. There were few women in those camps, still fewer Chinese women. What children there were worked like their parents. My mother and Wai Ling were lonely. When my father could not bear their unhappiness any longer, he decided that it was time for us to settle. He had heard about a fishing village in Monterey, built by Cantonese immigrants who had grown tired of mining and railroad work. It had been there since the fifties, and by the time we arrived, it was thriving. Many of the fishermen had brought their families from China. Best of all, they had no resident doctor. They took us in readily, and no one dared to call me unlucky.

"The village always smelled of smoke and drying fish, but soon it became the smell of home. I think all of us loved it there equally. The houses were built right on the seashore, which reminded us of our old home in China. There was always something happening, whether it was simply the coming and going of the fishing boats, or the arrival of the train that took the fresh catch to San Francisco, or the huge junks that came to take dried American fish back to China…"

The mellowness of Siu Fai's voice had grown suddenly threadbare. He looked at Meredith, who looked back at him anxiously. She had noted the change of tone, and the past tense in which he spoke of his family, and she dreaded whatever was coming. But instead of going on with his story, he smiled and took the pictures from her.

"You are tired now." Meredith shook her head. "You can't hide it from me. Remember, you have only just begun to recover. Your body needs rest to heal. There will be time enough for the story, later."

Meredith could not deny that she was sleepy. Sighing, she turned over and gave way to it. The last thing she was aware of was Siu Fai pulling the quilt up over her shoulders.

8

The next time Meredith awakened, she was ravenous. It was dark, though, the only lights the dull red glow of the stove and a small yellow pool on the desk, where Siu Fai sat. Meredith lay watching him for a long time, trying to work out what he was doing. He had a row of the ceramic jars on the desk in front of him. Working from the left, he would take a jar from the row, scoop something out of it into a large jug, and then put it back. When he had measured out enough of whatever was in the jars, he stirred the contents of the jug and then poured them into a clean jar, wrote something on a slip of paper, and pasted it to the lid. Then he put it aside and began the process again. As he worked, he spoke to himself in an undertone, in a language Meredith guessed must be Chinese.

Meredith didn't want to interrupt Siu Fai, but her hunger was becoming painful. Carefully, she pulled herself to sitting and wondered how to get Siu Fai's attention. Then she saw a shadow separate from the darkness at the base of the stove as Siji rose, stretched, looked for a moment at Meredith and then went to her master, nosed his arm. Siu Fai looked down at the dog, smiled as he touched her head. When she turned to look at Meredith, he looked too. His smile widened. He put the lid back on a jar he'd left lying open, and then brought the lamp over to the bed.

"You are awake! Do you know, you have slept twelve hours? You must be hungry."

Meredith nodded. But rather than go to the stove, Siu Fai studied her face intently. Then he said, "May I please take your pulses?" She looked blankly at him. "I need to feel your wrist."

She held out her arm, her blue sleeve falling back. Siu Fai took her wrist between his thumb and two fingers and held it like that for what seemed to Meredith many long minutes. Sometimes he changed the pressure or moved his fingers slightly. He did not look at her but at the dark window, his head tilted slightly and his eyes squinted, as if he were listening hard to a very faint sound. At last he let go of her hand, putting it gently back in her lap, and then he lifted the lantern near her face. Looking slightly embarrassed, he said, "Would you mind showing me your tongue?"

Meredith raised her eyebrows, but she stuck her tongue out for him. He looked at it for a few moments, and then he nodded as if it confirmed something. "There is nothing too far amiss. But your tongue is pale, and your pulses are weak. You need eggs, I think, and more chicken broth, while you are waiting for them."

Meredith nodded and accepted the bowl of broth he gave her. As she sipped it, Siu Fai lit more lanterns until the room was almost bright. Then he opened the cupboard, took out a basket of eggs and began to crack them into a bowl. He had just begun to ladle some of the chicken broth into the eggs when there was a faint scratch at the door.

Meredith jumped, but Siu Fai looked unsurprised. He set his mixing bowl aside, spoke a few foreign words to Siji who, apparently following orders, went to lie on her rug by the stove. Then he went to the desk and took up the jar he had just filled and labeled and went to answer the door. A woman stepped into the cottage. She was heavily swaddled against the cold, so Meredith could not judge her age or appearance – only that she was many months pregnant. Siu Fai handed her the labeled jar and spoke to her softly for some moments. Meredith could not hear his words, but she saw the woman nodding as she listened. She also saw the woman stealing glances in her direction.

Siu Fai saw it too. "This is Meredith," he said to the woman. "She was caught in the storm last week, and I am treating her for exposure." Perhaps embarrassed by Siu Fai's forthrightness, the woman thanked him quickly, handed him a basket, and then took her jar and hurried out the door.

Siu Fai was smiling when he turned back to Meredith. "That will give the good ladies of the valley something to gossip about for at least a month." He considered this, then he added, "Or perhaps not. To report your presence, she would have to admit to having come here."

Meredith raised her eyebrows, questioning.

Siu Fai shrugged. "They need me, but they don't like to admit it even to themselves." He saw Meredith's look turn toward pity, and shook his head. "I am happy with my life, happy to know that I am helping them even if it is by their own terms. Besides, it is a fertile valley. They pay well." He uncovered the basket and tilted it toward Meredith. It held carrots, potatoes and a plucked chicken.

Siu Fai put the basket into the larder and went back to mixing the eggs. When they were well blended with the stock, he took out a large, round-bottomed pan and poured hot water into it. He placed it on the stove, then put the bowl on a rack over the water, and covered all of it with a lid. He put rice on to cook beside it, and then he brought one of the lamps to Meredith, setting it on a shelf above the bed.

"Are your hands and feet very painful?"

Meredith tried moving them. They ached, but it seemed to her that the pain was diminished from what she'd felt that morning. She shook her head.

"I believe that the swelling is abating, too," Siu Fai said.

Meredith nodded, but she wasn't thinking about her discomforts. Her mind had turned back to the history Siu Fai had begun earlier. She wanted to know how he had ended up so far from that Californian fishing village, but she didn't know how to steer him back to the subject. At last, she sat up and gestured to the shrine, in which Siu Fai had replaced the pictures of his family.

"You want to know what happened to them," he said.

Meredith nodded. He studied her with pale, calm eyes, and then he sighed. "I wonder if it is really for the best? It is a sad story, and it seems to me there is too much sadness in you already."

Meredith shook her head.

"Well…" Siu Fai sighed. "You eat something. Then, if you are not sleepy, I will tell you more." He went back to the stove, checked his pots, and moved them off of the heat. He took a bowl from the shelf, scooped a helping of rice into it, and then ladled in some of the egg mixture. He brought the bowl to Meredith with a deep, oval-shaped spoon. The egg was soft, almost like custard. Meredith ate it all quickly, and Siu Fai refilled her bowl without comment. When she had finished the second helping, Meredith looked at him expectantly.

He laughed softly. "You are certainly tenacious." Meredith shrugged, and Siu Fai sighed. "Very well," he said. "But first, tea."

He went back to the kitchen and measured tea leaves into a blue and white ceramic pot. He poured hot water into the pot and then brought it, along with two handle-less cups, to the bed. The tea was light-colored, with a subtle, floral scent. Siu Fai sipped from his cup, then said, "I told you that we were happy in the fishing village." He looked at Meredith, apparently for affirmation, and yet it seemed to her that his expression sought more than that. Confirmation – as if he could not quite believe that this statement had ever been true.

She nodded hesitantly. Siu Fai nodded as well, and then sighed. "And yet, there was a shadow over our lives. Though we were a self-contained community, we were still foreigners. We were permissible in the eyes of the locals as long as we could be ignored. By the time my family moved to Monterey, however, the Chinese village was well off: not wealthy by any means, but comfortable. This irritated the locals, many of whom were poorer than we were. But what really infuriated them was the fact that we had made our fortune out of a resource that had always been at their feet, and with which they had done nothing. They could not forgive us that, because they could not forgive themselves for having missed the opportunity."

He paused for a moment, drinking his tea. "We did not own the village land; we had it on lease. So the first thing the locals did was try to pressurize the landowners not to renew our lease. But we paid the owners more for it than anyone else had, so they didn't listen. Next, they tried to frighten us away. A few of our people were attacked – beaten and threatened. When we still resisted, they destroyed nets, damaged boats and equipment, stole drying fish – anything to keep us from our work. But we were used to hardship. We mended our nets and patched our boats and carried on; and so they went to war.

"Or so I have to assume. Nobody saw who started the fire; nobody was ever arrested. But it was certainly set – they found a burned-out, punctured kerosene drum in the ruins of a canning shed. It was summer. Everything was tinder-dry. The fire started at night, of course, and by the time the alarm was raised, very little could be done. By morning, our village was a pile of ash." Siu Fai stared into his empty cup. His voice was not bitter, but it had gone very low and hard.

"I do not think," he began again, "that these men – or whoever they were – intended to kill anybody. I prefer to believe they didn't. But then, can one set a fire in the middle of the night in a dry season, believing that there will be no victims?" He shrugged, as if he truly didn't know.

"There weren't many, which is to say that most of us escaped with our lives. I escaped because our living quarters were situated above my father's dispensary, and too small to hold us all. I slept on the dispensary floor. The stairway was a wooden one running up the outside of the house. It was on fire by the time I woke up. I could see my family. They stood in the doorway, calling to me. I called back, trying to make them come down, but my mother was afraid to walk through the flames, and my father would not leave her there. So I tried to climb up – to lead them down. The stairway collapsed. That is the last I remember of that night."

He paused again, his eyes so fixed and faraway that Meredith worried he had slipped into some kind of trance. She reached out with one of her ruined hands, touched him on the arm. He started, looked at her, and then smiled apologetically.

"I am sorry. It happens whenever I think of it – the memory captures me with 'what-ifs'." He sighed. "I came out of my delirium in a white room full of beds and screams. It was the burn ward of the local hospital. They did what they could for me, I suppose, though my father could no doubt have done more. I wasn't told much. I don't suppose they expected me to live. I was burned over most of my body."

He put back his sleeves, revealing the scars Meredith remembered from the night he'd saved her. They covered his forearms, reaching right up into the palms of his hands, white ridges and red craters, like stone that had melted and congealed. "But I did live, and gradually I learned what had happened that night – that the village had been destroyed, and that ten people had died in the fire, including my parents and my sister. I learned that no arsonist had been caught, no one was to be prosecuted. The single repercussion of that fire was that the village lease was revoked, and its people told that they could not rebuild it. By the time I was able to leave the hospital, everyone I had known was gone, scattered in their search for new jobs and homes.

"For a long time I simply wandered. I don't remember much about those days except anger and bitterness. Perhaps there is nothing more to remember. I couldn't stay angry forever, though, and eventually I came back to myself. I remembered my father and all that he had taught me. I remembered how my mother and sister had left their home so that I could have a chance at a good life. In the end, they had sacrificed everything, but my life had been spared, and it would be a terrible dishonor to them to waste it. So I made my way to San Francisco, to Chinatown. I asked for the address of the best doctor. I told him who I was and what had happened, and I begged him to take me on as an apprentice. I count myself forever blessed that he accepted."

Meredith didn't realize that she was weeping until Siu Fai took her hand. "Please, Meredith, do not cry for me," he said. She lowered her head, the tears spilling faster. She could not stop them. "This life – " he gestured to the room around them " – it may look to you like exile, but it isn't. I could have stayed in San Francisco. I was respected there. I could have married and lived comfortably amongst my own people. But they didn't need me – not really – and when I no longer needed them, I went looking for a place that did. I found it here. I am content with this life."

And yet, Meredith thought, *contentment is not the same as happiness.* In the face of Siu Fai's stoic loneliness, she was suddenly and keenly aware of her own.

"Is it really me you are crying for, Meredith?" he asked after a moment, with a gentleness that told her he'd guessed some of what she was thinking.

She couldn't look at him. He put his hand on her head and said nothing else, only stroked her hair until her tears were spent.

Spiling

1

"You know that man under the tree?" Happy asked Silence one night at dinner. A hard November rain drove against the windows, but the kitchen was warm from the range, stoked to cook the supper that now lay on the table.

"Probably better than I know most anyone else," Silence answered, cutting into a pan of cornbread.

"How come he's the only Negro in this town?"

Silence looked up at her, considering. "I really couldn't say."

But Celia said, "Mostly colored folks stick together, somewhere out of the way of white folks."

"Why?" Happy asked.

"I guess because white folks have given them such a hard time. I know if I were one of them, I sure wouldn't have much time for us."

Silence sighed, anticipating a long debate. The flip side of Happy's talent for seeing the invisible was her inability to make sense of the lines draw by obvious differences. She couldn't understand why people failed to look Silence in the face or avoided Annie Newcombe, and she would spend hours minutely questioning anyone who might be able to provide a satisfactory answer.

This time, though, Happy didn't pester. In fact she looked as if her mother's answers had confirmed something she'd already believed. She said, "I want to meet him."

"I'm sure he'd be delighted," Silence answered. "You can stop after school Monday. Give him my regards."

"I want you to introduce us."

Silence looked at her over a forkful of pork and beans. "Since when do you wait to be introduced?"

"Since now."

"You knocked on Annie Newcombe's door all by yourself."

"This is different."

"Is it his light?"

"I haven't got close enough to tell."

Silence was suddenly curious to know what color Pascal's light would be. "All right. I'll take you tomorrow morning, if your Mama doesn't need you here."

Celia shrugged. "Just remember to order some seed potatoes, if you're going into town."

*

Going to town the next morning, Happy was jittery. She walked a few steps behind Silence, ignoring him when he called back to her to keep up. But when they reached the tree and she heard the music emanating from within the knot of listeners beneath it, Happy pushed right up to the front. Silence couldn't see her face, but by the angle of her head he knew that she was reading Pascal's light.

After a moment, the old man silenced the strings, looked up at her and said, "Well, *P'tite*?"

There was a long pause, and then Happy said, "Blue," her voice high and clear and certain. "Same as the sky around the full moon."

Pascal didn't ask for an explanation. He gave her a faint smile and said, "You got a pretty little voice, *P'tite*. You sing?"

"Sometimes," said Happy.

"You got a favorite tune?"

Happy considered this, ignoring the people waiting to hear how she would answer. "Green Rocky Road," she said at last.

"Green Rocky Road," Pascal repeated, and he began to re-tune his guitar. "Now that's a song I ain't heard in a looong time. Where on earth did *you* hear it?"

"Mississippi?" said Happy, pulling on one of her pigtails in concentration. "Or maybe it was Louisiana…"

Pascal looked up at that. Pain crossed his face like a wind-driven cloud, dark and certain but gone again in a moment. Then, shaking his head, he began playing soft cut-time octaves. Silence edged closer, along with a few of Happy's friends. The rest hung back, fascinated, not quite sure what they wanted to hear. Then Happy began to sing:

"When I go by Bal-ti-more,

Need no carpet for my floor,

Come – along with me

And we'll go down to Ga-li-lee

Singin' green, green, rocky road…"

Silence's heart twisted inside of him. He'd heard Happy singing to herself, but he hadn't really listened. It seemed to him now he'd never heard a sound as pure and bright. He

437

stood rooted to the spot until the last notes had been lost in the creaking branches, and even then he was reluctant to move, as if it would break some spell that had spun out between the child's voice and the guitar's.

At last Pascal nodded, and Happy nodded back. Then, with a sunburst smile she was off, shrieking and laughing into the brilliant morning with the other children. Silence sat down beside Pascal on the bench. Pascal shook his head.

"Your child's got a rare voice," he said.

"She's not my child."

Pascal gave him a canny look. "Oh yeah, she is. No doubt about it: whoever got her on her mother, she's yours now." He paused. "You did right bringing her here."

"She asked me to."

Pascal nodded. "Mother sing too?"

Silence smiled. "Not in a way you'd want to listen to."

Pascal chuckled, but his eyes followed Happy, thoughtful. "How come you haven't brought her by here til now? Or her mama either?"

Silence sighed. "I wasn't sure what you'd think."

"About what?"

"About them living with me. You being a God-fearing man…"

Pascal rolled his eyes. "Silence Ogden, don't you know me better than that?" Silence shrugged. "Well just to clarify, I don't believe in any God would find fault with a man for loving someone."

There was a fierceness in Pascal's words that took Silence aback. Still, he felt he had to set the record straight. "I'm not in love with Celia, and she turned down my proposal."

"Which was wise of her," Pascal observed dryly, "if you aren't in love with her. But you've got an affinity for each other all the same, otherwise you wouldn't be sharing a roof...or a child. Don't you try to tell me you don't love that child."

Silence thought of the twist in his chest when Happy sang. He thought of the way that her blue eyes never flinched from his face. He realized that Pascal was right. He wondered how her hadn't seen it himself, and why the simple truth of it terrified him.

"What did she mean," Pascal said after a moment, "about blue?"

Silence smiled, shook his head. "I'd be lying if I said I knew. But as I understand it, there's a light that shines around people. Most of us can't see it, but Happy can. When she meets someone new she reads their light, and that's how she decides whether or not they're worth knowing."

"Hm. So what does 'blue' mean?"

"Only she could tell you that. But you can be sure you passed muster, or she never would have given you the time of day."

"I'm glad to hear it. You tell her to come see me anytime – we can trade songs." Silence stood up to go, but Pascal added, "And you pay attention to her. That child has something to teach you."

2

After their meeting under the tree, Happy took up with Pascal as enthusiastically as she had with Annie. She didn't abandon her first friend, but now she spent half of the time that she used to spend trailing Annie on the bench beside Pascal, watching intently as he played the guitar or listening to his songs. She seemed to learn them effortlessly, singing them back to him perfectly after hearing them only a handful of times.

Silence never intruded on their meetings. He could see that Happy and Pascal were absorbed in each other as he and Pascal had once been. He wasn't jealous, but the sight of them together always gave him a sharp pang of regret that he couldn't quite account for. Still, Silence was used to feeling not quite right, and for the most part he was contented with his life.

Autumn turned seamlessly to winter. The first snowstorm came and went, blanketing the road down the mountain, sealing the hollow in its wintry keep. Time lost meaning as Heaven drifted, cut off from the world, and its people fell into their winter lull. Silence felt himself slipping too into the cocoon of the dark season, as he hadn't in many years. And then one Saturday afternoon he caught Happy emptying Pascal's dinner pail into the compost heap. The food appeared not to have been touched.

"What are you doing?" he cried.

Happy started and then looked up at him with guilty eyes. She opened her mouth, but nothing emerged.

"Don't you lie to me, Happy Gagne," Silence said, in a stern voice he used with her only rarely. "You tell me why Pascal didn't eat his dinner."

Happy looked toward town, as if Pascal might come and rescue her from her predicament, but the road was empty. Finally she looked back at Silence and said, "He told me he wasn't hungry."

A shade of dread passed through Silence then – except that he knew it was more than that. Not even a premonition: it was a conviction of coming darkness like he'd felt that day long ago when he knew, abruptly and absolutely, that his father would not live to finish the boat. He found himself trembling.

"How long has he been sending his dinners back?"

Happy's eyes were anguished, torn between two trusts. But she'd never been able to lie with any conviction. "A while," she said unhappily.

A while, Silence repeated to himself, passing a hand across his eyes. How long had it been since he'd visited Pascal? Panic wouldn't let him think. "Does he seem sick to you, Happy?" he asked, trying to keep the hard edge of worry out of his voice.

"He…he does cough a lot." Silence turned toward town. "No, Silence – you can't go! I promised not to tell you!"

Silence turned back to her, took her shoulders gently in his hands. "He should never have made you promise that, Happy. It was wrong of him, and you did right to tell me. But I know he's your friend, and he doesn't need to know you told me anything. I'll tell him I found the dinners you were throwing out, and worked it out myself."

Happy's face was still pinched with worry. Silence tried to smile before he turned again for town.

*

The bench was empty when Silence reached it, so he knocked on the church door. He had to knock three times more before Pascal finally answered it, and when he did he cursed himself for not visiting the old man sooner. He'd been thin before; now he was gaunt, his eyes sunken and shoulders stooped, collarbones standing like islands in the sea of drooping skin. He opened his mouth to greet Silence, but all that came out was a paroxysm of coughing.

"Christ, Pascal," Silence said, pushing past the old man and into the church so that he could close the door. It was hardly any warmer for that. "Why didn't you tell me?"

"Tell you what?" Pascal asked gamely, a spark flashing in his dark eyes still.

"That you're sick!"

Pascal shrugged. "It's just a cold. It'll pass."

"That cough's no cold, Pascal," he said grimly. "Besides, I know you haven't been eating your dinners."

Pascal drew back, his face shuttered. "That's *my* business."

Silence sighed. "Fine, call it a cold. Either way, it's freezing in here. You're not going to get better living in this place."

"It's my home," he answered querulously.

"It's not," Silence said, holding him in a steady gaze. "It's a drafty old church."

Pascal looked away, his mouth a stubborn line.

"A long time ago I invited you to come home with me. The offer still stands."

Pascal shook his head. "And so does my answer. I've been a travelin' man too long to stomach living in a house."

"What about an attic, then?" Silence countered.

"Ain't they part of houses?"

Silence shoved his hands into his hair. "Christ, Pascal, you are a stubborn old boot! Isn't there anything you'll let me do to help you?"

Pascal appraised the younger man. At last, something in his softened. "You're right about one thing: it is mighty cold in here."

"It's warm enough in my house," Silence muttered.

Pascal looked out the long window beside the door. Silence could almost see his mind working. "Haven't I seen a stovepipe sticking out of your barn roof?" he asked finally.

442

Silence began to smile. "You have indeed. My father put it in when..." Silence realized then that he'd never told Pascal about the boat in the barn. He didn't want to tell him now, for fear of him changing his mind again.

But Pascal didn't seem to have noticed the dangling sentence. "Well, I guess that might do," he said. "Give me a day or two to settle things with the reverend."

3

In fact he took five, but Silence knew better than to pester him. He was alone in the kitchen on a bitter white morning when he heard the hesitant knock at the door. He opened it to find Pascal on the other side, wrapped, apparently, in the sum of his clothing and carrying his guitar case on his back.

"Come in," said Silence, standing aside.

But Pascal shook his head. "Let's look at this barn of yours before we go any further."

"Is there any way I can convince you to live inside with the rest of us?"

"Believe me, son," he said, "I'm not too old yet to know my mind."

"All right," Silence sighed. "But let me carry the guitar."

Silence gathered a basket of logs and kindling. With that in one hand and the guitar in the other, he led Pascal across the yard to the barn and rolled back the door. Celia had reclaimed some of the space for the horse and the cow, but for the most part the barn was as John Ogden had left it on his last night on earth.

Pascal stopped dead when he saw the boat frame looming out of the interior twilight. "What on God's green earth is *that*?" he demanded.

"It's a boat. Well, it's the beginning of one."

Pascal succumbed then to a coughing fit. When it subsided, he croaked, "Silence Ogden, how come you never told me about this?"

"I guess it didn't seem relevant."

He shook his head. "Didn't it seem relevant to me movin' in?"

Silence sighed. "Does it really make a difference?"

Pascal gave him a shrewd look. "I guess that depends on why it's here."

"It was my father's idea. Well, I suppose it was mine first – it was something I used to talk about as a kid ..." And Silence found himself telling Pascal the whole story, from his earliest sea dreams, to Annie's stories, to the discovery in the attic, and finally his father's gift. As he spoke, Pascal made a slow circumnavigation of the unfinished vessel. Silence noticed a tiny hitch in his step that hadn't been there before – not as obvious as his own limp, but there all the same.

"I guess my father thought it would cure me," he concluded.

"Christ, son," Pascal said when he arrived back at the barn door. "That's a mighty big cure for a bout of melancholy."

"It was a mighty big bout of melancholy."

"So, when you planning to finish it?"

Silence smiled wryly. "Never."

Pascal looked up with keen eyes. "Well now that seems a shame, seeing as you've done so much already."

"What would be the point? I wouldn't know how to sail it, even if we weren't a million miles from the sea."

"More like three hundred."

Silence felt a spark of interest despite himself. "You mean you've been there? To the coast?"

Pascal shrugged. "I been just about everywhere this side of the Rockies."

Silence paused before the next question, a sudden anticipation churning in his stomach. "Have you been to sea?"

"Lord, no! Crossing the Mississippi was enough for me. Truth be told, I don't much like boats."

"Why not?"

Pascal paused for a long moment, and he answered into the dust-spun hollow of the boat's frame. "The best friend I ever had," he said slowly, his fingers running restlessly over non-existent strings, "the best man I ever knew...he lost his love on a sea crossing. Lost the better part of himself at the same time. It was the saddest thing I ever saw, the way he stumbled through life... I guess it's no wonder he couldn't bear the sight of a sailing ship. Well, some of that rubbed off on me."

Pascal lapsed into ruminative silence, his eyes somewhere in his distant past. Silence waited for more, intrigued by all that Pascal hadn't told him, but he didn't dare ask him to elaborate. The old man's voice when he spoke had dredged as deep a pain as any Silence had known.

"Anyhow," Pascal said, surfacing from whatever recollection had snared him, "that's nothing to do with you. Whatever your daddy had to do with it, you started this boat for a reason, and you need to finish it."

"I already told you – " Silence said, beginning to be irritated.

"And I'm telling *you*," Pascal interrupted, pointing a bony finger into his chest, "you need to finish that boat, no matter what you know and don't know, no matter how far we are from the sea. It's calling for you. I can hear it, clear as those souls in the tree. Can't you?"

Silence ignored the question, since they both knew the answer. Even now, the boat's voice hung like harmonics in the air, keening for its own unfinishedness. He sat down on the stool his father had converted to a work-box and faced the skeleton head-on.

"The truth is," he said, "I'm not capable of finishing it. It was my father who knew wood."

Pascal considered this, fingers moving ruminatively on his imaginary guitar. After a moment he asked, "Do you know what he was meaning to do next? On the boat, I mean – before he died."

Silence smiled sadly. "I don't think I could ever forget it. They were his last words to me: 'Tomorrow we'll begin planking.'"

"And you know what he meant?"

Silence looked from Pascal to the frame, the frame to the neat pile of ripped planks under the window. "More or less."

Pascal didn't admonish Silence as he'd expected. Instead he nodded, looking at him with earnest eyes. "Listen to me, Silence. I know you've known a lot of pain for your years. Pain and disappointment, and they can douse the fire in a man like nothing else. But the flame's still there in you somewhere, and if you mean to keep it going, you're going to have to do some work, because the fastest way to put it out is to let those things stand between you and what you love."

Silence gave him a dubious look, and Pascal sighed.

"I'm telling you, *P'tit*: God gave you those sea dreams for a reason, just like your daddy gave you this boat for a reason. Hell, he even gave you the means to go on with it once he was gone, if you weren't too stubborn to see it!"

"Now just wait a minute…" Silence began, and then stopped, because he couldn't think of a valid argument against what Pascal had said.

"You go back to work on that boat, and you'll find your way. I know it."

Silence gave him a long look. "How about a deal, then: I'll work on the boat if you'll give up this crazy idea about living out here, and move into the house."

Pascal glowered, and Silence grinned.

"See, I'm not the only stubborn one around here!"

"I just don't feel right in a house," Pascal grumbled.

Silence shrugged. "It's up to you. Celia will be glad enough to have me helping on the farm, rather than banging away in here on a fool's project."

Pascal sighed. "Did you say something about an attic?"

4

W.P. Stephens had acquired a recriminatory layer of dust in the year he'd lain untouched on the barn's worktable. Silence wiped it on his trousers and then took the book to an upturned crate by the stove, which he'd stoked with old straw and offcuts. He opened to the page marked with a sliver of wood, trying not to think of his father's fingers placing it there.

As soon as he began to read, though, a calm enveloped him. Stephens' words were comforting as those of an old friend, even if he didn't understand all of them: "While but few of the many different methods of building are adapted to the purpose of the amateur, a description of the principal ones will enable him to understand the entire subject more clearly. Of these, two are by far the most common, the carvel, and the lapstreak, also called clinker or clincher. In the first, usually employed for ships' boats, yawls, Whitehall and other boats, where lightness is not of first importance, the planks (six to eight on each side) are laid edge to edge, not overlapping, and nailed to the ribs or timbers that make the frame, the latter being spaced from nine to fifteen inches apart."

Silence couldn't remember how his father had intended to lay the planks, if he'd ever spoken about it at all. Also, the boat's ribs were spaced considerably more than fifteen inches apart. He was relatively certain that lightness was not of first importance, but to be sure he skipped ahead to the description of the lapstreak method. It sounded more complicated, but what finished it for him was Stephens' warning: "Three objections are made to this mode of building – liability to leakage, difficulty of cleaning inside, and the obstruction that the laps offer to the water."

"Carvel it is," he said to nobody, his breath making clouds despite the roaring stove. Having made the decision, he felt almost confident: with the planks already made, surely it was only a matter of nailing them to the frames, and even he ought to be capable of doing that.

But when he skipped to the section on planking, his heart sank. "Perhaps the most difficult part of boat building," said Stephens, "certainly the most difficult to make plain to a novice, is the planking." With increasing despair, Silence went on to read about the many ways that planking could go wrong, from bringing unnecessary strain to the understructure, to wrenching it completely out of shape. Getting it right all seemed to come down to mastering a process called "spiling", which involved making a lot of measurements and exact cuts in each plank. That, however, was as much as Silence could glean from Stephens' description.

Tossing Stephens aside, Silence went looking for the trusty dictionary, which he was certain he'd left in the barn when his father died. Eventually he found it in an empty feed bin, not much worse for the wear. Taking it back to the crate by the stove, he looked up "spiling", and found nothing. Next he tried "spile" which, apparently, could mean a small plug used to stop a cask, or a spout put into a tree to draw off sap.

Sighing, he put the dictionary aside and turned to the boat frame itself. He picked up one of the planks and laid it experimentally along the ribs just below the keel. It seemed flexible enough to bend across them, but because of the keel's curved line, its edge wouldn't lie flush against the keel's. One thing on which Stephens had been clear was that the planking process had to leave as few gaps as possible. Obviously the plank would have to be trimmed so that its edge matched that of the keel, but how to get the exact curve?

Silence put the plank down again and regarded the keel. He thought about the table of offsets, all of the calculations he and his father had needed to scale MacFarlane's drawings up to full-size paper patterns. A pattern of some kind seemed a logical solution here, too, but as he was no longer working on the flat he couldn't see how he'd make it. Even if he were careful, a pattern made by laying paper over the frame would be terminally flawed. He needed to find a way to draw the cut lines directly onto the wood. He leaned his head on the boat's transom: the only finished piece of it. He was aimlessly angry, stymied before he'd even begun.

"This is mad," he said to the mute wood. "I have no idea what I'm doing."

The wood beneath his forehead gave a slight shudder then, like the muscles of a dreaming dog. Silence sprang back, staring at the boat and then peering around the barn. Nothing moved in the dim light of the stove and the single window.

"Hello?" he called.

There was no reply, but he thought he heard a rustle and a faint intake of breath. He walked down the length of the boat, toward the dark end of the barn, where a ladder led up to the hayloft. He climbed the ladder, up into the sweet, dusty region under the beams. Winter had only just begun, so the loft was still mostly full of hay and straw, leaving only narrow alleys to navigate within it. Silence pushed into the midst of the prickling mass, looking into the tunnels and alcoves. Then, in a little cleared space just above the boat's transom, he found Happy.

"What are you doing here?" he cried.

"Please don't holler at me, Silence." Her eyes were a supplicant's. "I just wanted to see you build the boat."

He laughed ruefully. ",There's not much to see. Does your mama know you're not in school?" Happy grimaced. Silence had to smile. "Come on. I'm getting nothing done here – I'll take you to town and explain to Mr. Marsh, and your mama never needs to know."

"Oh, no!" Happy drew back into the prickly recess. "I am *not* going to school!"

Silence raised his eyebrows. "What's Mr. Marsh done to offend you?"

"Don't make fun," Happy said darkly.

"I'm not."

"You are."

"Happy."

"You are!" Happy could glower as well as she could plead.

"Very well; you tell me what happened. But first, let's get out of the hayloft."

They worked their way back through the hay and down the ladder. Silence fed more scrap wood to the stove, and then they sat down in front of it. "Well?" he said.

Happy sighed. "It isn't Mr. Marsh. I like him just fine. It's Mrs. Marden I don't like."

Silence felt his face go hot, his body cold. "You mean Jenny Lindquist?"

Happy gave him an odd look. "No, I mean Mrs. Marden. The pretty one with the yellow hair."

"That's Jenny," Silence said sullenly. Since his erstwhile fiancée had married the shopkeeper's son the previous summer, he had tried even harder than before not to think about her, and he didn't like being reminded now.

"Well whoever she is, I don't like her."

"That makes two of us. What did she do to you?"

Happy made a face, shaking her head. "She tried to make me sew."

"Sew? Don't you already know how to do that?" Silence had seen Happy darning socks and letting down hems with her mother plenty of times.

"Yes. But Mrs. Marden came in to teach us girls to do fancy sewing. Pictures and letters and things."

"That doesn't sound so bad…?"

"I guess it wouldn't be," Happy answered, "if it was someone else teaching. But Mrs. Marden has absolutely no imagination."

Silence had to work hard to suppress a laugh. "How so?"

"Well, we were supposed to make a sampler with a motto. She had this big book of mottoes with her for us to look through. She said we should pick something that expressed our innermost heart. It hardly took me any time to find the perfect one. I drew it on the cloth in pencil just like she said, and I did that stupid chain stitch just like she said, and the letters even came out pretty straight. The ones she let me finish..."

"She didn't let you finish?"

"No. She took it away from me and threw it in the stove."

Silence wouldn't have thought Jenny had the gumption. "Why on earth did she do that?"

"Well," Happy answered, clearly beginning to enjoy relating the story despite herself, "she was coming around to all of us in turn, to see if we were doing our stitches right. She kept saying how wonderful they all were – until she came to me. She stood there and watched me for a while, and then in this real mean voice she said, 'Little girl, give that to me.' So I gave it to her, and she looked at it, and then her face went white, and she started shouting about how I was a horrible little girl, making a mockery of her."

"A mockery? What was your motto?"

"'Home is a woman's workhouse and a girl's prison'," Happy recited solemnly.

Silence could no longer keep from laughing. "So she threw it in the stove?"

"Not then. See, I wasn't too sure what a mockery was, but I thought it was something like crockery, and that didn't make too much sense, so I asked her about it." Silence laughed harder. Happy gave him a dirty look but continued, "After that, her face got all red instead of white, and she shouted a lot of things that got all jumbled together. The only part I could really hear was how it was no wonder I was bad, with a harlot for a mother."

Abruptly, Silence's laughter died. "She said that?"

Happy shrugged. "Lots of people say that; Mama says just ignore them. But then she said you were bad too – you were a bad influence on me. I thought it was real mean of her to say that about you, Silence, and I told her so. I told her you were the nicest man I ever knew, and my best friend, and she wasn't even good enough to say good things about you, never mind bad things."

Silence was quiet for a moment. "You said all that to Jenny Lindquist? I mean, Mrs. Marden?"

"Yep."

"What did Mr. Marsh do?"

"He gave Mrs. Marden a glass of water and a handkerchief, and he made me write lines on my slate."

"I guess he had to."

Happy nodded. "And at least he didn't rap my knuckles."

"Indeed," Silence said, recalling his handful of run-ins with Mr. Marsh's ruler.

"He also said he wanted to talk to you."

"To me? Not your mama?"

"He said you."

Silence sighed. "All right." They sat for a while listening to the stove wood crackle. Then Silence said, "Happy, I'm sorry, but I'm going to have to take you back to school."

"I know," she sighed.

"But I'll have a word with Mr. Marsh. As far as I'm concerned, you're excused from Mrs. Marden's sewing class forever."

Happy's face bloomed. "Thank you, Silence!"

"You're welcome, Happy."

"You know," she said as they stood up, "there's an easy way to make that piece of wood fit."

It took Silence a moment to realize what she meant. "Oh?" he asked. "What's that?"

"Use a compass," she said, making a right angle of her thumb and forefinger to illustrate. "I know you've got some on that work table. Hold the wood right under that bit," she pointed.

"The keel," Silence told her.

"Right. Put the metal part of the compass against the keel, and the pencil part on the board."

"Plank."

Happy waved his correction aside and continued, "Trace along the keel like that, with the pencil on the wood, and the line will be exactly right."

Silence blinked at Happy in astonishment. "How on earth did you work that out?"

She shrugged. "It's kind of like sewing."

5

It took Silence eight hours and seven ruined planks to hang the first one fair. After that, the process began to go more smoothly, especially after it occurred to him to make two copies of each plank – one for each side. This worked until he got far enough down the hull that a single plank no longer reached the distance between bow and stern. Then he faced another problem: how to join two planks without leaving a gap for leaks.

MacFarlane's plans made off-handed mention of something called a "butt block joint", but failed to explain what this might be. Stephens, with his focus on canoes, which took shorter, thinner planks, was no help at all. The dictionary didn't have an entry for "butt block", but it did have "butt joint": "a joint made by fastening the parts together end-to-end without overlap and often with reinforcement." Which was all well and good, but without knowing what to use for reinforcement or how to apply it, Silence was no further along.

At a loss, he rolled the barn door shut and crunched through the frozen rime of snow to the house. The kitchen was empty except for a burning pot of coffee someone had left on the range. Silence threw it out and brewed another, and then he took two mugs out to the attic. He could hear Pascal coughing before he even opened the door and wondered whether it would be possible to get a doctor to the hollow before spring. He wished that he'd insisted rather than suggested before the snow began to fall.

Sighing, he pushed the door open, expecting to find Pascal still in bed. Instead, the old man was up and dressed and sitting with his guitar in a rat-bitten velvet armchair beside the crate of decrepit weaponry. It was so cold his breath hung around him like an aura, but he seemed unperturbed by it, smiling up at Silence.

"Well, ain't that a welcome sight," he said when Silence handed him the coffee. He'd been careful to make it *au lait*, as Pascal called it. Silence knew no French, but he'd learned by trial and error that *au lait* meant so watered down by milk it was hardly worth drinking. He took his own coffee black.

"You can sit in the kitchen, you know," Silence said, perching on an old Florida orange crate.

"My music grates on Celia."

"It doesn't," Silence lied. "But anyway Celia's not there, and you're never going to shake that cough if you don't get warm."

Pascal picked up his guitar, ran a thumb over the strings and then began to play a quick, quiet little melody. "Once," he said, speaking into the guitar, "I passed by a fancy sanitarium for rich folks who'd got consumption. The yard was all full of tents. When I asked how come, I was told the tents was where the sick folks slept – and that was in the dead of winter! Oh, they wrapped up to keep their bodies warm, but the doctors thought the cold air helped clear their lungs."

Silence sighed. He never knew whether these timely anecdotes were fact or whether – like his music – Pascal pulled them out of thin air in order to shut him up.

"Anyhow," Pascal said, "how come you're in here worrying me, and not working on your boat?"

"Because I've come to a dead end."

"What folks call a dead end," Pascal retorted, "is really just a sign that you've gotta step off the beaten path."

"There's not much of anywhere to step off to, in winter, in Heaven."

"Lord, I never knew such a man for excuses," Pascal muttered to his guitar.

"Excuses! It's the truth! Unless you happen to know how to make a butt block joint, in which case, I'm listening."

Finally Pascal looked up at Silence, though he didn't stop playing. Silence was irritated to see that he was smiling: a small, covert smile, as if this were a card game and he held the flush. "Why don't you tell me a bit about this blocked butt, and we'll see what we see."

Silence shook his head. "The problem is, the boat's gotten too long for the planks."

"Well then, it seems you gotta put two together."

"I'm not *that* ignorant! But seeing as it's a boat, and it's got to be watertight, and the planks have to fit measurements and align to curves and all the rest, you can't just bang them together any old which way."

"Your philosophers got no suggestions?"

Silence scowled at him. Though he'd never attempted to discuss his reading material with Pascal after the first failed attempt, Pascal still jibed him about it.

"Oh, all right," Pascal sighed, laying his guitar down. "So let's get this straight: you need a way to put two pieces of wood together so as they don't let in water."

"Right."

"And you think the way to do it is this blocked – "

"Butt block joint!" he cried, and then, sighing, "Yes – that's what the plans say."

"Well, didn't those plans come with any kind of instructions?"

"Of a sort. But they seem to presuppose you've been apprenticed to a shipwright. Or at least grown up with some working knowledge of sailboats and how they're put together. And seeing as I've never even set eyes on one..." He shrugged.

"That does sound like a dilemma," Pascal agreed and lapsed into a reverie, staring at the newspapered wall beside him. Silence was about to take himself off to brood, and perhaps re-attack Schopenhauer (about whom he wished he'd followed Mr. Marsh's advice) when Pascal spoke again.

"It's true, there's no sailboats in these parts. But there sure are a lot of things made out of wood." He knocked on the wall he'd been eyeing up. "If your daddy could make sense of those plans from a lifetime building barns and houses, there must be someone else in this town can do the same."

"No doubt you're right," Silence said glumly, "but there aren't many of them would welcome a drop-in visit from me these days."

"You sure about that?"

"The only people around here who still speak to me are you and Celia and Happy and Mr. Marsh and – " He came up short against the answer, staring him in the face, as it so often seemed to, with Annie's agate-blue eyes. "Ah," he said, as much in wonder as in realization.

Pascal smiled. "You're a smart boy, Silence. You just gotta learn not to think so much. It kicks the hell out of your good sense."

6

When Silence came into her yard, he found Annie up on the roof of her cottage, hammer in hand and her mouth full of nails, fixing shingles. She raised her free hand to acknowledge Silence, and then she went back to work. He sat down on the step to wait, and after a time he heard her creaking down the old loft ladder, then crunching through the frozen snow to the front of the house. Her cheeks burned red with cold and exertion; her eyes snapped bright and clear as the winter sky.

"Silence Ogden," she said. "I hope you're not looking for a story. I'm not in a fictitious type of mood."

"No," he said, standing up. "This time it's bare-bones practical."

"Oh?" she said. "Well that's unusual, coming from you." She opened the door and held it for him. It was warm and smoky in the house. A frame with a half-finished quilt on it took up most of the room. It looked like a spray of abstract color, but Silence thought that might just be because it wasn't finished yet. Annie poured two cups of coffee, and they sat down at her tiny table.

"Well?" she asked, after she'd swallowed some.

"Do you know how to make a butt block joint?"

She blinked at him in apparent disbelief. She was silent so long he thought she must not have understood. He was about to tell her never mind, when she asked, "Why do you want to know that?"

"I thought I told you already – I'm building Ian MacFarlane's boat."

Annie didn't lose her composure, but her flushed face blanched. She looked at Silence for a long time before she spoke. "You told me all right. But I was under the impression you'd given that up."

Silence didn't bother asking her how she knew that. Annie always knew what she needed to know; except, apparently, in this case. "I did give it up, when my daddy died. But Pascal talked me into going back to it. The thing is, I don't know what I'm doing, aside from the little bit my daddy taught me before he died. And now I'm stuck because I don't know how to make a butt block joint."

"And you think I do?" she asked, with a hard edge to her tone that Silence was too preoccupied to notice.

"Well, you built this house, didn't you?" He gave her a direct look. "Rather like Sweet Angelina built hers, in that story of yours…"

"You don't use butt block joints building a house," she said stubbornly, looking out the window.

"So then it's something specific to building boats?"

Annie pressed her lips together, her eyes moving rapidly over the birches beyond the glass, as if searching for something hiding among their bare striped trunks. Silence searched her face for anger, but what he found was plain, stark fear.

"Sweet Angelina didn't die in the sea, did she," he said, with a pain that surprised and confused him.

"She did," Annie said firmly.

"Fine," he said, suddenly angry. "But not in the way you've let me believe all these years."

"It's not my business what you choose to believe."

"Can't you ever just speak plain?"

"I've told you the truth," she answered coldly, "as well as I could."

"You've told me nothing!" he cried. "And now I'm dreaming of smashed boats and sea storms and a half-drowned girl, and it's starting to make me crazy!"

"And you blame me for that?" Annie answered after an over-long pause, her voice suddenly low and savage. "God knows I've tried to help you, Silence Ogden – "

"Have you?" he asked bitterly. "Or have you always been helping yourself?"

She looked as though he'd slapped her, recoiling slightly before she rejoined, "It isn't my job to tell you what your life means, nor what to do with it."

"Just admit to me that you're Sweet Angelina MacFarlane," Silence said, unaware of the plea in his voice.

Annie shook her head. "That *would* be a lie."

"Fine! Then admit that once, however long ago, you were her."

Annie was looking back out the window, her jaw working. "Why on earth does this matter to you?"

"Because if you are her, then there's a chance that I'm not mad! There's a reason for these dreams that haunt me."

"A reason?" she repeated, shaking her head. "You of all people should know there are no reasons, Silence. Things are the way they are. Sometimes it seems too much to be coincidence, but in the end it's just fate. Fate – or serendipity I suppose. If it's going your way."

"Fine," said Silence, standing up. "Just tell me one thing: is it fate or serendipity that keeps showing me your daughter trying to kill herself?"

In the wake of the words Silence felt as shocked as Annie looked. Until that moment, he hadn't realized that was how he'd read the dreams, but now he was certain he was right. All at once Annie's face was ablaze, her fury pushing against him like a storm wind. She picked up the hammer and nails she'd laid on the table, and a square scrap of wood; laid the block of wood over two abutting planks on the table; and then drove a nail into each corner, the final one so hard that the block split.

"That," she said, pushing it into his hands, "is your butt block joint. Now get out of here, and don't you ever come back!"

Silence stared at her in disbelief.

"Go!" she repeated, in a voice as terrible as the storms in his dreams. He went, without looking back.

7

It took Silence a few days to recover from his run-in with Annie enough to go back to work on the boat. When he did, he couldn't help wondering if she'd given him the wrong information out of spite: the joint she'd demonstrated looked far too bulky and crude to fit into the elegant lines of the emerging boat. But when he hung the first jointed plank, and it looked from the outside more or less like the whole ones, he decided that her demonstration, if brutal, had at least been accurate.

Silence thought about Annie as he worked. He was as certain as he could be that she was Sweet Angelina, or had been once, but that knowledge did nothing to explain or reconcile him to the dream of the beleaguered girl on the beach. She hadn't appeared to him again, but in his nightmares now he felt her presence. They were confused dreams, no longer of the sea but of paths through dark woods; of hunger and haunted places and unrelenting pain. Often he would find himself trying to run from some nameless terror on feet that felt as if they were being stabbed by knives with every step, like the hapless little mermaid in the terrible story he'd once read as a child.

Most nights he stayed up late talking to Pascal, or reading philosophy if Pascal wanted to sleep, trying and failing to escape the lingering despair of the dreams. Waking too early, he would take a lantern out to the barn and hang planks by its frail light as his fingers slowly went numb, and his worry with them. And so the winter passed uneasily for Silence, but nonetheless fairly predictably, in a procession of bad dreams and wooden strips, until Celia's premonition.

*

For a woman who set so much stock in her daughter's talent for divination – never mind her explanation for her own dreamlessness – Celia was remarkably skeptical when it came to other manifestations of the supernatural. It was an attitude that put her further at odds with a community in which nobody spoke of a bad dream before breakfast in case it came true, and a dog's midnight howl would provide terrified speculation over portended death for weeks to come, and the town's only calico cat had a bald patch on her back from being so often petted for luck.

Celia had been appalled to learn that even Silence followed some of these old-time rituals. She'd laughed, for instance, when she found his tally of August fogs; more so when he explained that it would predict the number of winter snows. She had flat out refused to put off planting the winter rye until the new moon, since the fine weather was bound to turn by then. And so Silence was justifiably surprised by her explanation when he came into the kitchen one afternoon in early March to find her sitting tight-lipped at the table, her knuckles white around a cup of forgotten coffee, a half dozen biscuits on the floor.

"Celia, what's the matter?" he demanded, wondering if she'd taken ill.

"A stranger's coming," she said, looking up at him with haunted eyes. "A stranger bringing evil."

Silence poured himself a cup of tepid coffee and sat down beside her. "What makes you think that?" he asked.

She looked at him for a moment, as if sizing him up. Then she answered, "All day, my nose has been itching."

Silence studied her, wondering if she was playing a trick on him. Her eyes, though, were deadly serious, daring him to scoff. "All right," he said. "But the hay is pretty dry by now."

"It is," she agreed, "but I've never been troubled by hay fever before. And then, while I was washing the breakfast dishes, the rooster came to the door and started crowing."

"Isn't that just what roosters do?"

"And *then*," she persisted, "just now, I dropped the biscuits."

Silence shrugged.

"You must know that dropping a biscuit while taking it from the oven is a sure sign that unwelcome company is coming. But dropping *six*..."

Silence waited to hear more evidence of impending disaster, but Celia had lapsed back into thin-lipped silence, her dark eyes wide and unblinking and fixed on him with what looked disturbingly like desperation.

"Celia," he said, "how many times have you told me that you don't believe in those old sayings?"

She shook her head. "Normally, I don't," she said. "Any one of those things is bound to happen in the course of a day. So is a stranger, or for that matter, a death. But *three* warnings in one day – I'd be a fool to ignore them!"

"All right," Silence said. "But 'evil' is a mighty strong word. A lot stronger than 'unwelcome'."

"Yes," she said. "But I have a feeling."

"A feeling," he repeated. "That an evil stranger is coming to Heaven..."

"Don't you mock me, Silence Ogden!"

"Sorry," he said, half-smiling. "I just can't quite believe I'm hearing this. I mean, who would bother coming all the way to Heaven to do evil?"

Celia's eyes flickered across the kitchen, as if taking stock. Then they settled on Silence. She drew a breath. "My husband," she said.

8

After that Silence hardly slept at all, and when he did it was with his father's old shotgun, oiled and loaded, under his bed. By virtue of Celia's panicked certainty, he expected her erstwhile husband to knock on the door the next day, or at most the day after, but everything remained quiet. New snow fell, further clogging the path to the valley road, and in the end even Celia began to entertain the possibility that she was simply being paranoid.

Still, Silence couldn't quite settle back into his old routine. His feeling of being watched, which had begun when Celia mentioned her husband, hadn't subsided. He didn't speak about it because he didn't want to frighten Celia, particularly when it might be a simple matter of his imagination running away with him. But the feeling didn't dissipate; rather it began to seem to him that people were acting peculiar in general.

Celia, for instance: though she no longer looked hunted, she also hadn't gone back to her straight-talking self. She was often quiet, and Silence would find her staring off into the woods or muttering to herself as she worked in the kitchen. Once or twice, when she seemed particularly lost in her own thoughts, he'd asked her flat-out what was going on in her head. But she just sighed and went back to work.

Happy, meanwhile, had turned inward and brooding, and she also refused to talk about why. At first Silence wondered if she had overheard the discussion about Celia's husband, but when he asked her point-blank if she'd been eavesdropping lately she denied it. Then he began to worry that she was having more trouble at school. This time when he asked, Happy's answer was equivocal.

"No," she said, "no one bothers me now."

There was a hesitancy to her answer that Silence didn't like. "Not even Mrs. Marden?"

She looked pointedly at the dish she was drying when she answered, "Mrs. Marden doesn't come anymore."

"You must be glad of that," Silence said, wondering why she didn't sound glad at all.

Happy gave him a hard look. "Silence, did you ever go have that talk with Mr. Marsh?"

"I'm sorry Happy," he said. "It slipped my mind. I'll go after school tomorrow – I promise."

She nodded dubiously, but as it turned out Silence didn't get the chance to forget again. He came in from the barn for dinner the next noontime to find a wheelbarrow full of books parked by the porch and voices coming from the kitchen. Sidestepping the wheelbarrow, Silence pushed the door open. Happy and Mr. Marsh sat with Celia at the table. Celia clutched a cup of coffee in shaking hands, her eyes flashing and lips pinched with anger. Mr. Marsh looked dejected; Happy, oddly triumphant.

"What's going on?" Silence asked.

Celia opened her mouth to speak, but nothing got past her quivering rage. Mr. Marsh gave her a sympathetic look and then said to Silence, "I'm afraid there's been a bit of an...event..."

Happy shook her head, rolled her eyes and announced, "We were fired."

"*I* was fired," Mr. Marsh corrected. "You, Happy, were expelled."

"Can someone explain in plain English?" Silence asked, exasperated.

"That's about as plain as it gets, Silence," Mr. Marsh said. "I've lost my job, Happy has been asked not to return to school, and it's all down to the machinations of your erstwhile fiancée."

"Of course it is," Silence said, slumping into a chair as the pieces began to fall into place. When his boots ran up against something that turned out to be an ancient leather valise with an irate cat peering out of it, he began to be angry. "You've lost your house too?"

Mr. Marsh shrugged. "Part and parcel of the job."

"And all this is because of Happy's sampler?"

"To be fair, one *could* argue that the fault is mine – "

"You're too generous by half," Celia interrupted sharply. "She sure damned well got you fired, and my daughter denied an education into the bargain, all because you were man enough not to whitewash the truth!"

"So it isn't about the sampler?" Silence asked wearily.

Mr. Marsh shrugged. "I suppose it did begin with the sampler."

"And me making a mockery of it," Happy added.

Mr. Marsh shook his head, but he couldn't resist a smile at the memory. "You didn't make a mockery of anything, Happy. You made an honest mistake, and Mrs. Marden simply lacks the imagination to realize it. But even if Happy had intended to mock her, it's a bit much to demand the child be expelled as punishment."

"Jenny Lindquist doesn't have the authority to expel children from school," Silence scoffed.

"Actually, she does," Mr. Marsh said wearily. "She's the newest member of the Ladies' Moral Improvement Society, and they act in lieu of the school board during the months of the year when we're is snowbound."

"But it was only an embroidery project!" Silence cried. "Happy does just fine at her other lessons."

"Well yes, that's true, but there was a bit more to it…" Mr. Marsh glanced sideways at Celia, who met his eyes squarely.

"Believe me, Marsh," she said grimly, "that woman can't have said anything that we haven't heard before."

He sighed, and nodded. "Well, she claims that Happy's – ah – family situation makes her a detriment to the morals of the other children, the sampler being proof of her ungodly upbringing. I went to speak to the Society, to try to explain, but unfortunately they had several examples of what they called Happy's 'undesirable influence'. Still – " he said, as Celia turned her glare on Happy " – I've never seen anything of the sort myself, and I can't see why a child shouldn't be denied an education because of pranks she pulls in her free time. However," he sighed, "the board doesn't agree."

"That explains Happy," Silence said, "but why did they fire you?"

Mr. Marsh gave him another beleaguered smile. "Arrogance – my own, sadly. I told them that if they kept Happy out of school, then they need not expect me back either."

Nobody needed to ask what the Society's response had been.

"But where are they going to find another teacher in snow season?" Celia asked at last.

"The Society has taken it upon themselves to run the school until summer."

"And you? What will you do?" she asked.

"Well, Happy has very kindly invited me to stay the night, as I was required to leave my house immediately. If you have a bed to spare," he said to Silence, "I'd be most obliged to borrow it. Tomorrow, I shall see if I can't find someone with the means to take me down the mountain, and then – "

"Oh, no!" Silence cried. "You aren't going to give up *that* easily."

"Silence, I really don't think – "

"Mr. Marsh," Silence interrupted, "Thomas – there aren't many teachers with your qualifications who'd teach in a backwoods school like this. There are even fewer I imagine who could help a farmer's son win a place at college. I think you belong here, and if you think differently, that's your choice to make. But you can't let Jenny Lindquist's temper tantrum drive you off."

Mr. Marsh sighed. "In an ideal world, Silence – " he began, and then he stopped, and sighed again. "But it isn't an ideal world. Every one of us at this table knows that only too well. Mrs. Gagne – "

"Miss!"

"Very well – I imagine you can get Happy back into school with some perseverance. But Jenny Marden's had my card marked ever since I started keeping Silence late for extra lessons and he stopped walking her home."

"I don't think so," Silence said with sudden conviction. "She did this to get back at me."

"For what?" Happy asked.

"For failing to make her a lawyer's wife. And I for one don't intend to let her get away with this. Thomas Marsh, I invite you to live in my house for as long as it takes us to get you your job back."

Mr. Marsh met his eyes, but shook his head. "Surely, Silence, you have too many battles to fight already."

Silence shrugged. "If so, then what's one more?"

God's Lanterns

1

Meredith was confined to her bed for another week. Siu Fai continued to treat her with the teas and the needles, but he also cooked her an array of strange, wonderful food, which more than made up for the discomfort. Once a day he put on his warm clothes and smoked glasses – his pale eyes were sensitive to the glare off the snow – and took Siji out for a long walk. He also tended the horse.

But Meredith wasn't satisfied with his reports that the horse had recovered perfectly, and so one morning he brought her into the yard to settle Meredith's mind. Meredith stood at the window, watching the horse's breath make clouds in the cold air, and longed to be on her back, with the sun at her left hand. Despite Siu Fai's kindness, she felt herself imprisoned, and her eyes filled with tears.

By the time he came in, Meredith had control of herself again, but Siu Fai seemed to sense some of her restlessness, and that evening he began telling her stories. It quickly became a ritual. After dinner Meredith would settle on the bed and lie with her legs up on bolsters while Siu Fai told her about San Francisco, or anecdotes from his long journey east, or more rarely about the river delta in China where he had been born.

When he saw Meredith looking tired, he would put out all the lights but one and go to work at his desk for a while before he retired to the lean-to off the back of the house for the night. Meredith found herself dreading the time when he would shut the door between them. She told herself that it was because she had grown used to the horse's company, that she didn't know how to be alone. Nevertheless, she woke each morning eager for Siu Fai to emerge from the lean-to, to kneel by the shrine and make his silent prayers.

This ritual also fascinated Meredith, and when he realized this Siu Fai put her in a chair beside the shrine and began to explain. "In China there are several religions, but whatever our other beliefs, all of us pray to our ancestors." He lit three sticks of incense and put them in the jar of sand in front of the shrine. "To us, family is everything, and family includes the dead. We believe that the deceased are still with us in spirit, that living or dead, we remain a family."

Siu Fai went to the table by the window, picked up a small bowl of rice, and then returned to the shrine. "I make offerings of earthly things to honor them, but also to provide them with things that they might not find easily in their spirit lives." He scooped a little pile of rice onto each of the three plates in front of the altar. "In return they bless me with their wisdom and guidance and love." He paused, studying the pictures and then turning to Meredith, his blue eyes earnest. "Since they died, I have shared a house with no one but Siji." He stroked the dog's head. "And yet, I have never felt alone. Does that seem strange to you?"

She shook her head, and she meant it. Though she had never considered it before, she realized then that she could say the same about her long journey with the horse.

Siu Fai smiled, and then, turning back to the pictures of his family, he sighed. "The truth is, these pictures should not be here. They are meant to stay on the home altar for forty-nine days after a person has died, and then to be replaced by ancestral tablets." He indicated three small rectangles of wood at the back of the shrine, covered in Chinese characters. "Memory is meant to be enough to keep them alive for those left behind. Perhaps I am weak; perhaps I am not a good Buddhist. Yet I have no other family, no neighbors who share these traditions. I don't even have a grave to visit, and so I have given myself a dispensation." Siu Fai shrugged and sat back, watching as the sweet smoke curled up toward the ceiling.

Meredith wondered if he were praying then, and if so, what shape those prayers might take. She thought of Vasilisa's painting, which her mother had called sacrilege and which the people of Belmonte now worshipped as a miracle. She thought of the Shakers, with their plain ways and convoluted incantations. She wondered whether she would ever believe anything so completely.

2

With every day that passed the swelling in Meredith's hands and feet decreased, and the ache diminished. The blisters burst and then flattened and began to heal. When the last of them had closed over, Siu Fai said, "Now, you must bathe."

Meredith knew that Siu Fai was right, but she didn't relish the idea. She knew that he'd undressed her at least once, in the days of her delirium, but this was another matter entirely. She watched him apprehensively as he heated water and filled the zinc tub he brought in from outside. When the tub was full she put her feet on the floor and tried to stand. It didn't hurt as much as it had the first time she tried it, but it was still painful. Her legs felt strange and unsteady, her feet leaden, and she stood swaying until Siu Fai came and pulled one of her arms across his shoulder, steadying her with the other. He was half a head shorter than she was: a fact that surprised her.

"You can try to walk," he said, "but go slowly. You will no doubt have lost some feeling in your extremities."

Meredith nodded. Drawing a deep breath against the pain, she put her right foot forward. It trembled, but it held her. Slowly, she tottered her way across the room, clinging to Siu Fai all the time. He walked beside her patiently, praising her efforts, and reaching out for a chair with his free hand when they were beside the tub. Meredith toppled gratefully into the chair.

"You have a strong will," he said, looking at her with admiration.

Meredith shrugged.

"Still," he said, "I do not think you can manage this on your own."

She frowned.

"I understand," he said gently. "Try to put your mind elsewhere."

Meredith nodded. Siu Fai knelt down and unfastened the ties on her robe. Then he eased it away from her shoulders and carefully over her damaged hands. He held her under the elbow as she shrugged it off, stepped into the tub and slumped gratefully under the water. Relief at having the worst of the ordeal behind her dulled the pain of the warm water on her hands and feet.

Siu Fai left her for a few minutes as he added the dirty robe to a pot of laundry he had simmering over a fire outside. When he came back in, he picked up a cloth and a bar of soap and a pitcher, and came to sit on the chair by the tub.

"Let me see your hands," he said.

Obediently, Meredith lifted them from the water. They were scabbed and livid, but Siu Fai didn't seem displeased with their appearance. He wet the cloth, put soap on it, and then began gently rubbing at the dead skin.

"Does it hurt much?" he asked.

Meredith shook her head, though the cloth felt like sandpaper on her tender skin.

Siu Fai laughed softly. "For a woman with no voice, you lie quite proficiently. If it becomes too much, just take your hand away."

But Meredith continued to watch with a pathological interest, ignoring the pain as the skin came off her hand in sheets. Although it stung when Siu Fai finally laid it back in the water, it felt like a part of her again. She offered him the other hand. He looked at her with raised eyebrows.

"You are very brave."

Meredith shook her head. Siu Fai said nothing more, just went back to work. When he'd finished he turned his attention to her feet, and she sat staring at her flayed hands. She thought of how they had looked when she came out of the sea – thin and wrinkled and white, like a corpse's hands. She wondered if she would recognize that woman if she saw her now.

When Siu Fai had finished her feet, he scrubbed her back, and then her hair, and gently wiped her face. By the time he was finished Meredith was too exhausted to worry about what he saw when she emerged from the water. He held a clean robe open for her, looking tactfully over her shoulder as she pulled it around her. When she returned to her bed, she lay down and fell immediately asleep.

3

Meredith awakened the next morning to an absence she could not immediately place. She lay looking up at the knots in the wooden ceiling until she recognized it: for the first time in weeks, nothing hurt. She lifted a hand, spread it above her. Though the skin was still rough and red, it looked like her hand again rather than a separate, alien thing.

The cold, clear weather held, and if Meredith had not been sedentary she would have noticed little difference day to day.

As it was, she saw that the sky through the window held its light a little bit longer each evening, and the sun at midday was strong enough to send rivulets of melting snow dripping from the eaves.

"The storm that caught you was the last of the season," Siu Fai told Meredith when he saw her studying them. "Spring is coming."

She looked doubtfully out the window at th frozen world. Siu Fai came to the window, pointed toward the trees at the perimeter of his yard. "See the buds swelling? They do not lie."

Meredith looked out at the trees, and she knew that he was right. But she didn't share the joyful anticipation she heard in his tone. She was dressed in her own clothes again, and she could hobble around the cabin if she leaned on him or the furniture. She was healing, surely as the trees were wakening. It would not be long before she could ride, but she couldn't feel anything of the old pull of the road south. She felt only an amorphous sadness.

"Come outside," Siu Fai said, sensing her melancholy.

Meredith raised her eyebrows. He had not yet allowed her outside, saying that she was still too vulnerable to the cold.

"You are ready. You won't fit into your boots, but we will wrap your feet."

He bound them first in strips of flannel, then covered the bandages with two pairs of woolen socks. There was pain when she stood, but nothing like what it had been. It was more of a dull ache, a reminder not to push her fragile body too far. Siu Fai helped her on with her coat, and then wrapped one of his own woolen mufflers around her head and neck. He put socks on her hands as well, wary of irritating them with anything closer-fitting. Then he called to Siji, put on his dark glasses, and opened the door.

The cold hit Meredith like a wall, snatching at her breath. She gasped, reached instinctively for Siu Fai. His hand was already there to meet hers; he guided her arm around his shoulder.

"You have been so long indoors," he said, "you have forgotten how to face the cold. It will come back to you."

Meredith nodded and then simply stood, bewildered.

"Would you like to see your horse?"

She smiled. Siu Fai let her go for a moment, in order to close the door, and before she could panic Meredith felt something come under her hand. She looked down into Siji's almond-shaped eyes. Her hand rested on the dog's back. It was the first time Siji had allowed Meredith to touch her. The cold seemed to recede at the contact with the dog's warm fur.

Siu Fai took her other hand, and they stepped off the porch. Meredith took a few awkward steps forward, turned to look back at the house, and then stood staring in astonishment. She had assumed that Siu Fai's cabin would look like any other on the outside, as it did on the inside. In fact it was like nothing she'd ever seen. The planks of its wooden walls were laid vertically instead of horizontally; the roof sloped downward in a graceful curve, shingled with rounded, grey tiles. It overhung the narrow porch at the front, supported at the bottom by square wooden pillars. The windows had latticed wooden shutters carved in intricate patterns.

"It's like the Cantonese houses," Siu Fai told her. "Do you like it?"

Meredith thought that it was the most beautiful house she had seen on all her long journey. She wished she could tell him so. Instead, she smiled and nodded.

"I'm glad. Come, now."

He took her hand from Siji's back and drew her arm across his shoulders. They made their way slowly toward a path that led into a stand of leafless oaks. There, he stopped. Siji came up beside Meredith, and once again she rested her hand on the dog's back to keep her balance as Siu Fai stepped away. He pulled one of the lower tree branches downward, and pointed to the tip of one of its twigs. Meredith counted five little conical, reddish bumps.

"See them?" he asked. "Spring really is coming." And he smiled as he released the branch.

They walked farther into the wood. Meredith was ashamed of her ponderous pace, and how heavily she had to lean on him, but the only comments Siu Fai made were encouraging ones. At last the trees thinned again, opening into a small clearing bordered by a crumbling stone wall. At the far side of the clearing was a shed with an open front. The horse stood inside of it, browsing a pile of hay.

As they approached, her head came up and she turned, ears forward and hay dripping from her mouth. When she saw Meredith she trotted a few steps forward, and then she stopped. Her ears twitched backward, and Meredith's elation turned to despair. She looked at Siu Fai with stricken eyes; he was looking at the horse.

"Come now," he said to her, "that's no way to treat your mistress! She would have come to you sooner, if she could."

The horse stood watching them, her ears falling further back. Siu Fai took a carrot from his pocket and gave it to Meredith. Then he led her toward a gap in the wall, which he had blocked with an old gate. He moved the gate away from the opening, and they stepped into the paddock. Meredith held the carrot on her outstretched palm. The horse's ears flickered in interest. She took a few more steps forward, then stopped again.

Why are you angry with me? Meredith asked her.

The horse turned her head away. Meredith's eyes filled with tears and she swiped at her eyes, furious with herself and with the horse. She took a few lurching steps toward the horse on her own. The horse pretended not to look at Meredith, though Meredith could see the edge of her black eye, half hidden in her long forelock, following the movement. When she was a few feet away, Meredith offered the carrot again. The horse stretched forward, still not meeting Meredith's eye, and sniffed at it. Meredith stood perfectly still. At last, the horse stepped forward and took it. Meredith pulled the sock off her hand and reached to stroke her nose, but her fingers barely brushed it before the horse turned and went back to her hay. Meredith felt near tears again.

"Do not be unhappy, Meredith," Siu Fai said, coming up beside her. "She is angry with you because she loves you, but it's not a horse's way to hold a grudge. It will pass."

Meredith shrugged, but she was glad when Siu Fai's arm came around her shoulders again.

4

When they returned to the house, Siu Fai sat down at his desk with his jars of herbs, and Meredith sat down to write. She had been practicing for several days, trying to regain the dexterity she had lost. She wrote in a blank book that Siu Fai had given her, with fine cream-colored paper and a cover of blue brocade in a cherry-blossom pattern. The book had seemed too fine for offhand conversations, and Meredith had stared at its first blank page for several days before she dipped the pen and put it to the paper.

Even then she hadn't known what she meant to write. When she looked down to see, in the wake of her hand, the words: "My first love was the wind," she was so shocked that she almost put a line through them. It was Siu Fai who had stopped her, saying, "If your hand and heart have something to tell you, it's best you listen." And that was how she'd begun to lay out the scattered pieces of her memories, to commit them to the solidity of ink and paper.

Once she'd begun, she found that she couldn't stop. She was driven to record the facts of her life with an abstract need as potent as the one that had led her implacably south and west for so many months. She suspected that it had something to do with having come, once again, very near to dying. Wrenching her body back from the cold that had tried to claim her had left her with a lucid awareness of the distance between herself and the battered girl the sea had cast back months before. She was also aware that the beginning of her journey had become as vague and dreamlike as those memories she'd recovered since. She knew that she had to make them concrete, or lose them altogether.

She didn't know why she was suddenly so desperate to record and remember what she'd once tried so violently to forget. Siu Fai might have been able to speak to the value of preserving even a painful past, but he kept himself scrupulously apart from Meredith's struggle. It was, at times, brutally difficult for him to refuse her offers to read what she had written. But he knew from his own hard experience that no one could help her in the battle she was fighting. So he kept his silence and tried to keep his distance.

5

One evening, just after sunset, there was a pounding on the door. Siji leapt up, stiff and growling until Siu Fai spoke a few words to her and she sat back down. Still, she watched him with quivering attention as he went to answer the door. A wild-eyed, white-faced man stood on the porch. At first Meredith took his expression for anger, and her throat squeezed with fear. But when Siu Fai greeted him calmly and asked him his business, the man answered in a shaking voice, and Meredith realized that he was not angry but terrified.

His wife was in labor with her first child, and something was wrong. The midwife was attending a birth in another valley; the nearest doctor was a day's ride away. Siu Fai nodded as if none of this was news to him, and Meredith guessed that the woman in labor was the one who had come to him that night for medicine. He made the man sit and drink a cup of tea while he gathered supplies into a bag. She was preparing herself for a long, lonely wait when Siu Fai said, "Meredith, do you think you can ride?"

She looked at him, questioning. Siu Fai glanced back at the man, and then said, "Mr. McIvor, I think you had best start back now. It is a long walk. I will take my guest's horse and meet you at the farm."

The man nodded dazedly and went back out the door. When he was gone, Siu Fai turned to Meredith and said, "I cannot go there alone."

Meredith found her pencil and a bit of paper and scrawled, "I know nothing about childbirth!"

Siu Fai sighed heavily. "I do not need you for a midwife, only to bear witness to what happens."

"Why? What is going to happen?"

"All I know is that this labor is unlikely to end well, and I will be charged with the outcome either way."

At last, Meredith understood. Humbled and appalled at once, she nodded, pulled on her coat and then eased her boots over her feet. They were only a little bit tight now, and though she walked slowly, she could do it without support. Taking a lantern, Siu Fai shut Siji into the house and then walked the path to the horse's paddock.

She was standing at the gate, her ears forward as if she had been listening for them. She stood patiently while Meredith bridled her, and she didn't balk when Siu Fai climbed up behind Meredith on her back. As they zig-zagged down the mountain, Siu Fai explained to Meredith what he knew about the case.

"It's been a difficult pregnancy," he said, "and the child is big. Quite possibly too big, but that is the least of my worries, since it is also breeched. It is not difficult to turn a breeched child with the needles, if you do it before labor begins. But when I suggested it…well, it was hard enough convincing her to swallow the herbs."

Meredith sighed, wondering where he found the grace to accept the ignorance of the people he was trying to help.

"I think that Mrs. McIvor has known for some time the child would give her trouble," he continued, "but she has pretended otherwise, even to herself. She is her husband's second wife. He lost his first in childbed."

They rode the rest of the way down the mountain in silence. At last they saw the lights of the settlement, and a few minutes later the path joined a road that ran between the farms of the valley. It had begun to rain; soon they were all soaked and shivering. At last, Siu Fai pointed to a house with all of its windows blazing.

"There," he said.

Meredith turned the horse into the yard. They climbed down, and Meredith handed the reins to a pinched-looking boy who emerged from the barn. She gave him an admonishing look, but he took the horse with a gentle hand and led her toward the barn, speaking softly to her all the time. Meredith was glad to have one thing less to worry about.

Mr. McIvor had not yet made it back to the house. The door was opened by an older woman – by the look of her McIvor's mother – who pressed her lips together at the sight of Siu Fai and Meredith and glared at them as she held the door. Siu Fai nodded to her politely nonetheless, and made introductions. The woman remained silent.

"Very well," he said. "You've heated water? Good. Meredith – " he handed her a small bundle wrapped in paper " – you remember how to boil herbs? Boil these twice, and then bring the infusion to me. Be careful not to burn them – it's all we have."

Meredith took the packet and looked at the woman. "Kitchen's that way," she said grimly, pointing down the corridor to the right.

"And Mrs. McIvor is…?" Siu Fai said.

"Up here." The taciturn woman started up a narrow stairway as a piercing scream resounded through the house. Meredith shuddered, and turned away.

The kitchen was dim and full of dogs, but there was a large kettle of water simmering on the range. Meredith put back her sleeves and got to work, trying not to listen to the anguished cries of the laboring woman. The kitchen filled rapidly with a pungent steam, from which the dogs fled, to her relief. When the decoction was ready, Meredith poured it into a pitcher, took a cup from the draining board and started for the stairs.

By the time she reached the landing, the screams had given way to low, despairing moans. The narrow corridor smelled of blood and fear, and also of strong spirits. She didn't understand the latter until she stumbled over a dark lump in the shadows: Mr. McIvor, passed out with his hand around a half-empty bottle of whiskey.

Stepping over him, Meredith walked toward the skewer of light falling from the cracked door at the end of the hallway. As she reached the door, Mrs. McIvor fell abruptly silent. She could hear Siu Fai and the older woman involved in a low-pitched altercation. Taking a breath, she pushed the door open.

The room was small, the atmosphere hot and close. A pile of bloody sheets had been tossed into a corner, and those on the bed were little cleaner. Siu Fai's scarred arms were bloody to the elbows, and the grim old woman wore an apron stained crimson. Mrs. McIvor herself seemed to have slipped into unconsciousness, her face white as death.

Siu Fai looked up, clearly exhausted, and relieved to see Meredith. "Thank you," he said, taking the pitcher and cup and setting them on the bedside table.

"And what do you mean to do with *that*?" the older woman snapped, looking at it.

"That depends on whether or not I operate," he said, wearily.

"You ain't cutting her," she answered.

Siu Fai sighed, and then said, in a voice that told Meredith he'd said the same thing too many times already, "Mrs. McIvor, there is no hope that your daughter-in-law will give birth normally. Even if the placenta wasn't blocking the birth canal, the child is lying sideways." He glanced at Meredith, his eyes full of quiet despair. "If I don't operate, both of them will die."

"It's *you* who'll kill her," said Mrs. McIvor venomously, picking up a rusty black shawl from a chair in the corner. "I'm going for the doctor, like we should have done to begin with!"

"Very well," Siu Fai said, watching her calmly.

"I don't want you in here with her while I'm away."

"Would you have me leave her here alone?"

"Where's my son?"

Meredith pointed toward the hallway. Mrs. McIvor looked out the door, and then back at Meredith, with little change of expression. Meredith guessed that Mr. McIvor's state wasn't an unfamiliar one.

"*You* can sit with her," the old woman said, pointing at Meredith. "Don't let him touch her." She swept out the door, beckoning to Siu Fai to follow.

Meredith listened to their retreating footsteps and then turned to look at the woman on the bed. She had never attended a birth, or none that she remembered. She felt no affinity to her; in fact, the smell of blood and desperation had begun to sicken her. Wrapping her arms around herself, she sat in the chair from which the elder Mrs. McIvor had taken her shawl, resigning herself to a long, bitter wait.

No more than a few minutes had passed, however, when she heard footsteps on the stairs again. A moment later the door opened. Siu Fai came into the room, his expression hard and determined and so far from its usual gentleness that Meredith leapt to her feet. Taking little notice of her, he began to unpack things from his bag that Meredith had never seen in his house: a rolled pouch of small, sharp knives; a tiny case that looked as if it might contain more needles; a strange-looking spool of thread.

When the things were laid out, he looked up at Meredith. He saw her reaching for the paper in her pocket and answered before she had the chance to ask: "I can live with the consequences of failing, but not of doing nothing."

Meredith found she was trembling. Still, she made herself nod agreement.

Sighing, Siu Fai said, "Do you think you can get the whiskey bottle away from McIvor without waking him?"

Meredith raised her eyebrows. She had never seen Siu Fai drink.

"To clean the instruments," he explained.

Meredith crept into the hallway, gingerly lifted the bottle out of McIvor's flaccid grasp, waiting all the while for him to wake and snatch it back. He muttered a few unintelligible words and then recommenced snoring. Meredith turned her back on him in disgust.

"You don't need to watch this, Meredith," Siu Fai said when she brought him the bottle. When he looked at her, she saw fear in his eyes along with the exhaustion. She shook her head firmly.

"I admit, I would be happier if you stayed," he said. "But it won't be an easy thing to watch. The surgery aside, there is every likelihood that the child is dead already."

Meredith reached out and clutched Siu Fai's hand, holding it until both of their hands were steady.

"Very well then," he said when she let go. "Will you half-fill that bucket with live embers?"

He indicated the ash bucket beside the fire. Meredith tipped the ashes from the bucket onto the hearth, and shoveled embers into it. Siu Fai thanked her when she brought it to him, and then he poured a generous amount of the whisky into a wide dish, placing the knives into it. After that he folded his hands and stood looking down at the woman's deathlike face for a long moment. Meredith wondered whether he was praying, or pleading with her.

At last he took out his box of needles and began placing them at various points around the woman's body. "Take this," he said, handing Meredith a clean towel. "When the child is out, I will hand it to you. If it's breathing, then wrap it tightly and hold it by the fire. If not, rub it all over with the towel and hope that it starts. Are you ready?"

Meredith nodded, although she doubted she could ever be ready. Siu Fai turned back the woman's bloody shift, washed his hands in the whisky and then swabbed her swollen belly with more of it. He took one of the knives from the sterilizing dish and made a slow, careful incision down the center of her abdomen. He held a towel where the blood sprang up and stuck a blunt knife in the bucket of hot coals. When it was heated he applied it to points on the woman's wound. Smoke rose along with the smell of burning flesh, and Meredith kept the contents of her stomach only by sheer force of will.

"Open the window," Siu Fai said, and Meredith was happy enough to oblige. She took several gulps of clean cold air before turning back to the bed.

The bleeding had slowed to a trickle, and Meredith found after an initial moment of queasy horror that if she didn't think of the woman as a woman, if she focused only on Siu Fai's hands, then she could watch what was happening. Layer after layer he cut through the woman's flesh, stopping to cauterize blood vessels when the bleeding was too quick, and again to allow a gush of clear fluid to drain, until at last he arrived at something purplish and solid. He put his knife aside, and slipped his hand into the cavity he had made. When he began to lift the purple thing, Meredith finally understood that it was the child.

She held her breath as he brought it forth. Her: the child was a girl. Siu Fai looked into the still violet face for a moment, his fingers on the baby's neck. Meredith's nausea began to return. But then Siu Fai took his finger from the child's neck, opened her mouth and cleared it of mucus. He brought the child close, sucked something from her nose and spat. To Meredith's astonishment, the child wriggled weakly in response and offered a frail cough. There was a faint upturn to the corners of Siu Fai's mouth, if not quite a smile, when he handed Meredith the baby and turned his attention back to the mother.

Meredith gazed at the child in her arms. She seemed an alien thing, blotched blue and pink, sticky and bloody and smelling vaguely of the sea. It was revolting; she wanted nothing more than to put it down and run from the room. But she had promised to help Siu Fai, so she wrapped the infant in the towel and sat down with her by the fire.

Gradually, as they sat there, the baby's skin lost its blue tinge. With a corner of the towel, Meredith wiped the blood from her face and head, from fingers that curled at the contact like a sweet-pea's fragile runners. Some instinct in her stirred; she offered the baby a finger, and smiled as the tiny hand grasped it with surprising strength. And then, without warning, the baby began to wail.

Meredith leapt up in panic, nearly dropping her, but Siu Fai's hands came under hers, took the baby from her. He smiled down at the screaming baby. "That's right," he said. "Scream with all your might." To Meredith he said, "Only the angry ones survive."

Meredith stared dumbfounded at Siu Fai, still beaming at the screaming child. A moment later the door burst open, and Mrs. McIvor entered, alone. She glanced at her daughter-in-law, who lay now chastely covered on the bed, and then crossed the room, arms outstretched for the baby. She took her with surprisingly gentle hands, the anger and exhaustion on her face replaced by wonder.

"The doctor could not come," she said softly, her eyes never leaving the baby's face. "There," she cooed, "there now…" And the child began to settle.

Siu Fai said, "It does not matter now. Your granddaughter is strong and healthy, and her mother may well survive."

"I suppose you cut her after all," she muttered.

Siu Fai didn't flinch from her hard look when he answered, "As I told you, it was that or watch them die."

Meredith expected reproach, or worse, but Mrs. McIvor only gave him a curt nod and went back to gazing at the baby. Looking as if he would rather not, Siu Fai took a breath and spoke again. "I assume the doctor will come as soon as he is able?"

"He'd better," the old woman answered.

Siu Fai nodded. "When he comes, you must tell him that it was an obstructed birth. The placenta had grown over the birth opening. It did not come away easily, and the womb has not closed down as it should. Your daughter-in-law has lost much blood, and she is bleeding still. I have given her medicine to stop it, and I will leave more with you. I cannot promise that she will recover, but she will have a better chance if she takes it."

Mrs. McIvor looked dumbly up at him, vitriol and scorn burned at last to blank defeat. "Tell me what to do," she said.

"Give her a cup of this, three times daily." He gestured to the pitcher Meredith had put on the bedside table. "Keep her warm. When she is ready to eat, give her eggs, chicken broth, beef broth. Black beer if you have any. No milk or anything made from it. After a week I will bring you a different medicine, to build her blood and help her recover her strength. Most importantly, do not stop her from feeding the baby. That is better than any medicine for helping the womb to heal."

The woman nodded meekly, hanging on Siu Fai's words.

"Make sure that her wound and her bedding are kept clean and dry. That is the best that you can do, for now. Send for me if you need anything more."

Again the older woman nodded.

"I wish you luck," Siu Fai said as, gathering his things, he prepared to leave.

He and Meredith were half way down the stairs before she said, "Mr. Jyu!"

Siu Fai turned back. Mrs. McIvor was a shadow against the dim light of the bedroom. "Thank you," she said.

6

It was bright morning by the time they arrived back at Siu Fai's house. He made breakfast, which Meredith ate as if she had not eaten in years. When she had finished, though, a melancholy descended on her. She reached into her pocket for pencil and paper, but she sat looking at the blank sheet for a long time before she decided what to write.

She turned the paper toward Siu Fai. "Will the baby live?"

He sighed. "I hope so," he said. "She will have a better chance if the mother survives."

"Could she?"

Siu Fai shrugged. "If they don't allow the doctor to undo what I have done." He finished his cup of tea, and then he looked at Meredith with tired eyes. "But there's no good in thinking of that. It's beyond me, now."

He stood and turned toward the lean-to. Despite having just saved two lives, he seemed beaten. Meredith watched him, stricken. She couldn't bear the thought of him lying down in the cold room, alone with his looming defeat. She wondered how often he went to sleep like that; more than anyone should have to, she suspected. And so, when Siu Fai reached for the door handle, she crossed the room, put her hand over his.

He looked at her, his blue-grey eyes surprised and curious. He released the door handle, but Meredith didn't release his hand. She closed her own hand more firmly around it, and Siu Fai's eyes widened. He half-shook his head.

"Are you asking me what I think you're asking me?"

Lord, I am! she thought, shocked even as she nodded.

Siu Fai shut his eyes for a moment, and then he opened them, and smiled at her, and slipped his arms around her waist.

*

By the light of the oil lamp, Meredith traced the scars on Siu Fai's chest with one finger. Earlier, when she had opened his shirt, he had not been able to look her in the eye. But she saw nothing shameful about his scars. There was even a strange beauty to them, the way that they swirled down his chest to the unburned skin like a river's path to the smooth white lakes and seas of some secret country.

"You don't have to touch them," Siu Fai said to her.

Meredith wrote, "Why wouldn't I?"

"I have never met the person who wasn't disgusted by them – least of all the very few women who have been persuaded to share a bed with me."

"Then they have been hypocrites, every one."

Siu Fai raised his eyebrows. "How so?"

"I've met many people in the past few months, but none who is not equally scarred, or whose scars don't make up a part of their beauty. Yours appear on your skin, but they are no less beautiful for that."

Siu Fai laughed with disbelief. "This, from the loveliest woman I have ever set eyes on!"

It took Meredith a long moment to decide that he meant it. Then she wrote, "You are mad. I'm tall as a man and thin as a stick, never mind that I'm shedding my skin like a snake."

He looked at her, bemused. "You truly have no idea how beautiful you are? Has no one ever told you?"

Meredith shivered, hearing an echo of similar words in a very different voice. "One person," she wrote. "But I put no stock in his opinion."

Siu Fai touched her cheek. "I am sorry," he said.

She shrugged, asking, *What for?*

"For whatever he did to you."

If Meredith's estimation of Siu Fai could have risen higher, it would have then, for the simple fact that he didn't ask what it had been, only slipped his arms around her and held her close.

7

There was no question of leaving Meredith behind when the McIvors' stable boy came a few days later to fetch Siu Fai. Likewise there was no question in Siu Fai's mind that he was about to face somebody's wrath over what he had done, and so both of them were shocked when Mrs. McIvor greeted them with a smile and ushered them straight up to the bedroom. Siu Fai's face broke into a smile as well when he found the younger Mrs. McIvor pale and feeble but alive, and nursing her baby.

Her husband sat by her, red-eyed but sober. When Siu Fai and Meredith came into the room, he jumped to his feet and shook both of their hands. "I don't know the words to tell you how grateful I am for what you done," he said, "though she says you're like to poison her with that medicine."

His wife nodded, and Siu Fai smiled at her. "It may not taste good, but it's the reason why you're sitting here holding your baby."

"I know it," she said in a thin voice, but she offered him a sincere smile. "I want to thank you, too."

"You are welcome," Siu Fai said, inclining his head. "How are you feeling this morning?"

"Like I've been trampled by a slew of horses," she answered.

Siu Fai smiled. "Unfortunately, that is to be expected. But I'm hoping you will feel better before long." He paused, and then asked, "Has the doctor been?"

"Been and gone," said McIvor. "He said there was nothing for him to do that you hadn't already done. I guess he didn't think much of your medicine, but he said it probably wouldn't hurt."

Siu Fai hid a smile at that. "Did he inspect the incision?"

All three McIvors looked at him blankly.

"The wound," he said.

"Oh," Mr. McIvor said. "I guess he did, but he didn't say much about it, did he, Angel?"

Mrs. McIvor shook her head. Siu Fai said, "Might I...?"

"Of course," she answered.

"There's wood needs splitting," her husband said, and hurried from the room.

"I guess with another lady here, there's no need for me," his mother said, following him almost as quickly. Siu Fai hid another smile.

"Now," he said, "if you give the baby to Meredith, I'll see if you are healing properly."

Reluctantly, the woman offered Meredith the baby. She looked very young and frightened. Meredith wondered how much she remembered of the ordeal the other night. She certainly seemed to be anticipating further pain. Meredith sat down in the chair her husband had vacated, and shifting the baby to her left arm, she reached out for Mrs. McIvor's hand. It closed around hers convulsively as Siu Fai put back the bedclothes and lifted the woman's nightdress.

Meredith had been too busy with the baby on the night of the birth to watch Siu Fai closing the incision. Now she saw that a line of stitches ran down Mrs. McIvor's abdomen, swollen skin straining against them, its edges crimson in the pale morning light. No wonder the woman was terrified at the thought of someone touching them.

Siu Fai's own dismay registered only as a faint ripple across his features. "Is the wound giving you much pain?" he asked.

"It's giving me plenty," Mrs. McIvor answered grimly.

Siu Fai put the woman's nightdress back over her and covered her again with the quilts. For some reason this made her clutch Meredith's hand even harder. "I will not lie to you, Mrs. McIvor," he said gently. "There is an infection starting in the wound; possibly in the womb itself."

Meredith was impressed by the stoicism with which she took this news. "Well," she said, "can you cure it?"

Siu Fai looked out the window for a few long moments before he turned back to her. "I can try. There are medicines for this type of infection…and I'd like to use the needles, if you'll allow it."

She sighed. "You got us this far, I guess."

"Very well: Meredith, will you go to the kitchen and put these herbs on to boil?"

Meredith nodded, but she looked questioningly at the baby dozing in the crook of her arm. Siu Fai's face softened. "Give her back to her mother. There is no better medicine for the illnesses of birth than its product."

It was true, she thought, handing the baby back to the other woman: a little color came back into her cheeks as soon as she held her daughter again. Meredith wondered with a sudden pang if her own mother had ever looked at her like that; whether she had even survived her birth. Quickly she took the packet of herbs and turned away.

When she returned with the decoction an hour later, Mrs. McIvor was lying back against the pillows with the baby tucked against her, dozing. There was still more color in her cheeks, and she took the glass of brown liquid Siu Fai poured, swallowing it without protest.

"I almost forgot to ask," Siu Fai said as he gathered his things to go, "what have you named her?"

Mrs. McIvor shook her head. "I haven't, yet."

"Ah well, there's plenty of time for that."

Meredith hoped that this was true, for the sake of both mother and child. Mrs. McIvor was looking hard at Siu Fai. "I guess 'Siu Fai' is a man's name?" she asked tentatively.

Siu Fai smiled in delighted surprise. "It is. And anyway, if you called her that, she'd have to spend her life explaining why."

"You got any other names?" Mrs. McIvor asked after a moment's thought.

"My family name is Jyu."

He laughed again at the woman's expression, but she persisted, "Does it mean anything? In English I mean?"

Siu Fai's expression turned contemplative. "Yes, in fact, it does – it means 'pearl'."

The woman's face lit up. "Pearl...now that's a real pretty name. Pearl McIvor. What do you think?"

Siu Fai looked toward the window. Meredith saw the faint tremor as he drew breath. "I think," he said at last, looking back, "that it would be the greatest honor anyone has ever paid me."

8

By the time Pearl was two weeks old, the last of Meredith's peeling skin had shed, leaving new, white skin behind. The oak buds that Siu Fai had shown to her had burst open, and the green tips of bulbs began to poke through the earth at the margins of the yard. It was spring: a reticent mountain spring, with nights that still felt like winter and a sharpness beneath the noontime warmth.

Still, the horse danced in her paddock, high on new grass, and Meredith tried not to see how she turned her head south, her ears pricked and nostrils wide. Likewise she tried to ignore the quickening pull in her own blood, which she'd assumed was dead. It was only that she had grown used to moving, she told herself. She couldn't bear to think otherwise, because the pull toward Siu Fai had grown almost as strong as the pull of the road.

Meredith wondered what he thought, but she didn't dare ask him. She hoped that he couldn't sense the battling desires in her. There was no reason why he should – she had never made any mention of them to him. Still, she caught him looking at her sometimes with a strange expression, less scrutiny than certainty. She came to dread that look, and at night she held on to him as if she might wake to find that he had only been a dream.

Instead, she woke one morning to find Siu Fai cooking. This was far more than his usual breakfast – the table was covered with different ingredients, the stove with simmering pots.

Meredith pulled on her clothes quickly and wrote, "Are you expecting company?"

Siu Fai read the note, smiled and shook his head. "Tomorrow is *Ching Ming Jit*." He handed her a bowl of rice, checked a pot, and then took a bowl of his own. He cleared a small space on the table and they sat down.

"What is it?" Meredith asked.

"Tomb Sweeping Day – a festival to honor the dead."

"How?"

"You will see."

All that day Siu Fai cooked, with Meredith helping when she could. The next morning he rose early. "Put on all of your warm clothes," he said to Meredith "and your boots."

"Where are we going?" Meredith wrote.

"You will see," he repeated.

The sun was just rising when they left the house. The air smelled sharp and clean and new, and it seemed to Meredith that the trees' new leaves had doubled in size overnight. Siji trotted along between Meredith and Siu Fai with her violet tongue hanging out, and her mouth curved into what could only be described as a smile.

They took a narrow path down the mountain, on the opposite side from the McIvor's village. It ran through dense woods, the conifers' black branches blocking the sun so that the winter's cold lingered beneath them. Even so the north face forest betrayed tiny signs of spring: silvery fiddleheads in a clearing where a tree had fallen; brilliant green moss blanketing a grey tree trunk; feathery clusters of ground pine pushing up through the damp brown needles. And then there was the sound of running water. It was this that Siu Fai followed until they came to a small stream tumbling down the side of the mountain. He stood scanning the banks for a few moments before his face lit.

"There!" he said, pointing upstream.

Meredith couldn't see anything out of the ordinary, but she followed Siu Fai along the watercourse until he stopped by an old, leaning tree, its roots like a hand gripping a boulder on the stream bank. He smiled up at its draping, budding branches.

"This is the only willow I've ever seen on the mountain," he said. Taking a knife from his pocket, he cut four long, slender branches. "*Ching Ming* is a time when the spirits of the dead walk the earth. We welcome and honor those of our ancestors, but there are evil spirits abroad too on this day. The willow wards them off."

Meredith glanced at Siu Fai, uncertain how much of this he actually believed. His face was inscrutable. A moment later, though, he said, "I do not put much stock in demons and evil spirits," he said. "I think we humans are adept enough at creating evil and suffering. But this is part of the tradition," he nodded at the willow branches, "and so it seems important to me to keep it."

*

When they arrived back home, Siu Fai sat down on the front step and bent one of the willow branches, twisting the thinner end around the thicker to make a wreath. Meredith watched him for a time, and then she looked up and across the yard. A patch of brightness by the forest's edge caught her eye. She got up to investigate and found a little clump of late snowdrops. She picked a handful of them and offered them to Siu Fai, to add to his wreath. But he shook his head.

"They were my mother's favorite flower," he said. "Save them for her." He hung the willow wreath on the door and then opened it, following Meredith inside. "If I were in China," he continued, "this would be the time to visit my ancestors' graves." He set up the three remaining willow branches so that they curved over the shrine. "These should be set in the earth of my family's graves. But I do not know where they are buried, even if it weren't so far away." He studied the willow branches for a moment. "Still, I believe that they understand."

Meredith's throat felt tight, her eyes hot. To hide this from Siu Fai, she knelt down and arranged the snowdrops in front of his mother's portrait. He said nothing, but he gave her a small smile. Then he went to his desk, took something from one of the drawers. When he returned, he knelt beside Meredith and gave it to her. It was a packet of paper squares, so delicate they were almost transparent. Each had a gold square printed in the center, and on top of it, red Chinese characters.

"Spirit money," Siu Fai explained. "The characters are the same as those you would find on real bills." He took them back, placed them in an empty dish in front of the shrine. Then he lit a taper and touched it to the edges of the paper. They caught and flared, quickly curling in on themselves. "Burning them sends them to the spirit world, so that my family can use them there." He looked down, addressing the pictures in the shrine. "Mother and Father, Sister," he said, "this money is given by your son and brother to honor you on the day of the dead."

When the paper was ash, Siu Fai went to the kitchen cupboard and took a platter filled with small dishes of food, tea and wine. He set them in front of the shrine – eight in all, with a bowl of rice in the center. He stood an incense stick in the rice, and lit it. Then he knelt with his head to the ground. He did not need to explain the meaning of the gesture to Meredith. She did the same.

At last he sat up. He smiled at Meredith. "And now, we eat." He led her to the table, and then brought out more platters of food. He poured two glasses of wine he'd made from wild plums, and then he began to pass dishes to Meredith. She took some of everything. She had long since realized that everything he made, no matter how outlandish the ingredients, was delicious. For a time they ate in silence, but in the end Meredith's curiosity got the better of her.

Pushing her plate aside, she wrote, "Is there more to this festival?"

Siu Fai nodded. "*Ching Ming* also marks the beginning of spring. It is the time when the plowing begins and when courting couples declare themselves…"

He trailed off, looking into his lap, a flush on his white cheeks. Meredith watched him carefully. He had never spoken about the change in their relationship, only accepted it, apparently as philosophically as he accepted everything that happened to him. She wondered now what he really thought about it; whether he felt as pushed and pulled by emotions as she did.

At last he looked up again, with a slight, bemused shake of the head. "I have no fields to plow. But I do have a garden, and I normally give it some attention on this day…"

Meredith nodded, glad at the prospect of a distraction from the conversation that was becoming more and more difficult to avoid. She stacked the plates by the washbasin and then put on her coat and followed Siu Fai outside. The garden had been covered in snow for much of the time Meredith had been there, and so she hadn't paid it much attention. Now, standing at its margins, she saw that it was an orderly collection of cultivated squares, with stone paths among them. Some of them were already misted with green. A compost heap in a wooden frame sat at its far end, along with a shed. Siu Fai went into the shed and took out various tools, handing Meredith a spading fork.

"The three beds at the far end will be summer vegetables," he said. "All of them need to be turned and have compost dug in." Meredith pointed to the nearer beds with the green shoots, shrugging. "They are perennial herbs," he answered, squatting down to examine one of the beds. "I use them for medicines." He began poking at a row of shoots with a small fork.

Meredith took up her larger one and began turning the vegetable beds. The afternoon was mild, and before long she had shed her jacket and tied her hair up on top of her head. Still, by the time she was finished her shirt was damp and clinging to her, her face flushed. She stood up, brushing a wet strand of hair from her face. The sun hung just above the western ridges, its light low and golden. Siu Fai stood leaning on his spade, watching her. Meredith saw his expression before he could hide it: a sadness so profound it was like a stone thudding into her chest. She dropped her fork and dragged him into an embrace as if she meant to squeeze the breath from him.

Meredith didn't realize that she was crying until Siu Fai pushed her gently back, and the tears turned cold on her face. The sun had set, and his own face looked like stone in the sudden twilight.

"You are going to leave me," Meredith managed to scratch onto her scrap of paper.

Siu Fai barely glanced at it, and then he shook his head. "No. It is the other way around."

She rubbed at her eyes, but the tears wouldn't clear. She couldn't see to write; she could only shake her head. Siu Fai took her face between his hands, and when she was still, he said, "Yes, Meredith. You are leaving, and that is how it's meant to be."

Meredith covered her heart with her hands, and then she covered his. Siu Fai took them in his own. "And I love you, too. But it isn't enough."

Meredith turned away from him, the tears still streaming down her face.

"Come," he said after a moment, putting an arm around her shoulders. "Please. We'll go inside and talk."

Meredith wished bitterly that she could, that she could sound the words that would make him believe that he was mistaken. Instead she followed him inside and sat shivering on the edge of the bed while he lit a lamp. Siu Fai put a blanket around her shoulders, but Meredith pushed it off. Sighing, he put it back, and this time Meredith didn't fight him, likewise when he sat down beside her and began stroking her hair. It felt to her as if all of the fight had run away with her tears. Now, beneath his fingers, the anger slipped away too. It was gone before she knew whether she was angry with him or herself, leaving her cold and sad.

"Do you know that I've loved you from the moment I pulled you out of the snow?" Siu Fai asked her.

Meredith missed a breath; then she turned to face him. His cloud-colored eyes were stricken, and she was shocked to see wet streaks on his face. He had wept without uttering a sound.

"That's the truth," he continued, "even though I cannot explain it. It's true also that I've never loved any other woman. I didn't think that I could. I thought that what happened to my family had somehow damaged that part of me..."

Meredith began to search for paper, but Siu Fai reached up onto the shelf and brought down her book and pencil. She opened the book to a blank page and wrote: "If it's the truth, then why do you want me to leave?"

Siu Fai smiled sadly. "I don't want you to leave. I am simply trying to accept it."

"Have I said that I'm leaving?" she scrawled. "Do you think that I'm fickle?"

Siu Fai sighed. "I think that you are true to your core, and therein lies the problem: just as you would never betray me, you cannot betray your heart."

"You don't know my heart."

"I know that it doesn't belong to this mountain," he said softly, patiently, "and if you stayed here, sooner or later you would realize it too. Then, you would be forced to choose between betraying yourself and your promise to me. Either way, you would begin to hate me, and that would be far harder for me to bear than your leaving now."

"You can't see into the future!" Meredith wrote, suddenly furious. "You can't know!"

Siu Fai was silent for a few long moments, looking into his lap. Then he looked back at Meredith and said, "It's true, I can't know the future. I can only guess, by virtue of the present. But there's something I do know that no amount of time will change. Your heart, Meredith – or your soul, or whatever it is that's at the center of us all – it's full of the sea." He held up a hand against her protest. "I know that you were hurt, and that the sea was tangled up in it. But I also know that it wasn't the sea that hurt you. If anything, it tried to save you. It's trying still."

Meredith shook her head, spattering tears across her hands, but Siu Fai persisted: "You've told me about the journey that brought you here. Has it not struck you that a common thread runs through it?" Meredith looked stubbornly away, and Siu Fai sighed. "Meredith, when I first saw this place it was no more than a snowy ridge like a hundred others, but I knew absolutely that it was where I was meant to be. Can you say the same?"

505

Meredith stared at her hands while a string of defiant answers ran through her head.

"And yet," he persisted, "there is a place where you've felt like that, isn't there."

It wasn't a question, and even Meredith's fury couldn't quite obscure the truth. She saw the lick of green water on a springtime beach. She remembered the way that it enfolded her, like a mother, or a lover. It seemed so long ago, so far out of reach. She shut her eyes, beginning to cry in earnest, though she didn't know what she cried for. Siu Fai pulled her close again, resting his cheek against her head.

9

It was dark when Meredith's tears finally stopped. Siu Fai released her then and stood. Meredith was instantly panicked. She sat up, reaching for him, but he smiled gently. "Don't worry," he said. "I'll be right back."

He lit more lamps, and then he went to his desk, reached into a bottom drawer and brought out a small box covered in red silk. He came back to the bed and handed it to Meredith. She sat looking at it for a long time, wary of what it might contain. Siu Fai said nothing, only waited with her. Even Siji watched from her rug by the fire, still as the stone lions after which she had been named, until Meredith mustered the courage to put back the lid.

Inside the box, two silver bangles lay on a white silk cushion. They were of identical design, simple circles figured with a long-tailed bird facing a beast with a snakelike body and a lion-like head. Meredith picked one of them up. She could tell by the tarnishing around the figures that it was old, and by the weight, that it was valuable. She put the bracelet back, looked at Siu Fai.

"They are called Phoenix and Dragon bangles. When a Cantonese couple becomes engaged, the boy's mother gives a pair of them to her future daughter-in-law to wear on her wedding day. They symbolize the unity between man and woman." He picked up the bracelet Meredith had put down, pointing to the bird's head. "The phoenix represents the *yin*, the female energy; the dragon is the *yang*, the male. These were my mother's. She gave them to me just before she died. Now they are yours."

Meredith looked at the bracelets for a moment longer, and then she shut the box and picked up her book. "I cannot take these," she wrote. "You will want them one day for your wife."

Siu Fai smiled sadly and shook his head. "I would not want any woman but you to wear these bracelets."

She took a deep breath, to keep herself from beginning to cry again. "Someday you might change your mind," she wrote.

Siu Fai shrugged. "Even if I did, there is little chance that I would find a wife here. The world is changing fast, but not so fast as that." Meredith looked at him, still unconvinced. He sighed. "Besides, these bracelets are more than a token of engagement. They are a promise from the groom's family to the bride that she has become a part of their family. And that is my promise to you."

He opened the box, and Meredith looked at her hands, still not trusting herself to look at him. Siu Fai took out the bracelets, clasped one around each of her wrists. Meredith looked down at them, wishing that she had something to give him in return. And then she realized that she did. She went to her coat hanging on the back of the door, took out a small wad of black cloth from the pocket, and brought it back to Siu Fai.

"What is it?" he asked, puzzled.

Meredith wrote, "I know nothing about Cantonese customs beyond what you have told me. But I imagine that the bride's family also presents gifts to the groom."

His forehead furrowed. "That isn't what I intended. "

"Of course you didn't," Meredith wrote.

Siu Fai unfolded the grubby cloth. The three pearls that were all that was left of Stella Maris rolled into his cupped palm. He raised his eyebrows in surprise. "What are these?"

"Consider them an offering," Meredith wrote, and then, putting the book aside, she took the pearls from his hand and brought them to the shrine. The snowdrops were limp and faded in the flickering light of the candles. She swept them aside and replaced them with the pearls, one in front of each of the photographs of Siu Fai's family.

She heard him come up behind her, and she was suddenly afraid that she had done something wrong. But Siu Fai knelt beside her, a smile lighting his pale face. "In China," he said, "crushed pearls are sometimes taken to soothe an unhappy mind. And legends say that they are worn as protection against fire." He inclined his head. "Thank you, Meredith." She nodded. His eyes fixed on the pearls, he said gently, "Tomorrow morning I will go and visit Mrs. McIvor. She will have run out of medicine by now."

Meredith understood. She stared hard at the flickering candles, unable to look at him.

"I do not want to end this night sadly," he said.

Meredith knew that he was waiting for her to agree, but she couldn't make herself do it.

Drawing a deep breath, he said, "There is one more tradition that I would like to show you. It's not quite the right time, but it's near enough."

She nodded absently, and Siu Fai stood up. He went back to the lean-to he'd abandoned, and Meredith realized with a pang that she had never been inside it. Her throat tightened around all of the things she didn't know about Siu Fai; that she hadn't asked or told him. *Stop it*, she told herself, and then tried to think of nothing. She had almost succeeded when she heard a rustling.

Looking up, she saw Siu Fai holding an orange fish made of delicate paper, and a string of small, round, red paper lanterns. She raised her eyebrows, and Siu Fai smiled. "Wear your coat, and bring the lamp and a taper." He went outside, followed by Siji. Meredith collected the things he had asked for and followed him.

Siu Fai sat on the porch step and lined up the lanterns in a row, putting little candles in them. She handed him the lamp and the taper, and he began to light the lanterns. When all of the candles were burning, Siu Fai picked up the paper fish, attached a spool of string to a hook in its mouth. He took the fish down the yard, and then released it into the breeze. At last, Meredith understood: it was a kite. The fish disappeared quickly into the dark sky. Siu Fai continued to feed out more string, and Meredith saw the lantern nearest her twitch. It too was attached to the kite string.

"Will you launch the lanterns, Meredith?" Siu Fai called back to her.

Meredith picked up the first globe. The flame within fluttered like a heart, but it stayed alight as the lantern left her hands and floated up into the night. She saw each of them into the sky like that, and then she walked down to where Siu Fai stood holding the kite string. His silvery hair obscured his face. That and the tiny chain of airborne lights were all that she could see in the perfect dark.

"We call them God's lanterns," he said after a moment.

God's lanterns, Meredith repeated silently.

Siu Fai took something from his pocket, pressed it into Meredith's hand. It was a knife. "You must cut the kite string."

Meredith put a hand on his arm, asking why.

"Setting the kite free brings good fortune," he said.

Still, Meredith hesitated.

"The fish is a carp," he said. "It is strong and brave enough to swim against the current; it will make its way to where it is meant to be."

And where is that? Meredith wondered as she brought the knife down on the taut string. *How can he be so certain?* She looked at Siu Fai. His upturned face was calm as the moon. There was no answer in it, because there was no question. And so Meredith turned her own face upward and watched God's lanterns grow ever smaller, until even their memory faded.

Chain of Angels

1

Meredith shed no tears on the trip down Siu Fai's mountain. She was raw with missing him, scoured by the sweep of her own loneliness. To have wept, though, would have been to negate what had been between them, and she knew that the necessity of leaving, and of what she was feeling in the wake of it, was as much a part of that as the joy had been.

In the end she found it easiest not to think of him at all. As she rode she paid careful attention to the landscape, to the horse's gait, to the slow track of the sun across the sky. She was even able to ignore the cool silver circles on her wrists, but at night, she couldn't help dreaming of him. The dreams were so vivid sometimes that she woke, certain she heard him breathing beside her, and then it took all of her strength to open her eyes, to shed her blankets and get on the horse and not look back. There was pain even in that familiar routine, in the tacit confirmation of all that Siu Fai had said in the horse's eager step. For the horse had never taken her anywhere she wasn't meant to go.

And yet, they couldn't go on forever – not as they were. Their country, however vast, was in the end an island like every other. Sooner or later they would run up against the sea. Sooner or later, unless they stopped: and neither possibility was one that Meredith wanted to consider. Nor, however, could she push them from her mind – not when every unfurling leaf and blossom confirmed a spring far earlier than any in her body's memory. She had no idea how far south she'd come. For all she knew, she might have crossed the line long ago – the boundary between running from the sea, and towards it. For the first time since the night in the cannibals' graveyard, she wondered whether the horse had any plan or destination. She could not bring herself to ask.

2

Meredith might not have been able to point out her position on a map, but she had nevertheless become attuned over time to the subtle changes in the territory through which she rode. She knew when she had left one place and entered another. A couple of weeks after leaving Siu Fai's mountain, the undulating ridges among which he lived grew higher, their valleys deeper, until it became a different country altogether. By the strangeness in her head as she traversed the ridges, by the incandescent clarity of the light, she knew that its mountains were at least as high as those of Anis and Tomah's country. But these black, brooding hills had none of the northern ones' jagged ostentation. They were all drops and curves, dark with the spruce and fir that covered their higher slopes, putting Meredith in mind of water.

The comparison haunted her, becoming more persistent the more she tried to forget it. A ridgeline against an evening sky took on the shape of a static river; a valley full of early morning mist was a white lake. And then, looking west from a bald top one evening, Meredith saw the sea. *It tried to save you...it's trying still...* She shivered as she forced the words away, made her eyes redesign the blue-grey dips and loops unfurling to the horizon as the stacked ridgelines they were. Nothing, though, would make them shed their attitude of water; nothing until the sun set, and night erased them.

3

In the valley, Meredith found the season even further advanced. The leaves looked like leaves rather than hatchling butterflies, meadows were knee-high with wildflowers and berry bushes starred with blossoms. The nights were barely cold enough now to merit a fire, though she lit one all the same, for comfort as much as anything else. The horse's winter coat came out in dark clumps when Meredith stroked her, and she scrubbed her back and sides along the ground or a tree trunk at any opportunity. Meredith wished that she had a brush to soothe the horse's itching. She wished she had one for herself: her hair was a tangled, knotted mess. It was the longest she had yet gone without someone offering her a bed and the other trappings of civilization.

She supposed she could have found one if she'd put her mind to it. She'd passed logging camps and rugged smallholdings. Yet though she no longer feared these places, she also had no desire to seek out company and – aside from a hairbrush – still less need. The streams in the valleys were full of fish, and Siu Fai had given her several bags of rice, which stretched much further than flour or potatoes. Added to the leaves and roots he had taught her to scavenge, these provided adequate sustenance, and there was plenty of new grass for the horse.

Though she didn't stop, she studied the towns she passed. They were like the other farm towns she'd seen, but just as the mountains showed different faces in different territories, so did their settlements. Here, in contrast to the red farms near Siu Fai's mountain, no one seemed to paint their houses or outbuildings. Only the ubiquitous little stub-steepled churches were whitewashed. Every other wooden structure blended into the forests surrounding them. These little communities folded into their deep valleys seemed worlds unto themselves, cut off from the larger one. Meredith met little traffic moving between them, though the roads were often decent, and when she passed close to one, its people would stare at her unabashedly, as if the sight of a stranger was a novelty.

Often groups of children would come running from these villages to demand sweets or pencils or simply her name and where she'd come from. Meredith quickly became used to this, and to the small pang she felt each time she had to disappoint them. But they were generally good-natured about it, as if they hadn't really expected anything, and were happy simply to pat the horse and then wave her on her way.

At first Meredith didn't mind. Gradually, though, she became aware that that the horse did. Whenever a gang of children approached, the horse would slow down, lift her head and prick her ears as she peered at them, almost as if she were searching for something among them. This worried Meredith for no reason that she could explain.

Who is it you are looking for? she asked the horse after one of these encounters.

The horse didn't answer for a long time, and Meredith thought that she had decided to ignore the question. Then at last she said, *I will know when I find her.*

Meredith wished she hadn't asked.

4

With every day, the weather grew warmer. Meredith put her coat into her rucksack, and still her winter clothing seemed too warm. On the first day that she could justifiably call hot, Meredith decided that it was time to wash her winter things, and herself, and she began to look out for a suitable stream. Around midday she found it. She had followed a narrow brook up a gentle incline for half a mile or so, when the woods opened out into a clearing. In the middle was the stream's source: a large pool with a gravel bottom at the base of a small waterfall. She slid off of the horse and removed her bridle, then she shed her pack and sticky clothes. She moved to the edge of the pool, drew a breath and dove.

The water was icy, and seemed somehow less dense than her scattered memories told her water should be, but there was a familiarity to the enveloping coldness nevertheless. For as long as her breath lasted, she explored the bottom of the pool, its multicolored pebbles and schools of flashing minnows. When her chest began to burn, she turned upward toward the sun, and then froze as a dark silhouette came across it.

She burst from the water, drawing a ragged breath. Confused images tumbled through her mind; her hands went to her throat. But the figure on the bank was not a grinning man with a golden face. She was a woman, tall and serious in a red calico dress and white headscarf, with skin like polished mahogany. She held the rein of a white mule with brightly embroidered saddlebags, which stood beside her, sucking water from the pool.

"I am so sorry to have intruded on you," the woman said in a voice as deep and rich as the red of her dress. "But Jesse's gone all morning without water, and nothing moves this mule when he's set his mind to something." She said it fondly. "Just let him drink his fill, and we'll be on our way."

Meredith stared at the woman; she couldn't look away. There was something mesmerizing about her, as if she was subtly brighter than everything around her. She wore some kind of garland or charm necklace that jingled as she moved, equally enticing.

"Or," the woman said to Meredith's silence, "I'll wait like this, if you want to get out."

Meredith turned and swam to the far bank of the pool, where the horse stood by her things, watching the mule with ears pricked and nostrils flared. She reached into the pack, took out the first pieces of clothing that came under her hand: a blue cotton tunic and black trousers, faded and softened by years of washing. Siu Fai had given them to her, along with several others, for the summer ahead. She hadn't meant to take them out, let alone wear them, thinking that it would be too painful. But as the scent of the mountain cabin drifted out of them – woodsmoke and incense, bitter herbs and ginger – she felt no sadness. For the first time since she had left him, Meredith believed that it had been the right thing to do.

When she turned around, she saw that the horse had joined the mule, and they were grazing together. The sun was halfway down the afternoon sky, and she knew that she should be moving on, but she couldn't make herself think how to do it. The other woman seemed to realize this.

She came to stand by Meredith. "You lost, honey?"

Meredith shook her head.

"Where're you headed?"

Meredith took the paper and pencil from her pack and wrote, "Can you read?"

The woman raised her eyebrows and said, "Yes, I can. But can't you speak?"

Meredith shook her head.

"Well, that's tough," she said, gazing off over the water, golden now in the horizontal sunlight. "But I get the idea that you are, too."

This surprised Meredith. She'd never thought of herself as tough.

"So, where are you headed, anyway?"

"I don't know," Meredith wrote. She noticed that the garland the other woman wore was a chain of little birds, each a different color and shape, made from various materials.

"You're just wandering for the sake of it?"

Meredith sighed. "If you're really interested, this explains it, more or less." She took out the blue, silk-covered book and offered it to the woman.

"I tell you what," the woman said. "There's a plucked hen in my saddle-bag. You make it into dinner while I read this book of yours, and we'll see if I can't help you out of whatever trouble it is you're in."

Meredith wanted to tell the woman that she wasn't in any trouble, but she was afraid that if she did, the woman would leave. For some inexplicable reason, she didn't want that to happen. She wrote, "That's fair. My name's Meredith."

"Saint Catherine."

It wasn't until the woman nodded that Meredith realized this was her name. She nodded back, and then she went over to the mule's saddle and took the chicken from the saddlebag. It was wrapped in burlap and looked fresh. She jointed it and put it aside to start a fire. Then, after a moment's consideration, she went to her own pack and took out the small bag of seasonings Siu Fai had given her, which she hadn't had the heart yet to use. Before she could think too hard about it, she filled her cooking pot with water and set it over the flame on three flat rocks. She added sugar and cinnamon, a generous shot of soy sauce, slices of dry ginger root, and a single pod of the star anise she had considered too beautiful to cook, before she tasted it. When the mixture came to a boil she put in the chicken, and then she sat back to wait.

Saint Catherine was reading intently, one long finger resting on her indigo lips. She seemed to Meredith to be carrying on a silent conversation with the story she was reading. Sometimes she shook her head or furrowed her brow. Other times she uttered soft exclamations: "No!" or "True enough," or, more often, a non-specific "Um-um." The sunlight turned honey-colored and then bronze. A cloud of insects shimmered in the syrupy light over the pool, as the little clearing filled with the smell of Siu Fai's house. The warmth of the smell, the touch of the soft cotton on her skin, made her think of gentle hands; of benediction. Leaning against her pack, watching the veil of insects, Meredith drifted until Saint Catherine closed the journal.

"That's some story, Meredith," she said. "But it doesn't tell me how you learned to cook Jamaican."

Meredith was confused until Saint Catherine pointed to the pot. Then she wrote, "I didn't. It's Chinese."

Saint Catherine gave her a long look, focusing on her clothes. Finally she said, "I didn't know there were any Chinamen in these hills."

"There aren't," Meredith wrote. "He lives three weeks ride north and east of here."

"That explains it. I don't often get up as far as Shenandoah."

"Doing what?" Meredith wrote.

Saint Catherine's face took on a look like Siu Fai's had when he spoke about his medicine: a mix of peace and pride. "Preaching," she answered.

Now it was Meredith's turn to raise her eyebrows. "You're a minister?"

"I guess I am," Saint Catherine answered.

"I've never met a lady minister," she wrote.

"And I've never met a white girl who dresses like a Chinese man. So as I see it, we're even."

Meredith stared at her for a moment and then smiled.

"Now, is that chicken ready?"

Meredith looked into the pot. The water had almost boiled away, and under the skin, the meat was white. She lifted it out onto her tin plate, and then put rice in the remaining broth to cook. Then she looked at the other woman and wrote, "You've read my story. What's yours?"

Saint Catherine smiled, but there was something in it that went against her aura of serenity. "I guess you're within your rights to ask," she said. Then she nodded to herself and continued, "I was born the same day Lee surrendered to Grant at Appomattox. But by then my parents were already settled on St. Catherine's Island, thanks to Sherman."

Seeing Meredith's blank look, Saint Catherine said, "Field Order Fifteen The one that split up the plantations and gave the land to the freed slaves. You know: forty acres and a mule?"

Meredith shrugged. Saint Catherine shook her head and sighed. "Well, why would you? I guess you weren't even born then, and whatever his good intentions, Sherman's plan didn't pan out. Still, it lasted long enough for me to be born on St. Catherine's. My mama insisted on naming me after the place she saw as the beginning of our good fortune. Too bad it didn't last."

Meredith stared at Saint Catherine, while Saint Catherine stared at the backlit sunset woods. Without shifting her gaze, she continued, "Lincoln's high hopes died with him. No matter that Negroes were free; we still had to eat, and the only work that most of us could get was the work we'd always done. So I grew up on a plantation just like my mama and daddy did. In return for an old slave cabin and a patch of land to grow his own crops on – if he could find the time and the strength – my daddy worked twenty acres of cotton and gave it all to the white boss in the big house.

"Still, no one owned him, and no one could sell his family, and to him that meant more than I could ever understand as a child. All I knew is that I worked hard in the fields all day, and then again at the kitchen table at night. Mind work." She tapped her head. "My daddy could read, and he taught us kids and our mama. He taught us from our only book, which was a ratty old Bible he'd been given by the do-gooder Yankee who'd taught him, back when it was a crime. He said it was the best book anyone could learn from, because you learned the Lord's word the same time as your letters." Saint Catherine smiled at the memory.

"Anyway," she continued, "that was the way it was til I was about twelve. By then, our house was bursting at the seams. My mama had eleven babies in all, and every one of them lived. There was never enough of anything, so when we were old enough we were sent out to work. I got a job tending an old, blind, white lady whose children didn't want the care of her. When I first heard that, I felt sorry for her. I felt mighty smug, too: I thought an old, blind lady couldn't be too much work. Mama didn't tell me different. All she said was, 'You're going out on your own now, Saint Catherine. Once you leave here, you'll have nobody in the wide world to look to but God, so don't you forget about Him.'

"I admit, those seemed strange words for her to speak to me. She wasn't a woman given to that kind of gloomy thinking. But I didn't worry too long about it – I was too proud of myself, a big girl with a job, out on her own. I remember walking to that old lady's house in town like I was going to a fair." Saint Catherine chuckled, shook her head.

"Well, it was clear soon enough why I'd got that job: no white girl would have it. Mrs. Mason was the meanest, most ornery woman you're ever likely to meet. It wasn't just cooking and cleaning. I had to feed her, and take her to the toilet, and sit up entertaining her all night long when she couldn't sleep. And if I missed a word of a novel I was reading her, or if she missed the pot she peed in – and I still swear she did that on purpose – she would beat me.

"Well, I resented that. My parents brought us up proud, and they never raised a hand to us. Too much of that done in slave times, my daddy would say. I don't know if it was right or wrong of him. All I know is the anger grew up in me, until the day that awful old woman wet her bed. She said it was because I didn't come fast enough to help her to the pot, but she gave me a twisted smile when she said it, and I knew she'd done it just because she could. She raised her hand to slap me, and something in me broke. All that rage that'd been building in me burst out. I had just enough sense not to slap her back, but not enough not to turn around and walk right out of that house, leaving her in her stinking wet bed.

"I thought my mama would be glad to see me, but she looked angry. She didn't soften any when I told her what happened. For the first time in my life she looked at me with cold eyes. She said, 'I always thought your daddy raised you kids too soft. If you're gonna survive in this world, Saint Catherine, you're gonna have to get yourself a thick skin. And sure I don't know what we'll do now – we needed the money from your job, and ain't no one else gonna hire you for house work after this story gets out.'"

Just in time, Meredith recalled her rice and took it off of the fire. A thin layer was stuck to the bottom of the pot, but the rest was all right. She divided it between two plates that Saint Catherine produced from her saddlebags, but Saint Catherine scraped half of hers back into the pot and took only a small piece of chicken. She ate all of it hungrily, but refused more when Meredith offered.

"There's plenty," Meredith wrote.

"I see more clearly," Saint Catherine said, "when I eat less."

"See what more clearly?" Meredith wrote.

"God," Saint Catherine answered. Meredith scrutinized her, but her face was sincere. After a moment she took up her own story again: "In fact, it wasn't long after leaving Mrs. Mason that I had my first vision.

"See, I was miserable when I realized how I'd disappointed my parents. Just like my mother said, there was no chance of me getting work in town again. I moped and wept until my mother shooed me out of the house. Then I wandered in the fields and woods, not knowing what to do with myself. I couldn't eat when I thought about my little brothers and sisters going hungry because of my selfishness. I got thinner and weaker all the time, but Mama was pregnant again, and I made my own penance of taking on all her work. I wouldn't let her lift a finger, even though my head was always spinning with hunger. I felt like I was turning into a ghost. I stopped feeling the ground beneath my feet. Everyone looked at me so strangely, I could have believed that I was changed into something unnatural. Can you imagine that?"

Meredith could. More than that, she remembered it; one more puzzle piece dropped into place.

"This went on until the night I lay down on my pallet in the kitchen, knowing I was going to die," said Saint Catherine. "I admit I was scared. I figured no one would forgive me, not even God. I remembered then what my mama said to me when I first went away, about looking to God, and I wished I'd remembered it sooner. I started to pray then, anyway, the best that I could. I tried to say psalms, but my head was too mixed up to remember them, so I just thought my own prayers. I pleaded with God to forgive me. I promised that if I lived through the night, I would change. I would devote my life to doing His work.

"There was no answer, just that terrible mix-up in my head, like it was full of swirling water, and the water was there to drown me. But just as I felt it pulling me down, I heard a voice calling, 'Rise up, Sister, and pray!' Strength flowed through me; my head cleared. I got up on my knees and started saying the Lord's Prayer. A light started up in the corner of the room. It got brighter as I spoke, purer and brighter than the summer sun. All the kitchen was full of it, all of the kids' faces glowed, so I thought they must wake up, but they just slept on while the light turned into a man, and the man took me by the hand and said, 'Come with me.'

"I was scared as I was awed. Still, I had sense enough to take the hand he offered me. I felt his light and love flowing into me, and he led me upward until we came to the door of heaven. It was open. I could see all the saved souls there beyond it, and I heard a voice saying, 'Do you wish to join them?' I answered, 'I do, with all my heart.' The light changed then. It moved outward and downward until I saw all the world below me, all its wickedness and misery. The voice said, 'Then you must show that you are worthy. You must go down there, and root out iniquity, and call the people to repentance.' I said, 'Father, I will do it,' because I finally understood who it was I was speaking to. He said, 'I know that you mean those words now, but you got to mean them down there too, where people will laugh and insult you and set their dogs on you for trying to bring them the light. Remember, though: while you work to spread my word, I won't ever forsake you.' And then I was back on my hard pallet in my mama's kitchen. I was thirteen years old, but it was then my life began."

Saint Catherine went quiet. She looked for a moment at the dying fire, and then threw a few more sticks of wood onto it as Meredith waited, riveted, for more of the story. When Saint Catherine didn't break her silence, Meredith wrote, "What happened next?"

Saint Catherine stared at the words for a long time before she looked up again, and when she did there was something speculative, even hopeful in her face. "That's a long story, Miss Meredith," she said. "But if you care to share your road with me for a time, I'll be happy to tell it."

Meredith smiled, and Saint Catherine smiled back.

3

The next morning was the first since she'd left Siu Fai that Meredith didn't wake wondering if she'd made the right decision. She opened her eyes to see Saint Catherine mixing something in a bowl with her hands, her bird necklace looped over her shoulder. Peace spread through her like the spring sunrise spreading across the horizon. She sat up as Saint Catherine dropped lumps of sticky batter into a pan of hot fat, and the smell of cooking filled the clearing. Meredith came and looked into the pan, then sat back again as the fat popped and spattered.

"Careful," Saint Catherine smiled. "They'll be ready soon enough."

"What are they?" Meredith wrote.

"Calas. Or near as you can get out here. They make them down in Louisiana, from leftover rice. They ought to be sweet, and the mixture should have sat longer – it gives them the right taste – but…" She shrugged, and lifted the browned fritters out of the oil, and handed the plate to Meredith. She dropped the rest of the batter into the pan before taking the bowl to the pool to wash it.

When she returned, drying the bowl on her skirt, she took the remaining fritters out of the oil. Meredith had finished the first lot – they had been delicious, despite Saint Catherine's protestations. Now Saint Catherine gave three of the new batch to Meredith, and put two on her own plate.

"You have to eat more than that," Meredith wrote, trying to give them back.

But Saint Catherine only smiled. "I told you, I don't eat much. I'm so used to it now, I couldn't hold more than this." She picked up one of her calas and took a delicate bite, chewing slowly. When she swallowed, she pointed to a little pot sitting by the fire. "I'd be mighty glad of a cup of coffee, though. You?"

Siu Fai had not been able to stomach coffee, even as far as the smell, and Meredith had almost forgotten what it tasted like. She nodded, and Saint Catherine poured steaming black liquid into two tin cups, handing one of them to Meredith and sipping from the other. They ate and drank in companionable silence, and when they were finished, Meredith washed the dishes while Saint Catherine went to the animals.

The mule and the horse had spent the evening making faces at each other, but they seemed now to have come to an understanding. They stood quietly together while the women packed the camp away, and onto their backs. When it was finished, Saint Catherine stood by the mule's head, looking for a moment at the pool and waterfall. The night's thick mist was rising off the water, golden in the morning light; the rush of the falls was glass-green.

"Surely, God has touched this place," Saint Catherine murmured, and Meredith wished that she had the voice to say "Amen".

*

For a time they rode in silence, and Meredith began to worry that Saint Catherine had thought better of her promise to continue her story, or, worse: she had changed her mind about riding with company at all. But when they emerged from the woods, and the horse turned south without guidance, Saint Catherine said, "That was the way I went, too."

Meredith looked over at her, raising her eyebrows.

"When I began my work," Saint Catherine explained. "The morning after I had that first vision, I told my parents that I'd had a call from God, and I meant to use my life to spread His word. I expected an argument, but they gave me their blessing. Maybe it was because they knew that I had no chances if I stayed where I was, or maybe God's light had touched them too. Anyway, my father told me about a place he'd heard of, a convent in New Orleans for Negro nuns called the Sisters of the Holy Family. They dedicated their lives to helping the poor Negro people of that city, and they ran schools for their children.

"Truth be told, I wasn't too sure about becoming a nun. It seemed to me a dull kind of life, full of rules and closed doors. But then those sisters' mission sounded a lot like what God had told me in my vision. If nothing else, I thought, they'd point me in the right direction. So I tied up the few things I called my own in a spare apron, and I set out to walk to New Orleans."

Saint Catherine lapsed back into silence, her eyes on the blue-black ridges in the distance, a considering kind of expression on her face. Meredith had a hundred questions, but she couldn't write and ride at once. So, nudging her horse up beside the mule she reached across and touched Saint Catherine's arm.

Saint Catherine smiled and said, "I haven't bored you yet?" Meredith shook her head. "Well, I won't tell you about that journey, because then I just might. Besides, the most important thing about it is that I never made it to the Sisters. I never even made it to Louisiana."

Meredith twitched her shoulders upward: *Why?*

"Because God called on me again before I got there. I was walking a road near a stand of woods one night, looking for a place to camp, when I heard singing. It was so beautiful, so joyous, I thought for a minute it was the beginning of another vision. But then I rounded a bend in that road and I saw a big camp, too many tents to count, all ranged around a three-sided shelter lit up like midday.

"Inside the shelter there was a man – a white man – who looked to be leading the singing. When it ended he got up on the middle of that platform and started sermonizing. He took a text from John 3, the one about the wonderful love of God. How no one can possibly describe it. I don't remember the whole of it now; I don't suppose it matters. What matters was that he was saying it at all, and *how* he was saying it, and that all those folks had come to listen and be guided by it.

"I'd never even heard of a camp meeting before, but I knew then and there that I would never join those sisters in New Orleans. I was meant for big, joyful gatherings like that one. But I didn't know where I'd ever find another, so I worked my way around the crowd, trying to get closer to the speaker. It was pretty tight though, and mostly white, and no one prepared to make room for me. Then, round about the back I found a separate, smaller gathering of people in front of a crowd of tents. All of them were Negroes. They spoke to what the preacher was telling them, answering with 'Amens' and 'Hallelujas', and when I came up to them, a woman my mother's age smiled at me and moved over to make room on the blanket she was sitting on.

"Well, that meeting lasted a good three days, and all that time I stayed with that woman, who was called Addy, and her family. They were good, kind people – freed slaves trying to make better lives for their children, just like my own parents. Or like my parents might have been if they'd had just four children instead of eleven, and more time for seeing to their souls. I watched the way they seemed to take sustenance from that meeting. How, when it was time to pack up and go home, they seemed brighter, like they'd been touched with some of the angel's light from my vision.

"I knew I had to be a part of that. I asked Addy how you got to be a camp meeting preacher. She laughed, and then she stopped when she saw I meant it. 'Honey, that ain't no life for a child,' she said, 'and though I've seen a few Negro preachers in my time, I ain't never seen a woman. If God's calling you, you better follow him down to New Orleans like you planned.'

"I thanked her and wished her family well, and then I hunted out one of those white preachers as he was leaving and followed him. He rode north, toward the mountains. He went slowly, but I was too scared to approach him out there in the middle of nowhere. I waited til we came near to a town, then I caught up to him and pretended it was chance we met up on the road. I figured he might not talk to a Negro girl, but he was a friendly kind of man. Besides that he was full to bursting with God's word, and I guess two days with no one to tell it to was about enough for him. He started sermonizing to me, and he seemed surprised that I knew all the verses he was talking about. He was even more surprised when he heard I could read. When we came to the town proper he asked me where I was going, and I told him I had no fixed plan, except that I wanted to learn to be a preacher like him.

"I guess there must have been a lot of kindness in him, because he didn't laugh at me. In fact he seemed kind of sad when he explained that even though that was a noble idea, it just wasn't possible, because the Bible said women couldn't be preachers. I didn't know about that verse, but he opened his Bible and showed me, and there it was in First Corinthians: 'Let your women keep silent in the churches, for they are not permitted to speak; but they are to be submissive, as the law also says.'

"Now, I didn't quite think that meant what he thought it meant. From what I'd seen women spoke plenty in church, and sang too. Besides, lots of books in the Bible say it's just fine to own slaves, too, and we'd just got done proving *that* wrong. I thought I'd better ask someone else." Saint Catherine paused and sighed and shook her head. "I got the same answer from all of the preachers I spoke to, until I gave up asking. For a while I just walked the country with no purpose, caught between God's calling and the facts of life. And then one night I had an idea.

"I was at another camp meeting, up by Baltimore. I was the only colored person there – or so I thought. As I made my way around the edge of the crowd, I saw an old Negro woman leaning on a stick, trying to see over the people in front of her to the preacher on his platform. When she saw me, she shook her head and said, 'I would so like to hear that man's words, but I fear neither you or I's gonna get any closer than this.' She pinched her lips together and turned away, and that's when it came to me. I said, 'Hold on, ma'am,' and that old lady turned back to look at me. I said, 'Do you live around here?' and she said, 'Near enough,' and I said, 'Have you got your own house?' She smiled a little, like I'd said something funny. 'I got a room,' she said, 'but at least I can call it my own.' I said, 'That's perfect,' and she said, 'What for?' and I said, 'You gather your friends together, and we'll have a prayer meeting of our own.'

"Well, that old lady – her name was Hepzibah Straw – she looked me up and down, hard. But she didn't look at me like I was crazy, and for the first time in a long, long time, I felt a weight lift off me. I knew she'd said yes even before the word came out of her mouth.

"Hepzibah was a war widow, and her room was in a tumbledown house in one of the lowest streets in Baltimore. But it was clean, and Hepzibah seemed to light it up with the joy she felt at hosting her very own prayer meeting. She called on her friends, and the next afternoon I found myself sitting in that room, surrounded by a half dozen colored women of all shapes and ages. They looked to me the way I'd seen people look to those camp meeting preachers, and in that moment, for the first time since my vision, I felt at peace.

"We each took a turn praying, and when they'd all said their piece, they asked me to close the meeting. I started to speak about one of the Gospels we'd prayed on, and that shabby little room filled up with light – the same light I'd seen in my vision. I fell on my knees to give thanks, and then, just as quick as it came, the light was gone. I was there on my knees in the dark and someone was pounding on the door.

"Well, Hepzibah got up to open it. It turned out to be a watchman. He said he heard there was an illegal meeting going on. I didn't know it then, but in some towns colored folks could only have meetings in church. In some towns it's still that way." She pursed her lips and shook her head, and then went on, "All those sisters were shaking and pleading, but I was still full of God's light. I got up and faced that man and put my hand on his shoulder and opened my mouth, and God spoke through me. He said, 'How do sinners sleep in hell, after slumbering in their sins here? Is the cause of God to be destroyed for this purpose?'

"Well, I guess that watchman had never heard those kind of words come out of a colored girl before, or else maybe he knew it really was God speaking. Either way he went whiter, and he shook like the sisters and begged my pardon. He said he hadn't meant to interrupt us, and he would never break up a meeting like that again. Then he wished us all well and tipped his hat and left." Saint Catherine laughed at the memory.

"I guess that night made me," she said. "Partly it was because the story of it spread like a prairie fire, and before I knew it, I had people all over asking me to preach to them. But more than that, I'd stood up to a white man, and God had backed me. I knew then for certain that I was through that strait gate, walking on the narrow way."

She paused again, with a look that said she was remembering. "The road's been at least as hard as Matthew warns," she said at last. "For every time I manage to gather a congregation and speak God's word, there are five where I'm laughed right out of town. They call me an enthusiast, or unnatural, or downright blasphemous..." She trailed off, looking at the path ahead padded with last year's leaf fall, and the new spring leaves blazing out above.

Meredith fumbled in her pocket for her paper and dropped the reins long enough to write, "How can you stand it?"

Saint Catherine read the words, and then smiled at Meredith; a calm smile that reminded her of Siu Fai's. "There's nothing to stand," she said. "I've held the hand of God."

"You never doubt it?" Meredith wrote. "Your calling?"

Saint Catherine smiled again, this time sadly. "When the road's full of snow and no town will have me. When the mule goes lame and we have no choice but to sit it out in the middle of nowhere. I guess I wouldn't be mortal if I didn't doubt, then. That's why I have this."

She fingered her bird necklace. Meredith saw then that the ends weren't fastened – it was a chain rather than a loop, wound twice around Saint Catherine's neck and the ends crossed loosely to keep them out of the way. Meredith shrugged her question.

Saint Catherine answered, "Each bird is a saved soul." Seeing that Meredith didn't understand, she explained, "They're sparrows. A sparrow is a symbol of God's love: it's a lowly bird, but it's still God's creature, same as any other. '…even the lowly sparrow was invited to make her home in the Lord's temple…' Just like the least among people are invited with the greatest."

She paused, considering the words, and then continued, "And then there's a story. It isn't in the Bible, so it isn't well known, but it's still about Jesus. How once as a child, He made a dozen sparrows out of river clay and then breathed life into them, and they flew away." Saint Catherine's dark face tilted sunward, misted gold by the hazy light. "I don't think there's a better way than that to describe a conversion."

Again, Meredith shrugged, and Saint Catherine explained: "A non-believer is like a clay man. Lifeless. Soulless. Anchored to this coarse earth. But when he takes in the light of the Lord, his soul grows wings, like those clay sparrows." Saint Catherine moved her long fingers in a graceful upward motion, so that Meredith could almost see a lifting soul. "It is the most beautiful thing you could ever hope to see, and just as rare. So when it happens, I add a sparrow to the chain, to keep a little of it by me always." She looked from Meredith down to the birds on her breast, smiling fondly. "I can tell you the name of every one of them."

They rode then in silence after that, Saint Catherine contemplating her chain of saved souls, Meredith awed by the strength and beauty of the woman's vision. Also, very slightly, disconcerted by it. As with the Shakers and Siu Fai and the other believers she'd met along her road, Saint Catherine's faith made her both uncomfortable and slightly envious. Still, she would rather be traveling with the other woman than not. Her serenity was a palliative to Meredith's disquiet. She didn't know how it worked, only that in Saint Catherine's presence she felt different, lighter, disconnected from the things that had weighed her down before with sadness and fear.

When they stopped at midday to eat and rest the animals, Meredith wrote down the question she'd been avoiding since they met: "Where are you going?"

Saint Catherine looked at the question, picking at a small helping of last night's chicken. "Well now, that's a good question." As if to prove it, she considered it a long time before she spoke again. "I guess the best way to think of it is, I'm like one of those old-time Methodist circuit riders. I go to the places that aren't likely to have churches, or if they do, then they can't get a minister to preach in them. Saddlebag preachers – that's what they called them, because they carried all their worldly goods in here." She patted the mule's saddlebags. "Their worldly goods and God's word.

"I don't put much stock in color, aside from what the law says," she continued, "but I guess it makes sense that I usually find myself preaching to Negroes. For one thing, they're less likely to have churches and preachers of their own, especially out here. For another, they're more willing to listen to me." She thought about this, chewing, and then added, "Then again, white folks sometimes come along just for the entertainment of seeing what a skinny black lady might have to say about salvation." She smiled, touching her necklace. "Pride's a sin, but I can't help feeling a little bit of it for the white birds on here."

Meredith raised her eyebrows.

"Oh yes – I've converted a few of them in my time, even baptized a white baby once, though the mother made no bones telling me it was only because he was sick, and she couldn't find a 'real' preacher to do it on account of the child being a bastard."

Meredith was surprised to find that the word touched a nerve somewhere deep inside her. She wondered suddenly whether she had been baptized. She wondered why it mattered to her. "Is that allowed?" she wrote.

Saint Catherine shrugged. "Is a colored lady preacher allowed?"

Meredith had to smile.

"Well, anyway, to answer your question, I go where the Lord guides me. Every few nights He comes to me in a dream and tells me where to go next. Sometimes it's a place I've been before; more often it isn't."

"What if you can't find it?" Meredith wrote.

"That's never happened."

"How do you know how to get there? Do you dream a map?"

Saint Catherine laughed. "I dream a destination, and I wake with a direction in my bones. I know I've arrived when the world lights up...like God loans it some of His light." She glanced at Meredith and added, "Just like it lit up yesterday afternoon. The water in that pool glowed fine as gold, same as I saw it in my dream."

Meredith looked at her, incredulous. Saint Catherine met her eyes with calm certainty. "Did you think God had no hand in us meeting?"

Meredith didn't know what hand had pushed her toward Saint Catherine, but she was certain that someone's had. It was a troubling certainty, far as it was from the way she was used to looking at things. More troubling was her growing feeling that Saint Catherine was keeping something back amidst all of her open-handed confession. This feeling deepened, though she couldn't have said why, when Saint Catherine resumed speaking on an abrupt tangent.

"One day," she said, "I'm going to open an orphanage."

Meredith felt that a comment was expected of her, but she couldn't think of one.

"An orphanage and a school," Saint Catherine continued. "There aren't too many of those for colored children."

Meredith wrote, "That seems like a fine ambition."

"It's not ambition," said Saint Catherine. "It's my destiny. I've dreamed it often enough to know."

"Is that where you're going now?"

Saint Catherine shook her head. "Not yet." She glanced at Meredith, and then said, "I'll settle on the day I make this chain into a circle." She fingered her necklace. "The day I save my last soul."

"But how will you know which is the last?"

Saint Catherine only smiled and said, "It's time we were going."

4

That night Saint Catherine had a vision. There was a settlement to the south of their campsite where God told her she was needed. Since it wasn't out of her way – or so she told herself – Meredith decided to go with Saint Catherine. She couldn't quite admit to herself that she wanted to see whether all of the business about visions was true, and if it were true, what Saint Catherine would do about it.

Half a day proved it. An hour after they'd stopped for lunch, they rode into a rocky little valley with a clutch of old buildings at its heart. They were crooked, warped wooden structures, most of them looking nearer falling down than standing up. For the most part they were windowless, with drystone chimneys leaning at precarious angles. None looked like they could contain more than a single room, yet clusters of people gathered in the packed dirt dooryards and sagging porches to watch as Meredith and Saint Catherine rode in, from great-grandparents down to tiny babies. All of them were Negroes, and all wore the same look of weary suspicion when they realized that Meredith wasn't. More than one woman took a baby or a small child into a house and shut the door.

Saint Catherine wasted no time. "Brothers – sisters – " she called out when they'd reached the center of the tiny village, "I'm come here to bring you God's word!" Her voice rang like a churchbell in the little clearing. She looked like an ancient goddess, Meredith thought, sitting straight and proud on her white mule, in her crimson dress, in the center of that shabby town.

But the watching people didn't appear impressed. "Ain't never heard of no lady preacher," Meredith heard one old man say to another.

"Maybe she's one o' them mistin...missing...what's that word, Matty?"

"Missionaries," a younger woman answered in a sharp voice. She shook her head, looking Saint Catherine up and down before she added, "I don't think so. Missionaries is white."

"Sure, then, maybe that one's the missionary," said the first man, pointing at Meredith.

"We don't need no convertin'," another woman said to Meredith, jiggling a baby on her hip. "We're Christians already. And anythin' you might want to sell us, we don't need and can't afford anyhow, so you best be on your way." She turned back to her child.

Unperturbed, Saint Catherine said, "I'm not a missionary, and nor is Meredith. I'm here to speak God's word, not force it on you."

"You a preacher?" asked Matty.

"I am," said Saint Catherine.

People were shaking their heads, exchanging looks. A few of them laughed. Saint Catherine didn't seem to notice.

"And the white girl dressed like a boy," Matty continued, "what does *she* do?"

Saint Catherine smiled gently at Meredith. "She listens."

"She ain't tied to no plantation, is she? Because we all tried sharecropping already, and it didn't agree with us."

This seemed to interest Saint Catherine. "You were tenants? All of you?"

"Um-hm," said Matty, her mouth hard. "Til we decided it was better to starve out here than break our backs makin' some fat, white man's money for him."

Saint Catherine looked at her speculatively. "How long since you left the plantations?"

"Abe?" said Matty, turning to one of the old men.

He ruminated on his fingers for a moment, then answered, "Five years? Six?" Then he shrugged. "Not much point in keepin' time, here."

Saint Catherine smiled at that, but it faded quickly. "And you've never had a preacher in all that time," she said. It wasn't a question, and nobody seemed to feel the need to answer it. "Well, I'd be honored to be your first, but like I said, I don't force the Word on folks who don't want to hear it. I'll leave it up to you, but either way, Meredith and me, we'd be glad to camp here tonight. That all right?"

After a moment, Abe gave her a fraction of a nod. Saint Catherine nodded back, then she got off the mule and led him to a flat place on the bank of a little stream farther down the valley. The stream was shallow there, the water whispering over a bed of smooth stones. Meredith followed her reluctantly as the people gathered in a knot behind them and fell into discussion.

"What if they tell us to leave?" Meredith wrote, standing with her pack still on.

"They won't," Saint Catherine answered.

"You dreamed it?"

"I don't dream people, remember? But I've been doing this long enough to read them. These ones aren't mean, and what's more, their souls are starved for God's word. But if they've been tenants, it's no wonder they're wary of us."

"It's me they're wary of."

Saint Catherine shook her head. "There's plenty of their own people would sell them down the river given half a chance."

Meredith took off the horse's halter, but she didn't open her pack. She sat on top of it, watching the play of the water over the stones in the stream as Saint Catherine brewed coffee. The villagers were still debating when Saint Catherine handed her a cup, but by the time she'd finished it, they'd gone back to their chores – all except Abe, who was wobbling toward them on scarred, barefoot legs.

When he reached their campsite, Saint Catherine poured another cup of coffee and handed it to him. He took it from her with a kind of reverence, sipped, shook his head and smiled, wrinkles radiating outward from it like a child's drawing of the sun. "Now *that's* something I ain't tasted in a *long* time!" He tapped the cup with one callused finger. "Just about the only thing I miss from the plantin' days. Ain't got nothin' but chicory here."

Saint Catherine smiled, took a packet out of her saddlebag and handed it to him. "Well then, you have the rest of this," she said.

Abe raised his eyebrows in surprise, tipped his hat back. "Why now ma'am, you don't gotta do that! We already fixed on lettin' you speak."

"I'm glad to hear it," Saint Catherine said, her face lighting. "But the coffee's a gift, regardless."

Abe nodded and tucked the packet carefully into his threadbare waistcoat. He drank down the rest of his cup, and then he said, "Now come on with me, ma'am – I got somethin' to show you." He paused, his eyes flickering over Meredith. "You too, Miss, if it pleases you."

With the village's eyes heavy on her back, Meredith stood and followed Saint Catherine, who followed Abe as he crossed the stream over a row of stepping stones and walked into the woods. Saint Catherine showed no hesitation, and as Meredith walked she wondered about her own, and whether she would have felt the same if Abe had been white. She tried hard to push the thought out of her mind and was properly ashamed of it when the path ended in a clearing, at the center of which stood a tiny split-log chapel. It had oilpaper windows and a white, wooden cross on its squat, wooden-shingled steeple. There was none of the village houses' rickety tenacity about it. Clearly, Abe's people had put the best they had into their church.

Saint Catherine stopped in front of it, her hands over her mouth and tears standing in her eyes. For a long moment she stood like that. Then she turned to Abe, took his hands in hers and said, "Sir, I am honored. In all my preaching days, I've never seen such a beautiful chapel."

He smiled. "It is pretty, ain't it?" he said. "When we came here, we hoped to get ourselves a preacher before too long." He shook his head, sighing. "I guess preachers got better things to do than live in the woods with a bunch of ex-sharecroppers. We come here to pray on our own, but I guess it ain't the same."

Saint Catherine shook her head. "God hears you, Mr. Abe. I'm sure He does. But even so, you tell everyone to come here at sundown – we'll have ourselves a proper meeting!"

5

"'Now faith,'" Saint Catherine read from her battered Bible, resting on the chapel's lectern, "'is the substance of things hoped for, the evidence of things not seen.'"[8]

She put the book aside and stepped out from behind the lectern. She stopped in a shaft of evening sunlight, mellowed by the windows' oilpaper panes, turning her face to it. For a moment she just stood there, eyes closed and face to the sun, as if listening. Then the sun slipped behind a tree or a cloud, and as the light slowly faded, she stepped down to face the congregation ranged on the polished wooden benches. She looked at Meredith, sitting alone in the back row, and smiled; then she began to speak.

"Faith – it's an easy word. It slips from the tongue like a fish through a pool. But it's a hard word too – hard as that same fish to catch and keep. It hides like that fish hides in the reeds and rocks and shadows, such a little light in a world full of the darkness of hatred and fear and bald-faced injustice. And there's no one knows that better than the Negro."

There was a ripple of murmured "amen"s. Saint Catherine glanced at Meredith as it rose and then died away, a question in her eyes Meredith couldn't read. She shook her head slightly, and Saint Catherine looked away with the ghost of a smile.

"Yes, brothers and sisters: we know what it is to suffer. We remember our years of work without profit – some of us are still living them." Another murmur of affirmation. "In those dark times so many of us lost the light. We forgot how to hope, how to believe in something that

---

8 Hebrews 11:1

couldn't be seen. So here we are now, free men and women but living still in the darkness, without path or purpose. I'm here to remind you of the truth of Christ's words, to show you that hope is the path back to faith, and faith is the light in the darkness that will turn injustice inside-out."

Saint Catherine's voice, which had risen, was soft again when she continued after a pause: "Are you with me, my brothers and sisters?"

A murmur of affirmation. The golden light fell on Saint Catherine like a benediction. "Then let us begin…"

*

Saint Catherine drifted through the next few days in a dreamy euphoria, saying almost as little as Meredith. Only once did she mention the service in the sharecroppers' church, and that was to ask Meredith what she'd thought of it.

"I've never heard truer words," she wrote.

"Honestly?" Saint Catherine asked. "What did they mean to you?"

Meredith thought for a long time without coming up with a response. She put her pencil to the paper in desperation, and found herself writing, "You made me see the security of surrendering everything." She looked at the sentence, confused, because she didn't remember thinking those words. She was sure they weren't what she'd intended to write, but when she tried to recall what she *had* intended, her mind was blank.

"I mean," she tried again after a moment, "while you were speaking, I felt the courage to pull light from the air, colors from the flowers and plait them into something that explains…" Her pencil hovered. She had no idea what it explained; she only knew that it had meant everything to her in the moments that she felt it, listening to Saint Catherine speak. She passed a hand over her face, shook her head. "I think that I am going mad," she concluded.

Saint Catherine laughed softly. "No, honey. You're just waking up."

"From what?" Meredith wrote.

But Saint Catherine was lost again in her reverie.

*

That night, they camped in a meadow at the foot of a mountain that dwarfed all of the others around it. Meredith pushed through the long, flower-starred grass and into a stand of red spruce. She poked around at the winter's deadwood until she found a piece that wasn't too wet or too dry, which fit neatly in her closed hand. She took it back to camp and started whittling it in the last of the light, trying not to think too hard about what she was doing, or her sudden, driving need to do it.

Saint Catherine didn't ask about it. She sat stirring a pot of black-eyed peas and salt pork, although Meredith doubted that she'd even taste it. She'd eaten nothing all day – a sign, Meredith thought, of an impending revelation. It made her wary of the project she'd begun, but her hands seemed to work on their own, driven by something beyond reason. She dug at the wood with her dull knife until most of it lay in chips on the ground, and the nugget that was left was no bigger than a pecan, but the form within it was visible at last.

"Beans are ready," Saint Catherine said, and Meredith shoved the unfinished carving gratefully into her pocket, taking the plate the other woman offered. She ate her dinner absently, while Saint Catherine watched the moon rising over the mountain. When she'd finished, Meredith took her lone dish to the stream at the edge of the meadow and washed it. When she returned, she found Saint Catherine lying back against one of her saddlebags, counting off the sparrows on her necklace like a rosary as she sang softly:

"I've got peace like a river,

I've got peace like a river

I've got peace like a river in my soul…"

Meredith sat down by the fire. It was little more than a flicker among the embers, but the night was warm and the moon was bright enough to carve by. She took the wood back out of her pocket, and went to work on it again as Saint Catherine sang, her sweet low voice settling over the meadow like a favorite quilt.

"I've got love like an ocean,

I've got love like an ocean,

I've got love like an ocean in my soul…"

The falling wood chips were only slivers now. Meredith had the feeling that she wasn't creating the bird so much as freeing it, each scrape of the knife cutting another fetter. She wondered if this was how the child Jesus had felt when he made his birds of river clay; whether it had been a true act of creation, or simply the ability to see that they were there already, waiting. She wondered whether any act of creation was ever more or less than a recognition.

Saint Catherine was singing about joy like a fountain, and Meredith felt that joy, though she knew what the bird in her hand meant. And though Saint Catherine fell silent when the song ended – slipping easily as a child into waiting slumber – the essence of it remained over the meadow, closing Meredith in its arms so that she felt no fear or sadness when she scraped the last of the wood from the sparrow's wings. She stood up, placed the bird into Saint Catherine's upturned palm. The other woman's eyes were moving beneath her closed lids; seeing, Meredith knew, the road that would mean their parting.

She drew a breath. The moon drifted in the hazy springtime sky, full of infinite possibility. Then she lay down by Saint Catherine, curled against her warmth, and followed her into dreamless sleep.

7

When Saint Catherine shook Meredith awake the next morning, she'd already added the wooden sparrow to her necklace. Its two spreading wings joined the ends of the lariat, making a loop. Saint Catherine smiled and said, "Thank you, Meredith."

Meredith nodded. She could see divinity in the ecstatic light of Saint Catherine's face. She sat up, took out her paper and pencil and wrote, "Are you leaving now?"

Saint Catherine looked at her for a long moment, and then away, toward the mountain. "Today, our roads part, but not yet. We'll ride together a little longer."

Part of Meredith was relieved, part of her troubled by this. But the morning was warm, the air still and sweet. *The first day of summer*, she thought, and memory surged with the sharp smell of the sea, warm sand bounding water still winter-cold, the sun disconnected by a shimmering green roof. She shook her head against the sudden longing.

"Come," said Saint Catherine. She handed Meredith the reins of the horse, which she'd bridled while Meredith slept, and gave her a leg up. They rode out of the meadow, the grass and flowers closing behind them, hiding the signs that they'd been there. They rode into the woods, along a deer path that loosely followed the bank of the stream in which Meredith had washed her supper plate, before the two diverged, and the woods thinned and gave out onto a road. It looped like a silver ribbon down the valley until it rounded a curve of hill and was lost. It was a dirt road, but well-packed and wheel-rutted as if it were frequently traveled.

Despite this, they met no other traffic. The world seemed to have emptied, as it had at the very beginning of Meredith's journey. Sometimes smaller roads diverged from the big one, leading up into the hills on one side or the other, though there was no evidence of settlements there. Each time they approached one of these forks, Meredith's heart beat a little faster as she wondered whether this was the crossroads where Saint Catherine would leave her.

It was evening before it happened, and then there was no warning beyond the residual glow of the sun on the high face of the hill above them, and the moment when Meredith wondered if that was the color of Saint Catherine's visions. Then they'd rounded the hill and stumbled into a band of angels. Or so they seemed to Meredith: backlit, dressed in white, with their dark skins casting the sunset back in bronze and copper. They sang in sweet high voices, with hands joined and eyes closed, a song whose words Meredith heard only later, in her memory of that night, though the meaning of them burned cleanly into her:

"As I went down in the valley to pray
Studyin' about that good old way
And who shall wear the starry crown
Good Lord, show me the way.
Oh fathers let's go down
Let's go down, come on down.
Oh fathers let's go down,
Down in the valley to pray…"

They weren't angels; Meredith saw it as the sun finally set and their brightness faded, and they lost the gauzy inconsistency of distance. They were children, boys and girls of various ages, though none yet into their teens. They wore travel-stained white pinafores; the girls' hair was neatly braided and tied with strips of white fabric that fluttered like wings in the evening breeze. They stood in front of an overturned wagon, the horse that had pulled it no more than a memory and a broken leather harness. A woman's arm protruded blue and rigid beneath one splintered wheel.

Meredith looked over at Saint Catherine. She'd got down off of the mule, her face glowing as if it held onto the sunken sun. The children sang:

"Oh mothers let's go down,
Come on down, don't you want to go down?
Come on mothers and let's go down,
Down in the valley to pray…"

Meredith slid down from the horse's back and grasped Saint Catherine's hand. The woman gave her a rapturous smile, gently disengaging it. "This is my road, Meredith," she said, indicating whatever lay beyond the overturned wagon. "Mine alone."

Meredith felt tears in her eyes. She shook her head.

"Honey, you don't need me anymore." Meredith looked at her through the slipping tears. "Don't you understand? Yours was the last soul." She fingered the white wooden bird hanging against her breast. "It's time for me to move on, and you too."

Meredith shrugged: *Where?* Saint Catherine pointed. In the shadows behind the wagon, Meredith saw a thin ribbon of road leading up the hill to her right.

"Last night, I dreamed you riding up that road," Saint Catherine said.

Meredith looked at it in despair. She didn't want to find another stricken village or lost soul. She didn't want anyone else to need her. She felt suddenly exhausted; she shook her head.

"Love has saved your soul," Saint Catherine told her, "but you still haven't found your path."

Meredith shook her head again, but Saint Catherine had already turned back to the children. Two of them let go of each other's hands, offering them to her. She took them, turned and called back to Meredith: "Don't you cry over me, Miss Meredith. We'll meet again one day – I know it!" She joined the song as she led the children around the wrecked wagon and disappeared into whatever was beyond it.

"Come on sinners and let's go down,
Let's go down, oh, come on down!
Come on sinners and let's go down,
Down in the valley to pray…"

A cloud burned red on the horizon. Saint Catherine and her children seemed to be walking into it, their figures catching and burning until they were only wisps of smoke, and then those were gone too. Meredith stood weeping, despite Saint Catherine's admonition, until a sudden flock of birds startled her, lifting past the sunset into the bare, blue sky. When they were gone, Meredith dried her tears. Turning the horse's head, she started up the hill.

Caulking

1

Not long after Mr. Marsh moved in, Silence realized that Pascal was watching him. At first he thought that it was just Pascal's way of alleviating his boredom – his cough had worsened with the last snowfall, and he complained of pain in his hip, so he spent a lot of his time in bed, or in a chair by the parlor window. But the intensity of his eyes through the attic panes, and the way he ducked out of sight when he realized Silence had seen him, gradually convinced Silence that there was more to it.

As such he wasn't entirely surprised on the morning when he went to bring Pascal his *café au lait*, and instead of waving him away again, Pascal motioned to him to sit down. Given the gradual decline in the old man's health, Silence thought he knew what was coming. He put his coffee aside and waited for the worst – until he realized that Pascal was smiling.

"Silence," he said, taking the younger man's hand in his and looking at him with earnest eyes, "I want to be the first to congratulate you."

Silence blinked at him, wondering if senility was finally setting in. "Well – thanks," he said. "But I don't think I've done anything lately that's worthy of congratulations...unless you count finishing *The World as Will and Representation*."

Pascal grimaced. Silence had read him a few passages of Schopenhauer, which were more than enough for him. "*That* deserves commiserations," he said. "No: I'm congratulating you on the end of your celibacy."

"*What*?" Silence demanded, mortified.

"You heard me."

"Christ, Pascal. What kind of thing is that to say?"

"The truth," he answered, shrugging, and took a sip of his coffee. "Or it will be soon enough."

"You can't be serious."

"Why would I joke about this?"

"I don't know. Maybe – "

"What? You think I'm crazy?" He crossed his arms over his quilt-swaddled chest.

"It had crossed my mind," Silence grumbled and then, seeing Pascal's glower, he sighed. "All right. If you're serious, you'd better tell me what makes you think I'm going to...I mean that someone's going to...oh, Lord, Pascal this is absurd!"

Pascal shrugged. "No, it's not. When you get to be my age, you just get a feel for these things."

"Right," Silence sighed. "So, who's the lucky lady?"

"I don't know. I only know that she's comin'."

"Coming?" Silence repeated, a chill suddenly running up and down his spine as he recalled Celia's fallen biscuits. "You mean she isn't from here?"

"Nope. She's traveled a long way."

Silence had a sudden flash of a sea-wet girl walking toward a dark wood. "What does she look like?" he asked in a low voice.

But Pascal only shrugged. "How would I know that?"

"How indeed," Silence sighed.

Pascal peered at him. "You don't believe me."

"It's not that. It just seems awfully...unlikely."

"How's that?" Silence turned his scarred cheek toward Pascal, who shook his head and rolled his eyes toward the newspapered ceiling. "When are you gonna realize that scar ain't your be all and end all?"

"When people stop treating me like it is."

"Me," said Pascal, beginning to count off on his fingers, "Celia, Happy, Annie Newcombe, Thomas Marsh – "

"All right, all right! But even if this mysterious lady does overlook my ruin of a face, what would she see in me to make her...well..."

Half-smiling at Silence's flush, Pascal said, "You must know one or two things about wooing women. You were engaged to that stuck-up, yellow-haired girl, after all."

"Don't remind me."

"And you get on fine with Celia."

"Yes – as a friend."

Pascal shook his head again. "You are one stubborn so-and-so, Silence Ogden."

Silence shrugged. "I'm sorry. This just doesn't make any *sense*..."

"Sense? Love isn't supposed to make sense!"

Silence raised his eyebrows. Pascal sighed, studied the ceiling, and then his coffee, and finally looked back at Silence. "Look: I'm gonna tell you something I didn't ever mean to tell you."

"Oh?" said Silence, instantly intrigued. "Why not?"

"Because I thought you might not see me the same way if you knew. It's not something most folks would understand. But you, Silence – well, I'm hoping you'll be different. And I'm hoping it will convince you to look at this thing with an open mind." He drew a deep breath, let it out slowly. "Anyhow, you gotta promise to think long and hard about it before you pass judgment." His face was as serious as Silence had ever seen it.

"All right," Silence agreed, his heart suddenly beating hard.

"I've only ever been in love once," Pascal began.

"Oh?" Silence said again. "Who was she?"

Pascal's eyes flickered away for a moment. "I'll get to that. But first, you gotta know that once I was a slave."

"I do know that," Silence said quietly. He also thought he knew where Pascal was going.

"Yes – but what you don't know is that I was a house servant. I was one of the lucky ones: I never broke my back hauling cotton out of some white man's fields. But still, I was property. I had no choice but to do what I was told, and the older I got, the more I resented it. Sure, none of us liked it, but I resented it all the more because I had an ambition.

"See, the daughter of the house played the piano. This wasn't no simpering coquette learning love songs. Sidonie was a hard little thing: never showed she felt much of anything, except when she played. That girl played the piano like the devil was in her, even as a child. I was only a few years older than her, and I used to listen at the music room door. I thought if I could play music like that, I would be happy. But it was impossible as freedom. Sure, some of the other slaves could play the banjo or fiddle, and I guess they could have taught me, but all they knew was dance music or religious songs. I wanted to play Beethoven."

He paused, and Silence's mind ran ahead to what he saw as the inevitable conclusion to this story. But Pascal's next words weren't what he'd expected.

"Things went on like that for a time – and then they got Sidonie a teacher. He was a foreign man, came from Scotland, and he was different from any of the white folks I knew. They had no slaves in his country, and he didn't know any better than to treat us as equals. He even brought a piano out to the quarters and played it at night for us – said the big house made him too nervous to play.

"Well, I saw my chance with Allistair. I asked him to teach me to play, and he did teach me – but not then, and not the piano. The year I turned twenty-one, he gave me my fiddle." Pascal paused, looking out the window at the yard, where the bright March sun ate away at the rotting furrows of snow. "He'd had it a long time," he said at last. "Once it belonged to his friend…the one who came from Scotland with him. The one who died on the crossing and broke his heart…"

Pascal paused again. Silence didn't notice; he was busy trying to remember where he'd heard that story before, about the man who died at sea, poisoning it forever for the friend who'd watched him die. He remembered at the same moment he realized there were tears on Pascal's cheeks, and then he began to understand.

"You weren't in love with Sidonie," he said.

Pascal burst into laughter amidst the tears. "Sidonie? *Mon Dieu*, son, she *owned* me!"

"And yet her teacher…you…" Silence trailed off, waving his hand around the words he couldn't quite speak.

"Loved him," Pascal said, his black eyes level on Silence, his voice unwavering. "Still do."

"And he…"

"Yes, Silence," Pascal sighed. "He loved me, too."

Silence didn't know what to say. He didn't even know what to think. One of Mr. Marsh's books had been *The Symposium*, but though he'd read it with an anthropological interest, the ideas in it had seemed to belong to a different world from his. He certainly never imagined they would materialize under his own roof. Pascal watched Silence struggle with it for a few moments longer, and then he began to speak again.

"There's another thing you gotta know if you're gonna understand this at all: it was Allistair bought my freedom."

"So…you were grateful to him?"

"Of course I was," Pascal said, "but don't you go usin' that to explain the rest to yourself. Gratitude wouldn't have kept us together for twenty-two years."

"Twenty-two *years*?"

He nodded. "We criss-crossed this country more times than I can count. We could never stay long anywhere, or someone might get suspicious, but I didn't mind. Maybe because I'd spent my whole life before that in one place, I couldn't get enough of new ones. We scraped by on what we could earn playing revivals or dances or suchlike, but to a man who grew up expecting to die as someone else's posession…well, it seemed to me my life was blessed. I don't know if Allistair felt the same, but if he didn't, he loved me enough never to let on."

There was a long pause as Pascal's eyes roamed the past, and Silence tried to make himself accept these revelations. At last he asked, "How did it end?"

Pascal smiled sadly. "The way all true loves end, I guess: I buried him."

Silence looked up at him. This revelation shouldn't have shocked him after all the others, but the simple, unrequited grief with which Pascal spoke the words drove home the truth of the rest.

"Remember that song you heard me sing the night we met – 'Where the Southern cross the Dog'?"

"Of course I do."

"Well, his grave's not far from the place where those tracks cross." He took a breath; this one shuddered. "I've been without Allistair McCune longer now than I was ever with him, but I never stopped feeling like I buried my heart in that railroad town." He turned to Silence, his eyes boring into him. "A white man and a black boy: that's how blind love is, Silence Ogden."

Silence could only gaze at him.

"You still speakin to me, *P'tit*? Should I pack my things?"

Silence uttered something between a laugh and a sob. "Don't be an idiot, Pascal!" He reached out and took his frail hand. "I admit, you threw me for a loop – but I'm still glad you told me."

Pascal nodded, his eyes drooping, as if the effort of revealing his secret had exhausted him. "You're a good boy, Silence. And don't worry: whoever it is that's coming for it, your story can't possibly turn out as strange as that."

2

At the beginning of April the plough horse foundered.

It began with a slight lameness after the first day in the fields, which Celia only mentioned to Silence as a second thought. "It's been a long winter," she said, shrugging at Silence's concern. "He just needs to work out the kinks, like the rest of us."

"Charlie's old, though," Silence said. "He's been here as long as I can remember."

"Maybe you should let him rest," Happy said anxiously. She had an affinity for all animals, but she particularly loved Charlie. Silence often found her seated on the stable rail, holding a one-sided conversation with him.

"And who'll pull the plough then?" Celia shook her head. "He's old, but he's tough. He'll be all right after a few days steady work." And she flashed Silence a look that told him to keep his mouth shut.

The next day, though, Celia came into the barn where Silence was caulking seams, her eyes wide and worried. It was barely mid-morning – she should have been at work for another two hours.

"What's wrong?" asked Silence, setting aside his mallet and iron.

"Charlie won't move," she said.

"What do you mean?"

"I mean he won't move! He just stopped in the middle of the field, wouldn't take another step. I couldn't even lead him back here."

Despite his dearth of agricultural knowledge, Silence realized that this was serious. If the horse wouldn't pull the plough, there would be no crop. With no stores left from the last wasted summer, they'd be hard pressed to make it through the following winter. He left his caulking and followed Celia back out to the field. Just as she'd said, Charlie stood in its midst like a dejected statue, head hanging and back humped. His hind legs were tucked unnaturally beneath him and his forelegs splayed too far out front.

"Do you know what's wrong with him?" Silence asked.

"Founder," Celia said grimly, "plain and simple."

Silence felt a stab of guilt. "Was it because of the green oats?"

Celia sighed. "With founder, you never know. The effects can show up a long time after the cause. It might be the green oats, or he might have got into something in the paddock last week that he shouldn't."

Silence knew how unlikely this was. "I'm sorry, Celia."

"Apologize to *him*," she snapped, and then she sighed and touched Silence's hand. "I didn't mean that. You didn't know any better, and we'll never know for sure what caused it. It's only that now…"

He didn't ask her to finish. She'd only be repeating what he knew already. "Is there any hope of saving him?" he asked.

"Not much." She considered this, and then she said, "But Happy will never forgive me if I don't try. Let's get him inside."

After a good deal of chasing and coaxing, Charlie hobbled into the barn. When he reached his stall, he lay down, staring at nothing. Celia felt his hooves, then the pulse in his legs, and frowned. "The fores are worse than the hinds, but that's not saying much. First thing to do is cool them off."

"How?"

"Cold water. I doubt he'll agree to stand in four buckets, so we need towels, and water, and all the ice we can spare."

Silence went to fetch them. He had no qualms about hacking a big slab off the last remaining block in the ice-house. When he returned to the barn, he found Celia standing at his worktable, wearing a pair of garden gloves and chopping what appeared to be a pile of nettles with a draw-knife.

"Is he going to eat that?" Silence asked.

"Not without some encouragement," she said grimly, "but first things first. I'll start on his feet; you bring me a bucket of hot water and the jar of molasses."

By the time Silence returned with the water and molasses, Celia had wrapped the horse's hooves in cold, wet towels. She stood leaning on the rail, watching him. "He hasn't tried to kick them off," she said.

"Isn't that a good thing?"

She turned and smiled sadly at Silence. It was all the answer he needed.

"I've got the things you asked for," he said.

Celia turned back to the work-table. She poured a large measure of wheat bran into the bucket of water, added some of the molasses and the chopped nettles, then mixed them all together into a steaming mush. She brought the mixture to the horse, who raised his head when he smelled the molasses and began to lap halfheartedly at the mixture.

"The nettles are for the heat and swelling," Celia explained to Silence. "They'll also help soothe his gut if he's eaten something he shouldn't. Likewise the bran. Of course, it would work better with prickly ash bark, hawthorn and meadowsweet...I suppose I might be able to find some of them growing wild, though nothing will be in flower yet..." She sighed.

"Is there anything else we can do?" Silence asked.

"Pray," she said, and smiled thinly.

3

Happy was devastated when she came in to dinner and heard what had happened. "Why didn't you come get me?" she wailed.

"If you stayed nearby like I told you to, I might have," Celia answered sharply.

Happy gave her mother a wounded, blue look, and then she stormed out, heading for the barn. Celia untied her apron, clearly meaning to follow her, but Silence said, "Don't. It's my fault – I'll talk to her."

When he reached the barn, Happy was sitting stroking Charlie's head. "You've got to get better," she was saying to him. His brown ears, still tipped with winter fuzz, flickered to the sound of her voice. "You've *got* to!"

"I guess he's doing his best," Silence said. He'd meant to comfort her, but she looked coldly at him.

"Don't you tell me about him, Silence," she said. "If you cared about him at all, he wouldn't be sick in the first place."

"Happy," he began.

"*Don't*, Silence!" She'd begun to cry, infuriating herself. Silence turned and left the barn.

*

The next morning the horse wouldn't eat his mash, even when Happy offered him portions from her own hand. "Mama," she said, her eyes welling.

"Is there anything else we can do?" Silence asked Celia.

She regarded the horse for a long moment, and then taking Silence aside, she said, "There is one thing, but it's drastic. I've only ever seen it done once – I've never done it myself – "

"Do it!" Happy cried.

"Happy, stop eavesdropping!"

"You've got to save him, Mama!" Happy cried, ignoring the admonition.

"Happy, you have chores to do," Celia said, but her voice lacked conviction. Happy didn't move from Charlie's side, and Celia didn't ask her to again. Instead, she turned to Silence and said, "Do you have anything here that'll cut a groove?"

"A rabbet," Silence said automatically.

"Pardon?"

"Sorry," he said, moving to the toolbox and beginning to rummage. "In boats, a groove is called a rabbet. And yes, I have plenty." He offered her a selection of hook-bladed knives in varying sizes.

"Perfect," she said, selecting one of the finer ones. "It's sharp?"

Silence shrugged. "I haven't used that one since my father died."

"It'll have to do."

"What exactly do you plan to do with it?"

"Groove his hooves. It releases the pressure, and eases the pain. It'll also help them grow back properly – if he survives."

"You're sure this is a good idea?" Silence asked dubiously.

"I'm not sure at all. But it's my only idea. I don't suppose you have any spirits?"

Silence shook his head. "My parents never kept anything stronger than damson wine, and I'm afraid that's long gone."

"Soap and water then," she said. "Happy – "

"I'm going!" she cried, flying out the barn door before her mother could even finish the request.

When Happy returned with the soap and the bucket of water, Celia carefully washed and dried Charlie's hooves. "Happy," she said, "you go outside now."

"But Mama – "

"I mean it," Celia said sharply. "He's not going to like this, and I won't have you getting kicked!" When Happy didn't move, she said, "Or would you like to have Silence take you in for an arithmetic lesson with Mr. Marsh?"

Glowering, Happy ducked under the stall rail, but she hovered just on the far side of it.

"Silence," Celia said, "you stay near. I may need you to hold him."

Silence nodded and slipped his fingers under the chinstrap on the horse's halter, bracing himself for a fight as Celia approached the first foot. But the horse barely shifted as she drew the blade down the length of the hoof, leaving a curl of blue horn a quarter inch wide. After the first one she worked faster, cutting more grooves, an inch and a half apart. When she was finished, she washed Charlie's feet again, dried them carefully, and then bound them in strips torn from an old sheet. The old horse looked on, his dark eye full of the profound patience of an animal that has resigned itself to suffering.

"Now what?" Silence asked.

"Now we wait," Celia answered, sweeping up the curls of horn.

*

At first, it seemed that Celia's operation had helped the horse. He stood up for a few minutes the following morning, and longer still the day after. When he began to eat his mash again, everyone began, cautiously, to relax. And so it was doubly devastating when Happy brought him his breakfast on the third morning and found him prostrate again, his breathing shallow and his eye dim.

"They're infected," Celia said dejectedly, after examining his feet.

"What does that mean?" Silence asked.

Celia's quick glance at Happy was all the answer he needed.

"So that's it? There's nothing more you can do?"

"He's an old horse, Silence," she said. "Doing any more would be a cruelty, not a kindness."

"Mama?" Happy said tentatively.

Celia drew a breath, and looked at her daughter. "Happy Moon," she said gently, "Charlie's very sick. He's also in pain, and that will get worse before it kills him."

"Mama…" she whimpered.

"He's spent his life serving people," Celia plunged on, though the tremor in her voice betrayed the difficulty of it, "and the best way to thank him for that is to put him out of his misery."

"You want to *kill* him?" Happy cried.

"I don't *want* to, Happy – "

"If you kill him," Happy interrupted, her voice dull and certain, "I'll hate you forever."

"You can't hate your mother, Happy," Silence said, before Celia recovered from her shock. "If you have to hate someone, let it be me."

"Silence – " Celia began.

"This is my doing," he said, "and so it's mine to finish. You take Happy out of here."

"Silence!" Happy shrieked, but Celia took her firmly by the hand and led her toward the house.

When Silence came in for his father's shotgun there was no sign of Happy, but Celia was waiting for him. "Take this," she said, pressing one of the last of the stored apples into his hand. "I think he'll walk, if you offer it. Take him to the oatfield. I'm rotating it out this season, and we can bury him there…"

Silence accepted the apple, glad that she'd had the presence of mind to think of it. He hadn't considered how they would remove a dead horse from the barn, nor what they would do with him once they had. He couldn't think of anything beyond the immediate task of loading the shotgun.

Celia had been right: the horse dragged himself to his feet at the sight of the apple. Or maybe, Silence thought, he knew. There seemed to be an understanding in his dim, black eye as he followed Silence out to the oat field; perhaps even gratitude. He crunched the apple philosophically, and he didn't flinch at the snap of the hammer.

Silence didn't remember pulling the trigger. He was only aware of the world dissolving into grey fuzz, returning him briefly to the moment the boiler's shrapnel tore his life to pieces. Then he was back in the fallow oatfield. He knelt in the mud, his ears ringing with the gun's report, so he didn't hear Happy until she was beside him, flinging herself, weeping, over the horse's neck. Celia stood half way between the house and the field, her hands twisted in her skirt and head bowed. Mr. Marsh stood beside her, his right hand hovering by her left shoulder, irresolute. For a moment, their little world seemed consumed by its mundane disaster.

And then Silence saw something, a flicker of movement in the band of woods that ran along the far side of the field, dark against its somnolent winter brown. Then there was a flash of white, followed by a sudden, piercing whinny. He wondered briefly if he was losing his mind. Then the dark shape parted from the trees and raced toward them, slowly resolving into a running horse, black with a scribble of white on its side and on its muddy legs. It ran straight toward Happy, trailing the broken ends of a crude rope rein.

Silence recovered himself at last and moved to push Happy out of the animal's way. But she slipped his grasp and ran toward the horse, her sobs now mixed bizarrely with cries of something that sounded like, "Pony! Pony!" Silence could do nothing but watch in horror, but just as it seemed the black horse would trample the child, it checked its headlong gallop, cantering in a circle around her, then trotting, before it finally stopped. Happy reached out her arms, and the horse pressed its big head into her chest, exactly as if it sought and welcomed her embrace.

"I can't believe it," Celia said, arriving breathless at Silence's side, with Mr. Marsh following a few paces behind.

"What?" Silence asked, still dazed.

"That's Epona!" She turned to look at Silence and Mr. Marsh, her eyes shining in a face still wet with tears. "Our horse, the one who was stolen from us. Where could she have come from? And how on earth did she know?"

She was off again before the men could answer, walking toward Happy, who was leading the horse by the broken rein. Silence watched as the horse, Epona, greeted Celia with the same head-nudge she'd offered Happy. His mind was incongruously full of Pascal's premonition, but surely, he thought, the old man couldn't have been speaking of a horse?

"The world's gone mad," he said softly, only realizing he'd spoken when Mr. Marsh answered, "The world was always mad, Silence."

Silence turned to him. "How do you explain this?"

"I wouldn't even try," he said, without the hint of a smile.

They stood watching as Happy and Celia led the horse back toward the barn, both of them talking to her at once. After a moment, Mr. Marsh shook his head and turned back toward the house, but Silence held his ground. Something still felt strange, as if there were a discordant note in the birdsong, or a spot of unexpected color in the grey April sky, yet he couldn't see or hear anything out of the ordinary. He turned in a slow circle, stopping to look at the wood from which the horse had appeared.

Nothing moved among the bare trees, though their trunks hazed in the film of mist rising from the warming earth. Still, he was certain that it was the source of his premonition. He took a few steps toward the trees and then stopped again, certain that he saw something: a faint pale spot that could equally have been a face, or the scar from a recently-fallen branch. He walked forward again, trying to keep it in his line of sight, but the distance was too great. His vision swam, bright sky colliding dizzily with dark forest. By the time he reached the trees, it was gone, if it had ever been there at all.

4

"Epona," Mr. Marsh mused. "An ancient Celtic goddess, if I remember correctly."

"A *horse* goddess," Happy amended. "It means 'Great Mare', and she is. She's the greatest horse there ever was." Her face was ecstatic, difficult to reconcile with the misery only a few hours past.

"She's a good carriage horse, all right," Celia said, dishing out lunch. "I just hope she doesn't think she's too good to pull a plough."

"Well I don't care if she pulls the plough or not," Happy said defiantly. "I'm just glad she came back."

"I've heard of cats locating their owners miles away," Mr. Marsh mused, looking at his own cat, who had taken up residence in the log basket. "But I never knew horses shared the talent."

"As far as I know, they don't," Celia answered, her face troubled. "It sure is strange her turning up here, and just at the moment we needed a horse...it seems more than luck can account for."

"That's 'cause there's no luck involved," said Pascal. "It's serendipity."

Silence started, remembering how Annie had used the same word. "Not God's will?" he couldn't help asking.

Pascal shrugged. "Who says they aren't one and the same? Truth is, Silence – " But he never had the chance to enlighten Silence on that particular truth; he began to cough, and once begun he couldn't stop, the paroxysms strengthening until he

567

shook with them. The others concentrated hard on whatever they were doing. They'd learned that it was futile to try to help Pascal during these coughing fits; any attempts angered him and made the coughing worse. When the spell was past, even Happy was subdued.

"Well," Celia said after a few long moments' silence, "serendipity or not, I guess we're going to have to ask around and see if anyone knows anything about how Epona came to be here."

"Mama!" Happy wailed, but Celia set her mouth firmly.

"It's all well and good saying she was stolen from us," she said, "but she'll have passed through a few hands at least to wind up here. And she was wearing a halter. Someone might have bought her believing it was all on the level, and I don't much like the thought of being taken for a horse thief." At which everyone lapsed again into gloomy silence.

But all of their inquiries in town that afternoon proved Pascal right. No one knew anything about a horse of Epona's description; certainly no one had bought one. It seemed she'd come to Heaven of her own free will, and so there was nothing to stand in the way of Celia claiming her back.

*

For a few days life was quiet again. Epona appeared to have no objection to her new job, and she and Celia made short work of the ploughing. Silence went back to his caulking, working his way steadily along the boat's seams with oakum and putty, iron and hammer. It was repetitive work, not requiring much thought, but in its way it was soothing, and he welcomed the break from wrestling with planks and minute calculations.

He was working late one clear evening, taking advantage of the lingering light, when Happy came into the barn with a mug of coffee. "Mama said to bring you this," she said, setting it on his stool.

"You tell her I said thank you kindly," Silence answered, sipping gratefully from the cup.

Happy climbed onto the stool and watched him work for a time. Abruptly, she said, "Silence, do you believe in fairies?"

"Fairies?" he repeated, looking up from his seam. "I can't say I've ever really thought about it."

"Me neither," said Happy, "until this morning."

"What happened this morning?"

"I saw one."

"Oh?" Silence glanced at her, thinking this was the beginning of some new prank, but her face was serious, even slightly perturbed. "What makes you think it was a fairy?"

"Because she was in the woods, sleeping inside a ring of bluebells. That's called a fairy ring – I know from one of Mr. Marsh's books. Besides, she looked just like the pictures in that book."

"How's that?"

"She had long yellow hair, and her face was shaped like a heart." Happy traced the shape in the air with her finger. "The only thing is, she wasn't wearing a long, see-through dress, only these clothes that looked kind of like a man's pajamas. Also she didn't have any wings – but I guess they could have been hidden under the pajamas."

Thinking of Epona's broken rein, Silence had a sudden terrible thought. "Are you sure she was sleeping?"

"I'm sure. See, at first I thought she might be dead, so I got a stick and poked her. She didn't wake up, and I thought she really *was* dead, but I poked her harder to make sure, and then finally she did wake up."

"Well didn't you ask her who she was?"

"Of course I did!" Happy said with a withering look. "But she didn't say anything. She just looked scared and kept shaking her head, even when I tried to give her some of my dinner. It was black-eyed peas and cornbread. But she just looked at me. I guess fairies don't like cornbread and black-eyed peas."

The hammer and iron had hung forgotten in Silence's hands for several minutes. Now he laid them aside and leaned against the transom, studying her. "Happy," he said at last, "I can see why you think what you think, but couldn't it as easily have been an ordinary girl you saw rather than a fairy? A vagrant, or something?"

Happy sighed, as if she'd expected him to ask just such a stupid question. "That's one thing I'm sure about: she isn't an ordinary girl."

"But how do you know?"

"Because she's got no color. She's got no light around her at all."

Silence felt a creeping premonition. "Happy," he said, "do you think you could find that place again? Where you saw her?"

"Sure," she said.

Silence nodded. "I need to help your mother in the morning, but how about if we do some fairy hunting in the afternoon?"

Happy grinned.

5

All through the morning, Happy hung around Celia and Silence, allegedly helping and actually getting in the way. "What on earth's got into her?" Celia grumbled as Happy lifted her second bag of seed corn by the wrong end, spilling it at her feet.

"She's trying to hurry us up," Silence told her.

"Well she sure is taking an interesting approach." All at once she focused on Silence, her dark eyes dubious. "What's she plotting?"

"She thinks she found buried treasure in the woods. I told her that when we were finished, I'd have a look." Silence had no idea why he'd lied to Celia, particularly when he was no good at it. He only knew that he was suddenly wary of alerting anyone to the possible presence of Happy's fairy.

But Celia accepted his explanation without comment. "Why don't you take her now," she said in a voice worn thin by irritation, "before she ruins the whole crop?"

Silence nodded and shouldered his tools. Happy skipped behind him on the way to the barn, demanding, "Can we go *now*?" the moment he'd laid the tools down.

Silence looked down at his stained shirt and muddy trousers. "I guess so. I hope your fairy isn't afraid of sweat and dirt."

"She was a lot dirtier than you," Happy said cheerfully.

He followed her across the fallow field where they'd buried Charlie, heading straight for the place where he'd seen what might have been a face on the day Epona returned. He'd never told the others about it; Happy couldn't have known. Silence was filled with a sudden, jittery sense of something impending.

Drawing a deep breath to steady himself, he followed Happy into the woods.

Among the trees, the sunlight slanted in dusty shafts, like the light through church windows. The sharp smell of crushed pine rose up from the ground beneath their feet. Happy led Silence down to the river and then along the bank, past the cave and deeper into the trees, where the riverbed narrowed and the water turned deep and dark, slipping between blue-black firs. Silence could not help thinking of the far-away sea, drawing the stream like a magnet.

"So where exactly did you see this fairy, Happy?" he asked when they'd been walking for about ten minutes.

"It's not far now," she said.

A few minutes later they came to a clearing dwarfed by an ancient hemlock, whose lower boughs swept the ground. The ring of bluebells was there beside it in the yellow grass, but it was empty. Nearby were the remains of a small fire, carefully banked around embers which were still warm, as if someone meant to stir it back to life in the not-too-distant future. Aside from the fire, though, there were no signs of human habitation.

"What about that?" Happy asked, pointing to the tree.

Heart beating faster, Silence pushed a swathe of branches aside to reveal a cool, green cave, high enough at its center for Happy to stand straight. On one side of the space, a pile of bracken and pine boughs had been arranged into a crude mattress, with a tattered old blanket spread over it and a hunting jacket rolled like a pillow. A mountaineer's pack leaned against the tree trunk. Silence was debating whether or not to open it when Happy interrupted in a hushed voice:

"Mr. Marsh's book does say fairies can live in trees."

Silence sighed, "I don't know, Happy. These things look pretty mundane to belong to a fairy."

"What's mundane?"

"Normal."

"I guess," Happy said doubtfully. "But there isn't too much normal about living under a tree."

"Well one thing's for sure: fairy or otherwise, she wouldn't have left all of these things if she wasn't meaning to come back, and I don't think she'll much like to find us in here."

"You want to *leave*?" Happy cried in disbelief. "Without even seeing her?"

"No," said Silence. "I just don't want to terrify her. Come on – we'll wait for her outside."

They crawled out from under the tree again and sat down beneath a cluster of blooming hawthorn bushes at the edge of the clearing. Happy busied herself plaiting a crown from its spiky green twigs, while Silence tried not to think about Celia's superstition and Pascal's bizarre prediction. Most of all, he tried not to think about Epona's broken rein.

They waited for a long time. The sun turned westward and slipped behind a blue-grey bank of cloud, painting its edges brilliant gold. The air grew chilly. Happy wriggled impatiently, and Silence's doubts began to take hold. Then, just as he was about to give up and go home, he heard the faint brittle crackling of footsteps coming from the direction of the river. The birds paused in their singing. The whole world seemed to hold its breath.

Silence turned in the direction of the footsteps just as she emerged from the trees. She had two gutted fish slung over her shoulder, and the legs of her trousers were wet to the knees. Happy sat up, her eyes bright and mouth open, but before she could make a sound, Silence clapped his hand over it and shook his head. They pushed back into the thicket and watched the girl from behind the screen of hawthorn.

Silence could see why Happy had thought she was a fairy. She was tall and slender, and she walked like someone used to listening: with grace and little extraneous movement. Her hair hung down in a golden Rapunzel's-rope to her waist, leaking wavy, golden tendrils and full of tiny white petals, as if she'd brushed against a blossoming tree on her way through the woods. Her face was obscured by her shapeless brown hat, but her arms were bare to the elbows where she'd rolled her jacket sleeves, exposing two lengths of sunburned skin and wrists like fragile branches, each circled by a silver bangle.

She came around the side of the hemlock, laid the fish by the banked fire, took out a knife and began peeling a stick into the embers. Before long, a tiny flame licked up among the curls of wood, picking up lights in her hair that the deepening cloud cover had hidden. Bangles glinting, she wrapped the fish in sassafras leaves she took from her pockets, pinned them shut with sticks, laid them by the fire, and wiped her hands on the grass. Then she sat back on a fallen log, took off her hat, and pushed the stray hair from her face.

With that gesture, she wiped Silence clean. All that he had been, the sacred beliefs and bitter resolutions of a lifetime crumbled the moment he saw her face. It wasn't simply that she was beautiful, though she was, with a serene, timeless kind of beauty that Silence had glimpsed once in a charcoal drawing of a Renaissance princess in one of Mr. Marsh's books. It was the fact that he recognized her with a deep, profound certainty, as if he'd always known her. And perhaps, he thought vaguely, he *had* always known her. She had always been there in his sea dreams – he knew it now – whether he'd seen her there or not.

A finger of sunset light shot through a break in the clouds, through the hemlock and oak branches and ignited her profile; the wind lifted her loose strands of hair again, shattering them into threads of light. Silence had long since let his hand drop from Happy's mouth, but for once she was silent, transfixed as he was by the woman's uncanny beauty. Then the cloud closed in again, and Silence regained his wits. He grabbed Happy by the hand and dragged her up with him as he stood.

"Ow!" Happy protested.

The woman looked up. For a moment her eyes caught Silence's; a moment that seemed to him to stretch a thousand years. And then she was turning and running back into the trees, ignoring his pleas for her to stop, to listen. "Damn it," he muttered and began to run after her, Happy trailing behind. He knew at once that it was hopeless. The woman was gone, lost in the shadowy forest. Silence stood still and listened for retreating footsteps, but he heard nothing. It was as if she really was a supernatural being and had dispersed in a cloud of vapor.

Heartbroken in a way he never could have imagined an hour before, he and Happy made their way back to the clearing, where the little fire flickered cheery irony before his miserable eyes.

"Well," Happy said, kicking stones at the fire, "now do you believe me?"

"I always believed you."

"But do you think she's a fairy?"

"I think she's going to be my undoing," Silence muttered to the fire.

"Well I don't think she's a fairy anymore."

"Why not?" he asked, only half-listening.

"Because if she was, she'd have *flown* away."

Silence smiled wryly. "She might as well have." Then, after a moment of deliberation, he took a piece of paper half covered with boat calculations out of his pocket, and a stub of pencil from the other. He wrote, "We are sorry to have frightened you.

We mean you no harm. If you need anything, come to our farm, Heaven Homestead. It's the one just south-east of here."

He had no idea whether or not they were the right words. He didn't know whether he should even leave a note at all. But it was written now, and Happy was tugging impatiently at his hand, and night was closing in. So Silence weighed it down with Happy's hawthorn wreath, tossed a few more sticks on the fire, and then he let Happy drag him home.

6

The following morning, Silence couldn't eat. Nor could he work. After breaking three lengths of mahogany veneer by sheer lack of concentration, he gave up on trying to do anything constructive, and took to pacing circles around the boat. As he walked, he turned the past evening's events over and over in his mind. No amount of prodding made him anything less than certain that the woman in the woods was the one from his dreams. But the implications of that, the possibilities that opened if all that he had come to suspect about her were true, frankly overwhelmed him.

At last he did the only thing he could think might help: he went back to the woods to confront her. All the way to the clearing he rehearsed the many things that he could say to her, but when he reached it all of his reasoning evaporated. She was gone: so thoroughly gone that not even a bent blade of grass remained to attest that she had ever been more than a figment of his imagination.

And so Silence went home again, in the blackest mood he'd known since his father died. He couldn't eat or sleep, and communicated with the household only in monosyllables. He spent his time in the barn, allegedly working but actually brooding. After several days of this, though, Silence wearied of his own company. He returned to the house to find Celia in the kitchen, thinning a tray of seedlings. Silence slid into a chair across from her.

"Celia, you've got to help me."

She gave him a wry once-over, and then went back to her plants. "What with?"

"I think I'm going crazy."

"Rest your mind, Silence," she said. "You already were crazy."

"That isn't a joke!" he cried. "That woman in the woods, she's got into my head, like a...I don't know, a disease. I can't even think anymore!"

"Melodrama," Celia said, meticulously extracting two thready tomato sprouts from either side of a third, "never got anyone anywhere."

"*Melodrama?* I might be losing my mind, and you call it melodrama?"

"Melodrama and moping, plain and simple!" she snapped. "Silence, I've got a whole goddamn farm to plant in the next two weeks if we aren't going to starve next winter, so if you're not going to help, then go talk to Pascal, or Mr. Marsh, or Annie Newcombe, or *anybody* who isn't me!"

Silence looked at her with hopeless eyes, but he stood and moved toward the kitchen door. "And I hope to God one of them can kick some sense into you," Celia called after him as he pushed back out onto the porch.

He found Happy there, drawing with a piece of charcoal on the warped silver canvas of the porch steps, clearly trying to disguise the fact that she was eavesdropping. Nevertheless, she'd done a decent rendition of the house's residents. All of them looked out of the picture smiling, except for Silence, who was looking over his shoulder.

"It's all right, Silence," she said, meticulously drawing a scar on his charcoal face. "*I* believe you're crazy."

She smiled brightly up at him, and shaking his head, Silence walked back to the attic. It was a fine, mild day, and the double doors stood open. Pascal sat just inside them in the moldering armchair, wrapped in a crocheted blanket, reading a pre-war broadsheet. In the bright light, the bones of his face showed starkly, and the skin on his hands looked paper-thin. His eyes had sunk so far beneath his brows that their glint was barely visible. As Silence approached, he tucked something quickly into the folds of the blanket, but not before Silence identified red spots on white cloth. A wave of shame stopped him in his tracks, but Pascal put down his broadsheet and smiled, beckoning Silence over.

"Well, *P'tit*?" he said as Silence sat down beside him on an upturned bucket.

"You taking your medicine?" Silence asked, to have something to say. He already knew that Pascal poured Celia's foul herbal concoctions into the flowerbeds when she wasn't looking.

"Now, is that all you came to say to me?" He sounded stern, but Silence was certain he saw a mischievous glint in the shadowed black eyes. "I ain't seen much of you these last few days, Silence Ogden. Could lead a fellow to think you're avoiding him."

Silence ran a hand over his face. Three days' stubble covered it, except where the scar ran down through it like a poison river. "All right," he sighed. "I've been avoiding you."

"Now why would you do a thing like that?"

"Because you were right, as I'm sure you're perfectly well aware."

"Right?" Pascal repeated, blinking innocently.

"*Right*," Silence confirmed. "About the woman. And now you better help me, because I think I'm going crazy."

Pascal reached down into the shadows by his chair and pulled out a cobalt medicine bottle. He took a sip from it, then offered it to Silence.

"What's that?" Silence asked dubiously.

"The cure for whatever ails you," Pascal said.

Silence took the bottle, sniffed it and then said, "Jesus, Pascal! That's pure rye whiskey!"

"Hu-ush!" Pascal said. "Or Celia will hear you."

"Where'd you get this?"

"The schoolteacher. Turns out he's a right liberated fellow, even if he does talk in riddles. I told him rye whiskey's the best thing for a cough, so he scared me up some. I hear it helps too with troubles of the heart."

Silence took a couple of long pulls from the bottle, spluttered as they burned their way down his throat, and then passed it back to Pascal.

Pascal laughed softly. "I guess she must be as pretty as Happy says."

"Happy told you about her?"

"Mm-hm. The whole thing. Except she seems to think it was some kind of haint you saw...or an angel."

"No," said Silence wistfully. "She was a flesh-and-blood woman, all right."

"Any idea who she is?"

"One. But if I tell you, you'll think I'm crazy."

"I always knew you were crazy, *P'tit*." Silence wondered if there was anyone left who didn't think this, until Pascal continued, "Just like me. Remember, we both seen those spirits in the tree. We're even in the crazy stakes, so to speak. So you may as well spit it out."

Silence nodded, squinting into the sun, and said, "I guess it begins with Juniper Barrens." Before he knew it, he'd told Pascal the entire story, even his speculations about Annie and the fight they'd had. "Do you think she's her daughter? And that's why she's here? But if it is, why was she just hiding in the woods?"

Pascal considered it for a while, sipping from his bottle, and finally he looked back at Silence. "It seems to me," he said, "that the only thing you really need to know right now is where she went. Until you find her, the rest is gonna stay a mystery."

"I wouldn't know where to begin looking."

"Hm," said Pascal speculatively. And then, "Maybe you're not s'posed to. Maybe *she* gotta find *you*."

"That's absurd! She has no reason to want to find me!"

"You sure about that?" he asked, glancing at Silence. "There's no reason she might want to track you down?" Pascal's eyes rested on the horse lipping grass in the bald paddock.

"Epona?" Silence said. "But if she meant to claim her, wouldn't she have done it by now?"

Pascal shrugged. "All I know is, things that's meant to be together, they got a way o' findin' each other, sooner or later."

"I hope you're right about that."

"You ever known me to be wrong, Silence Ogden?"

Silence only sighed.

"Meantime, you need somethin' to occupy yourself, or you really *will* go crazy." He reached behind the chair and pulled out his guitar, then offered it to Silence.

"I'm really not in the mood."

"Well then hold onto it until you are."

"I can't take your guitar, Pascal."

"It's not mine, Silence," he said gently. "Or if it is, well, it was always a temporary arrangement. The man who gave it to me, he told me a guitar is like a good horse – it'll pass through many hands before it's done, and if it's passed wisely, that will make it better. The truth is, Silence, I'm tired. Played out. It's your turn now."

Silence took the guitar hesitantly, and only because Pascal's arm was beginning to shake. Something about the handover struck an ominous chord. "I don't know, Pascal. Now it's spring, you're sure to start feelin' better – "

"I need it back," Pascal interrupted, "I'll let you know. But in the meantime, I want you to start teachin' that child to play."

"Happy?" Silence asked, puzzled. "Really? You think she has the patience for it?"

"I know she does," he said. "More than that…"

But his eyes wandered off with his thoughts, and then they shut, and he was asleep.

7

Between Pascal's guitar and the spring planting, Silence at least managed to keep himself busy while he was miserable. After a while, Mr. Marsh's philosophical quips, Celia's pragmatic lack of sympathy and Pascal's blood-spattered handkerchiefs even slapped him back into some kind of equilibrium. But it was Happy who offered him the first slim hope that the woman in the woods hadn't disappeared forever.

She came out onto the porch one rainy afternoon a couple of weeks after the woman had vanished. Silence was sitting in a cane chair thumbing the guitar, while Pascal dozed in another. Celia had gone to town for dress fabric, and Mr. Marsh had accompanied her for no clear reason, which seemed to be happening more and more frequently of late.

Happy sat down on the first step, just beyond the rain's reach, with her arms around her knees: a caricature of Annie in calico and pigtails. She pulled a wad of spruce gum out of her pocket, wiped off some lint and then put it in her mouth. After a few moments' vigorous chewing, she spat a stream of yellowish juice into the rhododendrons. Silence watched her repeat the process twice more before he broke down and asked, "Happy, what are you doing?"

Happy looked at him earnestly. "Spitting," she said.

Silence sighed. "Obviously. But why?"

"Mr. Harris and Mr. Marden do it when they sit out on the front porch of the store when there's no business," she said. "They chew and they spit, and their spit is brown. I never knew why, so I asked them the other day how I could make my spit brown like theirs, and they looked at each other and laughed and said, 'Girl, you get yourself a plug.' So I asked Mama what a plug is, and she thought about it, and then she told me it's spruce gum. Want some?"

Silence regarded the wad she'd disgorged from her mouth, clearly in preparation for dividing it between them. "Thanks... you keep it."

Happy shrugged and replaced the gum. "Only, I think it's from the wrong kind of tree. My spit doesn't look like theirs."

"Could be," Silence agreed, trying not to smile.

"Also, it doesn't help me think," she added.

"And why would it?"

"That's what Mr. Marden said when I asked why he chewed a plug. He said it helps him think."

"Right. And you need help thinking about...what, exactly?"

"You, Silence."

Silence raised his eyebrows. "Me? What about me?"

"Something's wrong with you."

"Go on."

"Ever since we saw that fairy in the woods, all you do is sit out here with your guitar and...and *malinger*."

"Malinger! Jesus – does Mr. Marsh teach you words like that?"

"One a day. He says they'll improve my mind."

"No doubt he's right," Silence answered, "but we've digressed. Have you learned 'digressed'?"

Happy considered it. "What your stomach does with pork and beans?"

"Not quite. It means 'strayed from the original point'. Which was, according to you, that something's wrong with me."

"Something must be," Happy agreed, "since you never work on your ship anymore."

Silence smiled sadly. "That's true, Happy. I'm afraid the boat and I are at an impasse."

"Impasse?"

"No way forward or back."

Happy looked puzzled. "What about those little strips of wood?"

"The veneer?" He shook his head. "That's the impasse. I can't seem to touch it without breaking it, and it costs about a thousand dollars a strip, so it seemed wisest not to touch it at all."

"But the ones you put on so far look all right."

He shook his head. "I haven't got any of the veneer on yet."

"Yes you do," Happy insisted. "It goes half way up one side."

Silence felt a ghost of the jittery portent he'd felt when they went fairy hunting. "You sure about that, Happy?" he asked slowly.

She sighed. "Come on – I'll show you."

Silence put his guitar aside and followed Happy to the barn, telling himself the entire way that it was nothing, that Happy was mistaken, that the sudden anxious hope in his chest was unfounded. But his admonitions fell away as Happy rolled the barn door open, because, once again, she was right. Someone, somehow, had laid almost all of the veneer on the boat's starboard side. More than that, they'd done it well: the curves were fair, the seams so tight they were barely visible. Silence ran a shaking hand over the smooth side.

"Who..." he began, and then trailed off as the barn wavered around him. Because he knew who, and yet, he couldn't believe it.

Happy, who had been following silently behind him, suddenly flitted past him and bent to look at something on the floor. A fine layer of sawdust lay on the dark packed earth, pristine as the winter's first dusting of snow, except for a single footprint in the center. It was barefoot, narrow and high-arched, curved like a seashell. It was clearly a woman's, but it was too big to belong to Happy or Celia, and that Annie could have done this work – barefoot, no less – was simply too preposterous to imagine.

"It's the fairy's," Happy whispered.

"I think you might be right," Silence said.

They looked at each other for a long moment, then Happy asked, "What are you going to do?"

Silence sat down on a crate, sighing. "I have absolutely no idea."

Happy studied the boat, head cocked to one side. "She did a good job, didn't she?"

"A better job than I ever could."

"Well then," said Happy, "you have to write her a thank-you note."

Celia called for Happy then, and she skipped out into the rain, leaving Silence to brood. Maybe Happy was right, and he ought to thank the woman for what she'd done, but writing a note was no simple matter. He knew nothing about her – not even whether it was really she who'd fixed his veneer. He began five different letters, some of them long, some of them philosophical, all of them fire-fodder before they were half done. The one he eventually settled on was little better than the others, but as far as he could tell, there was nothing in it that could possibly frighten or offend. It said:

To the Girl from the Woods:

Thank you for what you've done here (assuming it was you) and I'm sorry about scaring you the other day. Ever since then, Happy and I have been worrying about you. If you're happy living in the woods, then so be it. But if you need anything, please come to the house. We have plenty to share, and I sure could use your help with the boat.

Sincerely,

Silence Ogden

He tacked the note to the planking where the veneer ended and then, reluctantly, he went back to the house to wait.

8

The next morning, Silence ran out to the barn as soon as the sun was up, heart pounding right up into his throat, only to find everything exactly as he'd left it. By the middle of the week, his heart no longer pounded. By the end of it, he didn't even bother checking. He was despondent and irritated, and sometimes late at night he wondered if Happy had been right, and the woman in the woods hadn't been a woman at all, but some kind of apparition. The more rational explanation – that she was a woman, but a mad one – wasn't one he could bear to contemplate.

As it was, though, he didn't have much time for contemplation. Coming into the kitchen one morning, he found Celia sitting at the table, staring at her hands. Celia was never idle unless something was very wrong.

"Celia?" he said. When she looked up at his, he could see that she'd been crying. "Celia, what is it?"

She reached into her apron pocket and took out a handkerchief stiff with dried blood. He didn't have to ask whose it was. His legs shaking, he folded into a chair.

"I didn't know it was so bad, Silence," Celia said in a wavering voice. "And I think it's been this bad for a long time. He's been hiding them under the bed."

"I'll go for the doctor right now."

Celia sighed, looking out over the half-planted fields. "I watched two of my sisters die of consumption," she said. "When it's this bad, it's beyond doctors."

Of course Silence had known all along what lurked behind the persistent cough and hastily-hidden handkerchiefs, but he hadn't dared to think the word. He'd lost too much, too quickly. But now Celia had spoken it, the lines were drawn.

"I'm going anyway," he said, and he tried not to see the resignation in Celia's eyes as they followed him out the door.

*

The doctor was a mistake: Silence knew it the moment he led the man into Pascal's attic room. He was a young man, not much older than Silence himself; too young, Silence would have thought, for the war's divisions to leave their mark on him. But he hadn't thought about it. It had never occurred to him to mention that Pascal was colored, until he saw the look on the doctor's face when he stepped up to the bed.

"There's nothing that I can do," he said after a cursory glance at the old man.

"It doesn't look to me like you've tried," Silence answered, knowing that it was futile to argue, but refusing to let the doctor wriggle away so easily.

"I told you I didn't want no doctor," Pascal whispered, his glassy eyes baleful on the man.

"And you should have listened to him," the doctor said.

"This man is my best friend," Silence said stubbornly, planting his feet firmly across the top of the narrow staircase that led to the sleeping loft. "If it weren't for him, I doubt I'd be alive today. Now he's the one that needs me." He sighed in exasperation at the doctor's stony silence. "Look, you're here already. I've got money to pay. What is there for you to lose by examining him?"

Reluctantly, and with a meaningful sigh, the doctor set his bag down. He listened perfunctorily to Pascal's chest, examined the hip that was swollen now and too painful to move. Then he stood up, wiped his hands deliberately on a towel, and said, "Late stage tuberculosis. It's spread to that the hip joint, which it has no doubt destroyed. If the patient should by some chance survive the pulmonary infection, he will nevertheless be permanently lame."

"Is there no medicine that can help him?" Silence asked, dazed.

"Laudanum, I suppose, for the pain," the doctor said off-handedly. "If you think he needs it. But frankly, these people are like animals – they bear pain far better than we do."

"We'll take it," Silence said through clenched teeth.

The doctor rummaged in his bag and handed Silence a dark glass bottle. With that, he clicked his bag shut. Silence returned from seeing him out to find Pascal lying on his back, his eyes fixed on the newspapered ceiling. He lay so still he might have been dead, except for the tears slipping from the corners of his eyes into the pillow beneath his head. Silence sat down beside him.

"You shouldn't have bothered," Pascal said in a low, toneless voice.

Silence sighed, looked out the tiny window. "There are plenty of times you shouldn't have bothered with me."

Pascal said nothing.

"I meant it, you know," Silence said after a moment. "About you being my best friend."

Pascal offered him a twitch of a smile. "You really oughta get out more, *P'tit.*"

"Pascal...don't mind what he said. He was just a small-minded bigot."

Pascal sighed. "He was that, Silence. But you and I both know, what he said was the truth."

Silence wondered which part he was talking about. He didn't dare ask.

"And that's why I didn't want no doctor," pascal continued. "In my experience, all they do is make it impossible to hope."

*

Pascal's words proved all too true in the following days. It seemed to Silence that the supercilious doctor had taken the better part of Pascal with him when he went, leaving a shell to lie in bed staring at the ceiling or sit wrapped in quilts on the porch, looking at nothing. He'd answer questions listlessly, eat when Celia pleaded, smile occasionally at Happy. Sometimes Silence tried to engage him in conversation. Daily, he offered him the guitar, but Pascal would only push it away and mumble about the ghosts in the tree crying out for him and how he didn't need the instrument anymore to answer.

The only thing for which he showed any enthusiasm was the laudanum, to which he'd taken as if he'd been a lifelong addict.

It left him serene and silent until it was time for the next dose, at which point he'd start hollering for it.

Finally one night, as Pascal grabbed for the glass of tincture, Silence burst out, "Christ, Pascal, don't do this!

Pascal turned slowly to look at him, smiling beneath wretched eyes. "Why, son – it's already done." And that was all he would say.

9

If he was powerless to help one friend, Silence thought, at least he could try to help another. Two perhaps: Happy's and Mr. Marsh's plight had slipped to the back of his mind in the past few weeks, but with Pascal calm and the boat still stalled, it came back around to the front again. Knowing that Mr. Marsh would try to talk him out of it and Happy would demand to come along, he picked an afternoon when everyone else was occupied to slip out the back door and into the woods. He met the road near town, made his way to the school and then waited at the edge of the yard until all of the children had gone.

He hadn't known who he'd find running the place, but it didn't surprise him much to see Jenny's willowy silhouette in the doorway. She eyed him up and down coolly as he approached, making no move to come meet him or to retreat. When he stopped at the bottom of the steps, she crossed her arms over her chest and said, "What business do you have here, Mr. Ogden?"

"Come on, Jenny," he said, "you know why I came."

"In fact, no – I don't see any reason for it."

"Look," he said, shoving a hand through his hair, "you've made your point. Both of us know that Happy's sewing project was an innocent mistake. You can't be serious about keeping her out of school indefinitely."

Jenny gave him a long, hard look, in which Silence saw his defeat. Nevertheless, he followed her when she retreated into the schoolhouse.

"Jenny – "

"Mrs. Marden," she said coldly.

"Very well, Mrs. Marden – I know that you're doing this to punish me."

"That's conceit if ever I heard it," she said, pushing papers and books into orderly piles on the teacher's desk. "Why would I ever think about you at all?"

Silence slumped dejectedly onto a front-row desk. "Christ, Jenny – Mrs. Marden. You can't pretend that there was never anything between us."

She shot him a spiteful glance. "In fact, I can. I'd prefer to forget all about it."

All at once, Silence understood something. Before he could think better of it, he said, "So you'll push a child out of school and a man out of his job, just so they aren't here to remind you of what you can't have?"

She gave him a longer look this time, smoothing her hands over her skirt in a way that made it obvious she was expecting. Silence hadn't realized, and it shocked him despite himself. By the glint of triumph in her eyes, he knew that she'd meant it to.

Jenny sat down at the desk. "The members of the society made it quite clear to those present that your – lodger's – daughter was being expelled because she posed a moral threat to the other children. Likewise Mr. Marsh, in taking her part. So you see, Mr. Ogden, it has nothing at all to do with you."

"If Happy's situation is really so dire, wouldn't it be the moral thing to do, to keep her in school and try to educate her about the error of her ways?"

He'd spoken ironically, but Jenny answered with cold conviction, "I have nothing to say to a bastard, and I'll have nothing to do with one."

In his sudden fury, it was all Silence could do not to remind Jenny that only a few years since, she was eager enough to conceive a bastard of her own. "How dare you judge her?" he demanded instead. "How could you possibly know what Happy is?"

"It's clear enough," Jenny answered with a dry little laugh. "Even ignoring the fact that they live unchaperoned with you, her mother doesn't wear a wedding ring."

"And have you ever asked her why not?"

"Isn't it obvious?" she asked, but he could see a flicker of interest in her eye.

Silence paused. He hadn't come to the school planning to divulge Celia's secret, let alone to Jenny Marden, but he'd also never agreed with her keeping the truth from Happy. If Celia's pride was all that stood between Happy and the future she deserved, then there was only one choice to make.

Looking Jenny hard in the eye, he said, "I'm going to tell you something, but you have to promise me that it will never go further than these walls."

"Why would I promise you anything?" she snapped.

"Because I know a few of your secrets, too."

"Are you threatening me, Silence Ogden?"

Silence sighed. "No, Jenny. I'm trying to make you see reason."

She rolled a pencil back and forth across Mr. Marsh's desk. "I'm listening."

"Celia's married. Happy was born in wedlock."

He'd expected Jenny's jaw to drop, but instead she gave him a sugary smile. "That's absurd. No married woman would choose to be seen as a...well." She cleared her throat.

"She might if she was running from her husband."

He could see Jenny fighting the urge to beg for details, and stifled his own scornful smile: Jenny had never been able to resist a piece of gossip.

This time, though, she surprised him. "That's a mighty big claim, Mr. Ogden," she said. "Still, the Society would be worthless if we didn't live by our own laws. If you can prove to me that Happy Gagne is legitimate, then I'll personally escort her back to school."

By the way she smiled, Silence knew that she had no fear that this would ever be required. "I'll look forward to it," he said as he got up to leave, hoping that she wasn't right.

10

Silence didn't know whether to blame Fate or Serendipity or Jenny Marden's loose tongue when Happy looked up from her lessons the day after his trip to the schoolhouse and asked, "Do you know who my daddy is?"But he did know whom he blamed.

Cursing Celia inwardly, he tried to sound sincere when he said, "No, I do not." It wasn't entirely a lie, after all. Celia had never told him the man's name.

"Okay," she nodded, as if she'd expected this answer. "I just thought Mama might have told you."

"Why do you want to know?" he couldn't help asking.

Happy looked at her copybook for a long moment, and then she sighed. "I just thought if I could find out who he is, maybe I could hunt him down and make him marry Mama, and then I could go back to school."

Silence was shocked. He hadn't realized that she understood so much about the reasons for her exclusion. "You really miss school that much?"

"I do," she said. "But I also don't much like being a bastard."

Silence had to look away then. When he'd composed his face, he said, "Happy, even if your mama had told me who your daddy was, it wouldn't be right for me to tell you. That's up to her."

She gave him a dubious look.

"But either way, don't you ever let anyone call you a bastard."

She thought about this, and then she aksed, "Why do you think she won't tell me?"

"I don't know, Happy," he sighed. "But let me try and find out."

"That's none of your business," Celia said sharply when Silence repeated Happy's question later that night.

They were sitting on the porch. In the dim light, Celia's eyes looked too bright, but Silence knew that if she were crying, she wouldn't want him to know it. So he let the tears slide on into the dark, if there were tears at all, and looked out over the still fields. The first of the summer's white moths fluttered languidly around the lantern by the door. Though the barn was lifeless as it had been every night since he left the note, Silence couldn't help wondering if another quiet creature was moving somewhere out there in the dark.

Finally he said, "I'm sorry to upset you, Celia. But as long as you and Happy are living here, I think it *is* my business."

"Then we'll go," she said without hesitation.

"You don't mean that."

"Don't I?" Her voice was steely.

"Celia, I don't want you to go. Truly, I don't. But I do want Happy to be…well…happy."

"You think knowing about *him* would make anyone happy?"

"Well, actually – yes. I think it would help, anyway. Look, if that damned Ladies' Society knew that you were married, they'd let Happy back into school."

She uttered a despairing laugh. "Not nearly good enough."

"But how is she ever going to find her place in the world if – "

"That's *enough*, Silence!" Celia stood up, her slight body stiff with anger. "You might be smart, you might know what all those dead philosophers say, but there's still a few things you don't know anything about!" She wiped a hand across her eyes and then stalked off down the steps into the night.

595

Silence looked at the place she'd been, trying not to give in to his own anger. "Well why *shouldn't* Happy be miserable?" he asked the moths battering the lantern. "If I were her, I'd hate us all. Who wouldn't?"

But the moths kept their own counsel.

Hawsing

1

Silence hadn't seen Annie at anything but a distance since the day that he'd confronted her about her past, and so he was startled when she marched up to the porch one night, dragging Happy by the hand.

"Happy!" he cried. "What are you doing out of bed?"

"I might as well ask *you* the same thing," Annie snapped. "You and Celia'd better get your act together, Silence Ogden. Even in Heaven, more harm than good's going to come to a little girl wandering around in the dark."

"What were you doing?" he asked Happy. She only kicked the dirt.

"I found her down by the barn," Annie answered for her. "And this isn't the first time I've seen her there after dark – it's just the first time I've caught her."

"Happy?" he said, looking at her. She still wouldn't meet his eye.

"You think on what I've said, Silence," Annie chided. Then she turned and walked back into the night, before Silence could think to ask her what *she'd* been doing at his barn in the dark.

For a few moments he blinked into the place where she'd been, wondering how she always seemed to get the better of him. Then he grabbed Happy, who was trying to sneak around him into the house. "Not so fast, Sweet Pea," he said. "What were you doing at the barn?"

Happy glowered and kept her mouth stubbornly shut..

"You tell me what you're up to, or I'll wake up your mama."

She held out for another few moments, and then, sighing, she relented. "I was watching that lady from the woods."

"*What*?" Silence cried.

"I saw a light on in the barn from my window, and I thought it was you. I went out to see you because I couldn't sleep. But it was her, not you. She was building your boat for you, but don't get cross because she's doing a real good job – "

"Wait here," said Silence, wild-eyed. "I'll be right back."

Ignoring her plaintive, "But Silence…" he sprinted.

When he reached the barn and found it empty aside from a single burning lantern, he let out a yell loud enough to wake Pascal from his opiate doze, back in the attic. Then he collapsed onto his storage stool, raging with frustration, until he noticed three things. First, the horse, which had so far appeared a docile animal, was pacing and grumbling in her stall. Second, the note he'd tacked to the bow of the boat was gone, the nail hole neatly filled with putty. And third, the veneer was complete. It wasn't a huge change, but it was enough that instead of looking like the poor-man's lunacy it was, the boat looked, for the first time, like a boat.

Stepping outside, Silence cleared his throat and spoke into the inky darkness: "Ma'am, if you can hear me…well…thank you.

And I wonder if maybe, sometime, you could come back when I'm here. I don't really know what I'm doing, as you can see, and I surely could use your instruction…" Silence trailed off, realizing how absurd he must sound, if the woman was even listening. He wrote a thank-you in the sawdust by the bow, and then he blew out the lantern.

When he returned to the house, Happy was dutifully waiting where he'd left her, looking small and forlorn in the smoky light of the porch lantern. "Did you catch her?" she asked.

Silence smiled ruefully, showing her his empty hands. "I'm afraid not."

"Oh."

He sat back down on the step with a sigh. "Look, Happy – how long have you been watching her?"

"Only tonight. It's the only time she's been there. But I think she must come other times, because the boat looks better every night."

Silence wanted to demand why she hadn't told him this before, but he knew that if he put her on the defensive, she'd tell him nothing. Taking a deep breath, he said, "So you've been going out there at night, hoping to find her." Happy nodded. "Why?"

"So you'd stop being grumpy," she answered.

He had to laugh. "I don't suppose you spoke to her."

She shook her head. "I wanted to – but I was scared."

"Why?"

"Because of her not having a light."

"What do you think that means?"

Happy shrugged.

"You ever seen anyone else without a light?"

"Yes. But they were dead."

Trying not to think too hard about that, Silence asked, "Did she do anything interesting?"

"Not really. She just did what you do – only better. She must have built a lot of boats. Or wrecked some. Maybe she's a siren. I bet sirens don't have lights."

"A siren?" Silence asked. And then, "Mr. Marsh has you reading Greek mythology?"

Happy nodded. "Only she didn't sing. And anyway, if she was used to wrecking boats, why would she be fixing yours?"

"Good question. What else did she do?"

"Well, when she was done sticking on those little bits of wood, she stood there staring at the boat for a long time. And then she started crying. I knew she was crying, because there were tears running down her face, and she kept on wiping her nose on the back of her hand, but she didn't make noise or yell like I do when I cry."

"Then what?"

"Then a bony old monster hand came up out of the dark and grabbed my arm, and another one covered my mouth, and I thought I was about to die, but it was just Annie. She said, 'Now don't you make a sound and scare her,' and I tried to say okay, but I couldn't because her hand was in the way. And then Annie unclapped my mouth, and I started asking her how come she snuck up to scare me like that, and she just shook her head like Mama does and dragged me away. Then she said, 'You shouldn't spy like that, Happy Moon,' and I said, 'Yeah, but I had to make sure she wasn't messing up Silence's ship,' and Annie said, 'She isn't.' How do you think she knew that, Silence?"

"I can't imagine," Silence muttered.

Happy thought for a moment, and then she said, "There was one more thing."

"Oh?"

"Just before we got to you, Annie stopped me and she said in this kind of yelling whisper – you know that yelling whisper? –

she said, 'That girl's here for a reason, Happy Moon. Now you just let her be.' And there was a funny look on her face…"

"What kind of funny?"

"Like someone stuck her with a pin."

Silence sighed. "Okay, Happy. I guess we don't need to tell your mama about this, as long as you promise to stay in bed at night from now on. Deal?"

Happy shrugged, and Silence knew that was the best he would get.

2

Once again, the mysterious woman seemed to disappear. Although Silence watched from the darkened hayloft night after night, nothing disturbed the barn's stillness. He couldn't begin to guess at the woman's motivation for working on his boat. It seemed that she had none, and that in itself was troubling, because there was nowhere to go with it but the direction in which all the clues clearly pointed: the direction the dead-eyed dream girl had taken when she turned her back on the sea.

"That way madness lies," Silence said to himself, alone in the hayloft. Then he laughed, and laughing, knew that if he didn't let her go, he would follow her on that path.

"But how can I?" he asked Pascal, who himself was half way to madness on a road of morphine and fever and pain. "How can I forget her when I can't stop dreaming of her? When she put the skin on my boat? When I still feel her watching me?"

"You're not supposed to forget her," Pascal said, with languorous conviction.

"Then what am I supposed to do?"

"Wait and pray. Turn this town upside down..."

"Well, which?"

"*Je ne sais pas, Petit...*" he answered, and then he began to sing a Creole love song. Silence dropped his head into his hands.

*

A few days later, Celia went out to work as usual, and then came immediately back, her face flushed and eyes wild. "Silence, the horse!" she cried. "She's gone!"

A calm descended on Silence then, like the calm before a summer rainstorm, when the wind dies and the leaves hang limp under a yellow sky. He headed for the door.

"Where are you going?" she asked.

"To get your horse back."

"But you don't know where – " she began, and then an echoing gunshot silenced her. It came from the direction of town. Silence's face paled. He turned back, disappeared through the hallway door and returned with his father's shotgun.

"Silence?" Celia's eyes were filled now with fear.

"Was that gunfire?" Mr. Marsh asked, coming in from the attic, where he'd been reading to Pascal.

"It was," Silence said grimly as he strode toward the door. "Stay here."

"Thomas," Celia said, her voice frightened now, "go with him."

Thomas? Silence wondered, as Mr. Marsh fell into step beside him. But he let it go. It would wait; whoever had fired the gun wouldn't.

*

By the time they reached town, a crowd of men had gathered under the oak tree, loud and incoherent. Jenny Marden and a handful of other women watched from the store's porch, their eyes coldly anticipatory. Jenny's husband was at the edge of the crowd, struggling to hold onto Epona. The horse danced and pulled against her rope halter, whinnying shrilly, but no one seemed to pay her any mind.

With his guts in his throat, Silence pushed into the crowd. The woman from the woods was at the center, as he'd known she would be; kneeling, with her mountaineer's pack on the ground beside her and her hands tied behind her back. She looked up at Silence from beneath the shapeless hat, her eyes raincloud grey except for three black flecks in the right one. They widened when she saw the gun in his hands, but she didn't flinch.

The men, who had quieted when Silence Ogden pushed in to their midst, began to murmur. "I never saw a horse thief quite as pretty as you," one of them said clearly, reaching out from behind Silence to touch her cheek. The girl didn't move a muscle, but she glared at him with such intense hatred that his hand faltered. The rest of them laughed, shifting nervously until another spoke up:

"A horse thief's a horse thief."

And then another: "Only one thing to do with a horse thief."

"Have you all gone mad?" Mr. Marsh cried. "This isn't some godforsaken frontier town – "

But his protests were drowned out with objections. Someone threw a rope over a low branch. Someone else pulled the woman to her feet, and yet her eyes stayed fixed on Silence's, the still point in his spinning world. He felt sick, but moreso he felt a wild fury that these farmers he'd known all his life could so easily become a violent mob.

"Let go of that woman," he said coldly, raising his gun to the man with the rope.

"I can't do that, son," said the man holding her bound hands. Silence realized he was Joe Neville, his father's old friend who'd gone for the doctor after the accident. "We can't just let a thief walk free."

"And who's calling her a thief?" Silence asked.

Joe Neville narrowed his eyes, took a long pull off his cigarette. "Are you saying that's not your horse she was making off with?"

"And wasn't that horse stole from Celia once before?" someone else said.

"It was," Silence said. "But plenty of horse thieves steal to sell. There's nothing to say she didn't come by that horse fair and square in the meantime."

"That's a lot of maybes."

"It is," Silence agreed. "So I guess one of you knows the real story?" A hush fell over the crowd. Silence nodded. "Well then, let's find out." Silence looked at the woman. "You want to tell us what happened?"

The woman looked back at him. There was no supplication in her eyes; if anything, there was a glint of defiance.

"Help me out here, ma'am," he said in a low voice. "They will do what they're threatening." But she simply continued to stare at him.

"See?" said Joe Neville. "She can't even think up an alibi."

"There's one way to find out for sure if this is her horse or not." Amidst their protests, Silence handed the gun to Mr. Marsh. Then he took out his pocketknife and cut the ropes binding the woman's wrists. Her hands fell to her sides. Silence took one of them – it lay in his own hand like wood, like she didn't care what he was planning. But he knew that she cared. He could feel her heart thundering in the core of himself as he pulled her through the crowd.

When they were past its fringes, he told Jenny's husband, "Let the horse go."

"What?" Marden cried.

"As the man said," Mr. Marsh spoke up from a few paces back, gun trained on Mr. Marden.

Reluctantly, he let go of the horse's halter. She shook her head and blew, looked around as if judging which direction to run. And then her eyes fell on the woman, and she stilled. Her ears went forward, as if she were listening to something, although the woman stood perfectly still and silent. It could only have been a few seconds before the horse took a hesitant step forward, though it seemed to Silence to go on for many long minutes. Then the woman stepped forward too, closing the gap. The horse touched the woman's outstretched hand with her nose, and then nudged her in the chest. The woman wrapped her hands in the long black mane and looked unflinchingly back at the silent crowd.

Silence couldn't help smiling then. "Looks like Celia and I are the horse thieves."

The men began muttering again, this time with a distinct tone of uncertainty.

"You'll want to get her out of here, I think, Silence," Mr. Marsh said in a low voice.

"Will you come with me now?" Silence asked the woman.

She looked at him for a long moment before she nodded once, decisively answering the prayer Silence hadn't realized he was making. He gave her a leg up onto the horse, and then Mr. Marsh helped him up behind her. The girl sat the horse as if she'd done so all her life. She clucked softly, and Epona moved off on a tide of whispers. Silence wouldn't allow himself to look back. He focused on the sound of Epona's hooves falling steady as a heartbeat on the soft spring road, until at last they rounded a bend, and the crowd disappeared, and he let out the breath he'd been holding.

Thank you, Meredith told the horse. But the horse said nothing in reply. Her debt to Meredith had been repaid.

3

When they were far enough away from town, but not too close to home, Silence said, "Can you stop her?"

Meredith shifted her weight subtly, and Epona stopped in the middle of the road. Silence slid down and looked up at Meredith. She looked back, emotionless except for her hands, which quivered slightly as she gripped the horse's mane. Something about this touched Silence more deeply than her beauty ever could.

"Silence Ogden," he said, taking off his hat. "Pleased to make your acquaintance."

Meredith looked at him for another long moment, and then she tilted her head, barely perceptibly, down and then up again.

At last it dawned on him, and with it the enormity of what she had just escaped. "Can't you talk?" he asked.

She shook her head. Her silver bracelets sparked in the light coming through the new leaves. Silence could see now that they were intricately worked with what looked like animal figures, and no doubt valuable. He wondered what would make her risk taking a horse, even one she thought she owned, rather than sell them to procure one honestly. He wondered why she had waited.

"Well," Silence said, letting the word out slowly, intrigued and daunted. "But you can hear."

She nodded again.

He sighed. This was stranger even than the madness he'd imagined. "All right. I know that you didn't steal this horse, but I also know that Celia has a claim on her. More to the point, we just lost our only plough horse, and we don't have the money to buy another. So you can see I'm in a bit of a bind."

The woman shrugged. At first he thought it meant she didn't much care about his bind, but her face was open, her eyes expectant. He realized that she was asking him a question.

"I don't know what to do," he said, "if that's what you're wondering. But if you'll come home with me, I'm sure we can work something out."

Meredith looked off into the trees. At last, softly, she sighed, and nodded.

Silence nodded back. "You know," he said, "you could have just come to the house. You could have told us…"

She looked away quickly, frowning.

"All right," he sighed. "Forget I said it."

*

Celia and Happy were waiting white-faced on the porch. They leapt to their feet when they saw him with Epona, and then, seeing Meredith, they stopped.

"Wait here," Silence said to Meredith. "And don't even think of trying to run off – those men will never let you go a second time."

Meredith slid to the ground, but she didn't let go of the horse's mane. Silence looked at her for a moment, as if to fix her in place. Then he went in to the porch, where Celia's shock had turned to distrust.

"What in God's name is going on?" she demanded. "Who is that?"

"It's her!" Happy cried suddenly. "The lady from the barn!"

Silence caught her as she made to run toward Meredith and Epona, holding her firmly by the arm.

"The *barn*?" Celia hissed. "Do you mean to say she's been prowling in the barn, and you and Happy knew about it, and you didn't tell me?" Then she made the connection. "She's the one who took Epona! What do you think you're doing, bringing her back here?"

"Saving her from our neighbors," he said, "and our neighbors from committing murder. They were going to hang her for a horse thief."

Celia's face was hard, her eyes narrowed. "In some places, that's no more than the law."

"Well this isn't one of those places," Silence retorted. "And besides, she didn't steal Epona."

"Then who did?"

Silence sighed, exasperated. "Yes, she took the horse. But that's because she thought *we'd* stolen her."

"Epona's mine! I broke that horse myself!"

"She might be yours," Silence said, "but she's hers too. I mean, look at them!"

Grudgingly, Celia looked. Meredith was still standing by the horse, one hand on her withers, and the horse stood by her solid and still, though no rope held her.

"Well, maybe they're acquainted," Celia said grudgingly. "Did she tell you how?"

"She didn't," Silence admitted.

"Didn't you ask her to?"

"There wasn't any point. She can't talk." Before Celia's anger could reignite, Silence continued: "She's not simple, and I don't think she's crazy, either. She can hear, and she understands what I'm saying to her, but as for why she can't speak…" He shook his head. "Well, hopefully she can write, and then we'll know – "
What? he interrupted himself. What could the woman possibly tell them that would resolve the issue at hand? What could he offer in exchange for a horse for whom she'd risk her life?

"Anyway," he concluded, "we owe it to her to hear her out. If we don't, we're no better than that mob in town."

Celia conceded with a sigh. "But if I catch that woman making off with my horse again, I don't plan to wait for an explanation." Which made Silence glad that the shotgun was out of reach. "Well," she said, "it's too late to start work now. I guess Epona can go back in the paddock."

Happy skipped off toward the horse before anyone could stop her. The horse turned to her call and pulled away from Meredith to follow her. Silence saw the look of utter desolation Meredith cast after her. And though Meredith watched her until she rounded the corner of the barn, Epona never looked back.

4

When Celia and Happy were gone, Silence led the woman into the kitchen. He felt like he walked in the midst of a madman's dream, unable to make himself believe that she was real, even when she sat across from him at the kitchen table looking into a cup of coffee.

"Are you hungry?" he asked – the first sensible question that came to mind.

Meredith twitched her shoulders in reply. Choosing to construe the gesture as affirmation, Silence took a plate from the drying-rack and began to fill it with leftovers from breakfast. When he put the plate down in front of her Meredith looked at it, and then at Silence. He thought that she might start to cry, and since he knew he couldn't stand that, he got up, rummaged in a drawer until he found Happy's tablet and a pencil, and pushed them across the table to Meredith. She looked at them for a moment, apparently as overwhelmed by them as she was by the plate in front of her. Then she picked up the pencil. Her hand moved deliberately across the paper, as if she were weighing her words, but the writing in its wake was clear and solid.

"I don't mean to seem ungrateful for what you did today," Silence read when she pushed the tablet toward him. "But without the horse, I am lost."

Silence looked at her. She looked levelly back. Rather than resume a fruitless argument, he asked, "How did you come by her?"

He pushed the tablet back to her. Meredith looked at it, turning the pencil over and over in her hands. Finally she began to write again, and then she pushed her answer over to Silence.

"I saved her," it said, "from a man who wanted to shoot her because she wouldn't help him fell a forest."

Silence nodded as if this made perfect sense. "And when was this?"

Meredith looked out the window for a long moment, and then she wrote: "Sometime between summer and autumn."

That surprised him. He wondered if she really could have been living as he'd found her living for the better part of a year. "Well," he said, "maybe we could find you another horse."

"I don't want another horse."

Silence sighed. "And neither does Celia, never mind Happy. To tell you the truth, I think that Epona's the only reason she's still speaking to me after what happened with Charlie."

"Happy?" she wrote. "Epona? Charlie?"

"Happy is the little girl."

"Your daughter?"

Silence shook his head. "Celia's daughter. Epona is their horse...your horse. Charlie was our plough horse."

"The one you shot in the field."

This threw Silence for a moment, though it shouldn't have. He'd known, deep down, that the face he'd seen in the woods that day hadn't been a figment of his imagination. He'd known whose it was. "I guess Celia might sell Epona for the right price," he said, though he doubted it. "And if we let Happy choose the next horse – "

Meredith was already shaking her head. "I have nothing to pay you with," she wrote. Silence's eyes fell inadvertently on the silver bracelets. Meredith saw it, and folded her hands under the table, her chin lifting beneath her direct stare. He sighed again.

"All right," he said. "Let's leave it for the moment. Why don't you eat something? You can't tell me that you're not hungry."

Meredith picked up a piece of cornbread and took a small bite, then a larger one. Once she was eating, she seemed to relax a little. Gambling on that, Silence said, "Why did you work on the boat?"

Meredith looked up at him, the half-eaten piece of cornbread suspended from her fingers. After a moment, she put the bread down and wrote, "Because it was needed."

"But how did you know that it was in the barn in the first place?"

"I didn't," she wrote. "I was looking for the horse." Then, seeing his bemused look, "I'm sorry I interfered."

He smiled, shook his head. "I'm not. You got me out of a jam. But tell me: why didn't you answer my notes? In fact, why didn't you just come here and explain about the horse, rather than trying to steal her?"

She looked at him long enough to make him uncomfortable, and then she looked back at her tablet. Happy's shrieks and laughs drifted in waves through the open kitchen window. At last she wrote, "I knew that it would be pointless."

Silence sighed. He couldn't argue with that. "Tell me," he said when she'd eaten uninterrupted for a few minutes, "if I can't get Celia to give you the horse back, what will you do?"

For the first time since he'd led her from the crowd under the tree, Meredith looked frightened. After a moment, she shook her head.

"Well, where were you going?" Silence asked. "There might be another way to get there."

She smiled wryly.

"All right," he said. "I guess we'll just have to see if Celia will compromise."

Meredith sighed.

"She won't be in until supper time. Is there anything you'd like to do until then?"

Meredith thought about it, and then she wrote, "Wash. Sleep."

Silence smiled. "That, I can manage. Come on, there's a spare room upstairs." As Meredith stood to follow him, he turned back and said, "I'm sorry – I don't even know your name."

She took the tablet, wrote, and then gave it back to Silence. He read it, and then, across the spinning room, he looked into the girl's steady eyes. They were frank and open; she was telling the truth. Her name was Meredith MacFarlane.

5

There were two beds in the room to which Silence showed Meredith. Once they had belonged to his twin maiden aunts, who had died in them in perfect symmetry, the first-born expiring exactly four and a half minutes after the second, in reverse order to their birth. But that was before Silence's time, long before Meredith's, and whether or not their spirits remained in the room, he was running out of spare beds.

These beds had ancient cast-iron frames, their white paint chipping to reveal strata of pale green and blue paint and, in places, the original rusting metal. Between the beds was a rag rug, its once bright calico plaits long since faded to pastels;

likewise the quilts on the beds. The yellow walls were bare except for a darker oval above the washbasin where a mirror had hung before John Ogden's purge, and a few framed pictures, their glass dirty and their matting discolored with age.

Meredith put her pack down on one of the beds, and after she'd washed in the cold water she'd insisted on, she went to study the pictures. The first was a tarnished daguerreotype of a woman wearing quarter-sized, wire-rimmed spectacles and the stern expression imposed by the long exposure times of early photographs. Someone had written "Mother" on the moldy cardboard frame.

Beside the daguerreotype matriarch were two paper photographs of a later vintage, but old enough to have come free of the tape that had once anchored them, so that they slouched in their frames. One was a wedding portrait of a smiling, curly-haired man and a woman with dark hair and a deer's gentle eyes. The other was a picture of a baby who must have been Silence Ogden. He had the groom's dark curls and the bride's eyes, and the same reticent smile as the man he would become, though he lacked the scar.

Meredith turned away from the photographs and lay down on the bed beside the window. A young birch tree stood not far from it, mellowing the light. She watched its new leaves flutter until her eyes shut, and she woke with the setting sun in her face. The light sent filigreed shadows of the tree's branches wavering across the raw boards of the floor. Against the flood of light, Meredith felt immaterial as the shadows, as if it could erase her. She reminded herself that she had very nearly died that morning, but it piqued no more emotion than anything had since the day she had watched the man, Silence, shoot the lame horse, and her own horse abandon her for an older, stronger love.

Since then she had lived in a kind of suspension, unwilling to stay in this tiny hilltop town, but unable to leave. It wasn't simply that she'd lost the horse. She'd walked before, and she could do it again. Perhaps, as Silence had suggested, she could even have bought another horse. But her answer to Silence's suggestion had been more fundamental than he realized. She didn't want another horse, because her purpose was tied to Epona. She had followed her lead so long that she'd lost her own sense of direction, and after the horse had run from her, she had forgotten where she'd wanted to go, or why, or if she'd ever had a destination at all.

What was worse, the horse wouldn't speak to her, although she'd stolen into the paddock to plead with her many times over the past weeks. Wouldn't or couldn't. Meredith didn't want to believe the latter, but those weeks had gradually eaten away at her certainty until she had little choice but to believe it. The horse's eye was clear and innocent when she spoke to her, her gaze sweetly oblivious. Whatever grace had allowed them to converse was gone. Or perhaps, Meredith thought as she hid in the trees, watching the child laugh and chatter to the animal, it had been transferred.

Therefore she'd determined to take the horse away from that place, those people. She needed her in a way they never would, and she could never explain, even if she possessed a voice. Still, she knew that it would be a blow to them, so to soothe her conscience she would find a way to pay them back. And then, the night she crept into the barn to work out a way to escape with the horse, she'd known how. She didn't like it, but she would do it to have the horse back. A half a side of veneer seemed a reasonable exchange.

What she hadn't calculated was the vigilance of a tiny town, and so here she was, imprisoned by the kindness of a peculiar family in the middle of nowhere, indentured to work at the one thing she'd come so far to avoid. The little room seemed suddenly stifling. Meredith grasped the sash and pushed the window open, then leaned out into the warm springtime breeze. It was steeped in the smell of new grass and the sharp, dark heart of the pine forest. The leaves of the birch tree beckoned, fluttering brilliantly against the sky.

I could go now, she thought. *Nobody would know, and nobody could follow. I could wait until dark to take the horse and go through the woods…*

"If you want to leave," said a woman's voice behind her, "you can use the door. We have three of them, and no one will stop you."

Earlier, preoccupied with the horse, Meredith had given the woman a single cursory glance – not enough to record any details beyond the fact that she was tiny and dark-haired. Now, when she turned and saw her standing in the doorway, she froze. Her hands curled around the bedstead with a white-knuckled grip. She couldn't think anything but *How?*

The woman's harried look changed slowly to suspicion as Meredith gaped at her. "You look like you've seen a ghost," she said, but Meredith only continued to stare at her, because the woman was right: she *was* looking at a ghost, another puzzle piece from her disjointed past. The woman was older now, her face marked by hardship, but her eyes were the same; likewise the way she stood, straight and certain, framed by the slanting doorway with its cast of sepia light, not unlike a cardboard frame around a flimsy tintype print.

"I'm Celia," she said.

It was clearly a prompt. Her eyes were distrustful. Meredith made herself let go of the bed frame. She raised her hand, touched her throat.

"Yes," Celia said, "I know you can't speak. No need: I came to tell you that dinner's almost ready."

Meredith nodded, still dazed.

"Though if you'd rather go, I won't stop you," Celia said. "As long as you don't try to take my horse with you." She turned on her heel and left.

Meredith drew a breath and let it out again. She didn't know what she would do without the horse, but taking back to the road on her own suddenly seemed far more appealing than staying in this house, with a woman who would constantly remind her of the man she'd come so far to forget. Picking up her pack, she went out into the hallway. Its walls were unfinished, and the old wood, warmed by the westering sun, let off a maple-sugar smell that Meredith knew well. It beckoned with its promise of a time before the beach, a time before betrayal, but she wouldn't let it comfort her.

She walked down the stairs carrying her boots and emerged into a whitewashed hallway that led to the kitchen. There were sliding glass-paned doors on the outer wall, presently open to the evening sun. Two steps led down from the doors into the yard beyond. On the top step two cats, one grey and one orange, lapped their supper from a chipped willow bowl. Meredith could hear voices in the kitchen, someone coughing, a child laughing. Something about the chorus of human sounds caught at her, as the smell of the warm wood had done. She felt suddenly dizzy and sat down on the step by the cats to steady herself.

Outside, the air was golden as clouds of tree pollen caught the light. The trailing ends of a honeysuckle vine just coming into leaf tapped at the glass around the open doors; a hydrangea shook its papery brown pompoms in the wind. Further out, toward the barn, a stand of apple trees dropped showers of petals. Meredith sat there, watching the petals fall, trying to summon the courage to walk away into that soft spring evening.

"There you are," Silence said behind her.

Meredith jumped; she hadn't heard him enter, and she couldn't readily see where he'd come from. He stood behind her, a reticent half-smile on his face. The first time he'd smiled at her, she'd thought it was the scar that stopped it short. Now she realized that he stopped it himself: wouldn't allow himself to complete it. Despite herself, she wondered why.

The smile faded when he took in the pack and boots. "You're leaving?"

He couldn't hide his disappointment, though she saw him try. It pierced and slivered her certainty. *Maybe,* she thought, *I can still convince them.* She shook her head, negating her own thought and inadvertently answering his question. The hope that dawned in his face was almost painful. Sighing, Meredith opened her pack, brought out a pencil and the book Siu Fai had given her, and showed them to him as if this was what she'd intended to do all along.

"Ah," said Silence, his relief obvious.

Meredith followed Silence into the kitchen. Everyone stopped talking when they saw her, and she wished that she'd at least attempted to comb her hair. Celia still regarded her with suspicion; the child with fascination. The man who'd been with Silence in town was there now too, peering at her curiously through spectacles resting on the end of his long, patrician nose. Only the old Negro seemed glad to see her, pushing out the chair beside him and patting it.

"Sit, *P'tite,*" he said in a peculiar accent: part French, part long, rounded vowels that dredged even deeper into her past.

She sat. The Negro nodded once and then went back to his cup of milky coffee. Celia frowned and began taking dishes from the stovetop and putting them on the table. The child stared unabashedly at Meredith, alternating between suspicion and fascination. Silence smiled apologetically and said, "You've already met Celia and Happy. This fine man beside you is Pascal McCune, and this other one is Thomas Marsh."

Meredith nodded to both of them. Pascal smiled; Mr. Marsh said, "Pleased to make your acquaintance on happier terms than we met formerly."

Celia shot the man a look that Meredith would have called jealous if it had made any sense. When she bent to put a plate in front of Meredith, Meredith reached for her book and wrote, "Please tell your daughter that she's welcome to ask me whatever question she's stewing over."

Celia turned back to the stove, smiling wryly. "Go ahead and say it, Happy."

"Are you going to try to steal Epona again?"

"I'm sorry Miss MacFarlane," Silence said, coloring. "She didn't mean it like it sounded."

"Yes I did!" Happy cried.

"Happy," Celia warned, though Meredith could tell that she was suppressing a laughe.

Taking her book back, Meredith wrote, "She has a right to ask."

Celia took her place across from Silence, passed a bowl of early greens to Meredith and said, "Well then, since she's brought it up, what do you think we ought to do about this issue with the horse?"

"There is no issue," Happy said sternly. "Epona is ours."

Nobody said anything for a moment. Then Silence said, "That's true, Happy. But Miss – I mean, Meredith bought her in good faith, and so she's hers, too."

"But she was ours first! Besides, she tried to steal her." She glared at Meredith, her eyes cold as meltwater. "And besides *that*, how do you know she's not lying about how she got her?"

Meredith sighed, pushed her untouched plate aside and wrote, "Happy is right, on both counts. The horse was hers first, and you have no reason to believe me." She pushed her response to the middle of the table so that all of them could read it.

Pascal was the first to look up at her. With earnest black eyes, he said, "*I* believe you."

Meredith looked at each of them in turn, her eyes settling on Happy. She took her book back and wrote, "It's true, I would do almost anything to have Epona back. But I never considered her mine. If she taught me anything, it's that a horse belongs to no one. She chose me once; now she's chosen you. I'll go. You don't need to worry that I'll try to take her." Tearing the page from the book and leaving it on the table, she hurried from the room.

*

Silence found her in the corridor by the cats' empty dish, strapping on her pack.

"I'm sorry," he said. "Celia could have handled that better, and I should have – "

Meredith shook her head decisively.

"You can't be planning on going back out there," Silence pleaded. "Sleeping in the woods, hiding…"

The look on her face told him that this was exactly what she was planning.

"I can't let you do that!"

The manifestations of her anger were subtle, but clear. She pressed her lips together, cinched a strap with a sharp jerk and walked down the steps. Later on, Silence was certain she would have done it, too – walked right out of his life and never looked back – if she hadn't looked at her arm, first. The arm, which she'd lifted to settle the pack, bore the clear marks of the ropes that had held her that morning, circling her wrist like a purple shackle. She stood, looking down at the bruise with an expression Silence remembered well enough, from the first time he'd seen his scar in the mirror. It wasn't the scar that had terrified him, not in those first few visceral moments. It was the realization that he had been on touching terms with death, and it had let him pass.

"Those men won't have forgotten what happened," he said into the space between her hesitation and decision. "They'll be waiting for another chance."

Meredith looked at him, her eyes wide, and Silence felt a twinge of guilt for using her fear against her. He pushed it aside and added, "You don't need to stay forever. Just until they've had a chance to see that you and Celia have made it up."

She looked at him for a moment longer, and then away, letting out a long breath. Then she took out her book and wrote, "How can I stay here, with Happy and Celia looking at me like they do?"

Silence shrugged. "Happy's a child – she'll have forgiven you by tomorrow. And Celia might be a hard-headed woman, but she's a fair one too. She won't hold a grudge. Besides, it's my house, and I'm inviting you. It'll work out, you'll see."

Meredith raised her eyebrows.

"Look," he said, trying not to plead, "I don't know what's happened to you, but something has. Something that changed everything. Believe me, I know what that's like." Silence touched his scarred face. Meredith didn't avert her eyes – she didn't even blink – by which she grew miles in his estimation.

"I'll bet you've seen a lot of the world since you got on that horse," he continued, "but we aren't much like the rest of the world, as far as I can tell. I've come to think the people who find their way to this house find their way precisely because they aren't."

Meredith was looking out the doors now, twisting the hem of her shirt in her hands. Her jaw was clenched too tightly. Silence felt failure settle in him like a shipwreck. No longer caring how desperate he sounded, he tried one last time.

"All right...all right. If you're really set on going, I'll help you. I can get you down to the main road in a couple of hours, and no one else will be any the wiser."

Meredith looked up at him hopefully. He tried not to let his devastation show.

"The thing is," he added slowly, "I'd really rather you didn't. You see, it's not just that those men might re-think their decision not to string you up. It's not even that you look like you could do with a place to stop and rest for a while. The truth is, I need you. That boat in the barn – I've been building it since I was twelve years old. Up until a couple years ago, it was only in my head, but still, you could say it's always been the purpose of my life. The problem is, I have no idea what I'm doing. I know nothing about wood. I've never even helped raise a barn."

Meredith shrugged, *Why?*

Silence smiled wryly. "Because I was going to be a lawyer."

Meredith's brow furrowed at this, though her eyes lit with grudging interest.

"Yes, well," Silence continued, "that's a long, depressing story you can't really want to hear. The point is, I know nothing about building, let alone building boats. I've never even seen the ocean. But you have, I'd bet my life on it, and you already proved you know what you're doing with the boat. So don't you see? You were meant to come here and help me finish it."

Meredith scrutinized Silence, while he stood wracked by paroxysms of certainty that he'd alienated her for good. He sounded like a lunatic even to himself; he couldn't imagine what she must think. It was all he could do to keep standing there as slowly, deliberately, Meredith lifted her book again and began to write; all he could do to believe the letters unfolding in the wake of her hand.

"I'll stay," said her neat, firm script. "But only until you know enough to finish on your own."

6

Meredith sped up time. Days that had once dragged now ran together like an hourglass continually upended. Despite Silence's constant anxiety that she would disappear some night, Meredith was there at the breakfast table every morning, and gradually he started to believe that she meant to keep her promise.

Yet that knowledge wasn't as satisfying as it could have been. Even though Meredith worked diligently at the boat, even though she was neat and clean and helpful, she never lost her bereft look. She drifted through her days only half-present, and Silence often found her with tools forgotten in her hands, gazing toward the southwest horizon. He wondered what it was that called her there. He couldn't bear to ask her.

Nor could he discuss his worries with anyone. Between the fevers and the drugs, Pascal was less than present himself. Mr. Marsh had taken inexplicably to melancholic brooding. Celia, meanwhile, had decided that she didn't like Meredith. She never said it, but it was obvious to Silence by the way she went quiet and tight-mouthed whenever Meredith came into the room.

"I can't settle her," was her explanation when Silence finally asked her why. "I can't even settle on *why* I can't settle her." She stabbed viciously at her knitting.

"Are you still afraid she'll steal the horse?" Silence asked, disappointed that he'd been wrong about Celia holding a grudge.

But she shook her head. "I don't think she's bad or underhanded. In fact, I trust her for no good reason. I just can't like her. Maybe it's the not speaking. Sometimes it seems... studied."

"Studied?"

Celia nodded. "I'd bet my eyeballs she wasn't born mute. That it's something she took up later."

"Took up?" Silence repeated, shaking his head. "I didn't take you for petty, Celia."

Celia didn't rise to the bait, though, because she guessed that Silence had thought something similar himself. And she was right. He could see the words written on Meredith's face, clumped in the corners of her eyes and the curves of her rare smiles, so clear it seemed impossible that she really couldn't speak them. His discomfort wasn't confined to her silence, either. Sometimes he caught her looking at him as if she were looking into him – as if she heard all the thoughts in his head – while she herself gave nothing away. She answered questions about her past only in the most general terms, and she never asked any of her own. Even her movements were guarded, right down to the way she sat, with her limbs bent in tense angles that suggested she was about to bolt.

Yet despite it all, the boat grew, throwing Meredith's stasis into relief. It marked the passing days and weeks in strips of wood and oakum, and the tension that grew with them out of the knowledge that something had to give. And finally, something did.

*

The light was nothing more than a faint wash across the grass, but it was enough to convince Silence that he wouldn't sleep as long as it was burning. There was only one person who'd have a light on in the barn after midnight. He dressed quickly and went out into the soft May night. Bats dipped and swerved against the deep blue sky. Somewhere in the woods, a hunting owl cried.

Meredith was inside the boat, which now stood upright on the sleepers she'd constructed. She looked up when Silence appeared at the top of the ladder, offering him a wan smile that only unsettled him further. It was a gesture that would normally have prefaced speech, and it played like a wrong note against her muteness.

Silence forced a return smile, wondering what she saw, looking at him. Wondering whether the scar arrested her eyes' traverse of his face just like it did others', and she was only better at hiding it. He was immediately embarrassed by the thought. He'd never caught her staring, or even with the hastily downcast eyes of a near miss. More to the point, it assumed that she thought of him with interest, when he had no reason to think she thought of him at all.

Meredith must have seen the unhappiness on his face, because her own look softened, and she took out a pencil. "I couldn't sleep," she wrote on one of the hull planks. It was a habit they'd fallen into, being easier than locating her notebook every time they needed to converse. Now the inside of the boat was covered with halves of conversations.

"Neither could I," Silence said, dropping down onto the deck.

"It's coming along well," she observed.

"Is it?" Silence asked, because he honestly didn't know.

Meredith studied him for a moment, and then she pocketed her pencil and stood up. She offered him a more genuine smile than the first and then, hesitant as a flame taking damp wood, her hand. Silence blinked at it for a moment, certain that he was dreaming. When it closed over his, though, he knew as surely that it was real, because he could never have dreamed the intricate rasp of calluses, the ragged nails he'd watched her break on the skin and bones of his boat over days and weeks which seemed now to collapse into the present moment.

He could have traced the details of that hand indefinitely, but she was tugging with it, leading him to the bow of the boat. Letting go of his hand, she took her pencil back out, knelt down and began to draw. It took him a moment to decipher what she was doing, but at last, kneeling beside her, he understood. She was blocking out spaces on the deck and labeling them: locker, berth, hatch, head, galley, bilge, icebox, stove. As he followed the line of her pencil the specters of these spaces rose before him, as if she were transmitting what she remembered, and he could only imagine. And for the first time since the night when his father had tempted fate, Silence allowed himself to believe that his Idea would become reality.

When they reached the stern, Meredith sat back on her heels, setting the lantern down between them. Her face shone, her hair was a fuzzy halo. It seemed there was no world beyond the circle of lantern light, no room in its sacred sphere for any troubled realities. Her eyes, momentarily unguarded, asked him, *Well?*

An image slipped the locked safe of Silence's childhood memory: a summer dawn when he had awakened for no reason, and for less reason still, gone outside. Once there he'd understood why: a doe stood alone in the fallow field in the loose-woven light. She was young, her baby spots just fading, but she showed no fear of Silence. If anything, she seemed to invite him to touch her, her dark eyes still, her nostrils flaring as she tolerated his hand on her neck for a few seconds before she turned and dipped back into the woods.

Meredith was looking at him like that now: with infinite possibility. Taking courage from that, Silence said the words he'd been thinking since he first set eyes on her: "Meredith, when this boat is finished, please don't leave. Stay and launch it with me."

Meredith looked at him for a moment longer, and then, on the floor between them she wrote, "I can't."

"Why not?"

"I'm through with the sea."

"I can't believe that! Not when I've seen how you touch this wood…like you're saying your creed." Her eyes were black, haunted. "What happened, Meredith?" he asked softly.

She turned her head stubbornly away.

He nodded, and drew a breath and said, "Very well: keep your secrets. I love you despite them, and I always will."

He stood there listening to the words settle, not quite believing that he'd spoken them. Meredith watched him for another moment. Then she turned with a tearing that went through Silence like fire, and she ran, stringing his heart behind her.

Fairing

1

Silence was still sitting in the boat the next morning when Celia came to find him.

"Silence," she said from the top of the ladder, her eyes full of pity he didn't want.

He looked bleakly up at her. "I've made a terrible mistake."

"I don't think so," she answered, lowering herself down onto the deck, and brushing sawdust from her skirt distastefully.

"I told her I love her."

"I know."

"She told you that?"

Celia smiled wryly. "No. She won't come out of her room, so I knew it had to be something drastic. And given the way you've been looking at her lately – well."

"I've been an idiot."

"Possibly."

"How could I have ever thought that she could love me?" He shook his head bitterly, ran his hand down his scar. "She made me forget. She never looked at it, you see…"

Celia's smile died. "Listen to me Silence Ogden," she said. "You have got to stop letting that scar run your life for you."

"I don't let it run my life!"

"Of course you do! You've been hiding in this house since the day you got it – you try and tell me different!"

"Well what about you?" he retorted. "You'd rather let your daughter suffer than face up to the fact you married a bad man!"

Celia blanched, her eyes went dark and dangerous. He waited for her castigation but instead, Celia sighed. All of the fight went out of her. "All right Silence," she said at last, "you have a point. But that's a whole other conversation. I came here to talk to you about *your* problem."

"Well?" he said, when she didn't go on.

Sighing more deeply still, Celia cast a baleful eye on the dusty deck, and then sat down beside Silence. "I didn't plan to tell you this," she said, "because I didn't want to give you false hope. But rather than have you sitting here thinking a patch of lumpy skin is to blame for your troubles with Meredith…well, I'm pretty sure you're wrong on all counts."

"Which counts are those?"

"I've seen you looking at that girl, but I've seen her looking at you, too. Oh, it's when you don't know she's looking – women are good at that. The point is, it isn't the way a woman looks at a man who disgusts her."

"Do you mean…you think she might…" He couldn't bring himself to finish the sentence; it seemed too absurd after Meredith's clear rejection.

"I wouldn't presume to know what goes on in her head," Celia said, her voice taking on a sharp edge again. "All I know is you've got her attention, and I'm pretty sure she's got a soft spot for you."

"Then why did she run?"

"Lord knows."

"It makes no sense!"

"Love never makes sense."

"That's what Pascal says, too," he grumbled.

"There you are, then. *Everyone* thinks they're the only one who ever got sideswiped by their own heart. Everyone thinks their pain is the only pain, when really it's the one thing we all have in common." Her voice hardened again. "Only sometimes, I think men don't know the half of it, because they can take it and leave it."

"What do you mean?"

"I mean, when a man falls in love he holds the reins. Don't you argue – this is one thing I know more about than you. You see, men are in charge from the very beginning, when a woman has to sit and wait for one to declare himself. Then we have to hope our fathers will consent, and our husbands will treat us kindly, and so on and so on – and that's just when it works out. If it doesn't – if you realize the person you married isn't who you thought – what then? If you're a man you can turn and walk away, right on into a brand new life if that's what you want. But a woman? If she leaves, she leaves everything behind – her money, her pride, her reputation. And if she's left, she's left to clean up the mess. Pay the debt. Bear the shame. Raise the child alone." Celia's eyes bored into the deck beams over their heads, her cheeks were flushed with emotion.

"Celia?" Silence asked tentatively.

"Have you ever wondered why I never liked your boat?" she demanded.

"Of course I've wondered. But you more or less told me not to ask."

"Happy's father loved boats," she said, still not looking at him. "He was a river gambler, spent his life hopping between steamboats, cheating rich men out of their money and then drinking it all away again.

"Of course, I didn't know that when I met him. He told me he was a steamboat steward, and I believed him. Why wouldn't I? I used to blame myself for not seeing through him from the first, but over the years I've met others like him, and now I don't think I ever had a chance. He was golden. I don't just mean handsome: there're plenty of handsome men in the world wouldn't have made me lose my head. But he had that gambler's gift – that quality that made men keep betting against him even while they were losing, and women believe whatever lies rolled off his tongue."

She shook her head. "I met and married him inside of a few weeks. Gave him all of the money I'd saved to start new in the city. He said he was saving too, to buy a steamboat of his own. He said that he'd make his fortune once he was captain of his own ship. He'd tell me stories about the glorious life we'd live on that boat, and I believed them. I believed them even after I realized there was no job, and he never saved anything but his own skin. I made myself believe, because I'd given him everything, and by then I was pregnant too."

Finally, she turned to Silence. He'd expected fury, but her eyes were immeasurably sad. "And then one morning he was gone," she said. "I looked everywhere, asked everyone, but there was no trace of him. Then, a few days later, I saw a story in the papers, about a missing man: the son of a tobacco planter who was wintering on his sailboat. Last anyone saw of him, he was playing cards in a sailor's bar on the levee. It seems he lost his pants to a river gambler. A few men remembered him pleading with the card sharper; a few more remembered them leaving together. Next time anyone saw that boy, he was floating facedown in the river. They never did find his boat."

"And you think – " Silence began.

Celia smiled wryly. "Honey, I *know* – just like I knew they'd come after me in the end. So I ran. I went home first, but when my daddy heard what happened, he wanted no more to do with me. And so I started walking, looking for a place that might take in a penniless, pregnant girl. I'd never have made it through that time if it hadn't been summer in farm country – there was plenty of casual work, and when there wasn't, there was plenty to steal. I was lucky too to find that witch in the woods to deliver Happy, jut like I was lucky to find you. But I guess you can see why I'm not too fond of boats, never mind charming strangers."

Silence drew a deep breath. Celia and her whims suddenly made a lot more sense; still, he didn't feel any better. "I'm glad you told me that," he said at last. "But to be honest, I still don't know what to do."

"For Christ's sake, Silence! Finish your boat and sail away, or sell it for firewood and go to college like you meant to. Find religion, be a hermit, raise goddamn show chickens for all I care! Just don't waste another moment fretting over a girl who locks herself in a room when you offer her your heart."

Silence stood up quickly, hit his head on a deck beam and let out a string of curses. When they ran out, he said, "All right, Celia, I understand."

She peered closely at him to make sure that he did, and then she said, "I'm glad to hear it, Silence. And since I believe you, I'll tell you something I promised myself I wouldn't."

Silence was in no mood for another dramatic revelation, but he knew he owed it to Celia to listen. "Well?" he sighed.

632

"Don't give up."

"What?"

"On Meredith."

"But you just said – "

"Not to let it rule you. I didn't say don't try."

"If only I knew anything real about her..." he sighed.

Celia looked at him speculatively. "Maybe it's time we find out."

"How?"

"By asking her."

"Celia, I really don't think – "

But Celia had made up her mind.

2

Meredith watched Celia from her bedroom window as she marched back from the barn, face set and determined, and braced herself. Even so, she underestimated the force of Celia's resolve. Within moments, she was pounding on the bedroom door; it rattled as if in a storm wind.

"Open the door, Miss MacFarlane," Celia demanded. She'd never conceded to calling Meredith by her given name. "You and I have matters to discuss."

Trembling despite herself, Meredith opened the door. Celia breezed in, locked the door behind her, pocketed the key and then sat down on the chair. She indicated to Meredith to sit on the bed opposite, but Meredith remained standing, not wanting Celia to know how much she intimidated her.

"Suit yourself," Celia said with a weary shake of her head. "Now, let's begin with why you won't talk, because I know you weren't born dumb." She waited for several silent moments before she took a sheaf of old store receipts and a pencil from her apron pocket and extended them to Meredith.

Sighing, Meredith accepted them and wrote, "You're right, I wasn't. But if you think I am deliberately silent, you are very much mistaken."

"I haven't yet met the malady that takes a voice – at least not for more than a few days."

"I woke up this way one day," Meredith wrote, "about a year ago. It's been like this ever since."

Celia gave her a skeptical look, and then she sighed. "Miss MacFarlane, what are you doing here?"

"Someone took my horse," Meredith wrote. She shoved the page at Celia, her eyes unapologetic.

Celia swatted it away with an impatient hand. "Yes, but how on earth did you end up in the one place in all these mountains where she might let herself be taken? It seems a mighty fine coincidence."

"I've stopped believing in coincidence," Meredith wrote.

"Christ," Celia muttered, "you're as bad as Silence. Still," she said, her eyes direct and voice purposeful, "I've seen the way you look at him."

"What way is that?"

"Not the way a woman looks at a man if she plans to run when he declares himself."

Meredith turned away, feeling her color rise, but her eyes landed on the window, which framed Silence as he stood at the yard gate, looking down the empty road. She turned back to Celia.

Celia's eyes narrowed. "If it's another man you're pining for, I hope you know you'll never find one better than Silence."

"I'm not pining for a man," Meredith wrote.

"Well then, why won't you have him?"

"That's a very long story."

Celia raised her eyebrows. "I've got nothing pressing. I've also got the key." She patted her pocket.

Sighing, Meredith sat down on the bed. "What do you want to know?" she wrote.

"Let's begin at the beginning. Who are you?"

"I'm Meredith MacFarlane," she wrote grudgingly, "just like I told you."

"Well," Celia sighed, "that's a promising start. How about telling me where you come from?"

Meredith wrote, "A long way from here."

Celia snorted. "Well that clears everything up." She looked at Meredith, and finally, taking in her misery, she relented. "I think this might take a while," she said. "Can I sit beside you, so we don't have to keep handing this paper back and forth?" Seeing Meredith's hesitation, she added, "I promise not to bite."

Meredith shrugged, but she stayed put when Celia sat down.

"So," said Celia, "how long is a long way from here?"

"A year's ride north," Meredith found herself writing, "more or less."

"You could be clean up to Canada in that time..." Celia said speculatively. "You aren't running from the law, are you?"

Meredith couldn't help a slight smile. "No," she wrote. "And I've never been to Canada. At least, I don't think I have." Seeing Celia's suspicion deepen, she continued, "Everything before

I woke up on the beach is jumbled. Some things I remember clearly, others I don't."

"You woke up on a beach?"

"Yes. My boat was wrecked in a storm."

"Christ! And the other passengers?"

"There were no other passengers. It was only a little boat."

Celia's sympathy turned back to suspicion. "Why on earth would a girl go out to sea alone in a little boat, never mind in a storm?"

Meredith thought about this, and then, hesitantly, she wrote: "I was to be married, but something terrible happened."

"Ah," Celia said, studying her. "I don't suppose you remember what it was?"

Meredith shook her head, and although Celia saw dissimulation in her averted eyes, she let it pass. "And your people? Wouldn't they help you?"

"They tried," Meredith wrote. For the first time, she felt a stab of guilt at the truth of this. "But I couldn't bear to let them. They'd warned me."

Celia studied her for several moments, and then she sighed. "Is that when you stopped talking?"

Once again, Meredith's eyes flashed anger. "Why won't you understand? I didn't choose silence. I didn't choose any of this. I sailed into a storm hoping to disappear, and instead I woke up on a beach. I woke up, but most of me was gone. I was numb. I couldn't hear, I couldn't speak. I couldn't remember anything, not even my own name. I only knew that I had to get away from the sea, and so I started walking."

It was Celia's turn to gaze speculatively at the window. Following her eyes, Meredith saw that Silence had gone, and the yard was empty. She had the sudden urge to run outside, to find him, to beg him to forgive her. But she was locked up, and Celia held the key, and she knew that there was no avoiding what was coming. She'd known it since the first time she set eyes on Celia.

"All of this," Celia said at last, bitterly, "for the sake of a man." Then, pinning her dark eyes on Meredith, "Do you really expect me to believe you don't remember what happened?"

Meredith wouldn't look at her.

"You can't run from the past forever. Trust me, I've tried."

Meredith stared down at the paper in her hands. She took out a new page and began to write, trying not to think about Celia reading over her shoulder. "My father is a boat builder, and my fiancé had one of his boats. He was a rich man's son. He meant to sail to Europe, and he brought his boat to my father for repairs before the journey. All the way up from New Orleans."

Meredith paused, allowing Celia time to digest this. She didn't dare look at her, but she could tell by the sudden quickening of her breath that Celia had begun to suspect. "I should have known what he was. I *did* know, I think, although I convinced myself otherwise. I knew from the moment I saw your picture tacked to his wall."

At last, Meredith looked up. Celia had blanched, her mouth hardened. She seemed to be summoning the right words to answer with, but when she spoke, it was only to whisper, "It couldn't have been him."

"Jacob Devereaux was my fiancé," Meredith wrote. "Mine, and yours."

The two women looked at each other for a moment, and then Celia began to laugh, like the grating of rusted clockworks. "You have it wrong," she said. "You don't know how wrong you have it."

Meredith stared at her, waiting.

"Jacob Devereaux was never engaged to either one of us. He was found floating in the Mississippi off New Orleans with his throat cut, going on eight years ago. The man you were engaged to is called Jim Swain, and he's no rich man's son. He's not even from Louisiana."

"How do you know that?" Meredith wrote, her hand shaking.

"Because," Celia answered flatly, "he was my husband."

"I don't understand," Meredith wrote.

"No," Celia answered, her eyes venomous and voice suddenly cold, "you wouldn't. Because you escaped. You never had to pretend to believe he'd earned his money honestly or watch him drink it away while you went hungry. You never felt the back of his hand when he came in after losing a game, looking for someone else to take the blame. And you never had to make a child believe she's a bastard to save her from the truth that her daddy's a cold-blooded killer, or lie awake nights terrified that he'd find a way to take her from you, like he took everything else. Really, Meredith MacFarlane, you don't know how lucky you are."

Meredith looked at Celia. In her eyes, she saw herself dragging a red shroud from the sea and flinging a white dress back in its place. Once again, she felt the full force of Jacob's brilliant, dissembling smile. Her chest tightened, her heart beat like a cornered animal's. She leapt from the bed, made for the door, forgetting that Celia still held the key.

"Where are you going?" Celia demanded.

In a trembling hand, Meredith wrote, "I thought you wanted to get rid of me."

"So did I. Now I'm not so sure."

"What do you want from me?"

"I don't want anything from you. It's Silence I'm thinking of, and I won't let you break his heart for the sake of Jim Swain."

Anger punched through Meredith's fear. "You can't make me love him!"

Celia smiled sadly. "That's true. Luckily, it's only a matter of making you see that you already do."

"You don't know me! You don't know how I feel."

"Actually, I do. I know exactly what it feels like to have loved Jim, to have believed in him, and then have him betray you. I know what it's like to run from him, from whatever he did to you or took from you or made you think you had become."

Meredith glared at her with wet, furious eyes.

"I also know what it feels like to finally stop running. That's what Silence is offering you, same as he offered me. Don't waste it, Meredith."

Celia reached in to her pocket, then, and offered Meredith the key. Meredith took it and wrenched the door open. She ran out the kitchen door, past Happy in the garden, past the barn where Silence sat waiting, past the grazing horse, without a glance. She ran until she reached the woods, and then she stumbled on a tree root and sprawled. She lay where she'd fallen, one cheek against the earth and her heart battering her ribs, her mind like a sea storm.

Through the chaos, though, came one clear and inescapable truth: Celia was right.

3

Meredith was still sitting at the edge of the forest when the wind changed. Without warning it swung around to the northeast, spinning the weathervanes on Heaven's barns, herding in belligerent clouds bruised purple and grey. It raised Meredith's head from the tree she leaned on. It tugged at Happy's pigtails and sent the hens squawking and fluttering to shelter under the porch. It swept away Celia's righteous anger, leaving her open to doubt, and whistled forlornly to Silence through the empty shell of his boat. The old men on the porch of the store turned irrefutable eyes to the sky and predicted trouble.

That night, Celia tossed in her bed until Happy woke shrieking from a nightmare. "He's d-d-dead!" Happy told her. "My daddy's d-dead! That's h-how come you don't t-tell me about him!" And Celia was surprised to find herself crying, too. So she took Happy into bed with her and began to tell her the story of a man with a gambler's charm and a girl too young to know any better.

That night, Meredith sat writing in her room as the wind howled around the storm-bound house, filling page after page in a hand that was no longer slow and neat, until the truth began to take shape. Silence sat on the porch in the deranged light of the wind-rocked lantern, reading and re-reading the pages Meredith had thrust at him before locking herself away again, until he'd memorized them. All the while he thought of his fever dreams; of the grey-eyed girl who turned her back on the sea; of the solitary woman who'd once told him stories; of the connection between them that looked no less like lunacy whichever way he turned it.

And Pascal, ensconced in his terminal half-sleep, dreamed that God was shaking Heaven's oak, and the ghosts were falling from its branches. Disengaged, they flocked to him, their banshee screams circumscribing the house as they tried to reach their negligent keeper. Then God narrowed His eyes, filled His cheeks and issued one mighty gust.

The ghost wails echoed for a moment, like the pieces of a broken mirror in their own slivered silence. Then it was only the wind howling, and soon enough that, too, began to die. The full moon peered around a selvage of cloud; silver light settled over the town, soothing the battered fields and houses, and finally Heaven slept.

*

Silence woke to sun through his window and the sense he'd walked a thousand miles. He got out of bed, stood for a moment in a stream of sunlit dust motes, and then he opened the window. The wind that came in was cool as autumn, but at the same time full of the burgeoning trees and damp, tilled fields and something else. A scent he didn't recognize, mineral with a note of decay, both repellant and compulsive. He drew a long breath and let it out. The chaos went with it, leaving him weightless, his head full of the color of the sky.

When he came into the kitchen, Celia was waiting for him with a tight, anxious face. His first thought was, *She's gone.* And so he was confused when Celia said:

"The tree came down in the night."

"What tree?"

"The *tree* – Pascal's tree, by the church. The wind blew it down, tore the roots right out of the ground."

All at once, Silence felt those gaping roots as if they'd been his own. He sat down heavily. "Who's going to tell Pascal?"

"No need," Pascal said, making Celia and Silence jump. He was standing at the porch door in a clean white shirt and dark trousers, his eyes clear of the opiate haze for the first time in weeks. "I know the tree came down in the wind, and if God meant for it to be like that, ain't my business to question Him."

Celia looked her ambivalence at Silence. He shrugged.

"We've gotta go to town first thing though," Pascal continued, "before someone else gets their hands on it. One thing I know, that old soldier deserves better than to end up stove wood. But first, I need sustenance. What's for breakfast?"

Silence and Celia looked at each other again, both of them wondering if Pascal had finally lost his mind. Then Celia got up to make him a plate.

While he was eating, Silence went up to Meredith's room, fearing the worst. When he reached it, though, he found the door ajar, and Meredith asleep on the old rag rug, a pen in one hand and her head resting on a pile of old store receipts, filled with her writing.

"Come on, Silence!" Pascal hollered up the stairs then. "We gotta get to town before someone gets your tree!"

"*My* tree?" Silence said to no one in particular. Then he shut Meredith's door, and went back downstairs..

The tree had come down neatly, falling away from the bench and breaking only a few branches in its collapse. Silence had thought that it would make him sad to see it, but it was more like looking at an old man in his coffin at the end of a long, full life.

A small crowd had formed, staring into the gaping hole in bewilderment. "Don't you all worry now," Pascal told them. "We'll have this cleared up in no time."

"You?" snapped Jenny Marden, bouncing her squalling infant on her arm. "Why should *you* have this wood? It's our house it stood nearest to."

Pascal gave her a cold look. "It's not for me. It's for Silence. After all, it was his great-granddaddy founded this town, and it was this tree gave him the inspiration." Jenny opened her mouth to argue further, and Pascal added in a low voice which nevertheless carried across the crowd, "I'd say you owe him at least that much."

Celia hid a smirk. Jenny flushed red, turned on her heel and marched back to the store, her husband following sheepishly in her wake. The crowd began to disperse, though a few men offered to help Silence cut up the wood so that it would be easier to transport.

Once again Pascal interceded. "Thank you gentlemen, but no. We need this tree in one piece. I guess the loan of a few horses wouldn't be unwelcome, though." Silence watched in astonishment as the men nodded agreement and walked off toward home, presumably to harness their horses.

"I'll get Epona," Celia said and started back along the road.

When they were alone, Silence turned to Pascal. "All right – are you going to tell me what all this is about?"

Pascal smiled faintly and nodded to the bench. "Let's sit."

It was strange to sit on that bench in the full light of the sun, without the ghosts' whispers drifting down. He thought of all of the lunch hours he'd spent there growing up, and all of the times he'd come there for comfort after the accident. He had the sense of a loss that would take a long time to feel fully, longer still to understand.

"Oak burns well," he said at last, "but there's plenty to be had nearer home."

Pascal frowned at him. "Would you burn a dead friend, Silence Ogden?"

"I was being rhetorical," Silence told him.

"What?"

Silence sighed. "Just tell me plain, Pascal: why are we bringing this tree home?"

"Because a tree ain't like a man. Its life doesn't have to end when it dies."

Silence waited for him to elaborate.

"For a long time this tree's been the heart of Heaven, just like your family has," he continued, his hands in his lap moving over imaginary strings. "But nothing lasts forever. You're the last Ogden in Heaven, and soon you'll be taking your leave. But there's a way to bring a little of Heaven with you when you go."

"But – "

Pascal smiled ruefully. "No 'buts'. Plain and simple, *P'tit*: you're going to use this tree to finish your boat."

"Oh," was all that Silence could think to say. But he felt the first stirrings of inspiration as he realized the peculiar logic of Pascal's words. "It's true I need a lot of wood still to finish the boat. It's quite a coincidence, isn't it?"

"When are you gonna learn there's no such thing as coincidence?" Pascal said. "It's serendipity."

"Really? That's it?"

"What?"

"You're not going to try to tell me how it's God's doing, and Fate helped out, and all of it was part of someone's grand plan for the destiny of Silence Ogden?"

Pascal only smiled, and patted Silence's knee. They sat for a time, saying nothing.

Then Silence said, "I figured you'd be more cut up about this tree coming down."

"I thought I would be too. But now, I'm just plain relieved."

"Relieved?"

"That I don't have to listen to those ghosts anymore. I don't have to play their music. After waitin' so long, I can finally rest…"

A cold wash of panic went through Silence then. "What do you mean by that?" he asked.

Pascal glanced at him. "You know what I mean, Silence."

And Silence wished he didn't.

4

,Silence had managed to put the business with Celia and Meredith out of his mind while they were in town. Once he got home, though, he went looking for Meredith with a distinct feeling of dread.

The last thing he expected was to find her with Happy. She'd never quite taken to Meredith, although she watched her with a kind of morbid fascination that made Silence wonder whether she still thought Meredith was some kind of magical creature. He wondered also whether Happy had ever located her missing aura, but he didn't ask her. He didn't like to admit to himself that he was afraid of the answer.

But they were together in the attic when he found them, Happy wearing a crumpled velvet bonnet and cape and leaning over Meredith, who sat on the floor with an old election poster spread face-down in front of her, drawing something. Happy was rapt, Meredith's face lit like a Christmas window. Silence turned to go before he disturbed them, but at that moment Meredith looked up. Her smile broadened when she saw him.

"Silence!" Happy cried. "Did you get the tree?"

"It's coming," he said. "I hope you weren't bothering Meredith."

"I wasn't," she answered with a withering look. "I just went upstairs to see if she was awake, and I found her sleeping on the floor. So I woke her up and asked her if she was going to leave."

"Oh?" said Silence, his eyes on Meredith, and hers steady on him. "What did she say?"

"She said not anytime soon," Happy answered, and despite the ambiguity of the answer, Silence felt himself beginning to smile, too. "So I asked her if that meant you'd really finish that boat."

"And she said?"

"She said if you got hold of that tree and worked real hard, it would be ready by the end of summer."

"Really?" Silence asked Meredith, wondering how she'd heard about the tree and come so quickly to the same conclusion as Pascal. "You mean that?"

Meredith nodded.

"I told her I didn't believe that thing in the barn would ever look like a real sailing ship, so she made me this," Happy said. She took the paper from the floor and held it up. Just like his childhood dream, a schooner with billowing sails bounded across an open sea. Though it was sketched in charcoal, Silence's mind supplied the white of the sails and the contrasting blues of sea and sky, the varnished brown of the hull and the shine of the brightwork.

Happy beamed from inside the bonnet. "That looks like a real boat, all right." Then she turned toward the door. "Horses!" she cried. Shedding her cape and hat, she ran out the door toward the road. But a moment later she reappeared. "Silence," she said, her eyes bright as the sky behind her.

"Happy?"

"I was wrong." She nodded at Meredith. "The light was only hidden. It's white – same as yours." And she disappeared again.

Silence turned back to Meredith, who'd written on a scrap of paper, "What light?"

"It's a long story," he answered. He started back toward her and then stopped half way, shy at finding himself alone with her for the first time since his disastrous declaration. "But tell me, how did you know about the tree?"

Meredith held his eyes for a moment, her own eyes wide and clear and a paler shade of grey than he remembered. Then she wrote, "I dreamed it."

"Of course you did." Silence took another couple of steps forward. "And the wood – you really think I can use it?"

Meredith wrote, "Oak is a fine wood for salt water. It'll do for deck planks, the rudder and tiller – even the spars and mast, if it's sound and straight enough."

"But a whole tree," he said, shaking his head. "I've only used cut lumber. I don't know where to begin."

"I do," Meredith wrote. She watched him with steady eyes as he read it.

"So…you really do mean to stay and see it finished," he said. Meredith nodded.

"I'm glad," he said, trying not to show his elation. "I thought that after yesterday…after Celia…" Silence stopped, not knowing how much would be too much to say.

Meredith was biting her lip. At last she wrote, "I'm sorry, Silence."

"What for?"

"For the way I've been. I've been traveling so long – " she crossed out "traveling" then and replaced it with "running" " – that I've forgotten how to stand still. I thought that I was choosing to keep going, but really I kept going because I didn't want to choose. So when the horse made that decision for me, to stop, I was angry. I was angry at her, but I took it out on all of you. It was wrong."

Silence nodded, though in fact he was baffled by half of what he read.

"It will take a lot of work to finish the boat by the end of summer," she wrote. "But it isn't impossible."

Silence finally found his voice. "Thank you," he said, and then they stood in the sunlit dust-eddies, the papers on the walls whispering softly in the drafts. "About the other thing," Silence said at last, because there really was no sidestepping it, "what I said to you the other night …"

He trailed off as Meredith looked out the open door, held his breath as she watched the wind riffle the grass and trees, and trace fine, smoke-blue lines of cloud across the sky. At last she turned back to him. She took her blue notebook from her pocket, wrote something on the fly-leaf, handed it to him, and then left.

Silence looked down at the page. "Read this," she'd written in the charcoal with which she'd been drawing, "and then decide whether you mean it."

5

Meredith went to work as soon as the chains and harnesses were off of the tree, stripping bark, assessing the limbs and trunk for strength and straightness. From the porch, as he read, Silence stole intermittent glances at her. The journey that her book described was almost unbelievable, yet that wasn't what drew his eyes. Something subtle but fundamental about her had changed. It was clear in the way she held herself, in the way she moved as she worked, that the job was no longer something she was suffering through, but something she'd chosen.

It was evening by the time Silence had read and re-read Meredith's history enough to feel he understood it. He pocketed the book and walked out to meet her. She was in the barn putting tools away, but she stopped when she saw him coming, her eyes wide and luminous, her mouth trembling. He realized then that she was actually afraid of his reaction.

"Did you really think that anything in here could make me change my mind?" he asked, handing her the book.

Meredith shrugged almost imperceptibly, her hands shaking now too as she accepted the book and clutched it to her chest.

Silence shook his head, smiled his crooked smile. "Yes, Meredith. I mean it. That book – your journey – well, your courage is impressive. But the fact is, it has no bearing on what I feel. I've loved you all my life."

Hesitantly, Meredith smiled. Equally hesitant, Silence reached out across the twilight with its first frail web of stars. Meredith met his hand and grasped it.

*

It was dark when they returned to the house. The parlor window stood open, and voices spilled out: Pascal and Happy, Celia and Mr. Marsh, and one more, too low to identify. Still, Silence wasn't entirely surprised to find that it belonged to Annie. She fit seamlessly into the gathering in the parlor, sitting in a chair by Celia, her swarthy face split between shadow and the lantern's soft light. She looked up as they came in, her eyes catching on Meredith for a moment before she looked away again.

"Happy invited a dinner guest," Celia said.

"I'm glad," Silence answered. "It's nice to see you, Annie." Annie regarded him with a quizzical half-smile. He met it head-on, saying, "I hope you'll forget about the last time we talked. Things are clearer now."

"So I see," said Annie, her eyes flickering to Silence and Meredith's linked hands.

"I'd like to introduce you to Meredith MacFarlane," he continued, watching carefully for her reaction. Annie nodded tersely to Meredith before turning back to Celia, her face set in its usual expression of detached calm. But Silence was certain there had been something in the pause when Annie first looked at Meredith. A minute flicker; whether interest or alarm, it was impossible to say.

"Silence," Happy called, "look what Pascal showed me!"

Silence dragged himself back from his rampant speculations to see that Happy was holding his guitar. She stretched her fingers across the strings and strummed a G chord. She switched position, played C, and then looked up, beaming. Everyone applauded.

"I'm impressed, Happy," he said. "I guess it won't be my guitar for long."

"If she can learn music," Mr. Marsh mused, "she can surely learn Latin."

Celia shook her head and said, "You'll be sending her to college next!"

"Well, and why not? Many women go to college these days." He paused, looking at her. "I could teach you both...if you wanted to learn, that is."

"Oh, Thomas!" Celia cried, coloring, and hurried out to check something in the kitchen.

Thomas again? Silence thought, and then, seeing the way that Mr. Marsh's gaze rested on Celia's empty seat, he understood. Given Celia's predicament, he wondered whether congratulations or commiserations were called for.

"Supper's ready," Celia said, re-appearing in the doorway. "We'll eat in the dining room, I guess – there are too many of us for the kitchen table."

It was the first time since Esther took ill that the dining room had been used; the first time in more years than Silence could count that all of the chairs had been filled. Sitting in his father's place, with Meredith on his right side and Annie on his left, he felt vaguely disjointed, as if the scene couldn't be real. Two nights ago, he'd been certain that he would never make good on any of his dreams, that he'd never be happy again. Now, he couldn't imagine being happier.

Still, he couldn't help wondering what Annie knew or how to reconcile the riddle of her stories with the present reality. He couldn't believe that she'd come to his house tonight purely on Happy's account. Nor could he believe that he'd imagined that pause when she first laid eyes on Meredith, but there was no way now to question it. In coming to his house, she'd forced an apology; in apologizing, he'd relinquished his right to question her.

Sighing, Silence poured more of the blackberry wine Annie had brought and tried to pay attention to the current conversation. Pascal was re-telling his dream of the tree's fall, and how it must have been serendipity.

"No," Annie said quietly, her fingers like tree roots themselves around her wine glass, "it was an act of god – but no Christian god." She stared into the dark puddle left at the bottom of the glass as if it were a magic mirror. Her eyes were dark as ink in the frail candlelight. "Once, people worshipped trees. They believed that a tree links the earth to the heavens and the underworld, that it speaks to the gods of those places and relays their messages. And of all the trees, the oak was the most sacred. It symbolized the center of the universe, and so every village was built around an oak tree."

"Like ours," Happy said.

"Like ours," Annie agreed.

"But now ours is gone…"

Annie shook her head, her eyes catching the candles' glow the way stones in a riverbed catch the sun. "It isn't gone; it's only finished one stage of its life. Thanks to Silence, it will live on for a long time to come."

"And to Meredith," Silence added. "I'd get nowhere with that tree without her help."

There was a moment's silence, and then Annie said, "If there is a god, it must watch over this place." She raised her glass in a silent toast and drained the last few drops. Then she stood up. "Thank you," she said, to no one in particular, and in the time it took to blink she was out the door.

The others paused for a moment in the wake of her leaving, each feeling that they'd been given, and didn't quite understand, something vastly important. Meredith caught Silence's eye, her own clearly troubled.

"We'll clean up," he said to Celia, "if you want to take Happy to bed."

"Not yet!" Happy cried.

"It's long past time already," Celia contradicted, but her voice was soft. "If you hurry, I'll tell you a story. Let me just help Pascal to bed first."

"I'll do that," Mr. Marsh said.

"Oh, but – " Celia began, and then her eyes caught Mr. Marsh's, and once again she looked away, coloring. "Thank you," she mumbled, and then, "come on, Happy."

Mr. Marsh helped Pascal to his feet, and they followed Happy and Celia out of the room, leaving Silence and Meredith alone. She looked at him, and for a moment he felt that he could see the words in her, jammed together and clamoring for freedom. But still, something stopped them. Sighing, he asked, "What's wrong?"

Meredith took out her book to answer. When she pushed it across the table to Silence, he read, "There's something familiar about Annie. As if I've seen her before. Where does she come from?"

Silence looked at the words for long time, trying to decide whether or not to tell her what he suspected. It had seemed so obvious when Meredith had been no more than a dream, but the reality of her muddied the waters, so that he was certain one moment and uncertain the next.

"I don't know," he said at last. "She's not from here, but as far as I know, she's never told anyone where she lived before."

"So she could have lived up north, once," Meredith wrote.

"Maybe. But I was a small child when she came here. You'd never have remembered her. Maybe it's just that she reminds you of somebody. Couldn't there still be things from the past that you don't remember?"

Meredith paused, and then she wrote, "There could be. But it's *her* I remember, not just someone like her."

"How do you know that?"

"I just know."

"Well," Silence said, even as his gut told him he shouldn't, "you could always ask her."

"Yes," Meredith wrote. "I could."

They sat in the resonant stillness wondering what, if anything, had been agreed. Silence's thoughts strayed, and he didn't even realize that Meredith was writing again until she pushed the book into his hand.

"There's enough wood in the tree to finish the boat," it said.

Silence looked at the page for a long time. It was no more than he'd suspected, but it wasn't until he saw the solid words that he believed it. "It's strange to think of it finished," he said.

"Dreams are strange," Meredith wrote. "When they come true, they're both greater and lesser than what you imagined."

"You've had a dream like that?" Silence asked, intrigued.

Meredith wrote, "I used to dream that I had a mother." The look on her face told Silence that she understood longing – and, perhaps, the sudden dislocated feeling of its object's realization – better than he ever would.

"I think," he said, "you'd better talk to Annie."

Meredith wrote, "I think you're right."

6

She didn't go right away, though. Instead, she threw herself into her work. Pascal's tree had proved sound to the heartwood, and under her hands it diminished quickly, feeding the rapidly-growing boat.

"You work like you're on a mission," Silence said to her once, as she laid deck planking.

"I am," she scribbled on the underside of one plank, and then she hammered it into place.

"What is it?" he asked.

"I don't know," she wrote on another plank. "It's as if the boat has a mind of its own, and it knows something is going to happen soon, and it wants to be ready for it."

Silence didn't ask her to elaborate; it already sounded too much like Celia's dropped biscuits for his liking. He was even more unnerved when Meredith jerked back one day from a porthole she was cutting, clutching her hands in front of her as if she'd cut herself. But when he asked to see it, she shook her head.

"I'm not hurt," she wrote on the oval offcut from another porthole. "But when I looked down just now, it was Ian's hands I saw, not my own." Seeing Silence's bewildered look, she added, "Sometimes these days, I feel that he's here."

After that, Silence began to sense Ian's presence, too. The more he worked, the more real it felt, until it filled the old barn with the ghosts of whistled sea-chanteys and revenant drifts of pipe smoke. And then one night, working late, Meredith dropped her hammer and turned, her face lit with expectation. Silence came up beside her, looking where she looked, into the dark beyond the doorway. A minute passed, and then another, and nothing broke its void. Slowly Meredith's face dimmed until it ran with tears. Silence put an arm around her, and she leaned into him.

When the tears were finished, she sat down on the stool, took out her book and wrote, "There was somebody watching. I <u>know</u> there was."

"Meredith," he sighed, "if your father was here, why would he hide from you?"

She pressed her palms against her tired eyes. Then she blinked, wiped a hand over a wet face suddenly grim, and wrote, "Maybe I have it wrong. Maybe it isn't his body that I'm sensing, but his spirit."

"You mean...?"

"I don't know," she wrote. "It's been a year, after all. What I do know is that I have to write to him."

*

Meredith discarded all of the letters she wrote that night, and then the ones she wrote the next morning. She couldn't find words to express her shame for having abandoned her family, or her sudden fear for them. Even when she finally chose one and sealed the envelope, she knew that it was inadequate. Still, mailing it gave her a temporary peace.

Meanwhile, summer bloomed with the boat. By June its exterior was finished, the woodwork varnished to let the perfect grain of the mahogany and oak show through. Silence and Meredith spent their days now in the hot, cramped interior, making good on Meredith's old pencil drawing as they laid paneling on the walls and built the frames of the berths, partitioned off the head and set in tanks to store water.

When the interior was finished, they turned their attention to the mast and spars, which, Meredith told Silence, might well prove the most difficult part. The mast had to be made from a single piece of wood, and as such the obvious choice was a pine trunk. But the mottled heartwood of the fallen oak was long and straight, if not as elastic as pine.

"With some work, it would serve the purpose," Meredith wrote, "if you want it to." It took Silence a long moment to realize that Meredith was asking his advice, and he was even more surprised by the certainty with which he answered, "Yes, I do."

Sometimes they worked long into the night and slept in the barn. Other times Meredith left early and wrote in her journal in her room until the short night faded into another morning. When she was too tired to write and too restless to sleep, as seemed to be the case more and more often, she came to Silence's room and lay down beside him. Together, they listened to the night until sleep captured them.

Beyond the occasional, accidental brush, they didn't touch each other. It was a tacit agreement: as long as Meredith couldn't speak, they could make no mutual declaration, and without that, Meredith wouldn't let Silence commit himself to her further than he had already. He tried not to draw unhappy conclusions from her continued silence, while she tried not to doubt herself and the intricacies of time.

Still, Meredith couldn't help wondering why her voice hadn't come back with her purpose. She wondered if it ever would. And then one morning in early August, her letter was returned.

7

"Dear Miss MacFarlane,

"I regret to inform you that Ian and Hunter MacFarlane are no longer resident at the address to which you posted your letter. The younger Mr. MacFarlane left nearly a year ago; the elder has been absent roughly a month. I have tried and failed to locate a forwarding address. The most that I can tell you is that the property has not been sold, and so I assume that one or both men intend to return. As such I will keep your address on file, and alert them to it should they do so. Other than that, I am afraid that I can be of no service to you.

"Most regretfully yours,
Miss Margaret W. Pritchett, Postmistress
Bryce's Landing, ME"

When Meredith finished reading the letter, she burst into tears. She wept with abandon, head down on the breakfast table in front of everyone, not bothering to explain. Celia and Silence exchanged horrified glances. Mr. Marsh, terrified of female emotional outbursts, discovered pressing business on the porch. Pascal looked at Meredith, with an incongruous half-smile. And Happy looked at the letter.

"Don't worry," she said, as Celia snatched it from her, too late. "Your daddy's on his way here."

"Happy," Celia warned.

"Well, where else would he go?"

"Happy, I think you need to weed the garden. Right now."

"Why won't you listen to me?" Happy cried. "It *has* to be that! Meredith's brother must have written to him and told him – " Happy clapped both hands over her mouth. The room was suddenly, deathly silent.

"Well, Happy," said Celia, "we're all listening now."

"Never mind."

"It's too late for that, Happy," Silence said. "You'd better explain yourself."

Happy looked at Meredith, her eyes wide, repentant and defiant by turns. "All right. But it's Annie you should really ask, not me. She's the one that saw him." When nobody said anything, she sighed and continued, "It was a few days back. Everyone was working, so I went to read in my cave. Only, when I got there, I found Annie. She was crawling around on her hands and knees with her eyes all squinted up, and I thought she was having histrionics."

"Histrionics?" Silence repeated.

"Wasn't that the right usage?" Happy demanded of Mr. Marsh, who'd just decided it was safe to return.

"Perfectly correct," he answered faintly as Celia glared at him.

"Go on, Happy," she said. "No need to embellish it with fancy vocabulary."

"Well," said Happy, "I was about to go away again when she sat up and looked at me. She said, 'What've you been doing out here, Happy Moon?' and I told her, 'Nothing,' because it was true; I hadn't been there in weeks. So she looked me over, and I guess she believed me, because she nodded. So then I said, 'What are *you* doing here, Annie?'

"Well, at first she just looked at the river and didn't say anything. Then she said, 'I'm looking for someone,' and I said, 'Who?' and she said, 'Someone who's come looking for Meredith,' and I said, 'How do you know someone's looking for Meredith?' and she didn't answer, she just opened up her hand. She was holding a long, black hair. I said, 'Is that from the lady who's looking for Meredith?' and she said, 'It's not a lady looking for her,' and I said, 'Is it her husband?' and Annie laughed and said what made me think Meredith had a husband? And I told her about how you have a husband, Mama, one that no one knows about, and how you pretended you didn't because you were afraid he'd come looking for you."

Celia's attempt at nonchalance was ruined when Mr. Marsh looked over at her, and she blushed to the roots of her hair. Faintly, she asked, "What did she have to say about that?"

"She just said she was glad you finally told me. And then she said, 'No, Happy Moon, this doesn't belong to Meredith's husband. It belongs to her brother,' and I said, 'How do you know that?' and she said, 'Because I used to know him,' and I said, 'Did you used to know Meredith too?' and she said, 'Yes, I guess I did.' And then she got that far-looking way in her eyes, and I started to think she was going to have some more histrionics."

His eyes on Meredith's stricken face, Silence asked, "Did Annie say anything else?"

"Welllll…yes," Happy admitted sheepishly.

"What was it?"

"She told me not to tell you. She said when the time was right, he'd tell you himself."

Everyone looked at Meredith then. Meredith's eyes were fixed on the window over the draining board, but a moment later she looked back at them. Taking up her book, she wrote, "Thank you for telling me, Happy. Please, don't anyone punish her. She was only trying to keep a promise no one should have asked a child to make."

Then she pocketed the book and stood up, her face a battleground for what she wished and what she feared. No one had to ask where she was going.

*

Meredith found Annie waiting for her, or so it seemed: she sat on her front step, looking down the path toward the road, and she showed no surprise or even anxiety as Meredith approached. Her blue-green eyes were serene. She watched for a moment as Meredith fumbled for her book and pencil, and then laid a hand on her arm to stop her.

"There's no need," Annie said. "I know why you're here."

Meredith raised her eyebrows.

"The child told you what I found. You want to know if it's really him…and how I knew."

Meredith was perplexed, but Annie smiled. It lit her face and the air around her like a match bursting into flame. "Don't worry, I don't read minds," she said. "I just know Happy."

Meredith nodded vaguely. The wind washed through the trees, echoing a wave's reach and retreat. Annie's smile faded as her eyes seemed to zero in on something in the distance. "Come with me," she said.

By the time Meredith registered the words, Annie was five strides into the woods behind her house, and Meredith had to run to catch up. Annie didn't speak again until they reached the banks of the river. "It's not far from here," she said and then walked on, her eyes intent on the ground.

Meredith hadn't been in the woods since the morning she tried to take the horse back. Those few months away had made a foreign land of her old refuge. The trees, no longer winter-bare, murmured to one another in an intricate tongue. Their trunks creaked softly in the breeze like a boat rocking in its slip, their branches broke the pale-yellow light into shards. Jays chased and scolded in the branches; high above and hidden, a chickadee called out and was answered by another.

After a time they came to a lazy bend in the river, where a moss-covered windfall diverted the stream. Eddies swirled in its lee, and at its far end, a blue heron balanced on one leg, close enough that they could see the curled feathers on its crest.

"Now that's a rare sight in these hills," Annie said.

They stood watching the bird. It watched them back, prehistoric eyes unblinking, pink half-smile unwavering. They didn't move, yet Meredith could have sworn that their stillness wasn't the reason that the bird didn't startle. It seemed to have no fear of them, but rather to be sizing them up. At last, it tilted its head at them, spread its wings, and lifted off of the rotting tree trunk. It made its stately way out of the clearing, spiraling up into the blue until it was a speck, and then a memory.

"A rare sight," Annie repeated speculatively, turning back to Meredith. "The Indians say that the blue heron is a sign of self-reliance…a message to stand on your own two feet, and let them take you where your heart guides." By the stump of the fallen tree, Annie knelt down. "Here," she said, and shifted to the side.

Kneeling beside her, Meredith saw two pairs of footprints in the mud. One was lug-soled, long and broad, the other flat-soled and narrow. Her heart beat fast, but not as fast as it did when her eyes caught on something pale, half-covered in mud. She knew what it was even before she picked it up, but still she gazed at it in disbelief, a tide of memories swelling around her. At last they drained away to one: a little carved boat on a dusty mantle above a crude stone fireplace. The same carved boat she held now in her hand.

"It's them," Annie said softly, her eyes flickering shadows.

Her voice broke through Meredith's reverie. She slipped the boat into her pocket, and then she took out her book and wrote: "Who are you to me?"

Cool, green light drifted into the river; the river drifted towards the far-away sea. With her eyes on the water, Annie said, "I'm a woman who once was greedy; I held onto myself so tightly that no one else could hold me for long. Three times, life offered me unconditional love, and three times I denied it." She paused, her eyes narrowed to two black lines. "I haven't been unhappy, but I'm not without regrets. No day passes when I don't think about how things might have been different. No day passes when I don't wonder about the ones I left. Except that now I wonder if I ever really left them at all."

Annie laid a hand over the footprints, and then she stood up abruptly, began walking back along the riverbank towards home. Meredith opened her mouth to release the cry paused there – but it fell back, choking her as it toppled inward. She didn't bother to watch Annie disappear. Her eyes filled with tears.

But they didn't spill. All around her, the tree-filtered sunlight wavered like light sifted down through layers of water. She closed her eyes and let it run over her face. The river's whisper ran through her like a silver thread. And then a shadow passed over her, eclipsing the sun. She opened her eyes and found Silence looking down at her, his face the color of the varnished boat in its warm, sunlit nimbus. He knelt beside her.

"Are you all right?" he asked, looking at the footprints in the drying mud by the fallen tree.

The wind swirled down through the trees and broke around her; she thought, *I am*. When Silence stood up, offering a hand to help her, she took it, and stood, and kissed him.

Axis Mundi

1

At the end of August, the boat was finished. Silence was the first one ready on the day they chose for the christening, and he paced the kitchen in a suit he hadn't worn since his father's funeral. It wasn't the boat he was anxious about, but a decision he'd come to gradually over the weeks since he'd first kissed Meredith by the windfall in the river. He had learned all of her in those weeks, from the ladder of her ribs that still showed, despite Celia's cooking, to the precise number and position of black flecks in her right eye. And the more intimately he knew her, the more wrong it began to seem that he didn't even know his own face. So as Celia argued with Happy over a dress that was too small, and Annie swept Meredith upstairs with a mysteriously shrouded parcel, Silence went into Celia's room and closed the door.

He paused for a moment, trying to steady himself, but he was trembling when he turned to face the dresser. His breath came fast as he saw the dusty wooden frame of the mirror above it:

the only mirror left in the house. Clutching the top of the dresser with white-knuckled hands, he leaned toward the small glass oval so that his face filled it.

For a long time, he could do nothing but stare, unable to believe that the face he was looking at was really his own. He had been little more than a child the last time he looked himself in the eye; it was a man who looked back at him now. The change was so profound that if it hadn't been for the undeniable evidence of his mother's dark brown eyes and his father's jaw and unruly hair, he wouldn't have believed it was his own face at all.

The scar, too, had changed beyond recognition. The skin was still raised and shiny where the wound had closed, but there was no red left in it. Standing a few feet from the mirror, it was hardly visible. Likewise, the fist-like contraction of his features had relaxed as time soothed the wound's angry memory and the muscles adjusted. Still, to test it, he smiled. The tightened skin of the scarred cheek drew that eye down a little lower than the other one and kept that side of the smile from reaching quite as far, but it was nothing like the travesty he'd imagined for so long.

"See?" Celia said from the doorway. He whirled around, flushing, but her smile was gentle rather than triumphant. "Didn't I tell you you're a good-looking man?"

"Sure, you did," he grumbled, turning even redder.

Celia laughed at his embarrassment. "Well, if you're done admiring yourself, everyone's ready."

Silence followed her down to the kitchen where, indeed, everyone was waiting for him. Pascal, leaning on Mr. Marsh's arm, had folded himself into a dusty old suit that he'd found in the attic. Mr. Marsh wore his ubiquitous dark jacket and schoolmaster's glasses, but he seemed to have taken greater care with them that day: the coat was brushed and the glasses polished. He kept stealing glances at Celia, resplendent in a red calico dress she'd remade from one of Esther's old ones, and apparently victorious in her argument with Happy, who was wearing her own new dress, despite the lace collar she complained was scratchy.

Silence looked around the crowded kitchen for Meredith and found her at last, hovering behind Annie. Annie stepped away and pushed her forward with a little smile and a look that seemed suspiciously like pride. Silence thought she had a right to be proud: whether or not there was a blood tie between her and Meredith, she had transformed the younger woman. For the first time since Silence had met her, Meredith was wearing a dress. It was an elaborate swirl of pale blue sateen, its cut a good quarter-century out of date, and yet it fitted Meredith as though it had been made for her. Meredith seemed mortified by it, plucking at the ruffles, her eyes unable to meet Silence's. But when he stepped forward and took her hand, she seemed to relax.

"Let's go," he said, and he and Meredith led the way out into the bright morning.

It was the kind of day, Silence thought, when things were meant to happen. Everything looked newly washed, the late summer colors humming brightly against the pristine sky. When they reached the barn, he and Meredith each took hold of the door and pulled. It grated open on its protesting runners, and light flooded in.

Silence stood for a moment, looking at his boat with an awe that hadn't yet faded. Its gleaming sides tapered down to the crisp edge of the keel; reflected sunlight blazed from the glass and brightwork. The mast and spars lay next to it on a tarpaulin, waiting to be set in place when they launched it. As yet, they had no sails, but Meredith assured him that they would find a dozen willing sailmakers in any good-sized port town.

"Well, Silence," said Celia, stepping inside for a better look, "even I have to admit it's a beautiful thing."

Pascal had his hat tipped back, pride all over his face. "That it is," he said, "and I thank God I got to see it."

Before Silence could process that ominous addendum, Happy cried, "I'm going to look inside!" She was half way up the ladder before anyone had a chance to object, with Meredith climbing up after her to make sure she didn't fall off.

"Does it have a name?" Pascal asked.

Silence looked at Meredith, but she only shrugged. "We haven't had much time to think about it…"

"I know that look," Celia said. "Out with it, Silence."

"Well," he said sheepishly, "I did have one thought. Seeing as it keeps coming up, what about 'Serendipity'?"

While the others looked at each other for opinions, Happy said, "That's a good name, Silence."

"Do you even know what it means?" Celia asked her.

"A fortunate accident."

Celia raised her eyebrows at Mr. Marsh. He shrugged, and said, "Happy does have a keen memory for vocabulary."

Silence looked at Meredith. She smiled, and gave him a small nod. "Well, if we're agreed," he said, "then I guess it's time to do the honors. Annie, do you have the champagne?"

Annie handed him a bottle of her potent homemade cider.

"Meredith?" he said.

She stepped up to the bow with him. Silence laid his hand on it for a moment, and then, with Meredith's hand on top of his, he drew the bottle back.

"Hold on a moment, lad!" someone called.

Meredith turned and then blanched. Silence lowered the bottle and followed her eyes to the two men standing in the doorway. One was tall and broad, his chestnut hair and beard gone mostly to grey; the other was nearly as tall, but slender, with long dark hair pulled back from a fine-boned face. With a ragged cry, Meredith flung herself into her father's arms. He squeezed her tightly, the tears in his eyes belying his nonchalant words. But they were nowhere near as astonishing as Meredith's real, loud, wracking sobs.

After a moment she struggled to free one arm from her father's embrace, in order to wrap it around her brother. And after another moment she turned to Silence. Her eyes were no longer grey, but blue as a June sky, the black spots turned to gold. He had barely had time to process the change when she opened her mouth, and said, "Don't just stand there! They came all this way, now do it!"

Silence was too stunned to heed her words. But Happy cried, "Silence! Smash the bottle!" Silence looked at Happy, and then at the bottle in his hand, and without further ado, he smashed it against the exact place where once he'd pinned a letter beginning "To the Girl from the Woods…" He said, "I christen you 'Serendipity'." He turned to Mr. Marsh. "Anything to add?"

"*Qui audet adipiscitur*," he said.

"What on earth does *that* mean?" Celia asked.

"It means, 'I told you so'," Silence said.

Ian laughed, and pointing at Silence, he said to Meredith, "I like this one. No arrogance."

"Indeed not," said Meredith, holding out a hand to draw Silence forward. "Pa, I'd like to introduce you to Silence Ogden."

"Pleased to meet you at last," said Silence, shaking his hand after wiping the cider from his own.

"At last?" Ian asked.

"It's a long story," Silence told him.

"And his friends," said Meredith. "Our friends. This is Celia Gagne, her daughter Happy, Mr. Marsh and Pascal McCune, and Annie. Annie?" Meredith peered at the empty place by the workbench where a moment ago, Annie had stood.

"She's there!" Happy cried, pointing at the figure slipping toward the loft ladder at the back of the barn. Annie froze; Ian squinted, and then it was his turn to pale. "It couldnae be…" he murmured.

"Mama?" Hunter said.

With an audible sigh of defeat, Annie threw up her hands and came back to the front of the barn.

"God almighty," said Ian, his eyes fixed on her, "it *is* you! Sweet Angelina, what on Earth are *you* doing here?" Now Silence marked his accent: full of the stops and cadences that sometimes, faintly, worked their way into Pascal's.

"Same as you, I guess," Annie answered, and to her credit, she met his eye. "Trying to right a few old wrongs."

"But how did you – "

"When were you – "

"Did you and Meredith – "

The sudden tangle of competing questions silenced them again. For a moment, nobody knew what to say.

At last, Celia broke the silence. "Well that's Serendipity, all right! But I think it'll all be a lot easier to swallow with some of Annie's hooch. Luckily, she brought a few extra bottles. They're in the house. Shall we?"

2

That night, Heaven Homestead blazed like a lighthouse. Every curtain and door was open, every room lit, and even though the night was mild, a fire roared in the parlor hearth. Silence sat listening to the string of questions chase its tail around the room, wondering how he'd ever make sense of any of it. Then Happy cut into the confusion with her clear, bright voice, addressing Hunter:

"But how come you went looking for Meredith when you thought she was dead?"

"Because I never *really* thought that she was dead," Hunter answered.

"Why not?" Happy persisted.

Hunter thought about this, and then he said, "I don't rightly know. But you see, the place where Meredith and I grew up, it wasn't like this. We lived miles from the next house, on an island miles from anywhere. We never had any playmates but each other. It got so we could pick up on each other's littlest changes of mood, finish each other's sentences. And when she disappeared – well, I knew it made no sense, but in that same way, I knew she wasn't gone forever."

"Oh," said Happy, but Hunter continued unprompted. "I also knew she couldn't have got far in that little boat – not in that storm – so I set off looking for a sign of her. I thought it would take a day or two at most." He smiled faintly and exchanged a glance with Meredith. "I underestimated you. After a week, I was coming around to thinking everyone was right and you'd drowned in that storm.

"Then I met a lobsterman on a little rocky beach away to the south. I thought he'd lost something, because he was pacing up and down, back and forth over the same stretch of sand. But when I asked him, he told me he was looking for a girl he'd seen on that beach, the morning after the storm: a grey girl who'd walked up, out of the sea and into the woods and left no trace. He said he was beginning to believe she'd been a ghost." Hunter looked at his sister. "I think that he'd fallen in love. I told him you weren't a ghost, but you were surely gone. He didn't believe me. Maybe he's there still, pining for you…"

"Oh, don't!" Meredith cried.

Hunter smiled, and shrugged. "Still, it's an effect you seem to have had on a lot of folks you passed on your way down here. Though the people came later. At first it was all little, silent things that told me I was on the right path. A barefooted print by a dried up puddle. That boat carving in a derelict hunting cabin. I admit, you had me flummoxed once or twice – but then I met a logging gang who remembered you. In fact, their foreman nearly burned my ears off, ranting about you stealing his horse – "

Meredith threw up her hands. "Why is it that everyone takes me for a horse thief? He was only going to shoot her – "

"Shoot Epona?" Happy screeched.

Meredith nodded. "So any way you look at it, I was saving him a bullet. But as it happens, I *did* pay him for the horse."

"You did indeed," Hunter said, shaking his head in disgust. "One of the older men told me you gave him a diamond ring in exchange. Lord, Meredith, do you have any idea how much that thing was worth?"

Meredith gave him a steady look. "It was worth Epona."

He conceded with a smile. "Anyhow, he told me you went off south-west, so I did too. Next time I stopped was in what

I thought was a ghost town. But as it turned out, it wasn't completely deserted. There was an old man – "

"Joseph!" said Meredith.

Hunter nodded. "Now there's a geezer who loves to talk! I can't imagine how he stands it up there, all alone."

"He seemed all right to me."

"That may be – but he said since you left, he'd been feeling lonely for the first time in years. Thought he might move in with his niece who kept asking."

"He didn't," said Meredith.

"Oh yes, he did. You charmed him, just like the lobsterman."

"I don't see how," Meredith said tartly. "I didn't speak a word to him." She paused, and then asked, "I don't suppose you met a girl – an Indian girl, living in a valley with her grandfather?"

"I met the girl. She was setting up a cross on a fresh grave under a cherry tree."

"Oh," said Meredith. "Then Tomah must have died…"

"If Tomah was her grandfather, then yes, he did. She said she was about to go to town, to get married, but she wanted to visit her grandfather one last time. She remembered you. Said you gave her her Bible, and she'd cherished it ever since. I never knew you had a Bible, Meredith."

"I didn't," she said softly.

Hunter shook his head. "Then I met the Shakers. They said that they pray for you every day, though from the way they rant on, I'm not certain this is a good thing!"

"It is," Meredith smiled.

"And there was an old woman who smelled like fish and spoke like a poet. She said you and your young man had stopped one night with her." He glanced at Silence.

"Not me," Silence told him, looking sidelong at Meredith.

"Elijah was a friend," she said. "A man who'd left the Shakers and needed help. We traveled together for a time, until he saved a woman called Evangeline from a pack of vigilates."

"Well, she's his wife now," said Hunter, "and they have a baby girl."

"Oh!" said Meredith, sudden tears springing to her eyes. "The baby was all right!"

"Alive and kicking," Hunter said, smiling. "Screaming, too. They sure remembered you, anyway: the baby's name is Meredith. Later," Hunter continued, pretending not to see Meredith's tears begin to fall, "I hopped a train in coal country. Someone else had had the same idea: a mother and daughter. Russian, I think. They'd had what the woman called 'an unexpected windfall,' and they were going to start a new life in New York City. The daughter was an artist – she showed me some of her paintings and told me all about a princess she was named after."

"Vasilissa spoke to you?" Meredith cried.

"Oh, yes. Her English was real good."

"When I met them, the girl was dumb," Meredith said.

"Well she isn't now. In fact, she told me to tell you thank you."

"Some time after that," said Hunter, "I met a colored man called Sox. He was going north, to try for a place at Howard University. He told me to give you his regards and to send you his cousin Chloe's as well. I guess she's training now as a teacher."

Meredith smiled, shaking her head. "I suppose you met Gabriella, too?"

"And every one of her friends and relations, as well as a painting of a goddess they swear is you. Although to me, it looked very like one of the Russian girl's paintings…"

"That's a long story," Meredith said. "But tell me, are they well?"

"They surely seemed it, by the amount of food they cooked and tried to make me eat!"

Then Meredith saw his face change, and she knew what was coming next, also why he hesitated. "Siu Fai?" she asked, trying to keep her voice even.

Hunter nodded. "It was strange – almost as if he expected me. As if he knew who I was before I even said a word."

"That's because I told him all about you," Meredith answered. "I stayed a long time with him. I nearly froze to death. He…he saved my life."

She looked at her hands, shy of what Siu Fai might have told him, but Hunter only said, "He told me to tell you to be happy."

Meredith nodded. "I don't suppose you met a woman called Saint Catherine?"

"No, but I heard about her plenty. It was in a town not far from here, all made up of colored folks. They couldn't wait to tell me about you and your friend – the white woman dressed like a man, traveling with an angel. From what I could put together, this 'angel' was a Negro woman – an evangelist. They said she gave them a sermon that shook them to their bones."

"She did," said Meredith, smiling at the memory. "And I think she really was an angel. She's gone now to start an orphanage, but she was the one who sent me this way…and here I am."

"Aye, and a true adventure," said Ian proudly. "It puts me in mind o' my sailing days."

"*Annus mirabilis,*" said Mr. Marsh.

"A year of wonders," Silence translated.

Meredith looked at them, wanting to tell them that what Hunter had related didn't even scratch the surface of what the past year had been to her; that the true wonders were the ones to which she couldn't put words. The human infant mothered by a wolf; the diamond highway with no one but her horse and herself to witness its beauty. The ghost climbing an eternal ladder of water; Gradlon's grief and Old Maggie's smoke. The Gettysburg ghosts marching into a blazing perpetuity; Sox's tears and Chloe's bitter beauty. Siu Fai's scars and Vasilissa's smile, and the incongruous evil that had sent her on this journey.

"I wonder what happened to *him*."

Meredith didn't realize that she'd spoken the words aloud until she heard the thick, ensuing silence. Hunter and Ian exchanged a look, and then Ian gave a tiny nod. Hunter reached into his coat and took something from an inner pocket. He handed it to Meredith. It was a piece of water-stained wood, the size of a small book. Two letters were carved into it, still showing vestiges of the gold leaf that had once picked them out: "TC".

"Where did you get this?" Meredith asked tremulously.

Hunter smiled wryly. "On the next beach down from the one where you washed up."

"Do you mean…?"

Hunter nodded. "I went to the county coroner to make sure. Seems Jacob's boat hit a shoal and sank in the same storm that wrecked yours. A lobsterman pulled his body up with a trap a few days later. Except it turns out he wasn't Jacob Devereaux at all. It took a while for them to piece it together, but apparently his real name was – "

"Jim Swain," Meredith finished for him, tossing the piece of wood onto the fire.

Hunter blinked at her in surprise. "Well, yes. How'd you know that?"

But Meredith's answer was precluded by a wrenching cry. Celia had her face in her hands as she wept great, wrenching sobs.

"Mama?" Happy asked, her eyes round and frightened. "What's the matter?"

Celia took her hands from her face. It was beaming. She wrapped her arms around Happy and said, "Nothing, honey. Nothing at all. Everything's finally right!" She clutched the baffled child as she dissolved again into tears.

"What in the hell is going on here?" Annie asked, looking from Meredith to Celia to Hunter and back.

"I sense," said Ian, "that it's another very long story, and I, for one, am knackered. Nae doubt it'll keep til the morning." He stood up as Mr. Marsh and Happy led Celia from the room.

"I'm afraid I'm out of beds," Silence told Ian.

"Ach – Hunter and I can kip in the barn." Nodding to the others, they took their leave.

"A hand, *P'tit*?" Pascal said to Silence, who helped him out of his chair and off toward the attic.

Meredith also stood to go, but Annie reached out and caught her hand. "Wait," she said.

"What is it?" Meredith asked, unable to keep her voice from wavering.

"I'm sorry. I know that words don't begin to atone for what I've done, but I fear my explanation wouldn't be much better."

Meredith studied her for a moment. The words themselves were final, but the tone held a buried plea. "Let me decide that," she said, sitting back down.

Annie nodded. Still holding Meredith's hand, she looked into the dying fire and began, "I haven't been settled my whole life long. I grew up without any people, and I guess by the time life finally provided me some, it was too late for me to learn how to belong to them. So I left them, without apology or explanation. Lots of folks would say that was wrong, but they don't know the despair I felt, and the terror that my despair would infect

my family too. Leaving was the only way I knew to save them…
but you…"

She paused, looking at Meredith, who looked back at her
squarely. Sighing, Annie continued, "I didn't know I was
carrying you when I left. By the time I *did* know, it was too late
to go back – well, that's what I told myself. So I kept you until
you weaned, and then I took you back to Juniper Barrens, where
you should always have been. I thought I was saving you, like
I thought I saved Ian and Hunter, from the burden of my own
unhappiness. Now I see I was foolish and selfish."

"It's true that as a child I pined for a mother," Meredith said
after a thoughtful moment, "and sometimes it was hard on me,
thinking I didn't know who I was…but the fact is, I always
knew. Ian and Hunter loved me without condition, without
reason, and that's more than many people ever have. They were
my family, and I was theirs, and if anyone's taken them for
granted, it's me."

Annie – Sweet Angelina – searched Meredith's face for
insincerity. At last, finding none, she nodded. "I hope your
brother and your father will be as forgiving to me," she said.

"Mother," said Meredith, "don't you know that they've
forgiven you already?"